Not Dark Yet

Also by Peter Robinson

Caedmon's Song
No Cure for Love
Before the Poison

INSPECTOR BANKS NOVELS
Gallows View
A Dedicated Man
A Necessary End
The Hanging Valley
Past Reason Hated
Wednesday's Child
Dry Bones that Dream
Innocent Graves
Dead Right
In a Dry Season
Cold is the Grave
Aftermath
The Summer that Never Was
Playing with Fire
Strange Affair
Piece of my Heart
Friend of the Devil
All the Colours of Darkness
Bad Boy
Watching the Dark
Children of the Revolution
Abattoir Blues
When the Music's Over
Sleeping in the Ground
Careless Love
Many Rivers to Cross

SHORT STORIES
Not Safe After Dark
The Price of Love

PETER ROBINSON

Not Dark Yet

HODDER & STOUGHTON

First published in Great Britain in 2021 by Hodder & Stoughton
An Hachette UK company

1

A CIP catalogue record for this title is available from the British Library

Hardback ISBN 978 1 529 34307 6
Trade Paperback ISBN 978 1 529 34312 0
eBook ISBN 978 1 529 34309 0

Typeset in Plantin Light by Hewer Text UK Ltd, Edinburgh
Printed and bound in Great Britain by Clays Ltd, Elcograf S.p.A.

Hodder & Stoughton policy is to use papers that are natural, renewable and recyclable products and made from wood grown in sustainable forests. The logging and manufacturing processes are expected to conform to the environmental regulations of the country of origin.

Hodder & Stoughton Ltd
Carmelite House
50 Victoria Embankment
London EC4Y 0DZ

www.hodder.co.uk

To Sheila

I

Zelda hadn't visited Chişinău since she had been abducted outside the orphanage at the age of seventeen. And now she was back. She wasn't sure how she was going to find the man she wanted – she had no contacts in the city – but she did have one or two vague ideas about where to begin.

As she walked down Stefan cel Mare Boulevard, she noticed that while many of the shops and their colourful facades were new, the wide pavements and road surface were still cracked and pitted with potholes, and the old ladies in peasant skirts and headscarves still sat under the trees gossiping and selling their belongings to make ends meet. Spread out at their feet lay everything from articles of clothing to children's toys and pink plastic hairbrushes.

The heat was oppressive, dry and dusty. Zelda felt it burn in her chest as she walked. And the smell of the sewer was never far away. She looked behind, not because she seriously believed someone might be following her, but because such caution had become a habit. All in all, she knew that she was much safer here in Chişinău than she was back in Yorkshire, or London. She had been worried that Petar Tadić would work out that she had been responsible for the death of his brother Goran, and that he would come to find her. But how could he, she asked herself in more rational moments? Even if he discovered that a woman had killed Goran, there was no reason why he should assume that was Zelda. Goran had abused a lot of women. Why would his brother think for even a moment of that young, frightened Moldovan girl they had raped and abused on a long drive across Romania over thirteen years ago?

The underpass Zelda took to get across the broad road was dark and scrawled with graffiti, mostly swastikas and erect penises. The concrete steps going down were cracked and missing huge chunks, making them awkward to negotiate. The passage was dark and smelled of urine. Zelda picked up her pace, and when she emerged, it was into an altogether different part of Chişinău, an urban wasteland of neglected grey Soviet tower blocks and swathes of sparse grass and spindly trees. A couple of children were kicking a football around, and a scrawny dog lifted its leg against a dead tree.

There were signs of construction – huge piles of dirt, concrete blocks, wooden rafters, metal bars – but the sites were deserted and the mechanical diggers idle. In the midst of all this stood a brand new shopping centre opposite the crumbling blank-eyed stare of the National Hotel. A luxury Intourist hotel in the Soviet era, and once the hottest party spot in town, the National had been built in the late seventies and had stood empty for as long as Zelda could remember. Its decayed grandeur was a cynical reminder of the faded glory of the old days. In front of the hotel stretched a sunken area of dried up and litter-strewn fountains, now overgrown with weeds and home to empty beer cans, broken bottles, used condoms, McDonald's wrappers, needles and whatever other rubbish people tossed into it.

Past the Beer House and a row of travel agents and car rental outlets, Zelda wandered into the backstreets off Constantin Negruzzi Boulevard, and before she knew it, she was standing on the very corner from which she had been snatched.

It was a narrow street by Chişinău standards, tree-lined, with a mix of older, more elegant Russian-style buildings and modern uniform Soviet blocks, what Zelda called Stalinist architecture. Everything was grey and pockmarked, chipped and pitted. Very few cars passed by as she stood fixed to the spot. The old bar on the corner was gone, turned into a brand new *farmacie*, complete with green neon cross, but the rest of the street was much the same.

There, all those years ago, with the dazzling promise of a great future, Zelda's life as she knew it had come to an end. She remembered seeing the small scuffed suitcase break open on the cracked road surface, spilling what few possessions and memories of her dead parents she had – her mother's music box, her father's scuffed leather wallet, the book Zelda was reading – *Bleak House* – her clothes and the scrapbook and diaries she had diligently kept over her years in the orphanage, and her father's chipped shaving mug, which broke into fragments when it hit the concrete.

And the photographs. It had hurt most of all to lose the photographs. While there were plenty taken with friends during her years at the orphanage, there were only three that showed her parents. It was too long ago to remember the details, but she did remember the day the suitcase arrived at the orphanage, only a few months after her parents' deaths in 1992. The contents of the case were the only remnants left of her life from those days.

One photograph showed her father, young and handsome with a shy smile, and another her mother wearing a bikini on holiday in Odessa, with the Black Sea in the background, pretending to strike a sexy pose and putting her hand over her mouth to stifle the laughter. The third showed a stiff and formal family group in a studio portrait taken when Zelda was about three. She sat on her mother's knee, wearing what must have been her very best dress, hair tumbling in ringlets over her shoulders, and her father stood, straight and serious, in his suit, one hand on her mother's shoulder and the other on Zelda's. None of them smiled. All stared directly at the camera.

Zelda had expected that she would feel angry or sad when she returned to the spot where she had lost everything, but all she felt was numbness. Whenever she had looked back on the life that had been stolen, she had simmered with hatred, but now, at the very spot where it had all begun, she felt nothing at all. She thought of all the cars that had driven by since then, all the people who had walked there oblivious, none of them knowing what momentous event had occurred there. Somehow, her own experience was lost in the ceaseless flow of quotidian life, as if she were Icarus falling into the sea, while all around him everyone went on ploughing their fields and tending their sheep.

Now it was just a place, a street corner like any other. Sometimes she wondered who had picked up the music box, her book, the diaries, the wallet, and what they had made of it all. Had anyone actually *seen* her get taken?

It wasn't until she approached the orphanage building itself that the full horror of the past hit her right between the eyes, and she began to tremble at the power of the memory. The building was still there, an early twentieth-century Russian construction in the classical style, of dark stone with rococo touches. With its broad steps, small arched portico and chipped columns, it formed a contrast to the monstrous towers surrounding it. The windows on the lower floor had been boarded up, but the upper ones remained uncovered, jagged frames of broken glass.

Zelda couldn't stop trembling, and the breath seemed to solidify in her chest. This had been her home between the ages of four and seventeen. This was the place that had made her what she was, or what she *could* have been. Now, though, it was a ruin, and so was she, and the irony didn't escape her. What the hell was she doing here, running away from the good life she had found, despite all the odds, and from a good man, who was more than she deserved, seeking God only knew what? Revenge? Atonement? Reconciliation?

There were very few people about, and those who were went about their business, heads down, not paying any attention to Zelda or to anyone else. Trying to push the knot of troubling thoughts aside and to control her shakes and breathing, she walked up the steps and, with a quick glance around her, shoved at the door. It didn't budge. She turned the heavy metal handle and pushed harder with her shoulder, and this time it made a screeching sound, like fingernails on a blackboard, as it dragged across the tiled floor. Again, Zelda glanced around to make sure no one had seen her, then she gave another shove and found herself standing in the hall.

She pushed the door shut behind her.

When the day of Tracy's wedding dawned, Detective Superintendent Alan Banks awoke early to the sounds of birdsong and the glare of bright sunshine through a chink in his curtains. Another perfect midsummer day in an unbroken run of nearly two weeks. He ate a leisurely breakfast of toast and marmalade in the conservatory, listening to the Brahms clarinet quintet on Radio 3 as he glanced over the *Guardian* review section, then took his second cup of coffee out to the garden to contemplate the day ahead.

He had offered to pick up his parents from their sheltered housing on the Northumberland coast but, fiercely independent as ever, his father had insisted that they would make their own way down. Banks knew better than to argue.

When the time came to get ready, he dusted off his dark grey suit – thank God it wasn't a morning-suit affair – and dressed. It was to be an old-fashioned C of E wedding at St Mary's church, at the far end of Market Street, not far from where the Banks family had lived when they first arrived in Eastvale. Old-fashioned apart from the 'obey' bit, Tracy had assured him, though he was to 'give away' the bride. He was nervous, as any father would be, but proud, too. His son Brian would be there, as would his ex-wife Sandra – Tracy's mother – with her husband Sean.

Finally, he was ready, and he went out to the car.

He drove the familiar road with a light heart listening to Mendelssohn's *Octet*, which lifted his spirits even higher. He arrived in good time for a quick glass of red at the Blue Monk before the bridal party was scheduled to meet at the church, just around the corner.

Outside the church, Banks met up with his parents and his son Brian. His mother fixed him a buttonhole, then Tracy's car arrived, and they decided they shouldn't keep poor Mark waiting too much longer. Everyone went inside except for Banks, Tracy and the two bridesmaids.

Needless to say, Tracy looked gorgeous, and Banks felt a lump in his throat as he walked down the aisle beside her and she smiled at him. Tracy had been the sort of child you always wanted to be happy, to keep her innocence. Of course, that was impossible, and though she had been a carefree child, she had lost her way for a while after university and veered towards the dark side, but she had made it back. Now, when Banks looked at her, he saw a grown-up woman, but he felt the same way as he had when she was a child. He could no more protect her from the world now than he had done before – he knew he had been far from a perfect father – but that was what he wished for her in his heart.

As he walked down the aisle beside Tracy, Banks felt as if he were floating through the moment, with faces drifting in and out of vision as guests turned in their pews to catch a glimpse of the bride. Everything seemed somehow unreal, in slow motion; even the swishing of Tracy's wedding dress sounded like soft waves against the shore. He saw Sandra from the corner of his eye, sitting with Sean on the front row. She flashed him a quick smile. Then he saw his parents, his mother already with her hanky out. Tracy gave his hand a squeeze when they got to the front and everyone took their places. Tracy turned to Mark and smiled. He looked scared as hell, Banks thought.

Everything went smoothly, everyone got their lines right and it seemed that in no time they were all walking back down the aisle.

After the photographs and confetti, the crowd dispersed. The reception was to be held over an hour later in the banquet room of the Burgundy Hotel, where most of the out-of-town guests were staying for the night.

Banks found himself walking close to Brian, Sandra and Sean down Market Street, past the end of the street where they used to live, and he was lost for words. To him, Sandra appeared hardly any different than when she had left him. She had kept her figure, and though her hair colour might have been bolstered with a few drops of one of Boots's concoctions, there was nothing false about its lustre. Her face seemed still relatively unlined, her dark eyebrows nicely plucked. She wore a powder blue skirt and jacket over a plain, silk white blouse. A St Christopher on a silver chain around her neck was the only jewellery she wore.

Sandra and Sean edged away to talk to Mark's mother and father, and Banks and Brian slipped away to the Queen's Arms for a quick drink before the reception.

* * *

The silence inside the ruined orphanage rang in Zelda's ears, interrupted only by the distant motor of a car, shout of a child, or bark of a dog. The place smelled musty with rotten wood, mould, dead leaves and stagnant water. For a while, Zelda just stood there as her eyes adjusted. Dust motes floated in the pale light that came in through the broken windows on the upper level.

Ahead of her, a broad staircase led to the first and second floors, mostly dormitories and classrooms. Down here, on the ground floor, had been the administrative offices, staffrooms, cafeteria and communal areas where the children could sit and chat, watch TV, play chess or table tennis. There was also an assembly hall, where they gathered every morning for hymns and prayers.

When Zelda could see clearly, she noticed that the plaster was crumbling from the walls, and in places was completely gone. The thick pile carpets that had once graced the stairs had rotted away to stained tatters, and their patterns had faded. There had been paintings on the walls – nothing special, just landscapes and portraits easy on the eyes – but they were all either gone now or lying torn and broken on the floor. Even in here there was graffiti, the usual sort of crudities, and the floors were strewn with rubbish. Somewhere in the distance she could hear water dripping. Then she heard something skittering down one of the corridors. It wasn't loud enough to be another person. Probably just a rat.

When Zelda moved, she realised she had been holding her breath so long she was beginning to feel dizzy. She grabbed a banister and took a few deep breaths. The wood felt as smooth under her palm as it had years ago, when she and her friends had slid down, strictly against the rules. Olga. Vika. Axenia. Where were they all now? She knew that the beautiful Iuliana had been sold, the same way she had, for they had met a couple of years later in a brothel in Užice, in Serbia. Iuliana, her body and spirit broken, had told Zelda about seeing Lupescu, the orphanage director, watching as she was taken in the street, and drawing back inside as soon as he realised she had spotted him. Nothing was ever said or done about it, and that was one reason Zelda thought he was to blame. Iuliana had killed herself soon after their talk. She was why Zelda was here today.

Zelda carried on up the stairs, wondering what she would find there. But it was just another scene of vandalism. More sunlight poured in through the broken windows and illuminated the clouds of dust Zelda kicked up as she walked. By instinct, she went first to her old dormitory, beds for twelve girls arranged into opposite rows of six, each with a cupboard and bedside table. She thought of the conversations they had had there after lights out, secrets shared, hopes and dreams, grief at the loss of their parents, plans for the future, crushes and loathings, mostly for the boys, who teased them mercilessly. But Zelda had experienced her first feelings for a boy there, she remembered. Radu Prodan. She had buried the memory for years, but now she remembered he had been beautiful, shy, quiet, intelligent, with an untamed shock of blond hair and a habit of trying to smooth it down. Perhaps she had loved him, as well as any girl could love a boy at the age of nine. She had no idea what had become of Radu. Had boys been sold, too?

The old beds had all been stripped down to their metal frames, the tables upturned and the cupboards smashed. There was more graffiti. Zelda wondered whether the vandals who had done all this had any idea what the place had been, what lives had been nurtured here – nurtured and then stolen, in some cases. It didn't matter.

She wandered the rooms and corridors in a daze until she came to an old storage room, which was still full of boxes and packing crates. It was in one of these that she discovered a damp, misshapen cardboard box full of old books, mostly water-damaged, mouldy and warped, with curled pages and stained covers. But they were the books she remembered, the English books: *Jane Eyre*, *David Copperfield*, *Five Go to Mystery Moor*, *4.50 From Paddington*, *The Sign of Four*, *The Lion, the Witch and the Wardrobe*. As she handled them, she felt tears burn in her eyes, and soon the sobbing wracked her body. She let herself slump on the filthy floor to cry. These were the kind of books that had filled her teenage hours with joy, romance and adventure.

When the whirlwind of emotion passed, leaving Zelda feeling numb and tired again, she put back the soggy book she had been holding – *The Wind in the Willows* – and made to close the box. As she did so, she caught sight of a label affixed to the corner of one of the flaps. It was faded and almost completely peeled off, but when she got closer, she was able to make out a name and address: Vasile Lupescu, the name of the orphanage director, and the address of the place she was in. But there was a second name, unknown to her. It was an English name, William Buckley, and the address was in Suruceni, a village on the shores of Lake Danceni, about twenty kilometres west of Chişinău.

Was this, then, the address of her mysterious benefactor? She had always wondered who it was, where the books had come from. Was he still alive? Still in Suruceni? She hadn't made any kind of plan beyond visiting the orphanage, hoping she might find some clue to Vasile Lupescu's whereabouts. Everything had depended on what she discovered here. And now she had something concrete to go on. The first person she would go to for information was William Buckley.

All the outside tables were occupied, but Banks didn't mind being relegated to the inside of the pub. They found a quiet corner and Banks fetched a pint of Theakston's bitter for each of them. Brian was moderately famous, as a member of the Blue Lamps, and one or two of the drinkers stared as if they thought they recognised him but weren't quite sure.

Cyril had recently installed some air-conditioning on the cheap, and it managed to send a blast of chill air across the room every two or three minutes. And then there was the background music, one of Cyril's never-ending sixties playlists, always full of surprises. There was something about that era of early sixties pop, before it became 'rock' and started taking itself seriously, that smacked of innocence and the sheer joy of being young and alive. It was epitomised especially by the song playing at the moment: The Crystals singing 'Then He Kissed Me'. It sounded just like that first kiss tasted.

'You all right, Dad?' Brian asked.

'Why? Don't I look it?'

'You seem a bit . . . I don't know. Distracted.'

'I suppose it was all the excitement of the wedding,' he said. 'The emotion. My little girl getting married. And seeing your mother again. It's been quite a while. I suppose I'm feeling just a little bit sad. And old.'

'Yeah, it was weird walking past where we used to live. Are you sure you're OK, though?'

Banks swigged some beer. 'Me? Course I am. Tough as old nails. It just feels like a momentous occasion. That's all.'

'It is for Tracy. What do you think of Mark?'

'He's all right, I suppose. Could be a bit more . . . you know . . . exciting. Adventurous.'

'He's an accountant, for crying out loud. What do you expect?'

Banks laughed. 'I know. I know. And he does like Richard Thompson. That's definitely a point in his favour. She could have done a lot worse.'

'She almost did, as I remember.'

'Yes.' Banks remembered the time when Tracy had taken up with the archetypal 'bad boy' and almost got herself killed as a result.

'So maybe a little dull isn't too bad?' Brian went on. 'What about you, though? Still living the exciting copper's life?'

'It's rarely exciting. But what else would I do?'

'Same as everyone else your age, Dad. Putter about in the garden. Get an allotment. Ogle young women. Drink too much. Watch TV.'

Banks laughed. 'I already do all those things. Except the allotment. Maybe I should write my memoirs?'

'You always said you hated writing reports.'

'Well . . . yes . . . but that's different. Enough about me. What about you? The farewell tour? How's it going?'

'Great so far. Mum and Sean came to the London show. Are you coming to see us?'

'Of course. Wouldn't miss it for the world. The Sage. I've already got the tickets. Ray and Zelda are coming, too.'

'No date for you?'

'Not these days, it seems. I think my allure must have deserted me.' The music had changed again. Neil Sedaka was singing 'Breaking Up is Hard to Do'. He managed to make even such a sad song sound almost joyful. At that moment, Banks's mobile played its blues riff. The number was withheld, but that happened often enough not to be a problem. He excused himself for a moment and went outside.

'Yes?'

'Banksy?'

It could only be Dirty Dick Burgess; no one else ever called him that. 'Yes?'

'Where are you? You sound funny.'

'I'm standing in the market square outside the Queen's Arms on my way to my daughter's wedding reception. So make it fast.'

'Sorry,' said Burgess. 'Give her my . . . you know . . .'

'Right.'

'Keeping busy?'

'Oh, you know. The usual.'

'Getting anywhere with the Blaydon murders yet?'

'It's still early days,' said Banks. 'As I said, I'm on my way to a rather important wedding reception. I'm guessing you've called for some other reason than to yank my chain?'

'Oh, you're no fun. But as a matter of fact, I have. You're not the only one working on a dead-end murder investigation.'

'Where do I come in?'

'I don't want to say too much over the phone, but I think we should meet and compare notes. Are you seriously busy?'

'No. Well, yes, but . . . we're trying to make a case against Leka Gashi and the Albanians for Blaydon's murder. Trouble is, we don't even know where they are.'

'Leka Gashi and the Albanians,' repeated Burgess. 'Sounds like a rock band. Anyway, the Albanians can wait. They'll be back. Don't worry. You'll nail them. Do you think your boss will let you come out to play?'

'You want me to come down to London?'

'I honestly can't get away at the moment. Not for longer than an hour or two, and that won't even cover the train ride. Meetings up to the eyeballs. Otherwise, as you know, nothing would please me more than a trip up north.'

Banks couldn't always figure out when, or if, Burgess was being ironic.

'I promise you it'll be worthwhile,' Burgess went on. 'And if you can get here by lunch tomorrow, I'll even buy. How's that?'

'An offer I can't refuse.'

'Excellent. Whenever you can make it. Pret on—'

'Hang on a minute. I'm not going all that way to be fobbed off with Pret A Manger.'

'Zizzi's, then?'

'You must be joking. Next thing you'll be telling me it's the NCA canteen.'

'Do we have one? Well, it's not going to be Gordon bloody Ramsay's or Michel Roux's, either, I can assure you.'

'I'm sure you'll find somewhere suitable. Text me in the morning.'

2

Zelda called at one of the car rental agencies she had passed earlier and managed to rent an old grey Skoda with a starfish crack on the windscreen and so many dents and scratches the young man at the counter didn't even make her sign off on them.

It was an easy drive to Suruceni, and after the outskirts of Chișinău – more ruined buildings and half-built tower blocks – she drove through pleasant, rolling countryside on E581, encountering very little traffic.

It was early evening when she pulled up in front of William Buckley's house in the southwest of the village, not too far from the lake. It was a small, detached bungalow of beige stucco with a matching pantile roof and white mouldings around the arched windows. The house was slightly raised, and there were four steps up to the side porch and door. The small garden was untended, with not much but stones, dirt and a few blades of parched grass. Even the weeds were struggling against the heat. Two fat crows sat on the pantiles. They didn't move as Zelda walked up the steps and knocked on the door.

At first, she thought there was no one home. The silence was resounding. But she knocked again and heard a slow shuffling sound from behind the door. Eventually, it opened, and a white-haired old man with what could only be called a 'lived-in' face peered out at her in some surprise. A book-jacket photo she had seen of W.H. Auden came to mind. His face was a road map of a life hard lived, but his eyes were a startling childlike blue, and by far his liveliest feature. They could have been the eyes of someone her own age, Zelda found herself thinking.

'Yes?' he said, speaking Moldovan. 'Can I help you?'

Zelda spoke English. 'Perhaps. Are you William Buckley?'

'Ah, a compatriot,' Buckley said. 'Yes. I am he. And call me Bill. Please, charming lady, do come in. Don't be afraid. I'm a harmless, toothless old man.'

Zelda smiled and followed him inside, taking in the framed Japanese-style paintings and drawings on the wall and the sunlight through the arched windows. Buckley shuffled ahead of her, a hunched figure, walking stick in his right hand. The bungalow was small inside, just a living room, one bedroom and kitchen/dining area, Zelda guessed, but it was cosy. Bookcases lined two of the living-room walls, and each was so stuffed with books they lay on their sides on top of other books. All in English.

'To what do I owe the pleasure?' Buckley asked, indicating that she should sit in a damask armchair at right angles to the matching sofa which, judging by the little table holding a tea mug and a copy of *Phineas Finn*, was his spot. 'May I fetch you a cup of tea?'

'I don't want to trouble you.'

'It's no trouble. As a matter of fact, I just made some. It should still be hot. Milk and sugar?'

'Just a little milk, please, then.'

Buckley shuffled off and Zelda glanced around at the books. They covered all subjects – fiction, history, poetry, music, art, literary criticism, theatre, architecture – and were of all shapes and sizes, from dog-eared paperbacks that looked as if they had been bought in used bookshops, to recent hardcovers in shiny dust jackets and oversized coffee table volumes.

She was still reading titles, her head slightly tilted, when Buckley came back with the tea. 'A keen reader, are you?' he asked.

'Yes,' said Zelda.

Buckley nodded slowly and handed her the tea, his wrinkled hand shaking slightly.

Zelda smiled. The room was stifling, and there was a slightly unpleasant smell of neglected hygiene and spoiled food, but she could put up with it. If Buckley lived here alone, it would be hard for him to deal with the myriad daily matters of simply keeping things ticking over.

As if reading her thoughts, he said, 'I do have a local lady who comes in once a week and cleans for me, but I'm afraid she's not due next until tomorrow. I do apologise for the air of neglect.'

'It's nothing,' said Zelda.

Buckley half reclined on the sofa and grimaced, as if the movement caused him pain. 'You wanted to see me for some specific reason? Do I know you?'

Now that she was here facing him, Zelda wasn't sure how to get things started. 'Yes,' she said. 'I mean, no, you don't know me, but I do want to see you. It's about the orphanage.'

'St George's?'

'That's the one.'

Buckley narrowed his eyes. 'Don't tell me you were there.'

'I was.'

'You poor thing.'

'Oh, no!' Zelda cried. 'Don't think that. I had a wonderful life there. Everyone was so kind. The books and . . .' She found herself on the verge of tears. Was this man truly her benefactor? Or could he have been her destroyer?

'I meant to lose your parents at such an early age. But I'm glad St George's was good to you. That was certainly the idea behind it. Yes, I do believe it was a place where much good was done in a time when such things were the exception rather than the rule. But how did you find out about me? I did my best to remain an anonymous donor.'

'I've been back there,' Zelda said. 'Just now. It's in ruins, but there was a box of books in a storeroom, and your name and address were on them.'

'Yes. I'm afraid St George's closed its doors in 2009. A real tragedy. In Moldova, as I'm sure you know, everything no longer used is simply left to decay at its own rate.' A mischievous smile crossed his features, giving Zelda a glimpse of what he might have been like as a young man. And while he wasn't exactly toothless, he wasn't far off. 'Even many things which are still in use are falling apart. We are great believers in entropy. We have a very cavalier attitude towards progress and development.'

'You say "we",' Zelda said, 'but you're English, aren't you?'

'If you want to be accurate, I'm Welsh, but as I've been here nearly thirty years now, the matter of my origins is quite academic. I have certainly retained my interest in British culture, if that's of any interest to you.'

'Thirty years? B-but, how? I mean . . . what . . .?'

'What have I been doing all that time? Why am I here?'

'Yes. All that.'

'It's a very dull story. I was what's called a cultural attaché to the Romanian embassy in Bucharest. A diplomat and cheerleader for the British Council. I moved here to Moldova during the civil war, after the Soviets left in the early nineties. I suppose the long and the short of it is, I fell in love.'

'With?'

'With the country, and with a woman. *Cherchez la femme*. It was a second chance for me, you see. My first wife had died some years earlier, and I had never expected to fall in love again. I was fifty four years old. She became my wife. Sadly, she, too, died five years ago.'

'I'm sorry.'

He waved his hand. 'Not for you to be sorry, my dear. Though I know what you mean, and I thank you for the sentiment. I'm surprised you don't ask me why I fell in love with the most undesirable country in Europe.'

Zelda laughed. 'Love is blind?'

Buckley smiled his approval. 'Yes. That would be the easiest response, and perhaps the most accurate. But there's a simplicity to the place, to life here, once you know the ins and outs. I'm happy to end my days here in Suruceni. There's still corruption everywhere, I know, but the people have a spirit and a strong sense of stoicism. We always managed to get by. We lived in Chișinău then, my wife and I, and our house was always full of artists, writers, musicians. I taught English whenever I was allowed to do so. I also supplemented my income by writing books and reviews.'

'Would I know your work?'

Buckley laughed. 'I hope not. No. I wrote under many pseudonyms. Potboilers in every genre you could imagine. Novelisations of movies or TV series, romance, crime, horror, science-fiction. You name it. I seem to have a talent for ventriloquism but no real voice of my own. But you're not here to talk about me.'

'I am in a way,' said Zelda. 'Besides, it's an interesting story.'

'Probably not half as interesting as yours.'

Zelda looked away. 'You wouldn't . . .' she said. 'You don't want to . . .'

'I've upset you, my dear. I apologise. It was a flippant remark. I can see there has been much grief in your life.'

Zelda shook her head. 'It's not . . . Oh, never mind. It's about the orphanage.'

'What about it?'

'The books, for a start. Did you send them?'

'I did. For many years. I suppose I was trying to spread my culture to a heathen land. No, that's not strictly true. Forgive me, I was arrogant. Moldova has her own poets. I wanted people – I wanted the charges at St George's in particular – to experience the same pleasures I myself experienced when I read those books as a child.'

'Were you an orphan, may I ask?'

'You may. And, yes, I was. Am. My parents were both killed during the Blitz, in London. I have no brothers or sisters or any other living relatives as far as I know. It gave me more freedom than I knew what to do with. I don't mean to belittle the grief and terrible sense of loss and aloneness, but did you have that experience yourself, a kind of odd relief that there was no one else to satisfy, to please, no one to make demands on you, to tell you what to do or in which direction to push?'

'I'm afraid I never got to experience the positive side of being an orphan. At least, not in that way. Kind as they were, the nuns were always all too willing to make demands and tell us what to do!'

Buckley smiled. 'Of course. I meant later.'

'There was no later.' Zelda leaned forward and clasped her hands on her knees. 'But the books. I must . . . I have to thank you. Without them, I don't know what I would have done.'

'I'm happy my gifts didn't fall on stony ground.'

'Oh, not at all! Those were some of the happiest times of my life, curled up in bed reading Enid Blyton or Charlotte Brontë. I felt as if I had always known English, as if it were my first language. I don't remember working hard to learn it. Even later, in my darkest times, when I couldn't make time to read, I always tried to summon up those memories. Peggotty. Jane. Julian, Dick, Anne and George. And Timmy, of course. And

Modesty Blaise. I loved Modesty Blaise. She became my benchmark if ever I was in trouble. Sometimes it worked. Sometimes they made me feel safe again, but . . .'

'It's a hard, cruel world out there, my dear. I know,' said Buckley. 'And there's rarely a Willie Garvin to charge in and rescue you.'

Zelda stared down at her clasped hands. She felt the tears struggling for release again. Held them back. This man could not have been her destroyer; she was certain of it.

'So you were born here?' Buckley asked.

'Dubăsari.'

'I don't know it.'

'There's nothing to know. It's a small place. In Transnistria. Near the Ukraine border. There's an amusement park.'

'And your parents?'

'Both killed in the civil war. They weren't participating, you understand. Just civilian casualties.'

'Indeed. There was plenty of "collateral damage". You must have been very young.'

'I was four.'

'And so you arrived at St George's.'

'Yes. It was very new at the time. Only in its second year, I think.' Zelda laughed. 'You could still smell the fresh paint.'

'For all that you have to thank a man called Klaus Bremner.'

Zelda frowned. 'Klaus Bremner. I've never heard the name.'

'You wouldn't,' said Buckley. 'Besides, he's long dead now. But for a while, in the uncertain days of the late 80s, when the Russian Empire was collapsing and a new Eastern Europe was struggling to be born, we were the best of friends. It was Klaus who put up the money for the orphanage and established the St George's Trust to keep it running even after his death. For a while, at any rate.'

'But why? Was he an orphan, too?'

'Klaus? No. And he was much older than me. He was a German soldier during World War Two. He fought in the Jassy-Kishinev Offensive.'

'I remember learning about that in history class.'

'It was an important battle. 1944. The Russians defeated the occupying German army and drove them out of Moldova. It was what Klaus witnessed in Kishinev, as it was known then – especially the number of orphaned children wandering the streets – that stayed with him. The guilt. He had never been a fully-fledged Nazi. Like many Germans, he was just doing his duty to save himself from being shot. He didn't do it with as much relish as some.'

'But what has that to do with St George's?'

'After the war, Klaus went to America, where he made his fortune in the engineering industry. I don't know all the details, but he was a very clever man, an industrial engineer before the war, and he came up with a few new ideas that were embraced by the new West Germany. I imagine he took a few of those secrets with him to share with the Americans. That way they could easily overlook his having been on the other side during the war. By the end of the Soviet era, when the Wall came down, Klaus, now called Claude, was a very rich man. He travelled to Moldova and Romania often and he even owned a winery here, near Cricova, but less famous.'

'When you were the cultural attaché?'

'Towards the end of my time in Bucharest. But that was where we first met, yes. Klaus was a very cultured man. We shared a passion for opera and symphony concerts. He and I travelled from Bucharest to Kishinev together on several occasions. He told me about the devastation he had witnessed, the scale of human suffering, the misery of the war. You won't remember, but there were also terrible stories about Romanian orphanages then, too. Abuse and neglect. I suppose you could say he had an epiphany. And he hatched a plan.'

'For an orphanage?'

'Yes. St George's.'

'Whose idea was the books?'

'Both of us. Believe it or not, Klaus was an anglophile. Teaching English was to be a priority. Other languages, too, of course, but particularly English. Your English is excellent, by the way, my dear. He saw it as the future, and none of us knew what lay ahead for Moldova or Romania. We both loved the English classics, and I was still able to get my hands on as many books as I wanted through my connection with the British Council and the newspapers I reviewed for. Also, I don't know if you're aware, but this village is famous for its monastery, the Monastery of St George. It's been here since 1785 and is home to a group of Orthodox nuns. Even the Soviets tolerated them. They still farm the land on the edges of the village. I had been coming here for years to get away from city life in Bucharest, for peace and quiet to write, and I had got to know some of them.'

'The nuns?'

'You remember, of course. Yes. These nuns helped with the orphanage. They taught lessons, cooked the food, did the cleaning, took care of you children.'

'I never knew,' Zelda said. 'Where they came from, I mean. Why they did what they did.'

'They did it because it was in their nature to do good.'

'They were kind. Distant, but kind.'

'So I heard. Not always the case with nuns, as I understand. Ask the Irish. So that was your lucky childhood.'

'Your books and Klaus Bremner's epiphany. Yes.'

'And the nuns.'

'And the nuns.'

Zelda swallowed. She felt overwhelmed by the information and the emotion it generated. But she knew she had to steel herself to find out what she had come for, even though the thought of doing so made her feel duplicitous. From all she had heard and observed so far, she was convinced that neither William Buckley nor Klaus Bremner had anything to do with her fate. She knew she might be wrong, of course. Often the nastiest of monsters lurk behind the most pleasing facades, and Nazis, of course, were among the nastiest. The whole orphanage, for example, could have been a scheme to raise young virgins for the sacrifice. But she didn't think so. Nor did she think they knew what went on. After all, both Buckley and Bremner had only distant connections with St George's. She had never heard of either of them the entire time she was there. They weren't involved in the day-to-day management of who was coming or going. That would have been Vasile Lupescu.

'Do you remember Vasile Lupescu?' she asked. The name almost turned to stone on her lips.

'Vasile? Of course. He was director from the beginning until the end.'

'Do you know what happened to him?'

'Nothing happened to him, my dear. It was 2009, the wake of the great financial crisis, the collapse of so many economies. The trust Claude had set up failed. Apparently, it wasn't quite as inviolable as he had intended it to be. It was all a terrible tragedy, a very sad time for us all. But there was nothing we could do. When the orphanage closed, Vasile was just about ready to retire. So that was what he did.'

'And now?'

'As far as I know he lives in Purcari. It's in the far southeast, not too far from the Ukraine border. Odessa. Good wine country. I think he has family down there.'

'I've heard of it,' said Zelda. 'Do you ever see him?'

'Not often. I rarely see anyone these days. You're probably the first person I've spoken to in ages, except for my cleaning lady, and certainly the first I've had any sort of conversation with in weeks, maybe months. And we weren't close friends, Vasile and I, even when we were both in Chişinău. The last time I saw him was when he travelled up to the city on business, and we met for lunch. But that was over a year ago. Why do you ask?'

'I just wondered, that's all. He was an important presence in our lives.'

'He certainly was. He took care of all the administrative details – admissions, transitions and everything. I'm sure he'd be very pleased if you were to tell him that. Are you planning on going to see him, too?'

'Yes, I might do. Can you give me his address? Would that be all right?'

'Of course. I don't see why not.' Buckley had a small diary on his table, and he leafed through it, then gave her an address in Purcari. Zelda glanced at her watch and realised she wouldn't be able to make it down there until well after dark. Instead, she decided to go back to the Radisson Blu in Chişinău and try to get a good night's sleep, if such a thing were possible after the conversation she had just had. She had one more day left in Moldova before her flight left at 5.35 the following evening, so she might as well spend it in Purcari.

At the door, they shook hands, and Buckley said, 'I don't know why you came here, my dear, and why you wanted to hear an old man's ramblings, but I sense some sort of mission on your part, some desire to reacquaint yourself with your roots, make peace with the past. Is that it?'

'Something like that,' said Zelda, hating herself for misleading him.

'Then let me thank you for your company and your conversation. And I wish you good luck in your quest.'

Zelda thanked William Buckley again for the books, for giving her a childhood and early adolescence, at least, then she took her leave.

Banks knew he shouldn't have done, but he drove home from the reception when the whole thing was fast becoming an endless DJ ego trip to a soundtrack of bad nineties synth-pop and electropop music.

Brian and two fellow band members who were with him had performed a brief unplugged set earlier, including 'Blackbird', one of Banks's favourite Beatles songs, even though it was McCartney and he had always regarded himself as a Lennon man.

The music had started to go downhill soon after Brian and his friends had left. Banks said farewell to his own and Mark's parents, all four still bravely soldiering on, and to Sandra and Sean, who were themselves just about to leave. Then he walked over to Tracy and Mark, embraced his daughter and shook her husband's hand. Tracy thanked him for his cheque, and he could tell by her tone that it had been enough. That was a relief.

Before leaving, he took Mark aside and said, only half joking, 'Break her heart and I'll break your neck.'

'Don't worry, sir. Mr Banks,' Mark replied nervously, his Adam's apple bobbing.

'Alan,' said Banks, patting him on the back. 'You're family now. But remember what I said, or you'll have me to answer to.'

Despite having had a couple more glasses of wine on top of the pint, enough time had elapsed that Banks felt perfectly sober as he got in the car. As a cop in the Eastvale region for many years, he knew well enough that there weren't any patrol cars out in the dale at this time of night, but he drove carefully. Not so much so that it seemed as if he were *trying* to drive carefully, but sticking to the speed limits and signalling properly. He made it back home in one piece, without incident.

There was a chill in the air, so instead of going out into the garden, he poured himself a glass of claret, sat in the conservatory and put on Dylan's *Time Out of Mind* to counteract the DJ's music that lingered like the aural equivalent of a bad smell.

Burgess's call intrigued him, and he wondered what it could be about. It was true that he didn't have a lot on his plate at the moment, but what he did have, the Blaydon case, had become much more complex and frustrating over the past few days.

A crooked property developer called Connor Clive Blaydon and his factotum Neville Roberts had been found murdered by Banks and DC Gerry Masterson in the swimming pool area of Blaydon's mansion just over a week ago. The postmortem revealed that both had been shot and that, while Roberts had died of his wound, Blaydon had subsequently been sliced open from the groin to the breastbone and his body dumped in the pool. Technically, he had drowned to death because the bullet hadn't hit any major organs and he had been using his hands to hold his intestines inside rather than to swim to safety.

The major suspect, Leka Gashi, a member of the Shqiptare, the Albanian Mafia, was a 'business partner' of Blaydon's. The 'business' included money laundering and county lines drug dealing, two activities that could easily result in violence. The MO matched Gashi's style, too. He was suspected of being behind the murder of a Leeds dealer called Lenny G, also gutted, who had previously managed a county line.

There was no clear motive, but Gashi and Blaydon were old partners in crime. Gerry had recently discovered that the two had met in Corfu some twenty years ago, much earlier than she had originally thought. Blaydon had owned a villa there since about 2002, and he had kept his yacht, the *Nerea*, moored at a marina near Kavos for a few years before that. A falling-out among thieves was not unusual, in Banks's experience.

Because Gashi and his cronies had an alibi and were now thought to be hiding out in the Albanian countryside, the case would have been languishing in limbo until they found him, as they had no other leads. But just a couple of days ago a cache of MiniSD cards and a wad of cash amounting to £30,000 had been found hidden in a special compartment at the back of the wardrobe in the factotum's cubbyhole. Apparently, what none of the guests at Blaydon's famous parties had realised was that several of the bedrooms were fitted with minicams, which were motion- or sound-activated. This discovery, of course, raised the possibility that it was Neville Roberts, and not Blaydon, who was the intended victim. On further investigation, it turned out that Roberts used to be an audio and video technician until he was jailed for his part in the illegal surveillance of a client's business rival.

DI Annie Cabbot and DC Gerry Masterson, Banks's 'team', were patiently going through and logging the material on the cards. So far, they had found that Roberts's victims included judges, a local MP, one ex-chief constable, a pop singer, an American evangelist keen to make property investments, an award-winning film director, a bishop, a premier league footballer and a Scottish rugby international, among others. No royalty appeared to be involved, except a minor baronet, who didn't really count. All had enjoyed Blaydon's parties, fuelled by vast amounts of alcohol and cocaine and the loving attentions of hordes of beautiful young women, many of them probably *too* young.

But the most recent development had occurred just the previous day, when they came across what appeared to be a video recording of a rape among a number of films that Annie Cabbot called 'married-men-who-should-know-better shagging young girls'. There was something wrong with the recording, a technical fault it seemed, and the images were dark and blurred. Neither the rapist nor his victim was recognisable. A video technician Gerry knew at County HQ was working on an enhancement. And that was where things stood. Two separate cases, perhaps, but occurring in the same house and separated in time by only five weeks: Blaydon and Roberts had been killed on 22 May and the rape footage was dated 13 April.

Banks ran his hand over his hair and stopped thinking about the case for a few moments to listen to 'Cold Irons Bound', then checked his watch and headed for bed. He needed to be up bright and early in the morning to catch his train.

Before he fell asleep, snapshots of Tracy, from childhood to the present, flashed through his mind, and the last image that came was of her beaming in her wedding dress just as the ceremony ended. She was beaming at Mark. Banks had given her away, and then, as he had stood beside her, he had felt that he had lost something, though his heart was filled with happiness.

3

Zelda got up early to prepare herself for her journey to Purcari. She had never been in the far south-east of Moldova before, though she knew of its reputation for fine wines and beautiful landscapes. As she sat over her breakfast of fruit and yoghurt, she looked at the map she had bought the previous day and checked it against the Google Maps on her laptop. It wouldn't be an arduous journey. The fastest route would take her straight south-east and should take no longer than a couple of hours. Moldova wasn't a big country. She also had to check out of her hotel before she left and arrange to leave the rental car at the airport.

Her visits to the derelict orphanage and to William Buckley had thrown her askew, brought back feelings and memories she hadn't known she had, but she had enjoyed a good night's sleep – no nightmares or sweats, for once – and she felt ready to go on and bring her quest to an end. Lupescu would be the last one; she was almost certain of that.

She finished her breakfast and refilled her coffee cup. Her room was fine, but there wasn't much of a view except the car park below, so she sat cross-legged on the unmade bed and watched the BBC World News on TV. There was nothing new, and certainly nothing pleasant. She checked her email and sent Raymond a quick upbeat message.

The address she wanted was on the northern edge of Purcari, which wasn't a big place. Zelda still had no idea how she would play the confrontation with Vasile Lupescu, and every time she tried to imagine it, it turned out differently. She hadn't done a great deal of forward planning, and she couldn't do much now. Nor had she planned any sort of fail-safe escape. If all went well, she would have no problem doing what needed to be done and getting to the airport in Chișinău in time to drop off the car and make her flight to London. *If all went well.*

But the best-laid plans, in her experience, often went wrong. She had learned from her past that murder was an unpredictable business. There were too many variables. What if he wasn't in? What if he was surrounded by family? What if he simply refused to see her, shut the door in her face? What if he lived on a busy street and there were lots of people around? In these circumstances, Zelda realised, she might well have to abort. Or at least postpone. If things went smoothly, then she simply had to make sure that there was no chance of discovery before she was well on the way to London. With a little judicious cleaning up and a certain amount of care in not appearing too conspicuous, or being seen by too many people, that should be easy enough.

She worried a little about William Buckley. If he heard about anything happening to Lupescu, he would no doubt remember Zelda's visit. He might tell the police if they asked him, but why would they? And the odds were that he most likely wouldn't hear about it anyway. Besides, there was nothing she could do about it now. She didn't know how good the detectives were in Moldova, but she doubted they were up to the same level as Alan Banks and his team; there was surely no way they could trace and arrest her within a couple of hours. They had done nothing to find or help her when she was abducted.

Zelda showered and dressed, amazed at how calm she was

feeling. She held her hands out. No shakes. She didn't want to get caught. She wanted more than anything for it all to be over so she could get back to Raymond and get on with their life together in Yorkshire. Explore the world of painting and sculpture in more depth. Cook dinners for friends. Learn to enjoy that dreadful sixties music Raymond played. Try to persuade his daughter Annie that she wasn't such a monster. But then, she realised, she *was* a monster, wasn't she? How could she fool herself into believing otherwise? She shrugged off the thought. Lupescu would be the last one. Then she would put it all behind her. But she had to do this. Until she did, the past would keep growing, like a cancer inside her, consuming or blotting out all that was good in her life.

One thing she had to make sure she didn't forget, she thought, as she packed her bags ready for checkout, was the knife she had bought in the shopping mall yesterday after her meeting with William Buckley. She held it in her hand, saw the blade glint in the sunlight through the window, then slipped it into her handbag.

That following morning on the train, Banks relaxed in his seat, his mild hangover fading under the ministrations of two extra-strength paracetamol. He listened to Abdullah Ibrahim's *Dream Time* as he watched the summer landscape of the English heartland flash by: bright-coloured canal boats, anglers casting their lines from the grassy banks of large tree-lined ponds, farmers out working the fields, distant green woodlands, squat church towers with gold weathervanes catching the light. It could be another age, he thought, another country, not the troubled and troubling one he was living in. He succeeded in relaxing to such an extent that he drifted off to sleep before the music ended, and the sudden arrival at King's Cross came as a shock to his system.

Banks took off his headphones as the train disgorged its passengers, and merged with the rushing river of humanity. Unintelligible messages crackled over the loudspeakers, and travellers dashed for connections, dragging enormous wheeled suitcases behind them, running over toes and bumping thighs, oblivious to everyone else. Others stood and stared at signs and noticeboards as if lost.

Banks threaded his way through the crowds and took the escalator down to the Underground, where it got hotter and more humid the deeper he went. He found the right platform and took the Victoria Line to Vauxhall, standing all the way, and walked up behind the MI6 building, famous from the James Bond movies, to The Rose on the Albert Embankment, where Burgess had arranged to meet him. It was a Victorian pub, or gastro-pub, as it was called now, with a view of the Houses of Parliament, warm gold in the early afternoon sun, over the river beyond Lambeth Bridge.

Burgess was already waiting in a booth, and Banks joined him, glancing around at the chandeliers and vintage furniture. 'Very nice,' he said. 'At least the decor beats Pret's.'

Burgess passed Banks a menu. 'The food's supposed to be good,' he said. 'And not too expensive. Let's order first. I'm having the homemade fish-finger sandwich.'

Banks scanned the menu and settled on a roast beef burger with smoky chipotle mayo.

'Drink?' Burgess asked.

'What are you drinking?'

'Krombacher Pils.'

Again, Banks glanced at the menu. 'Brixton pale ale, please.' Hair of the dog.

Burgess went up to the bar. The pub was crowded, obviously a popular lunch spot for both local office workers and tourists walking along the riverside. And what a day for it.

Banks glanced out of the window at the throng of people walking up and down the Embankment in the heat of the midday sun. Most wore sunglasses, shorts, sandals and T-shirts. Many carried cameras, pushed prams or held hands with small children. He found himself thinking how quickly things could change if a terrorist with a knife ran into the crowd and started stabbing people. Or a speeding van suddenly veered off the road on to the pavement. It was the police officer's curse, he told himself, to be so often imagining the worst. But things like that *did* happen. Had happened not so long ago, not so far away, and would certainly happen again. Relish every moment, as his poet friend Linda Palmer had told him.

Burgess returned quickly with the drinks. Banks remembered how good he was at bars; not for him any worries about who was first in line. It was all to do with who could push hardest and shout loudest. Banks sipped. It tasted good. They chatted briefly about Burgess's morning of meetings up the road at NCA headquarters and Banks's journey through the heartland. Now, though, he was back in the present in the thriving capital, just upriver from the centre of power. He tried not to think about what nefarious business might be going on in there. Backstabbing and prevarication, for the most part, he guessed. Perhaps politics had always been like that, but it seemed to him to have taken a turn for the worse over the last three or four years.

'So what is it?' he asked. 'You said you were working on something that might concern me.'

Burgess leaned back. 'Don't get your hopes up too high. But, yes, I think it might.'

'In what way?'

'In two ways. That bloke you've been after for so long. The one who tried to kill you, set fire to your house.'

'Phil Keane.'

'That's one.'

'And the other?'

'That young woman you've got a thing for. Zelda.'

'I'm intrigued,' said Banks. 'Do go on.'

'It's a bit complicated. I've been trying to put it all in order while I was waiting for you.'

'Give it a try. I'm sure I'll be able to follow.'

Burgess took a deep breath, then a few gulps of beer. 'Right,' he said. 'You know about Zelda's boss?'

'Trevor Hawkins, the one who burned to death in a chip-pan fire?'

'That's the one. Well, the two officers who've been investigating his death, Deborah Fletcher and Paul Danvers, haven't found any evidence of foul play, but there are one or two anomalies, and Danvers isn't quite convinced that it was an accident. It seems that your friend Zelda visited the street where Hawkins lived a couple of days after the fire.'

'I know that,' said Banks. 'You told me all about it the last time we talked.'

'Hear me out. Allow me my preamble. It's difficult enough as it is.'

'OK.'

Their food came, and they took a few bites in silence then carried on talking while they ate. 'Paul Danvers was suspicious enough to widen his inquiry a bit, ask questions around the street and so on,' Burgess went on. 'They talked to Zelda again, for example, but she was about as helpful as the first time. Mmm, this fish is good. How about your burger?'

'It's fine,' Banks said. 'Zelda couldn't be helpful because she didn't know anything.'

Burgess raised an eyebrow. 'Are you sure about that?'

'What do you mean?'

'Let's not forget how important Hawkins was. He was an agent of the NCA, running a special bureau compiling a database and facial recognition data of known sex traffickers. Your friend Zelda worked for him as a civilian consultant, using her special skills as a super-recogniser and her experience of the trafficking world to put names to faces. That way, they could track the movements of major players, keep an eye on who was climbing up the ladder, who was in, who was out, and so on. The long and the short of it is that a young bartender down the road in Hawkins's local pub, The George and Dragon, recalls a woman coming in one lunchtime shortly after the fire and asking questions about Hawkins.'

'Like what?'

'Whether he was a regular. Whether he had ever met anyone there.'

'And what did he tell her?'

'That Hawkins was a regular, but that he usually only dropped in for a quick half and the *Times* crossword after work.'

'Usually?'

Burgess took a bite of his sandwich before answering. 'He said he did once, quite recently, see Hawkins meet and talk with another man in the pub. Said it appeared as if they knew one another and the meeting was prearranged. Apparently, the woman showed Chris – that's the bartender – a photograph, and he recognised the man from it.'

'Who was he?'

'That we don't know. And Chris wasn't able to give us a clear description. You know – medium, medium, light brown hair, ordinary. He had a beard, too. One of those artsy type thingies. Van Dyke or goatee, whatever they call it. He didn't know the man's name, either.'

'Pity.'

'There was one tiny pinprick of light.'

'Yes?'

'He certainly remembered the woman, and he gave us a very detailed description of her. Sounded as if he was more than a little smitten, so Danvers told me. And I have to say, Banksy, that she sounds remarkably like your Zelda.'

'What if it *was* her?' Banks asked, spearing a fat chip. 'It doesn't necessarily mean anything.'

'I disagree. Where's your copper's instinct? Don't you think it's odd? I mean, I can just about swallow that she visited her dead boss's burned-out house because she was curious. But asking questions in his local about who he'd been meeting is going a bit too far. Don't you think so? Why? And who was it in the photograph she showed Chris the barman?'

'So you think Zelda's involved?'

'We *know* that she didn't kill Trevor Hawkins. She was out of the country at the time of the fire. And neither Danvers nor I can accept that she somehow paid for it or arranged to have it done.'

'Which leaves?'

'Danvers's theory is that she was suspicious of Hawkins's activities. For some reason, she suspected him of being in the pay of the enemy, the traffickers, or somehow in thrall to them. Does that make any sense to you?'

Banks drank some beer and thought for a moment. 'I suppose it does,' he agreed reluctantly. 'But what of it?'

'Surely it's significant if she had some reason to suspect him of being bent? She may have been watching him, observing him at work, even following him. Maybe his trafficker paymasters found out, and he started to become a liability?'

'Are you saying Zelda was responsible for Hawkins's death?'

'I'm saying that she was sticking her nose in where it wasn't wanted. The outcome was unpredictable. Though anyone with half a brain could probably have worked out it would end in tears.'

'But we don't *know* any of this. It's mere speculation on your part.'

'As is so much of our job. And you know that, too. Come on, Banksy. Are you so pussy-whipped you can't see the wood for the trees?'

Banks bristled, but he knew Burgess was right. Up to a point. There was nothing sexual between him and Zelda. She was Ray Cabbot's partner, and he respected that. Even if he believed he was in with a chance, which he didn't, he wouldn't make a move on her. He didn't do things like that to his friends. Not that she had given the slightest inclination of interest. But, yes, he liked her company, and yes, he lusted after her. What man wouldn't?

'I'm *not* pussy-whipped, as you so delicately put it.'

'Sorry, mate,' said Burgess. 'Maybe that was below the belt. But I need my Banksy back, not some mealy-mouthed apologist.'

Banks tried to think rationally. He had to get beyond his bias and see things straight. At worst, Zelda could be involved in something dodgy, and at best she could be on the side of the good guys and in danger from the same people who had hurt Hawkins. And it would always be a good thing to keep in mind that Phil Keane was a killer, and that his preferred weapon was fire. But quite where Keane came into all this, Banks still had no idea, except that Zelda had said she had spotted him in a photo with Petar Tadić, a known sex trafficker. And that also connected with Blaydon's murder. The police knew that Tadić had supplied Blaydon with girls for his parties. What did it all mean? Did Hawkins know that Zelda had seen the photo and recognised Keane? How was he connected with Keane? Was Keane the man he had met in The George and Dragon?

'As far as I can see,' Banks said, 'even if Zelda did do everything you say, she's done nothing illegal.'

Burgess sighed. 'Hardly the point. Nobody's saying she's bent.'

'Then what?

'She *is* involved, and you know it. She's up to her neck in it. Whatever *it* is. If just for her sake, try and focus that laser-sharp mind of yours on all that. I'm trying to help you save her from herself, not getting you to convict her.' He finished his plate of food, pushed it aside, gulped down some lager and burped. 'Besides, that's not all. It gets even more interesting.'

The drive to Purcari was easier than Zelda had expected, and she was passing a winery on the outskirts of the village before noon. It was a journey of low hills, soft greens and yellows, opening occasionally on distant panoramas; a journey of small villages, mostly neat and tidy and colourful, and with no one about except roaming cats and the occasional barking dog. Here and there, geese and chickens wandered the roadsides, and in some places, old women in traditional garb paused and eyed her sternly as she drove slowly by. Sometimes she imagined they knew what she was going to do. It was more like travelling back in time than in distance. The sun shone all the way, and she kept the windows of the old Skoda rolled down. Off the main highway, the paved roads were of variable quality, and she saw signs on them now and then that said, 'PAID FOR BY THE AMERICAN PEOPLE.'

At last, the chateau came into view, with its tower, white walls and orange roof against a backdrop of hillsides planted with rows of vines. Beyond the hills, Zelda knew, lay the River Dniester and Ukraine. She paused at a crossroads to breathe

the sweet air, and a gentle breeze wafted through the open car windows. She could smell manure and fresh-mown grass.

Lupescu's house, at some distance from any neighbours, was a contemporary construction in the Art Deco style, all white cubes and curves, topped with a large dome, like an observatory, and shiny, as if it were made out of plastic. It was hard to find a point of entry, but Zelda thought she discerned a door somewhere in the whiteness. There was no doorbell, so she knocked. She had realised a while ago that there was no point in trying to sneak up on Lupescu as he wouldn't know her from Eve. The last time he had seen her, she had been an excited seventeen-year-old girl on the verge of making her own way in the world.

At first, she thought there was no one home. Everything was silent except for the birdsong and someone hammering far in the distance. Perhaps Lupescu was old and slow, like William Buckley. Then the door opened abruptly and she found herself looking at the man himself. He was probably about five years younger than Buckley, she guessed, and had been retired for around ten years, which made him roughly mid-seventies. His skin was sallow, and the flesh on his cheeks and throat sagged into wattles and jowls. His hooded eyes, buried deep above the bruise-coloured bags, were pale and glaucous. He had very little hair, and what he had he wore in an absurd comb-over across his liver-spotted skull. But it was Vasile Lupescu, no doubt about it.

He spoke to her in Russian. 'Yes? Can I help you? What is it you want?'

'I was just speaking with William Buckley in Suruceni,' she said, also in Russian, hoping the speech she had rehearsed on her way came out right. 'He said if I was heading down south I should say hello. So here I am.'

'And you are?'

'You knew me as Nelia Melnic. One of the beneficiaries of Claude Bremner's largesse. And your hard work, of course.'

Lupescu frowned.

'The books,' Zelda explained. 'At St George's Orphanage.'

Lupescu's thin lips twitched in a smile. 'Ah, yes. The books. Please, do come in. Forgive my bad manners. I'm an old man and not much used to visitors.'

'Not at all.' Zelda stepped inside. In contrast to its bright exterior, she found the interior dark and dull, lightened only by abstract paintings sharing the walls with knock-off old masters and surrealist sculptures in nooks adjacent to ancient religious icons. Other than that, with its sepia and grey tones, it felt more like a tomb. She also got the impression that Lupescu's cleaning lady didn't come nearly as often as William Buckley's. How could anyone live here? she found herself wondering. Then she realised that it was probably more an indication of status than aesthetic pleasure, and that made sense. *This was a man who wanted to show the world that he had made money.*

Lupescu himself was wearing red carpet slippers, baggy grey trousers and a button-up maroon cardigan over his white shirt, despite the temperature, and he looked like nothing more than an old man near the end of his time who had no idea what to do or how to go about it. The cardigan was open and Zelda noticed a reddish stain down the front. Pasta sauce, she guessed.

'Would you care to sit down?' he asked, gesturing to a leather-upholstered armchair. Zelda sat and felt immediately as if she were falling backwards down a bottomless pit. The seat sagged under her, and she was sure she felt the prick of a spring where she least wanted it. She shuffled around a bit, rested her arms on the scuffed leather and managed to acquire a modicum of comfort. Lupescu sat opposite her in a similar chair. He didn't offer refreshments.

Zelda glanced around at the paintings. Most of the abstracts were probably original works. Some of them were quite good, she thought, though she would have been the first to admit she wasn't exactly the best judge of abstract art. For the most part they looked as if someone had stood near the canvas and flicked brushes dipped in various coloured paints in random patterns, which is probably exactly what had happened.

Zelda found herself wondering whether Lupescu liked this stuff or whether it was merely another instance of fortune-signalling. They made quite a contrast to the madonnas and classical scenes hung adjacent to many of them. The sculptures were better, she thought. Smooth, round, curving objects with surprising holes and twists in them, mostly made of wood, crying out to be stroked, though a couple seemed to be cast from brass. She ran her hand over a small wooden infinity figure within reach that seemed to languish over its base like Dali's watches melted over their surfaces.

'So you're a St George's girl?' Lupescu said.

'I was,' Zelda replied. 'A long time ago.'

'Yes,' Lupescu said. 'The old place has been closed for ten years or more now. A great loss. I was sorry to see it go. I was there right from the beginning, you know.'

'So I heard. Tell me, were you selling girls to sex traffickers right from the start, or did that come later?' She hadn't planned for it to come out that way, or so soon, but it did.

Lupescu seemed to freeze. He might have turned pale, but Zelda couldn't tell, as he was so ashen to start with. 'What do you mean by that?' he said, a quiver in his voice.

'Well, when I left St George's, two men were waiting for me at the street corner. They hit me and bundled me into a car and drove me across Romania, raping me all the way, until they dropped me off at a breaking house in Serbia. Do you know what a breaking house is?'

'But that's got nothing to do with me,' Lupescu spluttered. 'How can you assume I had anything to do with that?'

'It's a house where they break in the new girls. That means rape, day and night, beatings, humiliation, starvation, until you toe the line.'

'No!' said Lupescu, shaking his head so that his jowls wobbled, and half rising from his chair. 'I won't listen to this. That wasn't me. You can't blame that on me.'

'I'm not saying you're the one who did it, just that you're the one responsible. You're the one who made all the arrangements, who knew all the details, the one who spotted the pretty girls. I met others over the years, you know. In Pristina. In Zagreb. In Ljubljana. In Sarajevo. Girls who suffered the same fate in the same way as I did. Girls from the orphanage who were marked, chosen. One of them even saw you out on the street, watching as it happened. But you didn't call the police. You did nothing. That was Iuliana. Do you remember her? She killed herself. Slit her wrists. Nobody ever came looking for any of us.'

Lupescu shrank back into his chair. 'What could I do?' he said. 'These men were powerful gangsters. They had guns. You have no idea. You had a good life at the orphanage, didn't you? You were well taken care of. Taught. Fed. Coddled.'

'I suppose we were,' Zelda agreed. 'Like free-range chickens being fed and readied for the slaughter.'

'But what could I do?'

Zelda sat up and leaned towards him, half standing, her palms on the arms of the chair. 'You could have stopped it! You could have gone to the police. You . . .' She shook her fist at him. Then she made an effort and calmed herself down, subsided deep into the armchair again. 'I think it would be better if you confessed before your punishment, don't you?'

'Why? What punishment? What are you going to do to me? I'm an old man. I'm sick. I've got health problems. Heart. Diabetes.' Lupescu's eyes darted about the room, as if searching for a way out or for someone to come to his aid.

'You should have thought about your health problems back then,' said Zelda. 'Though I doubt anybody could have done anything about your heart, however hard they tried.'

Lupescu tried to get to his feet, but age had slowed him. In one smooth movement Zelda stood up, picked up the infinity sculpture from the table beside her and hit him on the side of the head. He sagged back in his chair, then slid to the floor, a trail of blood spoiling the symmetry of his comb-over.

'If there's more,' said Banks, 'I think I'll need another pint. You, too? My shout.'

'Go on, then,' said Burgess. 'You've twisted my arm. It's just a bloody boring security roster meeting this afternoon. I can easily sleep through that and nobody will notice.'

Banks went to the bar, his head still whirling with Burgess's story, connections spinning like plates on sticks. He wasn't quite as brash as Dirty Dick, but the bar wasn't too crowded, and he managed to get served quickly enough. As usual in London, he was gobsmacked at the price of two pints.

'You realise that we've probably consumed our entire weekly allowance of alcohol units this one lunchtime,' Burgess said when Banks got back. Then he contemplated the remains of the roast beef burger. 'Not to mention you being responsible for a few more icebergs melting in Antarctica.'

'It always puzzled me, that,' said Banks.

'What?'

'If cow farts are bad for the environment, how would stopping eating beef help?'

'If we didn't eat beef, we wouldn't need cows, stupid.'

'So what would we do with them to stop cow farts for ever? Kill them all and burn their bodies?'

'Well, no. Burning that many cows might cause environmental problems, too. Carbon emissions.'

'Not to mention that we'd be guilty of the genocide of a species. *Bovicide.* That can't be good, surely?'

'Talk to David Attenborough. I'm sure he'd put you right on the matter.'

'Or perhaps we should put them all in a big building where they can fart to their hearts' content, and we can use the gas to run the country.'

'We've already done that,' said Burgess. 'It's over there.' He pointed out of the window towards the Houses of Parliament.

Banks laughed.

'As I was saying,' Burgess went on, 'there's more. But first off, remember, I'm trying to do you a favour.'

'What's that?'

Burgess sighed and ran his hand over his lank hair. 'Danvers and Debs don't trust your Zelda for a number of reasons. You have to admit, she has a very shady past.'

'Shady?' said Banks. 'She was snatched off the street at the age of seventeen and forced to work as a prostitute for nearly ten years before she escaped the life.'

'I know that. But do you know *how* she escaped?'

'It's all a bit vague,' Banks admitted. 'Something happened in Paris, something big, something to do with the government, and it was hushed up. She obviously helped some very influential people with a problem. That's how she got her freedom and her French passport.'

'No details?'

'No.'

'Me, neither,' said Burgess. 'But don't you think it all sounds as fishy as that sandwich I just finished? Maybe she didn't *help* anyone; maybe she *blackmailed* them. You have to see it from the NCA's point of view. And from that of immigration. She *has* lived a nomadic life – she's never filled in any appropriate immigration or residence forms, she's filed no tax returns, her passport was not exactly official issue, and she spent most of her working life as a prostitute, which could reasonably be conceived as criminal. All in all, she's not the kind of person Britannia Unchained wants. We have plenty of prostitutes of our own without importing them from Europe, or anywhere else, thank you very much.'

'That's not *her* fault,' Banks argued. You make it sound as if it was *her* choice. She wasn't working as a prostitute, she was a sex slave, subject to rape, to violent beatings. Ever since she was abducted outside that orphanage, her life hasn't been her own. Until she came here. And now you're trying to take that life away from her.'

'*I* know all that, Banksy. And I'm not trying to take anything away from her. I'm just telling you how Danvers and Debs and their mates at the NCA and Immigration Enforcement might view things differently. She's on their radar now. I'm trying to keep her out of their hands and let you deal with it. I'm trying to do you both a favour, mate. But we need *some* answers from somewhere.'

'OK, so now I know. What am I supposed to do?'

'It's awkward,' Burgess said. 'And getting more so. They want to bring her in for questioning.'

'Danvers and Debs?'

'Yes. And someone else. There's more.'

Banks frowned. 'All right. Go on.'

'Ever heard the name Faye Butler?'

'I can't say as I have.'

'No reason why you should have. It's a case I took an interest in recently. It wasn't one of ours to start with. It was a Met case, and a Commander Barclay was in charge. I've known Ted Barclay for years, and after a few days he called me in. It's a strange one, all right. Disturbing, too. About a week ago, some young lads playing near the river down Woolwich way found a young woman's body snagged on a tree branch half out of the water. She hadn't been in there more than a day or two. At the post-mortem, it was discovered that she had died by drowning, but not in the river. The water in her lungs was tap water, not the Thames variety. It also turned out that she had been tortured. There was evidence of burn marks, as if from electrodes, of cuts, and significant bruising. Three of her teeth were missing and two fingernails. It was also clear to the pathologist that she had been sexually assaulted.'

'Bloody hell,' said Banks. 'The poor girl.'

'Indeed. Her name was Faye Butler, and she worked at Foyles on Charing Cross Road, in the art section. She was twenty-eight years old. Her body was found on 23 May. That was a Thursday.' Banks remembered. It was the same day he and Gerry Masterson had found Blaydon's body in the pool. 'Her flatmate in Camden Town had reported her missing.' Burgess paused to drink some pilsner. 'You know as well as I do, Banksy, what it's like with missing persons. You do your best to reassure the family or friends that nothing bad's happened, that it's perfectly normal for a young woman not to come home one night without phoning or anything. But it fucking isn't. We know it isn't. And from the moment you take the first call, you get that cramped feeling in your gut, and you just know that something's wrong.'

Banks knew the feeling. Missing persons were some of the hardest cases to handle if you let your imagination run away with you. Especially young girls. You could picture terrible things happening while you were reassuring the rest of the world that she would probably come walking in full of apologies at any moment, tell you that she'd stopped at her boyfriend's and just forgot to mention it to anyone. 'What happened next?' he asked.

'We made inquiries, but they didn't lead us anywhere. Naturally, the boyfriend came in for a bit of grief. Bloke called Grant Varney. They'd been together about three months. He said he hadn't arranged to see her that night and that she hadn't called around at his place. There were some of her things there – clothes, books, cosmetics, toothbrush – and apparently, she spent a fair bit of time there with him. They hadn't made any final commitment to live together or anything, but he said he was hoping she would agree to a more permanent arrangement. He knew she was still on the rebound at the moment, he said, and he was willing to wait. Varney was devastated. Ted said he thought he was a decent kid, and he was cleared pretty quickly. We did reconstructions of her route home, talked to people who took the same route, had seen her on occasion, but nobody noticed anything out of the ordinary.'

'How did she travel?'

'Faye usually walked home as long as it wasn't pissing down. She'd head up Tottenham Court Road, then Hampstead Road, and on a nice evening she'd cut through St Martin's Gardens on Camden Street. One witness thought she saw her talking with a man in the gardens, walking towards the road. She didn't get a good look at him, so we have no description except that he was stocky and was wearing a black T-shirt and ice blue jeans, but she did say that Faye seemed quite at ease, as if she knew him. You know, she didn't appear uncomfortable or scared, wasn't trying to get away. And the man wasn't in physical contact with her. He didn't grab her or anything. As far as our witness could tell she was just walking along chatting with a friend.'

'And that was the last time she was seen alive?'

'Yes. Except by her killer, of course. And he must have had transport of some kind. Her body was found some distance away from Camden. But nobody saw her getting into a car. We've had appeals out and done reconstructions, but no one's come forward with any new information and we got nothing from CCTV. It was as if she just disappeared into space.'

'He must have had a car waiting nearby,' said Banks. 'And maybe an accomplice.'

'We thought of that. I think you're probably right, but nobody remembers anything. It's also likely she got in the car willingly, if it was someone she knew.'

'I agree it's a nasty one,' said Banks, 'but where do I come in? And Zelda?'

'When we made inquiries at Faye's place of work, one of her colleagues told us that she was working the third floor about a week before the disappearance, and this woman came around asking for Faye. The colleague said she sent her to the ground floor, where we found out that she asked a lad called Lee Wong about Faye. Lee went and fetched her. The two of them chatted, then went upstairs to the cafe. Lee said he didn't know Faye well, but we talked to some more of her work-mates, and they all said the usual. You know, what a fine person she was – nice girl, always cheerful, helpful and so on. Ask about the dead and you'd think we were all saints. It was the flatmate, Agnes Hall, who told us that Faye had been a bit down in the dumps for a while after splitting up with her previous boyfriend. Apparently, she found him in flagrante with another girl.'

'Any idea who he was?'

'We couldn't get any further questioning Agnes or Faye's friends at work. No one remembered the ex enough to give more than the vaguest of descriptions. As far as Agnes knew,

Faye had never invited him back to the flat. At least not while she was there. Medium height, good-looking, light brown hair, small beard, no particular accent. Rather like the barman's description from The George and Dragon, I thought. Only she added she thought the hair was maybe just a bit *too* light brown.'

'Dye job?'

'Sounds like it. He'd been in the shop a couple of times, apparently, chasing after an art book, and that's how he and Faye first met. All her workmates knew was that his first name was Hugh. A couple of them told us they thought he was too old for Faye, despite the hair. Naturally, he became a person of interest very quickly.'

'Any luck?'

'No. Not at first. But when we searched Faye's flat, we found some printed selfies of her with a bloke taken in Regent's Park, and it wasn't Grant Varney. This bloke was medium height, good-looking, light brown hair, little beard.'

'Age?'

'In his mid-forties, maybe, but well preserved. Could've been older. Fifty, even.'

'Hugh?'

'The roommate confirmed it. The dates matched, too. They'd been taken around Christmas – you could tell by the lights and decorations – a few months after she took up with him, and not too long before they split up. Her mobile went missing with her, but we found her laptop in the flat, and there were emails from a bloke called Hugh Foley. We couldn't trace him from them, though, and the email address is no longer in use. There was no entry for him in her contacts list.'

'Anything in the emails?'

'Plenty,' said Burgess. 'All along the lines of, "I can't wait to suck your throbbing—"'

'I catch the drift,' said Banks.

'That's from her, by the way. The ones from him seem to involve agricultural metaphors, mostly to do with ploughing and irrigation. No addresses, mobile numbers or arrangements to meet.'

'I assume they did all that through texts, or maybe even over the phone. Again, I'm having a bit of trouble working out how I could be involved. Unless you've got something up your sleeve. Something you're not telling me.'

'Just two things,' Burgess said. 'First, the description of the woman asking about Faye Butler in Foyles bears a remarkable similarity to Chris the barman's description of Zelda, right down to the faint accent, and secondly, well, see for yourself.' Burgess dropped a photograph on the table in front of Banks.

Banks stared at it and his jaw dropped. Despite a few minor cosmetic changes – hairline and colour, the addition of a light beard – the man in the selfies with Faye Butler, the man who went by the name of Hugh Foley, was a ringer for Phil Keane.

'Jesus Christ,' Banks muttered, pushing the photograph aside. 'And what's the link with Zelda?'

'Ted Barclay would like to have her brought in to talk to her, too, and maybe find out the answer to that. Which is where you come in. I managed to persuade Ted to let you have a go first, told him you were familiar with aspects of her background and so on. I also lied a bit. Told him you were an excellent detective, and as you already knew her, and she trusted you, you'd be far more likely to get something out of her. He didn't like it, but he agreed to give us some leeway.'

'Why did you do that? Why are you being so helpful to Zelda?'

'For fuck's sake, Banksy. I might not be as soft-hearted as you – or maybe I *am* getting soft in my old age – but I'm not the cold and calculating bastard you sometimes paint me as. I don't know this Zelda. I've never met her. But a woman like her, what she's been through, what she's suffered, it almost beggars the imagination. You've met her, and you know her. And I trust your judgement, even if I do think it's a little biased by female pulchritude. God knows, I've made enough errors in that direction myself, over the years. But can you imagine the effect that being interrogated might have on her, not to mention any detention and imprisonment that might result? Does it sound so strange that I don't particularly want her put through the ringer with Danvers and Debs and Ted Barclay? If she's as fragile as many of the women who've been through what she's been through, it could do her permanent damage. I don't think she's killed anyone. Not Hawkins. Not Faye Butler. If I thought she had, I'd have her in before her feet could touch the street. But she *knows* something. It's all connected. I'm giving you the chance to find out what that is. And now Keane's involved, too. You know he is. And don't forget that photograph of him with Petar Tadić. Petar is certainly a person of interest, along with his brother Goran. These are people from Zelda's past, and now they're starting to figure in our present. It's all tangled up in a knot, and until we manage to sort out one or two threads, your lady friend is going to be a target. You can help her, Banksy. I'm giving you the chance. Talk to her. Loosen her up a bit. Are you going to take it?'

He was right, Banks knew. Zelda affected a tough veneer, but he had seen beyond that to the seething fears, anxieties and conflicting emotions underneath; the guilt and self-loathing, shame, despair and depression that she tried to suppress and overcome. He saw something else, too, a sort of steely purpose, a sense of quest or mission, perhaps.

Banks shook his head slowly, reached for his glass and murmured, 'Of course I'm going to bloody well take it. Of course I am.'

4

By the time Lupescu came round, Zelda had him trussed up on the sofa. As soon as he realised the predicament he was in, he asked for a glass of water and a bottle of pills from the kitchen table. Zelda checked the pills. They were sublingual nitroglycerin, for angina. He drank the water first then put a pill under his tongue. She used a damp cloth to wipe the blood from the side of his head. He winced as she did so.

'What is it you want?' he said. 'Money?'

Zelda took out her knife and glanced around at the paintings. 'Seems as if you have plenty to spare,' she said. 'It must have been hard buying all this artwork on an orphanage director's salary.' Zelda touched the knife to his throat. He flinched. 'You can cut the lies and excuses. We both know what you did. You sold me to the Tadić brothers. Me and the other girls.'

'Who?'

Zelda was thrown. Was she wrong about all this? Had she jumped to the wrong conclusion? 'The Tadić brothers,' she repeated. 'Petar and Goran.'

'I don't know them.'

Of course not. 'Just the drivers,' Zelda whispered, almost to herself. Then she prodded him again and drew a bead of blood. 'You dealt with their boss, didn't you? Who was he?'

'I still don't know who you're talking about.' She could tell from his eyes that he was lying now.

'The man you sold us to. Would you rather I went to the authorities and told them my story? Then they could investigate your actions and your finances, find other girls to testify against you. Send you to jail. Confiscate everything you own.'

'Or what? Or you'll kill me? You're going to kill me, anyway, aren't you?'

'Perhaps. But whatever happens, I want to hear you admit what you did to me and the others first.'

Lupescu paused, as if weighing his chances, determining which direction to go. He licked his lips. 'All right, then. Say I did what you're accusing me of. What then?'

'Don't you think you deserve punishment?'

'You've got it all wrong,' Lupescu said. 'I'm not a monster or a pervert. They forced me to do it.'

'Forced you? How?'

'They threatened my family.'

Zelda felt as if a trickle of icy water had run down her spine. 'They did what?'

'They threatened me. My daughters. The twins. They were thirteen at the time. *Thirteen.* And the man said if I didn't do what he asked, he would take them and my wife instead and put them in brothels so bad they would be dead within a week.'

Zelda let her knife hand drop, though she held on to the handle. She had known brothels like that but survived to tell the tale. Lupescu was shaking now, with tears in his eyes. If he was lying, she thought, he was a good actor. But how could she tell? She had assumed that Buckley had nothing to do with what happened, but she could even be wrong about that. Was she judging the man who gave the books against the man who sat in the office? But no. She must stop second-guessing herself. William Buckley had nothing to do with St George's apart from donating the boxes of books. Zelda had never seen or heard of him before yesterday. But Lupescu was there all the time, handled the day-to-day running of the place, knew who was leaving, when and how, where they were going. Maybe he was forced into it, as he claimed, but he was certainly guilty of it.

'What did they ask you to do?' she went on.

'Tip them off when a pretty girl was leaving. I didn't know what they were going to do with you.'

'I'll bet you had a good idea.'

'I didn't ask. I couldn't let myself think about it. My lovely twins . . . my wife . . .' Lupescu hung his head. 'Please believe me.'

Zelda passed him the water again. 'How many girls?'

He looked up, horrified, and after a brief silence whispered, 'Twelve.'

Zelda froze. *Twelve girls*. Sold into slavery like her. How many hadn't survived? How many had killed themselves or tried to escape and been beaten to death? How many had died of disease, drugs or violence? It hardly bore thinking about. How could Lupescu live with himself? She felt the anger rise in her, and her hand tightened around the knife handle as she raised it. Lupescu shuddered and cringed like a frightened reptile, edging away as best he could. 'No!' he said. 'It wasn't my fault. I had to do it. You must understand. I had to! For my family.'

'You could have gone to the police.'

'That wouldn't have stopped them. You know that. There are always more. And they buy the police.'

'This man who came to you. What was his name?'

'I don't know. Honestly. He was Hungarian. He was in charge. I just called him The Hungarian.'

'What about the money?'

'What money?'

Zelda gestured around the house with the knife blade. 'Come on. All this. The house, the works of art. Like I said before, you couldn't afford it on your orphanage director's salary. How much did they pay you?'

Lupescu hung his head again, and when he spoke he muttered so softly that she could barely hear him. 'Five thousand dollars for each girl.'

Zelda felt her muscles tense and the breath tighten in her throat. So that was what her life had been worth. Five thousand dollars. They had made more than that out of her in the first few months. Multiply that by twelve. And the years. She couldn't stop herself from slapping him backhanded across the face, hard. He grunted and his top lip split, spilling blood on to his chin. She hit him again.

'Stop,' he pleaded. 'I told you. They threatened my family. I'm sick. You'll kill me.'

'And I had no family,' Zelda said. She didn't know why she said it; the words just seemed to come out of nowhere. It hardly mattered whether she had a family or not. But she couldn't help herself. 'Like I wasn't worth anything to anyone except men like that. You bastard. You selfish, evil bastard!' She punctuated each syllable with another slap until his skin was raw and his nose was broken and bleeding.

'Please stop,' he sobbed. 'I'm sorry. I'm sorry. My heart.'

'You took their money. Admit it.'

'Yes. But only later. When they made me.'

'What do you mean? You told me they threatened your wife and your daughters.'

'They did! This was later. They made me take their money.'

'Why would they do that if they could force you to do what they wanted for nothing?'

'To make me complicit,' Lupescu said. He licked the blood from his lips and lifted his tied hands up to wipe his nose on his forearm. His voice was hoarse. 'Don't you understand? There was always a chance I might go to the police and tell them everything in exchange for protection for me and my family. Or that they might come around to St George's asking questions. I wouldn't have told the police anything, of course, but they didn't know that. I was too scared for my daughters. If they paid me, I couldn't tell the authorities without implicating myself. Don't you see? The payments went into my bank account. It was their insurance, their way of making certain I did what they wanted, that I was no different from them. There's not a day gone by when I haven't regretted it, but what could I do?'

'Well, you bought the house, didn't you?' Zelda flopped back in her chair and looked at Lupescu, shaking her head. The money they had paid him was her insurance, too, that he wouldn't talk. She had killed Goran Tadić, one of the brothers who had abducted her in Chişinău, and she had killed Darius, her vicious French pimp, and she didn't regret either murder for a moment. But she didn't consider herself a cold-blooded murderer. And this time, she just couldn't do it. Or didn't want to. She felt dirty and cowardly for beating this pathetic tied-up old man, whether he was telling the truth about his motives or not, and the whole encounter was fast making her feel disgusted and empty, even of hatred.

Lupescu had been responsible for her abduction from the street and her subsequent years as a sex slave, but she couldn't bring herself to kill him. He wasn't the one who had abducted her and sold her; he had only tipped off The Hungarian when she would be leaving the orphanage. That was the extent of his participation. She was still angry, twisted up in knots inside, but if she believed him – that they had threatened his family – what man wouldn't have done what he did in that situation? It wasn't that she forgave him; she could never do that. Twelve girls in his charge had been sold into lives of unbelievable humiliation, pain and terror at his say-so. But would it have been better if his thirteen-year-old daughters and his wife had suffered that fate instead? What kind of a bargain was that? How could you reckon such a calculation? No matter how you played the figures, they came out wrong.

So Zelda put her knife back in her bag, glanced down in contempt at the sobbing, bleeding old man hunched on the sofa, and left. Someone would find him and free him, or he would work his own way free eventually. Or maybe he would die of a heart attack. It was all the same to her. One thing she knew was that, if he lived, he could never breathe a word to another soul about what had happened here today without implicating himself.

'So what did this cost you?' DI Annie Cabbot asked, fingering the picture Gerry had laid out on her desk.

'More than you could ever know.'

'Seriously? Oh, get away with you. You didn't, did you?'

Gerry laughed. 'No, I'm joking.'

'So, what? You don't get this kind of service for free, in my experience.'

'He asked me out to dinner, that's all.'

'And you agreed?'

'Well, I had to, really, didn't I?'

'That's coercion, Gerry. You don't have to put up with it, you know. Haven't you heard of #MeToo? You should report him.'

Gerry blushed. 'No, it's fine. He's quite nice, actually.'

'Quite nice?' Annie rolled her eyes. 'That sounds like the beginning of a torrid love affair.'

'I'm not after a torrid love affair, but I'll be quite happy to go out for dinner with him. He didn't coerce me. As a matter of fact, I've had my eye on him for a while, so there.'

'You and Jared Lyall from tech support? Well, I never. Who'd have guessed it.' Annie paused. 'Still, I suppose he *is* rather cute, in a Justin Bieber sort of way.'

Gerry punched her arm lightly. 'Anyway,' she said, 'he told me there wasn't a lot he could do. The tech was right, there was some fault with the minicam. Something to do with fields and pixels and so on. Like sound sampling, missing bits out, only you can't always put them back. I'm afraid I'm not very well up on the technical language, but he said what he had done was mostly guesswork, trying to imagine what might be missing and replacing it. That's why it took him so long. It's quite a work of art. There was nothing he could do with the rapist. He never showed his face, or anything else, like one of those faces on TV they have to blank out.'

'Could it have been?' Annie asked. 'Tampered with? Blanked out?'

'Jared says not. It's all to do with his position and what little light there was. Besides, it would have been difficult for someone to get just the rapist's face blanked out and his victim's visible, no matter how distorted she is. I still think he's done a pretty good job with the girl. Jared also ran this reconstruction through our facial recognition software, too, but he came up with nothing. Still, we'd hardly expect *her* to be in the system.'

'Maybe it was because of the poor image quality,' Annie said. 'Couldn't Jared just enhance it more? I've seen them do it on TV. You make a square around the bit you want enlarged and keep pressing enter.'

Gerry laughed. 'Yeah, we tried that.'

'Well, what happened?'

'The bit we marked out got bigger and bigger and in the end you couldn't tell what it was. It was just a bunch of dots with spaces between them, like a piece of abstract art. Jackson Pollock or something.'

'Ray likes Jackson Pollock. Oh, well. So much for TV. I'll never believe anything I see in future.'

'It's not a video recording,' Gerry said. 'It was recorded on to a microSD card through a high-end mini spy-cam working on a motion sensor. The problem is that the bedroom was very dark, a room without windows, or so it seems. Usually the cams compensate for that, especially the expensive ones, but this one wasn't doing a good job. It just wasn't working properly.'

'I'm surprised Roberts didn't return it to Amazon.'

Gerry rolled her eyes. 'Jared worked from the original SD card, and he did his best with what he had.'

'I'm sure he did.' Annie held the image at arm's length. 'I think we may have a possible recognisable likeness here. It wouldn't stand up in court, but . . . maybe her own mother might recognise her.'

'As I said, it's the best Jared can do. I think we have to go with it. He said we could send the card away to a tech lab in London, and they *might* be able to salvage a sharper image, but that would take weeks, for a start, and cost a fortune, with no guarantee. What we've got now is a hell of a lot better than what we had. I'm pretty sure I could recognise her from that, if I saw her. If I knew her. We need to show it around to people who might have been at that party.'

'When we find out who they are,' said Annie.

The enhanced image showed a young girl in semi-profile. It was a segment from after the rape, when the rapist had gone and she had turned over on to her side and curled up in the foetal position. Her eyes were glazed and her jaw slack, but there was just enough definition to her features to make identification possible. The waifish look and the short hair were clear enough, and they had already estimated from the original footage, measuring her against the length of the bed, that she was maybe five foot seven or eight in height, or about 170 centimetres. It was impossible to tell her age beyond estimating that she was probably in her late teens.

Annie and Gerry watched the recording again, and it was even clearer that the girl was being raped, perhaps because they had a stronger idea of what she looked like. She had no chance. The man threw her down on the bed, ripped off her clothes and raped her. It didn't last long. Her struggles were weak and ineffective because she was clearly drunk or drugged, and after a while she didn't resist at all. There was no sound, so it was impossible to tell if she had screamed or called out, but when he left her half-naked among the rumpled bedsheets, she appeared to be sobbing.

And there the recording ended.

'Do you remember seeing the girl in any of the other videos?' Annie asked.

'No. Those women were all Tadić's hookers. Or at least we assume they were. None of them resembled her, at any rate, and they seemed to at least pretend they liked what they were doing.'

'It's true she doesn't look like a classy hooker.'

'Maybe she was working behind the scenes?'

'Possible,' said Annie. 'We need to find out how the parties were set up and organised. How people got invited. I know we've already recognised a few prominent figures from what we've watched, but there must have been other people there, ones we wouldn't recognise. Ones who might be more likely to talk to us. Someone must have seen something. Were any of the other films taken at the same party?'

'Only two,' said Gerry. 'I checked them out, and they were both fine as far as quality goes. Different rooms, too. So it was clearly just that one defective camera.'

'Who have we got?'

'One of them I recognise, but it's a woman.'

'Did Blaydon or Tadić supply men for fun, too?'

'Er . . . well, maybe,' said Gerry. 'But, I mean, it's not a man she's—'

'Another woman?'

'That's right.'

'Who is it?'

'Rosemary Vale.'

'No! You mean that actress? The one in that costume drama that's on at the moment?'

'That's the one,' Gerry said.

'She's gay? I don't believe it.'

'Well, you would if you watched the video.'

'OK. Who's in the other video?'

'Craig Lonegan.'

'What, that footballer with the big house out Swainshead way?'

'That's the one.'

'And what's he doing, or need I ask?'

'I'd blush if I told you,' said Gerry. 'But it involves rubber sheets and cooking oil, and whatever it is, he appears to be enjoying it.'

'We need to have a crack at them,' said Annie. 'One of them might have seen something. At the very least they might be able to fill out the guest list a bit.'

'Do you think it could have been Blaydon himself?'

'I suppose it's possible,' Annie said, 'but there's no way you could even guess from what we've got, let alone prove it. It could have been any one of a number of people.'

'What it amounts to, then,' said Gerry, 'is that we don't know who the girl is or who she was with. She's definitely quite young, and she's not the same type as the others, if that's not a terribly judgemental thing to say. But that's all we know about her.'

Annie smiled. 'I wouldn't worry about being judgemental,' she said. 'I'm the last one to judge you on your woke quotient. Besides, it's our job to make judgements about certain things. No matter what "type" she is, she's somebody's daughter, and it's our job to find out who she is and get the perpetrator behind bars. If there is a connection with Blaydon's murder, then all well and good, that might come out, too. What about guest lists for the parties? They must be somewhere.'

'There's that woman who used to work as Blaydon's personal assistant,' Gerry said. 'Remember her? She's on our list. Her name's Charlotte Westlake, and she lives near Leeds.'

'Right. If she was working for Blaydon back in April, she might be able to point us in the right direction.'

'Any more ideas?'

Annie shook her head, then said, 'Except that Zelda knows the Tadić brothers. I know she's talked to Alan about them, and in the photo of Keane she saw, he was with Petar Tadić. If they supplied the women for the parties, maybe she could shed some light on things?'

'Where is the super today, by the way?'

'London,' said Annie. 'Left early this morning. And very cagey about it. Some sort of mysterious appointment.'

'What about Timmy and Tommy Kerrigan?' Gerry suggested. 'I know we've interviewed them about the murders, but remember those photos taken around the pool in the cache, too? People having fun, letting their hair down. Timmy and Tommy feature in some of them. They don't seem to be doing anything illegal, unless smoking big cigars and drinking extremely large glasses of whisky is illegal now.'

'And wearing skimpy thong swimming trunks if you look like Timmy Kerrigan,' Annie added.

Gerry laughed at the image. 'Right,' she said. 'Well, it seems there are a few directions to follow up on after the weekend.

The assistant and the Kerrigans for a start. Maybe the Kerrigans will be able to tell us something about this Charlotte Westlake? First off, though, I want to have another trip to Blaydon's house and check out the actual room.'

Banks found himself with a lot to think about as he made his way back to Vauxhall Underground station. He had originally intended to do some shopping while he was in London, check out the big Waterstones on Piccadilly, visit FOPP at Cambridge Circus, but he decided he couldn't face it. Like everyone else, he did most of his shopping online these days. London was too hot and too crowded today; he just wanted to go home.

He wondered how he had managed to become such a recluse and homebody. He had always enjoyed trips to London before, as he had also loved living there with Sandra in Kennington in his early days on the force. The disenchantment seemed to have crept up on him slowly, ever since he had first moved into Newhope Cottage alone, after their divorce. There had been women since then, of course, but nothing that lasted. Commitment had never been a strong point with him after Sandra; he was dedicated to his job, and he tended to take up with women who were similarly dedicated to something other than hanging on to a partner. This meant, inevitably, that they drifted apart before long. Now he had women friends and colleagues, but not lovers.

He caught a mid-afternoon train, which would get him home by about six o'clock, in plenty of time for a little pottering in the garden and a good read. As he listened to Bach's Sonatas and Partitas for Solo Violin, played by Rachel Podger, he drifted and gazed at the passing landscape as he had done on the journey down, this time mulling over what Burgess had told him.

It seemed as if Zelda had been busy behind his back, if the accounts were to be believed. And he saw no reason why they shouldn't be. Why was she asking the barman questions in her dead boss's local? He had no idea. Was she becoming over-zealous in her search for Keane, or was there some other reason? Banks and Annie had warned her not to get too involved right from the start, told her that Keane was dangerous, but she seemed to have ignored them. Where had she come across the connection between Hawkins and Keane in the first place, and what was it? Was Keane now working with Tadić?

And how did Zelda get on to Faye Butler? That was a gigantic leap. The evidence pointed towards Faye being Keane's ex-girlfriend. Or Hugh Foley, as he called himself now. Why was she tortured and killed, and who did it? And what was Zelda's part in it all? Unanswerable questions at the moment, he knew, but they nagged away at him.

Burgess had asked Banks to talk to Zelda first and, if possible, avoid further action. He had agreed to try to find out what her meeting with Faye Butler was all about. But how was he to do that? Was he really going to bring Zelda into the station and question her, caution and all? If so, on what charge? Besides, that was one of the things Burgess had said he was trying to save Zelda from by letting Banks talk to her.

It would probably be best, he thought, to try an informal talk, but he had to be more probing and less willing to believe her than he had when they had talked before. He didn't think she had been playing him, but she *had* been holding out, and he was still worried about the possible danger to her. One only had to consider what happened to Faye Butler and Hawkins to worry about that. And he wondered about the man Faye had met in the park. Who was he? Keane? But Keane wasn't stocky. The only positive thing was that Zelda had been back up north when Faye had disappeared, as she had been in

Croatia when Hawkins had been killed in the mysterious house fire, so the police could hardly change tack and accuse her of those crimes. Her behaviour was suspicious, yes, but complicit, no.

The question of Phil Keane remained. He could be Hugh Foley. It would certainly make sense for him to change his name if he returned to England, especially to Yorkshire. Keane was fortyish when he and Banks had first crossed swords, so he would be about fifty now, definitely too old for Faye Butler, by her friends' standards. But Banks remembered that Keane was a smooth-talker and that he had been in youthful good shape. He seemed the kind of man who was attractive to women. He had taken in Annie Cabbot, after all. No doubt he still seemed younger than he was. Besides, Banks thought, the age thing was often irrelevant to the people involved in a relationship, such as Zelda and Ray, and was of concern mostly to prissy moralists who loved to pronounce judgement on other people's lives based on the view from outside. Superficial morality for superficial people.

Keane was good-looking, medium height. Ten years ago, his hair had been dark, with touches of grey, but he could easily have dyed it light brown. The beard would have been easy to grow, too, and a thinning hairline is natural for some people with the advance of years. The art book also made sense. Whatever he was up to now, ten years ago Phil Keane had been an art expert, not to mention a forger of provenances, and there was no reason to believe that his interest in art had lessened as his climb up the slippery pole of criminality had taken him higher and higher. So was Keane/Foley involved in sex trafficking now? It wouldn't surprise Banks. Even Zelda had pointed out early on that his document-forging skills would be every bit as useful in the world of people trafficking as in his previous enterprise.

The Bach finished, and Banks switched to Xuefei Yang playing music by Debussy, Satie and others arranged for guitar. How he wished he could play like that. He hadn't tackled any classical pieces yet. Truth be told, he hadn't even got beyond Bobby bloody Shafto in Bert Weedon's *Play in a Day*. That and holding down a playable G chord without breaking his little finger were pushing the limits of his patience and endurance these days. But he would get back to it.

The train rattled past the Darlington Arena and into the train station. The barriers were open, and Banks walked down the ramp and under the tunnel, then back up to the car park opposite the station exit, where he had left his car that morning. Behind the car park, a cattle auction was in progress, and he could hear the auctioneer's calls.

He was thankful, as always, to see the Porsche was undamaged. After half an hour of motorway driving, it was also a pleasure to turn off into the Dales along a winding road, lined with trees that opened every now and then on the magnificent vistas of rolling green hills dotted with bright yellow squares of rapeseed. And soon he was pulling up on the crunchy gravel in front of Newhope Cottage in Gratly. The sense of relief he felt as he turned his key in the door was only partly drowned out by the worries resulting from his conversation with Burgess, and where they might lead him.

It was the first time Gerry had visited Blaydon's house since she and Banks had found his disembowelled body floating face down in the indoor swimming pool. She felt some trepidation as she wound along the long drive towards the open area in front of the Tuscan-style grounds. When she turned off the engine and got out of the car, she felt the silence weigh down on her. The fountain out front was still turned off, the cherubim and seraphim surrounding the stone pond dry. Last time, she remembered, there had been a dead bird floating in the brackish water. That was gone now, and the water was covered in a greenish scum. The topiary was grotesquely misshapen, deprived of a gardener's ministrations, and the trellised arbours and wisteria groves overgrown with weeds, the roses in the rose garden all dead. Bindweed wrapped itself around whatever vegetation there was, strangling it, sucking the life out of it. Long shadows of trees fell over the gardens.

The bland house itself towered over her, three storeys of limestone, brick and stucco, with gables, shuttered windows and a low-pitched slate roof, its facade like a crudely drawn face. Gerry remembered the beginning of a film she had seen years ago with her parents, who loved old black-and-white movies, especially horror movies. She couldn't remember the plot or the title, but it was something about a house being insane, and the idea had terrified the twelve-year-old Gerry so much that she had experienced nightmares about it. Had Blaydon's mansion taken on the essence of things that had happened inside it? Was this house insane? She told herself not to be so silly.

The heavy front door was locked, and police tape warned any prospective trespassers to keep away, along with a lone constable on guard duty, having a quick smoke. Gerry knew that the house was still an official crime scene and that the CSIs and various scientific support officers came back to check on things from time to time. But there was no one else around today, except the bored constable, who checked her warrant card and had her sign his clipboard. She walked up the steps of the porch, with its stone columns, and gave a little shudder as she put her key in the lock and opened up.

Her footsteps echoed in the high-ceilinged entrance hall. She paused to gaze at the gilt-framed paintings on the wainscotted walls – a stormy seascape, harvest time, eerily lit docks at night. She was here to find and check out the room where the rape had been filmed, so she moved on through the corridors, following the diagram she had brought. Eventually she found it.

The small bed had been stripped and even the mattress taken away for forensic examination. The lampshade where the camera had been hidden had been removed, too, leaving a bare bulb. Gerry turned it on as the room had no windows, just as she had expected. A fairly wide-angle lens would capture the whole bed from above, but only from that one perspective. And the wide angle meant poor depth of field.

Gerry took some photos with her mobile. She was certain that the CSIs had been through the room and left nothing behind, but she looked around in any case – under the skeletal bed, in the empty wardrobe, in the drawers of the bedside table, also empty. As expected, she found nothing except traces of fingerprint powder here and there. It felt odd to be standing here, in the room where it had happened. She tried to imagine the poor girl's fear and panic, hoping only that whatever drugs the man had given her had dulled it to the extent that she hadn't suffered too much. Gerry remembered the final image of her half-naked body left among the tangled sheets, how the girl had turned on her side and curled up in a foetal position. Feeling a sudden surge of revulsion deep in her stomach, she turned and walked out of the door.

Before she knew it, she found herself standing in the doorway to the pool area. No traces remained there of Blaydon's gruesome death or Roberts's slightly less gory one, but standing there and smelling the ghost of chlorine brought it all back. Roberts had been over the other side of the pool, sprawled against the glass wall, which had been smeared with blood where he had slid down after being shot.

And Blaydon was like nothing she had ever seen before. At first, she had thought his body was some kind of sea monster from those old films she had watched with her parents. The water was tinged dark red around it, and a cloying sweet metallic smell mingled with the sharp chlorine. All she could make out was a dark tangle that looked like tentacles below the body, and his arms stretched out at the sides, like a cross. He was naked, and the whiteness of his skin stood out in contrast to the dark water. She shivered as she relived the sight.

But today, the bodies were gone, the pool empty, the sickening mix of chlorine, blood and severed bowels no longer cloying the air. Gerry hadn't expected to find anything new on this visit; she had just wanted to get a feel for the scene. But she hadn't expected it would have such an effect on her. She stood for a few moments until the waves of nausea and shock the recollection had brought on ebbed, then she went back to her car.

The drive was easy, with very little traffic, and Zelda made it to the airport with time to spare. With any luck, if her flight left on time, and if she took a taxi from Heathrow to King's Cross, she would be able to catch the last train home to Raymond. She felt nervous as she went through the immigration and security formalities. She had dumped the knife she hadn't used in a river on her way up from Purcari and was carrying nothing incriminating. She cleared all the airport hurdles without hindrance and settled back in her seat as the plane took off.

Zelda felt edgy and rattled, but she was glad she had handled Lupescu the way she had. Perhaps the guilt was enough, if he felt it as much as he had professed to do. A decent man with a wife and family didn't do what he had done and sleep easy at night. Perhaps it hadn't been so difficult at first to avoid thinking too much about what happened to the girls he picked out. They say some people lack empathy and can't imagine the suffering of others – the kind of thing that permeated Zelda's nightmares and kept her awake at night – and perhaps Lupescu was one of them. Maybe he did deserve to die, but that was out of her hands now; she would leave his fate to karma.

The plane landed and Zelda made her way through the busy terminal. If there was any air-conditioning it wasn't doing much good, because the air felt hot and sticky. When she got to the e-gate, she stepped forward when the green light came on, inserted her passport in the slot and looked up at the camera. It seemed to take for ever, and she began to feel nervous. Eventually the light turned red and her progress was barred. Her heart began to beat fast and hard. So much so that she was sure she was shaking. An immigration officer waiting on the other side let her through and led her over to a desk, where he pored over her passport and ran it through his computer.

The wait seemed interminable. Zelda did her best not to appear nervous, but there was nothing she could do about the beads of sweat on her brow. Perhaps Lupescu *had* called the police, after all, and they had informed immigration. Perhaps they were going to deport her. Or maybe it was nothing to do with Lupescu but something about her French passport, her settlement status. The hostile environment. She knew that she hadn't lived in France for long enough to gain true citizenship, or lived anywhere else for long since Chișinău, for that matter. But that wasn't her fault.

The real problem was her past. Danvers and Debs had certainly known that she had been a sex slave. How easy it would be for a hostile government department to translate that into the idea that she had worked as a prostitute. Definitely an undesirable alien. And much worse, she *was* a murderer.

Fortunately for Zelda, nobody knew about Goran Tadić, and the French authorities had even more reason for keeping the demise of Darius secret than she did. He had been pimp to a number of high-priced call girls, Zelda included, and had collected a great deal of compromising material on certain prominent French politicians, material that Zelda had been stealing when he had caught her, and she had killed him.

The fact remained that deep down she felt she didn't deserve to have a happy life in England with Raymond. Or anywhere. But she wanted it so badly. In her best moments she could justify what she had done – these were evil men who had done terrible things – but there were darker times, when her deeds haunted her and drove her to the brink of despair. Was the past to be her undoing? Could she ever get beyond it and remake herself into a decent, normal human being?

'What's the problem?' she asked.

'No problem, Miss. Minor glitch. The machine's sensitive.'

So am I, she was about to say, but stopped herself. These people weren't known for their sense of humour. She waited and chewed on her lower lip as the officer continued to study her passport and frown. He asked her where she'd been.

Zelda thought it should be obvious from her passport stamp, but there was no point acting the smart arse. 'Moldova,' she said. 'Chişinău.'

'What was the purpose of your visit?'

'Revisiting childhood places. I was born there.'

He gave her a sharp glance. 'How long were you away?'

Again, she thought of referring him to the stamp on her passport, but dismissed the idea. 'Three days,' she said.

'Not very long to visit childhood places.'

'It was long enough,' Zelda said. 'I had a deprived childhood.'

Oops. Nervous humour. *Big mistake*. But he simply failed to react. 'How long are you staying here *this* time?'

'For ever, I hope,' she answered, sounding as cheery and confident as possible. 'I mean, I live here.'

He didn't smile. He simply handed her passport back to her and said, 'Have a nice day.' She was going to inform him that there wasn't much of it left, but again her common sense kicked in before she opened her mouth, and she remembered that it was more sensible not to engage an immigration officer in conversation. Just get out of there. Fortunately, she had no checked luggage, so she could head straight for the taxi rank.

Not much more than an hour and a half later, she was settling into a first-class seat on a train heading north. Finally, she was on her way, though she was too tense to read. She still felt unsettled by her experience at immigration. Why had that happened? Was her passport flagged? Had Danvers and Deborah spread the word? Would the immigration police soon be knocking on her door in the small hours? Or would it be someone else, someone far more dangerous, who didn't even bother to knock?

She had got the passport quickly in Paris because her lover Emile had sway in the government, and because the powers that be had wanted both to reward her and get rid of her. So maybe it was dodgy, even though Emile had assured her it was genuine. But Emile was dead now, and she didn't think she could count on any further support from the French government. She had given them what they wanted, and they had no more use for her. She should count herself lucky that she had come out of it smelling of roses. There were times when she thought she was also lucky that they hadn't decided to have her eliminated instead. It must have been an option. And she clearly couldn't count on the British for anything, the way things were heading. But why now? She had used the passport several times since she had been living in England without any trouble at all.

Most of the journey she stared out of her window at the slowly darkening summer evening and listened to one of her three favourite symphonies. This time it was Tchaikovsky's *Pathétique*, and as she listened and rocked gently to the train's rhythm she thought about William Buckley, Vasile Lupescu and her immigration fears. When the train arrived at York, she felt better. It still wasn't quite dark. Midsummer evenings. The longest day wasn't too far off. She breathed a sigh of relief as she stepped on to the platform and walked to the taxi rank. Home, Raymond, and peace at last, she thought, as the taxi made its way along the A59 past Kirk Hammerton towards the A1.

5

Over the weekend, Banks had given a great deal of thought as to how he might get Zelda to 'loosen up'. First of all, he ruled out an interview room, or even his office, as too formal. Moving on from there, he counted out the entire police station, which reeked of authority. She could never relax in such a place, and nor could he. In addition to the personal trauma Zelda had been through, Banks thought she was, like many Eastern Europeans since Stalin's days, genetically terrified of the knock on the door in the middle of the night. And of the police in general. To them all cops were the FSB, KGB or Stasi, whatever, but Banks thought he had forged a bond with Zelda and that if he approached her in the right way, she would feel more at ease.

Finally he decided on a long walk interrupted by lunch at the Relton Arms with its spectacular views of Swainsdale below its spacious beer garden, and Zelda had agreed over the phone. There was plenty of room in the beer garden to get an isolated table, and perhaps with a little strenuous walking, the heat of the sun and a cold drink, Zelda might let her guard down. As Burgess had said, if they believed she had done something illegal they would have her in like a shot and interrogate her as long as the PACE rules allowed. But she hadn't. She wasn't a criminal, as far as Banks knew, but a victim, and perhaps a witness – to something, at any rate.

Zelda arrived in Banks's driveway at the appointed time. He had taken that Monday off, leaving Annie and Gerry to deal with the Blaydon murder and its assorted spin-offs. He had watched the rape video once more over the weekend, still searching for the telling detail, something he might have missed, and all that had happened was that it had sickened him all over again. How on earth, he found himself wondering, could one human being do something like that to another? But he knew he was being naive; he, of all people, ought to have some idea. The thing was, he knew that men did it, but he had no idea why. Unless it was, as one serial rapist had told him: 'Because I want to. And because I can.' Could it be as simple as that?

Human beings did far worse things to one another than what he had just watched. Men routinely raped women during war, as a strategy to unman and humiliate their opponents and signal superiority. It had been going on ever since man climbed out of the primordial swamps, and it would probably go on until his presence on the planet was nothing but a vague memory lingering like an unpleasant smell with no one to smell it. But such thoughts were not for a day like today, and he tried to push them aside, knowing that they only led to that one dark and lonely place he had found himself inhabiting too often lately.

It was another glorious, sunny day, and a light, cooling breeze alleviated the heat to some extent, which was a godsend to walking in such weather. He hadn't seen Zelda in a while, so there would be plenty to catch up on. She was wearing shorts, showing off her smooth tanned and tapered thighs, and a white shirt tied at her waist, sunglasses hooked over the top fastened button. Her dark hair hung in a ponytail down her back.

'Will I do?' she asked.

Banks looked at her feet and saw she was wearing short white socks and a sturdy pair of trainers. 'You'll do,' he said. 'Stylish but road ready.'

They walked through to the back of the house, where Banks strapped on his small rucksack.

'What have you got in there?' Zelda asked.

'Just essentials. Chocolate, apples, bottled water, mobile, Ordnance Survey map, compass, Bluetooth headphones, a book, portable first aid kit.'

'Which book?'

'*Flashman at the Charge*.'

'We had a Flashman book at the orphanage once. Not that one. It was about the Indian mutiny. It was very funny. What's this one about?'

'The Charge of the Light Brigade.'

'"Onward, onward, rode the six hundred."'

'That's the one.'

'Is it dangerous, this walk?'

'Of course not.'

'We are not likely to get lost?'

'No. I've done it dozens of times before.'

'Are you going to ignore me and listen to music or read your book?'

Banks laughed. 'No,' he said. 'I realise it might seem odd to be carrying these things, but I usually walk alone, and I always pack the same stuff. Fresh water and chocolate, of course, but the rest is automatic. Just habit. Sometimes I listen to music, but mostly I prefer the sounds of nature when I'm walking. And sometimes I like to have a rest and sit on the grass and read for a while.'

Zelda put on her sunglasses. 'OK. Lead on.' They headed out of the gate and over the stile on to the footpath up the slope to Tetchley Fell. Single file, with Banks leading the way.

Tetchley Fell could be a daunting climb, deceptively easy at first, but soon getting tougher with every step as the incline steepened. To get to the top, beyond about twenty-five feet of almost sheer limestone, you needed a few mountaineering skills and some basic equipment. But they weren't going that far.

'What did Ray have to say when you told him we were going for a walk?' Banks asked over his shoulder.

'"Have a good time,"' said Zelda. 'He's been involved in a new painting project these past few days, and he doesn't come up often for air.'

'And you?'

'Between projects. Resting, as they say.'

They walked over a patchwork of fields, saving their breath for the ever increasing gradient. Sometimes they disturbed a group of sheep, which scattered at their approach and stood at a distance, backs turned, as if somehow that would make any danger go away. After a few more stiles, they paused briefly and sat on a drystone wall to drink some water, eat an apple and look back at the view.

Already it was stunning, the huddled limestone houses of Helmthorpe below, its squat church tower, high street shops with racks of postcards out front and tourists browsing. Beyond the town, the river Swain meandered through the flatlands of the valley bottom, lush and green, speckled with blue, yellow and purple wildflowers. Further out, the opposite valley side began its ascent, green at first, then culminating in the long grey-gold limestone edge of Crow Scar, like a skeleton's teeth bared against the clear blue sky, where only a few wisps of white cloud twisted through the air like chiffon scarves.

'It's magnificent,' Zelda said. Her cheeks were flushed with walking, and beads of sweat glistened above her upper lip and on her brow. Banks felt that he was sweating like a pig, and it took him a while to catch his breath. His ears were popping, too, though he didn't think they had climbed high enough for that.

'How's work?' he asked.

'They closed down the department. The others were all serving police officers – NCA, anyway – so they got transferred somewhere else, but I was just a civilian consultant, so my job simply ceased to exist. Made redundant. Unemployed.'

'I didn't know that,' Banks said. 'I'm sorry. I'd have thought they would want to keep a worthwhile department like that going.'

Zelda shrugged. 'Worthwhile has nothing to do with it. You should know better than anyone that it all comes down to budgets.'

'The NCA's never been short of cash, as far as I know,' said Banks. 'I doubt that's the only reason.'

'It's not,' said Zelda. 'Naturally the death of Mr Hawkins caused quite an upset, even though they say they don't suspect foul play. The temporary shutdown was the perfect excuse to cut the department completely.'

Banks passed her the water bottle. She tilted it and drank. Banks watched her throat muscles move as she swallowed. 'I don't think Danvers and Debs are convinced that there was no foul play,' he said, 'but they've got no evidence of any wrongdoing.' Zelda passed back the bottle. Banks took several swigs and a few deep breaths of fresh air, then said, 'Shall we carry on?'

Zelda slid off the wall. They were on the Roman road that ran diagonally down the hillside all the way to Fortford, which had been the main settlement in Roman times. It was a stony path, used as a drover's road now, and had low drystone walls running along both sides broken by the occasional farm gate. It was broad enough for them to walk side by side, which they did. Once they had to slow down when they got behind a farmer moving his sheep across the road from one field to another. He said hello to Banks and asked how he was.

'Do you know everyone?' Zelda asked when they had passed.

Banks laughed. 'Not quite. But it's surprising the people you get to know when you do my job.' He gestured over his shoulder. 'Take old Tibor there. He had some of his sheep rustled a while back. It was an organised gang, all over the county, so we were involved.'

'Did you get them back?'

'Not much chance of that. They were probably in Bulgaria by then. Or a butcher's shop window. Now we even have rustling gangs who butcher the sheep in the field in the dark and take only the meat.'

'How horrible,' Zelda said. 'Tibor? That's an odd name for a Yorkshireman, isn't it?'

'Tibor's family came over from Poland just before the war to escape the Nazis. We have a long history of immigration in this part of the world, quite a patchwork inheritance, a sort of international brotherhood of farmers. Working the land is a tough job.'

As they walked on, Banks noticed Zelda glance over her shoulder once or twice, as if to make sure they weren't being followed. Flies buzzed around their heads, along with the occasional wasp, but other than that, it was mostly silent save for their footsteps and a few birds singing. They saw rabbits running in the fields and, once, a hedgehog curled up among the wildflowers by the roadside. A curlew flew over their heads making its high plaintive trill, and Banks pointed it out to Zelda. Only one couple passed them, going the other way, giving the usual Yorkshire greeting: a nod and a grunt.

'Nice day,' said Banks.

The man pointed to the sky. 'Aye. Won't last, though, like as not.'

After about half an hour, Banks led the way over a stile and across a field to a winding lane. On the way, they got too close to a tewit's nest and set off a flutter of frightened and angry squeaking. They could see a cluster of low stone buildings ahead, and Banks pointed. 'Lunch,' he said.

Zelda wiped her brow with the back of her hand, smiled and said, 'In the nick of time.'

'Where did you learn your English?' Banks asked as they headed towards the Relton Arms. 'I'm not being patronising. I just mean you seem to have all the idioms and everything. Things people pick up over a lifetime.'

'I've always had a knack for languages,' Zelda said. 'I listen. Most of the nuns at the orphanage spoke English, and we had lessons from a very early age. I read a lot. When I was in London and later, at Raymond's commune in St Ives, I watched a lot of British television. Not so much now. But I write in English. I even *think* in English.'

'I had more than enough trouble learning French at school,' Banks said.

'Oh, French is easy.' Zelda put her hand to her mouth. 'Sorry. I didn't mean to boast.'

'No, it's all right. I just wish I had your language skills, that's all. I'm envious.'

They entered the tiny hamlet of Relton, halfway up the hillside, passed the small general store with its Walls ice cream board propped outside and approached the whitewashed facade of the Relton Arms.

'Ah,' said Zelda. 'Now it begins.'

'What?'

'You know. The interrogation. The grilling. The thumbscrews. The rack.'

'What are you talking about?'

'Oh, come on, Alan. You didn't bring me all this way just for the pleasure of my company. You want something. I can tell. You've been edgy and evasive all the way here.'

Banks could have complimented her on the pleasure of her company, but decided it wasn't appropriate. 'I do have a few questions for you,' he admitted. 'But that's all. No thumb-screws. No rack.'

'Promise?'

'Cross my heart.'

'And you're not going to arrest me?'

Banks laughed. 'Should I? Have you committed a crime?'

'Don't joke,' Zelda said. 'I'm serious.'

'No, I'm not going to arrest you. Now shall we go inside and order some drinks and food? I could murder a pint, myself.'

Annie made her way past the flashing screens, and the pings, screeches, bangs and screams of a video arcade in full flight at school lunchtime. Negotiating the narrow path between the machines felt like walking the gauntlet, and with so much sunlight outside, she wondered why it was always so dark in these places. Lack of windows seemed to be the answer.

'Excuse me,' she mumbled, pushing her way through a cluster of lads from Eastvale Comprehensive busy splattering aliens into millions of pieces as they stuffed themselves with Greggs sausage rolls. They shifted only grudgingly, and Annie heard one of them whisper, 'Pushy cunt, she must be on the rag,' as she passed by. The others giggled. She chose to let it go. That wasn't what she was here for. She did, however, turn around and have a quick glance at the speaker, committing his face to memory. Satisfied she would know him if she saw him again, maybe smoking a joint down Casper's Wynde, she moved on.

It was turning out not to be her lucky day. Tommy Kerrigan was the only one in the cramped office at the back. The Stan Laurel of the two. She had hoped it might be his brother Timmy, who, though much larger and thereby taking up more valuable office space, was marginally more pleasant. At least he was civil and didn't give her the creeps the way the long, lugubrious pasty-faced Tommy did, with his milky eye and all. He looked like a cross between a funeral director and a vampire, and though nothing serious had ever been proven against him, he was known to have psychopathic tendencies. He also suffered from halitosis, which was definitely a minus in such a confined space.

There was room for one small chair on the opposite side of his desk, and Annie shifted some papers and sat down.

'Well, well, look what the cat's dragged in,' Tommy said. 'Detective Sergeant Annie Cabbot. We'll have to stop meeting like this or people will talk.'

'Detective *Inspector*,' Annie corrected him. Even his voice was annoying, Annie remembered. An affected southern drawl with a nasal edge of Geordie.

'Well, *pardonnez-moi*.'

'You should do something about your clientele,' Annie said. 'They're an ignorant bunch of yobs out there, feeding their faces and insulting your visitors.'

'They're not supposed to bring food in the arcade,' said Tommy. 'There's a sign. But what can you do? I'm short-staffed.'

'How's business?'

'Fair to middling. Not that it would interest you much.'

'Club running OK?' The Kerrigans also owned The Vaults, Eastvale's only nightclub, on the opposite side of the market square.

'Like a dream. Pleased as I am to see you again, Inspector, I'm a busy man, so if you could—'

But Annie beat him to it and slid the enhanced image of the young girl across the desk. 'Recognise her?' she asked.

Kerrigan examined the photograph and passed it back to her. 'Should I? It's not very good, is it? I mean, I probably wouldn't even recognise my own daughter from that.'

'What daughter's that?'

'Figure of speech.'

'So the answer's no?'

'Sorry.'

'Only she was present at one of Connor Blaydon's parties that we know of, the one on 13 April, and we know you and your brother were also there.'

'We did business with Connor, as I've told you. It's only natural we'd socialise once in a while.'

'The party looked like fun. I saw you and your brother in some poolside snapshots. There were home movies, too, shot secretly in some of the bedrooms.'

A flicker of alarm crossed Kerrigan's features. 'What movies?'

'Oh, you didn't know? Seems your business colleague's butler, Neville Roberts, liked to film Blaydon's guests having a good time. Too good a time, in some cases, if you know what I mean. And you should tell your brother about those thong swimming trunks. Nasty. Constitute a public menace, they do.'

'I don't know what you're getting at,' Kerrigan said, 'but even if we were photographed, unbeknownst to us and against our will, we did nothing wrong.'

'*Unbeknownst*, eh? That's a long word. Don't worry, you don't feature in any of the videos, unless you've already paid Roberts off for one. But you *were* there. Did Neville Roberts ever attempt to blackmail you? Did he have any video recordings to sell to you?'

'Blackmail? About what?'

'Those trunks of your brother's, for a start. And the drugs.'

'What drugs?'

'Or maybe you were in bed with an archbishop?'

'What the fuck are you talking about?'

'Never mind. Back to the photo.'

Kerrigan glanced at the image again and passed it back. 'I still don't recognise her.'

'Never seen her in here, or the club?'

'No.'

'Are you also sure you never saw her or anyone like her at Blaydon's parties?'

'There were always plenty of girls around. But not like her.'

'So you *can* tell something about her from the photo?'

'Enough to know that if I'd seen anyone vaguely resembling her, I'd remember, and I haven't. Most of the girls were . . . well, models or escort types . . . if you know what I mean.' He sketched an hourglass figure in the air. 'Shapely. Curvy. Definitely enhanced, in some cases, if not naturally well-endowed. This girl looks quite natural. You can tell that much even from this photo. So if that's all . . .'

'Not quite, Tommy. How young were the girls at these parties?'

'You've seen the videos, so you should know.'

'Humour me.'

'They were all over the age of consent, if that's what you're getting at. Mostly in their twenties, I'd guess.'

'Check their birth certificates, did you?'

Kerrigan gave her a look. 'Oh, come off it. It was obvious. They weren't kids. Most of the girls were strippers and tarts, like, with big tits and legs up to here.' He lifted his arm. 'All right if you like that sort of thing, I suppose.'

Annie knew that Tommy didn't; he preferred young men, rough trade, if available. 'Heard of a woman called Charlotte Westlake?'

'Course I have,' he said. 'Charlie. She's Connor's personal assistant. Or she was. Took care of pretty much everything on the business side. Ran errands, organised events, booked entertainers. "Indispensable," he used to say about her. But she hasn't been around for a while.'

'Was there anything of a romantic nature between them?'

'Not that I ever noticed. But you never knew with Connor. I wouldn't put it past him.'

'What do you mean?'

'He played his cards close to his chest. Especially when it came to his private life. I couldn't even tell you which side he played for, if you follow my drift.'

'Is she married, this Charlotte Westlake?'

'Dunno. Never saw a husband around, at any rate.'

'Was she involved in any of the action?'

'Charlie? You must be joking. A bit of posh was our Charlotte, don't you know. Cheltenham Ladies College and so on. Didn't even like you calling her Charlie to her face.'

'What about Neville Roberts?'

'What about him?'

'What did you think of him?'

'To tell the truth, I always found him a bit creepy. You know, sly, shifty.'

Pot and kettle, thought Annie. 'Go on.'

'What's to say? Connor swore by him.' Tommy scratched his nose. 'I reckon he was a bit of a snob, Connor was. Liked the idea of having a butler, you know. Someone to keep the Aga burning. Though Roberts wasn't really a butler, more of a factotum.'

'Factotum,' Annie repeated. 'Good one, that, Tommy. Your command of the English language is definitely improving.'

'Fuck off.'

Annie stood up. The halitosis was getting to her. 'Turns out Mr Roberts was quite the expert in audio and video surveillance. As I said, he had a nice little sideline in filming Blaydon's married or respectable guests doing the naughty. Know anything about that?'

'No. But I'll tell you something for nothing.'

'What's that?'

'One or two of these "respectable" guests, if they found out they'd been secretly filmed, well, let's just say I wouldn't give tuppence for Roberts's chances.'

'Or Blaydon's, if they thought he was behind it?'

'Goes without saying.'

'Thanks, Tommy,' Annie said. 'You've been a great help. And if you remember anything at all about the girl in the photo . . .'

Kerrigan's eyes narrowed. 'Why's she so important?'

'We'd just like to talk to her. That's all.'

'You think she was a witness? That she saw what happened to Connor?'

'Like I said, we'd just like to talk to her.'

'It's those fucking Albanians I'd be after if I was you,' Kerrigan said as Annie turned to the door. 'You ask me, that's who did for Connor. Those fucking Albanians.'

'Mr Banks,' called the landlady Sally Preece when Banks and Zelda entered the Relton Arms. 'Nice to see you again.'

'You, too, Sally,' said Banks. 'Any tables outside?'

'Take your pick. What would you like to drink? I'll bring them out to you along with the lunch menus. We've got a lovely game pie on special today.'

'Drink?' Banks glanced at Zelda.

'I don't know,' she said. 'I'll have what you're having.'

'Right you are,' said Banks. 'That'll be two pints of Black Sheep bitter, then, Sally.'

'Can I have some water, too, please?' Zelda asked.

'Coming up.'

'You seem to know her as well,' Zelda said. 'What was that, a burglary?'

'No. It's just somewhere I come for a quiet drink sometimes on my walks.'

Banks steered Zelda towards the door that led into the back garden, a broad and undulating stretch of grass. Fortunately, there was no bouncy castle; Sally Preece didn't go in for family fun. They picked a table overlooking the valley, close to the low stone wall and a field full of sheep. The lawn was uneven, but they managed to get their chairs stable enough, and Banks didn't think their glasses would slide off the wooden table.

They didn't. Sally Preece arrived soon after they had sat down with the beers, water and menus on a tray and said to come back to the bar and put in the food order when they were ready.

Banks had thought a great deal about what to say, how to approach questioning Zelda. He hadn't come to any firm conclusions – a great deal of it had to be played by ear – but he had at least a general approach in mind, and he had already brought up the Hawkins investigation when they had sat on the wall.

'Why do I feel so nervous?' Zelda said, fingering her menu.

'You don't need to,' said Banks.

'Do you think I'm lying about something?'

Banks paused. 'Let me put it this way: I don't think you've told me everything. There's something you're holding back. Or some things.'

'Like what?'

'That's what I want you to tell me.'

Zelda lit a Marlboro Gold, and Banks took a long pull on his pint. It tasted especially good after the exertions of the walk. There's nothing like a good pint when you feel you deserve it.

Zelda tapped the menu. 'What do you suggest?'

'Depends,' said Banks. 'I'm rather partial to the steak and frites, myself, but I think it's going to be game pie today. You might want a salad or something.'

'Don't mistake me for Annie.' Zelda put the menu on the table. 'I don't like game, but steak and frites is fine with me.'

Banks went and ordered. When he got back, Zelda was stubbing her half-smoked cigarette out in the green ashtray. Her beer was still untouched, but the glass of water was empty.

'You might as well know,' Banks began, 'that I already know you walked past Trevor Hawkins's burned-out house and questioned the barman at The George and Dragon about him.'

'How do you know that?'

'It doesn't matter,' Banks said. 'The point is that *you* didn't tell me.'

Zelda turned sulky. 'I don't have to report to the police every move I make or conversation I have, do I? It's not a police state yet.'

Banks smiled. 'Not yet. But I thought we were supposed to be working together. Like partners. Remember?'

'I'm not your "partner",' said Zelda. 'That's Annie.'

'You know what I mean. You said you wanted to help us find Phil Keane.'

'You told me to be careful.'

'But you weren't, were you?'

'Well, I'm still here, aren't I?'

'Is survival your only criterion of success?' Banks immediately noticed the pain in her expression. 'I'm sorry. Maybe that was insensitive of me after all you've survived, but what I mean is, partners are supposed to share. Why didn't you tell me?'

'Because it was all so vague,' Zelda said. 'I didn't really find out anything that would help you. What I found only complicated the situation I was in to start with.'

'Then why don't you tell me about that now, and we'll try to make sense of it all? Together.'

Sally Preece walked across the lawn with their meals. They already had the condiments and cutlery on the table. Banks thanked her and she left. 'Better eat before it goes cold,' he said.

He immediately felt lucky that Zelda didn't tell him he sounded just like her mother. Then he realised she probably didn't remember her mother. Zelda sawed at her steak, head down. Banks took a few mouthfuls of pie and washed them down with beer. It was good, plenty of pheasant and rabbit, and a touch of venison.

'Let's go back a while,' Banks said. 'Remember that dinner Annie and I had with you and Ray up at your cottage late last year? Remember when you told us you'd seen a photograph of Phil Keane with someone you recognised in connection with your work?'

Zelda finished chewing a piece of steak. 'I remember.'

'You were going to keep an eye out for anything else of interest, but you never came up with anything.'

'That's right. What did you want me to do, make something up? There was nothing. Just that photograph.'

'Of Keane with Petar Tadić?'

'Yes.'

'But you weren't even going to tell me about that, were you? I heard it from Superintendent Burgess.'

'Well, if he's so all-knowing, why don't you ask him?'

'Zelda, stop being petulant. It doesn't suit you. Talk to me.'

Zelda pushed her half-full plate away and studied a spider spinning its web in the drystone wall beside her. 'All right,' she said. 'All right. I didn't tell you because I thought you'd be angry with me for pursuing it when you said I shouldn't. OK?'

'I'm not sure that's the reason.'

'What, then?'

'I think there's something else you're not telling me, but I think it shocked you more than you said it did when you saw Keane and Tadić together in the photograph. It was two worlds coming together, or colliding, and one of them was yours. You didn't want to let me in on that, did you?'

Zelda fingered another cigarette out of her packet and lit up. 'What if that's so? What Petar Tadić and his brother did to me is not an experience I care to remember so often.'

'But why the sudden interest in Hawkins? I didn't ask you to spy on *him*. How was he connected with all this?'

Zelda took a deep drag on her cigarette and blew the smoke out slowly. 'All right,' she said. 'I'll tell you. Something happened. I was going to tell you before, at Christmas, but I lost my nerve.'

'Why?'

'Because I thought I was on to something, and I thought you'd take it off me and go charging in like a bull in a china shop, scattering all the pieces.'

'You don't have a very high opinion of me, do you?'

Zelda smiled and touched his hand briefly. 'I didn't mean it that way. Just that, in my experience, when the police get fully engaged, as a force, as an institution, then they have their own rules to follow and justice isn't always done. Remember, I grew up in the Soviet bloc.' She paused, then said, 'I saw Hawkins and Keane together once and had reasons of my own for wanting to know what they were doing together.'

'And did you find out?'

'Not really. I'll admit I went a lot further than you wanted me to. That's another reason I didn't tell you. I followed Mr Hawkins after work on a couple of occasions. One time he went into a restaurant in Soho, and I waited in a pub across the street, where I could see the place. After a while he came out, and he was with two other people. One was this Keane, and the other was a woman I didn't recognise. I took some photographs.'

Banks thought he might like to see these photographs, but he didn't want to interrupt the rhythm of their conversation by asking for them. 'And then when you went to The George and Dragon, you found out that Hawkins had met Keane there, too? It was him, wasn't it?'

'Yes.'

'Christ,' said Banks. 'You found out that Hawkins was meeting with Keane, who you already knew was connected with Tadić and who had once tried to kill me. For crying out loud, why didn't you tell me? Or someone. Hawkins could have been selling NCA information to Tadić's gang. Or he could have been in trouble. You knew what Keane was. Annie and I told you. A killer. A pyromaniac. And you know Tadić, too, from painful experience.'

'Yes. I was curious, that's all. They parted company, and I followed Keane and the girl.'

'Where did they go?'

'Just window-shopping on Oxford Street. Then they got a taxi on Regent Street and I never saw Keane again.'

Banks just shook his head slowly. 'Another drink?' he asked.

Zelda gave him a thin smile. 'Some more water, please.'

Banks went to the bar and got himself another pint and Zelda a large glass of tap water. His head was spinning with information. What did all this mean? What might he have done if he'd known six months ago or more? But somehow, he didn't think Zelda's story was over.

She was sitting as he had left her, gazing over the broad valley, smoking. The spider was still spinning its intricate web beside her. 'I'll miss this place,' she said softly.

'You're going somewhere?'

'Oh, I think so, don't you?' She sipped some ice water. Her beer was still untouched. 'Thank you.'

'With Ray?'

As Zelda told him about her experiences with immigration and worries about the pre-settlement form, he sensed a deep sadness in her, almost a sense of defeat, as if she felt no matter what she did, what happiness she found, it was bound to be snatched away from her before long, either by sex traffickers or immigration officials. She went on to tell him about Danvers and Debs hinting that her French passport didn't quite cut it, and that her past actions left a lot to be desired.

'It hasn't happened yet,' he said when she'd finished. 'And if it's of any comfort, I don't think you'll be going anywhere. Not if you don't want to. Ray's a wealthy man. He can take care of you. It's not as if you'd be a burden on the state. You're not poor.'

'I don't want to be a burden on Raymond, either.'

Banks laughed. 'I hardly think that's possible,' he said. 'Ray adores you.'

Zelda flushed. 'I've made money from my work, too,' she said, then paused. 'I mean my art work. The jewellery and sculptures, maybe not original paintings, but some copies I have made for people. But I haven't paid tax. I haven't filled in the proper forms. Not ever. I just came here from Paris and started living in London, doing that pavement art thing and living in a squat with a group of other immigrants. I didn't register or fill in any forms. Then Raymond came along and . . . You know the rest. They'll get me if they want me. What is it they say? I'm *undocumented*.'

'Is that another reason why you didn't tell me anything? Because you're afraid of immigration?'

'You can't understand this if you are not a stranger here. How it feels. It might have put me on their radar. As it happens, this Danvers and his woman have done that.'

'No,' said Banks. 'You did it yourself. They were only doing their jobs.'

'Ah,' she said. 'There you go. You're all the same, covering each other's bottoms.' She stubbed out her cigarette viciously. Sparks flew. 'I did nothing to draw attention to myself. I just did my job, made sculptures and jewellery and lived a quiet life with Raymond.'

Banks couldn't help but smile. 'Calm down,' he said. 'Believe it or not, I'm on your side. And it's arses, not bottoms.'

'It doesn't sound like you're on my side.' Zelda sulked for a moment then drank some water. 'There's more,' she said. 'You might as well know it all. Do you want to hear?'

'Of course. Go on.'

'The girl who was with Keane.'

'Faye Butler.'

'My God, you know about her, too!'

'I heard just the other day. Burgess again. She was Keane's girlfriend back then.'

'I'd like to meet this Burgess who knows everything.'

'I don't think so,' Banks said. 'But he's on your side, too, or we wouldn't be here having this nice friendly little chat right now.'

Zelda put her head in her hands and sighed, then took a deep breath and ran the backs of her hands over her eyes. Her fingers were long and tapered, like a musician's.

'Do you know what happened to her?' Banks asked.

'She's dead. Murdered. I read about it in the newspaper.'

'Yes.'

'The waitress in the restaurant knew where she worked. I went back there and asked about her. She was a regular customer. After that it was easy.'

'You went and talked to Faye Butler at Foyles?'

'Yes. I thought I might be able to get to Keane through her, but I hit a dead end. They had split up. She hadn't seen him for months. She didn't know where he lived. He was going by the name of Hugh Foley. I would have told you then, honest, if I had been able to find him for you.'

'And that was it?'

'That was it. I know I was going against what you told me, but I thought that if I could locate Keane for you it would be good for us all. I would find the Tadićs and others like them and just maybe you would be able to arrest them. Maybe even Annie would start to like me, too.'

'Annie doesn't dislike you,' he said. 'She's jealous, that's all, and protective of her father. Forgive the amateur psychology, but her mother died when she was very young, and she's felt responsible for Ray ever since.'

'Must have been quite a life,' Zelda said with a smile. 'Feeling responsible for Raymond.'

Banks laughed. 'I should imagine it took a lot out of her. But things will improve. Believe me. She'll accept you in time.'

'Do you really think so?'

'I do.'

Banks finished his drink and they left with a passing goodbye to Sally Preece. They walked back to Gratly mostly in silence, with heavy steps, each lost in thought, and as he gazed on the rolling hills, drystone walls, grazing sheep and flimsy white clouds snaking across a clear blue sky, Banks had the strangest fleeting feeling that they were leaving some sort of paradise behind and danger lay ahead. He shivered despite the heat of the sun.

6

It was early that Monday evening, and Banks was pottering about in his garden out back to a soundtrack of Schubert lieder sung by Anna Lucia Richter when he heard a car pull up in front. Curious, he walked through the house and opened the door to find Ray Cabbot standing there, hands on hips.

'What the fuck's going on?' were Ray's first words.

Banks gestured him inside and shut the door. 'What do you mean?' he asked.

'You know damn well what I mean,' said Ray, following him along the corridor to the back door. 'You and Zelda. I might be an old hippie, but I can still knock you into the middle of next week.' He stood in the conservatory with his fists clenched.

'Calm down, Ray. Come on outside and calm down. Tell me what's up.'

'Zelda is what's up. As if you didn't know. She's upset. Ever since she came back from her talk with you this afternoon she's been in a right state. What the fuck did you say to her?'

'I can't see how that was anything to do with me,' Banks said. 'We talked, yes, but I didn't say anything to upset her. What did she say to you?'

'She wouldn't explain. She just said you interrogated her, humiliated her, as if she was a criminal. We had a row. Then she just went off to her studio and banged around. I've got a bloody lecture to give at Leeds Art Gallery tonight, so I left her there to stew. What's it all about? You must know something.'

'Ray, sit down.'

Ray sat on one of the spindly chairs around the table on Banks's lawn. Birdsong filled the brief silence, and Banks hoped it would help to inject an atmosphere of calm. 'Drink?' he asked.

Ray shook his head, then said, 'Go on, then. Just the one won't do any harm. Got any beer?'

'I think I might have a couple of bottles of Stella in the fridge.'

'That'll have to do, then.'

Banks went and fetched Ray a bottle of Stella and a glass of iced water for himself.

'Not indulging?' Ray asked.

'Just thirsty from messing about in the garden,' Banks said, then leaned forward. 'I didn't interrogate Zelda,' he said. 'We talked about some of the things she's done to help us find Phil Keane and where it led her. And some of the things she hadn't told me. Maybe I was a bit annoyed that she hadn't shared this with me before, but I can't see why it would upset her so much. I'm sorry if it did. She was a bit quiet and jumpy when she left me, but that's all.'

'What was it all about?'

Banks sipped some ice water. 'Believe it or not, Ray, I was trying to help her out. There are some cops down in London who would dearly like to talk to her about various things, but an old mate gave me the chance to get in first. The softer option. Believe me, they wouldn't have been as easy with her about it all as I was.'

'About what?'

'I can't tell you that. But take it from me – Zelda may have made one or two foolish moves, but as far as I know she hasn't committed any crimes.'

'Well, thank the Lord for that.' Ray buried his face in his hands. 'I don't know,' he said. 'She's been having a hard time lately. I'm worried as hell about her.'

'But why? I thought things were going well for you.'

'They are. Or so it seemed. I don't know what it is. That's why I – I'm sorry, I shouldn't be blaming you. I just thought you might have an explanation for her moods.'

'What moods?'

Ray slouched in his chair and guzzled beer from the bottle. Banks listened to a blackbird singing and admired the view of Tetchley Fell while Ray collected his thoughts. He could make out a couple of tiny figures way up on the top of the fell, walking the edge. Banks had been up there on a number of occasions and remembered how pure the air was and how invigorating the exercise. Even a climb as far as the Roman wall, where he had gone that morning with Zelda, was exhilarating.

Ray took some Rizla papers from his pouch of Drum and rolled a cigarette. He glanced up at Banks as he did so and said, 'Just tobacco.'

Banks shrugged.

Ray lit the cigarette with a disposable lighter. Condensation was forming on his bottle, pooling at its base on the table. Banks hadn't seen him for a few days and thought he was looking tired. Even so, you'd never think he was in his seventies, despite the straggly grey beard, bandana and grey hair tied back in a ponytail. He resembled Willie Nelson, but with fewer wrinkles. Normally he had the drive and energy of a man twenty years younger, but not today.

'Come on, then. Give,' Banks said. 'What's up? What's the real reason you wanted to see me, apart from the pleasure of knocking me into the middle of next week.' Banks could hear faint strains of Schubert's 'Das Heimweh' coming from inside the cottage. Ray was clearly too distracted to notice or he would surely have made some comment on the choice of music.

Ray looked sheepish. 'Sorry about that,' he said. 'Bit of hyperbole. I'm a pacifist at heart.'

'Not to worry. Is it a police matter?'

'With Zelda? Maybe. I don't know.'

'Tell me, then.'

Ray took a drag on his cigarette and a pull on his beer. 'She's got something on her mind, Alan,' he said. 'This past month or so, ever since I got back from my big American trip. Since she got made redundant. She's been distracted, paranoid, jumpy, on edge. Anxious. She disappears into her studio for ages.'

'She said the same about you.'

'That's different.'

'Any idea what the cause is?'

'Not really. I've been thinking it might have something to do with Immigration Enforcement. You know she has to apply for this pre-settled status because she's been living here under five years? Can you believe it? She has to fill in some long form, and it's been giving her a lot of grief. They want stuff like P60s or P45s, utility bills, council tax receipts, passport stamps, proof of where she's been and when, bank statements and so on.'

'Well, surely that's not a problem? The NCA would be able to supply details of her employment.'

'She thinks they'll just wash their hands of her now the unit's been shut down.'

'No. They don't work like that. Besides, she should still have plenty of evidence to show how long she's been over here.'

'Everything's in my name,' Ray said. 'The payments just come out of the bank automatically. Before we met she was practically living on the streets.'

'Surely they would understand that?'

'You and I might think so. But she's been trying to live under the radar.'

'She said the same thing, but I didn't understand why.'

'Circumstances. It's partly her past, the Soviet legacy. Lists, interrogations, secret police, all that sort of thing. It's anathema to her. She's got a dodgy French passport, but she's from Moldova. I didn't know it, but Moldova isn't even a member of the EU. That means she's not technically an EU citizen. She's not sure how well her French passport would hold up to scrutiny. She assures me it's not forged or anything, it's the genuine article, but she's still not comfortable about it. I try to talk her down, you know, tell her not to worry, but it's not easy. She's convinced they're looking for a reason to chuck her out of the country, especially now she's unemployed. And not only because of all this Brexit rubbish. She thinks those two coppers who hassled her about her boss's death are behind it, took a dislike to her, dug into her past and didn't like what they found.'

'Paul Danvers and Deborah Fletcher? Yes, I got an inkling she wasn't too happy with them when we talked this morning. They've got nothing to do with Immigration Enforcement.'

'Zelda's got a bee in her bonnet about them. Thinks they're all in cahoots. Like I said, she's been acting paranoid. She thinks people are following her. She said they know things about her past, about the sex trafficking and all, and they could make it seem like she was a prostitute, an undesirable alien. She doesn't like to talk to me about the old days, so I don't push it. Oh, I know the big picture, what happened to her, and I know something big happened in Paris that changed everything, but I don't know what. Even when I can get her to talk about the past she's vague about it. Always skimpy on the details. Croatia, too, and Serbia.'

'You can't blame her, can you?' said Banks. 'The things that happened to her. She probably wants to forget, put the past behind her as best she can, the way our parents did with the war. It just sounds like she's having a bout of uncertainty and anxiety, what with Brexit and losing her job. I'm sure it will work itself out in time.'

'Easy for you to say.'

'Maybe she'll run into problems with Immigration Enforcement and maybe not,' said Banks. 'I've heard the Home Office can be pretty nasty when they want. Or even stupid. Sometimes they don't do anything when they really should. But it's not as if she's likely to be a burden on the state, is it, even if she is unemployed? And she did work for the government. They owe her something. Think about it. We're not exactly a nation without a heart.'

'I wouldn't put anything past those fascist bastards these days.'

'Ever the sixties firebrand, Ray.'

'Someone has to be.'

'I read the *Guardian*, too, Ray, but I don't take it that seriously. Maybe you should try the *Mail* or the *Telegraph* as well and get a different perspective, figure out perhaps the truth lies somewhere between.'

'Traitor. I think I'll stick with *Private Eye*.'

Banks laughed. 'There you go again.'

'She's even been talking about wanting to move to Italy or Greece.'

'And you?'

'I love Italy and Greece, but I love Britain more. It's my home. Besides, I just moved from Cornwall to Yorkshire. I don't want to move again. I'm too bloody old. And there's Annie to consider. We've had a couple of arguments over it, Zelda and me.' He paused and rolled another cigarette. 'But if they treat her badly . . . I've considered getting an Irish passport, you know, to make travel easier if we do have to move or spend more time out of the country.'

'How can you do that?'

'My mother was Irish. Annie's grandmother. Country girl from County Clare.'

'I never knew that.'

'Hell of a woman,' said Ray. 'Tough as nails. Ask Annie. They adored one another.'

'I will.' Banks drank some more water. It was already too warm. 'I really don't think Immigration Enforcement are after Zelda, though I could be wrong. They don't confide in me. More likely it's just a figment of her imagination.'

'Is there any way you can find out? Put our minds at ease.'

There was one way Banks could think of: ask Dirty Dick Burgess.

'I'll see what I can do,' he said. 'In the meantime, just try to carry on as normal. Whatever her problem is, she needs your support more than ever.'

Charlotte Westlake lived on a quiet tree-lined street of large detached houses in Adel, near Alwoodley in North Leeds. Gerry parked the car on the opposite side of the street, and she and Annie walked up the path by a well-kept lawn surrounded by colourful flower beds. It was early Monday evening. The house itself, half hidden by a fat old oak tree with a gnarled trunk, was an ordinary enough combination of stone and red brick, with a bay window on the ground floor and a dormer in the slate roof.

Annie rang the bell, and a few seconds later a woman answered. She was casually dressed in tight-fitting designer jeans and a white fuzzy top with a scalloped neckline. She was slender and tanned with expensively coiffed blonde hair tumbling in bouncy corkscrew waves over her shoulders. Sometimes Annie found herself wondering why some women paid a fortune to arrange their hair in exactly the kind of tangled mess her own naturally aspired to. This was one such moment. Annie pegged Charlotte as about forty, with smooth skin, high cheekbones and the kind of figure she would have had to work out at the gym at least three times a week to maintain. Annie felt immediately aware of her own failed determination to lose the ten pounds she had put on recently.

They showed their warrant cards, and Charlotte Westlake invited them in. Annie noticed gold embroidery around the shield-shaped back pockets of her jeans as she led them through to the back of the house. A glassed-in area like a conservatory, but still an integral part of the large open-plan living room, it overlooked a lush and rambling garden, complete with birdbath and gazebo, on to Adel Woods, a vast expanse of woodland, open meadows and heathland popular with walkers, cyclists and joggers.

'What a lovely view,' said Annie.

Charlotte inclined her head regally. 'Yes,' she said. 'One never tires of it, no matter what the season. Please, sit down.'

Annie and Gerry sat in comfortable armchairs facing the windows, and Charlotte sat opposite them.

'Can I ask you what this is about?' she said.

'Of course. It's to do with Connor Clive Blaydon.'

'Ah, yes. Poor Connor. Such a sad loss.'

Annie was surprised by the comment but held her tongue. As far as she was concerned there was nothing 'poor' about Blaydon, and he was no great loss to humankind. 'We understand you were Blaydon's personal assistant,' she said. 'What exactly was your role?'

'Just what you'd expect, really. Pretty much whatever came up. I helped him organise his busy schedule, reminded him of appointments and meetings and so on. Fielded requests I thought he wouldn't want to be bothered with. Smoothed ruffled feathers, oiled creaky wheels, calmed troubled waters.'

'Good Lord,' said Annie, 'I wish I had someone like you to organise my life for me.'

Charlotte laughed. 'Maybe you should try it?'

'On a copper's salary? You must be joking. What about Blaydon's parties?'

'Them, too. Invitations, catering, drinks, performers sometimes – you know, a string quartet, DJ or a rock band, that sort of thing. I used to be an events organiser. Am again, as a matter of fact.'

'Do you have any of these old invitations?' Annie asked.

'No. I'm not speaking literally, you understand. I didn't exactly address envelopes and lick stamps. We never sent anything by post. It was all fairly casual. Connor would give us a list of names, then my secretary would either phone, text or email.'

'Pity,' Annie said. 'Do you remember the names of any of the people who attended?'

'It varied. I remember some of the more famous people, of course, and I can name you a few media people and local politicians. Tamara took care of most of it.'

'Tamara?'

'My secretary.'

'Is she still around?'

'I suppose so. She lives in Eastvale, I think.' Charlotte paused. 'Why do you want to know? The parties *were* pretty exclusive, but some of the most valued guests brought friends or colleagues, business people they wanted to impress. You could hardly refuse them entry. And there were gatecrashers on occasion, or people who had fallen out of favour trying to sneak back in. I suppose what I'm saying is there's no real written record of everyone who attended them. There was a lot of word of mouth. Connor's parties were very popular, sort of like an exclusive luxury nightclub.'

'I'll bet they were,' said Annie. 'Who manned the door?'

'Roberts. He could be quite diplomatic when required to be.'

'Did you usually attend?'

'Me? Hardly ever. My job was done by the time the parties started. I had staff members working behind the scenes making sure everything went smoothly, and some making sure everyone's drink was topped up, the canapés didn't run out and nobody was stuck alone in a corner. They chatted with guests, worked the room, helped make people feel at home.' She laughed. 'Glorified waitresses, really. I was usually in touch by phone over the evening in case there were any glitches, but there rarely were. Sometimes I'd drop by if there was a special event, like live music I wanted to hear, or a theme night.'

'Theme night?'

'Yes, Connor had themed parties, too, sometimes.'

'Fancy dress?'

'Sort of. Roman times, sixties, twenties flappers, that sort of thing.'

'Fancy dress and period behaviour?'

'Who knows what they got up to? If I did drop by, it would never be for long.' She twisted a ring on her middle finger. 'And certainly not to spy. Why are you asking me all this? What's going on?'

'Who made sure that the cocaine dishes remained full?' Gerry asked.

'So that's it.' Charlotte spread her hands. 'I'd be a liar if I said that I didn't know there were drugs around, just as there were sexual favours being given, and taken, but I can assure you I had nothing to do with either. I've told you. My work was behind the scenes.'

'Boys will be boys,' Annie said.

Charlotte shrugged.

'But were you ever present when drugs were taken?' Gerry asked.

'Surely you can't arrest me for that?'

'I'm sure we could find a charge without resorting to making something up if we wanted to.'

'Connor *was* my employer,' said Charlotte. 'It wasn't my place to criticise his habits. You may judge me wealthy on the basis of this house, but I'm not a rich woman. I needed to work. Still do.'

'You mentioned events organising?' Annie said, in a move to get Charlotte off the defensive.

'That's right. I'm a partner in an events organising company.'

'What kind of events?'

'All sorts. Mostly corporate. Product launches, gala dinners, parties, retirement dos, presentations, AGMs, conventions. You name it. Pretty much anything except weddings. I hate weddings. They're too much of a nightmare, and there are plenty of other companies around to deal with them.'

'How did you get into the business?'

'I suppose I drifted there. It was something I found I had a knack for – finding the right venue, the right band or DJ if either was required, working with a chef on a menu, keeping costs down – whatever was required.'

'Was that your background?'

'Good heavens, no. I was fortunate enough to attend Oxford. I studied Economics and Management at St Hilda's. I suppose you could count that as a bit of a background.'

'Cheltenham Ladies College?'

Charlotte laughed. 'Where on earth did you get that idea? No, nothing like that. Just a Halifax comprehensive. Though I did get a scholarship.'

'So you went into the business straight from university?'

'Not quite. After three years of studying I felt I needed a break. Let my hair down. I went travelling with some like-minded uni friends.'

'Where did you travel?'

'All over. First the Far East. Thailand, Vietnam and Cambodia. Then we spent some time bumming around the Mediterranean.'

'Sounds exotic. Are you married?'

'Widowed. Five years now. Leukaemia.'

'Yet you still live here alone?'

Charlotte played with her ring again and glanced around the room. 'In this huge mansion. I know it's too big for me, but I couldn't bear to leave,' she said. 'I know it would make sense. I could sell this place for a tidy sum, buy a nice little flat in Headingley or somewhere and live off the profit. But it's my home. Gareth and I lived here all our married life. And it's mortgage-free now. I can just about afford the upkeep as long as I keep working.'

'How long were you married?'

'Just ten short years, but I wouldn't change them for anything.'

'How did you come to work for Mr Blaydon?' Gerry asked.

'I helped organise a gala dinner for him when I first got in the business. I'd known him vaguely on and off for a while. He used the company I worked for before frequently for his business events.'

'So you go back a long way?'

'Well, not *that* long,' said Charlotte. 'I'm not that old.'

'Was he a friend of your late husband's?'

'No.' Charlotte paused. 'Truth be told, Gareth disapproved of him, of his business practices.'

'It's true they left a lot to be desired,' said Annie. 'But you gave up event organising to become Blaydon's PA?'

'I needed a break, a change. A challenge, even. It seemed like a good opportunity. After Gareth died I had what you might call a fallow period. I needed to get back to work. Connor offered me a job. There was a fair bit of foreign travel involved, which I enjoy, and the duties weren't too onerous.'

'Where did the foreign travel take you?'

'All over. Sometimes Connor had parties or business meetings at his villa on Corfu. I organised meetings in America sometimes, and a convention once in Cape Town.'

'Sounds like fun,' Annie said.

'Yes. I enjoyed it.'

'Did you ever meet someone called Leka Gashi in your travels?'

'That animal? Towards the end, Connor was mixing with some seriously undesirable people. He said they were important to his property development plans, but if you ask me, they were just using him.'

'For what?'

'Contacts, mostly. He'd built up a lot of contacts within the community and the establishment over the years.'

'What about money laundering?' Gerry asked.

'I don't know anything about that.'

'I understand that he invited people from all walks of life to his parties,' Annie said. 'At least the higher walks. Judges, senior police officers, politicians, clergy, actors, footballers, the odd rock star or two.'

'Connor collected people. And he liked to be among the movers and shakers, the stars and entrepreneurs. He liked to be seen with them. Photographed.'

'And Gashi?'

'He wanted to appear respectable. I would have said it was impossible for a man like him, but he thought that with Connor's contacts and prestige, some of it would rub off on him. Like the others, he probably thought that knowing Connor would make him appear respectable.'

'But instead some of Gashi's criminality rubbed off on Connor?'

'I don't know about that. I wasn't his business manager. He had other people to deal with all that stuff. I never saw him do anything illegal. I just didn't like Gashi. He was a crude pig of a man.'

'Was he sexually aggressive?'

'Not towards me, except with his eyes. But I would imagine so, yes. He was a man used to getting what he wanted, no matter what.'

'As we understand it, they were old friends. Blaydon had known Gashi for years. Did you know that?'

Charlotte blinked and gave a brief shake of her head. Her hair danced over her shoulders.

Gerry glanced at Annie and raised an eyebrow. 'What about Petar Tadić?' she asked.

'Another of Connor's gangster friends. Fortunately, I didn't have much to do with him.'

'We think Tadić supplied the girls. What did you know about the sexual favours?' Annie asked.

'Nothing. That was purely Connor's domain. As I said, I did the food, sometimes the entertainment, the ambience, but the drugs and women were nothing to do with me.'

'You didn't help Tadić supply girls for him?'

'God, no. What do you think I am?'

'You must have known what was going on. Couples disappearing into bedrooms, girls hanging around naked by the pool.'

'I know there were always plenty of pretty girls about, models and so on, but beyond that I didn't inquire. And I was rarely present. It wasn't my business. I just assumed they were WAGs, as I believe they're called. Many of Connor's guests had beautiful models or actresses as girlfriends, and some of the wealthy and powerful men had young attractive wives. And the last time I heard, sex wasn't illegal.'

'Depends on how old the people involved are,' Annie said.

'And how willing,' Gerry added.

'Are you saying the girls were underage?'

'Some of them look that way,' said Gerry. 'Didn't you notice? Didn't you think so at the time?'

'Like I said, I wasn't there often. And when I was, I hardly paid them any attention. They were just decoration. I had other things to think about.'

'Of course,' said Annie. 'Like making sure everyone's glass was full.'

Charlotte stood up. 'I've had enough of this. I think you should go now.'

'I must say,' Annie went on, 'this seems rather naive of you, assuming they were wives and girlfriends. You don't strike me as a particularly naive woman. Didn't you feel uncomfortable, being involved with all those orgies? It wasn't what you signed up for, was it?'

'I told you, I wasn't around for any orgies. Maybe I was burying my head in the sand, not wanting to know why the women were there, or where they came from. But things changed, slowly, subtly. I was starting to feel uncomfortable with Connor's new friends and ways. When I first started three years ago, things were far more civilised, before Gashi and Tadić appeared on the scene. In fact, I left at the end of April, before . . . before Connor died. I had the opportunity to return to my old line of work in partnership with a friend.'

'Mrs Westlake,' said Annie, 'Connor Blaydon was murdered. He didn't just die. Someone helped him on his way. Let's call a spade a spade.'

'Gashi.'

'Why do you say that?'

'He seems like the sort of man who would do . . . that.'

'Kill someone?'

'Yes.'

'Did you ever hear him talk about killing people?'

'Good Lord, no. He wouldn't talk like that in front of me. But I'll bet you he was involved. Either him or one of his little gofers.'

'Can you help us prove it?'

'No. I told you, I was involved in getting back into events planning. I didn't like the company Connor was keeping, the way things were going. There seemed no more . . . moral centre, for want of a better term. Things were spiralling into chaos.'

'Fair enough,' said Annie. 'Please sit down again. We've got a few more questions.'

Charlotte sat down slowly but remained on the edge of her seat, as if she were going to get up and leave the room at any moment.

Gerry consulted her notebook. 'There was a party at Mr Blaydon's house on 13 April, this year,' she said. 'Were you present?'

'It's highly unlikely. As I said, I rarely attended. Let me consult my diary.'

'Would you do that, please? And while you're at it, perhaps you could also let us know where you were on 22 May.'

Charlotte left the room for a couple of minutes and returned with a large desk diary. 'No,' she said, holding it open for them to see. 'I thought so. I was out of the country the week of 13 April.'

'Where were you?'

'Costa Rica.'

'Costa Rica,' said Annie. 'Very nice. Why were you there?'

'Connor sent me. I was organising an international business conference.'

'Was that normal?'

'Perfectly. I told you my job involved a certain amount of travel. Connor was a partner in a new hotel complex development there, and he wanted to bring the investors together with the ideas men and the architects. They all needed to be wined and dined.'

'Naturally,' said Annie. 'Would you have any idea at all who might have been at that party?'

'I'm afraid not.'

'Who might know?'

'Someone who *was* there, I imagine. Maybe Gashi?'

'He was there?'

'Sometimes.'

'Ever heard of someone called Phil Keane? Might have been a friend of Blaydon and Tadić.'

'It doesn't ring any bells.'

'Hugh Foley?' Annie said, remembering what Banks had told her about Keane's relationship with the murdered Faye Butler.

'No. Sorry.'

'And the 22 May?'

'Nothing specific,' said Charlotte. 'Though I think we had a book award dinner to organise in Bradford. I remember it was towards the end of last month.'

'Would anyone be able to corroborate that?'

Charlotte gave her a puzzled glance. 'Corroborate? Why?'

'Would anyone?'

'Maybe. I don't know. I'd have been back and forth, setting things up. Someone might have seen me.'

Annie took the enhanced photo of the girl from the SD out of her briefcase and passed it to Charlotte. 'Do you recognise her?'

Charlotte examined the photo through narrowed eyes and passed it back. 'No, I'm afraid I don't. Though I'm not sure I'd recognise my best friend from that. She looks rather the worse for wear.'

'We think the girl was drunk and possibly drugged,' Annie said. 'And though the images are hard to distinguish, the video clearly shows that she was raped.'

'Raped!' Charlotte repeated. 'I don't know what to say. What video is this?'

'It appears that Blaydon's right-hand man Neville Roberts left a small collection of X-rated movies behind.'

'From the parties?'

'Mini spy-cams in the bedrooms.'

'My God. I had no idea that Connor filmed his guests without their permission.'

'Not Blaydon,' Annie said. 'Neville Roberts. Do you know anything about him?'

'Not much. He was a bit of a dark horse, clearly. I hardly ever talked to him. He was around often, yes, but he was a rather taciturn person, quite surly, and our worlds rarely crossed. He was more of a manservant, really, a sort of butler. Connor liked the luxury. But Roberts had nothing to do with Connor's business dealings.' She tapped the photograph. 'I have to say I've never seen anyone in that state at Connor's house. Not while I've been there.'

'But you're so rarely there,' Gerry reminded her.

'Yes. Even so. I always thought that whatever went on, they still remained fairly wholesome and civilised.'

'A sort of Playboy Mansion thing?'

'If you like. Not that I've ever been to a Playboy mansion.'

'You're doing it again. Pardon me, but isn't that a little naive? Especially as you mentioned things spiralling into chaos.'

'Perhaps. As I said, I *was* fast becoming disillusioned. Even so, I'm honestly shocked by that picture. This is appalling.'

'Hardly surprising,' said Annie. 'As I said, she'd just been raped. We have the whole thing on a MiniSD card.'

'No,' Charlotte whispered, hand at her throat. 'I still don't believe it. Did Connor do this?'

'Why do you say that?'

'I don't know . . . I . . . you said it was one of his parties, you're asking me about it . . . I don't know . . . I just . . .'

'Unfortunately,' Gerry said, 'this is the closest we can get to a likeness of the victim. As you say, it's not very good. And there are no usable facial images of the man involved. Was this an ordinary party or a themed one?'

'Ordinary, I think. At least I don't remember any mention of a theme.'

'You're sure you don't recognise her?'

'I'd tell you if I did.'

'She didn't work for you behind the scenes or anything?'

'I honestly can't tell from that photo.'

'We'd really like to find out who this girl is,' Annie said, 'and it goes without saying that we'd like to catch the man who raped her. If you remember anything, however insignificant it seems to you, please let us know.' She passed Charlotte a card. 'And we'd appreciate a list of names. Any guests you might remember, especially badly behaved ones, and the names and addresses of your employees who attended that party.'

'Of course.' Charlotte stood up again and touched her hair.

She showed them out and they saw her standing at the bay window watching as they got in the car. 'What do you think?' Gerry asked.

'For all her shock and outrage,' said Annie, 'I don't think she was telling us everything she knew.'

'I got the impression that she was holding back, too. Maybe I should have a look into her background?'

'And there was something else,' Annie said.

Gerry headed for the ring road. 'What?'

'She never even offered us a bloody cup of tea.'

'So you're absolutely sure no one from the NCA or Immigration Enforcement is following Zelda, or making enquiries about her past?'

'I told you, Banksy,' said Burgess. 'I'd know. And they're not. Danvers and Debs aren't convinced that Hawkins wasn't bent, but they don't think Zelda had anything to do with his death. They just want to know why she was poking around asking questions about him. What you've just told me about the Phil Keane problem should settle that line of inquiry for them. She was clearly doing it to help you.'

'Have they been talking to immigration about her?'

'Not their style.'

'So I can tell Ray there's nothing to worry about?'

'Yes. At least nothing that I know of.'

'OK. Thanks.'

'No problemo. See you later.'

At least he didn't say 'alligator', Banks thought as he hung up. Burgess's Americanisms were a bit hard to take sometimes, especially when they were archaic, too.

So that was that. First Banks had told Burgess the details of his talk with Zelda, then Burgess had told him how he was certain she wasn't being targeted. He would find time to pop by and see Ray and Zelda together tomorrow morning and give them the good news. If Zelda was suffering from paranoia about the immigration process, nothing he said would cure that completely, but at least it would set Ray at ease and put him in the right state of mind to be there for her.

It was almost eight o'clock. After the phone call, Banks got in his car and picked up a Chinese takeaway in Helmthorpe, and before doing anything else, he tucked into his spring rolls, chicken fried rice and garlic shrimps in the kitchen, drenching them with lashings of soy sauce and washing it all down with simple tap water.

It was another mild evening. After dinner, Banks took George MacDonald Fraser's *Flashman at the Charge* outside, along with a glass of Côtes du Rhône Villages, and sat in his lounge chair facing Tetchley Fell to read for a while.

At first, it was enough just to sip his wine and feel himself unwind as he gazed on the fellside with its criss-cross patterns of drystone walls and enjoyed the gentle breeze on his skin. The breath of wind took the edge off the heat and carried the sweet, dry smell of fresh-mown grass with it, along with a hint of wild garlic and mint. The green fields on the gentle lower slopes slowly gave way to sere grass higher up, where he had walked with Zelda, and finally to outcrops of grey limestone at the top like Henry Moore sculptures shining with an unexpected golden hue in the evening sunlight. Occasionally a sheep bleated way up on the hill, and the swifts made their graceful loops and spirals in the sky. There seemed to be fewer of them this year, he had noticed.

Often when Banks watched the aerial ballet, he thought of Bob Dylan's line about a bird never being free from the chains of the sky. He had also been recently discussing some of Dylan Thomas's poetry with his informal tutor, Linda Palmer, over Sunday lunches up at Low Moor Inn. As far as he was concerned, the jury was still out on the boozy, bardic Welshman, but he had loved the music of 'Fern Hill', whatever the words meant, and the line 'I sang in my chains like the sea' had stuck with him. It was similar in meaning to the other Dylan's observation, he thought.

But it didn't do to overanalyse too much. He had learned that from Linda. Poetry wasn't something to be translated or decoded into a 'message', the way it had been taught at school. True, some poems were overburdened with learning and literary allusion, and they needed some level of exegesis, but most poems meant what they said and said what they meant in the best way, often the only way, possible.

It had certainly been an interesting day. First the walk with Zelda, then Ray's angry visit. He knew that Zelda had gone away annoyed at him for pressing her on matters she would rather have kept to herself, no matter how hard he had tried to be understanding. The thing was, he still wasn't certain that she had told him all she knew. She was holding back about something, but he didn't know what it could be. She had told him only things she thought he already knew, or might suspect. Yes, she had come clean about seeing Keane with Hawkins and asking questions about her late boss, and she had told him about finding Faye Butler, and how that had led to a dead end. But had it? For some reason, he thought, there was more. And he couldn't forget that Faye Butler had ended up dead – tortured and murdered – not so long after Zelda's visit to her.

Ray's concerns also worried him. It was natural enough that Ray would see possible immigration and residence problems as the main source of Zelda's anxiety and depression, but Banks wasn't convinced. Yes, she was worried about being deported back to Moldova, but he didn't believe that was all that was worrying her. He remembered the times during their walk when she had looked over her shoulder to make sure they weren't being followed. Who else did she think was after her? Her old abductors and abusers? But why? Surely they had lost track of her by now. It was also unlikely that Tadić and his like would even remember Zelda, let alone recognise her after all these years. She was the super-recogniser, not him. But until she was willing to talk even more openly, he realised that he wasn't going to find out anything else. And he was still no closer to Phil Keane than he had been when Zelda had first mentioned seeing the photo of him with Tadić, before last Christmas.

Banks opened his book and slipped back into Harry Flashman's version of the disastrous Charge of the Light Brigade as he sipped some more wine. Colonial Britannia at her best. And so the evening passed, quietly and pleasantly as the sun made its way down in the western sky, below the hills, painting an abstract design first of grey and pink behind the slow-moving strata of long thin clouds, then of crimson, orange and purple under the darker, heavier ones. In the distance, a car's rear lights followed the winding road over Tetchley Pass into the next dale.

Banks sat on, sipping his wine and enjoying the nature show, until the evening's chill made him shiver and there was no longer enough light left to read by. Then he took his wine and moved back inside. He checked his phone to see if he had missed any messages. He hadn't.

When the evenings stretched out as they did in summer, he rarely watched television or movies, unless it was raining. He didn't even listen to much music. Sometimes he played the guitar Brian had bought him, wondering when he would get the fingering of even the basic three chords exactly right. And that reminded him: it was only two days until the Blue Lamps' farewell concert at the Sage. Tracy and Mark would be going with him, along with Ray and Zelda. It promised to be a fine evening. Maybe they would all manage to get together with Brian for a drink or two over the river afterwards.

He wondered how Tracy and Mark were getting on in Tenerife, where they had gone for their honeymoon. He was glad they had decided against a destination wedding, unlike so many other young couples these days. It was selfish in the extreme, he thought, going off to Cyprus or Malta to get married when half your family either couldn't afford to attend, or were too old and ill to travel. Healthy and independent as they were, Banks's parents wouldn't have been willing or able to travel so far for their granddaughter's wedding.

Tonight Banks felt restless for some reason, and he couldn't settle down with the guitar. He was sick to death of playing 'Bobby Shafto' but seemed unable to move beyond it. He searched through YouTube for interesting music and ended up watching a few Grateful Dead concert clips.

Halfway through a fine 'Scarlet Begonias', Banks's mobile played its blues riff. He was in half a mind not to answer, but habit kicked in and he put the TV on pause and picked it up. It was going on for eleven o'clock, and he always felt a tremor of apprehension when the phone rang so late. Had something happened to Tracy? Or Brian?

He recognised the number as Ray Cabbot's. Puzzled, he answered, but couldn't make out what Ray was saying at first. He asked him to repeat it, and this time it came through loud and clear: 'She's gone,' Ray said. 'It's Zelda. She's gone.'

7

Lit by Banks's headlights, the B-road to Lyndgarth unfurled like a ribbon over the moorland, passing by fast-flowing becks and grassy hillocks, until the lights of the village came into view, nestled in a hollow and scattered around the lopsided village green. It stood at the junction of Swainsdale and Lyndsdale, where the river Lynd joined the Swain. Just a couple of miles to the north, the valley sides rose steeply on either side to form two curved limestone scars. It never got completely dark at that time of year, and a three-quarter moon made the scars stand out like bands of light floating above the darkness of the valley.

Banks drove along the high street, beside the green, past the chapel, two of the village's three pubs and the Spar general store, then turned left and carried on west for another mile or so until he pulled up at the short turn-off for Ray Cabbot's cottage. All the lights were on. Ray must have heard the car coming, or seen its lights, as he was standing in the doorway smoking and waiting.

When they went inside to the living room, Ray stubbed out his cigarette and poured himself a generous measure of single malt. He offered the bottle, but Banks declined. Ray's hands were shaking as he lifted the glass to his mouth.

'I don't know what to do,' he said. 'I should never have left her.'

'Calm down and tell me what happened,' said Banks.

'I don't *know* what happened. All I know is she's gone.'

'There's no note or anything?'

'No.'

'What time did you get back from Leeds?'

'Around half ten. The lecture finished at nine so I headed straight back after a few questions. I was worried about Zelda. I told you we'd parted on bad terms. She was upset, angry. I wanted to . . . I mean . . .' He put his glass down and hung his head in his hands. 'Oh, Christ, Alan, what am I to do?'

Banks touched his shoulder. 'Try to stay calm, Ray. Did she take anything with her? A suitcase, clothing?'

'I don't know. I haven't checked. But her car's still here, round back.'

'She can't have got far then. Are you sure she isn't at a friend's house in the village? Or in the pub?'

'She wouldn't do that. I mean, she doesn't really have any close friends in the village. People are still a bit frosty. We do go to the pub. Mick Slater, the landlord, is a decent guy. But I don't think she'd go there by herself, especially not at night. You don't understand, Alan. When I said she was *gone*, I didn't mean gone as in she'd left of her own free will. I meant she's gone as in she's been *taken*.'

'How do you know?'

Ray jerked his head towards the back of the house. 'Her studio. It's a mess. Like . . . I don't know.' He put his hand to his chest.

'OK?' Banks asked.

'Fine. I just get a bit breathless sometimes, a bit of tightness in the chest, especially when I'm upset.'

'You should go see a doctor.'

'Bah. Waste of time.'

Banks brought him a glass of water from the kitchen, touched his shoulder and said, 'Stay here. Take it easy.'

Then Banks walked out back and across the stretch of grass to the large garden shed that served as Zelda's studio. The door was wide open and the lights on. Inside, there was enough room for her to set up an easel to paint, or tools to sculpt, and a workbench where she crafted jewellery, but not much more.

In the far corner, undamaged, stood a stack of canvases and sketches, mostly imitations of famous artists – Magritte, Modigliani, Hockney, Dali. They were good copies, though mostly unfinished. Zelda was a skilled imitator, but she wasn't a forger. She had never tried to pass any of them off as originals. On the other hand, if you wanted a competent version of *A Bigger Splash* or a Modigliani nude to hang on your wall, she could knock one off for you, for a price.

Banks saw what Ray meant about thc mess. There had clearly been some sort of struggle near the door. A wine glass lay shattered on the floor, its contents splattered all over the threadbare carpet. The easel had been knocked over, paints spilled, a work in progress ruined, and Banks saw what he thought to be a smear of blood on the workbench, though he supposed it could be paint or red wine. There was a smell of turpentine and oil. On her workbench, Zelda had a small vice and set of tiny engraving tools for her delicate jewellery work. He leaned forward and examined the vice closely. There was no blood on it, and it didn't appear as if it had been used to crush her fingers or toes. That was something to be grateful for. Banks left the workshed as it was and went back to the main house.

'See what I mean?' Ray said. 'Someone took her against her will.' He was smoking another roll-up, taking short, nervous drags.

'Are you sure you didn't have a fight and throw stuff around and she walked out?'

'Of course not. Don't be so bloody silly. You saw the state of her studio. You surely can't believe *I* did that? Or Zelda herself? I told you we had an argument earlier, but not a stand-up, drag-down fight. I've never once been violent towards her.'

'It looks like there was some sort of struggle,' Banks said. 'Have you checked the rest of the house to see if she's hiding anywhere? Or hurt.'

'First thing I did. She's not here.'

'Let's check her clothes,' said Banks. 'You can tell me if anything's missing.'

Ray stubbed out the cigarette. They went upstairs and Ray led him into a small bedroom. 'This is hers,' he said.

'You mean you . . .?'

'We have separate bedrooms,' Ray said.

The room was neat and tidy and showed no traces of a struggle whatsoever. The walls were painted in pastel greens and yellows, hung with random sketches and paintings, and the duvet was burgundy. Banks and Ray searched through the wardrobe and drawers. When they had finished, Ray said, 'No. As far as I can tell, everything's where it should be. But I don't . . . you know . . . I didn't keep an inventory. I'm not saying there isn't a T-shirt or a pair of knickers missing. But she didn't have a lot of clothes. It seems normal to me.'

'What about the surrounding countryside? Have you been out searching for her?'

'No. I haven't had a chance yet. I phoned you pretty much straight away, soon as I'd seen the studio and checked the house.'

'We'd better have a look,' said Banks. 'She might be out there, not far away. She may have run off, or simply gone for a walk. She might be hurt. Trapped.'

'I never thought of that,' said Ray, jumping at the idea that Zelda might be nearby after all.

'Got a torch?'

They went downstairs and Ray fetched two torches from the utility room under the staircase. 'They're not much cop, I'm afraid, but it's all I've got.'

'That all right,' said Banks. 'The moon's pretty bright. We might not even need them.'

To the east of the cottage, a grassy slope ran down to the edge of Lyndgarth village, about half a mile away. It was a wide-open space and hardly a likely spot for concealment. As far as Banks could see, it was uninhabited. On the other side, however, the cottage stood on the edge of moorland which stretched for miles to the west. It was rough terrain, covered in heather and gorse, with a number of dangerous bogs, several wooded areas and deep gullies. The natural light was almost enough to see by, but they carried their torches in case they came to a gully or pothole. About a mile to the south-west stood the dark ruins of Devraulx Abbey, suitably Gothic and ghostly in the moonlight.

As they walked, they called out Zelda's name, but got only silence or the cry of a frightened bird in return. After a while, it became clear that they needed their torches to illuminate the tangle of roots under their feet, which slowed their progress.

After almost an hour's wandering with no success, they returned to Ray's cottage and flopped down on the living-room chairs. Ray rolled another cigarette and lit up again. 'What if she's further away, bleeding, or she broke her leg or something? Shouldn't we go out again? Further, this time.'

'I don't think it's very productive to start thinking along those lines, Ray. She's not bleeding to death. There was no great amount of blood in her studio, if it's even blood. And if she is out there hurt, it's a mild night, and she'll have no trouble lying low until morning. You know how quickly it gets light here in summer. By then I'll have a search party organised.'

'I can't help thinking something terrible's happened to her. Maybe she's unconscious. Or dead?'

'She'll be fine, Ray. Zelda's a lot more resourceful and resilient than you imagine. Think what she's endured over the years. And think about this: if someone wanted to kill her, or hurt her, they could easily have done it here and just left her body in the studio. Don't you think that's what they would have done?'

'Probably. But what's happening to her? Do you think someone might be hurting her?'

Banks knew that the worst thing about dealing with missing persons was imagining the terrible things they might be suffering, such as torture – right down to fingernails being pulled, teeth extracted, electrodes attached to private parts, limbs smashed, bloody beatings and, especially when women were involved, rape. There was no way of stopping such images for an empathetic person, which Ray clearly was. Banks felt empathy, too, but he had learned to control it over the years. Such imaginings could cloud his judgement and the procedures that had to be followed in these cases. The thing to concentrate on was finding the missing person alive and not to be distracted by what he or she might be suffering in the meantime. It was hard, but he had learned to do it most of the time. The fears only came back in the dark hours, three or four in the morning, when he lay awake and terrible images crowded his mind. Ray was already at that stage.

'There's no evidence that anyone harmed her in the studio,' Banks said, 'and I assume if it was information they wanted, they could have got it out of her there.'

'But who could have done this? Might immigration have taken her?'

'Well, for a start,' Banks said, 'they haven't yet stooped to abducting people from their homes by force. Even they wouldn't go that far.' Though even as he said it, he wondered. Certainly if someone put up resistance, immigration officers might use the same sort of force as the police would to make an arrest in similar circumstances. He still very much doubted that was what had happened.

'Do you think she might have been kidnapped?'

'Maybe. The thing is, we don't know. All we know is that she's gone and that it looks as if someone took her against her will.'

'I've got money. I can pay the ransom. Up to a point. I can sell more paintings.'

'Let's not get ahead of ourselves, Ray.'

Ray stood up and started pacing. 'But we have to do *something*. We can't just sit here.'

'I need to call it in,' said Banks. 'Get a team set up. Lines of inquiry. Time can be crucial in these cases, and we've already wasted too much.' He didn't want to tell Ray that most murders occur soon after a person goes missing. On the other hand, it had made sense to check the house and the surrounding countryside thoroughly before gearing up for a full missing person investigation. 'Did you touch anything in the studio?' he asked.

Ray shook his head. Banks hadn't either. He had deliberately kept his hands in his pockets.

'Did you leave it exactly as you found it?'

'Yes. The door was open, the lights on.'

Banks reached in his pocket for his mobile. Nobody would appreciate such a call in the early hours, but it had to be done. When he connected with the comms room he asked for the duty officer and explained in clear terms what had happened, stating that, in his opinion, Zelda had been forcibly abducted by persons unknown and that AC Gervaise should be informed at once. All patrol officers should keep their eyes open for a woman matching Zelda's description, which he gave them, with a little help from Ray. He also asked that they organise a search team for the immediate moors as soon as it was daylight, and have AC Gervaise alert the CSIs to come and search the victim's premises. 'And tell them to be careful driving in,' he added. 'There might be tyre tracks and Lord knows what else out there. Fingerprints and trace evidence in the studio.'

Ray sat pale and shaking as Banks talked on. When he'd finished, Banks put his phone away and made some notes about timing. 'You need to know they'll be a lot harder on you than I've been,' he said. 'The first suspect in a missing persons case is always the one who reports it, along with the missing person herself.'

'But you know I'd never do anything like that,' pleaded Ray. 'Isn't it obvious? I love Zelda. I could never harm her.'

'Doesn't matter what I think. And to an objective interviewer, it won't be obvious. People kill for love as often as they do for profit or hatred. You need to tell them absolutely everything you think will help us find Zelda. And I mean everything. Don't gloss over the row you had because thinking about it makes you feel bad, or you think it'll make them suspect you more. Tell them. They'll also want to know her habits, haunts, friends and so on. Any problems or worries, too. Whether you thought she was having an affair. I know we think she was abducted from her studio after a struggle, and that's what it looks like, but she may have run off and gone to hide somewhere, or to be with someone. Maybe she wrecked the studio herself in a fit of rage, or she decided to disappear and the mess is a red herring or a cover-up.'

'She wouldn't do that,' Ray said. 'And there's nobody else. I'd know.'

'The point is that we *don't know* what happened. All we have to go on is guesswork. Just tell them what you know about the work she did and the people who abused and enslaved her. Her fears about Immigration Enforcement, her relationship with Annie. I know you say she didn't tell you much about her past, and it's possible I can fill in a few blanks myself, but tell them everything you *do* know. It may all be connected.'

Ray swallowed. 'What now?' he asked.

'I don't suppose you want to go to sleep?'

'No way. I need to stay awake. Someone might call. A ransom demand or something. Or maybe Zelda herself. Annie. My God, I should call Annie.'

Banks stood up. 'I'll do that,' he said. 'I need to talk to her. The officers should be here soon. I'll head to the station and start organising things from there.'

'No,' said Ray, reaching out and grabbing his elbow. 'Don't go. Stay here with me, Alan. Please. I'm at my wits' end and I can't be alone. I want you to head the investigation. I need to know you're on this a hundred per cent.'

Banks disengaged his arm gently. 'All right,' he said. 'I'll do my best. I don't think my being a friend will disqualify me from trying to find Zelda, and it may even give me an advantage in any search, but there's always a possibility my bosses might think I'm too close to things. I'll stay here for now and talk to the team when they arrive. There's one condition.'

'Anything.'

'Seeing as I won't be driving home for a while, you can clear some space on your sofa and pour me a large glass of that fine Highland Park right now.'

After he finished the whisky, sleep didn't seem to be an immediate possibility, so Banks left Ray and went to check out the studio again. This time he took a pair of latex gloves from the crime scene kit in the boot of his car so as not to disturb any evidence that the attackers might have left there.

First, he picked up Zelda's leather satchel-style shoulder bag, the one she always carried, from the chair. Its contents were as one would expect: mobile phone, keys, purse and cigarettes – but in addition she also carried a small digital camera, a black Moleskine notebook, a Kindle and a little white case of AirPods. There were a few other inconsequential odds and ends – paper tissues, tampons, a combination penknife/corkscrew, hairbrush, lipstick, a couple of rollerball pens and a charger for the iPhone.

Zelda had a desk in the far corner of the studio, which seemed untouched by the struggle, and on it sat her MacBook along with a small flat-top printer. Banks knew better than to touch the computer, even with his protective gloves on. The CSIs would rush it to tech support for a thorough check. It was easy to lose data inadvertently if you didn't know what you were doing, and Banks would have been the first to admit that he didn't. He wasn't tech-illiterate or a Luddite by any means, but the inner workings of the CPUs and vagaries of internal architecture and configurations of computers were way beyond his grasp.

He glanced over at the titles on the bookshelf above the desk. As he would have expected with Zelda, there were a lot of literary classics – Dostoevsky, Kafka, Dumas, Flaubert, Dickens, Hardy – along with an odd selection of children's books, mostly by Enid Blyton, Jacqueline Wilson and Roald Dahl, and a few Modesty Blaise novels by Peter O'Donnell. There was also, he discovered on further investigation, a half row of non-fiction books concerned with the stories of women trafficked and raped by terrorist groups such as ISIS and Boko Haram, especially Yazidi and Rohingyan women, including *The War on Women* by Sue Lloyd-Roberts, Dunya Mikhail's *The Beekeeper of Sinjar* and Nadia Murad's *The Last Girl*.

One of the desk drawers was filled with printer paper and spare cartridges, another with a selection of pens and pencils, rulers and other stationery items. But this drawer also contained some more personal items – photos of her and Ray in happier days, a few sentimental souvenirs from trips they had made together. There was a newspaper clipping about the discovery of Faye Butler's body, which made sense now that Banks knew Zelda had met Faye. There were also some official papers, including her French passport. It still had a few years left on it, and when he examined the stamps he noticed the most recent was from Chișinău, dated the previous Friday. He knew that was where she had grown up, and where she had first been abducted from, and he wondered what she had been doing back there so recently.

When he had finished, Banks stood at the centre of the room and opened the notebook. It wasn't a diary or a journal, but more of a catch-all. There were fragmentary shopping lists, titles of books she wanted to read, quotations from books she had been reading and memos to herself, as well as poems and story ideas, passages of self-analysis, descriptions of dreams and fantasies. There were also several lengthy descriptions of landscapes: an unnamed stretch of the Croatian coastline, the moorland around Windlee Farm, a view of London from somewhere on the South Bank near Blackfriars Bridge, a London hotel called the Belgrade.

There were flashes of memory, too, mostly bad – a vicious beating in Ljubljana, a john who threatened her with a knife in Pristina, a failed suicide attempt in Minsk. It made for harrowing reading. In addition, several pieces read very much like fantasies of revenge against people who had harmed her: a pimp in Paris called Darius, Goran Tadić and someone called Vasile Lupescu. These sections might also be notes towards a story, or stories, she intended to write someday. Zelda was an artistic type and a keen reader; perhaps she had ambitions towards fiction and this was a record of her imaginings.

Banks hoped the notebook might offer some clues to Zelda's whereabouts, and he would study it further for that very reason. But it also put him in a difficult position. At the moment, he was the only one in the possession of these private musings; if he didn't include the notebook with the rest of Zelda's possessions, he would be guilty of withholding evidence. But evidence of what? he reasoned. Fantasising about a murder isn't the same as committing one. Jotting down notes for a mystery story isn't a crime.

Besides, he couldn't, in all conscience, create more problems for Zelda when she was probably living in terror of her life. He would ask her about the notebook when he found her.

Without further thought, Banks slipped the notebook in the inside pocket of his jacket and went back to the main house.

Dawn broke early over Lyndgarth Moor, and by the time the sun was up, a semicircle of officers moved slowly west from the isolated cottage. Seen from afar, they could have been grouse-beating but for the police uniforms most of them were wearing.

Back in the house, Banks and Ray Cabbot sat drinking strong coffee with a fresh-faced AC Gervaise, who had only just arrived smelling of soap and shampoo. Banks had had a fitful night on the sofa and wondered if he looked as bad as he felt, while Ray, he imagined, hadn't slept at all. His clothes were wrinkled, his eyes blurry and red. Two detectives from the Northallerton HQ at Alverton Court – DS Flyte and DC Bharati – had appeared with the search team and CSIs, and they had already questioned Ray. No wonder the poor bloke was exhausted, Banks thought.

No one was yet any nearer to finding Zelda or to working out what had happened to her. She hadn't been seen by any of the night patrols, and though her description had gone out nation-wide, the general thinking was that she couldn't be that far away. No one would want to risk a long journey with a kidnapped woman and all the possible encounters with police cars and CCTV cameras that might occur. Whoever took her had probably planned it all out in advance and had a place already prepared somewhere in the Dales. Perhaps a deserted farmhouse or ruined barn, Airbnb, or a remote cottage rental. It wasn't as if there was any scarcity of isolated spots and abandoned buildings out there. It depended on what her abductors planned to do with her, of course. And when they planned to do it.

The CSIs agreed there had been a struggle in the studio but found no immediate evidence of harm being done to Zelda. The suspect bloodstain turned out to be paint. They were still working out there, collecting trace evidence, fingerprints and anything else that seemed relevant. The search team had first gone through the house and grounds, even though Ray assured them he had already done so. They were just doing their jobs, Banks told him, and it paid to be thorough, but Ray complained anyway. He must have smoked a whole pouch of Drum, and the front room stank of smoke.

One positive outcome was that the CSIs were able to determine the direction in which a car had travelled by the pattern of fresh tyre tracks – and it had turned on to the moorland road, an unfenced track, heading westward, deeper and deeper into the wild heathland dotted with tiny hamlets and remote farms. West wasn't the best way out of the area if the abductors wanted to link up with any of the major motorways. They would have about a two-hour drive over rough moorland terrain to get anywhere, and they probably wouldn't want to be so exposed for that long. They could have no idea when the hue and cry over Zelda's disappearance would go up.

'So what's next?' Ray asked.

Gervaise glanced at Banks. 'You're SIO, Alan,' she said. 'What do you think?'

'We'll see if the early search teams turn up anything,' Banks said, 'then we'll start a door-to-door in the village and out in the dale, asking if anybody saw or heard anything unusual. We'll also talk to Zelda's friends and try to find out about anyone who might wish her harm. We don't know what actual time she was taken yet, do we?'

'You know I was over at your place late yesterday afternoon,' Ray said. 'About half five, six. Then I drove to Leeds, gave my talk and got back here by about half past ten.' He glanced at Gervaise. 'Soon as I realised something was seriously wrong I phoned Alan and he was here in, what, twenty minutes?'

'If that,' Banks said. 'And it was about a quarter to eleven when Ray phoned.'

'So any time between about five o'clock and ten-thirty,' said Gervaise.

Ray nodded.

'Tell me, why did you call Superintendent Banks rather than the police station?'

'The other blokes asked me that, too. I would have thought it was a no-brainer. I know him. He lives nearby. He's a mate. And he's a detective. Made sense to me.'

'What about your daughter?'

'Annie? Dunno. I didn't think of her at first.'

'Why not? Just because she lives further away?'

'Not really.'

'Because she's a woman?'

'No. Because she's my daughter.'

'You might as well know,' Banks said, 'that Annie and Zelda don't get along too well.'

'Oh?' said Gervaise, glancing at Ray. 'And why's that?'

'None of your—'

Banks cut Ray off. 'Plenty of reasons,' he said. 'You know families. They just got off on the wrong foot, that's all. It's hardly relevant. You don't think Annie had anything to do with this, do you?'

'It pays to be thorough and not discount anything,' Gervaise said. Then she smiled. 'But no, I don't think DI Cabbot is a suspect. Though I do think she's too close to the case to work it in an objective manner. She's a relative.'

'Zelda and I aren't married,' Ray said.

'A mere technicality,' said Gervaise. 'I'm going to keep her on the Blaydon rape case for the time being. DC Masterson, too. You can have DS Flyte and DC Bharati, Alan. Let's see how this goes today before we have another meeting and decide whether to raise the investigation to another level and bring in more troops.'

'I think it's pretty obvious something's happened to Zelda, don't you?' said Ray. 'Why wait? What do you lot need to get you started, a dead body?'

'Ray,' said Banks. 'Everything that can be done is being done. When we see where we're going, we'll know whether we have to allocate extra resources. What we hope is that we'll have Zelda back safe and sound long before we need to make that decision.'

Ray rolled another cigarette and gave him a look that said, 'Bullshit.'

8

'How's Ray really doing?' Annie asked over a late lunch in the Queen's Arms. 'All he told me was that he was coping and not to come over because the house was full of cops already.'

They were sitting outside, in the shade of a large umbrella, Banks munching on fish and chips and Annie picking away at a quinoa salad. The landlord Cyril stopped short of vegan sausage rolls and plant-based burgers, but this was his one recent gesture towards the rise of healthier eating. Annie was drinking fizzy water and Banks was trying one of the no-alcohol beers, another gesture to modern times. He was surprised how good it tasted.

'Not so well,' said Banks. 'He's smoking like a chimney and hitting the bottle pretty hard. But it's true the CSIs are going to be at his house for a while longer. You know what they're like. I just dropped him off at my place and left him there with a bit of Pink Floyd in the background to calm his nerves.'

'No ransom demands or anything?'

'No. Nothing. He's got his mobile with him, just in case. Besides, Flyte and Bharati are still at the house, and they're trained to deal with situations like this.'

'I should go and see him.'

'Maybe. Give him a little while to decompress first. I wish Winsome wasn't still on maternity leave. I don't know Flyte or Bharati well. They seem OK, but . . . let's just say I could do with DS Jackman.'

'I know what you mean. I paid Winsome a visit yesterday.'

'How's she doing?'

'She's in excellent spirits. And the baby is a real sweetheart.'

'I'll bet she just can't wait to come back to work, can she?'

'Dream on.' Annie paused. 'You know Zelda and I have our problems, but this is terrible. I hope nothing awful's happened to her.'

'Whatever it is, it's not likely to be good.'

'What do you think it's all about?'

Banks paused for a moment and heard a snatch of 'Be My Baby' coming from inside. Phil Spector's 'Wall of Sound'. It reminded him of better times, listening to music on the front step on a Sunday afternoon with his school friends. How good the old Dansette had sounded then. And how exciting the music had been, heard for the first time. Now Spector was in jail for murder and Ed Sheeran was topping the charts. 'Either it's a set-up and she's done a bunk,' said Banks, 'or someone's taken her.'

'Why would she fake her own abduction?'

If Zelda *had* killed Goran Tadić and felt that his gang had found out about it, that might be one good reason, Banks thought, but he couldn't tell Annie that. Besides, he still wasn't convinced by her writings that she had done anything of the kind. More than anything else, she seemed to have been questioning her ability to commit such an act, something even Banks himself had wondered about from time to time. He had killed plenty of people in his fantasies. 'I don't know,' he said. 'Last time we talked she told me a few things I didn't know, about seeing Keane with her boss, and finding his ex-girlfriend, Faye Butler. Remember, I told you he was going by the name of Hugh Foley? But I still got the impression that she was holding back. That there was something important she *couldn't* tell me, or wouldn't. And she seemed anxious, on edge. I didn't think our conversation was strained, but Ray said she was pissed off when she got home, and they had a row. Maybe I hit a nerve. I think she may be in big trouble. If she did do a runner, it was probably because she felt things were closing in on her and she needed to escape. She might also have been worried about Ray, about him getting dragged into whatever it was. He's a bit of an innocent, your father, in a lot of ways.'

'Always was. In his own world. What things might Zelda need to escape from?'

'I think it's something to do with what she wouldn't tell me. Someone was after her. She was always looking over her shoulder.' He laughed. 'You know what they say: just because you're paranoid, it doesn't mean there isn't somebody following you.'

'Who?'

'That I don't know. I have my suspicions. It was probably someone from her past. Tadić, maybe. But I've no idea *why*. She's either crossed someone, or she knows something they're afraid she'll tell. The only good news is that they *took* her alive. They didn't leave her in her studio beaten or dead, and they didn't appear to have tortured her. That means there's a good chance that she might still be alive. I'm hoping the door-to-door and forensics on the studio will give us some sort of a lead. The only trouble is that forensics can sometimes take a long time, and time is one thing we don't have. All we know right now is that there was a struggle and they drove off to the west, on that unfenced moorland road. That's an awful lot of area to cover.'

'Did they take anything?'

'Not that we can tell. Her computer was still in the studio, and her shoulder bag with her phone, purse and so on. Passport, too, in a drawer.'

'Odds are if she did a bunk she'd have taken her passport and money,' said Annie. 'She wouldn't get far without them.'

'What I thought,' said Banks.

'So they've probably not taken her out of the country.'

'Depends who we're dealing with,' said Banks. 'No doubt her old traffickers know safe routes out, as well as in. And if Keane, or Foley, is in with them, he could probably fix up a fake passport quickly enough.'

'Any forensics yet?'

'Not much. One of the CSIs found six cigarette ends in a hollow within good viewing distance of Ray and Zelda's cottage. They're not Marlboro Gold, which was Zelda's brand, or Ray's roll-ups, so whoever took her might have been staking the place out for a while. They're being analysed.'

'Have you considered that if Keane is with them, he might also be up here, and you might be in danger. What if he wants to finish what he started?'

'No, I hadn't thought of that,' said Banks. 'Thanks for reminding me.'

Annie slapped his arm. 'I'm just saying you should be careful, Alan, that's all. And remember, he's not alone this time.'

'Thanks.'

'Think nothing of it,' said Annie. 'Just because I'm not officially allowed near the case, it doesn't mean I can't help you if you need me.'

'Of course not,' said Banks. 'I know that and I appreciate it. Just watch yourself, that's all. AC Gervaise is bound to have her eye on you. And as you know, with Zelda missing and probably in danger, not to mention Ray on my back, I'm going to have to live and breathe this case, but keep me informed on the rape investigation, too. Anything new?'

The music jumped forward a few years to Tim Hardin's 'Hang on to a Dream'. Another tortured soul and heroin casualty.

'We still haven't identified the victim,' Annie said. 'According to Charlotte Westlake, there were no guest lists for the parties, so we're still stuck with finding out who was there on the night in question.'

'Do you think this Charlotte Westlake was involved?'

'I don't think she's telling us everything. Though she could hardly be the rapist – that was a man – and I doubt that she facilitated it. She said she was in Costa Rica at the time of the party, and it's true. We checked. She says she doesn't recognise the girl in the photo, but that's not surprising, given its poor quality.'

'Could she be lying?'

'I think she could. There was something a bit suspicious about her reaction to the whole mention of the rape and the minicams.'

'What do you know about her?'

'She used to be plain old Christine Pollard from the local comprehensive in Halifax – though I doubt she was ever plain. Then she got into Oxford. Apparently, she was the one in her year to make it. She drifted into events planning, met Gareth Westlake at a function she helped organise for his construction company. That was when she became Charlotte Westlake. Charlotte was her middle name. I guess it sounded a bit posher now she'd gone up in the world and mixed with a different set. Gareth died of leukaemia five years ago, as she told us. No children. Then three years ago she bumped into Blaydon at an opening party for a new shopping development he was involved with – the one before the Elmet, out Selby way. She'd known him vaguely from before, apparently, and he needed a PA. She took the job and the rest is history.'

'No connections with Gashi or Tadić?'

'Not that Gerry could find. Not before going to work for Blaydon, at any rate. Not that we expected any.'

'No form?'

'None. Again, we didn't expect any.'

'So what next?'

'Gerry's arranged to talk to her ex-secretary this afternoon. Tamara Collins. She took care of the actual party invitations by text or email. She works for that solicitor's firm on Market Street now. You know the one, just a few doors down from the Costa Coffee.'

'I know who you mean,' said Banks. 'Proctor, Maddox and Reaney. I used to walk past there every morning on my way to work, back when Sandra and I were together.'

'Apparently there were a lot of word-of-mouth invitations, too,' Annie said. 'If we can just track down some of the invitees and show them the girl's picture, someone might remember seeing her and know who she is, or who was with her that night.'

'I doubt anyone will talk.'

'But they can't all have been involved, can they? It was a big party. You've seen Blaydon's mansion, how many rooms there are, with the swimming pool and all. Not all the guests were rapists. It was very late at night. There must be quite a few who don't know what happened and would be as appalled by the news as Charlotte Westlake said she was. Probably most of them. Maybe they saw the victim around the pool or somewhere, noticed who she was talking to or hanging out with. Maybe someone was bothering her. Maybe she said something to someone.'

'It's worth a try,' said Banks. 'Good luck.'

Ray Cabbot sat in Banks's back garden, where they had talked just the previous evening, which seemed a lifetime ago now, and rolled another cigarette. How his whole world had fallen to pieces in such a short time. Shifted and crumbled. He was oblivious to the sunshine, the birds and the beautiful view.

Even the muted strains of David Gilmour's 'Shine On You Crazy Diamond' coming through the open windows of the conservatory failed to move him or console him in any way. Ever since Banks had left him alone at Newhope Cottage, he had been fighting the urge to attack the collection of single malt whiskies, but had resisted so far. He didn't know how much longer he could hold out. Only oblivion could take away the pain of losing Zelda and save him from the terrible images that filled his mind.

Faceless men ripped off her clothes and pawed at her; they stuck knives in her until the blood flowed; they beat her face until it was misshapen and unrecognisable. His beautiful, vulnerable Zelda lay dying with no one to help her, no one to hold her as her last breath ebbed. But it wasn't just the pain and the violence, it was what she must be feeling that also tore at his heart. The loneliness, the fear, the despair. After all she had been through, had she found herself a captive again in the hands of people who lacked any semblance of empathy? Was she going to die alone and in agony?

Ray had never felt so impotent, so useless, in his life. And their last words to one another had been angry ones. He would never forget the sound of the studio door slamming. Zelda was so rarely angry. Why hadn't he gone after her? Surely, she would have let him in if he had knocked? Then he could have apologised and comforted her and taken her to Leeds with him and none of this would have happened. She had listened to his lectures before and said she enjoyed them. They could have gone for dinner afterwards, perhaps booked in at the Dakota and made a night of it. Instead he was exiled to Banks's garden while heavy-handed coppers went through his home and belongings.

He could just imagine their reactions to some of his work: 'Hey, have a look at this one, Joe. Got a right set of knockers on her, she has.' 'I'll bet that's his missus.' But what could he do? For better or for worse, they were the only people he could rely on to find Zelda. And Alan. Where was Alan? Organising things, he had said. Yet it all seemed so disorganised. He couldn't see what sort of plan they were following, how they hoped to get anywhere closer to finding Zelda by going through his things. They would be in her drawers, too, fingering her underwear, her personal stuff. Making crude comments, holding things up for everyone to see.

Ray stood up and walked over to the back fence. He felt caged. Maybe he should go for a walk up Tetchley Fell? But the mere sight of it made him feel out of breath. He was in no fit shape to go hiking. He stubbed out his cigarette, went inside and stared longingly at the bottles of Macallans and Highland Park. He knew Banks wouldn't mind if he helped himself to a tipple. The thing was, he felt like shit already, having drunk too much the previous night instead of sleeping. And he needed a clear head in case Zelda called.

But his head wouldn't clear. Maybe a little drink would help. He took out his mobile for the umpteenth time and checked for missed calls. Nothing. The music finished, and he couldn't be bothered putting anything else on. Images of Zelda terrified and bloody filled his mind again. He sat back down and put his head in his hands. He wished he were painting. Usually everything else went from his mind when he took a brush in his hand. But perhaps even that wouldn't work this time, even if he was allowed back in his studio. This was too serious to permit easy escape, if only for a second.

He rolled another cigarette, pictured the bottles on the shelf inside. Then he heard a car pulling up out front and jumped up. They'd found her. Surely that's what it was. Alan was hurrying to give him the good news. He left his roll-up burning in the ashtray and dashed through to the front of the house with visions of Zelda running into his arms.

Costa was usually busy after work, but Gerry and Tamara Collins managed to find a table for two in the back. After Gerry had brought the lattes, they settled down to talk amid the hubbub of conversation and the hoarse gurgling of the espresso machine. Tamara was probably about Gerry's age, late twenties, and pretty in a sharp-featured, no-nonsense sort of way. Her clothes were conservative – white blouse, navy skirt and jacket – as one would expect from a legal secretary.

Gerry took her notebook out. 'How do you like your new job?' she asked.

'I'm very glad to have it.'

'It's a bit different from working for Mr Blaydon, I should imagine?'

Her expression darkened. 'Yes.'

'How long did you work for him?'

'Three years. But I was working for Mrs Westlake.'

'Technically, I know, but Blaydon employed both of you. Was he a good employer?'

'The pay was OK, the hours not bad.'

'And the boss?'

'To be honest, I didn't see very much of him. I worked at his office in Leeds. Mrs Westlake was his personal assistant. She didn't have anything to do with the property developments or the estate business, but she had an office there. Mind you, she wasn't there all the time. Well, it makes sense, doesn't it? If she was supposed to assist him, she probably had to be out and about a lot. And Mr Blaydon himself was in and out, here and there. We didn't see him very often. He travelled quite a lot. I think he had a yacht or something. It wasn't as if we were all together in one big room. And he wasn't a grabber, if that's what you mean.'

'He never behaved inappropriately?'

'Oh, Lordy me, no.'

'Why did you leave?'

'I had this job in my sights for a while. It's closer to home and the pay's much better. The work's more interesting, too. The opportunity finally came up about a month ago.'

'Did you ever get invited to one of Mr Blaydon's parties?'

Tamara laughed. 'Me? Lord, no! Why would he invite me? I don't think he even knew I existed. The parties were just to impress important people – friends, influencers, business colleagues and so on.'

'I understand he liked to have a few pretty women around, too.'

Tamara blushed. 'Well, I certainly wasn't one of them.'

'Where did he get them from?'

'How would I know? I just worked in the office. Basic secretarial duties for Mrs Westlake.'

'Where do you think?'

Tamara held her coffee cup in both hands. 'I heard things, like you do.'

'What things?'

'Just the usual. Office gossip. You know, that he hired models to be nice to his guests.'

'Models or escorts?'

'I wouldn't know about that.'

'What about drugs?'

'Again, I heard rumours. I can't say they interested me very much.'

Gerry leaned forward. 'Tamara, we think – in fact, we *know* – that Mr Blaydon used a lot of girls from Eastern Europe, probably supplied by sex traffickers. His parties were also well known for their cocaine use. Did you ever meet a friend of his called Leka Gashi?'

Tamara shook her head. 'I'm not saying he was never in the office. People came and went. But I was never introduced to anyone by that name.'

'Petar Tadić?'

'No.'

'We also know that Mr Blaydon used, or allowed to be used, a number of his properties as pop-up brothels. Did you know that?'

'Pop-up brothels! God forbid. Of course not. Like I said, I had nothing to do with renting out properties or anything like that. I worked for Mrs Westlake organising travel, accommodation, dinners, meetings, events and that sort of thing. That was all.'

'I understand you sent out the party invitations.'

'Well, I sent out texts and emails sometimes, yes. Made phone calls.'

'Were you working on 13 April this year?'

'I suppose so.'

'Do you remember sending out invitations to a party for that date?'

'They would have been sent out about two weeks earlier. That would make it the end of March, or thereabouts. I can't remember the exact date. I mean, it was a pretty menial task, to be honest, and it usually didn't take very long. I just got it done and out of the way as soon as possible. Sometimes it was fun seeing a name I recognised, like a pop star or footballer, but that's all. It was pretty boring otherwise.'

'I can understand that,' said Gerry. 'Do you remember any names from that specific party?'

'I'm sorry, I can't,' said Tamara. 'Maybe that means there weren't any I recognised. Nobody really famous.'

'Would you try and write down any names you do remember?'

'Yes, of course.'

'For any other parties that you can think of, too.'

'All right.'

Gerry fished out the digital image of the rape victim and passed it to Tamara. 'Do you recognise this girl?'

Tamara held the photo and studied it from different angles. 'Do you know, I . . . She looks very upset and dishevelled here, very different, but maybe . . .'

'Maybe what?'

Tamara handed the photo back. 'I think maybe I saw her in the office once.'

Gerry felt her pulse quicken. 'When was that?'

'Before 13 April, that much I know. February? March?'

'What was she doing?'

'She wanted to see Mrs Westlake.'

'Can you remember what it was about? It might be important.'

'No. But Mrs Westlake interviewed people for jobs and wrote cheques or made some payments in cash. Sometimes people dropped by to pick up their payment. Not everyone likes electronic bank transfers.'

'And this girl came for cash or a cheque?'

'I'm just saying that she might have done. Or maybe she was after a job. She didn't tell me. I mean, there was nothing unusual about her. I do remember she was very pretty. Quite tall, long-legged, short reddish hair, maybe hennaed.' Tamara dabbed at a latte moustache. 'Mrs Westlake put the personnel together for the events Mr Blaydon held, including the serving and kitchen staff and people to coordinate them on site. She didn't trust most outside caterers. Not just for the parties, but business events, too, gala dinners, retirement parties, employee of the month awards and so on. She liked to use her own core team. I don't know for certain why this girl came to the office, but that would be my first guess. For a job.'

'So there would be records in Blaydon's business files? Bank details, name, address?'

'There should be. It was all above board. But accounts handled all that.'

'Are you sure she came to the office to see Mrs Westlake?'

'Yes. That's why I remember her. She came up to my desk and asked if Mrs Westlake was in, and if she could see her. Said she had an appointment but she was a bit early. She waited in the reception area for a while, glancing at a magazine. I do remember she seemed nervous. You know, not really concentrating on what she was reading, just flipping the pages, looking at the pictures. Putting it down and picking up another. Then when the time came I showed her into the office myself.'

Gerry thought it odd that Tamara had recognised the girl from the photo when Charlotte Westlake, who must have had far more dealings with her, hadn't. Was Charlotte lying? They would have to re-interview her. 'I don't suppose you remember her name, do you?' she asked.

Tamara thought for a moment and said, 'Do you know, as a matter of fact I do. I asked her, you know, so I could tell Mrs Westlake who was here to see her. Announce her, like.'

'And?'

'Her name was Marnie. I'm afraid I can't remember her second name, but I remember her first name struck me as odd. It's not often you come across someone called Marnie.'

'No,' said Gerry, scribbling away in her notebook. 'No, it isn't.'

'It's from an old film, isn't it?'

'Yes,' said Gerry, who had seen just about every 'old' film there was with her parents when she was growing up, and had a surprisingly good recollection of most of them. 'Alfred Hitchcock. Tippi Hedren and Sean Connery. It's about sexual violence. And Marnie was a sexually repressed kleptomaniac.'

DC Dev Bharati was a keen young detective from County HQ, handsome, slim and casually dressed, and he was clearly excited to be involved in such a high-profile case. He was a bit too deferential for Banks's liking, but that probably wouldn't last. Still, it made a change from the easy familiarity of Annie, Gerry and Winsome, with whom he was more used to working.

'I thought you'd want to know right away, sir,' Bharati said as he drove Banks into Lyndgarth. 'DS Flyte is still with him.'

They pulled up outside the Black Bull in the high street. Bharati had to duck as he walked through the doors. The beams inside were also low, and he had to watch where he walked. DS Samuel Flyte was sitting at a rickety table with the pub's landlord Mick Slater, a grizzled old denizen of the public house trade. Banks had met him before on a number of occasions and found him gruff but sound enough.

Flyte was a few years older than Bharati, fat but not obese. He reminded Banks of his old oppo, DS Jim Hatchley, now long retired and by all accounts practically taking up residence at Eastvale Golf Club. Hatchley had resembled a rugby prop forward gone to seed, but Banks guessed there was more muscle than fat in Flyte's bulk. He was also bald, with a shiny head, a small moustache, a red face and a slow, countryman's manner of moving, along with the habit of appearing to think for a moment before answering any questions. He stood up when Banks entered and shook hands. He was wearing a tight-fitting navy suit, already a little shiny around the elbows.

There were plenty of people in the pub, and Banks had no doubt most of them were talking about what had happened on the edge of the village. He recognised a couple of reporters from the local papers, but the London press hadn't turned up yet. As soon as they got wind of what had happened, they'd be up the M1 quickly enough, and Zelda's dirty laundry would be spread all over the front pages of the national media. Another good reason for hanging on to the notebook.

Banks sat down with Mick Slater, Flyte and Bharati. Slater offered drinks, but they all refused. The two detectives did so because Banks was present, he assumed, and Banks declined because he didn't want any alcohol and rarely drank tea or coffee in the afternoon.

'Let's get straight to it,' he said. 'I know you've probably told DS Flyte already, but I'd like you to tell me exactly what happened. Start with when.'

'It was three or four days ago,' said Slater. 'Just before the weekend.'

'What time of day?'

'About now.'

Banks saw DC Bharati make a note of the time. 'And what were the man's actual words?'

'He asked if I knew of a young woman living in these parts. Said he was an old friend and he hadn't seen her for some years, but he'd heard she was living in Lyndgarth. A place called Windlee Farm. He didn't have a full address and his satnav was going wonky. Well, they do that a lot around these parts. Then he described her. Her appearance, the slight accent. It sounded to me as if he was talking about Mrs Cabbot.'

It sounded the same way to Banks, though it was strange hearing Zelda described as Mrs Cabbot, especially as she and Ray weren't even married. 'So you got the impression that he didn't know exactly where she lived?'

'Right. It's easy enough if you have a street address in a small village like this, but Windlee Farm isn't exactly in the village, as you know. It's over half a mile away from any other houses here. I don't even know what the address is, myself, or even if there is one. I think it's on Lyndsdale Road, but that could be wrong. The road changes its name every hundred yards, it seems. And I don't think there's a number. Must be a postal code, of course, but I'd be hard pushed to tell you that, either. It's just known as the Old Farm around these parts. Anyone who wants it knows that. And knows where it is.'

'It's like my place,' said Banks. 'Newhope Cottage. In Gratly. No street address. No street. What did he look like?'

'Medium height, stocky, fortyish maybe, cropped black hair, five o'clock shadow – the kind you get with those special razors – thick lips, fleshy nose and beady eyes. Moved like the sort of bloke who probably thinks he's God's gift to women, if you catch my drift. Flash clothes, too, just a bit too gaudy, if you ask me, and jewellery. You know, gold chain, big rings, that sort of bling. He looked like a bit of a thug, to be honest. And he had an accent.'

'What sort of accent?'

'European. Not French or Italian. Maybe Bulgarian or Polish or something like that. Could've been Russian. Who knows? Bit of a harsh edge to it. Guttural. Just the sort we voted to get rid of.'

'What did you tell him?'

'Nothing. Like I said, I didn't like the look of him, and I don't like to give out that kind of information about my customers on spec. You never know who you're telling, do you? Could be planning on burgling the place. Or raping her or something. I don't know Ray and his missus very well, but they come in here for a drink or two now and then, and they always seemed nice enough to me. This bloke looked like trouble, and Mrs Cabbot, well, she's an attractive woman, out there on her own sometimes . . . you know. Like I said, you never know what someone has in mind.'

'That was good thinking,' said Banks. 'You did the right thing.'

'Seems as if he found her, anyway, doesn't it? Maybe I should have reported it straight away. At least told Ray and Zelda, given them a chance.'

'Not your fault.' He must have asked someone else, Banks thought, or driven around until he saw the name on the front of the cottage. Then when he'd found it, he staked out the place from the hollow over the weekend before making his move, probably after seeing Ray leave in the late afternoon. There would be an accomplice somewhere, too. Maybe someone had seen him out on the moorland? You tended to get quite a few ramblers out there on weekends.

'Did you see his car?'

'No.'

'I did,' came a voice from the left.

Banks turned. 'And you are?'

'Kit. Kit Riley.'

'Kit's a regular,' Mick Slater said.

Banks looked more closely. Kit was an elderly man, a bit dishevelled in a grubby, striped rugby shirt, baggy brown cord trousers and a leather gilet, despite the weather. His white hair stuck out at all angles, and he clearly hadn't shaved in a week. He had the weather-beaten complexion of a lifelong farmer.

'You saw the car?' Banks said.

'Aye. I were just leaving, like, and he pushed past me, rude as can be. *Foreigners*. Sooner we're shut of 'em, the better.'

'But you did see his car?'

'Oh, aye.' Kit paused and glanced down at his glass, which was almost empty.

Banks sighed. Everyone had watched too much television these days, it seemed, and expected something in return for whatever information they gave the police.

Banks nodded to Mick Slater. 'Give him what he wants.'

'Ooh, ta very much. I'll have a whisky, please, Micky, my boy. A double.'

Slater poured the drink. When Banks reached for his wallet, the landlord shook his head, as if to indicate he'd bear the expense. 'No, it's only fair,' said Banks, passing some money over. Slater shrugged and got the change from the till.

'Right then, Kit,' said Banks, after Riley had taken his first sip and smacked his lips. 'What kind of car was it?'

Riley sipped some more whisky theatrically before saying, 'It were a Ford Fiesta.'

'You're sure?' Banks asked, heart sinking.

'I know my cars,' said Riley. 'I tell you, it were a Ford Fiesta.'

Only the most popular car in the country, with about 100,000 registrations last year alone. 'What colour was it?'

'Dark green. Or blue. Hard to tell.'

'You didn't get the number, by any chance?'

'Stopped writing down car numbers when I was twelve,' Riley replied.

Banks felt a memory rise up from deep in his mind. Sitting on the secondary modern school wall by the main road junction with his best friends, Steve and Paul, writing down the makes and numbers of cars that went by. He must have been about ten or eleven. Why on earth had he thought to do something as pointless as that? Probably because his friends did. But it wasn't even as serious a pastime as train-spotting, standing at the end of a windy platform in the rain jotting down train names and numbers, then going home and neatly crossing them off in your book with pencil and ruler. There was no book of car numbers, as far as he knew, only pictures and descriptions of models in the *Observer's Book of Automobiles*.

It was a pity that Kit Riley had given up the practice so early. Inquiries about a dark Ford Fiesta wouldn't get very far. It was clear that whoever was looking for Zelda had made no effort to hide the fact. He had gone into the pub on the village high street, obviously rather exotic in his bling, and described Zelda to the landlord. So he clearly wasn't worried about his description being circulated. Why? Did he think the police were too stupid to trace him? Was he so confident and arrogant that he could afford to do what he wanted right under their noses? Banks had known plenty of criminals who were, who would think nothing of walking into their local, shooting someone they had a grudge against and walking out again. And how did the man know what Zelda looked like unless he knew her? He must have seen her somewhere, or at least seen a photograph of her.

'Is that all?' he asked Kit.

'Aye. Oh, there's one more thing.' Kit glanced down at his empty glass.

Banks ignored the gesture. 'Go on. Tell,' he said.

Riley seemed disappointed, but he knew when he'd gone too far. 'There were another bloke with him. Waiting in the car, like. I didn't get a good look at him, but it wasn't someone I'd care to meet in a dark ginnel, I can tell you that much.'

9

Ray looked terrible, Annie thought, when he answered the door to Banks's cottage. And it was hard not to feel hurt at the expression of disappointment that crept over his features when he saw her. She wouldn't deny that there were 'issues' between her and Zelda, but that didn't mean she wished her any harm. Whatever Annie thought of Ray's choice of partner, he clearly loved Zelda, and it was good for him to have someone to share his life with. If only she weren't so damned young and attractive. It was hard to trust anyone as beautiful as her, and Annie lived in fear that she would run off with some young stud and break Ray's heart. Literally.

'Annie,' he said. 'I thought . . . Is there any news?'

'Sorry.'

For a few moments they just stood there staring at one another, then they hugged, long and hard, Ray sobbing on Annie's shoulder. A little embarrassed, they moved apart and Annie followed Ray through the front room and down the hall, watching his elbows move as he rubbed his eyes with the backs of his hands, then through Banks's kitchen and conservatory. 'I was sitting out back,' he said.

'Mind if I join you?'

'I'm not very good company right now, but you're quite welcome.'

Annie smiled. 'Oh, Dad, I didn't expect you to be good company. After all, it's not often you are.' She hardly ever called him 'Dad' or 'Father', but he didn't react when she did this time. Nor did he react to her little tease.

'My house is swarming with coppers,' he said.

'Don't worry. I'm sure they'll be respectful.'

They sat down. 'Want a drink?' Ray asked.

'No, thanks. I'm not stopping long. Alan told me you were here, and I wanted to see how you're doing.'

Ray spread his arms, then started rolling a cigarette. 'Well,' he said, 'as you can see.'

'We'll find her,' Annie said.

'I think I might have one. A drink, that is.' He left his unlit cigarette on the table and disappeared inside, emerging a few seconds later with a tumbler of whisky.

Annie felt like telling him to take it easy with the booze, but she held her tongue. It would only antagonise him. And maybe a drop or two of whisky wasn't such a bad idea for him at the moment. 'I know you think I don't like Zelda,' she said, 'and I know we got off on the wrong foot, but just put it down to me being silly, my silly feelings. And being overprotective of you. You know I want you to be happy, and if she makes you happy—'

'She does,' Ray said. 'You have no idea. Since your mother . . .'

'That's a long time ago,' Annie said.

'I haven't forgotten her, love, you know that. I never could. Zelda's not a replacement, she's . . . I don't know . . . a new start for me. Something I thought was way behind me. And beyond. You can't always be prepared for when things like that happen.'

'I wouldn't know,' Annie said.

'I'm telling you. It's true.' Tears welled up in his red eyes again. 'I don't know what I'll do if anything happens to her.'

'Oh, Dad.' Annie reached out and touched his arm. 'There is *some* news,' she said. 'And another reason I'm here. I just talked to Alan on the phone, and he told me Mick Slater from the Black Bull said there was a bloke in the pub asking after Zelda the other day, or at least someone who resembled her very closely. Said he didn't tell him anything. Didn't like the look of him.'

Ray picked up the cigarette, rolled it around between his fingers for a while, then put it in his mouth and lit it. 'They think that's the man who took her?'

'We don't know,' Annie said. 'But we'll definitely be checking into it.'

'Any idea who he is?'

'No.' Annie paused. 'But Alan said it might be a good idea, if you're up to it, if maybe you could go up there and help with a sketch. Mr Slater can give a pretty good description for you to work with. Only if you feel up to it. I'll drive you.'

Ray stood up so fast he knocked his tumbler over on the table and whisky flowed over the sides. 'Do I feel up to it? You bet I do. Come on, what are we waiting for?'

'No, the nose isn't quite right. A bit broader. And there's a sort of bump.' Mick Slater touched his own nose. 'Right here, about halfway up. As if it was broken or something. And the lips were a bit thicker.'

Ray got to work with the rubber then put pencil to paper again.

'That's it,' said Mick. 'Now the eyebrows. A bit thicker, too. Not bushy or anything, but not quite so thin. Dark and heavy, and nearly meeting in the middle. A heavier brow. Hairline back a bit. That's it. That's him.'

They were in a small office behind the bar, and there was just enough room for Ray and Mick inside, while Banks leaned against the door jamb gazing on from the sidelines. It was always fascinating to watch a master at work. Ray was a serious artist, not a police sketch artist, but he had helped Banks out in that capacity before, and he was good at it. It had seemed only natural to ask Annie to try and get him to help sketch a description of the stranger, with Slater's help. So far, things seemed to be going well.

Banks turned and glanced around the pub. He had accepted Slater's offer of a pint of shandy when Ray arrived and was glad that he had. It was getting hot in there, and the sweetness of the lemonade and the bitterness of the beer made a perfect antidote to the heat of the day. The Black Bull was an odd sort of place: dark and dingy on the inside, with an uneven flagstone floor, scratched tables and rickety chairs, but a great summer draw outside with its tables looking out on the village green and a beer garden out back. Unlike the Relton Arms, it had a small playground area and a bouncy castle for the kiddies. Banks could imagine the interior on a dark winter's night, the locals sitting silently around a blazing fire, dogs dreaming at their feet, while the wind howled and the rain battered at the windows outside. Lock-ins would be common there, and the local bobby would probably be on the inside of them.

Finally, Ray put down the finishing touches and passed the sketch to Banks.

'It's as good as I can get,' said Slater. 'I'm not that great at detail.'

'It's fine,' said Banks, then glanced at Ray. 'Thanks. Look, I have a pretty good idea of who this might be. I'll show it to a couple of colleagues who will know for certain and get back to you.'

'Is it bad?'

'I'll check it out, Ray. If I'm right, it'll help us with the search.'

'Why won't you tell me now? What don't you want me to know?'

Banks turned to Slater. 'Thanks for your time and trouble, Mr Slater,' he said. 'And thanks for not giving this stranger any information. I'd appreciate it if you'd keep quiet about this until I've had the chance to check a few things out.'

Slater nodded, and they returned to the bar with their drinks.

'Why won't you tell me what you think?' Ray persisted. 'Who is it? Why would he want to take Zelda?'

'Because I'm not sure yet,' Banks said.

'But if you're right, is it bad news?'

Banks took a long pull on his shandy and said, 'Yes, Ray. You want me to tell you. All right. If it's who I think it is, it's bad news.'

'It's Petar Tadić, all right,' said Burgess, just seconds after Banks had emailed him Ray's sketch. 'Where did you get it?'

Banks told him about Mick Slater and Ray collaborating.

'Brazen bastard, isn't he?' said Burgess. 'If you need any help on this, we've got trained experts here we can send up. Negotiators and the like.'

'Thanks, I might take you up on that if we don't find her soon,' Banks said. 'But right now there's nothing to negotiate. I'd appreciate it if you could find out whether Tadić is back in London, though. And if you find him, bring him in for questioning.'

'We can try. We have a pretty good idea of some of his haunts, but they keep changing. I'll see what I can do.'

'By the way, talking about haunts, have you ever heard of the Hotel Belgrade?'

There was a brief pause before Burgess answered. 'It used to be one of their hangouts, the Tadićs and their crew. Why?'

'No reason. It's just something that came up.' Banks could hardly tell Burgess that the hotel was mentioned in Zelda's notebook. 'Used to be?'

'Yes. It seems they've moved out en masse. We're not sure where yet.'

'When was this?'

'Less than a month ago.'

'One witness from the village says there was another man waiting in the car for Petar. What about the brother, Goran? Anything on him?'

'Goran hasn't been seen lately,' said Burgess. 'He must be lying low. Probably on holiday in Split or somewhere. These people are always on the move. That's how they keep a few steps ahead of us.'

'Thanks. Have you got an up-to-date photo of Petar? That might work better than a quick sketch.'

'I'll check.'

'Great. If you find one, can you send it directly to Adrian Moss?' Banks gave him Moss's fax, phone and email. 'In the meantime, I'll have Adrian get the sketch out to the news media, as well as on Facebook, Twitter and so on. Adrian's already blasted them with Zelda's disappearance, so they'll all have their tongues hanging out for more. And we'll get copies to patrol cars, beat officers, PCSOs, the lot.' They said their goodbyes and Banks hung up.

Adrian Moss was their media liaison officer, and though he was a bit of a trendy prat, with his wet-look hair and shirt hanging out, Banks had to admit he was very good at his job. If anyone could saturate the media with Zelda's disappearance and give the press a good story, Moss could. The photo of Zelda that Ray had given them wouldn't do any harm, either. Most men who saw it would certainly be motivated to find her, and quite a few women, too.

Moss's only problem was that he didn't appreciate his own talent for blowing smoke and always seemed to want to give away far more than Banks was comfortable with. He would have his work cut out when the national media horde arrived the following day. Which reminded Banks that Ray would need to be protected from them. The CSIs had finished for the day at Ray's house, and he had gone straight home from the Black Bull, so Banks had Newhope to himself. He was willing to take Ray in again tomorrow, if necessary, when the CSIs would no doubt turn up again.

On his way home, Banks had made a detour to the station. Moss had already got one of the TV crews set up in the press room, so Banks had recorded a brief impromptu appeal on television for any sightings of Zelda. Now he sat outside his cottage in the mild evening warmth, a glass of wine on the table in front of him.

Why had Tadić abducted Zelda? And why now? Banks wouldn't have been surprised if Tadić didn't even remember what he had done to her thirteen years ago. So why was she now suddenly so valuable, or so dangerous, to him?

Banks flipped through the Moleskine notebook again. The last entry concerned a visit to Chişinău at the end of the previous week to see someone called Vasile Lupescu, another demon from her past. There were several lengthy descriptions of the Moldovan countryside, complete with its wineries and peasants in traditional dress, along with old memories of Chişinău. On her flight home, she had written about their conversation, how Lupescu had at first denied setting her up for her abductors, then admitted it and finally insisted that he had been forced into it by threats against his family. It was a tense and dramatic scene, and it confirmed Banks's suspicions that the notebook was most likely a record of feelings and inquiries about her past, perhaps noted down for use in a story or memoir of some kind. Zelda clearly felt very strongly about the people responsible for ruining her life – and quite rightly so – and this notebook must be one of her ways of expressing all that, including fantasies about what she would like to do to some of them.

But it *could* get her into trouble. The disjointed meanderings might mean nothing to most people, but some police officers took everything quite literally, made no allowance for wishful thinking and fantasy. It could get Banks into trouble, too. He was beginning to think that taking it might have been the first step on a slippery slope to career suicide. At the very least it was misappropriating evidence. What on earth did he think he was doing? Protecting Zelda? From what? Whatever his rationale, Banks knew he should have left it where it was, let it become an exhibit in whatever followed. But it was too late for that now. There was no way he could explain hanging on to it to his superiors, and he knew as well as anyone that what might seem like a minor transgression could quickly blow up into a full IOPC investigation, meaning at least temporary suspension, and possibly being fired.

The Hotel Belgrade, Burgess had said, used to be a hangout for Tadić and his cronies until recently. How had Zelda found out about it? From Faye Butler? And had she gone there searching for Keane, only to find Goran Tadić instead? How would she have reacted to that? By fantasising about killing him? What had happened at the Hotel Belgrade? In their talk at the Relton Arms yesterday, Zelda hadn't mentioned anything about finding the Tadićs in London.

Just in case, Banks phoned the hotel, identified himself and asked if a woman matching Zelda's description had checked in recently. The answer was no. Had someone of that description ever stayed at the hotel? They couldn't possibly remember something like that. Guests came and went, many attractive women. Had she been seen there around a month ago? There was no way of knowing that. CCTV? Overwritten by now. Besides, there had been personnel changes, too, and changes in management. It was a fast turnover business. Tadić? No, they had never heard of anyone by that name.

Frustrated by the lack of response, Banks considered arranging for a team to search the place, but he had no real evidence for ordering such an action. And what would they find? As Burgess had said, the Hotel Belgrade *used to be* the Tadićs' hangout, but they had moved on, and no one there admitted to having heard of them. In any case, they would be unlikely to be keeping Zelda there.

Blue tits and goldfinches flitted around his shrubbery, ate at the feeder and splashed in the birdbath, until a local cat jumped over the wall, arched its back and mewed at Banks, then loped on. Only a robin, intent on searching the grass for worms at the bottom of the garden, was unflustered and didn't fly off. The other birds returned, and bees sucked on fuchsia that hung from branches like teardrops of blood.

Banks yawned. It had been a long day, and he hadn't had much sleep the previous night at Ray's. There wasn't anything more he could do tonight, and if he was going to be of any use in the search for Zelda tomorrow, he was going to have to be on the ball. So instead of pouring another glass of wine, he picked up Ray's overflowing ashtray from the table and went back inside, where he dumped its contents into the waste bin and went to bed, taking his mobile with him. Some Brian Eno ambient music might see him off to sleep early tonight.

Zelda woke up with a dry mouth and a terrible headache. When she found the nerve to open her eyes, she thought at first that she was in complete darkness. As her sight adjusted slowly in what little light there was around the boarded-up window, she realised she was in a room, lying on a floor that felt like bare boards. When she tried to move, she found that she was chained by her right ankle to a heavy old iron radiator fixed to the wall. She tried to jerk free a number of times but quickly realised that she couldn't. Then she shouted out, but her voice merely echoed in the empty room.

As her eyes adapted further, she came to see that the room she was in was more like an office than anything else. All the furniture had been removed, desk and filing cabinets, and she couldn't make out the colour of the walls. They seemed to be partially covered in that material with holes in it. She had seen it before in offices. The ceiling seemed high, and there was only the one window. Her hands were tied together with plastic handcuffs that only tightened if she tried to escape from them.

So what had happened? Zelda tried to piece it all together. Why was it all so vague? She and Raymond had argued and she had shut herself in her studio drinking wine and working on a painting. Angry brushstrokes. Red slashes. Why was she angry? Alan, that was why. He had pushed her into telling him certain things that she hadn't wanted him to know. Maybe enough for him to find his way to the truth. And Raymond had hardly been sympathetic. Raymond. What happened to him? He had gone out, of course. The Leeds Art Gallery lecture he had been so nervous about. But would they leave someone to wait for him and hurt him when he got back?

As far as she could tell, she seemed OK in herself, apart from the dry mouth and headache. They had injected her with some sort of anaesthetic, she remembered; that was what was making her feel this way. Nausea, too, perhaps because the room was so hot and stuffy. But there was no pain in any of her limbs, and everything felt intact. She hadn't been raped or sexually interfered with in any way. She would know.

She hadn't heard their car. All she knew was that suddenly the studio door burst open and there stood two men. One of them was Petar Tadić, of that she was certain – she would recognise his stocky body, his near non-existent neck and his beady eyes anywhere, even after all the years – but she didn't recognise the other one. As far as she could tell, Tadić didn't recognise her.

Had they found out what she had done to Goran and tracked her down? That could be the only explanation. It was as she had feared; they had resources, contacts and methods that the police lacked. Something might have led them to poor innocent Faye Butler, and under torture Faye might have given them enough clues to lead to Zelda. They wouldn't have reported Goran's death to the authorities, but would most likely have got rid of the body themselves, perhaps in several pieces. She had thrown her glass at them and struggled when they grabbed her, but the needle went in and its effect was quick. She remembered nothing more, not even how much time had passed, how long she had been out.

Now here she was, shackled in her prison. What was their plan? What were they going to do to her? If they wanted her dead – an eye for an eye – then surely they would have killed her by now. Or did they intend to kill her slowly? Starvation, perhaps? Just leave her here, chained to the radiator, until she died.

She hadn't eaten since her lunch with Banks, and she was starving already. How long ago that seemed. How petty her irritation with him. She wished he would walk through the door right now. She could do with a Willie Garvin to rescue her. What would Modesty Blaise do? Try to escape, obviously. But how? She looked around her in the darkness, but it was hopeless.

Zelda tugged at the chain again; it was still securely fastened to the radiator. And the iron chain was padlocked tightly around her foot. A heavy, strong lock, by the feel of it. She pulled at it, but it did no good. Though her hands were cuffed in front of her, rather than behind, they still weren't much use. The cuffs were tight and hurt whenever she tried to reach out. She wasn't going to escape trussed up like this. Somehow, she had to get free of her chains. But how?

As she was thinking of possibilities, she heard footsteps coming closer down the hall outside her door.

IO

Banks was in his office early the following morning, having made his way past the crews of two TV vans parked in the market square and a knot of reporters on the front steps of Eastvale Regional HQ.

While Stephen Hough played some late Brahms piano music in the background, Banks pored over Ordnance Survey maps, but he was distracted by mulling over whether he should cancel his outing to see the Blue Lamps' farewell concert at the Sage that evening. Mark and Tracy could easily get there by themselves. Though he had arranged to have a meal with them beforehand over the river in Newcastle, they would surely understand that he had a crisis on his hands. He also had tickets for Ray and Zelda, but they would have to go unused unless he could find someone in the station who wanted them.

But if he stayed at the office or at home, what would he do but worry? He could take his mobile to the concert with him, set on vibrate, even in the hall; he wouldn't be far away, and he could respond immediately to any breaks in the case. It wasn't as if he was expected to be out crawling over the moors with a magnifying glass and a deerstalker looking for clues himself. But could he even pay attention to his family and the music if he went? That wasn't the issue, he realised. He mustn't let his son down just because leaving the investigation for an evening made him feel as if he were playing truant. This wasn't about him; it was about Brian. Wherever Banks's mind was, at least his physical presence should be there in the Sage concert hall while his son played one of his last gigs with the band he'd been with for years.

Eno's *Reflection* had done the trick the previous night, and Banks had slept well. First, he called Ray to find out how he was doing. Ray was hungover and depressed and told him the 'bloody forensics blokes' had just turned up again to make his day even worse. Banks told him that the media would probably arrive in Lyndgarth soon, and he could go and hide out at Newhope Cottage if he wanted. But Ray said he was going to lock himself in his studio and try to immerse himself in work and music. It was the only way he thought he had any chance of surviving this whole business. He had just taken delivery of a rare vinyl copy of Jan Dukes de Grey's 1969 debut album *Sorcerers* and that should get him through the morning. Even Banks didn't have that one, only *Mice and Rats in the Loft* and *Strange Terrain*.

Next, Banks phoned Adrian Moss and asked him to organise a press conference for later that morning. Zelda had been missing for a day and two nights now, and they were no closer to finding her, so the more publicity the better. Surely someone had seen something?

His last call was to the Croatian authorities asking them for help in locating Tadić. It appeared they knew all about Petar and Goran and said they would be only too willing to help if either was foolish enough to return to Croatia any time soon. But they had no idea where the brothers were.

AC Gervaise had talked to Assistant Chief Constable Ron McLaughlin and the chief constable himself, and Zelda's disappearance was now an official Category-A investigation, with a budget to match. They would need it, too, with the extra men drafted in, then the Swaledale Mountain Rescue

Team, based at Catterick Garrison. Banks had heard that it cost around a couple of thousand just to get the SAR helicopter up in the air. Still, with its heat-seeking capabilities, it could help isolate a living human figure in a vast landscape.

Despite their name, the search team didn't restrict themselves to Swaledale, but also carried out operations in Wensleydale and Swainsdale. They had worked on the Claudia Lawrence search back in March 2009, when Claudia, a chef at the University of York, had disappeared. Sadly, Claudia still hasn't been found, though various theories of her murder have been brought forward, including the possibility that she was a victim of the serial killer Christopher Halliwell. The search team had also helped out in recent flood relief efforts, including the collapse of Tadcaster Bridge.

Frustration began to set in quickly, as it so often did with missing persons cases. Things just weren't happening fast enough. Every moment Zelda was missing Banks felt the tension in him rack up a notch. It was partly the impotence, of course, and the not knowing, but also the fear of what might be happening to her and, as time went on, the fear that she might already be dead.

Banks shuffled the papers on his desk. There was a lab report informing him that the cigarette ends found in the hollow near the cottage were Ronhill, a popular Croatian brand, and that they would yield DNA if required. Again, it was all pretty brazen, or careless, on Tadić's part. DNA tests were expensive, but flushed with his newly approved budget, Banks ordered one.

Radio 3 was playing Weinberg's 'Kaddish' Symphony, No. 21. It was close to the end when a melancholy keening female voice entered. The strange melody was so moving that Banks stopped what he was doing for a few moments and just listened. He didn't know the composer's work well but had read about him recently in *Gramophone* and liked what he was hearing. Amazing to know there were at least twenty more symphonies out there waiting to be heard. Weinberg had also written quite a lot of music for viola, one of Banks's favourite instruments, up there with the oboe. He had known a very beautiful violist years ago, and had almost had an affair with her. Almost.

When the symphony finished, the announcer mentioned that the wordless singing was performed by the conductor of the City of Birmingham Symphony Orchestra herself: Mirga Gražinytė-Tyla. Even more impressive. Banks only wished he could learn to pronounce her name.

As his thoughts began to drift, he was struck with an idea he thought might produce some positive results. Zelda, Banks was almost a hundred per cent certain, was being kept somewhere in the area. But where? It seemed unlikely they would keep her in a village or small town, as newcomers would draw too much attention in such places – especially newcomers like Tadić and Zelda – where everyone knew everyone else's business. But given that Blaydon owned dozens of vacant properties all over Yorkshire, and that Tadić had been connected with Blaydon, wouldn't these be logical places to search, along with recent holiday cottage lets, Airbnbs, converted barns and so forth?

The problem with this line of thinking was that Blaydon was dead. But that didn't have to be a game-stopper. Tadić had used Blaydon's properties before as pop-up brothels, so he probably had a good idea of what was available out there. In the same way, Leka Gashi had used them for his county lines operations. The connection might seem obvious, and something to be avoided by a cautious criminal, but as Banks had already seen, Tadić was far from cautious: he was brazen and arrogant. Perhaps he might also be careless or stupid enough to use one of Blaydon's empty properties to keep Zelda.

Banks phoned through to the squad room and talked to Gerry, who assured him that their files on the Blaydon murder investigation contained comprehensive lists of all the properties on his books. Ever since he had become more interested in speculation and property development – projects like the Elmet Centre – rather than mere ownership, Blaydon had let many of the places he already owned go to seed, or had simply rented them out and forgotten about them. Now he was dead, his daughter would inherit them, along with everything else, but she had already indicated that she had no interest in her late father's businesses and would rather just sell the whole kit and caboodle and go live in St Kitts and Nevis.

Banks asked Gerry if she could make time to come up with a list of vacant, isolated Blaydon properties within a radius of, say, twenty miles of Windlee Farm, and she said she would.

'So Charlotte Westlake is lying about not knowing the girl?'

'So it would appear,' said Gerry. She was sitting at her desk in the squad room of Eastvale Regional HQ the day after talking with Tamara Collins. 'The interesting question is why.'

'We both felt there was something she wasn't telling us,' Annie said. 'And this is probably it. She's more involved than we thought.'

'It's not much, though, is it? Mistaken identity. Poor photograph. Easy to explain away. Maybe she genuinely didn't recognise this Marnie from the photo, especially if she didn't know her well?'

'It's a connection. That's what's important. And it tells us she's a liar. You specifically asked her if it might have been someone who worked for her at the parties, and she had every chance to come up with a possibility or two. Remember, she didn't study the photo closely. She just rejected it out of hand. Fair enough, it's not a great photo, but if you'd hired the person depicted in it, there's a reasonable chance you might recognise her from it, don't you think?'

'I suppose so.'

'Why should we trust anything she tells us? For all we know she might be in cahoots with Tadić on supplying the girls. Maybe she's a madam with a ready-made stable.'

Gerry smiled. 'Hang on a minute . . . It *is* still possible that Charlotte was telling the truth and she didn't recognise Marnie from the picture.'

'I know. I know,' said Annie. 'Maybe I'm exaggerating, making too much of it. But we have to consider that Charlotte Westlake *might* be lying, out of loyalty to Blaydon, or to cover up some involvement of her own. In exactly what, I don't know. Remember she said she knew him vaguely before she went to work for him. Maybe he's the rapist, and Marnie told Charlotte about it, cried on her shoulder? What would Charlotte do about that? At the very least she ought to be able to supply us with the victim's last name now we can tell her the first one, which is a hell of a lot more than we have right now.'

'True enough,' Gerry agreed. 'But are you also thinking Charlotte might have had something to do with Blaydon's murder because of what he did to Marnie?'

'Or Marnie herself,' she said. 'But I can't see either of them going that far. And gutting him . . .? No. Charlotte's already told us she was finding Blaydon's behaviour harder and harder to take. That's why she left.'

'If she's telling us the truth about that.'

'Fair enough. But Marnie was just another employee. And what about Gashi? Maybe *he* was the rapist? Maybe he killed Blaydon because he thought he had something on him, or he found out about Roberts filming it? Don't forget, we've always leaned towards the theory that the Albanians killed Blaydon. We just lacked any evidence. Maybe this is it? At least it gives us a clearer motive. Perhaps we should go and have another word with Charlotte, push her a bit harder.'

'We could have the local force pick her up and bring her in,' Gerry suggested. 'Use an interview room. Give her the full treatment. Be more intimidating.'

Annie thought for a moment. 'Good idea. We've got Tamara's statement that Charlotte met with the girl in her office. That gives us something to confront her with, more ammunition.'

'Sounds like a plan,' Gerry said, sliding off the desk. 'I'd better get back to work on Blaydon's empty properties for the super first, see if we can find a suitable property Tadić could be using to keep Zelda prisoner.'

'It's as good an idea as any.'

The door opened and the bright light of a heavy-duty work lamp flooded in. Zelda blinked at the onslaught. When her eyes adjusted, she noticed Petar Tadić standing there with a scruffy, thuggish man she didn't know. She retreated to her corner and pulled up her knees. She could tell from the way Tadić looked at her that he still had no idea who she was, that they had met before, that he had raped her. The light elongated and distorted their shadows on the walls, so they resembled deformed creatures from a horror film. Freaks. Dracula in his cape. Nosferatu.

'Sit up straight against that wall by the radiator,' Tadić said.

Zelda didn't move.

Tadić stepped forward and kicked her on the hip. She cried out.

'Against the wall.'

Zelda shuffled herself into position.

Tadić turned the light full on her, and his sidekick took a digital camera from his pocket and squatted in front of her.

'Hold your head up. Don't smile for the camera,' Tadić said and grinned.

That was easy to do. The sidekick took several photos of her head and shoulders. 'Done, boss,' he said.

'Give the camera to Foley. He'll know what to do.'

He picked up the light and they left without another word. Zelda breathed a sigh of relief as she was once again consigned to darkness.

The interview room wasn't especially designed to scare the shit out of anyone questioned there, nor was it created to inspire a sense of calm and well-being. The walls were either institutional green or dishwater grey, depending on the light, which came in through a tiny high window covered by a grille. The furniture consisted of a metal table bolted to the floor, along with two hard-backed chairs on each side. Against one wall stood another table laden with tape-recording equipment, and high in one corner, the CCTV camera looked down on the proceedings and recorded every twitch and tic. The room's starkness was symbolic of its purpose: to get down to the bare bones.

The day Charlotte Westlake was led inside, the walls were decidedly pale grey in contrast to the bright sunshine outside, and to Charlotte's yellow blouse and green skirt. There was no air-conditioning, and the heat rose steadily throughout the interview. At the end, everyone was sweating, not only Charlotte Westlake.

When she was brought in, she first leaned, palms down, on the table and addressed Annie and Gerry: 'I want it on record that I very much resent this intrusion into my life for no apparent reason.'

'Sit down, Mrs Westlake,' said Annie. 'The sooner we get started, the sooner we'll be finished.'

Charlotte sat slowly, the anger still etched into the hard lines of her face. She wore her hair pulled back, fastened in a loose bun at the nape of her neck, and the tightness of her hairline accentuated her high cheekbones and narrow jaw. Her sapphire eyes were blazing with rage. 'Should I be sending for my solicitor?'

'Up to you,' said Annie. 'As far as we're concerned, this is what we call an "intelligence interview" and you're here simply to answer a few questions about a crime. You haven't been arrested or charged with anything.'

'I know you lot,' she said. 'You're sneaky. You'll get me to admit things.'

'Admit to what things?'

'You know what I mean. You're at it already.'

Annie leaned forward and tapped her pen on the table. 'This could be very simple,' she said. 'You answer a few questions, tell the truth, and it's all over. Call your solicitor and, well, things can get very long and drawn-out from that point. We could fix you up with a duty solicitor, but somehow I don't think that's what you want. You complained to the officers who brought you here that you have tickets for Opera North tonight. If you simply let us do our jobs, there's no reason why you shouldn't be there to enjoy the show. Believe me, we're not trying to trap you into admitting anything criminal. This entire conversation is being recorded for your sake as well as ours, and you haven't been cautioned. We can go through all the motions if you want, and perhaps we can charge you with wasting police time, or impeding an investigation, but believe me, it'll be far more binding on you should anything more serious come of our little chat. And it'll take time. So what's it to be?'

'I'm not being held on any charges?'

'No.'

'So I'm free to go?'

'Yes.'

She stood up. 'Then what's to stop me?'

'Nothing,' said Annie. 'Go ahead, if you like. All you need to know is that we think you have information we would like to have in our possession, too, and we don't give up that easily. You either lied to us or you were mistaken the last time we talked to you. This is your chance to put things right. Maybe your last chance. So walk, if you wish. We can't stop you. But we're not going away.' She paused. 'And you would be obstructing us in our investigation.'

Annie held eye contact with Charlotte for what felt like a long time before the latter slowly subsided back into her chair and said, 'Fine. Let's get on with it, then, get it over with. What do you want to know?'

Gerry, who had been sitting quietly taking notes of anything that might not be obvious from a sound or video recording, slid over the photograph of Marnie. 'Last time we talked to you,' she said, 'you told us you didn't know this girl.'

Charlotte glanced at the photo, then quickly turned away. 'That's right,' she said, her voice hesitant and shaky.

'Her name is Marnie. Does that help at all?'

'Marnie . . . I . . . I . . .'

Annie took over and tried to set her at ease. 'Easy to be mistaken. We admit it's not a very good image. But take another look. Go on. Take your time.'

Charlotte studied the picture, then said, 'Well, it *could* be her . . . I suppose. She *does* seem sort of familiar on closer inspection.'

'So you *do* know a Marnie?'

'I . . . er . . . yes.'

'Is this her?'

'It could be. Who told you that?'

'It doesn't matter. The point is that we found out. What's her surname?'

'Sedgwick. Marnie Sedgwick. If that's who she is. Is this the one . . .? I mean, God, I'm so sorry about what happened to her.'

'How old is she?'

'Old enough. Nineteen.'

'Old enough for what?' Gerry asked.

'To do the job I employed her for, of course, which might have included serving alcohol at some events.'

'Did it?'

'No. She turned out to be better suited to behind-the-scenes work.'

Annie picked up the questioning again. 'How did you become acquainted with her?'

'If it is the person I'm thinking of, then she's an employee. An occasional employee, I should say.'

'Gig economy?'

'Has to be, in my business. I can't guarantee her full-time or even part-time employment. It's on an event-by-event basis. I used her as and when she was available and when I needed someone.'

'For Blaydon's parties?'

'Yes. And his other events – sales conventions, retirement parties and so on. The usual sort of events most businesses have to cope with.'

'Did you first meet her when she applied for a job?'

'Yes. I don't advertise. At least, only by word of mouth. It would be one of the other girls who suggested her.'

'Which one?'

'I have no idea. As I said, I don't know her well. All I know is she came to me looking for a job, I interviewed her, and she seemed satisfactory, worth taking a chance on.'

'Perhaps you can furnish us with a list of all your employees, however casual they may be? I do believe we asked you for this last time we talked. We haven't got it yet.'

'I know . . . It's just . . . I don't know. What about privacy?'

'Theirs or yours?' said Gerry. 'We're not interested in tax avoidance, if that's what you're worried about. We don't care how many jobs they're doing on the side, or whether they're claiming benefits at the same time. Nor do we care whether your business is registered in Jersey or the Isle of Man. Not our department.'

Charlotte gave her a sour smile. 'Yes, of course.'

'So Marnie's one of your regular helpers now?' said Annie.

'Yes. She was.'

'Is she not still with you?'

'No. That was when I was working for Connor.'

'And now?'

'I'm afraid I have no idea where she is.'

'You let her go?'

'She could have come with me, but she chose not to.'

'Where did she go?'

'I have no idea. She didn't confide in me.'

'Any idea why she left?'

'I assumed she'd found something else. Something better paying, better hours, or steadier work, perhaps.'

'Did she say what?'

'No.'

'How was she as an employee?'

'She was a bit reticent, shy, when it came to the hostess work, and she made it clear that she didn't like doing it. That's why she didn't work out on the service end. She'd worked as a waitress in a family restaurant, but this was different. There was a lot of alcohol involved, and the men . . . Well, I'm sure you know what I mean. Her attitude might have made her seem stand-offish. But she was good at the practical aspects of the job, the backroom stuff. She was no slouch. And she was reliable. Always turned up on time. You'd be surprised how rare that is these days.'

'Just not so good at chatting up the men at front of house?'

'That wasn't part of her job. And it's a strictly hands-off policy with my serving girls. Connor knew that. It's not as if there weren't enough of the other kind of women around recently. Marnie's an attractive girl, it's true, but she isn't the type to display her cleavage and a bit of thigh. She's a very serious girl, a thinker rather than a talker. She's also good at being invisible when she needed to be. I liked that about her. And mostly she was stuck in the kitchen. You have no idea how much cleaning up, restocking and ongoing maintenance there is to be done at events like those parties. They don't run as smoothly without a lot of skilled help, you know.'

'Maybe all of Blaydon's guests didn't know about your hands-off policy,' Gerry cut in. 'She certainly wasn't invisible to one particular person on the night this image was captured. Sometimes people want what they can't have, more than what's on offer. Perhaps someone thought she was too stuck-up and wanted to bring her down a notch or two?'

'I wasn't there. I told you. I'm sorry about what happened. It's terrible. You can't believe how sorry. Maybe if I'd been there . . .? But it wasn't my fault. I was in Costa Rica.'

'Yes, we know,' Annie said. 'But the point remains that you *do* know Marnie Sedgwick. You employed her to work at that party on 13 April, as you had done before, even though you weren't present yourself.'

'Yes, but I don't see how you could possibly hold me responsible for anything that occurred at that party.'

'Who said anything about holding you responsible? We're after information, that's all, not to apportion blame. Do you *feel* responsible?'

'No. I'm just upset. You're twisting my words. I knew this was the sort of thing you'd do.'

'Why did you lie to us about knowing Marnie?'

'I didn't lie. I just wasn't sure. It's a bad photo. Maybe I didn't look closely enough. I don't know. I just didn't want to get involved.'

'Involved in what? Did you already know what had happened to Marnie? Did you lie about that, too?'

'Know? About the rape? Good Lord, no. But when the police come calling, you don't think it's about your TV licence being overdue, do you?'

'Is it?'

Charlotte just stared at Annie.

'Joke,' Annie said.

'Does it surprise you, what happened to Marnie at the party?' Gerry asked.

'Of course it does. It appalls me. I organised *parties* for Connor, not orgies. The guests were thoroughly vetted. I know they could get a bit wild sometimes, but every one of them was a trusted—'

'Oh, come off it!' said Annie. 'He invited people he wanted to be seen with, people he wanted to impress and people who might do him some good in business, make him more money. Do you really believe he wouldn't bend over backwards to give one of them what he wanted if it was important to him? They were no more vetted for their morality than the American president. For crying out loud, you had Petar Tadić supplying trafficked girls, and Leka Gashi brought bowls of cocaine. So who saw Marnie Sedgwick and thought she was part of the package, too?'

Charlotte sat forward and placed her palms flat on the table again. 'I've told you, I don't know. I wasn't there. I didn't even know there'd been an incident until you came along.'

'Are you sure about that?' Gerry asked.

Charlotte glanced sideways at her. 'Yes.'

'Blaydon never told you?'

'I don't even know if *he* knew. And if he did, he didn't tell me. Why would he? Isn't it the kind of thing you cover up? He's hardly likely to tell me that something so terrible happened in his house to one of my staff, at an event I organised, even if he didn't do it. People were always slipping off to bedrooms, as I told you. I was getting tired of it, the atmosphere was becoming poisonous.'

'But you said you only rarely attended the parties,' said Annie.

'One hears things. And I popped in from time to time. Some of these things are hard to miss, even on brief acquaintance. I'm not that bloody naive.'

'You also told us that you thought these girls were wives and girlfriends, not professionals brought in for the purposes of sex.'

'That was certainly true in the earlier days.'

'When did it start to change?'

'Around the end of last year.'

'Any ideas why then?'

'Connor got involved in a major new development. A shopping centre and housing estate.'

'The Elmet Centre?'

'Yes. And that's when he brought in Tadić and Gashi, along with a whole host of new business colleagues and hangers-on. That's when his behaviour started to worry me, and the parties started to change in character.'

'So you're not too surprised that something like this might happen? The rape,' Annie said persistently.

'Perhaps not. Seeing as you put it like that. But I'm still shocked.'

'Well, surely it would fall on someone to keep the girl quiet, slip her an extra bob or two, tell her it was an unfortunate incident best put behind her? Who better than you?'

'Well, I didn't. I knew nothing about it.'

'Perhaps she came crying to you, and you comforted her? She told you Blaydon had raped her. One of *your* girls. You saw red. Maybe you killed him?'

'That's ridiculous.'

'Is it? Where were you on the afternoon of 22 May?'

Charlotte seemed knocked sideways by the question. 'Is this a trick question? I've already told you. I'm not sure. We were working on a book award dinner in Bradford, but I was back and forth. Where were you?'

'We're asking you.'

'Bet you don't remember where *you* were.'

'We may ask you to come up with a bit more detail at some point. Something solid we can check.'

Charlotte said nothing.

'Where does Marnie Sedgwick live?' Gerry asked. 'We'd like to talk to her, get her side of the story. Maybe find out why she didn't report the rape.'

'Lots of women don't report rapes because of the way they get treated by the authorities.'

'What way?'

'As if *they're* the guilty ones.'

'OK. Point taken,' said Annie. 'But we'd still like to hear it from her.'

'I don't know her address.'

'Come on, Charlotte. Don't be coy with us now we're

getting along so well. She was on your books. An employee. You must have an address and phone number for her.'

'No. I mean it. I did know. I mean, yes, I had an address for her before, along with her other details, but I heard she'd moved on after that party. Left the area. I don't know where, honestly. And I don't know why, though I suppose I can guess now.'

'Where are your old employment records?'

'With Connor's stuff, I should imagine. I assume you've got it somewhere.'

'You could save us a lot of time. I'm sure you probably kept a note of it in case you wanted her to work for you again.'

'I could probably dig it up,' Charlotte said.

Annie clapped her hands together. 'Good. Now we're getting somewhere. Soon as you get home, please. Along with that list of employees. Didn't you ever wonder why Marnie moved on after the party?'

'Not especially. Girls come and go.'

'Like buses, there'll be another one along in a minute?'

'If you must put it so crudely. I'm a businesswoman. Marnie was one of my employees. That's all there was to it. Now can I go?'

Annie leaned back in her chair. 'You know,' she said, 'it took us a while to get this much out of you, and I'm still not convinced you're telling us the whole story, or the whole truth. But we'll leave it at that for the time being. You probably do remember a lot more than you've admitted to, including names. In which case, if I were you, I'd be very careful from now on.'

'Oh, why's that?'

'Marnie Sedgwick was raped at a party held by Connor Clive Blaydon. A party you organised, no doubt attended by a number of famous faces and up-and-coming Jack-the-Lads that Blaydon had some reason to want to impress. Now, if Blaydon himself didn't rape Marnie, the actual rapist probably has a great deal to lose if he's caught. We don't know who he is. Not long after this party, Blaydon and his so-called butler Neville Roberts were murdered in a particularly nasty manner. I'd worry about that, for a start. We were thinking that maybe it was Gashi's gang, or even Tadić's – after all, they're both international gangsters with about as much respect for human life as Godzilla – but what if it wasn't them? What if it was something to do with what happened to Marnie Sedgwick? Revenge? Self-protection? What if her rapist killed Blaydon? If you do know something you're not telling us, that could put you in a rather dangerous position, couldn't it?'

Charlotte had paled. 'Are you telling me that my life is in danger?'

'We're just warning you to be careful, that's all,' said Gerry. 'Seeing as you employed Marnie and supplied her for the party, another possibility is that some people might have got the impression – the wrong impression, of course – that she was part of the entertainment, and that what happened to her was partly your fault, that you should share some of the blame with the rapist and with Blaydon himself. Maybe Marnie told her father, or her boyfriend, what happened? Maybe one of them killed Blaydon? People jump to conclusions sometimes and act before they think. That's what makes our job so difficult.'

'So what are you suggesting? That you give me police protection?'

'Love to,' said Annie, 'but we're stretched to the limit right now. Still waiting for those twenty thousand new coppers we've been promised.'

'So what *are* you saying?'

'OK, here's the deal,' Annie said. 'You go away and have a good think. A good long think. And you see if you can remember what you haven't told us, then come back and put that right. Especially if you've heard rumours of anyone Marnie may have hung around with at the party, or anyone who'd been bothering her. Say, perhaps, one of the other girls working that night noticed something. If it was Blaydon who raped Marnie, you can tell us. You don't have to worry about him. He's dead. But if it was someone else, someone still alive . . . well, time becomes an issue.'

'But how can I? I don't know anything.'

'You know some of the characters involved. Names. Maybe some of the same people were at previous parties? Maybe you noticed someone expressing an unusual interest in Marnie when you dropped by? Perhaps this person asked Blaydon for a special favour, and Blaydon had good reason to grant him his wishes. Who was he trying to win over, or impress? Perhaps you stood in the way? Maybe that's why he sent you to Costa Rica, to get you out of the picture, clear the decks so to speak. Have you ever thought of that?'

'No, I haven't,' said Charlotte. 'But thanks for putting the idea in my mind. I can try to think back, if you like, but what about in the meantime? What am I supposed to do?'

'In the meantime,' said Gerry, 'you can send us the information we asked for, then take our advice and be very careful.'

On the second visit, Tadić stood over Zelda. 'You know why you're here?' he asked.

'No,' said Zelda. 'I don't even know where here is.'

Tadić laughed, a hoarse, phlegmy sound. 'That doesn't matter. Do you know who I am?'

Again, Zelda shook her head.

'My name is Petar Tadić. Does that help?'

Again, Zelda said, 'No. I'm hungry and thirsty. Can I have—'

With surprising speed, Tadić gave her a backhander that sent her head sideways into the cast-iron radiator. She could taste blood and her head was ringing, starting to throb with pain. She thought she could feel blood oozing into her hair and over her ear.

'Does that help your memory?'

She was about to say no again, but realised what would happen if she did, so she kept quiet. Tadić was a man who liked the sound of his own voice, she remembered.

'Let me tell you, then,' he said, squatting in front of her. 'You're the bitch who murdered my brother.' He put his face so close to hers that she could smell curry on his breath. It almost made her sick. 'Eh, my beauty? Am I right?' He caressed the side of her face where he had just hit her. 'Am I right?'

'I don't know what you mean,' Zelda said. 'I haven't—'

But before she could say any more, he hit her again, in the same place. Her head reeled, and she tasted burning bile in her throat. Luckily, this time her head didn't crash into the radiator.

'It's no use denying it,' Tadić said. 'I saw you on the hotel CCTV. The sexy red dress. Yes? Oh, I saw you. My men are very good. They talk to Foley's girlfriend, Faye Butler. She tells them plenty before she dies. They find restaurant where you saw her with Foley and Hawkins. They find taxi driver who drove you back to your hotel after you kill Goran. They find out your name and where you live from hotel. But not quite, because you give no street and number, do you? Just house name Windlee Farm and that village. Lyndgarth. But we find it. And now we have you. What do you think of that? Good detective work, yes?'

Zelda vomited down the front of her T-shirt.

Tadić jumped back up so fast he almost fell over, but he couldn't escape getting a few flecks on his polished leather Italian shoes.

His partner lurched towards Zelda, but Tadić held him back. 'No,' he said. Then he took a handkerchief from his pocket, cleaned off his shoes and tossed it in a corner.

'Kill her now, boss,' the man said. 'Let *me* kill her.'

'No. That is too easy.' Tadić towered over Zelda. 'Why did you kill him?' he asked. 'Why did you kill Goran?'

Zelda tried to control her breathing, raised her head and looked him in the eye. 'You and your brother abducted me outside an orphanage in Chişinău many years ago.'

'I don't remember you. Or Chişinău. Is that why you killed my brother?'

'Yes,' Zelda spat.

Tadić kicked her again, this time in the stomach. She doubled up in pain. They stood looking down on her as she struggled to hold back more vomit. When she could trust herself to speak again, she asked, 'What are you going to do to me?' Her voice felt thick. She probed a broken tooth with her tongue, tasted blood and vomit.

Tadić grinned. 'Do? I could sell you to the Albanians. They know what to do with a *kurva* like you. But no. Like killing you, it is also too easy. No. I have a friend who tell me about special house in Dhaka. Do you know where that is? Bangladesh. Long way. Sick old men who go there like young girls or boys best, but a white woman like you will be novelty. For a while. Do not worry. You will not survive for long. If the diseases don't rot your pretty little *pička*, the drinking water will poison you. But it will be a slow death. Long and slow and painful. You will have much time to remember what you did to Goran.'

Zelda felt panic rush through her. She jerked and tugged at her chains again and tried to drag her hands apart so much the plasticuffs bit into her skin.

Tadić and his friend just stood there laughing. 'You can scream as loud as you like,' Tadić said. 'There is no one to hear you.'

When the strength went out of Zelda's struggle, she was aware of the light disappearing and the door closing. She lay in the darkness alone again, her face and her teeth aching, head throbbing, and the thought came to her that she would not be able to bear the future they were planning for her, however short it was likely to be. Not only that, but she *couldn't* let it happen. And the only way she knew of stopping it was to kill herself before they got her to Dhaka.

II

According to Charlotte Westlake's records, Marnie Sedgwick had lived in York on a cul-de-sac terrace of tall, narrow Victorian brick semis. It wasn't far from the city centre, and most of the houses were divided into flats and bedsits. Though it was some distance from the university, it looked like student housing, and Annie wondered if Marnie had been a student, working part-time for Charlotte.

They walked up the steps and Annie rang the bell with the empty nameplate beside it. They had phoned ahead and the landlord said he would meet them there. They heard someone coming down the stairs and Duncan McCrae, the landlord, opened the door for them.

'Right on time,' he said, rubbing his hands together.

'We don't like to disappoint,' said Annie, stepping forward. 'Shall we go up?'

'There's nothing to see, like I told you on the phone,' said McCrae, 'but be my guest.' He led the way to the first floor, at the back, where Marnie's tiny bedsit overlooked an alley full of wheelie bins and the backyards of the houses opposite. Beyond them lay train tracks. McCrae hovered in the doorway as if he was worried they'd steal the silverware. Only there wasn't any silverware. There wasn't anything except an empty three-shelf homemade bookcase built of bricks and boards.

'Exactly when did she leave?' Annie asked.

'End of April.'

That worked out at a couple of weeks after the rape, Annie reckoned. 'Did she take all her stuff with her?'

'There wasn't much to take. That's the thing. She just left one day and left the mess to me. As far as I could tell, she probably didn't take more than a suitcase with her. Clothes and some personal stuff. She left the rest. A few books. Some cutlery, dishware, pots and pans. Household things. That's about all. Here one day, gone the next. But her rent was up to date.'

Annie managed to hold her tongue before saying how happy she was to hear that. 'What about a forwarding address?'

McCrae just shook his head.

'Previous address?'

'No.'

'You didn't ask for her details?'

McCrae shifted from foot to foot. 'Well . . . er . . . no.'

'What happened to her things?'

'Bin bag in the cellar. I thought I'd keep it a little while, you know, in case she called back for it.'

'We'll look at it when we're done here,' Annie said as she started wandering about the small room. She peeled back a moth-eaten curtain and saw the hot plate with two shelves above it, both bare. There was nothing else in the room.

'Where did she sleep?' Gerry asked.

'Mattress on the floor, under the window there, and a ratty old sleeping bag,' said McCrae. 'I threw them both out.'

Annie sniffed the air. It was stale and foisty, as one would expect in a room shut up so long in warm weather. She tried to open the window but couldn't budge it.

'Bloody painters,' said McCrae. 'Only painted it shut, didn't they?'

'What was Marnie like?' Gerry asked.

'Like? Well, just ordinary really. Quiet. She never said much. Seemed a serious sort of girl. Used to have posters on the walls – save the planet, that sort of thing. Always polite, though. A smile and a hello. Well brought up. You could tell. I never had much to do with her, really, so there's not a lot I can tell you beyond that.'

'What happened to the posters?' Annie could see the bare patches where they used to be.

'I took them down, dumped them.'

'Did you notice any changes in her behaviour or demeanour?'

'Eh? Come again.'

'Anything different about her around the time she left?'

'I didn't talk to her much the last few weeks she was here. I don't live here, of course, so I wouldn't know. But I don't think she went out much. I mean, if I was around fixing something, I didn't see her coming or going. Like I said, she left at the end of the month.'

'Did you *see* her at all?'

'Once or twice.'

'How did she seem on those occasions, the last two or three weeks?'

McCrae seemed stumped by the question. 'Tired, mostly,' he said. 'Her eyes, you know. Puffy. With bags under. As if she hadn't been getting enough sleep.'

'Or crying?' said Annie.

'Aye, maybe that, too.'

That made sense, Annie thought, given what Marnie had been through. Why had she not sought help? What had been going on in her mind? 'Was she a student?' she asked.

'Miss Sedgwick? No, I don't think so. You'd have to ask the others, though.'

'How did she get around?'

'She had a car. A Fiat, I think.'

'So Marnie was wealthy?'

'No, I'd hardly say that. You wouldn't, either, if you saw the car. But she had a paying job. Two, actually.'

'What jobs?'

'A cafe in town. Waitress. One of those chains. Ask. Zizzi. Pizza Express. Something like that.'

'You can't remember which one?'

'I think it was Pizza Express, but I can't be certain. She gave me a slice once. Pizza, that is. She brought some home from work with her and I happened to be in the hall. I think the box was Pizza Express but I wouldn't swear to it.'

'And the other?'

'Catering of some sort, or helping caterers. That one was occasional. Just when she was needed, like.'

'Did she have any close friends among the other tenants?'

'I did see her chatting with that Chinese lass from 3b once or twice. They seemed quite close.'

'OK. I think we've seen enough here,' said Annie. 'Can we go and see the stuff she left behind her now?'

'Follow me,' said McCrae. He led them down to the ground floor, where he fumbled for a key in his pockets and opened a door to the cellar. It was more of a basement, really, Annie thought, having imagined a grim and sooty old coal cellar, and she was surprised McCrae hadn't done it up a bit, given it a lick of paint and rented it out as a basement apartment. Instead, it was full of junk.

McCrae took them over to a black bin bag in a corner. 'This is it,' he said.

Gerry went back to the car to get the proper bags to store the stuff as evidence. There wasn't much, as McCrae had said. Books, mostly philosophy and psychology as far as Annie could tell; two plates, cups, glasses, knives and forks; and a pan and kettle she would have heated on the hot plate. That was it. No personal items – notebooks, diaries, lists of addresses, letters, nothing like that.

'What about post since she left?'

McCrae walked over to a battered chest of drawers, opened the top one and took out a bundle of envelopes fastened with a rubber band. 'I keep the mail of any tenants who leave for a while, if they don't arrange a forwarding address, just in case there's something important. You'd be surprised. Over the years I've had cheques, passports, you name it. These are just junk mail.'

Gerry took the bundle. They might hold some clue as to where Marnie had gone. 'Thanks,' she said. 'We'll take these, too.'

After they had carried out Marnie's stuff and stored it in the boot of the car, they tried the door to 3b, occupied by a student called Mitsuko Ogawa, who was definitely not Chinese, as even Annie's rudimentary grasp of foreign languages told her. But there was no one home. She scribbled a little note, added her mobile number and said they'd be back later, then she grinned at Gerry. 'If you ask me, it's lunchtime. Fancy a pizza?'

Zelda still couldn't tell whether it was night or day. At one time, she thought she could hear traffic beyond the boarded-up windows, or an airplane fly over, but even then she thought she might be imagining things. One thing she wasn't imagining was that nobody was coming to rescue her. No Willie Garvin. No doubt the police were trying to find her, but they clearly had no more idea where she was being kept than she did. And there was no way she could see of getting a message out.

She spent a lot of time trying to figure out ways of killing herself before they could take her to that brothel in Dhaka.

She tried to wrap the leg chain around her neck to strangle herself, but it wasn't long enough, so she only managed to strain a muscle in her thigh. She tried holding her breath, and swallowing her tongue, but found she could do neither. She always gasped for breath on the verge of passing out and never got as far as putting her fingers in her mouth to push the rolled ball of tongue down her throat. She couldn't face trying to bash her brains out against the radiator.

She was a coward, she had to admit. If she were to die, she wanted it to be as easy and painless as possible. Pills, preferably. There was no way she could stand Dhaka, so she had to do it somehow. Maybe there would be more opportunities along the way? Maybe she could even catch somebody's attention and get free – at an airport, for example, or on a flight. It would be a long journey; they would have to escort her through at least one airport, if not more. She was certain that even Tadić didn't have a private jet. Or did they plan on travelling overland, smugglers' routes? No doubt that was why she was being kept here so long, so that they could work out the routes and phoney visas. She had already figured out that the photographs they had taken when she first arrived were for a fake passport, no doubt to be supplied by Keane, the man she thought had killed Hawkins and who had once tried to kill Alan Banks.

Alan. Raymond. She thought of them often; sometimes she thought she would burst with grief when she pictured Raymond alone and desolate at Windlee Farm. He would be a complete mess. That would be one way to die, she supposed. Grief. And what was Alan doing? He would do whatever he could to find her, of that she was sure. But it was hopeless.

Despite the fear and the will to suicide, Zelda was hungry again. As long as her body survived, it would demand sustenance, just as it needed movement and air. She could stand up, but she couldn't move far in her leg iron. She marked time every now and then, just to keep her circulation going.

After that second visit, Tadić's sneering sidekick had returned to deliver a chamber pot and throw a plastic bottle of water and a Big Mac at her. She had seen the way he looked at her, and knew that only fear of Tadić stopped him having his way. That and the vomit on her T-shirt, perhaps.

The Big Mac was cold, but she had gobbled it down. The water she tried to make last. The chamber pot was a blessing, as she imagined the only alternative – short of squatting on the floor – would be for one of them to accompany her to the toilet whenever she needed to go. A chance to wash and change would be nice, though. Surely, they would want to clean her up before they travelled? A bath, perhaps? Fresh clothes. But what was the point of any of it if she was going to die anyway, either before she got to Dhaka, with any luck, or soon after she arrived there, if the worst happened?

Sometimes she thought that she couldn't take her own life because she still had dreams of escape, hope of being rescued. It was true, these things *could* happen, though they grew less likely hour by hour. If she didn't eat, then perhaps she would get ill and die of malnutrition, rather than by her own weak hand. But she thought that would take much longer than they planned keeping her here.

Also, in some of her darkest moments, she had a strange feeling of elation out of nowhere. It was like a smell – not of the sea, but of the seaside – and a vague image of being a little girl walking with her hand in her father's at Odessa flashed through her mind. A sense of safety and warmth. But it was also neither a smell nor an image; it was an inchoate memory of total happiness she had perhaps never experienced. How could you have a memory of something you had never felt? But that was what it felt like.

In the embrace of that perfect happiness, she had not a care, not a worry, not a thought, but the sheer pleasure of being. No fear of what was to come or regret for what was past. It was pure and simple happiness, the ghost of childhood's essence.

But it was rare and fleeting. Most of the time she felt a deep and paralysing sense of fear and dread, edging into despair, that no amount of reason or epiphany could dispel.

Driving in York was an absolute nightmare, Gerry thought as she steered her way along narrow streets lined with parked cars, braked sharply for pedestrians and missed a turning that forced her to make a long detour. But parking was even worse. Finally, in frustration, she pulled into the forecourt of York Explore Library and Archive and threw herself on the mercy of the woman in charge, who told her she could leave the car there until they were finished.

'Next time we'll take the bloody Poppleton Park & Ride,' Annie said as they crossed the road and walked the short distance down to Pizza Express. The city was bursting at the seams with tourists and locals out enjoying the fine weather, and this area around the bridge was always crowded. It led ultimately up past St Mary's and the library to the Minster, which stood at the top dominating everything, a magnificent Gothic construction, its main tower obscured by scaffolding.

Pizza Express was in an old building with a high ceiling on Museum Street near the bridge and opposite the Museum Gardens. The large dining area reminded Annie of a banquet hall in some ancient stately home. They flashed their warrant cards, and Annie asked the girl who showed people to their tables if she might talk to the manager. The girl disappeared through a door to the back and came out moments later with a tanned young man in a suit and tie. He didn't look old enough to be a manager, Annie thought, but what did she know about the hospitality industry? He introduced himself as Mark Baldini.

She showed him the photograph. 'Do you remember a woman called Marnie Sedgwick? Does she still work here?'

'Marnie. Yes, I remember her,' he said. 'She left around the beginning of May.'

'Do you remember the circumstances of her leaving?'

'It was so sad,' Baldini said. 'Marnie was a good worker. She'd been here about a year, but towards the middle of April she changed. She wasn't concentrating, seemed to be dragging her feet. She wasn't attentive, she mixed up orders, delivered things to the wrong tables.'

'What did you do?'

'I liked her. And as I said, she was a good worker, so I took her aside into the office and had a word with her.'

'How did she react?'

'She didn't react much at all. She agreed she wasn't doing a great job, said she wasn't sleeping well, that she couldn't concentrate. I asked her if she was ill or if there was anything wrong, anything I could help with, and she shrugged and said no. I asked if she thought she could attain her previous high standard of work again, and she said she'd try.'

'Did she?'

'Nothing changed. I hated to do it, but I knew in the end I'd have to give her notice. I was going to tell her she could come back when she was better, like, and I'd do my best to make sure she got her job back, but she couldn't go on as she was.'

'How did she respond?'

'I never got to tell her. The next day she got an order wrong, and the customer was very snappy with her. He was one of those pushy, loud-mouthed blokes. You know the sort. Always right, always angry. He shouted at her, called her a stupid cunt, and Marnie dumped the pizza on his lap and ran out in tears. That was the last I saw of her. I made sure we paid her what we owed her, into her bank account, like, a standing order, and that was it. What was it? What was her problem? Do you know?'

'That's what we're trying to find out, Mr Baldini,' said Annie. 'Was she close to any of her colleagues here? Anyone who's still here?'

'Yes,' said Baldini. 'Mitsuko. In fact, it was Marnie brought her to us, got her the job. I think they shared a flat or lived in the same house or something.'

'Mitsuko Ogawa?' said Annie.

'Yes. Lovely girl. Terrific waitress.'

'Is she here now?'

Baldini glanced around. 'She should be.' Finally, he pointed to a table in the far corner where a petite young woman was serving pizza and salad. 'That's Mitsuko.'

'Can you do us a favour?' Annie asked.

'Depends what it is.'

'We're going to have some lunch here, so could you give Ms Ogawa an early tea break or whatever and ask her to join us at our table? We won't keep her for long.'

'Of course. Take as long as you like. We're not too busy right now.'

It was mid-afternoon, and the place still seemed fairly full to Annie, though she and Gerry had no difficulty getting a table for four. Busyness in a place like this was all relative, she supposed.

When their waitress came by, Annie ordered a margherita pizza and side salad, and Gerry picked a Diavola. Both ordered Diet Cokes to accompany their meals. They had barely got their order in before a young woman joined them at the table. She introduced herself as Mitsuko Ogawa and sat down. Annie guessed that Mitsuko was around Marnie's age.

She was small, with shoulder-length black hair drawn tight from her forehead and fastened at the back. Her eyes shone with concern as she sat down and smoothed her dress over her knees.

'Mr Baldini said you wanted to talk to me about Marnie,' she said, with a slight Geordie accent. 'Do you know where she is? What's happened to her?'

'I'm afraid we don't know where she is,' said Gerry. 'That's one problem we were hoping you might help us with. I understand the two of you were close?'

'I thought so,' Mitsuko said.

'What do you mean?'

'Something changed. I don't know what it was, but she just wasn't the same after. Did Mr Baldini tell you what happened here?'

'Yes. He said her work went downhill and she left in tears.'

'That's about right.'

'Do you have any idea why? What was wrong with her? He said he thought she might be ill.' They had a very good idea of what was wrong with Marnie, but they couldn't tell Mitsuko; they were hoping she might be able to tell them more than they knew already.

'She wasn't eating properly,' said Mitsuko. 'Or sleeping very well. But I don't think there was any illness as such. Just a sort of malaise, you know, weariness, depression. She lost interest in everything. But I don't know why. We used to be friends. When she first moved into the house a year ago, we spent a lot of time together, you know, just talking, listening to music. We'd go out to the pub, the cinema, concerts. Marnie likes art-house movies – Bergman and Kurosawa, that sort of thing. And she likes goth rock. You know, old weird stuff like Joy Division, Nick Cave, Sisters of Mercy. All that dark stuff. My taste is a bit more mainstream and upbeat. Action thrillers and Marvel. And I prefer music you can dance to. But we liked each other.'

'So you'd say you are close friends?'

'Yes,' said Mitsuko. 'Yes, I would. I've been beside myself since she left. Has something happened to her? *Please* tell me if it has. I've been worried sick.'

'Not that we know of,' said Annie. 'We're just trying to find her. What's she like?'

'Marnie? I suppose she struck me as fairly complicated, really, serious, sensitive, deep-thinking, but she can also be pretty happy-go-lucky a lot of the time. She's great fun. We had some laughs. She loves life, but that doesn't mean she doesn't see the problems in the world. She's especially serious about climate change. That Greta is a real hero of hers. Or should I say heroine? She's generous, thoughtful, interested in people. I got the impression she was maybe a bit secretive. Like, you'd spend an evening with her and realise you'd told her your deepest darkest secrets but you hadn't learned much about her in return. Enigmatic, I guess. But I suppose we all are, to some extent.'

'Did she tell you about her life?' Annie asked.

'Not much,' said Mitsuko. 'Bits and pieces over the time we knew each other, I suppose. But that's how it happens, isn't it? I mean, you don't usually sit down and tell your new friends your whole life story at once. You find out about people slowly, over time. Bits and pieces come out when something reminds you of a particular incident or sparks a memory. That's what it was like. She comes from down south somewhere, but I don't remember where, if she ever even told me. It was near the sea, I think. I know she missed the sea. But she could be annoyingly vague on details. She'd just moved up here when we first met a year or so back. Wanted a change of scene. I could relate to that.'

'Did you make such a change?'

Mitsuko smiled. 'Yep. All the way from Sunderland. My dad came over here to work for Nissan when they opened the plant in 1986. He and my mother liked England so much that they stayed. I was born here.'

'Why did Marnie move to York? Was she a student here?'

'No, she wasn't at uni. And I don't know why she moved – except for that change of scene I mentioned.'

'I see. Are you sure you can't remember where she came from? We're really keen to find her, and anything to speed that up would help us a lot.'

'I'm sorry. She talked about her father quite a lot, what a great guy he was, how kind and gentle. Hang on, though. She did say something once about it being Hardy country. Her dad liked Hardy. We did him at school. That's Wessex, isn't it?'

Annie had no idea. She shot Gerry a glance.

'That's right,' Gerry said. 'Well, Wessex isn't a real place, but Hardy based it mostly on Dorset. Plenty of sea around there.'

Annie rolled her eyes at Mitsuko. 'The benefits of a public-school education.'

'We never did Hardy at school,' Gerry protested. 'Far too risqué. I read him off my own bat one summer holiday when I was at uni. *Tess of the d'Urbervilles*. You should try it.'

'Life's too short,' said Annie. 'I'll stick with Martina Cole and Marian Keyes.' She turned back to Mitsuko. 'What did Marnie have to say about her childhood?'

'She said she had been happy growing up. I got the impression it was a pretty ordinary childhood. You know. Caring parents, and all. Like mine, really. Did well at the local comp. She was all set for uni, and she said she'd done her first year at Nottingham, studying History, I think. But she soon realised she simply couldn't afford to finish it, that she'd end up so much in debt she'd never get it paid off. I mean, History might be fun, but it's hardly a passport to a high-paying job, is it? Not that I think that's what uni should be about or anything. Her folks were great, she said, but they didn't have a lot of money, and she wasn't going to even ask them to help her out. So she dropped out.'

'And came here to work at Pizza Express?'

'Yes. That's about it. I suppose you could say both of us are trying to figure out what to do with our lives, where to go next. I mean, this job isn't meant to be permanent for either of us.'

'And you?'

'I'm at uni,' Mitsuko said. 'English Literature. Also pretty useless for the job market.'

'Did Marnie ever tell you anything about the other job she had?'

'You mean the posh parties?'

'Yes.'

'Well, I think she only worked a few, but she said she got paid as much for one of them as she did in a week working here, so that was a big incentive to do more. She didn't care much about all the celebs and so on, but I think she kind of liked the job in a way. She said most of the time she was in the kitchen, or driving back and forth from base. It was like some sort of industrial kitchen on *MasterChef*, she told me. She did talk about a footballer she met – she knows I'm a big Sunderland fan – and what an egotistical jerk he was. And a guitarist from a band I liked who didn't have anything much to say to anyone. Little vignettes like that. There were a lot of boring old politicians and businessmen there, too, but she didn't have a lot of contact with them. She worked behind the scenes.'

'Can you give us their names?' Gerry asked. 'The footballer and guitarist. We may have heard of them.'

Mitsuko looked puzzled but said, 'Sure,' and told them. Gerry had heard of the footballer but not the guitarist. Annie knew of neither.

'What about the man who threw the parties,' Annie asked. 'The man whose house it was? Connor Clive Blaydon?'

'Was that his name? She never said. Just that she was working for an old friend of her boss.'

'Did Marnie say exactly what she did there?'

'A bit of everything. Dogsbody, she said. Loading and unloading the dishwasher, arranging trays of canapés, opening wine bottles and tins of caviar. She'd lend a hand with just about anything if they got busy or someone didn't turn up.'

'What about meeting the guests, serving drinks and so on?'

'She got to serve drinks occasionally, but she didn't like it much. Mostly they had a bunch of scantily dressed women to do that.' Mitsuko lowered her voice. 'She did say there was stuff going on, you know. Escorts and that sort of thing.'

'Did she mention anyone in particular, anyone who had shown interest in her?'

'I don't think so.'

'What about unasked-for attention?'

'Uh-oh. Well, that's always a given, isn't it, for someone like Marnie? Even here. She isn't exactly beautiful, but she's definitely striking. And sexy, I suppose. In that innocent sort of way, you know, without realising it, or at least without emphasising it or playing it up at all. She just *is*, you know.'

'Natural?'

'Very.'

'Anything serious? At the parties.'

'She got offers, you know. A thousand quid if you spend the night with me. That sort of thing. Some old wrinkly who liked young girls. Maybe the occasional pat on the bum.'

'How did she react?'

'Shrugged it off, mostly, like you do.'

'Did she mention any names?'

'Apart from the footballer and guitarist? Not really. Not that I remember.'

'The name of anyone who propositioned her?'

'No. I don't know if she even knew their names. I mean, I'm not saying it happened a lot, just that she thought it was a bit of a laugh, that's all.' Mitsuko paused and frowned, as much as her tight forehead would let her. 'Is this going somewhere? Why are you so interested in the parties? Did something happen to Marnie there?'

'I don't know,' said Annie. 'Did something?'

'It wasn't long after her last party gig that she . . . you know . . . Did something bad happen to her there?'

'Did she talk to you about that particular party?'

'No. That's when she . . . she went strange. We never got to talk about it. Oh, my God. That's what this is about, isn't it? Something happened to her. Is she hurt? Is she dead?'

'Nothing like that.' Gerry rushed to reassure her. 'We're just trying to find her, that's all.'

'But something happened, didn't it? Please tell me. Was it drugs?'

'I'm sorry, Mitsuko,' Annie said. 'We can't give you any information. Right now it's confidential. You mentioned escorts. Did she talk to you about the things that went on at these parties? Sexual things, or other stuff.'

'She said there were drugs. Mostly cocaine. But she never took any. She wouldn't do that. And she thought some of the women with impossibly big boobs were hookers. They would sometimes disappear with a guest for a while. Apparently, the place had a lot of bedrooms. Sometimes people got lost, she said, and wandered into the kitchen and got embarrassed. And once she saw some naked girls swimming in the pool.'

'Sounds pretty exciting,' Gerry said.

'Marnie didn't think so,' said Mitsuko. 'She just thought it was sad. Or funny. But it paid well.'

'Did she ever mention Charlotte Westlake?'

'Her boss?'

'Yes.'

'Once or twice, just in passing, like.'

'Did she say how she first heard of Charlotte?'

'No. She didn't tell me. And I never thought to ask. It was just a job, you know, like this. I did . . . never mind.'

'What were you going to say?' Annie prompted her.

'Nothing. It was just an impression, but from the way she talked, I sort of felt she'd known this Westlake woman from before.'

'From before? When?'

'I don't know. But don't you just get feelings like that sometimes, from the way someone talks about someone? I don't know, body language, a facial expression. It was just a passing fancy.'

'Did Marnie drink much?'

'She liked a drink – white wine was her favourite – but she didn't overdo it, no. I've only seen her drunk about once or twice in all the time I've known her.'

'How did it affect her?'

'First she'd get very funny, silly, then she'd fall asleep.'

'You mentioned drugs. Did Marnie take any? You said she didn't touch coke; what about others?'

Mitsuko looked away.

'You can tell us,' said Annie. 'We're interested in finding her, not arresting her for smoking a spliff or whatever.'

'Ecstasy a couple of times, at parties. And maybe the occasional smoke. But that's as far as it went. Never the hard stuff. Like I said, she wouldn't have taken any of that stuff at those parties she was working.'

'Did she have a boyfriend?'

'She went out a few times with Rick, one of the guys from the pub we hung out in. The Star and Garter. He's nice enough. Fancies himself a poet, and Marnie was a sucker for artistic types. All that goth darkness and stuff. But I don't think it was serious.'

Gerry made a note and Annie asked, 'Is Rick still around?'

'Sure. Should be. But I don't think he'll be able to tell you anything. They split up around the same time she started getting strange.' Mitsuko paused. 'I'm still really worried about her, you know. That she might do . . . you know . . . might harm herself. She was soooo depressed when she left.'

'Do you know if she saw a doctor?'

'I suggested it, but she just shook her head.'

'Did she give you any idea at all of what might be going on, what caused her state of mind?'

'No,' said Mitsuko. 'And in the end, I just learned to stop bothering her. She'd get mad, tell me to shut up and leave her alone. I couldn't get through to her. And it hurt, you know.'

'I can imagine it did,' Annie said. 'Do you know where she went?'

'No. She just took off after that incident at work. I was working here that day, too, and Mr Baldini said I should go after her and make sure she was all right. He's very nice. So I did, but when I got back to the house, she was packing a few things in a suitcase. I asked her where she was going, and she said she was just going away for a few days to be by herself. I asked her what was wrong, but she told me it was nothing, not to worry. And that was it. I was dismissed. She drove off and she never came back. I left emails and messages on her mobile but got no response. I've been worried about her ever since. It's been over six weeks now and not a word. When you find her, please let me know. I won't try to see her or anything if she doesn't want. I just need to know that she's all right. Will you tell me?'

'Yes,' said Annie. 'Do you have a recent photograph you could share with us? The one we have is very poor quality.'

'Sure. I think.' Mitsuko pulled out her mobile from her back pocket and searched through her photo library. 'We went for a cheap city break to Rome last October,' she said. 'It was amazing. We saw the Sistine Chapel, the Colosseum, the Pantheon, everything. Here.' She turned the phone so they could see a clear picture of Marnie with a Roman ruin in the background. 'That was taken in the Forum.'

'Thanks,' said Annie. 'Can you email it to me?'

'I can AirDrop it,' Mitsuko said.

In a few moments Annie was asked if she was willing to accept the photo. She clicked yes, and there it was. She held out the phone and Gerry bent forward to see it too. It was the first time they had seen what the person they were after looked like. The image from the SD card did her no justice at all. Marnie was a lot more attractive than Annie had been able to tell from the video capture. And no doubt the fact that she was enjoying a weekend break in Rome, and hadn't just been assaulted, helped a great deal. Her big dark eyes stared directly into the camera, her complexion was pale and flawless and her short hair definitely hennaed. She wore a simple white T-shirt, no make-up or heavy jewellery, and had no tattoos on her arms or neck, but there was something of the goth in her appearance, both challenging and defiant. It was perhaps more of an attitude than a style, Annie decided, something in her stance and the seriousness of her expression.

Their pizzas arrived. Mitsuko asked if there was anything else, and they said they didn't think so. Not for the moment. She said she would be around the restaurant if they thought of anything, and went back to work.

As they tucked into their lunch, Annie thought about Marnie and remembered her own experience. After she had been raped, she had wandered around in a depressed haze of guilt and shame, wondering how she could ever have let such a thing happen to her. But it was her anger that ultimately saved her. She never let go of the fact that it *wasn't her fault*; it was the fault of the bastards who raped her. And clinging to that idea was probably what saved her from Marnie's fate, whatever it was. Annie had clawed her way out; Marnie seemed to have gone under.

She completely understood why Marnie hadn't been able to tell her best friend what happened. She had never shared what happened to her with a living soul until she told Banks in a moment of weakness on their first case together. It was a long time ago now, but the pain and shame would never completely go away; they were deep down, rooted in her very being. But that didn't mean she couldn't live a normal life, couldn't function properly. She did. She wanted to find Marnie and tell her that she could do it, too, even if at first she wouldn't believe it.

As soon as she got back to the station from York, Gerry got on her computer. A search through the databases revealed that a Marjorie Sedgwick lived in a place called Wool, in Dorset. According to Gerry's information, that came under the Purbeck North policing area. She made a note of the address, then phoned the Purbeck police.

A youthful-sounding PCSO answered her call, saying he knew the Sedgwick family by name and that they did, indeed, live in Wool, though he was very careful to point out that he didn't know them because of any criminal activity, suspected or real. When Gerry pressed her case and asked why he knew the name, he grew evasive and muttered something about a tragedy. Even though he had verified who Gerry was by calling back the Eastvale number she had given him, he still seemed reluctant to say more.

'If you can't or don't want to talk to me,' said Gerry, 'can you please put someone on who will?'

There was silence, then the sound of the handset being set down on a hard surface. Gerry tried to picture the location. Many of these police stations were much like the ones in rural Yorkshire, nothing more than the local copper's living room with a filing cabinet and a few wanted posters on the walls. She imagined a thatched roof cottage with a blue POLICE sign over its door and opening hours noted down the side.

'Sergeant Trevelyan here,' came a new voice at the other end. 'Who am I speaking to?' Gerry thought Trevelyan was a Cornish name. Still, Cornwall wasn't that far from Dorset. His accent didn't give anything away; it was pure RP.

'My name is Geraldine Masterson,' she said. 'I'm a DC at Eastvale Regional Police HQ in Eastvale, North Yorkshire. I'm making enquiries about a local girl called Marnie Sedgwick, and the database has led me to a Marjorie Sedgwick in Wool, Dorset. Your PCSO seemed to recognise Marnie's name.'

'Not many who wouldn't around these parts,' said Trevelyan.

'Oh, why is that?'

'Not the best of reasons, I'm afraid. Poor Marnie Sedgwick only went and killed herself, didn't she? The tragedy's still fresh in everyone's mind.'

Gerry felt her skin prickle. 'Killed herself?'

'Aye. Jumped off Durdle Door.'

'When did this happen?'

There was another pause, then Trevelyan said, 'May. Seventeenth May.'

About a month after the rape, Gerry realised, and five days before Blaydon's murder. She made a note on her desk pad.

'Can I send you a photo of her, then we can be certain we're talking about the same person?'

'Go ahead. Text it to my mobile.' He gave her the number. A few seconds after she had sent the image, she heard a ding and Trevelyan came back. 'Aye,' he said. 'That's poor Marnie, all right.'

Christ. Gerry felt a chill flutter in her chest. 'You said she jumped off Durdle Door?'

'It's a limestone arch in the sea near Lulworth Cove. The water's worn a hole in it over the years, so it's like an open door in the rock. The beach there is a popular tourist spot.'

'I've seen pictures,' said Gerry. 'Would you mind if my colleague and I come down to see you? We'd like to talk to the family, too, if possible.'

'It's all right by me,' said Trevelyan. 'Hell of a long way to come, if you ask me, though, and I won't have any more to tell you than I have right now.'

'Will you arrange for us to see this Durdle Door and to speak with Mr and Mrs Sedgwick?'

'Easy enough. I'll certainly ask them. You understand they might not wish to dredge it all up again. It's still raw.'

'We can be very gentle. Please try, Sergeant. It's important.'

'I'll do my best. See you soon then?'

'We'll talk to you soon.'

Banks hadn't heard the Blue Lamps live for quite a while, but they were every bit as good as he remembered, their bluesy feel, rhythmic complexity and subtle use of harmonies as strong and as familiar as ever. To Banks's ears, it was CSNY meet the Allman Brothers, but with an unmistakable edge of more recent pop styles in the mix.

It was a nostalgic evening, and they played songs from their earliest albums mixed in with more recent work, along with a few covers they had revisited now and then over the years. At one point, Brian announced, 'I feel like I've been listening to this song since I was in my cradle. This is for my old man. He's here somewhere tonight. Love you, Dad!' The crowd cheered and the band launched into a bluesy 'Visions of Johanna', with Brian taking the lead vocal and a soaring lyrical guitar solo. Emotion fizzed in Banks's chest and almost made it to his eyes. As with most of Dylan's mid-sixties songs, he didn't understand a word of it, but it sure had a powerful effect on him.

The Sage was full, and the fans both enthusiastic and saddened by the occasion. Some waved banners saying 'PLEASE DON'T TURN OFF THE LAMPS!' but everything was good-natured, including the band members, and no one felt cheated when the show ended after the fifth encore.

Banks kept checking his mobile during the performance, but nothing new came in. When the show ended, surprised by how the music had allowed him to put Zelda out of his mind for a short while at least, he nipped outside to phone Annie, who had been in charge during his absence, and told her about a derelict hunting lodge he had remembered on the fells above Swainshead. It turned out that the place had already been searched and found to be empty. As had the Blaydon properties they had searched so far. The only news was that Burgess had come up with a good photograph of Petar Tadić, and Adrian Moss had pasted it all over the media.

Cursing their lack of success and his own inability to come up with any better ideas, Banks made his way to the backstage area, where Tracy and Mark were already waiting for him with Brian and the rest of the band. The dressing room was crowded with lucky fans, hangers-on and a few journalists. After all, the demise of the band was a major event. There were two more dates left on the 'farewell' tour before the absolute final performance, back in London again, but this one was close enough to home ground to make the news.

Banks managed a few brief words with Brian, who regretted being unable to come and spend the night at Newhope Cottage because the tight schedule called for an early start to Edinburgh the following morning. It was a pity, as Banks had looked forward to spending some time alone with him, listening to old blues and Bob Dylan and talking about everything under the sun. Banks would have driven him to Edinburgh in the morning under normal circumstances, but he couldn't take the time off, either. After London, Brian said, when the tour was over, he would have some time off before starting a trainee sound-recording job he had set up at a studio down there, so he would come up for a few days then. Banks was no lover of big noisy parties, no matter what their purpose, so he said his goodbyes to the other band members and made his way towards the exit. Tracy and Mark said they would stay on just a little longer and take a taxi home. They had just got back from Tenerife that day and were feeling tired.

In the afterglow of 'Visions of Johanna', Banks played *Blonde on Blonde* on the way home, arriving in the middle of 'Sad-Eyed Lady of the Lowlands'. He felt lonely when he pulled up outside his dark cottage. Normally, living alone never bothered him much, but spending even a little time with Brian and seeing Tracy so happy with her new husband reminded him of when he had a family, when home was a place of love and comfort, where there would always be someone waiting for him. These days, his life seemed to lack purpose – or at least any purpose other than putting bad guys away. Zelda haunted him, too. Not only what might be happening to her now, but what the future might hold. Not very much, he suspected, and none of it pleasant. They *had* to find her.

The outside light usually came on automatically when he approached the front door, but tonight it didn't. He made a mental note to replace the bulb tomorrow. He used the light from his mobile, managed to get his key in the lock and open the door. He stepped over the threshold, looking forward to a quick nightcap, but before he could shut the door behind him, he sensed a sudden movement, then felt something hard hit the back of his head. He pitched forward into the cottage, and after that, he felt nothing.

12

Banks first became aware of a throbbing pain in his head. When he opened his eyes, he saw he was in semi-darkness. It was a blessing. Bright light would have hurt. He also realised that he was tied up. He wasn't sure how, or how securely, only that when he moved his legs to try to straighten them out, something tightened around his neck like a noose. Trussed was the word that came to mind. Trussed like a Christmas turkey. Hog-tied.

He didn't know how long he had been like that before he heard a door open and someone placed a portable work light down beside him. He shut his eyes, but not quickly enough to prevent the pain of the light exploding inside his head. He couldn't even raise a hand to cover his face.

When he did open his eyes again, he could only see the shadowed and hunched profile of the man who stood before him, but that was enough for Banks to recognise him. He was looking older, his hairline had receded and he carried more weight around the middle, but Banks didn't have to be a super-recogniser to know it was Phil Keane. He also noticed that he was being kept in a cavernous space, an abandoned factory or control centre of some sort, with large rusted wheels, heavy pipes and valves, pumps, storage tanks, hanging wires and broken consoles.

'Well, well,' said Keane. 'We meet again. You cost me a lot, you know. Because of you I had to leave the country, get a new identity, find a new line of work. But perhaps I should thank you. It's proven even more profitable than my previous work.'

'You've got a funny way of showing it,' Banks managed to mumble with a mouth that felt full of treacle. Keane was holding something, and Banks saw it was a large can. The kind you carry petrol in. 'Where's Zelda?' he asked.

'The girl? She's nothing to do with me. Petar's taking care of her. He has a score to settle. He's made plans for her. Fortunately, he's agreed to let me settle my old score, too.'

'If either of you harm her—'

'Oh, stop it,' said Keane, unscrewing the can. 'You don't know how pathetic you sound. We're going to do exactly what we want, and you're not going to be able to stop us. This time I'll get to finish what I started.' He shook the can and Banks heard the petrol slosh inside it. Soon he could smell it, too. 'We're clearing out of here very soon,' Keane said. 'It's time to move on. A good fire is just the thing we need to make sure we leave no traces.'

Keane splashed the petrol on the floor around Banks's feet.

When Tadić came into her room again and set the light down on the floor, he came alone. Zelda sensed some new purpose in his visit other than mere torture or gloating.

'We are leaving soon,' he said. 'Mr Foley has your new passport in the car, along with sufficient funds for the journey. It will be a long and hard one, and perhaps not as comfortable as you would wish.'

'So let me loose to clean myself up a bit. At least give me a fresh T-shirt.' Zelda's top was still crusted with dried vomit from the time Tadić had hit her.

Tadić smiled. 'Yes. Of course. A good idea. All in good time. We have nice new clothes for you in the car. But you are right about the T-shirt. It is disgusting.'

He knelt before her and took a flick-knife from the pocket of his leather jacket. He held it close to her face and flicked the blade open to make sure she saw it glinting in the light. Then he slid it under the material of her top and started cutting until the T-shirt was in shreds on the floor.

So this is it, Zelda thought. This is when he takes his pleasure. Feeling half-naked and exposed was nothing new to her, but it had been so long that she found herself feeling embarrassed and shy. She wanted to protect herself from his gaze and raised her cuffed hands up to cover her breasts as best she could.

Tadić merely laughed. 'Very modest for a *kurva*,' he said, unfastening his belt and unzipping his trousers. The light cast grotesque shadows of him on the wall. He took off his leather jacket and dropped it on the floor, then grabbed her by the hair. 'On your knees.'

Zelda had no choice but to submit. But as she did so, an idea formed. When she was kneeling, and Tadić had his trousers down around his ankles, he put the blade of the knife to her neck, right by the jugular vein and carotid artery. It wouldn't take much to cut them, Zelda thought. Just a slip of the hand, a nervous tic even, and she would be free. Could she do it? She hadn't been able to swallow her tongue or hold her breath, but perhaps she could accept death this way. She closed her eyes, felt the cold steel on her skin, felt his hand press against the back of her neck, pulling her forward.

'Open your mouth.'

Zelda opened her mouth and felt him enter her. She almost gagged, but managed to stop herself. Instead, she offered a silent prayer to the God she didn't believe in and bit down as hard as she could.

* * *

In that moment, Banks was certain he was going to die. Then he heard sounds from somewhere deep in the building, upstairs, perhaps. Someone shouting, a banging noise, a chain scraping along a floor.

Keane smiled. 'Sounds as if Petar is having his fun. I must say, he's a bit of an animal when it comes to the fairer sex. I can't say I approve. Me, I'd rather wine and dine and seduce a woman than simply take her. Like I did with Annie. How is she, by the way?'

'Bastard.'

'Doesn't matter,' Keane said, splashing more petrol over the floor between himself and Banks, who was still feeling too woozy to resist. Even if he hadn't been trussed up, he wouldn't have been able to offer much opposition.

'Tell me about Faye Butler,' he said. 'Why did you kill her?'

'Don't think this is going to be one of those long drawn-out confessions you get in movies when the hero is about to die,' Keane said. 'And don't think you're going to keep me talking until the cavalry comes. Nobody's coming. Faye was collateral damage, that's all. I didn't kill her. Maybe Petar got a little overeager to find out what she told your lady friend up there about his business. Like I said, he's an animal with women.'

'Did you kill Hawkins?'

'He was taking Goran and Petar's money and giving them crap in exchange. They lost a whole shipment of fresh girls because of him. You don't pull those kind of tricks on the Tadićs and live. They let me prove myself.'

'Bully for you. What happened to Goran?'

Keane paused. 'You don't know? You really don't know? Well, well. I'll tell you that, at least. Goran's dead. The girl killed him. Knife. Made a right mess. Petar and the others disposed of his body to prevent a police investigation. Then they carried out their own. Why do you think all this is happening?'

'Petar's revenge?' Banks said. 'But *you* don't have to do this. You don't have to be a part of it. You disappeared before. You can do it again.'

Keane paused. 'You don't understand. I *want* to do this. This is a favour granted me by Petar. And who knows, maybe I'll pay Annie another visit, too, before I leave here for good.'

Banks struggled against his ropes, but it was no use. He only felt them tightening around his throat. Keane stood in front of him holding the petrol can. The rest of the abandoned factory was quiet now.

'Just a little more, I think,' said Keane, and splashed some of the petrol over Banks's trousers and shoes.

Zelda had no idea what it would feel like when the knife cut into her neck. She had seen movies where the blood gushed out, but they conveyed no idea of the sensation. Would it hurt? How long would it take? What would dying feel like? Like going to sleep, she hoped. But surely she would find out very soon. His muscle would twitch and the knife would cut her open. The end.

She felt nothing. No pain. Nothing.

Tadić screamed, dropped the knife and clutched at his genitals with both hands. Stunned to still be alive, it took Zelda a moment to adjust her perspective. She had expected death, but perhaps now she had a chance to achieve freedom instead. He hadn't twitched in a reflex action but had instead dropped the knife and moved his hands to the source of the pain, thereby leaving himself open. But she had to act quickly.

Tadić fell to the floor and his grotesque shadow twisted and turned on the wall. Zelda saw the knife where it had fallen. She stretched her leg as far as she could with the chain still on and reached out her cuffed hands, but it had fallen just outside her grasp. She had no idea how long it would take Tadić to regain control, but she didn't think she had much time. He was in the foetal position on the floor groaning. It was awkward with her hands cuffed, but she managed to remove her belt, hold it in a loop with both hands and hook it over the knife like a lasso. It just reached. Slowly, she pulled the knife towards her.

Tadić's groans were less frequent now, but he was still sliding around on the floor in his own blood. Zelda tossed her belt aside and grasped the knife as best she could with both hands cuffed together. Tadić kicked out, either deliberately or still in agony, and his foot caught her on the shoulder. She almost dropped the knife but instead managed to lunge out with it. She felt it bury itself in his flesh. Now she got to her knees again and plunged the knife in and out of Tadić's chest and stomach until he stopped moving. It was only then that she saw her first cut had severed his femoral artery in his right thigh, and the blood was still gushing out. She slid back towards the radiator and landed against it, breathless, dazed and miraculously still alive.

Tadić lay unmoving in the pooling blood, and Zelda knew enough to be certain he would never move again. With some difficulty she tried to saw through her plasticuffs with the knife. It slipped twice and she cut her palm and thumb, but she got free. She rubbed her hands together to get the circulation going, then crawled towards Tadić's jacket, still lying where he had dropped it on the floor, dragging her leg chain with her. When she got close enough she went through his pockets. Eventually she found his keys, and after several tries found the one that fit the padlock on her leg iron. She was free. Alive and free. She massaged her ankle. But it wasn't over yet, she felt certain. Tadić hadn't been alone; there were others. She put on his leather jacket, wiped the knife on his jeans and crept towards the door, holding the blade before her.

The whole place stank of petrol. Banks felt his head swimming with the fumes, as if his consciousness were water gurgling down a drain. But the pain in his head kept him awake. For a moment, he couldn't remember who it was that stood in front of him, and why. Then it came rushing back. It wasn't a dream. He was in some sort of abandoned factory and Phil Keane was about to start a fire. He imagined the flames slowly creeping over his skin, through to the flesh and down to the bone. Like most people, he had only had mild burns in his life, but they had hurt enough. How long would it take for him to die? How much would it hurt?

'I think that's about enough petrol, don't you?' said Keane. 'Should be a nice little blaze. There's plenty of combustible material in the building. Probably bone dry after the recent weather. And we're far enough away from civilisation that there's not much chance of the fire brigade making it here until there's nothing left.'

As Keane talked, Banks fancied he glimpsed movement in the shadows behind him. It was out of the lamp's range, so he couldn't be sure. Maybe he was just imagining things. Or maybe it was Tadić come to watch the fireworks. But this shadow seemed to be creeping slowly, deliberately, up behind Keane. Surely Tadić wouldn't do that. Another wave of nausea and dizziness swept through him, and he lost track of the shadow, if there was one.

'I just have to make sure Petar and the girl get out first,' Keane said, 'then I'll be back.' He took a red disposable cigarette lighter from his pocket and flicked it so it flamed for a moment. 'Don't go away.'

There was definitely movement behind him. Silent. Slow.

Then suddenly, Keane seemed to jerk to attention. His hands went behind him and he dropped the can, petrol gurgling at his feet and over his shoes. Then he jerked again and dropped to his knees.

The next thing Banks knew, Zelda was stepping around Keane's body and cutting his bonds. Keane moved behind her and she turned around, blocking Banks's view, so that he couldn't be sure whether it was her or Keane who struck it, but the lighter flared briefly and Keane's petrol-soaked clothes went up in flames along with the floor around them. Keane screamed.

'Run!' cried Zelda, helping Banks to his feet and slapping out a tongue of flame that caught his trouser leg. 'Get out! Quick! Run! Run!'

Banks ran.

Running wasn't easy. Banks's head was bursting, and he kept tripping over himself as he made his way through the door and into the night outside, the flames at his heels. It was dark, but there was enough moonlight to see that he had been in an abandoned water treatment plant. The rectangular reservoirs stood before him empty of water and filled only with weeds, ghostly in the moonlight. He ran around the first one and headed for the woods beyond, with no idea of where he was going. He could hear the flames roaring behind him and turned to see how close Zelda was, then stopped in his tracks.

She wasn't there.

The flames were quickly engulfing the building, already eating their way through the roof, but he had to go back. He stood in the doorway and saw there was no way he could go any further inside. Parts of the ceiling were collapsing, the whole floor was blazing and the fire was spreading fast to every last corner. He called out Zelda's name but got only the roar of the flames in return.

He looked towards the spot where he had been tied up and thought he could make out Keane's burning body, but that was all. So what had happened to Zelda? Why hadn't she been right behind him? Should he have waited and made her go first? He hadn't been thinking clearly, couldn't think clearly because his head hurt and his thoughts were muddled. The heat was too much, and he staggered back towards the reservoir. Before he could stop himself, he fell backwards over the edge into the bed of weeds and felt his head jar against the hard bottom. And there, as the fire raged, he lost consciousness again.

13

When Banks opened his eyes, he had no idea who or where he was for the first few seconds. It was a fleeting sensation, but terrifying while it lasted. Then he saw he was in a white room, in a hospital bed with stiff sheets. He must have somehow got a private room because there was nobody else near him; nor was there another bed. He could see through the window that it was daylight, though what time it was he had no idea. Someone had removed his watch. But why was he there? What was wrong with him? How had he got here? Try as he might, he couldn't remember. Had he had a heart attack? A car accident? No, he could feel his heart beating more or less normally, and all his body parts seemed to be in working order except his brain. His head hurt and he felt sick and dizzy. Perhaps he'd had a stroke or cerebral haemorrhage? He could see that he had a line in the back of his hand with a tube leading to a drip of clear fluid on a stand, and there were the usual machines beeping away. Heart rate 80, blood pressure 145/83. That wasn't too bad, was it? Maybe his heart was beating too fast, but then it always had done.

He wished someone would come and explain what was happening. The only thing he knew about hospitals was that if there was nothing wrong with you when you went in, there would be when you came out. He also knew that despite all the criticism the NHS came in for in the media, when it came to an emergency, they couldn't be beat.

Was he an emergency? In intensive care? He was sure he must have work to do, a case to be getting on with. *A case*. That rang a bell. He was a detective. He had been on a case. Was that how he had got injured? He could feel bandages on his head. Perhaps some scumbag had coshed him. But why? What was it all about? He couldn't remember.

'Ah, good,' said a voice in the doorway. 'I'm glad to see you're back in the land of the living again.'

'Who are you?'

'Dr Chowdhury.'

He looked about twelve, Banks thought. Surely they didn't entrust serious injuries to twelve-year-olds yet? 'Where am I?' he asked.

'Eastvale General Infirmary.'

'What's wrong with me? Why am I here?'

'You don't remember?'

'No.'

'Can you tell me your name?'

'Alan Banks.'

'Address?'

'Newhope Cottage, Gratly.'

'What line of work are you in?'

'I'm a detective superintendent. A policeman.'

'What day is it?'

'No idea.'

Dr Chowdhury laughed. 'It's Thursday,' he said. 'You had a very lucky escape. You sustained a nasty blow to the back of your head – two blows, actually – and that sometimes causes short-term memory loss, along with other symptoms: dizziness, nausea, headaches. One of the head wounds required a few stitches, but that's all. Fortunately, there's no skull fracture, or we'd have whizzed you up to Newcastle or down to Leeds already.'

'I can't remember being hit on the head.'

'That's not unusual. You have a concussion. It should be only a temporary condition. Your memory should come back.'

'How long?'

'Before it comes back? Not long, I shouldn't think. Days rather than weeks. Maybe even hours. But you need rest.'

'How long have I been here?'

'You were brought in at a quarter past two this morning.'

'And now?'

'It's eight o'clock in the morning. You've been under observation regularly during the night. We're always especially careful with concussion patients where loss of consciousness is involved.'

Banks glanced towards the window again and saw his mobile and Bluetooth headphones on his bedside table. 'How did these get here?'

'A young lady brought them not long ago,' said Dr Chowdhury. 'Said her name was Annie. But you should know that mobile phone use is strictly prohibited in here.'

Bless her, thought Banks. 'Don't worry, I won't be using thc phone,' he said. 'What happened to me?'

'All I know is that you were brought in by ambulance with a head wound and minor burns to your ankles. There was also some bruising, most likely caused by a fall, and rope marks on your neck, wrists and feet, as if you'd been tied up.'

'Burns? Tied up?'

'Yes, I know it sounds strange. But the burns are nothing serious. We've dressed them. As for the rest, it's superficial.'

'Where was I brought from?'

'I believe it was a disused water treatment plant outside Eastvale.'

'I know that place,' said Banks. 'Not from last night. From before. I've driven past it dozens of times. I always wondered when they were going to knock it down and use the land for something useful.'

'Well, it's gone now,' said the doctor.

'Gone?'

'Fire. Burned to the ground.'

'Why was I there?'

'I have no idea.'

A vague memory of flames came into Banks's mind. It gave him a sudden feeling of nausea. 'Zelda,' he said.

'What was that?' the doctor asked. 'I didn't catch it.'

'Nothing,' said Banks. He wasn't certain of the importance of what he'd said yet, himself, so he could hardly explain it to a stranger. 'Who found me?'

'I suppose it must have been the firefighters. They were the first responders at the scene.'

Banks fell silent. Talking had worn him out already, and he was starting to feel sick and dizzy again.

'Nausea and dizziness aren't unusual in cases like this,' the doctor said, as if aware of what Banks was feeling. 'That, too, should pass soon enough.'

'Not soon enough for me,' said Banks. 'How long do I have to stay here?'

'We'd like to keep you in one more night for observation and to conduct some tests.'

'What tests?'

'Nothing invasive, don't worry. A severe jolt to the brain such as you have experienced can cause any number of problems. For a start, we need to test your reflexes and make sure there's no lasting physical damage. As far as other symptoms are concerned, it's mostly a matter of self-monitoring over time. I'll give you a list of things to watch out for. We'd also like to conduct an MRI scan, but for that we'll have to arrange to take you to the Friarage in Northallerton. We don't have an

MRI machine here. Until then, rest as comfortably as you can. Rest is very important in cases of concussion.'

'Always a pleasure to be here,' said Timmy Kerrigan, lifting the crease of his trousers at the knees as he eased his bulk into the chair and crossed his legs in interview room three. As usual, he was expensively and garishly dressed, this time in a navy bespoke suit over a psychedelic waistcoat, lilac shirt and green bow tie. Short golden curls topped his round head and, along with his peaches and cream complexion, made him appear quite angelic. Annie had decided to talk to Timmy instead of his brother this time, as he was marginally more garrulous and slightly less unpleasant to be around. But Timmy Kerrigan was a long way from being an angel.

Gerry was busy digging up whatever she could on Marnie Sedgwick's background. They had already talked briefly to the ex-boyfriend Rick, who had said he hadn't seen Marnie since the middle of April. She had become very unreliable and moody, he said, and he had decided to end the relationship and move on. He had a new girlfriend now, a drummer in a local rock band, and she confirmed that Rick had been with her almost constantly since early May. He also said he didn't know anything about the parties Marnie had worked, and he had certainly never been to one. There was no reason to disbelieve him as he was so far out of Blaydon's sphere of interest as to be almost non-existent. Unfortunately, they had had no success with the sparse list of guest and employee names Tamara and Charlotte had emailed. People either denied they were present, refused to talk or said they hadn't noticed anything. The footballer and guitarist Mitsuko had mentioned said they hadn't seen anything out of the ordinary and had spent most of the evening by the pool.

Annie was still worried about Banks. The doctor who wouldn't let her see him earlier that day had assured her he would be fine and his injuries weren't serious, but he was no more forthcoming than that. She had visited Banks's cottage as soon as she heard he had been taken to hospital and found his front door open, his mobile and keys lying on the hall carpet. She had picked up the mobile and grabbed Banks's headphones from the conservatory. She knew he would be insufferable in hospital without his music. The keys she would hang on to until he went home. There wasn't much more she could do except call the CSIs to check out the cottage.

For the moment, though, Annie tried to concentrate on Timmy Kerrigan. 'Timmy,' she began, 'first of all, you should know that this is simply an intelligence interview. You're not under arrest and you're not being charged with anything, OK?'

Timmy nodded and his chins wobbled. 'I rather thought so,' he said, glancing around the room, 'seeing as I haven't done anything. But why the dull decor?'

Annie smiled. 'You'd be surprised how it concentrates the mind. No interruptions. Can we start?'

'Whenever you're ready.'

'You were at a party thrown by Connor Clive Blaydon at his home near Harrogate on 13 April this year, right?'

'If you say so. We've been to a few of Connor's parties, Tommy and I. He's a good friend. Was. I can't remember the exact dates.'

'Now, we have evidence that a young woman was raped at that party, and we're trying to find out who did it.'

'Well, don't look at Tommy and me.'

'We know that Tommy has – what shall we say? – other interests, but as for you . . .'

'Whatever you've heard, it's a vicious lie,' Timmy protested.

Annie had heard rumours of his interest in young girls often enough to believe them without further proof, but she realised there was no point in angering him. It was clear from the video, poor as its quality was, that Timmy Kerrigan was entirely the wrong shape and size to have been Marnie's rapist. 'That's as may be,' she said, 'and it's not our concern at the moment, but what I want to know is whether you saw this girl at the party. Your brother said he didn't recognise her, but we only had a very poor photo to show when we talked to him.'

She slid over a print of the photo Mitsuko had AirDropped her. Timmy picked it up and studied it, then nodded. 'Maybe,' he said. 'I think she was there, but she wasn't . . . how shall I say . . . part of the entertainment.'

'She worked for the events organiser in the catering area, mostly back in the kitchen and behind the scenes. But apparently, she brought out drinks once in a while.'

'That must have been when I saw her. A very pretty girl. Gamine, I'd say.'

Annie ground her teeth. 'Yes.'

'I do hope she's all right.'

'As a matter of fact, she isn't,' said Annie. 'Not all right at all. In fact, she jumped off a cliff and died.'

'Oh,' said Kerrigan. 'That's a terrible tragedy.'

Annie almost believed he meant it; it was probably the closest to sincerity that Timmy Kerrigan got. Timmy linked his pink sausage-like fingers on the table. He was wearing a large gold signet ring, Annie noticed, so deeply imbedded in the flesh it looked impossible to take off.

'Do you know the events organiser?'

'Charlie? Yes, of course. Though she hates being called that. Charming lady. In fact, she's organised a couple of private dos for Tommy and I over the last three or four years. Retirement parties and so on. Extracurricular, so to speak. She organised the opening of The Vaults.'

'I thought that when you retired people, they were in no condition to have a party.'

Timmy cocked his head. 'Very droll. Have you considered a career in stand-up?'

'I'll stick with what I'm doing for the moment.'

'The stage's loss.'

'You were at other parties, weren't you? Earlier in the year.'

'I suppose you could say we were regulars.'

'Did you ever notice Charlotte Westlake introduce Marnie to anyone?'

'No. They seemed to know each other, though. I mean, I did see them talking together in the background on a couple of occasions.'

'It's a big house. Where did you hang out?'

'Tommy and I tended to stick by the pool except . . . you know . . . when nature called. I enjoy a swim now and then.'

Annie cringed at the mental image of Timmy in his thong trunks. Once seen, never forgotten. 'I suppose that was where most of the action was?' she said.

'The synchronised swimming and so on? Yes, I suppose it was.'

'I was thinking more of the naked women.'

'Can't say as I noticed.'

'Oh, come on, Timmy. You could hardly fail.'

'One gets used to these things. Besides, what's wrong with swimming as nature intended in the privacy of a friend's home?'

'So you and your brother sat around the pool, smoking cigars, drinking whisky and ogling naked women.'

'That last part is pure invention on your part. I don't ogle, and Tommy . . . well . . .'

'Tommy has no interest in naked women?'

'You could say that.'

'Blaydon was no doubt a very woke host. I'm sure he catered for all tastes and genders.'

Timmy giggled. 'Very good. Yes. Yes, he did that, all right.'

'So you saw Marnie on the evening of 13 April?'

'Yes. I've already told you that.'

'Did you see her with anyone?'

Timmy thought for a moment, or at least Annie assumed that was why his brow furrowed. 'No,' he said. 'That's about it. Except for Connor, of course.'

'Marnie spent time with Connor Blaydon?'

'Well, it *was* his party, after all, wasn't it?'

During the day, Banks slept as well as anyone can sleep in a hospital, but – even though he had the room to himself – there always seemed to be something going on somewhere, and it usually made noise. In addition, the nurse kept waking him up to make sure he could be woken up.

The paracetamol seemed to dull his headache for a while, and whatever they gave him for the nausea worked, too. Just after lunch, as he was trying to relax listening to the Pavel Haas Quartet playing some Shostakovich string quartets, he had more visitors. He didn't recognise the man with AC Gervaise, but they both looked serious.

'This is Superintendent Newry from Police Conduct,' said Gervaise. 'He'd like to talk to you. He has agreed to my being present during this interview, which I am assured is merely a preliminary. In no way are you accused or suspected of anything.'

'So why is he here, if there's been no complaints against me?'

'Standard procedure,' Newry said. 'Given the ... er ... unusual circumstances of your adventures.'

Newry was a small pudgy man in his fifties with thinning hair and a large round head. He looked angry. In fact, he looked as if he were permanently angry: red face, tight mouth, etched sneer. The hospital chair creaked as he sat down. His trousers tightened against the flesh of his thighs.

'Got your memory back yet?' Newry asked.

'No,' said Banks. 'It's still a blank. What's all this about? What's happened?'

'The fire investigation officers were able to enter the scene at the water treatment plant,' said Newry. 'They found two bodies. Now do you remember anything about how that came about?'

'Who are they?' Banks asked.

'We won't know until the post-mortems have been carried out. To be honest, there's not much left for her to work on. They were both very badly burned, and as yet we don't even know if they were male or female. But that's not the point. Do you remember anything?'

'No,' said Banks. *Zelda*, he thought. Please let it not be Zelda. Why did that thought flash through his mind? There was nothing in his memory to justify it, only that he connected what had happened, what he couldn't remember, with Zelda's disappearance, which was the case he had been working on. He remembered that. Had she been there, at the treatment plant? Had she been caught in the fire?

'How I hate these memory-loss cases,' Newry said. 'A person could say anything, or nothing, and we'd have no way of proving it. Any thoughts on the matter?'

'On your suspicions about my memory loss, or on what happened?'

'The latter will do for now.'

'I'm told I was knocked unconscious,' said Banks, 'and when I came round, I was here in hospital. As far as I know, I didn't go to the plant for any particular reason, by choice. Why would I? I must have been taken there. By whom, or why, I have no idea.'

'I understand that,' said Newry. 'And your DI Cabbot has already found evidence of your abduction back at your cottage. Your doctor also mentioned marks that ropes made on your wrists, ankles and throat. It's what the Americans call "hog-tied".'

'Perhaps that's why my throat's sore and my wrists hurt.'

'I should think so. And I'm sure you can understand why we're interested in any information we can get right now.'

'I know what you're after,' said Banks. 'A scapegoat. And it's not going to be me.'

Newry raised his eyebrows and glanced towards AC Gervaise. Banks could see she wasn't happy with what was happening.

'Any more questions?' he asked.

'Any guesses?' Newry went on. 'As to who it might have been? And why you were taken there?'

Banks took a deep breath before answering. 'As you probably know, we are involved in trying to find a woman who was abducted from her farmhouse near Lyndgarth on Monday. Her name is Nelia Melnic, though everyone knows her as Zelda. We think a Croatian sex trafficker called Petar Tadić was behind that abduction, in collusion with a wanted criminal called Philip Keane. We don't know why Zelda was taken, unless it was to settle an old score or to stop her from disclosing something incriminating she knew about Tadić, and I have no idea why they should want me, too, if that's what happened. Unless Keane felt *he* had a score to settle.'

'Was this Zelda being kept at the treatment plant? Is that why you went there?'

'I didn't go there. I was taken there.'

'Right. Could that be why you were taken there, then?'

'How would I know?'

'Was the woman there?'

'I have no memory of what or who was there. I don't even remember being there myself.'

'Your memory for some things seems pretty good to me.'

'Yes, it is. I can even remember my own name. But I don't remember what happened last night. It's called short-term memory loss, or temporary amnesia. At least, I hope it's temporary. Ask Dr Chowdhury. He'll be happy to explain it to you.'

'You have a history with this Keane, I understand?'

'He tried to kill me once, if you call that a "history". Drugged me. Set fire to my cottage with me inside it.'

'Something like that stays with you, I should imagine.'

'Surely the question is whether it stayed with *him*. Enough for him to want to repeat his attempt. And no, I haven't been dreaming of revenge for the last ten years.'

'Do you think Keane was the man who set the fire at the plant?'

'He has a history of arson, so it wouldn't surprise me, but I have no memory of anyone starting a fire. I don't even remember a fire.'

'You have burns on your ankle and legs. How did you escape?'

'I don't know that I did. I mean, I know I must have, because I'm here, but I don't know whether I was inside the building in the first place, or whether it was burning when I was. Or how I got out, if I did. Maybe I was always where the firefighters found me?'

'Surely if you were taken to the plant by someone who had a reason, you must have been inside at some point? And there are the burns.'

'They hardly prove anything. I told you, I don't remember being inside the building. I don't know where I was taken. Or why. I don't even remember *being* taken.'

'Yes. Of course. The memory loss.'

'Take or leave it,' said Banks.

'As a matter of fact,' Newry went on, 'you *were* inside the building. Forensic tests on your clothing show traces of petrol and dirt and grease from the floor.'

'You took my clothes?'

'Naturally. You'll get them back in due course.'

'I'm tired now. The doctor says I need rest. Please fuck off.'

Newry stood up and gestured towards AC Gervaise. 'I imagine we'll be talking again before too long,' he said. 'In the meantime, do get that rest, Superintendent Banks, and perhaps your memory will have come back by the next time we meet.'

'Is that some sort of thinly veiled threat?'

Newry managed to twist his features into what he probably thought was a smile. 'It's nothing of the kind. Good day.'

Gervaise waited until the door closed behind Newry before saying, 'Was that really necessary?'

'What? Arseholes like him give me a headache, and I've already got a big enough one to begin with. If you ask me, he's watched too many episodes of *Line of Duty*.'

'Even so . . . he's only doing his job.'

'He's already after handing out blame before he even knows what happened. Is that his job?'

'Are you sure you don't remember anything?'

Banks stared at her. 'Not you as well? Bloody hell. I don't believe this.'

'All right, all right, Alan. Don't get your knickers in a twist. I'd understand, you know, if you didn't want to tell Newry anything right now, until you're sure.'

Banks sighed. 'It's because I don't know anything, ma'am. Believe me, I wish I did, and when I do, you'll be among the first to know.'

AC Gervaise stood up and patted Banks's arm. 'You must be feeling unwell. You're calling me ma'am. I'll let you get some rest now.'

Banks breathed a sigh of relief once he was in the room alone again. Memory was definitely a funny thing, he thought. Little flashes came back, but he couldn't put them all together into a coherent narrative. At one point when he was talking to Newry, a wave of panic had passed through him, and he heard a voice in his head shouting, 'Run! Run!'

He did remember a fire now, and he also remembered that the voice telling him to run was a woman's voice. And when Newry had told him about the bodies, he had felt a tremor of fear that one of them might be Zelda's. But he couldn't say for certain that it had been her voice, or that he had even been inside the treatment plant, let alone seen her there. Nor did he know where the fire had come from, how it had started.

And when you can't remember something, it's like it never happened, and you can't believe your memory will come back, because you don't know you ever had it to lose in the first place, no matter what the doctor said. It was all too confusing. Even thinking about it made his head hurt again. He kneaded his pillows so they propped him up comfortably and leaned back to listen to the 'Lento' movement of Shostakovich's seventh string quartet.

14

'Wouldn't you just know it,' said Annie on Friday morning. 'We get a rare chance to visit a beauty spot and what happens? It fucking pours down.'

She and Gerry had arrived in Dorset late the previous evening, tired after a long drive, and were enjoying breakfast at the Castle Inn, West Lulworth. Annie, still trying hard to stick to the pescatarian course, if not total vegetarianism, had gone for the kippers, but Gerry was indulging in a rare full English. It was one of the things that annoyed Annie about her – not that she wasn't a veggie, but that she seemed able to eat whatever she wanted and not put on any weight.

Outside, the rain sluiced down the mullioned windows, blurring the view of distant hills. They had set off from Eastvale around lunchtime the previous day, after the Timmy Kerrigan interview, and though the weather had been good, the journey had taken them close to seven hours, including heavy traffic around the M18, a quick sandwich stop near Oxford and getting lost in the winding Dorset lanes. After a brief snack and a couple of glasses of wine at the bar, they had both been ready for bed, and Annie had just managed to stay awake long enough to make a couple of phone calls before drifting off to sleep.

First, she had spoken with AC Gervaise and learned that Banks was spending the night in hospital under observation and that he seemed to be having problems with his memory.

There was nothing she could do to help him right now, not from so far away, though she was glad that she had made time to deliver his mobile and headphones before she and Gerry set off for Dorset. Gervaise had also mentioned that the firefighters had discovered two unidentified charred corpses in the abandoned water treatment plant where Banks had been found. Now Annie was worried that one of them might be Zelda. Ray would fall apart if anything happened to her. She had asked Gervaise to call her again if there were any developments but had heard nothing yet. Last of all, she had called Ray to check up on him and tell him about Banks, without mentioning the burned corpses. Ray had sounded a little drunk, and there was loud music playing in the background: Led Zeppelin, 'Dazed and Confused', one of Ray's old favourites she remembered well.

Sergeant Trevelyan turned up outside the inn at ten o'clock on the dot, as he had promised. Annie and Gerry squeezed into his Land Rover, and what would have been perhaps, on a fine day, a pleasant twenty-minute walk, became a five-minute drive in the pouring rain. Luckily, Trevelyan was well-supplied with umbrellas, and when they arrived at their destination he handed one each to Gerry and Annie.

He was probably in his mid-fifties, Annie thought, maybe a bit old for a local sergeant. Most officers his age would have retired by then. He had a squarish face topped with grey hair worn in much the same style as Boris Johnson. His manner was brusque but friendly enough, Annie thought, especially as they were a couple of interlopers no doubt spoiling the rhythm of his day. She imagined that he was usually in uniform, but today he wore jeans and a light grey windcheater.

Once on the path, Annie felt the power of the wind as well as the rain. She held her umbrella close and kept her eyes on the muddy ground to make sure she didn't trip over any undergrowth or a half-buried stone. All this meant she didn't get to appreciate the beauty of the spot until they arrived at the cliff's edge, because she had been staring at her feet, but once she looked up, she was impressed. She couldn't believe she had never been there before, despite having grown up not too far away in St Ives, Cornwall. And somehow, in the grim weather, with a rough grey sea and white breakers below, it was even more awe-inspiring than she had imagined. They stood on the top of a rugged cliff overlooking a semicircular stretch of beach, deserted at the moment. 'Is this the spot?' Annie asked Trevelyan, raising her voice to make herself heard over the wind and the crashing waves.

Trevelyan pointed to the west. 'See that arch sticking out into the water there,' he said, 'the one with the hole in it?'

Annie saw it. From a distance it resembled a petrified brontosaurus, its long neck bent to drink from the sea. Still, she remembered, this area was supposed to be part of the Jurassic Coast, so why not? 'From there?' she said.

'Aye,' he said. 'She ran out there and jumped right off the end, bounced off the cliff and landed in the sea. It wasn't as rough as it is today, but it still took a while to find her. Too late, of course.'

They stood gazing at the spot, each lost in thought, the wind howling and raging around them. Annie tried to put herself in the mind of the young girl, humiliated and shamed by a rape that was no fault of her own, standing on that edge. What thoughts must have been whirling about in her mind? Was she already determined to jump, or did she suddenly decide to do it on the spot? Spur of the moment. Bad pun, she told herself, but unintentional.

After a few minutes, Trevelyan broke the silence. 'Seen enough?'

Both Annie and Gerry nodded.

'Right. I know a nice little tea shop not too far away that should be opening its doors just about now. Shall we go and have a chat?'

That same morning, as Annie and Gerry were watching the rain in Dorset, an ambulance took Banks over to the Friarage hospital, in Northallerton. He didn't think he needed it – he could have driven himself if someone had brought his car – but the rules were the rules. All his tests had shown good reflexes, and the MRI – noisy and claustrophobic, but otherwise painless – revealed no brain injury, so Banks was discharged.

Dr Chowdhury had already given him a list of symptoms to watch out for – including problems with speaking, walking or balance, numbness, blurred vision, fits or personality changes – and told him not to watch TV or use his iPhone, to lay off the booze, take paracetamol for his headache and to get in touch if his memory didn't return within a few days.

Most of all, he was supposed to avoid stress and get plenty of rest. But how was he supposed to do that, he wondered, with Zelda still missing, two burned bodies in the treatment plant and his memory of events scrambled beyond recognition? Superintendent Newry from IOPC would no doubt be on his case again soon. If you were a policeman, you didn't get to stumble out of a burning building leaving two bodies behind you and not remember a thing without at least a stiff interrogation.

The doctor also suggested that it might be a good idea to get someone to stay with him for the first forty-eight hours to watch out for any danger signs that may be more easily spotted by an outside observer, such as personality changes. As far as Banks was concerned, that was a no-no. He had had enough being woken up at regular intervals during his two nights in hospital. Besides, he didn't know anyone who would do it, or who he wanted to do it. Ray Cabbot probably would, but Banks knew that Ray was in no shape to play babysitter with Zelda gone. And Ray's presence would just make him feel edgy and guilty about not having found her.

It would be too awkward having Annie around, even if she wasn't away in Dorset. They had ended their relationship some years ago, mostly because they worked together, and he was of higher rank, but there were enough sparks remaining to make both wary of too close contact. Talk about stress. Anyone else, like Ken Blackstone in Leeds and Burgess in London, was simply too far away. Family was out of the question, too. He wasn't going to burden Brian with his problems when he only had two or three more gigs to play with the band, or intrude on Tracy's newly-wedded bliss with Mark. He figured he could probably keep an eye on himself.

Getting home was another matter, though, as his car was still in the drive outside Newhope Cottage. He had no qualms about asking a local constable to drop him off.

When he got there, three CSIs were still puttering around the front, and they gave Banks an embarrassing round of applause when he got out of the car. *Wonderful*, he thought, now even his home was a crime scene. He thanked the constable, and she drove off back to Northallerton.

'Found anything yet?' Banks asked Stefan Nowak, the Crime Scene Manager.

'Tyre tracks,' answered Nowak. 'Fingerprints on your door frame. Most of them probably yours. A few drops of blood, also probably yours, but hardly enough to cause anyone great concern. And cigarette ends. Whoever did it must have had a long boring wait. They're similar to the ones we found near Ray Cabbot's cottage a few days ago. Ronhill. Croatian. Go ahead and get some rest. You look terrible. We're done now.

We've got all there is to find. Oh, and maybe you should check your valuables, you know, just to make sure they didn't take anything. There's no evidence they even entered the house, but just to be on the safe side.'

'Thanks, Stefan. I will,' said Banks, trying to think exactly what his valuables might be. 'Though I very much doubt that was what it was about.'

'Seeing as it's not a serious crime scene, and the house wasn't broken into, you can go in. We won't seal the place up with tape.'

'You mean me getting bashed on the head and abducted isn't serious?'

'Well, if you put it that way. John! Bring that crime scene tape over here.'

'Away with you,' said Banks, smiling. 'On your way.'

Nowak walked towards the CSI van, grinned back over his shoulder and waved.

It was strange, Banks felt, that he could understand all the events Stefan was talking about – fingerprints, Croatian cigarettes, blood – but he still couldn't remember a thing about what happened to him two nights ago. Apart from a flickering image of flames and a voice – Zelda's voice? – telling him to run, it was still a blank.

He went into the cottage and saw that nothing appeared to have been disturbed in the front room. His computer was still intact. The entertainment room and kitchen were also untouched. Nothing was missing or out of place. They had come for *him*, not his possessions.

Besides, what other people might call valuables were just things as far as Banks was concerned: electronic equipment, books, CDs, DVDs and so on could all be replaced. Most of them, at any rate. The only true valuables he owned consisted of mementos of his own and his children's growing up: letters, old photographs, certificates, newspaper cuttings, and odds and ends from his grandparents, like a World War One bullet, a fragment of shrapnel and a tarnished cigarette lighter with a dent in it, which his grandfather had said saved him from a German bullet. Banks smiled. Everyone in the family knew that was a tall tale, but they all pretended they believed it for the sake of the old man's pride. After all, he had fought at the Somme and survived.

Thieves often took or destroyed things like this, with sentimental value for only the owner, but in this case, the box in which Banks stored them still nestled securely beside a similar box of his old *Beano* and *Dandy* annuals on top of his wardrobe.

Feeling tired, Banks thought he would go into the conservatory, have a glass of wine and maybe doze for a while. He remembered Dr Chowdhury's strictures against alcohol, but doctors were always saying things like that. One glass wouldn't do any harm. He opened a bottle of Languedoc and put on an old Bill Evans CD, the Half Moon Bay concert, then settled down in his favourite wicker chair, feet up on a low stool. He wasn't supposed to watch TV or work on his computer, or even play games on his iPhone, but he didn't feel like doing any of those things, anyway. Surely a little cool jazz wouldn't do any harm? It was good for the soul, as was the wine. Dr Chowdhury had cleared him for sleep, and the tests showed no serious damage. Which was just as well, as he started drifting off during 'Autumn Leaves'.

'Unfortunately, it's not the right time of day for one of our famous cream teas,' said Trevelyan, 'but if you're still around this afternoon, may I recommend that you sample one here?'

Annie wasn't hungry so soon after breakfast, but she thought they might stick around another night, as they had to go to Wool to talk to the Sedgwicks later. Tea time would be very late to set off on such a long drive back up north if the weather remained so bad. Was there anything in a cream tea she wasn't supposed to eat? Only calories, she thought. She wondered how Alan and Ray were doing back up in Eastvale. She didn't want to phone and spoil Banks's rest, if that was what he was doing, and she trusted AC Gervaise to call if there were any developments.

The three of them sat at a window table in a twee cafe in West Lulworth watching the passers-by hurry past, heads down, umbrellas up. The inside of the window was slightly steamed up, and along with the splattering of rain, it gave the view an Impressionist effect. And it was too hot in the cafe. Why did everyone have to turn the heating up when it rained? Annie sipped some tea and turned her mind back to the place they had just visited. Lulworth Cove and Durdle Door. Again, her heart weighed heavy at the thought of Marnie standing there, her life in pieces, then falling. No, jumping. And not standing. *Running*.

'It was a lovely day,' Trevelyan said.

Annie thought she might have missed something as she had been so lost in reverie. 'What? When?'

'The day Marnie Sedgwick died.' He gestured towards the window. 'It wasn't like this. The sun was shining, not a cloud in the sky, the water was all blue around the cove from the minerals in the rocks. There were boats out.'

'It was daylight?'

'Mid-afternoon.'

'I meant to ask you this before,' Annie said, 'but can you be absolutely certain that Marnie took her own life? There was no one else around?'

'There were lots of people around for a weekday,' said Trevelyan. 'That's why we can be sure. More eyewitnesses than you could shake a stick at. There was one group of Japanese tourists saw the whole thing. In shock, they were. We had to get an interpreter. They were on some sort of Hardy tour – Thomas, that is, our local celeb. One of his characters goes for a swim in the sea at Lulworth in *Far from the Madding Crowd*, and they all come by the coachload to see the spot. Can't understand it myself, as it never happened, it was all just made up.'

'Terence Stamp,' said Gerry.

Annie looked at her. 'Come again?'

'The one who swam out to sea, faked his suicide. Sergeant Troy, played by Terence Stamp. I've seen the film. Julie Christie as Bathsheba Everdene. There's a more recent version with Carey—'

'OK, Gerry. But remember, we're *not* on a Hardy tour.'

'Sorry, guv. My dad was a movie buff. I can't help it. And I was just thinking, you know, the suicide connection.'

Trevelyan smiled at the exchange. 'It's a good point,' he said to Gerry. 'Though Marnie Sedgwick wasn't faking it. At least twenty people saw her run out on Durdle Door and launch herself off the end. As you saw, the arch bellies out a bit and she hit the rock face as she went down. The pathologist says that was what killed her. A head wound. Fractured skull. After that she dropped in the sea and the waves battered her against the base of the arch until a boat managed to get close enough to haul her out. It was too late by then.'

Both Annie and Gerry silently contemplated Marnie's fate. 'Do you get a lot of people jumping off this Durdle Door?' Annie asked.

'Every summer. It's quite a popular sport among the young folk.'

'But they don't all die.'

'Of course not. We have the occasional serious accident, though, and the air ambulances are out there often enough, but there are spots where you can jump safely and avoid the outfling and the rocks at the bottom. The tides, too, of course.'

'But Marnie didn't do that?'

'No.'

'Would she have known the lie of the land?'

'According to her parents, Lulworth was one of her favourite spots. She loved the whole Jurassic Coast, no matter what the season.'

'Did she leave a note?'

'No. But there again—'

'Many suicides don't,' said Annie. 'We know. But there's no doubt in your mind that it *was* suicide?'

'None at all. Either that or she slipped and fell, but the majority of our witnesses say she definitely ran off the end.'

'Ran,' said Annie. 'You've mentioned that a few times and it strikes me as odd. Why was she running?'

'Nobody knows. Maybe she didn't want to give herself a chance to change her mind.'

'Or maybe she was being chased,' said Annie.

Trevelyan flashed her a stern glance. 'We're not the country hicks you might think we are down here, DI Cabbot. While there was hardly a major investigation, we did ask around. Marnie *had* been seen walking with and talking to a man in the car park and on the cliffs earlier. We couldn't get any sort of decent description except he was older, slender, medium height, with a touch of grey and, whoever he was, he was never seen again. The only unusual thing about him was that he was wearing a suit. You don't get a lot of that around here. There was certainly no one chasing her when she ran out on to the Door and jumped off the end.'

'What were they doing? Arguing? Holding hands?'

'Just walking and talking, as far as we know,' said Trevelyan. 'Nobody noticed anything unusual or potentially alarming.'

'Any photos or videos of him?'

'None that we saw.'

'Was there an investigation?'

'Only a cursory one, as I said, for the coroner's court.' Trevelyan took a tablet from his briefcase. 'And there's more. I don't want to upset you, but . . .' He turned the tablet on and went to the menu, then passed it to Annie. 'One of the Japanese tourists was taking videos of Durdle at the time.'

Annie held the tablet so that only she and Gerry could see it and pressed the start button for the video clip Trevelyan had selected. It began with a slow panorama of the sea and cliffs, the wind whistling in the microphone, white gulls swooping over the water's surface. Then there was an audible human gasp and the image jumped chaotically before it caught the end of Durdle Door and a human figure running. She didn't launch herself so much as fall like a rag doll and bounce off the cliff face. Annie felt sick and Gerry looked pale. But they watched it again. There was no indication that she had simply overbalanced or tried to dive into the sea.

'Sorry,' said Trevelyan, 'but that's pretty conclusive, I'd say. There's no sign of anyone chasing her. Naturally, we made sure the video was never shared on social media.'

'What about her stuff? Her mobile and so on?'

'The mobile must have gone with her over the cliff. We never found it. She had nothing else except a few quid and a set of car keys in her jeans pocket. Her car was in the car park. She'd even paid.'

'How long?'

'Two hours. She arrived at 12.27.'

'And was seen with the man when?'

'Around that time in the car park and about fifteen minutes later on the cliffs.'

'After that?'

'She jumped at 12.54, according to the timer on the video.'

'What happened to the man she was talking to?'

'Someone saw him get into a car at about ten to or five to one. They couldn't be certain.'

'What sort of car?'

'A posh one was all we heard. Maybe a Jag or a Beemer. Silver.'

'CCTV? ANPR?'

Trevelyan shook his head. 'It was too late by the time we heard all this. Recordings had been wiped over. To be honest, we didn't scour every possible source. There was no evidence that the man had anything to do with Marnie's suicide.'

'But he might have given her cause,' Gerry said.

'We'd still no reason to suspect him of any crime.'

'Isn't it a bit odd, though,' Gerry went on, 'that Marnie would bother paying for the parking when she was intending to take her own life?'

'People follow habit, as often as not,' said Trevelyan. 'If you're the sort of person who always pays your way, you'll just as likely do that even if you're planning suicide. Still, it's true that we don't *know* she was planning any such thing. It might have been a sudden decision – it might even have had something to do with the man she was talking to – but as far as we were concerned, her death did not involve foul play or suspicious circumstances. Maybe you see it differently.' Trevelyan put the tablet back in his briefcase and paused a moment. 'Now,' he said, 'I think you'd agree that I've been both patient and helpful so far. But you still haven't told me anything about *why* you're interested. Wouldn't this be a good time to tell me?'

'I'm sorry,' said Annie. 'You're right, of course. We have evidence that Marnie Sedgwick was raped at a party in the house of a man called Connor Clive Blaydon back on 13 April of this year.'

'Do you have any idea who did it?'

'No,' said Annie. 'The only evidence so far consists of a poor quality microSD recording from which we managed to enhance a picture of Marnie, but not of the rapist. We only found the recording some time after the event, while our CSIs were searching Blaydon's house. He was murdered in a particularly brutal fashion about a month later.'

'And you think that's connected with what happened to Marnie?'

'We don't think anything. We don't necessarily think Blaydon was the one who raped her. He could have been, but now we know for certain that Marnie didn't kill him. She died five days before he did. But everyone we've talked to has told us about the change in her after the date of the rape. How she became depressed, moody, anxious. Now you tell us – *show* us – that she took her own life about a month later.'

'You thought she might have been killed?'

'There was a possibility that the rapist might have feared his identity being revealed,' Gerry said. 'We had to consider that he might have decided the best course of action was to get rid of Marnie. That's why my ears pricked up when you mentioned she was talking to a man.'

'I'm sorry,' said Trevelyan. 'If I'd known any of what you've just told me before, I'd have made sure we tracked him down. But, as you saw, he wasn't anywhere near her when she went over the edge. Nobody was. And she didn't try to stop herself from falling. It seemed quite deliberate to me.'

'But she may still have been running away from him.'

'I suppose so.'

'It's not your fault,' Annie said. 'There was no way you could have known what had happened to Marnie back up north. Or her parents. She didn't tell anyone, as far as we know. We're still only just putting it together ourselves, and we don't know who raped her. Besides, this makes even more sense. I mean the suicide. Given her state of mind. Everyone says she'd been anxious and depressed ever since it happened.'

Trevelyan seemed lost in thought for a moment, then he said, 'It didn't make a lot of sense to us at first, even though her parents pretty much echoed what you say. But what you've told me just now at least puts it in context. There's more.'

'More?'

'Yes. We didn't want to tell her parents at first. They were upset enough that their daughter had killed herself. But they would have found out one way or another. Post-mortems and coroners' reports are a matter of public record, for a start. Not to mention the possibility of loose tongues.'

'What is it?' Annie asked, though she already had an inkling.

'The post-mortem revealed that Marnie was pregnant when she died.'

Banks awoke with a start when his phone played the blues riff. The Bill Evans CD had long since finished. It was late afternoon and shadows were lengthening across his garden and over the sloping stretch of land between the back of his cottage and the lower pastures of Tetchley Fell.

Banks answered. It was Ray Cabbot. 'Alan, I heard what happened. Annie told me you got hit on the head. Are you OK? Do you want me to come over?'

'No, Ray. I'm fine. It's OK. You're better staying there in case . . . you know, in case Zelda shows up.'

'Right. I don't suppose you've found anything new? She's been gone nearly four days now. I'm going crazy here.'

'Afraid not,' said Banks. 'But I've been out of commission all day and I don't remember anything. Annie would have told you, though, if there was any news. Just hang on.'

'Annie said something about a fire. I've tried calling her, but she's not been answering her phone.'

'No. She and Gerry are in Dorset following up a lead on a rape case. They're probably pretty busy.'

'Dorset? Are you sure Zelda hasn't been hurt? Did you find her?'

'People have mentioned fire to me,' said Banks. 'Unfortunately it's something I don't remember.' But as soon as he said it, he had the strange sensation that it wasn't true, that the state of his memory now was different from when he had drifted off to Bill Evans. That the pieces had rearranged themselves while he slept. He didn't want to risk saying anything to Ray, but he wanted to explore what that difference was. Could it have come back? Nobody really understood how memory worked. Maybe it was the music. Or a dream. He had no idea what triggered it, but he felt that it was all back, what happened two nights ago, and if he could just get some quiet time alone he could access it. 'I'm really knackered, Ray,' he said. 'And the doc says I've got to take it easy, so let's leave this for now, shall we? I can't tell you anything. I'm sure I'll be right as rain tomorrow. Let's get together then, OK?'

'OK,' said Ray. 'Sorry about . . . you know . . . Have a good rest.'

People kept saying that, but Banks was hardly likely to get a good rest until he had remembered what he could. The images were still fragmented, his memory in flux, but there were more of them now, and some were firming up into clear pictures. He found that it didn't take much effort to put them into a linear narrative. Waking with Keane looming over him, the smell of the petrol, a dark figure emerging from the shadows, Keane stiffening, stabbed from behind, spilling petrol, then Zelda stepping forward to cut his bonds. And the flames. It got a bit blurred again after that, with a sudden whoosh of flame and heat and Zelda shouting for him to run. Then he had woken up in the hospital bed.

There were still a few blank spots to fill in. The things Keane had said, for a start. There was something important in that, he remembered, without being able to grasp exactly what it was. He relaxed. It would come, and it was no good trying to force it. Perhaps some more music and another nap would help?

But it wasn't to be. No sooner had he put some solo Thelonious Monk on, than his phone went off again. He was tempted not to answer, as it was a withheld number, but he gave in at the last moment and paused the music. As he had suspected, it was Burgess on the line.

'How's the head?' he asked.

'Word sure gets around. It's fine, thanks.'

'Memory?'

'Still a bit untrustworthy.'

'I'd keep it that way if Newry's on your trail.'

'You know about that?'

'Sure. And him. He's a real bastard. Guilty till proven guilty.'

'Thanks for the warning.'

'That's not why I called you.'

'Oh?'

'No. We found an arm – at least, a recycling plant worker out Croydon way did. Severed just below the shoulder. Wrapped in a black bin liner. It fell out right in front of his forklift.'

'Whose arm?'

'No idea. And no other body parts yet. They're still scouring the area. The bad news is that there's no hand, therefore no prints.'

'Why tell me?'

'Thought you'd be interested. This arm, there's some decomposition, but it's not too badly preserved, and it's got a tat. A bit faded, but still readable with our technology. Looks like someone tried to scrub it off with bleach but didn't quite succeed.'

'Of what?'

'My experts tell me it's the insignia of some Croatian crime gang. "Loyal unto death" or some such codswallop.'

'Croatian?'

'Thought you'd be interested. I'll send up the details. And make sure you get plenty of—'

'I know. Rest. Believe me, I've been trying. Thanks. Talk to you later.'

Banks ended the call. An arm, he thought. Interesting. Then he started the solo Monk again and lay back in his chair.

There was a definite aura of mourning in the Sedgwick household, though the curtains weren't closed and neither Mr nor Mrs Sedgwick was dressed in black. There was a family photo taken in happier days on the mantelpiece, but no shrine to Marnie with candles burning and a vase of flowers. The mourning resided more in the general atmosphere and the numb, mechanical way Mrs Sedgwick – Francine, she asked them to call her – made tea and carried in the tray while her husband – Dennis, please – put out a gateleg table in front of the green velour sofa. It was an unremarkable house on an unremarkable street, and its view consisted almost entirely of other unremarkable houses, with just a glimpse of the rolling green Dorset countryside in a gap between two terraces.

The Sedgwicks looked older than Annie had expected, given that Marnie had been only nineteen when she died, but both seemed fit and trim despite a few wrinkles around the eyes and a touch of grey. Francine wore her hair long with a ragged fringe, and Dennis had his neatly cut with a side parting and a forelock that flopped over his brow. They were both casually dressed in jeans and short-sleeved shirts.

The rain continued to batter against the large arched window in the living room as they settled down to tea and the McVitie's chocolate digestives Francine had laid out on a plate. Annie took one, but Gerry and Dennis didn't.

'We're sorry to bring up memories that might still be painful for you,' Annie said, 'but we need to talk to you about Marnie. Is that short for Marjorie, by the way?'

'It is,' said Francine. 'Her name is Marjorie, but she couldn't pronounce it when she was young. It came out as Marnie, and it just kind of stuck. Especially when she got older and thought Marjorie sounded too old-fashioned.'

'Nothing to do with the movie then?' said Gerry.

Francine frowned. 'What movie?'

'Never mind.'

Annie gave Gerry a sharp glance and went on, 'We were wondering how long Marnie had been home until she . . . you know . . .'

'Committed suicide?' said Dennis. 'I know you're not supposed to say that these days. It's no longer PC, though Lord knows why, but that's what happened. How long was it, dear? Not long.'

'She came down at the beginning of May,' said Francine. 'I can't remember the exact date. The third or fourth, I think. But she was only home for a couple of weeks or so before she died.'

'And during that time how did her behaviour seem?'

'There was something wrong. She wouldn't tell us what it was, and we couldn't guess, but we knew things weren't right with her. She shut herself up in her room a lot, missed meals because she said she wasn't hungry. And mood swings. She had mood swings. We were starting to think we should try to persuade her to see a doctor when . . . it happened.'

'Did Marnie have any eating disorders? Anorexia? Bulimia?'

'No, never. She'd always had a healthy appetite, that's why it seemed so strange.'

'She wasn't drinking or taking drugs as far as you know?'

'No,' said Dennis. 'I'm not saying she might not have experimented while she was at uni or living up north, but not while she was here. I've done a drug awareness course, and I think I would have known the signs.'

'What kind of work do you do?'

'I'm a teacher. Local comprehensive. And Francie here works in human resources at the hospital. I started my summer break early, and Francie is still on medical leave. Her nerves are bad.'

'Sorry to hear it,' Annie mumbled. 'We'll try not to take up too much of your time.'

'There's no point pussyfooting around us,' Dennis said. Even though his wife looked alarmed, he went on, 'We know that Marnie was pregnant when she jumped.'

'Dennis!'

'Sorry, love.' Dennis leaned over and patted his wife's hand. 'But it's the truth.'

'We know,' said Annie.

'What we'd like to know,' Dennis went on, 'is why the police are coming around now, over a month after our Marnie killed herself. And why the North Yorkshire police?'

'Marnie lived in York,' said Gerry. 'That's not technically North Yorkshire – they're very much a nation of their own – but we think Marnie is connected with an incident that took place between Harrogate and Ripon.'

'What sort of incident?' asked Francine.

Gerry glanced at Annie, who gave her a slight nod. 'It was a rape,' Gerry said. 'At a party.'

'I told you,' said Mr Sedgwick to his wife. 'I told you Marnie wasn't the sort of girl to get herself into trouble.'

'But, Dennis,' she said. 'She was *raped.* Our Marnie was raped. Oh, God.' She wielded a handkerchief from beneath her cushions and started to cry.

Annie thought it was true that Dennis Sedgwick had made rape sound preferable to getting pregnant through consensual sex, but she didn't think he had intended it to come out that way. It had been a thoughtless statement, but not a cruel or brutal one. She distracted herself with her tea and a biscuit while the Sedgwicks settled themselves back down again, and said, 'It's more than likely she had no idea what was happening to her. It looks as if someone slipped something in her drink. Rohypnol, something like that.'

'She was drugged?' said Dennis.

'It appears that way.'

'Where was this party?'

'At the home of a man called Connor Clive Blaydon. Have either of you ever heard of him?'

They both shook their heads.

'What was she doing there?' Francine asked.

'She was working,' Gerry said.

'But I thought she worked at Pizza Express?'

'She did,' Gerry explained. 'But she had another job – part-time – working for an events organiser.'

'Doing what?' asked Francine.

'Backroom stuff. Mostly in the kitchen. Helping the caterers. Organising.'

'Then how did she become a victim?'

'We don't know. One of the guests must have had his eye on

her and managed to get her alone. He might have persuaded her to have a drink he had drugged.'

'She was always too trusting,' Dennis said. 'Even when she was a little girl.'

'We can't know for certain,' Annie said, 'because we haven't yet found any witnesses willing to speak to us, or anyone who admits to knowing anything.'

'Why not?' asked Dennis.

'Mr Blaydon, the host, was murdered about a month after the party. The 22nd May, to be precise.'

'And you think these events are connected? Marnie's rape and Blaydon's murder.'

'Not necessarily,' said Annie. 'We're just keeping an open mind. As you can no doubt work out, this was after Marnie's suicide.'

'Well, at least you're not trying to accuse her of murder.'

'No,' said Annie. 'But as I'm sure you understand, with both a rape and a murder occurring so closely together, on the same premises, we can't leave any corner unexamined. This Blaydon was involved with some pretty shady characters, and we think our best bet is that he was killed by a member of the Albanian Mafia.'

'Mafia?' gasped Francine. 'What was our Marnie doing with the Mafia?'

'Nothing,' said Annie. 'She was helping to organise the party, that's all. She had nothing to do with the guests. I doubt she even knew there were such dangerous characters around.'

'Until it was too late,' said Dennis.

'Yes.'

'Who was she working for?'

'A woman called Charlotte Westlake. She was Mr Blaydon's personal assistant, and her background is in events organising.'

'How did Marnie come to be working for her?'

'It seemed she just wanted another job. Needed the money. Mrs Westlake told us that most people who apply to her for jobs do so via word of mouth, so clearly someone who already worked for her, or had worked for her, suggested Marnie try it.'

'Who was this?'

'We don't know. We have a list of present and previous employees, so it's something we can find out if we need to. But it probably doesn't matter. The fact is that she was working at this party at Mr Blaydon's house when someone drugged and raped her. She didn't tell anyone.'

'Then how do you know?'

'There was a recording,' Gerry said. 'A very poor one – the cam wasn't working properly – but we managed to recreate an image of her face. Mrs Westlake's secretary had met her when she came for a job interview and identified her from that image as Marnie.'

'A *camera*?' said Francine. 'My God, are you saying someone *recorded* all this? Are you sure? Couldn't there be some mistake?'

'There could be,' said Annie, 'but we don't think so. As I said, we know that she was working at the house the night the attack occurred. Would you like to see the picture?'

'Is it . . .'

'It's just head and shoulders.'

Mrs Sedgwick nodded and Annie took out the photo and showed it to her. She put it down. 'It could be anyone, couldn't it?'

Her husband picked it up. 'Francine's right,' he said, tossing it back towards Annie. 'This doesn't prove anything.'

'We think it was Marnie,' Annie went on, 'and we think that was why people say she was behaving strangely after that party. Mood swings. Depression. Shutting herself away. She couldn't concentrate on her job at Pizza Express, so she left, then came home. That's when you were briefly reunited.'

'Did she know she was pregnant?' Francine asked, moving the hankie away from her face.

'We don't know,' said Annie. 'We don't even know for certain that the rape caused her pregnancy. If she knew, she never mentioned it to anyone we've talked to. All we can say is that she might have known, might have sensed the change in herself, even after just a month or so, while she was back with you. A missed period, perhaps, cramps, nausea, bloating, mood swings. And she was certainly upset enough by the rape itself for that to affect her behaviour. Do you know if she saw anyone in the two weeks she was down here? Old friends, perhaps?'

'They've all moved away. There's not much for young people to do around here. Most of them leave. Besides, she hardly ever went out.'

'Only the walks,' said Dennis.

'Yes, that's true. She went for long walks sometimes. Disappeared for hours. We were quite worried about her.'

'A witness saw her walking and talking to a man on the cliffs the day she died,' Annie said. 'Do you know who that might have been?'

'The police mentioned that to us, too,' said Dennis. 'We have no idea. Could it be important? Could it be the man who . . . who raped her?'

'There's no evidence that he had anything to do with what happened to her,' Annie said. 'And we don't know who raped her. But it's always good to talk to people who . . .' She paused. 'Well, I don't suppose we'll manage that now. Whoever he is, he'll be long gone. It probably isn't relevant.'

'We always told her not to talk to strangers,' said Dennis.

'It wasn't a stranger,' Francine said. 'That's what they're saying. If she was walking and talking with him, he was probably someone she knew.'

'We don't know,' said Annie. 'Did Marnie have any siblings, brothers or sisters?'

The Sedgwicks looked at one another in silence for a moment, then Francine said, 'No. Marnie was an only child. I . . . you see, we couldn't have children of our own, and . . .'

'Marnie was adopted?' said Annie, giving Gerry a puzzled glance.

'Well, yes. I assumed you knew.'

'Nobody told us.'

'It didn't make her any less our own. We couldn't have loved her more if I'd given birth to her myself.'

'No, of course,' said Annie. 'It's just that we didn't know. It never came up in any of our investigations.'

'There's no reason why it should, is there?' said Dennis.

'I suppose not. You just took us by surprise, that's all. How old was she when you adopted her?'

'Just a baby,' said Francine. 'They had to keep her in a while longer than usual because she was born early. But she was a beautiful tiny perfect baby.' She collapsed into sobs, and her husband embraced her.

Annie sat thinking and Gerry scribbled away in her notebook.

15

Banks felt a lot better the following morning after his first night at home. He was even hungry enough to scorch some toast to eat with his coffee. The headache was almost gone, as was most of the nausea. The dizziness still came and went, but the main thing was that he had got his memory back, or most of it, and had even managed to shuffle it into what seemed like the right chronology. The problem was what to do with it.

The missing fragments had fallen into place. He remembered Keane telling him that Zelda was being kept in the same building, and that she was with Petar Tadić, who was settling a score of some kind. Then Keane went on to tell him about Tadić torturing and killing Faye Butler, and his killing Hawkins, who was double-crossing the Tadićs. And he saved the best for last: Zelda had killed Goran Tadić, just as she had written in her notebook. So it wasn't fantasy. Now Banks really could be charged with aiding and abetting the murder, should it all come out.

Banks thought again of the severed arm Burgess had mentioned. What had Petar Tadić done with his brother's body? Could it be his? It wasn't every day they found severed arms in recycling plants, even in London, nor was it unknown for gang members to chop up dead colleagues and scatter the parts over a large area. No time for ritual or honour when you've got a body to get rid of. So it *could* be Goran's arm. On the other hand, there were other Croatian criminal gang members in the country, so it wouldn't do to jump to conclusions without more evidence.

Banks also now remembered Zelda yelling for him to run as the fire flared up. He had done so instinctively, without looking back, but when he got outside and turned to see her, she wasn't there. He had gone back to the doorway, he remembered, to see if she was still inside and whether he could get to her. The place was an inferno by then, and there was nothing he could do without sacrificing his own life, and his instinct for self-preservation had kicked in. He got the hell out of there. He had staggered away, half choked, then fallen in the weed-filled reservoir, hit his head on the bottom and passed out.

Now he was convinced that he should have waited for Zelda, even though the flames were quickly spreading, or at least made sure she went before him, instead of just running off without thinking. If she had been trapped by a falling beam or something and burned to death, he would never be able to forgive himself. He vaguely remembered brief snatches of consciousness, the firefighters picking him up, paramedics loading him on to a gurney, someone shining a light in his eyes, someone gently shaking him in the night, but most of it was blank until he woke up in the hospital bed.

But now that he had his memory back, he was stuck with a serious dilemma. He still didn't know where Zelda was, or even if she was still alive. Newry had simply said there were two bodies in the burned-out treatment plant. Keane was certainly one of them, but the other could be Zelda's or Petar Tadić's. It was also possible that there was a third body the search team hadn't yet found, and that all three were burned to a crisp in there. Burned human remains sometimes went undetected, or were damaged by firefighting and recovery operations. Fire scene investigators often couldn't tell the human remains from other fire- and water-damaged debris.

If Zelda had survived, though, she had probably run off through a different exit and gone somewhere she thought was safe. But things had changed. Now he knew she was a murderer – at least an *alleged* murderer, according to Keane – and he was a cop. He was supposed to catch murderers and see that they went to trial and, if found guilty, received their due punishment. But this was Zelda. *Nelia Melnic.*

He had read parts of her notebook, but he had brushed them off as fantasy at the time. What if it was true, as Keane had said? What if Zelda had killed Goran Tadić? What was he going to do about it? He had seen her kill Keane with his own eyes. A good argument for self-defence could be made for that killing. But Goran Tadić? Perhaps the same was true, but he knew nothing about the circumstances of what happened. Maybe Keane was lying; it wouldn't be the first time. But he had thought Banks was about to die, so why bother lying to him? To send him to his grave thinking a woman he cared for was a killer? Was Keane *that* cruel? Perhaps. The sensible, logical, moral thing to do was report what he knew to AC Gervaise, or Superintendent Newry, and leave it to others to track down Zelda, and to the jury and judge to decide on her fate.

But he couldn't do that.

So what the hell was he to do?

Annie and Gerry had skipped the cream tea and started out from Wool shortly after they had talked to the Sedgwicks, but not before Gerry had phoned the General Register Office and managed to persuade someone there to track down the birth details of Marjorie Sedgwick. They told her not to expect an answer until the following day as they were short-staffed. Now it was the following morning, and they were both tired. It had been a long journey back and a late night.

'We didn't dig deeply enough into Marnie's background,' Gerry said as she sat on the edge of Annie's desk in the squad room, coffee in hand. 'My mistake. I'm sorry. I should have found out what happened to her before we went to Dorset.'

Annie swivelled in her chair. 'Not to worry too much,' she said. 'We hadn't known her full name for very long. It's still early days, and we've got more to work with now. It probably won't make any difference in the long run. We're not racing against time.'

'I suppose the question we should ask ourselves is whether we still have a case to investigate now that the victim is dead.'

'Good point,' said Annie. 'We'll certainly have to scale down. The budget's bound to be cut. But let's carry on until we hear something from the AC. We can at least argue that we think the rape and Marnie's suicide could be somehow connected with Blaydon's murder.'

'Fair enough,' Gerry said. 'And if Charlotte Westlake was more involved than she's letting on, we may be on to something.' She glanced at her watch. 'We should find out what the registry has to tell us soon enough.'

'Let's not forget,' Annie added, 'there's still a rapist walking free out there.'

'Perhaps not,' said Gerry. 'I've been thinking. You know, maybe you were just being provocative the other day, suggesting that Charlotte Westlake might have killed Blaydon, but let me play devil's advocate here and suggest that Blaydon was the rapist, and Charlotte was keeping quiet either out of fear or some sort of misplaced loyalty. Why have we never seriously considered Blaydon for the rape before?'

'We did discuss it with Alan the other day,' Annie said. 'But we dismissed the idea. And it hasn't been very long since we found the cards.'

'Yes, but why? We never followed up. We never took it *seriously*. Maybe we dismissed it too soon?'

'It was hard to follow up. Blaydon was already dead. And we had no clear image of the rapist from the SD card images.'

'Fair enough,' Gerry argued. 'It's blurry and vague. But the image in the recording is as likely to be him as just about anyone else. Same size, shape and gender, at any rate. OK, maybe you can tell it's not a giant or a hugely overweight person, but other than that . . . You couldn't recognise your own father from it. Think about it.'

'We just never thought of Blaydon as a rapist, did we?' said Annie. 'A crook, yes, a gangster or wannabe gangster, yes, maybe even a killer, but a rapist? Maybe you're right and that was short-sighted of us.'

'We had nothing concrete to link him with Marnie until you told me Timmy Kerrigan saw him talking to her at the party.'

'True,' said Annie, 'but that doesn't necessarily mean anything.'

'I think it does,' Gerry said. 'It's the first time we've had any sort of evidence or witness statement linking Blaydon and Marnie *together*. Sure, she worked at his parties, at least a couple of them, at any rate, and he probably knew of her existence through Charlotte. But until you talked to Timmy Kerrigan, nobody reported having actually *seen* Blaydon and Marnie meeting and talking. Remember how Charlotte told us she was getting worried about how decadent the parties were becoming, how they were crossing boundaries of taste and morality? Perhaps we were seeing Blaydon in free fall, and that was where he landed. Rape. Take the boundaries away and you're left with moral anarchy. What he wanted, he took. And maybe he wanted Marnie.'

'You're suggesting that he drugged Marnie's drink and took her to the bedroom?' said Annie.

'Why not? It would have been easy for him. He was the boss. It was *his* house. He knew the layout. He had access to any room he wanted. All he had to do was get her alone for a while and give her a drugged drink. Apparently, he didn't know about the minicam with the motion detector that Roberts had set up. Think about it. End of the evening. Marnie's been working. She's tired. Her parents said she was always too trusting. Blaydon was an old friend of Charlotte Westlake's. Maybe Charlotte's been protecting him?'

'But she has no reason to do that. He was dead before we ever talked to her. She'd nothing to fear from him. I mean, why protect a dead man?'

Gerry shrugged. 'I'm not saying it's a perfect theory.'

'OK,' said Annie. 'Let's say we run with that for a while and see where it leads us. What happens next? Who killed Blaydon?'

'Well, it wasn't Marnie. She jumped off Durdle Door on 17 May and Blaydon and Roberts were killed on 22 May. The Albanians still look good for it, I'd say. The ballistics, the gutting. It's their style. But who's to say Blaydon wasn't also the rapist and that his murder had nothing to do with the rape? We shouldn't necessarily let one crime distract us from another.'

'So maybe we could go back to my original screwball suggestion,' said Annie. 'That Charlotte Westlake murdered Blaydon. Let's face it, she doesn't have much of an alibi for 22 May. Organising some book award in Bradford? Really?'

'What was her motive?'

'Anger at what he did to Marnie? Female solidarity? After all, Marnie was *her* employee, not one of Tadić's hookers.'

'Still, that's pushing it a bit as a motive, isn't it?'

Annie laughed. 'Like yours, it's hardly a perfect theory. Maybe Roberts was the intended victim and Blaydon was collateral damage? Roberts could have been blackmailing

Charlotte about something, and she uncovered his whole scheme, threatened to tell Blaydon. Maybe Roberts had a recording of her we didn't find? Maybe because she took it when she killed them?'

'Too many maybes,' said Gerry. 'We're going around in circles here. It's making me dizzy.'

'It doesn't mean we should stop searching, though, does it? Even though Marnie and Blaydon are dead. And I think we should definitely have a much closer look at Charlotte Westlake. We've interviewed her twice, and I don't believe she's been completely honest with us on either occasion.'

'I'll get on it.' Gerry's phone rang, and she grabbed the handset. She listened for a while and made some notes, then thanked the caller and put down the handset.

'Come on, then, give,' said Annie. 'You're like the cat that got the cream. What is it?'

'Marnie's father is listed as unknown,' Gerry said, 'but the mother's name is Christine Pollard.'

'No way!' said Annie.

Gerry smiled. 'Way.' They high-fived.

'Have you got an address?'

'The parents in Halifax. That was nineteen years ago, mind you. I'll talk to them if they're still there, then maybe we can haul Mrs Westlake in again. Arrest her this time. Suspicion of murder. The full works: caution, lawyer and all, if that's what she wants.'

Annie rubbed her hands together. 'Oh, goody,' she said. 'I'll oil the rack and sharpen the thumbscrews.'

There were still a few firefighters and CSIs at the old water treatment plant when Banks pulled up at the cordon they had erected around the main building, where all the damage had been concentrated. The control room took up the entire lower floor, and upstairs there had been a number of offices and a staff common room, where the second body had been found. Since then, searchers had looked again for any traces of a third victim, but found none. That was good news.

Banks showed his warrant card to the officer with the clipboard who guarded the scene and walked towards the entrance.

'Better take care,' said one of the fire investigation officers. 'It can still be a bit dodgy in there.'

Banks thanked him, put on the hard hat the officer handed him and went inside. The smell of wet ash and burned rubber was almost overwhelming inside the building. Its acrid, gritty texture caught in his throat. He also thought he could discern an undertone of petrol, which took him right back to the night it happened and set off a surge of panic that fortunately passed quickly. A man turned from collecting samples, pulled his face mask aside and said hello. Banks recognised the lugubrious fire investigation officer Geoff Hamilton. They had worked together on a narrowboat fire set by Phil Keane some years ago.

'Anything new?' Banks asked.

'Nothing startling,' said Hamilton. 'Your CSIs found evidence of a car parked at the side entrance, in the old staff park. The ground's concrete, cracked and weedy, and the tracks are too faint to tell us much, but there were some oil stains and skid marks. It was definitely there. And recently.'

'Anything else?'

'This is where you were tied up,' Hamilton said, pointing to an area not far from the main door. It was still possible to see what had once been ropes, now twisted and charred, on the ground, and chalk marks had been made around the area where Keane's body had fallen. 'You were lucky,' he went on. 'You can see where all the petrol was. Someone obviously cared whether you lived or died.'

'Yes,' said Banks, remembering Zelda's face close to his, her breath pungent with days of bad food, fear and a trace of vomit, the speed with which she worked at his bonds with the knife before the flames whooshed up around them. Then the shouted instruction: 'RUN!' *He should have looked back.*

'Is this our old friend again?' Hamilton asked.

'Doesn't it have his signature?'

'There are similarities. It's multi-seated, different spots connected by streamers. Not entirely as random as it might have seemed. I'll have to get more analyses done, gas chromatology and so on, and compare them with the records.'

'No need to bother, Geoff,' said Banks. 'It was Keane. I was there.'

'So I heard,' said Hamilton. 'Don't let it become a habit.'

'I promise. By the way, you might check with the Met fire investigation service on a fire at a house in the Highgate area a couple of months ago. It presented as a typical chip-pan fire, but . . .'

'Not his style, if this is anything to go by.'

'He may be versatile. I'd say it's worth a closer look, but as he was likely one of the corpses they hauled out of here, maybe there's not much point in pinning a crime on a ghost. But there are a couple of coppers I can think of down there who wouldn't mind knowing. Just one for the record books, maybe, if you've got a spare moment.'

Hamilton grunted. 'Chance would be a fine thing.' Then he put his face mask on again and knelt by a pile of charred rubbish.

Banks went upstairs to the other marked crime scene. There was tape across the doorway and most of the floor had collapsed, so he stood for a few moments and stared at the chain, darkened by fire, attached the solid metal radiator, half disappeared through the burned floor. Was this where Zelda had been kept? Though the fire had only spread up there later, it had done as much damage as it had everywhere else. The walls were charred and the ceiling partially collapsed. The firefighters had been a while turning up, mostly because there had been no working alarm and no one present had been in a position to call them. So how had they been informed? Banks wondered. Who had called them? The building wasn't very far from the A1, though it was hidden from the motorway by a stretch of woodland. The flames would possibly have been visible to a passing motorist once they had reached their apex.

He went back downstairs and found the side door that led to the small staff car park. He could see the CSIs had marked off an area with an oil stain and tyre tracks where someone had accelerated too quickly. Zelda? It made sense. She had cut Banks free then dashed off to save herself. She would have been in a hurry to get away before anybody found her. Maybe hurt and in pain, too. But where was she?

The road out wasn't much more than an unfenced laneway, but after curving a mile or more around the woods and running parallel to the A1 for a while, it came to a roundabout that fed into the main artery. From there, she could have gone anywhere. CCTV and ANPR would be no use because they had no idea what make of car she was driving or what the number was, and the A1 was always busy. It could be the dark Ford Fiesta that Kit Riley had told them about in the Black Bull, but there were thousands of dark Fiestas on the roads. They might be able to find out, given time, but it would probably be too late by then. She would have dumped the car as soon as she could and found some other mode of transport.

Banks went back through the building and stood by the rectangular reservoir. Its bottom was covered in weeds and shrubbery after years of neglect, and that was what had cushioned Banks's fall. If he had hit the hard bottom full on, he might have done himself even more serious damage. At least a broken limb, if not a fractured skull. He gave a shudder as he shouted farewell to Geoff Hamilton and the others and headed back to his car. Just before he got there, he turned and asked one of the investigators, 'It's a bit isolated around here, isn't it? Do you know who called it in?'

The investigator scratched his head. 'I can't say for sure,' he answered, 'but I do remember the boss saying it was a woman's voice.'

A thin drizzle had started when Gerry pulled up that afternoon outside Mrs Pollard's house on the outskirts of Halifax. It was a dark stone semi, millstone grit, probably, halfway up a hill, with a pub at the bottom and a fine view of the Pennines beyond, including a couple of enormous woollen mills with tall chimneys, now mostly converted into craft shops, art galleries, cafes and local theatre venues. Misty rain hung over the valley.

Tracking Mrs Pollard down had been easy enough – she was still at the same address listed by the General Register Office – but Gerry wasn't quite sure how to broach the subject of her visit. She certainly didn't want Mrs Pollard to think she was looking for evidence of her daughter's wrongdoing, yet she could hardly lie and say she was checking a job reference. Should anything she learned from this visit become important in a court case, then a lie like that could easily get it dismissed. The visit would have to appear to be related to Blaydon's murder, which it was in a way, but without even the vaguest of hints that Charlotte Westlake might be responsible for that.

When Gerry introduced herself, Mrs Pollard asked to see her identification, which she studied closely for half a minute before handing it back. 'You can't be too careful these days, love,' she said. 'I had a bloke on the phone the other day telling me my bank account had been hijacked and asking for my details. He even knew the last three transactions I'd made on my Mastercard.'

'It's very sensible of you to be cautious,' said Gerry, following her inside. 'These scammers are getting very clever these days.'

'Now sit yourself down and tell me what it's all about,' said Mrs Pollard – or Lynne, as she asked Gerry to call her. But first, unlike her daughter, she offered tea, which Gerry was happy to accept after her drive.

Lynne Pollard disappeared into the kitchen and fussed for a while, while Gerry took the opportunity to examine the living room. She didn't remember seeing many photographs at Charlotte Westlake's house, just one of Charlotte and a man she assumed to be Gareth, her late husband, but Lynne Pollard more than made up for it. There were framed photographs of Charlotte's graduation, her wedding, Charlotte as a child and as a teenager (Gerry guessed), not to mention Charlotte with Adele and Charlotte with Daniel Craig. How these meetings had come about, Gerry had no idea. She was glad she had discovered that Charlotte was an only child, because any sibling visiting this shrine would go away with an enormous inferiority complex, if that wasn't an oxymoron.

Lynne Pollard came back with a teapot, cups and all the necessaries on a tray and perched at the edge of an armchair upholstered in what resembled a Laura Ashley pattern. She was a short plump woman with a recently permed head of blue-grey hair. Her face was round and relatively unlined, with a smooth pinkish complexion, small nose and a wobbly double-chin. She wore brown slacks, moccasin-style slippers and a loose beige cardigan over a white blouse. Apart from a couple of rings, the only jewellery she wore was a cross on a silver chain around her neck. She wore a little lipstick and a touch of rouge, but no mascara or eyeliner.

'You've got a nice view,' Gerry said.

'On a good day, yes. Cradle of the Industrial Revolution. That's what my husband used to say.'

Gerry happened to have discovered in her researches that Mr Pollard had died not terribly long after Charlotte Westlake's husband, but she thought it only polite to ask after him. 'Is your husband deceased?'

'Yes. Cyril passed on three and a half years back. Heart. Just like that. Went to bed one night, dead by morning. Never smoked in his life, took a one-hour constitutional every day, hardly touched a drop of alcohol except a small dry sherry at Christmas. It just goes to show you, doesn't it?'

Exactly what it went to show her, Gerry had no idea. Maybe that life was fleeting and one should enjoy every moment. Well, she tried to do that already.

Lynne Pollard stirred milk and sugar into the tea. 'So what's all this about? It's not every day I get a visit from a police detective.'

Gerry gestured towards the photographs. 'You must be very proud of your Charlotte,' she said.

'Christine,' Mrs Pollard corrected her. 'She was always Christine at home. And, yes, Cyril and I were terribly proud of her. She got into Oxford, you know. Oxford! The only girl from her school to do it in the year.'

'What about her career?'

'Oh, wonderful. You know she mixed with some of the most important, famous people you can imagine. Politicians, pop stars – there's her with Adele – you name it. If they needed something organising, they asked for Christine. Well, Charlotte, I suppose, as it was her *professional* name.'

'How did you feel when she went to work for Mr Blaydon?'

'Is that what this is about? Connor Blaydon?'

'You knew him?'

'Met him on a couple of occasions. Perfect gentleman. You know, there's been a lot of lies and slanders slung around about him since his death.'

'It was murder, Mrs Pollard, and I'm one of the officers investigating what happened.'

'We all know what happened, love. And it's Lynne. Those foreigners killed him, that's who. Wanted him to be part of their evil crime empire and he wouldn't have it. Turned them down flat.'

'Did Char—Christine tell you this?'

'Yes. She knew him well enough. Why haven't you arrested them yet, that's what I'd like to know?'

'They're on the run,' said Gerry.

'Then you'd better hurry up and catch them before we cut ourselves off from the Continent for good.'

Gerry didn't see any point in telling her that Albania wasn't yet a member of the EU. Not that it mattered much any more. 'Yes,' she said. 'It's Connor Blaydon's murder I came to talk to you about. Christine has been very helpful – as you say, she knew him best – but we wondered if you too could shed any light on his background, maybe fill in a few blanks?'

'I don't see how I can help you, love. He was Christine's friend.'

'Yes, but you met him. You said so.'

'Only on a couple of official occasions.'

'How long had Christine known him?'

'I know she did some events for him early on, when she was first in the business after university. Then she cut back a bit on the events when she married Gareth and it was after he died that she went to work for Mr Blaydon. But you already know that.'

'When did she leave university?'

'When she was twenty-one. 1998 that would have been.'

'And after that?'

'She went off travelling with her friends.'

Gerry remembered Charlotte saying something about going to Thailand and Vietnam, then the Mediterranean. 'For how long?'

'Nearly a year. She'd saved up a lot from her summer jobs, and it was something she'd always wanted to do.'

'So she came home when?'

'July, it would have been. July 1999.'

'And she lived with you here?'

'No. She had friends in Oxford and she stayed with them until she got herself fixed up with a job. Surely she could tell you all this. Her memory's probably a lot better than mine.'

'I don't think there's anything wrong with your memory. Besides, it's useful to get a different perspective. I'm especially interested in the time she spent abroad. Do you know where she was last, say, June that year?'

'1999? They were in Greece then.'

'Whereabouts?'

'I honestly don't remember exactly. Greek names. I've never been very good with those. Tell you what, though, just hang on a minute.'

Gerry heard her go upstairs, then the sound of cupboard doors opening and closing. A minute or so later, Lynne Pollard came back down with a cardboard box and put it on the low coffee table. As far as Gerry could tell, it was full of envelopes and postcards.

'I've kept everything she's ever sent me,' Lynne said. 'Every letter, every card, ever since she went on her first school exchange when she was fourteen.'

Gerry looked at the treasure trove of Charlotte Westlake's past and smiled at Lynne. 'Where shall we begin, then?' she asked.

Banks pulled up in the car park of Eastvale General Infirmary at three o'clock that afternoon and headed straight for the basement. The high-tiled corridor echoed as he walked along towards the autopsy suite and Dr Karen Galway's office.

Dr Galway was sitting at her L-shaped desk, which was piled high with file folders. She was wearing a powder-blue blouse, and her white coat was hanging from a hook behind the door. She had bright green eyes, a rather long nose, thin, tight lips, and a high domed forehead over which hung a fringe of greying hair. A framed print of Rembrandt's 'The Anatomy Lesson of Dr Nicolaes Tulp' hung on the wall opposite her desk. While Banks admired the artist's skill, he could think of any number of Rembrandt paintings he would rather have hanging on *his* wall.

'Catching up with paperwork?' he asked.

The doctor rolled her eyes and spoke with a trace of Dublin accent. 'Like you wouldn't believe.' She swivelled her chair to face him. 'Sit down, please. I wasn't expecting you. I heard you'd caught a nasty bump on the head.'

Banks sat. 'Two. I'd say it's an occupational hazard, but it really isn't. Must be the first time in years.'

'You saw Dr Chowdhury here?'

'Yes.'

'He's very good.'

'He looks about twelve.'

Dr Galway laughed. 'I'll tell him you said that. Actually, he's thirty-three. A graduate of the Faculty of Medicine, Imperial College London. By the way, aren't you supposed to be resting? It's customary for concussion sufferers to rest.'

'It was a couple of days ago. And I'm sitting down, aren't I?'

'You know what I mean.'

'I suppose I should still be resting, but in reality, life gets in the way. Or in this case, criminal investigation.'

'You have short-term memory loss, don't you?'

'What?'

'Very funny.'

'Yes. That's true, but there's nothing wrong with the rest of my memory.'

'I just didn't expect you to be back at work so soon, that's all.'

'We still have a missing person to find as well as a rape and murder to solve. I can't afford the luxury of rest at the moment.'

'In that case, what do you want to know?'

'Have you completed the post-mortems yet?'

'I was in at six o'clock this morning. There wasn't a lot left to work with. I've been as thorough as I know how, but I'd be the first to admit I'm not well experienced with burn victims. As a matter of fact, of all the bodies I have to perform post-mortems on, they disturb me the most. I'm not shirking my duty or making excuses, you understand, just being honest. And if you think you need a second opinion, I wouldn't hesitate to call in an expert in the field I know in Edinburgh. He's worked in various war zones around the world, so he's more than acquainted with the properties of fire. I worked with him briefly in Iraq several years ago, and he handled most of the tough burn cases.'

'I hardly think that will be necessary. What have you found out?'

'The damage was quite advanced in both cases, and the remains are very fragile. Fire causes any number of changes to the human body – blistering, skin splits, exposure and rendering of subcutaneous fat. Then the muscles that overlie the bones retract when they're exposed to extreme heat. That's what causes the so-called pugilistic position often found in burn victims. What I'm saying is that kind of damage makes it almost impossible to identify any pre-fire trauma the victim might have been exposed to.'

'So you can't say if either of them was shot, stabbed or bashed on the head?'

'I didn't say that. The skin, flesh and fat are gone. So badly damaged by fire and by being transported here that they won't tell me what happened. But if the victim had been shot, I would expect to find a bullet – if not the hole it made – and if he was bashed over the head, as you so eloquently put it, I would expect damage to the skull indicating that, unless it exploded from the inside, of course.'

'Of course,' said Banks, feeling momentarily sick. 'Have you?'

'No. Stab wounds are particularly difficult, for example. Because the skin blisters and splits in fire, and the inner organs are consumed, any trace of an original knife wound in flesh would probably be erased. On the other hand, if the knife came into contact with a bone, then there could be evidence of that contact on the bone.'

'A notch?'

'That kind of thing, yes.'

'And is there?'

'On one of the bodies, yes.'

'Which one?'

'The one on the lower level.' Dr Galway twisted in her chair and pointed to a spot on her back. 'Fifth rib, posterior left.'

'Meaning?'

'There's a slight nick on the bone that could be a knife mark. I'll be further analysing and measuring it, of course, and may soon be able to tell you something about the weapon that caused it. But don't get your hopes up too high. It's a tiny nick and there could be other reasons it's there.'

'What would the result of such a wound be?'

'Most likely, depending on the angle and the length of the blade, it would have pierced the lung.'

'Would the killer, assuming there was one, have needed expert knowledge?'

'Not necessarily. He wouldn't have had to be a trained commando. It could have just been a lucky stab. Lucky for the killer, I mean. An expert would have known exactly what he was doing, of course, but that knowledge wasn't essential to the deed.'

It was Keane, Banks knew. Zelda had stabbed him twice in the back. He had witnessed it. 'And the other victim?'

'No sign of knife wounds, but I wouldn't rule it out.'

'Did they both die in the flames?'

'Impossible to say. They were both so badly burned that it wasn't possible to measure smoke inhalation. I'm sorry to be so vague, but it's well-nigh impossible to determine these things from the remains we had left.'

'Can you get DNA?'

'The sixty-four-thousand-dollar question.'

'Can you?'

'It's possible. Bones can be quite durable when all else is burned beyond recognition. The DNA may be degraded or contaminated, but there's a good chance it won't be. These bones are only semi-burned in places, especially the ones found on the upper level, not black or blue-grey, so there's still hope. The teeth, too, could be a possible source. I'm working on it with Dr Jasminder Singh from your forensics lab. There is just one more thing.'

It was probably the answer to the question Banks had been afraid to ask. 'Yes?'

'The pelvic bones were badly burned but still held their shape. Both victims were male.'

16

Banks had hardly been in his office ten minutes before a sharp rap at the door was followed by AC Gervaise and Superintendent Newry.

'What the hell are you doing here?' Newry demanded.

Banks turned down the Thea Gilmore CD he had been listening to. 'My job,' he said.

'I thought I made it clear to you that you were off the case until further notice.'

'You did nothing of the kind.'

'Don't play clever buggers with me, Banks. I already know you've visited the treatment plant, and talked to Dr Galway at the mortuary.'

'I dropped by both. True.'

'And asked her about the fire victims' post-mortems?'

'Also true.'

'I'm within a hair's breadth of suspending you from—'

'Superintendent Newry!' said AC Gervaise. 'A little restraint, please. There have been no complaints against Superintendent Banks. He hasn't been accused of any wrongdoing.'

'Not yet. But what if I accuse him? I've got two victims whose deaths are unaccounted for. There's a chain secured to a radiator in the upstairs staffroom, and it looks as if someone was restrained there. Ropes on the lower floor were most likely used for the same purpose. Your man here was found unconscious outside the building in question without any reasonable explanation.'

'You think I chained someone to the radiator, then tied myself up, stabbed someone and set the place on fire?' Banks said. 'When did I do all that?'

Newry turned to AC Gervaise. 'Detective Superintendent Banks can't account for his whereabouts or his actions during the time the events unfolded in the water treatment plant, and he was found on the premises by the firefighters, with forensic evidence to prove he was at some point *inside* the plant. He claims to have lost his memory—'

'Claims?' said Banks. 'You don't believe me?'

'Let's just say I have my doubts,' Newry snarled. 'I've told you what I think of these memory-loss cases. It's just a bit too bloody convenient, isn't it?'

'Not for me. And don't you think you should leave your prejudices at the door?'

Newry looked at Gervaise. 'Do you permit this kind of insubordination under your command, Chief Superintendent?'

Gervaise glanced between the two of them. 'Superintendent Newry,' she said. 'With all due respect, I expect any officer under my command to push back when unnecessarily provoked, and when it comes to the truth, I am still inclined to believe someone is innocent until proven guilty. All in all, I prefer to take the word of one of my most trusted detectives over that of a . . . a . . .'

'How about a jumped-up little Hitler?' Banks suggested.

Gervaise shot him a stern glance. 'That's enough from you, Superintendent Banks. That's not helpful. Let's just all calm down and have a rational look at this situation.'

Newry sneered. 'Well, fortunately, *with respect*, ma'am, what happens next doesn't depend on what you think,' he said.

'Then go talk to the chief constable.'

'Believe me, I intend to. I'm not letting go of this.' With a hard, angry look at both Banks and Gervaise, Newry pushed his chair back roughly and stalked out. 'We'll be talking again. Soon.'

'There goes a man in search of a heart attack,' said Banks. 'I hate to think what his blood pressure must be like.'

'Don't be so bloody flippant, Alan. Don't you understand what a predicament you're in? For Christ's sake, Newry wants you suspended. ACC McLaughlin and I are fighting in your corner, but we're running out of steam, and you're not helping by giving ammunition to the opposition, if you'll forgive me a mixed metaphor. I want you to take sick leave. As of now. Lord knows, you're due enough.'

'Gardening leave?'

'It's *sick* leave, Alan. Not suspension. Because you sustained an injury on the job. We'll leave the insurance claims and whatnot for later. This is the best compromise we can come up with right now. Even the chief constable is on side with this. You know as well as I do that an officer can be suspended for months, even years, without resolution, for no reason at all. Newry hardly needs a solid case to scupper what's left of your career. But sick leave . . . Your doctor also agrees it would be advantageous in combatting stress and shock.'

'But what about Zelda? She's still out there. I've got a responsibility to her. And to Ray. And what about the Blaydon—'

'You're not the only detective in the station. Don't you trust your team?'

'Of course I do, it's just—'

'You want to be in the know. You want to be in control. All right, I understand. We'll keep you in the loop.' She paused. 'Is that good enough?'

Banks sighed and gathered his things together. 'It'll have to be, won't it?'

Banks's headache and dizziness returned with a vengeance before he had even managed to pull the Porsche into his driveway. He hurried upstairs to his medicine cabinet, took three extra-strength paracetamol and went to lie down on his bed. The dizziness soon passed, but the headache persisted until the drugs wrapped it in cotton wool and pushed it away to a far, quiet corner of his brain.

It was too early to go to sleep, and he wasn't tired, so he got up and went back downstairs into the small study-cum-sitting room at the front, sat down at his desktop computer, answered a few long-overdue emails and browsed Apple Music for anything new. There wasn't anything he desperately wanted, so he went through to the kitchen, made himself a toasted cheese sandwich and went into the conservatory to eat. Outside his windows, the shadows were lengthening, and clouds blanketed the peak of Tetchley Fell. He could hear sheep bleating high on the hillside.

As he ate, he considered his position. He had to accept the sick leave. Chief Superintendent Gervaise, his area commander, and ACC Ron McLaughlin were going out on a limb for him, and it would be ungrateful to do otherwise, not to mention hammering another nail in the coffin of his career. Whether you were guilty or not, suspensions and IOPC investigations had a nasty way of sticking to your record like shit to a shoe. They guaranteed entry into a Kafkaesque world from which you were bound to emerge – if you emerged at all – a changed and probably broken man. The brass bullied and lied, cliques closed ranks, punishments were decided upon and meted out before judgement was passed, hopefuls queued up at the bottom of the greasy pole leading to your job, federation or superintendents' association reps objected and waved their hands in the air, and things marched irrevocably on towards that fateful gate where all who enter must abandon hope. The streets and shelters were littered with discarded detectives. You would have more hope of success as a refugee begging asylum from Priti Patel than you would as an honest copper dragged deep into the maw of an internal investigation.

So, sick leave. What was he going to do with himself? He wasn't going to sit at home and be sick, that was for certain. How did things stand right now? That was the place to start. Banks finished his sandwich and poured a glass of wine. Then he put on a Jerry Garcia Band concert from Lunt-Fontanne, New York, October 1987, and settled back to relax. The nice balance of versions of old Motown numbers, Hunter/Garcia originals and Dylan classics was just right, laid-back yet uplifting. And Jerry was in great form.

He was almost certain that he had his full memory of the lost night back now. Just to be clear, he ran through the series of events in chronological order several times in his mind until they felt right. He supposed he wouldn't know if anything was missing unless he sensed an absence, but as he didn't, he accepted this version as the truth.

What it meant was that Zelda was out in the wind somewhere. He had deliberately not told anyone yet about the return of his memory in order to give her as much time as possible to get as far away as she could. He knew he shouldn't approve of her vigilantism, that people taking personal revenge for ills done to them was the beginning of a very slippery slope, but he couldn't help himself. He also realised that in giving her time to get far away he was aiding and abetting a murderer escape, but he decided he didn't care.

If Zelda had killed Goran and Petar Tadić, she had had good reason, and she had killed Keane in order to save Banks's life.

She didn't have to do that. She could have crept out of some other exit, the way she had obviously done after she had cut him free and the fire started. But she had risked her own life to save Banks from Keane, just the way Annie and Winsome had done that first time, back in Newhope Cottage. Many more instances like that, he realised, and he'd be getting worried about his masculinity. Wasn't he supposed to be the one doing the saving?

The upshot was that he couldn't throw Zelda to the dogs, no matter what. And if he were honest with himself, he liked her too much to do that. And worried what it would do to Ray.

So should he spend his sick leave trying to find her? He thought perhaps not. Zelda was resourceful, and if she wanted to disappear, she would. No doubt, when he admitted to getting his memory back and told Newry as much of the truth as he could get away with, there would be a police search for her, perhaps involving Europol. How intense and long-lasting it would be, he had no idea. It wasn't only the police. The Tadićs hadn't worked alone; they weren't even the heads of their organisation. There might be other criminal gang members on Zelda's trail, too, and no doubt they would put a price on her head. The last thing Banks wanted to do was lead them to her. Zelda had her contacts; she knew how to disappear. And if she wanted to get in touch with Ray after some time had passed, then she would find a way.

When it came to the Tadićs, Banks realised there was one thing he could do. He remembered Burgess telling him about the arm they'd found with the Croatian gang tattoos, and the faint possibility that it might belong to the missing Goran Tadić. If Jazz Singh could get a DNA sample from the burned body in the upstairs room of the treatment plant, then it might be worth checking it against the arm.

He phoned the lab and found she was still there.

'Jazz, if you compare two DNA samples, can you tell whether the people were brothers?'

'Without going into a lot of complicated detail, yes, probably,' said Jazz. 'Full siblings share around fifty per cent of their DNA. Why?'

'Would you do me a favour and compare a sample from the body in the treatment plant, the upstairs one, with a sample I'll get Detective Superintendent Burgess from the NCA to send you?'

'I can do that, yes.'

'Thanks, Jazz.'

'Is this on the abduction case budget?'

'Yes.' Banks didn't tell her that he was on sick leave and wasn't supposed to be ordering DNA tests.

Next, he phoned Burgess, who agreed to get a sample sent up for comparison. At least that would tell them whether the bodies were brothers, which meant in all likelihood that they were Goran and Petar Tadić.

Banks let his mind drift back to the treatment plant to see if he could remember how Zelda had seemed. He hadn't been able to tell if she was hurt because he hadn't got a good look at her. She had crept up behind Keane from the shadows and stabbed him. After that, with the flames and smoke, it was soon chaos. She had come close enough to him to cut through the ropes that were binding him, close enough for him to smell her breath, and he hadn't noticed anything to indicate that she had been hurt, then she had shouted for him to run. And she had taken off by herself. But she had found time to phone emergency services about the fire, perhaps because she was worried about him. She could be anywhere now. Mostly, Banks hoped she'd had time to get out of the country. She would have a far better chance of disappearing in mainland Europe.

And what about Ray? Maybe there was a way he could let Ray know she was OK without giving too much away about what happened, but he didn't know how. However he did it, it would mean lying to his friend. If Ray knew the truth, he would fret that she would never come back to him, or that she would be caught and put in jail if she did. On the other hand, if he told Ray nothing, he would assume all was lost and sink deeper into depression.

But so much depended, Banks realised, on him keeping his cool. He would have to stop putting Newry off, simply tell him he'd got his memory back, submit to an official interview and give him a version that worked for everyone.

Especially Zelda.

Late that evening, Banks was listening to Jessye Norman singing French songs when he heard a loud knocking at his door. Edgy since the attack, he picked up a knife from the kitchen as he went to answer it, only to find Ray Cabbot standing there, not too steady on his feet. Ray lurched forward and almost fell into Banks's arms – not to mention the blade of the knife – when the door opened. As he helped Ray in, Banks glanced out front and saw his car parked at an awkward angle. The bloody fool had driven over, despite the state he was in. Or probably because of it, Banks speculated.

Once Ray was inside, he seemed to steady himself and followed Banks down the hall and through the kitchen to the conservatory where Banks had been sitting. He walked with the exaggerated gait of a drunk pretending to be sober.

'Got a drink?' he asked.

Banks certainly didn't think he needed one, but he was the last person to be moralistic or judgemental about drinking. Instead, he poured Ray a decent measure of Highland Park and himself a generous glass of Gigondas, his first of the day.

'Whass this music?' Ray asked.

'Debussy songs. Why, don't you like it?'

''S'all right, I suppose. Bit artsy-fartsy.'

Banks used his phone to change the stream. Instead of Duparc's 'L'invitation au voyage' there came Tim Buckley's *Blue Afternoon*. 'That do you?' he said.

'I suppose it'll have to.'

'What is it, Ray?' Banks asked. 'What's wrong?'

Ray took a hefty wallop of scotch. 'You know what it is. It's Zelda. I miss her.' He put his head in his hands. 'Oh, God, Alan, I miss her like I can't say.'

'I'm sorry, Ray. I'm sure she'll be back.' As he tried to reassure Ray, Banks went over his strategy in his mind. He could tell him only so much of the truth if he hoped to do him any good at all.

'You know what happened, don't you?' Ray said. 'You didn't tell me anything on the phone yesterday. You said you felt ill, and I gave you time to recover. But you know now, don't you? And I'm here, begging you. You remember, don't you? Tell me. Is she all right? Where is she?'

'I remember most of it now,' said Banks, 'and I'll tell you what I can.'

Ray handed over his empty glass and Banks went into the kitchen to refill it. His own glass was still over half-full. Back in the conservatory, they sat at right angles to one another by the round glass table. The twilit sky outside was indigo and a dim orange-shade table lamp provided the only other light in the room.

'Well? Is she all right?' Ray prompted him.

'Depends what you mean by "all right",' Banks said. 'I only saw her very briefly, and things were . . . a little hectic.'

'Was she hurt?'

'Not that I could see.'

'How did she look?'

'Fine, Ray. She hadn't been harmed in any way. Just kept there against her will for a few days. She'd had a terrifying experience. No doubt she'd have liked to be able to brush her teeth, change her clothes and have a nice long shower, but other than that . . . whoever it was hadn't hurt her.'

'Thank God for that. Did you talk to her? What did she say?'

'There was hardly time for conversation. The bloody building was on fire. We had to get out of there. But she said to tell you not to worry, that she'd get in touch, and she would be back when she could.'

'She's coming back?'

'I'm sure she'll come when she can. But don't tell anyone.'

'Why can't she come now?'

'I don't know. There are things she has to deal with.'

'What things?'

'She didn't say.'

'When will she be back? Did she say that?'

'She didn't. But her situation here, the people who took her—'

'Where are they? Are they still after her?'

'They're dead,' said Banks. 'In the fire.'

'Thank God for that. So why can't she come home?'

'She will. It's just a matter of time.' Ray reached for his tobacco, looked at Banks and halted. Banks just nodded. 'Go on.' Ray emptied his glass again and Banks went and poured him another refill, a smaller one this time. If he had anything to do with it, Ray wasn't driving anywhere tonight. Tim Buckley was singing 'I Must Have Been Blind'.

Ray lit up. 'I'll go anywhere she wants. You know that. Just tell her that.'

'I'm not in communication with her, Ray,' Banks said. 'I don't know where she is.'

'But she got away? You're sure of it?'

'Yes. She got away.'

'Where might she have gone?'

'I don't know. She might have gone overseas. It was getting a bit too hot for her over here.'

'Those two bastards from the NCA. And she was worried about immigration. But she's got friends there. All over the place. She'll be all right there. How long do you think? I'll go to her wherever she wants. France. Italy. Spain. Greece. Even fucking Moldova, if I have to.'

Banks couldn't help but smile. 'I have no idea. As long as it takes. I'm sure she'll be in touch when she can.'

Ray took a drag on his cigarette and drank some more whisky. 'Then I'll try to carry on as normal,' he said, nodding his head as if in agreement with some inner decision. 'Get on with my work. Right? Just wait for her to come back. It's what she would want.' He tapped his glass. 'And cut back on the drinking a bit.'

'That's the best plan. You've got to stop stressing yourself out. It'll make you ill.'

'What about these people who are after her?'

'They're dead, Ray. I told you. Don't worry about them.'

'Who killed them? Not . . . no?'

'No,' said Banks. 'Not Zelda. We think they went for each other. A falling-out among thieves.'

'You're sure she got away, got out of there?'

'Yes, Ray. Zelda saved my life. I was tied up. She cut me free. That's when she told me to tell you she'd be back. After that, the fire was starting to spread fast, so she pushed me towards the exit. She went out by another door and drove off. Their car must have been parked there. I heard her go. Simple as that. The CSIs found two burned bodies in the place, both male. They can tell by the bones.'

'Are they chasing her?'

'Who?'

'Anyone. The police. The other bad guys. There must have been more than two. She'll be terrified if she's on the run.'

'She's had plenty of time to get far enough away,' said Banks. 'Sure, the police would like to talk to her in connection with the fire, as they've been talking to me. But she didn't start it. Phil Keane did that. And I'll make it clear to anyone who questions me that Zelda and I were victims, that she didn't kill anyone. They'll come to their senses. And I told you, the bad guys are dead. Maybe there are more, but without their leaders, they'll scatter to the four winds. Zelda's safe, Ray. I'm sure of it.'

If Zelda had half the brains Banks credited her with, she would have dumped the car in a long-term airport car park, then taken a train or shuttle to another nearby airport and flown out. She might even have risked the Eurostar. If he were to guess, Paris would be her first choice of destination. It was the last place she had lived for any length of time before coming to England and meeting Ray, and she probably still had friends and contacts there. She would need money, transportation, an escape plan.

Ray stood up and attempted a sloppy embrace, then said, 'I'd better be off now. Thanks, mate.' He held up his tumbler. 'And for the whisky.'

'Off where?'

'Home, of course.'

'You're not driving anywhere, the shape you're in. You can either sleep it off in my spare room or I'll drive you home myself.' Banks still hadn't finished his first glass of wine. 'Or I'll call you a taxi.'

'Whatever,' said Ray. 'Though I think I should be at home, shouldn't I, just in case she comes back? I mean, as you said, she might come home any time. I wouldn't want her to get back to an empty house. But a taxi will take for ever.'

'I suppose you're right,' Banks said, getting up. 'I'll drive you. You can leave your car here. Get a taxi here and pick it up tomorrow.'

As he drove back home after dropping Ray off, Banks thought he would try to find out something about Zelda's life in Paris; maybe knowing more about her time there would help him find her. He didn't want to find her for the police, but for himself, and for Ray. He wanted what he had told his friend this evening to be true. He locked and bolted the front door and went back to his chair in the conservatory, put the Tim Buckley back on where he had paused it, at 'Blue Melody'.

As he sat and thought, he realised that already in his mind he was separating himself from the police, almost as if he were no longer one of them. Planning escape routes for fugitives was hardly something the old Banks would have done. What was happening to him? After all these years, had it come to this? In some ways it was as if a great weight had been lifted off him, but in another it was like dipping a toe into uncharted waters, not knowing where they would lead or what lay beneath their murky depths.

17

It was the first timc Banks had been on the other side of the interview table since his training days at Hendon. They had sent a car for him that afternoon, shortly after Ray had been back to pick up his car. Opposite him sat Superintendent Newry and beside Newry a female DI he introduced as Heidi Dunne. As far as Banks could gather, DI Dunne's role was to hand sheets of paper to Newry and to look disapproving, both of which she did very well. The conversation was between Banks and Newry, and even the solicitor sitting next to Banks kept out of it. Reg Courtenay was an old veteran of police affairs, and Banks wanted him there as a precaution. There were no charges against him, nor was he suspended, though this interview was being recorded, he wasn't under caution and was still being treated as a witness only.

'I understand you have regained your memory of the night in question,' Newry began, the sneer of disbelief clear in his tone, as if what he really meant to say was, 'Now you've got your story clear.'

'Bit by bit. It's still a bit blurry in parts, but yes, I remember most of what happened.'

'Perhaps you can help us, then?'

'I'll try.'

'I think you should know before we begin that my main concern, and that of DI Dunne here, who will be forming part of the active investigation team into this matter, is the discovery of two bodies in the burned-out water treatment plant on the eastern outskirts of Eastvale.'

'As I said, I'll help as much as I can.'

'Excellent.' DI Dunne shuffled some papers and Newry said, 'Perhaps you can begin by telling us about the events leading up to your abduction?'

'I was on my way home from a concert at the Sage in Gateshead. My son plays in a band and this was a part of their farewell tour.'

'I know about the Blue Lamps,' said Newry.

'That evening, they had played one of my favourite songs, Bob Dylan's "Visions of Johanna", at my son's instigation, and on my way home I listened to the original album, *Blonde on Blonde*.'

'I don't give a fuck what music you were listening to.'

If he hadn't guessed before, Banks knew at that moment there was no way he and Newry would ever get along. 'It helps if I pick up the threads,' Banks replied. 'If I jump in the story much later, it's far fuzzier in my memory for some reason. And you *did* ask for the events leading up to my abduction.'

Newry grunted. DI Dunne looked disapproving, not to mention disbelieving. 'Carry on,' Newry said.

'Thank you. *Blonde on Blonde*. Terrific album, by the way. You should try it some time. When I turned into my driveway and pulled up in front of my cottage, I noticed that the outside light wasn't working.'

'Someone had removed the bulb,' Newry said. 'There were fingerprints around the socket, but they're not on our files anywhere.'

'Probably Tadić or one of his minions,' Banks said.

'And another possible suspect,' Newry added. 'Minions have been known to murder their bosses from time to time.'

'I should imagine so,' Banks said. 'I used the light on my mobile, opened the door – or got the key in the lock, at least – and that's the last thing I remember before a sharp pain at the back of my head, then waking up in the plant. But even that was very hazy for the first couple of days.'

'Did you have any idea where you were?' Newry asked.

'Not at first, no. I'm no expert on water treatment, so I didn't recognise the purpose of the abandoned machinery, the pumps and pipes and so on. And it was dark. Not completely, but certainly not well-lit enough to recognise where I was. Only later, when I ran outside, did it become clear. But I get ahead of myself.'

'Sorry. Go on.'

'When I came to, I was on my side on a hard floor with my ankles tied together and my legs bent back at the knees. A rope from my ankles was also attached to my neck so that if I tried to—'

'A variation of the hog-tie, I understand.'

'Precisely. My hands were also tied behind me.'

'Were you on the upper level at any time, where the offices are?'

'No. Just down in the operating area.'

'Was anyone else present?'

'Yes. A man I knew as Phil Keane. He'd lately been going under the name of Hugh Foley, and he had been connected with a woman called Faye Butler, found dead in the Thames a few weeks ago.'

DI Dunne leaned over and whispered something in Newry's ear, never taking her eyes off Banks. 'Did you think this Keane was responsible for Faye Butler's death?' Newry asked.

'No. Keane likes fire. I put her death down to Tadić and his crew, the people Keane worked for.'

'I understand that Faye Butler wasn't your case,' Newry went on, 'but why do you think she was killed?'

'I think she was tortured for information, then raped and murdered.'

'What information?'

'Of that I have no idea. Something the Tadićs wanted an answer for, I'm sure.'

'What happened next?'

'Keane started splashing petrol around my feet and on the floor around where I was lying. While he was doing that he admitted to me that he had killed an NCA agent called Trevor Hawkins, who had been Zelda's – Ms Melnic's – boss at the department where she worked. He set fire to his house.'

'How did that come up?'

'What do you mean?'

'Did he just come out with it, out of the blue, so to speak, or was there a context?'

'I asked him. He'd mentioned something about the Tadićs, and I asked him what happened. Zelda had been getting a hard time about her boss's death from the NCA, so I wanted to know.'

'OK. So this Keane tells you he set fire to this man Hawkins's house, working on behalf of the Tadićs. Did he say why they had wanted this done?'

'Only that Hawkins was taking their money and giving them crap in exchange. It's my guess that he'd been tipping them off about possible raids, border checks and so on, but he'd either started to get cold feet, or he'd become greedy and given them dud information.'

'Quite the conversation you had.'

'You asked me. Some of it's conjecture. Besides, all the time he was talking, he was splashing petrol around. It was pretty obvious that it was meant for me, and I could hardly move. I figured my time was up and the best thing to do was keep him talking as long as I could. He knew this, so he said something about it not working, that he wasn't going to confess all just to keep me alive, even if I wasn't going to be around to tell anyone.'

'So what happened next?'

'That's all still a bit of a blur. Something happened. He stiffened. The fire flared up. I thought that was it, but the next thing I knew someone was cutting my ropes and telling me to run.'

'Someone?'

'Nelia Melnic.'

'Ah, the mysterious Zelda. Let me get this straight. She suddenly appeared in the room, incapacitated Keane and cut you free?'

'That's right.'

'How did she incapacitate Keane?'

'I don't know. Knocked him out, I should imagine.'

'But she had a knife.'

'She must have had, to cut me free. As I said, it gets a bit blurry. Maybe she took it from Keane?'

'Who started the fire?'

'I don't know that, either. I couldn't see. Keane, I should think. He was the one with the petrol and the lighter in his hand.'

'But you said this Zelda had knocked him out.'

'He wasn't completely out. Just dazed, I think.'

'Did you ever see Petar Tadić at any time you were in the plant?'

'No.'

'So he didn't suddenly come in and stab Keane and set the place on fire?'

'Not that I know of. If he did, I didn't see him.'

'Only there was forensic evidence of a knife wound on one of Keane's ribs.'

'So I heard. I didn't see a knife at the time. And I'm not sure the evidence of knife wounds on burned bones is conclusive.'

'Is that what Dr Galway told you? But we've already established that this Zelda must have had a knife to cut your bonds. And given the nick on the victim's rear rib, doesn't that seem to indicate that the one is connected to the other?'

'It doesn't necessarily follow. And Keane was hardly the victim, as you put it.'

'As far as I'm concerned he's a victim.'

'It's all a bit hazy, and it happened so fast. Zelda had her back to me. She was struggling with Keane. He'd lurched at her. I was disentangling myself from the last of my bonds that she'd just cut. Then the fire flared up.'

'So she still had the knife in her hand?'

'I don't know what happened to it, I just didn't see it. I had other things on my mind. Like getting the hell out of there. It was chaos. The fire was spreading. Keane was burning by then. Writhing and screaming.'

'By when?'

'By the time I was ready to run.'

'So he was still alive?'

'Yes.'

'The pathologist said it was impossible to check the body for smoke inhalation.'

'He was still alive when the fire started. He must have burned to death in the flames. Or he died of shock. I don't know.'

'Or this Zelda stabbed him.'

'I have no knowledge of any stab wound. But if she did, I'd say it was self-defence.'

'Well, unfortunately, you're not the one to be pronouncing on that.'

'But I was there. I know what I saw.'

'Come on, Superintendent. You can't have it both ways. Either it was chaos, and you don't know what happened, or it wasn't, and you do. Which was it?'

'I don't know. Both maybe. A lot of confusion.'

Newry scowled at DI Dunne, who continued to look disapproving. 'Are you sure you didn't see the woman stab Keane?'

'No, I didn't see anything like that. You keep going on about this knife. Did you find one at the scene?'

'No. She must have taken it with her. Are you sure *she* didn't start the fire?'

'I told you, she was struggling with Keane. I think she was trying to stop him. I couldn't see what he was doing because she was blocking my view.'

'Ah, yes, and the lighter went off mysteriously?'

'You must have found it, or what was left of it.'

'I'm afraid that doesn't tell us a great deal. Is it true that this girl is a friend of yours?'

'A friend of a friend. I know her. Yes.'

'You were searching for her, right?'

'Yes. She'd been abducted from her home three days before.'

'By these men Tadić and Keane?'

'A witness was able to give us a good description of Tadić in the vicinity of Zelda's cottage, but there's no evidence that Keane was involved in her actual abduction. Or mine. Talk to my team about it, or to AC Gervaise, why don't you? They know more than I do.'

'I'm not too sure about that, but I will, don't worry. You tracked this woman, Zelda, to the treatment plant, right?'

'No. You haven't been listening. I told you. I was knocked out and taken there. We had no idea where she was being held. We still had people out searching the moors.'

'Do you like this Zelda?'

'What kind of a question is that?'

DI Dunne gave Banks another disapproving glance. 'Just answer me, please,' Newry said.

'I admire her. Yes. She's had a difficult life.'

'And are you attracted to her? Is your interest in any way sexual?'

For the first time, old Reg Courtenay dragged himself out of his shell of silence and tut-tutted Newry. DI Dunne somehow managed to communicate even more disapproval. Banks said nothing.

'What happened to the girl?' Newry asked.

'I don't know. She must have gone out a different way. I think there was a car out by the side of the building, in what used to be the staff car park. Maybe it was Tadić's or Keane's.' He shrugged. 'I don't know.'

'So she stole a car to make her escape?'

'If you put it like that.'

'I don't know how else I should put it. Did you see this car? Did you know this at the time?'

'No. I'm just speculating. The CSIs found traces of a vehicle recently parked out there. Oil stains. It makes sense. Otherwise, where did she go?'

'That's what we'd all like to know. I was about to ask you the very same question.'

'I wish I knew,' said Banks.

'Why? So you could go and join her?'

Reg Courtenay tut-tutted again.

'Did you see or hear her drive off?' Newry went on.

'Listening for a car was hardly the main thing on my mind. I ran for my life, ended up in the reservoir unconscious again. I might have heard a motor running, but I can't be sure. The fire itself was noisy enough.'

'So the girl cut you free, but you just left her there, in the burning building?'

'It wasn't like that,' said Banks. 'I was still woozy from being hit on the head. She cut my ropes and yelled for me to run. I assumed she'd be running with me, or not far behind. When I realised she wasn't there, I tried to go back in, but I couldn't get any further than the entrance. The fire was raging too hard, and there was plenty of smoke by then.'

'What did you think had happened?'

'That she'd either got out by some other exit or that she was dead. It all happened so quickly. I wasn't thinking very clearly.'

'So you just ran off?'

'Yes. And I fell in the reservoir, where they found me. Hit my head again. If it hadn't been for the bed of weeds, I'd probably be dead. What the hell else was I supposed to do? Go back inside the plant and burn to death?'

Newry waved his hand. 'Sorry. I wasn't meaning to imply anything.'

'Like hell you weren't. The forensic evidence corroborates what I've told you.'

'Up to a point.'

'Is there anything else?'

'Not that I can think of. Not at the moment. DI Dunne?'

DI Dunne pursed her lips and shook her head.

Banks stood up. 'Right then. As I'm still on sick leave, and I'm feeling sicker by the minute, I'll go home now.' He nodded farewell to the others in the room and left.

18

Two days passed uneventfully, and Banks whiled away his time reading, gardening and listening to music – from Mahler's symphonies to Jon Savage's sixties compilation CDs. There were moments when he thought that if this was what not having to work was all about, then it wasn't such a bad thing at all. Other times he felt edgy and restless, longing for some obscure mystery he could sink his teeth into.

The missing persons search for Zelda was effectively over, and now the police wanted to talk to her in connection with the fire at the water treatment plant in which two people had died. Banks trusted that she was far enough away and well enough hidden that they wouldn't find her. Newry believed that she had killed both men, or that Banks had, but Newry wasn't on the investigating team. He was IOPC, and his job was over. The Homicide and Major Crimes team from Durham was tackling the case now. Banks had talked to them and told them what he knew, or as much as he wanted them to know, and it was out of his hands now. He was exonerated. Newry could gripe to his heart's content about the presence of a knife at the scene, a nick on a bone that might possibly indicate a stab wound and the matter of who struck the lighter that started the fire, but it no longer mattered what Newry thought, as what forensic evidence they had supported Banks's story and none of it implicated him. In addition, Banks's injuries, including the memory loss, were verified by Dr Chowdhury and proven to be commensurate with the physical circumstances of his abduction and incarceration.

From the bits and pieces Banks had heard, he got the impression that Zelda wasn't too high on their list of priorities; they seemed to be concentrating more on the Tadić gang's criminal concerns and on Keane's part in them. Gashi, too, was on their radar, his whereabouts unknown, and the disappearance of Goran Tadić was still an issue, albeit a minor one, as he wasn't regarded as much of a loss.

One interesting piece of information, supplied by Jazz Singh at Banks's request, was that a comparison between the DNA from the human arm found at the landfill site near Croydon and that from the body found on the upper floor of the burned-out water treatment plant gave a high indication that the two were siblings. Goran and Petar Tadić, Banks guessed, though there was no absolute proof, as neither was in any DNA database. The corpse's DNA also matched that of the cigarette ends found near Windlee Farm. As they presumably belonged to the man Mick Slater described and Ray Cabbot sketched, the corpse was identified by Superintendent Burgess as Petar Tadić.

But a man can only do so much reading and gardening, and on the second day of his sick leave, Banks made a few phone calls, and on the third, he took an early train from York.

'This is the second time you've had me brought up here,' Charlotte Westlake complained as Gerry tended to the recording equipment in the interview room and Annie settled down in her chair late that afternoon. 'I hope you've got a damn good reason.'

'Be careful, or you might get what you hope for,' said Annie.

'Wait,' said Charlotte. 'As the officer who *arrested* me and brought me here suggested, I requested my solicitor to meet me, so I would be grateful if you would please wait until she arrives. She won't be long.'

Annie and Gerry exchanged glances, then they left a young constable on guard and went down to the canteen for a cup of tea while they waited. Coffee at Costa would have been preferable to weak canteen tea, but they didn't want to leave the station. They had already planned the strategy of the interview, such as it was, the previous evening in the Queen's Arms. Gerry had uncovered more than enough information from her talk with Charlotte's mother and the box of letters and postcards Lynne Pollard had been only too happy to share. The rest had come from the General Register and the various databases available to her online. If she was right about some of the conclusions she had reached, based on scraps of information picked up here and there, Gerry was sure that Charlotte would paint herself into a corner from which the only way out was the truth.

As yet, Annie and Gerry didn't know what that truth was, and the possibilities kept shifting with the information coming in. When all they had was a number of inspired guesses, planning a strategy became that much more difficult. They would have to improvise from time to time. The basis for Charlotte Westlake's arrest – suspicion of murder – was probably a bit far-fetched, Gerry would be the first to admit, but it was a means of bringing her in and throwing her off guard. It would also allow them to keep her in custody for twenty-four hours if necessary.

Charlotte's solicitor, Jessica Bowen, turned up twenty minutes later and after a ten-minute huddle with her client, then they all settled down in the airless room. Gerry got the recording equipment working and made the introductions.

'Are we all sitting comfortably?' asked Annie. When the reply was silence, she said, 'Then I'll begin.'

Jessica Bowen gave her a stern glance for the frivolous *Children's Hour* opening.

'Mrs Westlake,' said Annie, 'was Marnie Sedgwick your daughter?'

Clearly, whatever Charlotte Westlake had been expecting, it wasn't this. She seemed like an animal desperate to escape its cage, squirming in her chair, turning pale, looking towards her solicitor one moment then back to her questioner the next. 'Wha . . .? How do . . .?' Gerry wondered how on earth she thought that they wouldn't discover this information. More burying her head in the sand? Naive or stupid?

'Simple enough question,' said Annie, ignoring the reaction. 'Can you please give me an answer?'

Charlotte took a deep breath and struggled to regain her equilibrium. Her lawyer gave her the nod to continue. 'Technically, I suppose, yes, she is,' she said.

'Technically?'

'I'm her birth mother, but as you clearly know already, I gave her up for adoption. Her true parents are the ones who brought her up.'

'The Sedgwicks?'

'I wasn't aware of who adopted her. It's not standard practice to give the birth mother such information.'

'Did you have any hand whatsoever in her upbringing?'

'None.'

'How old was she when she was adopted?'

'A baby. I never . . . I mean, straight away. As soon as possible. I never even held her.'

'Who was the father?'

'That's irrelevant.'

'Not to us it isn't,' said Annie. Then she turned over a page. 'Very well, we'll leave that for the moment.' She paused and went on in a weary tone. 'Why didn't you save us a lot of trouble and tell us this information right from the start?'

'I don't know. It didn't seem relevant somehow. It was a long time ago. Nineteen years.'

'Didn't seem relevant?' Annie repeated. 'That's one of the lamest excuses for lying to us that I've ever come across. Don't you agree, DC Masterson?'

'It's pretty lame,' said Gerry.

'She came back into your life,' Annie said, 'and not long afterwards, she was raped. And you didn't think any of this was relevant?'

'But there's no connection. It's just coincidence. I still don't think any of this is relevant.'

'Try again,' Annie said. '*Irrelevant*, *coincidence* – these aren't excuses we recognise. And this time, give us the *real* reason why you didn't tell us.'

'I've already told you. Besides, I didn't want to get involved. I knew you'd make too much of it.'

'Better. A little bit,' said Annie. 'But you *are* involved, like it or not. And this lie, or omission, makes you even more so. See, when people lie to us about one thing, we assume they might be lying about other things, too.'

'Why are you doing this to me?' said Charlotte, clasping her hands on the table. 'You're just being nasty. You must know that *I* couldn't have raped poor Marnie.'

'Nobody's suggesting you did.'

'Then why persecute me? Why don't you leave me alone? Any mistakes I've made I've had to live with. You've no right to sit in judgement on me.'

'There's no easy way of putting this,' said Annie, 'but things have taken another turn. I assume you know about Marnie's death?'

'Her . . . what?'

'Her death,' Annie repeated. 'I'm sorry. I thought you might have known.'

'How could I have known? Who was there to tell me?'

This had been a difficult part of their approach to plan. Either Charlotte knew what had happened to Marnie, or she didn't, and there was no easy way of finding out. In the end, they decided it was best to confront her with the truth. Gerry watched closely and believed that Charlotte's reaction was genuine, that she hadn't known.

'It's very important you tell us the truth about this,' Annie said. 'Did you know that Marnie was dead?'

'No.' Charlotte shook her head. 'I'm not even sure I believe you. You're trying to trick me. Tell me that's what you're doing.'

Gerry saw the misery etched in her features and knew she was telling the truth.

'I'm sorry to be the bearer of such bad news,' Annie said.

'What happened? How . . . I mean . . .?'

Annie went on. 'She took her own life just under a month ago, on 17 May. A few days before Connor Clive Blaydon was murdered.'

'A month,' Charlotte repeated. 'All that time. And I never knew. Where? Why? How?'

'Near home. In Dorset. As for why, who knows? I assume it was because she couldn't come to terms with what happened to her and she felt shamed, damaged, broken. Or that she found out she was pregnant.'

'Oh, my God,' said Charlotte. 'Things come full circle.'

'What does that mean?'

Charlotte started to cry and reached for a tissue from the box on the table and wiped her eyes. 'I'm sorry. I can't believe she's dead.'

'Take a minute,' Annie said. 'Can I get you anything?'

Charlotte held her hand up and gulped down some water. 'I'll be all right in a minute. Let's just get this over with.'

'It might take a while,' said Annie. 'We can take a short break if you need to. But if you're OK to carry on, we will.' She glanced at Jessica Bowen, who nodded.

'I'm OK,' said Charlotte. 'I want this all over with and I never want to see you again.'

'That all depends very much on your telling us the truth. You lied to us about your connection with Marnie Sedgwick, and that's why you're here. How did she find you in the first place?'

'The usual way. She applied for her birth certificate when she turned eighteen then tracked me down through one of those online hereditary sites.'

'When was this?'

'January. Just after Christmas.'

'Why did she wait so long?'

'She told me later that she wasn't sure she could go through with it. She'd been very happy with the Sedgwicks, and she didn't want them to feel they'd been inadequate or somehow let her down. It's not unusual for children seeking their birth parents to feel apprehensive, to hesitate.'

'And she came to see you this January?'

'Yes.'

'At the office?'

'No. She got my home address first.'

'How did the meeting go?'

Charlotte shifted in her chair. 'Awkward, as I'm sure you can imagine. But I think she understood finally, how the adoption was best for her, not only me. How I couldn't possibly have been a fit mother. I think she understood.'

'Was she angry?'

'No. She said she had been, at first, but it passed. She was just curious. She didn't want me to take her in or even develop any kind of maternal relationship. As far as Marnie was concerned, the Sedgwicks were her parents. She just wanted to see me in the flesh, so to speak, and for me to know that she existed.'

'Anything else?'

'Later, she came to me at the office. She wanted work. There was no special pleading or anything, she wasn't after any favours. She wasn't even asking for special treatment. She knew what I did and thought she could fit in somewhere. Simple as that. She already had a waitressing job at Pizza Express in York, but she wasn't getting paid very much, and she said she wanted to save to go back to university.'

'But she'd already dropped out of Nottingham.'

'Because she didn't have enough money, and she thought she was wasting her time studying History. She wanted to take on a practical subject like Management Studies or Hospitality.'

'And you encouraged her?'

'I told her I'd done fairly practical subjects at uni, that it was a good idea if she hoped to get a good job. That you can always read history and literature in your spare time, but it's not going to earn you a living unless you teach. I gave her work. It wasn't much, but she was well enough paid for what she did.'

'What about your relationship? Did it thrive?'

'I wouldn't say it thrived, no. There was always a distance. You'd expect that after so many years. As I told you, the Sedgwicks were her parents, no doubt about that. She made it clear and I accepted it. But it didn't degenerate, either. We got on well enough.'

'Why did you give her up for adoption in the first place?'

'The usual reasons. I was too young, too selfish, too irresponsible.'

'What about abortion?'

'I'm from a Catholic family. All right, so my parents were lapsed Catholics, and I've never been religious, but I just felt that abortion wasn't an option at the time.'

'Fair enough,' said Annie.

'I was living a pretty wild life. Free and easy. All the travel, sun and sand and everything. I didn't want to be lumbered with a child to bring up.'

'So what did you do?'

'When I found out I was pregnant?'

'Yes.'

'I went to stay with a friend in Herefordshire, near Hay, where they have the book festival. That was for my . . . what did they used to call it . . . *lying in*? That's what I did. I lay in and waited. The baby was born at the nearest hospital, a small one, and I gave her up for adoption. End of story.'

Annie consulted the notes Gerry had made. 'And after that you put your life back together, got on track, started a career in events planning? Met your husband?'

'Having a child shook me up. I grew up pretty quickly, I'd say, even though I didn't have the responsibility of child-rearing. So, yes, I threw myself into a new career. I happen to be a quick learner. The degree helped, too. Or at least, Oxford did. Connections. I also have some facility with languages. French, Spanish, a little Greek.'

'So what was your reaction when Marnie came to you and told you she'd been raped?'

'She never . . . I mean, I . . .'

'Come on, Charlotte. Don't start lying again. We were doing so well. Who else could she go to? Not her own parents. She wanted to protect them. You were probably more like a big sister to her than anyone else.'

Charlotte turned to Jessica Bowen, who leaned forward and whispered in her ear. Charlotte nodded a couple of times and turned back to Annie. 'All right,' she said. 'Marnie did come to my house when I got back from Costa Rica, and she told me what had happened. She was in a terrible state, emotionally. I . . . I did my best to comfort her. She wouldn't go to the police. I tried to persuade her, honestly, but she didn't want to go through the humiliation, the victim-blaming. She said she thought she could put it behind her. I wasn't too sure about that, but I realised my job, my *only* job, was to give her comfort and support right there and then. Which I did.'

'And now we come to the big question, Charlotte,' said Annie. 'Who did it? Who raped Marnie Sedgwick?'

By five o'clock that afternoon, Banks was sitting in the shade outside La Porte Montmartre, on the corner of the Boulevard Poissonnière and the Boulevard Montmartre, in Paris, with a large glass of excellent red Bordeaux in front of him, watching the world go by. It wouldn't have been true to say that he hadn't a care in the world – he had many – but at moments such as these, the cares receded, and it felt good to be alive.

His last-minute hotel, which went under the uninspiring name of Hôtel 34B, turned out to be a gem. For less than one hundred euros he got a comfortable room, decorated all in white, clean and spacious enough. It didn't have a balcony, but the windows overlooked the street below. The buildings on both sides of Rue Bergère were five storeys high, so it was like looking into a narrow canyon. Cars and motor scooters were parked by the pavements and even though it was only a little side street there was a constant flow of people. He could see three restaurants from his fourth-floor window: *Les Diables au Thym*, *Dr Auguste* and *Bio c'Bon*, an 'organic' salad bar, on the corner with Rue du Faubourg Montmartre, where there were many more restaurants and cafes, along with a *hypermarché*. The hotel was no frills and had no restaurant or bar, but Banks didn't need such luxuries when there were so many places to eat and drink in the neighbourhood. Like the cafe he was in now.

He was waiting for Jean-Claude Meursault, an old friend from the *police judiciaire*. They had first met at an Interpol conference in Lyon fifteen years previously and had stayed in touch ever since. Jean-Claude had retired the previous year, and Banks had attended his farewell party. If anyone knew anything about Zelda's time in Paris, and whether she was there at the moment, it was Jean-Claude.

A *commissaire* at 36 Quai des Orfèvres for many years, Jean-Claude reminded Banks of his hero Maigret, physically as well as in mind and attitude. The Rupert-Davies Maigret, of course. As far as Banks was concerned, Gambon was good, Atkinson was execrable, Bruno Cremer was the French choice, but Rupert Davies *was* Maigret. He was large and burly, and though he didn't smoke a pipe, one would not have seemed out of place in his hand or mouth. He also had that calm, slow manner of the deep thinker about him, though as Banks had once seen when they encountered some trouble in a bar, he could be remarkably quick on his feet.

Banks glanced around at his fellow drinkers: a group of tourists, a couple of old men sitting in silence together, a businessman trying to impress his secretary, an elegant woman sipping white wine and glancing nervously at her watch, perhaps waiting for her lover, two garrulous young Frenchmen sharing jokes. Gauloises smoke drifted over from the next table, reminding Banks of his school exchange with a boy from Lille when he was about fourteen. It was quite a discovery at that age to find out you could order a beer in a bar, then sit and drink it while enjoying a Disque Bleu and no one would think twice about it.

He watched the people passing by. Nobody seemed in much of a hurry. Suddenly, he saw the young Francoise Hardy, tall, willowy, with shiny long chestnut hair, stylishly dressed, carrying four long-stemmed red roses. She noticed him looking at her and flashed him a quizzical smile that for some reason made him feel like a dirty old man. But he wasn't dirty and he didn't feel old. He knew quite well that she wasn't really Francoise Hardy, but Francoise Hardy as she would have been over fifty years ago, when he was an awestruck schoolboy on his first trip abroad in the heady days of *Salut les copains*, Sylvie Vartan, Johnny Hallyday, France Gall and Richard Anthony. And he didn't feel any different now from that young man who had listened to her sing 'Tous les garçons et les filles' as he gazed at her photo on the album cover all those years ago.

He remembered a field outside Lille, surrounded by trees, a stolen kiss with Brigitte while the others immersed themselves in a game of boules. The scent of warm grass, the tang of wine, the softness of her lips yielding shyly. That was it. That was all. That was enough.

'Alain.' The familiar voice brought him back from the past in a rush. It was Jean-Claude. He had always used the French for his name, called him 'Alain'.

Banks stood up and they embraced warmly then sat down. The waiter drifted by and Banks ordered another Bordeaux for himself and whatever Jean-Claude wanted, which was a glass of Chablis.

'I was miles away,' Banks said. 'You know, I just saw a girl who was the spitting image of the young Francoise Hardy.'

Jean-Claude smiled indulgently. 'Always the romantic.'

'Is that such a bad thing?'

'For a policeman, I think it is.'

The drinks arrived and Jean-Claude took a sip. 'Excellent,' he said. 'You know, she was born not far from here. In the ninth, at any rate.'

'Francoise Hardy?'

'Oui.'

Banks's perspective shifted slightly, as if he were viewing the place from a different angle. 'How's retirement?' he asked.

'I'm not sure I know yet. It hasn't been that long, and I've been consulting with my squad on high-profile cases ever since.'

'So you're still working?'

'Basically, yes. But part-time. Less stress.' He tapped his forehead. 'Let the young men do all the running round and my little grey cells do all my work.'

The shadows were creeping across the pavement in front of the Grand Comptoir restaurant over the street, almost reaching the outside tables. Its pale cream facade was still lit in the late afternoon glow. The number of pedestrians passing by started to increase as the Metro disgorged more and more people on their way home from work.

The empty tables soon filled, and the buzz of conversation got louder. Banks and Jean-Claude chatted about old times, opera, football, books, Brexit and the future. Eventually, after the second glass of Chablis, Jean-Claude asked Banks, 'You wanted to talk about something? You were very cryptic on the telephone. Is it something I can help with?'

'Perhaps,' said Banks.

'Then I suggest we finish our drinks and discuss it over dinner. I know just the place.'

Charlotte paused so long that Annie thought she wasn't going to answer. Finally, she cast her eyes down and muttered so softly that Annie had to lean forward to hear her. 'Connor,' she said. 'Connor raped her.'

Annie slapped the table. 'Then why the hell didn't you tell us that from the start? Do you realise how much trouble you've caused; the resources you've wasted?'

'That's not my fault,' Charlotte argued back, her eyes brimming with tears again. 'I didn't tell you because Marnie didn't want anyone to know and Connor's dead, so what the hell does it matter? You couldn't put him in jail. How the hell was I to know there was a video and that you'd end up investigating the rape? I knew it would end like this, with you lot trying to find something to charge *me* with, lock me up and throw away the key. That you'd ruin the life I've worked so hard to build. That's why I didn't tell you the truth to begin with.'

'Oh, spare me,' said Annie. 'You're telling us you lied because you were surprised by the video? That you didn't expect to have to answer any questions? Is that why you also lied about not recognising Marnie from the first picture we showed you, leading us to waste hours of valuable time finding out who she was?'

'Yes.' Charlotte sniffed. 'And now Marnie's dead, too. They're both dead. It doesn't matter. Don't you see? None of it matters any more.'

'Perhaps if you had insisted that Marnie get the kind of help she needed, she would still be alive.'

Charlotte gave her a look of pure hatred. 'How can you?' she said. 'How dare you say that to me? You're a terrible person, a cruel person.' She started to cry again, and the lawyer passed her a tissue.

'Ease up a little, DI Cabbot,' said Jessica Bowen. 'You've just informed Mrs Westlake about the death of her biological daughter. She has reason to be upset.'

'You think I'm being too hard?' Annie said. 'Sorry. It's a sign of the extreme frustration this case has caused me.'

'We're all frustrated,' said Jessica Bowen, 'but let us please try to remain civilised.'

Annie glanced at Gerry, who also seemed dumbstruck by her last comment. Had she really overstepped the mark? Was she cruel? The only thing to do now was to press on to the logical conclusion.

'What was your relationship with Connor Blaydon?' she asked.

Charlotte blew her nose and looked up with reddened eyes. 'What do you mean, *relationship*? He was my boss.'

'Other than that?'

'Are you suggesting there was more to it than that?'

Annie turned over a sheet of paper. 'When Marnie's best friend, Mitsuko Ogawa, told us about her job, she said that you were working for an old friend. We thought it seemed like an odd thing to say at the time, as you'd told us you met Blaydon at a gala event a few years before. You never mentioned a friendship. But you also indicated that you had known one another on and off for some time. Only you were very vague about it.'

'Why should I mention a friendship? There wasn't one. We had a working relationship. I don't know what this Ogawa woman was talking about, but it was likely just a figure of speech.'

'How long *had* you known Blaydon, then?' Annie asked. 'Whether you were friends or not.'

'Like I said, a few years, on and off.'

'How many? Twenty?'

Charlotte turned away. 'I don't know. Maybe.'

Annie referred to the notes Gerry had made again. 'Isn't it true that you had known Connor Clive Blaydon since you were twenty-one, in 1999? You were a rebellious young tear-away gadding around the Greek islands with some wealthy friends you'd met at St Hilda's, cadging lifts and sleeping berths on yachts. Didn't you once cadge a lift on a luxury yacht called the *Nerea*, out of Corfu? And wasn't this owned by one Connor Clive Blaydon?'

Charlotte seemed to freeze. Jessica Bowen glanced from her client to Annie and back. 'DI Cabbot,' she said. 'Exactly where are you going with this?'

'Patience,' said Annie. 'Have patience, and all will be revealed.'

'I'm tired,' said Charlotte. 'And you've upset me.' She implored Jessica Bowen. 'Please, make them stop. It's my right. I'm entitled to a break. I want to go home.'

'Legally, we are entitled to detain you for twenty-four hours without charge,' said Annie. 'But you're right. You do have a right to breaks, meals and so on. Now, we have a destination in mind, and one way or another we're going to get there. If you're tired and need a break, we have a very comfortable cell in the basement. You'll be fed, made comfortable, and we can start again bright and early tomorrow morning.'

'This is a nightmare. I want to go home.'

'I'm afraid that won't be possible.'

'Why not?'

'Because you have to stay in custody until we're satisfied with your answers to our questions,' she said. 'It's the law.'

Charlotte glanced at Jessica Bowen again.

'You'll be all right,' the solicitor said. 'I'll be nearby. You'll be well treated. I promise you.'

But Charlotte didn't look happy in the slightest, least of all when two female officers marched her out of the interview room and down to the custody suite.

'You *know* Nelia Melnic?' Jean-Claude asked, clearly stunned by Banks's revelation of what he wanted to talk about.

'Yes. She goes by the name of Zelda now. She's a friend. Why, do you?'

'No. No. I've never met her. I just know the name. I'm surprised, that's all. I hear she's very beautiful.'

'Yes.' They were having dinner at a restaurant Jean-Claude knew, lost in the maze of backstreets of the 9th Arrondissement. The speciality was seafood, and both were enjoying the house platter along with a bottle of fine white Burgundy, chosen by Jean-Claude. They had been fortunate to get there early enough for a table out front.

'Why are you so surprised?' Banks asked.

Jean-Claude paused, a shrimp midway between his plate and his mouth. 'Because she is famous here, Alain. Perhaps not with the general population, though many will certainly have heard of her, but with the police for certain. She was a legend in the squad room. Did she not tell you?'

'I know something happened here,' Banks said. 'Something serious involving a pimp called Darius. But that's about all I do know.'

Jean-Claude gave him a serious look. 'Most of the story is classified, you understand. I could not possibly tell you all the names and positions of those involved. There was a scandal. Well, a narrowly averted scandal. Very few people know the details.'

'But you're one of them?'

Jean-Claude inclined his head slightly. 'I had some small involvement. To be perfectly honest, though, even I don't know the names of the major players. They were important people, that is all I know. Government people.'

Banks tussled with an extremely recalcitrant langoustine. 'She has a French passport.'

'Mm. You see, *I* didn't know that. Why are you interested?'

Banks told him about Zelda and Ray and the trouble with

the Tadićs, Keane and Hawkins, leaving out the murders and abductions.

Jean-Claude swallowed a mouthful of wine and said, 'So that's what became of her. Perhaps she is the sort of woman trouble follows around?'

'Perhaps,' said Banks. 'The Tadićs are from way back in her past. They abducted her outside her orphanage as she was leaving. But this Darius business is more recent.'

'It was just over three years ago,' said Jean-Claude. 'The month of March. I remember it well.'

'Did you work the case?'

'There was no case. And I told you, even I don't know the full details.'

'But you said you had some involvement. What happened?'

'Darius was a pimp. Or perhaps that does him an injustice. His girls were all beautiful, high-class, très chic and très expensive. With a Darius girl, it was strictly dinner at Maxim's, then back to a suite at the George V, if you know what I mean.'

'No matter what the price,' said Banks, 'the business is the same. I'd say he was a pimp.'

'You would get no real argument from me. We knew of him, of course. He was born in Algeria and came to Paris in his late twenties. A crook from the start. He very quickly made his way up the ladder through a mixture of brutality and business acumen. His rivals seemed to have a habit of disappearing, and he was not averse to hurting the girls when he thought it necessary to keep them in line.'

'A nasty piece of work then?'

'Very nasty.' Jean-Claude paused to finish the remains of his meal, ending with the last oyster, which he washed down with the Burgundy, then went on. 'What nobody knew for quite some time was that he had a little blackmail business on the side. You know, the usual: photos, sometimes film, famous or highly placed victims.'

It sounded very much like what Neville Roberts had been doing back on Banks's home patch. 'But I thought you French were more permissive than us lot about that sort of thing,' he said. 'Don't most Frenchmen have a mistress? Visit prostitutes? I seem to have read only recently about a Frenchman who died while having adulterous sex on a job-related trip, and it was classified as a "workplace accident".'

Jean-Claude laughed. 'So the Frenchman's workplace is his mistress's boudoir? Oh, Alain. What *have* you been reading? Or perhaps it is the films of Vadim, Rohmer or Truffaut that influence you? Yes, we are to a certain extent more liberal than you English as regards domestic arrangements and matters of the boudoir, but remember this was quite recent, and believe it or not, even France has been stricken by a plague of uber-morality in public life since the old days. *#BalanceTonPorc* – what you call #MeToo – has made its presence known here. Just look at the trouble with Roman Polanski, for example. That would never have happened a few years ago. The tide is turning. But if only that were all.'

'There's more?'

'Isn't there always? Dessert?'

Banks patted his stomach. 'I think I've just about got room.'

Jean-Claude caught the waiter's attention and ordered apple tarte tatins and Calvados for both of them. A couple of elegantly dressed French women took the next table. One of them, mid-forties, perhaps, with short, tousled brown hair, a pale oval face and full lips, wearing a cream blazer over a pale blue blouse, was particularly attractive. After they had adjusted their chairs and disposed of their handbags, she turned slightly and gave Banks a quick smile. Then they began speaking in French so fast that Banks couldn't follow at all.

'You were saying there's more?' he prompted Jean-Claude.

'Yes. Darius's clientele, customers, whatever you called them, were very mixed. They included men highly placed in government, ministers, prominent businessmen, even gangsters, Russian oligarchs . . . People in possession of closely guarded secrets. Men who, under the right circumstances, might find themselves talking out of turn.'

'I think I know where you're going,' said Banks.

'You are thinking of your Profumo affair, no doubt?'

'Yes.'

'Do you remember what President de Gaulle said about that?'

'No.'

'He said that's what happens when the English try to behave like the French.'

Banks laughed. 'But that was back in the Cold War,' he said. 'Russian spies and all that.'

'Well, it is true that the objectives have changed now that the Cold War is over, but the game remains the same. Darius had some highly placed customers, and some of his most beautiful girls were Russian. Trafficked girls, we suspect. Pillow talk is what it is, and money is always a good incentive for loose tongues. Only this time the matter exchanged involved business dealings, stocks and shares and takeovers, rather than weapons and military or political strategy.'

'And Zelda's part?'

'Your Zelda was one of Darius's favourites. Apparently, she was also very smart and she knew what was going on. And she spoke fluent Russian. Like your *Pretty Woman* film, one client came into her life and fell in love with her, what you would call a cabinet minister, with special responsibilities involving criminal intelligence and the police in general. My boss. Like your Home Secretary. He wanted her to change, wanted them to go away together. He was going to leave his wife and children for her.'

'Emile?' said Banks, remembering Zelda's journal.

'Yes. You know this? You know the full story?'

Banks glanced at the woman at the next table. She was in animated conversation with her friend and was paying not the slightest attention to him and Jean-Claude. 'No,' he said. 'Just a few fragments. Please go on. I promise not to interrupt again.'

'When this . . . Emile . . . had an idea of what was going on, he devised a scheme. If Nelia could somehow get to Darius's cache of blackmail material – especially the audio tapes – and either destroy it or hand it over to him, she would become a heroine of the French people. In secret, of course, as all the best heroes and heroines are.'

'And here's me thinking they were posthumous.'

'Cynic. Well, not in this case.'

'So how did it go wrong?'

'It didn't. Not until the end.' He glanced around to make sure nobody was paying attention. They weren't. 'None of this was for public consumption, but according to Nelia's statement *in camera*, Darius came in while she was removing the documents from his safe. He saw what she was doing and attacked her, tried to kill her. In the struggle, she managed to grab a knife from the table and stabbed him several times. Then, when he was weakened and incapacitated, she slit his throat, just to make sure he was dead.'

'And was he?'

'Oh, yes. According to someone I know who was at the scene shortly after it happened, there was blood all over the place. The girl was calm as anything, like a zombie. In shock, no doubt.'

'So what happened?'

'She disappeared. The rumour was that she had, of course, been pardoned for what happened to Darius and spirited away. Many, many people who would never admit it publicly were secretly more than glad that he was dead and his cache of blackmail material destroyed. Beyond, that, I don't know, except she was never mentioned again. You know more than I do about the aftermath and her later adventures. Emile must have got the French passport for her – he was certainly highly placed enough to do her that favour – and she cleared off, never to darken our shores again. It was to everyone's advantage that the whole affair was hushed up and forgotten. Much went on behind closed doors, you understand. A scandal was narrowly avoided. The documents and tapes were destroyed, of course, a few low-profile arrests were made, and the girl had her freedom . . . There was only one extremely tragic consequence.'

'Emile?'

'Yes. Three months later he was killed in a road accident on his way back from a meeting in Strasbourg.'

'Accident?'

Jean-Claude gave a very Gallic shrug. 'So they said. And there was no evidence to the contrary. No witnesses, no forensic indications that he had done anything except fall asleep at the wheel and veer off the road into a convenient tree.'

'Drugs?'

'Toxicology showed nothing in his system except a small amount of alcohol. Not even enough to get him charged with driving under the influence.'

'Darius's partners, no doubt?'

'Yes. Enforcers. But as far as we know they are all working for someone else now, peddling drugs in Marseilles. We keep an eye on them, of course, make sure they don't end up back here, but without their leader, there's not a lot of enthusiasm left in them for Paris.'

'They're not after Zelda?'

'Darius's women all drifted away after his death, some to other pimps, no doubt, and others to an escape from the life, and this Nelia was just one of them. It's unlikely they would still be chasing her after all this time. Loyalty among crooks only goes so far and lasts so long.'

'And Zelda hasn't been seen or heard of here since?'

'No,' said Jean-Claude. 'I will ask around, if you like. Get back to you tomorrow. But I still think the answer will be no.'

'You would know if she had been seen over the past few days?'

'Believe me, if she was here, I will know by tomorrow.'

'Thanks, Jean-Claude.' That didn't mean she hadn't been back in secret, but from what he had heard, Banks now doubted that she would have chosen Paris as the first stop on her escape route. He would have to search further afield, if he was to search at all. He had hoped he might see her here, get a chance to talk and clear some things up, but perhaps it was best to simply let her be, let her live the rest of her life the way she wanted. God knows, she deserved it.

'Tell me, Alain,' Jean-Claude said. 'This Nelia. Zelda. Are you in love with her?'

'I don't know,' said Banks. 'I realise that's an unsatisfactory answer to your question, but I've asked it of myself, too, and the answer is the same. I don't know. Besides, even if I am, it doesn't matter. There could be no future for us, for many reasons.'

Their Calvados and tartes arrived. The woman at the next table took out a compact and checked her face in the mirror as she refreshed her lipstick, catching Banks's eye briefly as she did so. He noticed a wedding ring on her left hand.

'And that, mon ami, is that,' said Jean-Claude. They clinked their Calvados glasses and drank. It was smooth as silk, but burned all the way down. 'And now I have a question for you, Alain.'

'What's that?'

'This Nelia. What is she really like?'

19

The following morning, Charlotte Westlake didn't seem well rested at all. Her eyes were sunken and had bags beneath them. Her cheeks were sallow and even her hair seemed lacklustre.

Annie, on the other hand, was awake and raring to go after a restful night's sleep. Gerry seemed bright-eyed and bushy-tailed, too.

'Good breakfast?' Annie asked Charlotte. She knew that the cells were comfortable enough and the food passable.

She got no answer.

'Service OK?'

'All right, all right,' said Jessica Bowen. 'Enough with the inappropriate humour. Just get on with the interview, if you don't mind. The clock's ticking.'

Annie picked up the threads again. 'Remember, yesterday evening we were talking about your relationship with Connor Blaydon?' she said to Charlotte. 'Would you care to tell us exactly when and how it began?'

'I don't know where you've dug up all this rubbish from, but I don't intend to dignify it with an explanation.'

'How well do you get along with your mother?' Annie asked.

'My mother? What's she got to do with all this?'

'Quite a bit, as it turns out,' said Annie. 'Were you always close?'

'I suppose so. I mean, she is my mother.'

'And I understand that your husband's and father's deaths occurred rather close together.'

'What is this? Are you trying to say I had something to do with my father's death now? My husband's? What is it with you?'

'Dear, dear,' said Annie. 'A night's rest doesn't seem to have made you any more helpful or better tempered, does it?'

'Rest? That's a joke.'

'Where are you going with this, DI Cabbot?' asked Jessica Bowen. 'I'm afraid you're losing me, too.'

'Just this,' Annie went on. 'In DC Masterson's conversations with Mrs Lynne Pollard we discovered—'

'You've been talking to my mother!' Charlotte sat bolt upright and glared at Gerry. 'You went to see my mother! How dare—'

'Mrs Westlake, calm down,' said Gerry. 'I talked to your mother. We had a nice chat. She made us a pot of tea. And a number of interesting points came up.' She opened a file folder on the table and took out two picture postcards. 'Most interesting of all were these postcards she received from you in June 1999. Your mother has kept all the correspondence she ever had with you. Surely it can't surprise you that she kept the postcards you sent her from your world travels? After all, you were doing what she never dared, never really had the chance to do. Travel. She was envious. She saw the world vicariously through your eyes.'

Charlotte regarded her incredulously. 'What are you talking about?'

'It's what she said. Your mother. Lynne.'

'I . . . well, no, I didn't know that . . . but I can't believe you just went there and talked to her behind my back. Surely you can't do that. There must be a law.'

She looked at Jessica Bowen. 'No law, I'm afraid, Charlotte,' Jessica said.

'Is nobody on my side here?'

'As your solicitor says,' said Gerry. 'I didn't need your permission. I was doing my job.'

Charlotte just shook her head slowly.

'These are postcards from you,' Gerry went on. 'I'm sure we could verify the handwriting if we needed to. They're both posted from the island of Corfu, two days apart in mid-June. In the first, you refer to meeting up with a wealthy landowner from Yorkshire called Connor Clive Blaydon, and in the second, you refer to a big farewell party he threw for you and your friends on his yacht, the *Nerea*. Is this true?'

'I did a lot of things I don't remember clearly back then,' said Charlotte. 'At risk of getting arrested for past behaviour, I was either drunk or stoned most of the time.'

'Like Marnie Sedgwick at Blaydon's party,' said Annie. 'Only that wasn't *her* choice.'

Charlotte ignored Annie, but Jessica Bowen gave her a warning glance.

'But is it true, Charlotte?' Gerry repeated. 'Your mother thought it all sounded quite glamorous. Like so much of your life. She's very proud of you and your achievements, you know.'

'I don't need you to tell me that. And if I wrote it on a postcard I suppose it must be true.'

'So you don't deny it?'

Charlotte folded her arms. 'What would be the point?'

'May I see these postcards?' Jessica Bowen asked.

Gerry passed over the cards. The solicitor picked them up, glanced briefly at the photograph of Kavos on one and a view of the Albanian coastline on the other, then turned them over one at a time and read. She passed them to Charlotte, who glanced at them in passing and dropped them on the table. Her body seemed to have tensed up now, Annie noticed. The skin stretched taut over her forehead and cheeks, lips a straight narrow line. She was playing with her ring again.

'Do you admit to writing and sending these?' Gerry asked.

'Yes,' Charlotte hissed. 'So what?'

'These postcards are evidence of your presence on Connor Blaydon's yacht, the *Nerea*, at Kavos, Corfu, on the week of 15 June 1999. What happened during that week, Charlotte?'

'What do you think happened? We partied. Sex, drugs and rock 'n' roll.'

Gerry checked her files. 'You gave birth to Marjorie – or Marnie – on 13 March 2000. If you do the calculations, you'll see that's very close to nine months after 15 June.'

'So?'

'So,' said Gerry. 'Was Connor Blaydon Marnie Sedgwick's father?'

Even Jessica Bowen's jaw dropped at that question.

'How could you even think—?'

'Do the math,' said Annie, 'as the Americans say.'

'It's just a coincidence.'

'There seem to be an awful lot of coincidences in your life,' Annie said. 'But maybe this is stretching it a bit too far. Is it a coincidence if a woman sleeps with a man and nine months later has a baby?'

'You're reading too much into it.'

'Tell me how. Or let me tell you what I think happened. What if you met Connor Blaydon aboard the *Nerea* that June and slept with him? Why not? You've already said you were running wild and fancy-free, sleeping around, and Blaydon already owned the yacht before he bought his first villa on Corfu in 2002. You were twenty-one and he was around forty. Attractive older man, rich and handsome. So you slept with him and you became pregnant. Happens all the time. As you've already explained, an abortion wasn't an option for you, so you returned to England, hid away in the countryside during your pregnancy, gave birth and arranged to have the baby adopted. Marnie Sedgwick. You remained there for a brief period of recovery, then you returned to the normal flow of life with new energy, throwing yourself into building a career. Am I on the right track?'

'Apart from the business about Connor, yes. More or less.'

'Are you sure?'

'Of course.'

'So who was the baby's father?'

'I . . . I don't know.'

'Are you suggesting it could have been one of many?'

'I wasn't exactly celibate, if that's what you mean.'

'But it could have been Blaydon's.'

'You're putting words into my mouth.'

'Yes,' said Jessica Bowen. 'Do stop that, DI Cabbot.'

'A DNA test could prove it one way or the other. Are you willing to risk that, Charlotte?'

Charlotte shook her head.

'What does that mean?' Annie asked. 'Did you sleep with Connor Blaydon on his yacht in June 1999, and did you have a baby in March 2000?'

'Maybe. Yes. Maybe. No. I don't know.' Charlotte put her hands over her ears. 'Can we stop again now, please?' She looked towards Jessica Bowen with a desperate expression.

'Because if you did,' Annie went on, 'and if Blaydon *was* the father of your child, then it means he raped his own daughter, doesn't it? She didn't know who her father was, and he didn't know she was his daughter, but *you* did. And that, Charlotte, I think, gives you a pretty good motive for murder. Is that what you meant when you said things had come full circle?'

'*Murder?* What do you mean, murder?'

'Let's call a halt to this right now,' said Jessica Bowen. 'My client is clearly distraught, and things are taking a turn none of us could have reasonably expected. We'll need some preparation time before we continue.'

Annie sat back in her chair. 'Fine,' she said, dropping her pencil. 'Take as long as you need. I could do with a cuppa myself.'

That morning, Ray woke up from a vivid dream convinced that Zelda would be coming home before dark. He couldn't remember the details, but the feeling of hope and anticipation remained strong in him even through breakfast and a quick perusal of the bills the postman had delivered. Money wasn't a problem. His paintings were selling well and his reputation was gaining in stature day by day. He might not be at Hockney's level, but then few living artists were. Those kinds of millions were beyond him and always would be. Still, he was doing all right; he could pay the bills, and he could support Zelda.

But it had been just a dream. In reality, Alan was coming over tonight when he got back from Paris, Ray hoped with more news about Zelda. He would go out later and buy food, maybe the ingredients for a chickpea curry, along with some beer and wine, and he had already put aside a few LPs for their listening pleasure: Soft Machine's *Third*, Kevin Ayers's *Shooting at the Moon* and Gong's *Camembert Electrique*. They should keep the blues at bay for a while. Anything to chase the demons out, even if only for an hour or two. Perhaps some Edgar Broughton Band? No. The three choices would be enough, then they would move on to something a bit more mellow. Pity Banks didn't enjoy the occasional spliff, though. Ray always felt like a naughty boy smoking dope in front of him. Maybe he would smoke up before Banks arrived this evening, avoid any awkwardness.

After the second coffee, still not inspired to start work, he decided he needed to tidy the place up. First, he dealt with the sink full of dirty dishes, putting as many as he could in the dishwasher and washing the rest by hand. After that, he swept the hardwood floors and vacuumed the carpeted areas. He stripped the bed and put on clean sheets and pillowcases, stuffing the others in the washing machine. He had lived alone down in St Ives long enough to know how to do all these things, as well as cook for himself and anywhere up to ten guests. Hungry at lunchtime, he whipped up a cheese omelette and toast, then drove to the Tesco on the edge of Eastvale and bought what he needed for dinner.

By early afternoon he felt ready for the studio. He was working on a new painting. It started as a portrait of Zelda, but had soon become a sort of composite of all the elements he saw in her. Faces within a face, a collage of possibilities. In some lights, she was a classic Eastern European beauty, from another angle perhaps half Thai or Vietnamese, and from yet another Middle Eastern. Ray was trying to capture all these facets in one small portrait and together, viewed from a distance, they should ideally resolve themselves into a realistic head and shoulders portrait of Zelda against a slightly psychedelic background. He would be the first to admit that there was more than a hint of Love's *Forever Changes* album cover in the work. In fact, he had it propped up on another easel while he worked and had played it many times over the past few days.

After an hour or so, Ray felt tired, so he took a break and rolled a cigarette. His neck and chest ached from the stooped position in which he painted. A quick shot of Macallan and a few stretches soon had him back at the easel again, but now he needed music. He searched through his collection of old vinyl looking for something he hadn't played in a long time and came across *The Thoughts of Emerlist Davjack*, by The Nice. That had some pretty good Keith Emerson organ work on it, he remembered, so he put it on. He remembered seeing The Nice at the Marquee in their brief heyday, Emerson sticking knives between the organ keys to hold the notes down, shaking the thing and all but jumping up and down on it like Jerry Lee Lewis. He smiled at the memory.

There was still a lot of work to do, Ray thought, as he stood back and viewed the painting critically. It lacked a certain clarity in places, and several minor touches stood out just a little too much when viewed from afar, unbalancing the whole effect. He began to wonder whether he could even carry it off. It wouldn't be the first attempt to immortalise Zelda to be abandoned. He moved in closer, chewed on his lower lip and got to work.

Time passed. As usual, Ray paid no attention to it. But he noticed the light dimming, clouds obscuring the sun, and as he hated working in artificial light, knew it was almost time to stop. He also had to get the curry started. Alan wasn't sure exactly when he'd be back, but that was OK; dinner could simmer on low for a long while if necessary, and he could leave out the chickpeas until the last twenty minutes or so.

This time the discomfort in his chest was greater, and when he turned to put down his brush, he suddenly felt as if someone hit him with a piledriver. He sat down. His brow felt clammy with sweat and his stomach was churning. What was wrong with him? Something he'd eaten? The omelette had been fine. He knew the eggs were fresh because he had bought them from the farm down the road just two days ago.

Another blow from the piledriver struck him, this time hard enough to send a pain all down his left arm. He tried to get up, knowing somewhere deep inside that it was time to call an ambulance, but his legs felt too wobbly. His phone was downstairs, where he usually left it when he was painting. He thrust himself to his feet, gripping the chair arm, and stumbled forward. He was having trouble breathing now, and the slightest move made him out of breath. His chest felt as if it were being crushed.

He made it as far as the top of the stairs, where he dropped to his knees. The world was closing down, the pain gripping him tighter. He was aware of The Nice singing 'The Cry of Eugene' as he fell forward on to his face. He grasped at the banister to lift himself up, but he had no strength left. *Oh, God*, he thought. *Oh, God, please don't let it end like this.*

After the short break, both Charlotte Westlake and Jessica Bowen looked as if they had been put through the ringer.

'Are you going to charge my client?' the solicitor asked.

'We're still in the process of gathering evidence,' said Annie. 'She's still under caution. You've been here throughout the interview so far, surely you must realise we have a fair distance to go yet? If necessary, we'll apply for an extension of detention from the Chief Superintendent.' Annie knew that AC Gervaise would authorisc such a request.

'I'm not so much interested in the journey as the destination,' said Jessica Bowen. 'My job's a little different from yours, and right now I'm here to safeguard my client's rights and well-being.'

'Well, let's get on with it, then.' Annie opened her file folder. Gerry set the recorders going again.

Charlotte Westlake seemed puzzled and frightened, Annie thought, as well she might, now all her lies were being held up to the light. Annie still wasn't convinced that Charlotte was a murderer, but she was intending to pick and pull at the scab of her tissue of lies until the truth was revealed one way or another.

Annie couldn't see Charlotte Westlake creeping into Blaydon's pool area, shooting him and Roberts, then gutting the naked Blaydon and dumping him in the pool. But she could have done it. The CSIs and pathologist told her that the killer hadn't needed to be especially strong. There was the matter of acquiring the gun, of course, but Baikals are easy enough to pick up, and there were plenty of guests at Blaydon's parties who might have had access and procured one for her – Gashi and Tadić, for starters. But Annie still couldn't quite see Charlotte as a murderer. Surely, she must soon come to understand that if she hadn't killed Blaydon but she knew who did, then she had better give it up before she was charged with murder herself.

There was, however, another ace left in the deck: Leka Gashi.

'OK, Charlotte,' Annie began. 'Do you remember where we'd got to? You had Blaydon's baby – Marnie – he raped her, she told you and you killed him for it. Is any of that wrong?'

'It's all wrong,' said Charlotte. 'You've twisted it all up.'

'Put me right then. Untwist it. Are you saying that Blaydon wasn't Marnie's father?'

'Yes. All right, I slept with him. Once. And I slept with most of his friends. Sometimes more than one in the same day. I was a slut. OK? Let's get that out of the way. But I'm *not* a killer.'

'Why should I believe you now after all the lies you've told?'

Charlotte banged so hard on the table that it rattled. 'Because it's *true*. All right, I lied. I tried to keep things from you. Do you blame me, the way it's turning out, the way you've been treating me?'

'That's entirely your own fault, Charlotte. Lying to the police isn't an advisable route to take.'

They let the silence stretch for a few moments, then Gerry said, 'Did those men you slept with on Blaydon's yacht in Corfu include Leka Gashi? Someone you described as "a crude pig of a man" the first time we talked. Is that accurate?'

'Probably.'

'That you said it, or that you slept with him?'

'Probably both. Back then Leka was a kind of fashionable sexy gangster. Like someone from a Guy Ritchie film. He was exciting to be around. And like Connor, he was young, sexy, devil-may-care. Liked to flash his money around. I was young and impressionable.'

'So you slept with him?' Gerry repeated.

'Yes. Probably.'

'Could *he* have been Marnie's father?'

'Leka?' Charlotte looked away. 'You must be joking.'

'Why not?'

'We took precautions.'

'Doesn't always work. Surely you must know that.'

Charlotte pouted.

'There's no need to sulk,' said Annie. 'Come on, get it off your chest. Tell us what you know.'

Charlotte glanced at Jessica Bowen, who gave her a brief nod. Charlotte seemed to pull herself together, this time taking several deep breaths and relaxing as best she could in her hard chair. To Annie, she seemed like someone who was finally relieved to be unburdening herself. It happened often in interviews, just before the confession.

'It's true I knew them both back then,' Charlotte said. 'Connor and Leka. The summer of 1999. I'd just turned twenty-one and the world was my oyster. Or so I thought. I had friends, money saved – not a fortune, but enough – and there were good times to be had. We spent most of May and the first part of June sailing the Greek islands – Samos,

Santorini, Mykonos, Patmos, Rhodes, Kos – all this before the migrants, before they were the way they are now. And yes, there were lots of parties, sex parties, if you like. And drugs. Mostly cocaine. That's why I was coming to hate working for Connor so much lately. I could see it starting all over again. It was all starting to remind me too much of my misspent youth, the bowls of white powder, the casual sex. I thought I'd put all that behind me.'

'Yes, but you weren't participating this time, were you?'

Charlotte managed a brief smile. 'No. But I was exposed to it. Somehow that seemed enough. And then Marnie came along.'

'Another reminder?'

'If you like. But a breath of fresh air, too. There was such an innocence about Marnie that's hard to describe. She was no ingénue. I don't mean that. She wasn't naive. In many ways she seemed old beyond her years, but she had a special sort of aura. Connor picked up on it immediately.'

'The first time she worked at one of his parties?'

'Yes. Back in March. Nothing happened then, or I would have known, but I could see him when I dropped by, the way he looked at her. And he mentioned her later. I should have known what it meant, done something about it right away, but I didn't. I don't know why. Maybe because I was selfish. Maybe because I didn't read the signs properly. It's easier in hindsight. But I did warn her about Leka and Tadić. To stay away from them. Even before she started working for me. She said she wanted money, and the parties paid good money, but I warned her to just do her job and keep her distance and she'd be fine. The idea of rape never entered my mind. As far as I was concerned, they might be criminals, but none of them was a rapist. And when Connor sent me to Costa Rica, I was just so thrilled to be going somewhere I'd never been before that I never gave a moment's thought as to what might happen while I was away. Or why I was being sent so far away. How could I know? But I didn't kill anyone, honest I didn't. You have to believe me.'

'Go on. What happened next?'

'I'd only been back a couple of days and Marnie came to my house. She was in a terrible state. Like I said, not so much physically – she'd cleaned herself up – but that innocence, that special aura was gone. She was empty, dead inside. She told me what had happened. That Connor had come to see her in the kitchen when most people had left or gone off to their rooms and it was quiet. He persuaded her to have a drink. She soon started to feel dizzy and sleepy and he helped her to a room where he said she could lie down and have a rest. But then he raped her. It was all a blur to her at the time, but she said she remembered the shock afterwards, the inability to move, just lying there as he did it to her. And when he'd finished, he drove her home, dropped her off outside her house.'

'What about her own car?'

'One of his minions must have picked it up the following day and dropped it off. She said Blaydon phoned and told her she got drunk, or she'd taken something, and he was worried, so that was why he drove her home.'

'So what did you do?'

'I tried to bring her out of it, but you were right earlier, she needed the kind of help that only an expert could give her. And I failed. I failed her.' Charlotte started crying silently and Jessica Bowen passed her a tissue. 'Sorry,' Charlotte went on. 'This is all very upsetting. I still can't quite take in the news of Marnie's death.'

'Then what happened?'

'She stayed with me in Adel. We spent some days together, talking, walking in the woods. She seemed to improve a bit.

Then she went back to work, back in York, and after that I didn't hear from her again. I'd suggested she go home to her parents and tell them what happened, and she said she would think about it. I suppose I was trying to pass the problem on.'

'Did you know where her parents lived?'

'No. Why would I?'

'She didn't tell you?'

'I think she was protective of them. All I knew is it was somewhere down south. I kept thinking she might phone, but she didn't.'

'And you didn't phone her?'

'No. I had her mobile number, but no, I didn't.'

'Did she ever mention suicide?'

'Good Lord, no.'

'Or pregnancy?'

'No. But how could she, really, if it had only just happened?'

Annie paused. Charlotte had taken a hell of a bruising, from hearing about the suicide of her daughter to the dredging up of her own painful memories, but it wasn't over yet. Never again would she have Charlotte in such a raw, vulnerable state, readier than ever, perhaps, to tell the whole truth, if only just to get out of there. 'Charlotte,' she said. 'Tell me the truth now. Did you kill Connor Clive Blaydon?'

Charlotte looked her straight in the eye and said, 'No. I didn't.' Then she paused. 'I wanted to, but I didn't have the guts. Maybe I . . .'

'So who did?' Annie asked. 'Can you help us? Will you tell us?'

Charlotte nodded. 'Maybe I *am* responsible for what happened. I don't know. But I invited Leka over to the house one evening after Marnie had left. I told him I wanted to talk to him about something important.' She paused, as if for some brief internal dialogue, shaking her head from side to side as if in judgement on herself, then hurried on. 'I told him that Marnie was *his* daughter, from all those years ago, that time on Blaydon's yacht. That I'd put her up for adoption but she had tracked me down and come to work for me. Now she wanted to know who her father was, maybe even meet him. I said I wanted to get his permission first, before I arranged anything. I thought he'd be angry and just say no, but he wasn't. He didn't. He knew who I meant. He'd seen her at Connor's. Leka and I had had a bit of fling back then, more than just a one-off, unlike Connor, at any rate. Never since. And he has become a bit of a pig. I meant what I said. But back then he was handsome, gallant, vicious. But never violent towards me. There's not much point even saying this, but he could be gentle. He could be kind.'

'Did he believe you?'

'I think so. He knew I had no reason to lie to him. I made it clear that neither I nor Marnie wanted anything from him, not money, not commitment or anything, and he could just walk away if he wanted. He didn't even need to acknowledge her as his daughter.'

'Didn't he ask for proof or anything?'

'No. As I said, I wasn't asking him for anything. I made it clear she'd had a good family. I told him I just wanted him to know, that's all. He said he *did* want to see her. He quite surprised me. He said I should have told him a long time ago, but it wasn't too late. That he had a wonderful large mansion in the countryside outside of Tirana and all his daughters and granddaughters lived there. Marnie could come with him and join them, be part of his family. She would never want for anything again.'

'What did you say?'

'After I got over the shock, I said I didn't think she'd be interested, that she would be happy where she was again once she . . . Anyway, he wouldn't give up. He wanted to talk to her so he could try to persuade her to go to Albania.'

'What did you tell him?'

Charlotte turned away.

'Charlotte?'

Slowly, she looked up, tears in her eyes. 'I made a mistake,' she said. 'I gave him her mobile number.'

Annie looked at Gerry. 'The man she met on the cliffs,' she said. 'The reason she was running.'

'What?' Charlotte said.

'Nothing. What else did you say?'

Charlotte paused and glanced at Jessica Bowen, who whispered in her ear. Charlotte nodded and went on. 'I told him that she was very upset. I told him what happened at the party. I told him that Blaydon had raped Marnie. Raped his daughter. Leka was already paranoid enough about Connor's loyalty. It didn't take much to push him over the edge. His men had also seen Connor talking to a policeman – Banks – who wasn't on his payroll.'

'And then?'

'A few days later, Connor was dead. I honestly never imagined all this would happen. I thought they might beat him up or something, put him in hospital. He deserved that. And I was angry. I couldn't think of any other way to get back at him. All right, so maybe I was a little bit crazy, too. Marnie absolutely refused to bring the police in. She said she knew what it was like for rape victims. I wasn't strong or brave enough to do anything myself. I thought maybe this would work, if I stirred things up, that maybe Leka or his friends would beat Connor up or something. I never imagined that they'd murder him.'

'And Marnie? Did Gashi tell you that he found her?'

'No. I've no idea whether he ever met her. I never saw Marnie again, and I haven't seen Leka since.'

Annie wondered if what she was hearing was mere naiveté or whether she had been outflanked and outwitted. 'That's what Gashi is, Charlotte,' she said. 'A killer. And we think he might have been to see Marnie in Dorset on the day she died. Maybe he told her he was her father and tried to persuade her to go to Albania with him. We don't know, but she appeared to be running away from him. Witnesses saw a man getting into a posh silver car. Gashi drives a grey Mercedes. It's close enough.'

'He didn't . . .?'

'No, he didn't kill her. She took her own life, Charlotte. She jumped off a cliff.'

'Because of him?'

'I doubt it. Though I'm sure he contributed. If what you told me earlier is correct, I'd guess he was just putting the proposition to her.'

'But he couldn't force her, could he?'

'Maybe. But I don't think so. I think she was upset enough to start with because of the trauma of the rape, and the pregnancy. Gashi only increased her confusion. I imagine that she listened for a while, and when it all got too much for her, her resolve strengthened, and she ran. She didn't want to hear any more. That's why she was running when she reached Durdle Door. Not because he was going to harm her or anything. It was just all too much. She did what she had intended to do anyway.'

Charlotte put her head in her hands.

The Albanians, Annie thought. Dammit, it *was* the Albanians all along, even if not for the reasons she had thought. But she was right. And Charlotte's crime? They called it 'soliciting to murder', and it could carry a life sentence. Gashi certainly wouldn't be helping them, even if they could find him. He was hardly going to admit that Charlotte had more or less asked him to murder Blaydon and that he had done so. And it would be damn near impossible to prove anything; they would have their work cut out convincing the CPS that Charlotte had solicited Blaydon's *murder* merely by telling Gashi about the rape, and that he was the girl's father. Unless . . .

'Is it true?' she asked softly. 'Was Leka Gashi Marnie's father?'

Charlotte stared at her, wide-eyed, and said, 'No.'

'Are you sure?'

Charlotte simply reached for another tissue and nodded.

'Blaydon?'

'No.'

'Then who? Do you know?'

'It was after I got back to Oxford,' she said. 'The middle of July. There was an old boyfriend. His name doesn't matter. We got too carried away to worry about precautions.'

'But Marnie's birthday was 15 March. You say you slept with Blaydon and Gashi in mid-June. That works out at exactly nine months from . . .' Annie put her hand to her mouth. 'Oh, my God,' she said. 'Marnie was a month premature, wasn't she, born after only *eight* months?'

'That's right.'

Annie looked at Gerry. 'We should have known. Francine Sedgwick, Marnie's mother, told us the baby they adopted had been born early, kept in the hospital a little longer than usual.'

'Do what you want with me,' Charlotte said. 'I don't care any more. I've told you the truth and that's all there is to it.'

There was still 'soliciting to murder', which they might have a better chance of proving now that Charlotte admitted she had lied to Gashi about his being Marnie's father, but even then, there were so many extenuating circumstances, the CPS might easily refuse to prosecute. All that remained was 'wasting police time' or 'interfering in a police investigation' or 'obstruction of justice' – lesser charges, but still serious. But it was unlikely that anything much would happen to Charlotte Westlake, Annie thought. And maybe that was all for the best. What would be the point in locking her up in prison? As was so often the case, she would probably be far harder on herself than the law would be on her. After all, she had been indirectly responsible for three deaths: Connor Clive Blaydon, Neville Roberts and Marnie Sedgwick.

Jessica Bowen was busy making notes, and Charlotte was lost in her own grief. Then Jessica glanced up at Annie, questioning.

Annie just shrugged. 'Later,' she said. 'We'll consider all the options. But later.'

They gathered up their papers and left.

20

Banks got back to Newhope Cottage around six-thirty that evening, had a quick shower and changed clothes. He picked up a bottle of Cahors from the rack, then he was ready to set off for Ray's.

After ringing Jean-Claude and finding out that there hadn't been a hint or whisper about Zelda visiting Paris recently, he had spent the morning wandering the bookstalls beside the Seine on the Left Bank, where he had bought a hefty copy of *À la recherche du temps perdu* in the original French. He didn't know why, as he hadn't been able to get very far with it in English, but it had just seemed the thing to do. And it wasn't very expensive. He also bought what he guessed was a reproduction of a sixties poster for Francoise Hardy's debut studio album, *Tous les garçons et les filles*, the picture with the umbrella. She looked just like the woman he had seen on the Rue Montmartre with the four long-stemmed roses.

He had no real news to give Ray, but at least he could try to keep his friend's mind off his worries for a few hours. He sometimes felt a little guilty for contributing to Ray's optimism about Zelda, when he had no definite idea where she was or what she was doing, but then *he* also believed that she might turn up one day, when things had blown over.

He also had a vague idea where she might be, gleaned from the Moleskine notebook, and he thought he could probably track her down if he wanted to. But he would give her time to make the first move, if that was what she wanted to do. She would either return in her own time, or she wouldn't. He had no idea if it was fear of arrest that was keeping her away. The file was still open on the two corpses in the burned-out treatment plant, but given the lack of solid evidence, even that investigation would soon slow to a crawl.

The weather was changing and it was a windy evening when Banks drove over to Lyndgarth listening to Rhiannon Giddens on the car stereo. He pulled up outside Windlee Farm halfway through 'Little Margaret'. All seemed quiet there, except for the wind whistling around the buildings – no sixties rock blaring out of the open windows – but Ray's car was in the drive, and it was unlikely he had gone anywhere without it. Banks walked up to the front door and rang the bell. Nothing. He knocked hard. Still nothing. Next, he walked around the property to see if Ray was in one of the outbuildings, Zelda's studio, or even sitting on the edge of the moor contemplating sketching, as he often did. But he wasn't there, either.

He went back and tried the front door. It creaked open. Ray never was much of a one for security, he remembered, and without Zelda's recent paranoia to drive him, he had reverted to old habits. However, Banks was certain that even Ray would have locked up if he had gone out. There was no smell of food cooking, which was also odd. Banks decided that Ray was either in a deep, alcohol-induced sleep or he was so lost in his work he wasn't paying attention to anything else. He put the wine bottle down and prowled around the downstairs rooms, kitchen, den, living room. Where was Ray? Banks suddenly felt a chill of fear run up his spine. Had they come back? Whoever was left of the gang that had taken Zelda. Had they come back to take revenge on Ray for her escape? But there were no signs of any disruption. At least, not downstairs.

Banks called out Ray's name but got only silence in return. There were no lights on and the downstairs was in shadow. Banks opened the cellar door, flicked on the light switch and went down. Nothing there. Next, he headed for the staircase. As soon as he got to the bottom, he froze. He could see a shape there, a bulk, right at the top, and there was a hand hanging over the first step.

He took the stairs two at a time and knelt by Ray's motionless body, laid two fingers on the carotid artery in his neck. No pulse. The skin was cold, and when he turned on the light he could see discoloration already beginning to affect the flesh. Banks fell back against the wall and slid down, knees together, and held his head in his hands. It couldn't be. Ray dead? Just like that.

But there was no mistake. Banks glanced over the body but could see no signs of physical violence. That didn't mean anything, of course; even a fatal knife wound might not be visible to the naked eye. The only thing to do was not to disturb the scene further and to call in the police. They would need a doctor and a mortuary van, but there was no sense in asking for an ambulance. Ray was beyond ambulances.

Following his copper's instinct, Banks checked out all the other rooms upstairs. Nobody. Ray's studio door was open and soft gold evening light flooded through the large skylight and back windows, illuminating the canvas that stood on its easel. It was Zelda, Banks could see. When he walked closer he saw all sorts of details and realised that it was a sort of optical illusion – one large image incorporating many smaller ones, also of Zelda, or so it appeared. It seemed somehow unfinished, and it would always remain that way now. On his way out he noticed *Forever Changes* on another easel and the cover of The Nice's *The Thoughts of Emerlist Davjack* leaning against the turntable.

With a heavy heart, Banks stepped carefully over Ray's body, made his way back downstairs on shaky legs, then went outside for some fresh air and punched in the familiar numbers on his mobile.

Neither Banks nor Annie had any interest in attending Dr Galway's post-mortem examination. Annie had gone down to the mortuary with Banks to identify the body, and then she had gone home, said she wanted to be by herself for a while. Gerry, too, was devastated. She and Ray had started out on the wrong track, Banks knew, because Ray had teased her mercilessly about her being a nubile pre-Raphaelite beauty and said how he wanted her to pose for him in the nude. But after she had almost died taking down a murder suspect, he had presented her with a beautiful head and shoulders sketch of her that he had drawn from memory. She had it framed and hung it in the pride of place on the wall of her small flat. Since then, they had been the best of friends, and she had given as good as she got in the teasing department.

When it was all over, Banks was the one who walked down that tiled corridor to the doctor's office alone and found himself again sitting under 'The Anatomy Lesson of Dr Nicolaes Tulp' while he listened to Dr Galway's interpretations of the post-mortem results.

'I can state categorically,' she said, 'that there are absolutely no signs of foul play. Your friend died a sad but most natural death.'

'Heart?' Banks said. He had already heard from the CSIs that there was no evidence of a break-in or of any struggle at Windlee Farm, and his own brief examination had told him there was nothing missing, so robbery was not likely to be the motive. The people responsible for Zelda's abduction and his own near demise were all dead – Phil Keane, Petar and Goran

Tadić. Leka Gashi, the Albanian whom Annie had discovered was responsible for the Connor Clive Blaydon and Neville Roberts murders was still on the loose somewhere, but he had no connection with Ray or Zelda.

'Myocardial infarction. A massive heart attack. It would have been quick. He would hardly have known what hit him. A few moments of pain, perhaps, then . . .'

'"The anaesthetic from which none come round."'

She frowned. 'Quite. Well, I suppose you could put it like that, if you happened to be of a poetic turn of mind. What I'm trying to say is that he wouldn't have suffered greatly.'

'Thank you. But would he have known what was happening? It looked as if he was trying to get downstairs to his phone.'

'He would certainly have known something was happening. But not for long.' She paused. 'His arteries were in a bad way. The blood supply to the heart was cut off. The damage was so extensive that he must have had at least some chest pain and shortness of breath over the past few months to warn him that something was seriously wrong.'

Banks knew that Ray would simply ignore something like that, not think it worth mentioning. 'I do remember once or twice he complained of chest pains,' he said. 'Not that I don't have plenty of aches and pains myself.'

'It's probably just your age. We often don't recognise symptoms.'

'And when we do, it often turns out that they're not symptoms at all but simply a result of sitting in the wrong position for too long. Or indigestion, heartburn.'

'There is that. But if you're worried about anything, maybe you should see your doctor and have a full physical?'

'Maybe. It's been a while. But I'm not worried. So a heart attack, then?'

'Yes.'

A heart attack. Pure and simple. Banks was glad it was a natural death. If Ray had been murdered, it would create a whole new set of problems, some for which he might even bear a modicum of blame. 'And the cause?'

'Hard to say exactly.'

'I know he didn't get much exercise.'

'That was quite obvious. He also drank and smoked too much and ate far too much fatty food,' Dr Galway added, with a pointed look in Banks's direction.

'I don't smoke,' Banks said, and she just smiled.

'I'm sorry about your friend, Superintendent Banks,' said Dr Galway. 'Sincerely sorry. But he was in his late seventies and he didn't take very good care of himself. Annie Cabbot's his daughter, isn't she?'

'Yes.'

'How is she doing?'

'About as well as you'd expect, which is not very well.'

'They were close?'

'I'd say so,' said Banks. 'Her mother died when she was very young, and he pretty much brought her up single-handedly. He just moved up here from Cornwall a year or so back.'

'With that young woman who disappeared, is that right?' Dr Galway asked.

'Nelia Melnic. Right.'

'He was upset about her?'

'Very.'

'That kind of stress won't have helped his condition much.'

'Can people really die of a broken heart?'

Dr Galway snorted. 'Only if you take a very poetic view of death, as you seem to do. Stress is a factor, yes, as can be depression, worry, anxiety and any number of mental conditions we don't fully understand yet. All those things put a strain on the heart and its function, but it wouldn't be entirely accurate to say that it breaks. A heart attack involves a kind of paroxysm rather than a snap. The human body is a complex mechanism, interdependent in so many ways. All I can give you is the doctor's viewpoint – the pathologist's, at that. I deal with the dead.'

'You really are very rational, aren't you, doctor?'

'Why, thank you. I try to be. That's the nicest thing you've ever said to me.'

Banks smiled and stood up, leaned over to shake her hand. 'Thanks for doing this so promptly,' he said.

'You'll be able to put his daughter's mind to rest?'

'I'll do my best. It won't be easy, but I'll try.'

'If she . . . I mean, if you think she's becoming seriously upset . . . there is help.'

'I know,' said Banks. 'And I'll make sure that Annie knows, too.'

'Well, then, I'll be seeing you.'

'Not too soon, I hope,' said Banks, and left. The Unicorn over the road from Eastvale General would be open now, and Banks could do with a pint. Or a double whisky.

On the day of Ray Cabbot's funeral, Banks drove to Harkside to pick up Annie, and for a while he thought she wouldn't come. She sat in her chair, still wearing her dressing gown, hair an unruly mass, unmoving, not speaking, her eyes puffy and red from crying, face tear-stained.

Banks sat with her in silence for a while, holding her hand. When he squeezed gently, he felt no return of pressure. What could he do? He couldn't force her to go. He spoke to her softly, telling her she should get ready. She looked at him, uncomprehending, then all of a sudden seemed to snap out of it.

'I must get ready,' she said. 'Dad's waiting.'

Banks helped her up and told her he would wait downstairs while she got dressed and ready, and not to worry, there was plenty of time.

It didn't take her long. In a few minutes Annie had managed to throw on a dark skirt, top and jacket suitable for a funeral, brush her hair and apply a little make-up to cover the ravages of her grief. She remained quiet as she got in the car and Banks drove to the funeral home in Eastvale. He refrained from playing any music. Annie might think it insensitive, even a requiem, and he honestly couldn't think of anything to play for the occasion.

Ray had left a will, as it turned out, and it stipulated that he wanted his ashes scattered in the sea below St Ives. He had also left a substantial amount of his estate to Zelda and the rest – more than adequate, along with the house – to Annie. He hadn't made any arrangements for his unsold paintings, but Banks imagined his agent would help Annie handle all that. He had left his collection of close to 2,000 vinyl LPs and Marantz turntable to Banks.

When Banks had revisited Windlee Farm a couple of days after Ray's death to make sure everything was turned off and locked up, at Annie's request, he had found a postcard among that day's post. It showed a reproduction of da Vinci's *Annunciation*, and on the back, next to Ray's address, a heart. Banks didn't think he needed to check the handwriting to know that the postcard was from Zelda. The postmark read Belgrade, but Banks didn't think that was where she was. She must have got someone to post it for her. He hadn't told Annie about it.

There was quite a crowd for Ray's funeral, and the small chapel was bursting at the seams. The arts crowd had come up from London, and most of the people who still lived at the artists' commune in St Ives, where Ray had lived for many years, turned up, along with some who had lived there only briefly and left years ago. They all remembered Ray's generosity and encouragement for young artists.

A vicar who had never even met Ray delivered a few platitudes and a prayer, and then the tears streamed down Annie's face as she sat through Banks's short eulogy, which Annie had said there was no way she could do without breaking down, and a reading by Gerry of Christina Rossetti's 'When I am dead, my dearest', which Banks had last heard at the funeral of his first love, Emily Hargreaves. Ray would have hated it, but funerals are about the living. As the service ended with The Beach Boys' 'I Just Wasn't Made for These Times', which Ray had once told Banks was what he wanted to be played at his funeral, there was hardly a dry eye in the chapel.

The funeral tea was held at Windlee Farm, and catered by the Black Bull's Mick Slater. It was nothing special, just sausage rolls, vol-au-vents, scotch eggs and slices of pork pie followed by Black Forest gateau, but it was enough. Slater had also brought a couple of kegs of beer, which most of Ray's friends seemed to prefer to tea. Banks chatted with some of Ray's old artist friends and also fell into conversation with a young woman who said she was a friend of Zelda's from her London days, and she had read about the funeral in the paper. She had come in the hopes that Zelda would be there and was disappointed when Banks told her they didn't know where she was.

Finally, the last guests drove off. It was still light outside, and Banks poured himself another glass of wine and went outside to enjoy the mild evening air and the open views of the moorland. Curlews flew high in the distance, and a lark ascended, singing. Banks thought of the Vaughan Williams music. Annie wandered out a few minutes later and joined him, linking her arm in his. The vast expanse of the moors at the back of the cottage spread out for miles under a thickening cover of dark clouds still in the distance. But there would be rain before long.

'So she didn't come after all,' said Annie.

'She probably doesn't know Ray is dead,' Banks said.

Annie removed her arm from his. 'There you go, making excuses for her again. I suppose you know it's all her fault. If he hadn't got involved with her, none of this would have happened.'

'Annie, Ray was ill. His arteries were blocked. He drank too much. He smoked too much. He ate too much red meat. He never went to the doctor's.'

Annie waved her hand dismissively. 'I know all that. You're a one to talk. But she's the one who brought it all on, the straw that broke the camel's back. You know what terrible shape he's been in since she disappeared.'

'It was hardly her fault she was abducted,' Banks said.

'I mean after. After the fire. When she saved you and ran away.'

'She was scared.'

'So was Ray. And she was supposed to love him. She didn't even bother to come to his funeral. Did you see that picture he was painting?'

'Yes,' said Banks.

'I hate it. You take it.'

Banks knew there was no point in arguing, and the last thing he wanted to do was upset Annie any further, which defending Zelda would most certainly do. It was one of those moments where he would have loved to light up a cigarette, but he made do with the wine.

Annie would get over it in time. Right now she was grieving and looking for someone to blame, and there was just enough truth in what she said to make that someone Zelda. There *were* certain aspects of Zelda's life that made her dangerous company. After all, if she hadn't become an important part of Ray's life, it would have saved him a lot of grief. But what about the love? What about the joy she gave him? The happiness they shared? Annie didn't see that. Banks had seen Ray and Zelda together and heard each speak separately about the other, and there was no doubt in his mind that they loved one another utterly, completely. Perhaps that kind of love can kill you eventually. He watched the distant birds swooping and weaving under the massing rain clouds. He couldn't make out what they were – lapwings, curlews, swifts – but that didn't matter. It was glorious just to witness the aerial ballet.

'We'd better go in,' he said. 'It's going to rain.'

Annie said nothing at first, then she tightened her lips and stalked off ahead of him towards the door. It was going to be a long haul.

21

Croatia was basking in late afternoon sunshine when Banks left his rental car at the bottom of the hill and started walking up the dirt path.

He hadn't got very far when a muscular young man with no neck appeared in front of him, cradling a Kalashnikov AK-47 in his arms. The man said something guttural in what Banks assumed to be Croatian, and Banks said he didn't understand, that he was English, his name was Alan Banks, and he would like to see Nelia Melnic. The man gave him a suspicious glance, pointed to the ground and said, 'You stay here,' then made his way up the hill. In case Banks had any fancy ideas about disobeying the command, another man, looking exactly the same as the first one, appeared, also cradling an AK-47. Banks considered asking him whether the weapon was legal but decided against it.

The first man came back, examined the package Banks was carrying and twitched his head in the direction of the summit. Banks followed him. They arrived at a high stone wall topped with broken glass set in concrete. The man opened the spiked wrought-iron gates and gestured Banks through. He was out of breath and paused for a moment to rest. In front of him stood a petite woman in her early sixties with short silver hair and pale blue eyes that had seen far more than anyone ought. Her wiry body looked strong, as if she had done much manual labour. She held out her hand in greeting and walked forward. Banks shook it. Her grip was firm and her hand calloused.

'Please forgive me if I ask for some identification,' she said.

Banks noticed that his guide with the Kalashnikov was lingering by the gate. Only when he had shown his warrant card and the woman nodded did he disappear.

'One can't be too careful,' she said.

'Is Nelia here?'

'She is.'

'You must be Mati.'

The woman raised an eyebrow. 'And you must be a very good detective.'

'I have my sources,' Banks said.

The woman started walking over the final gentle slope of grass past the side of the house. Banks walked in step beside her. 'Will you tell me why you want to see her?' she asked.

Banks paused for a moment. 'Her partner, Ray Cabbot. I'm afraid he died.'

Mati stopped in her tracks. 'Raymond? Dead?'

'I'm afraid so, yes.'

'When did this happen?'

'A few weeks ago. It took me a while to find you.'

'That's good. I mean that it took the great detective a long time. We depend on being a needle in a haystack. But this news. It is very bad for Nelia. She is not strong.'

'It's not something I've been looking forward to,' said Banks. 'But she should know.'

Mati started walking again. 'Yes. Of course she must know. Please, sit over there and wait.' She pointed to a white table with matching chairs on the edge of a promontory overlooking the Adriatic. 'Forgive me if I do not invite you into the main house, but some of the girls . . . they are not yet ready to see a man again. I have to keep my sons away, too, and they are the gentlest people you could ever hope to meet.'

Banks flashed on the neckless pair cradling their Kalashnikovs. Gentle wasn't the first word that had come to his mind, but he believed her.

Banks sat down at the table and faced the sea. The water ranged from pale green to deep blue and all shades in between. Small crafts and fishing boats bobbed between the islands, and far out to sea he could see the white bulk of a cruise liner. A light refreshing salt breeze blew up from the water. There was a bottle of Plavac on the table, already open, along with two glasses, and Banks saw no reason not to pour himself one.

'Pour one for me, too, please, Alan.'

The voice from behind startled him. He hadn't heard her approach. Instead of pouring, he stood up and faced Zelda again, at last.

She wore a simple, shapeless grey shift and her face was bare of make-up. Her hair was cut very short – not professionally, by the looks of it – and there was a strange pale luminosity about her skin and her eyes he had never noticed before. In an odd way, she reminded him of those old posters of Jean Seberg playing Joan of Arc. She was certainly a long way from the Zelda of Ray's unfinished portrait. Was this one face of her that Ray had never seen? She was still beautiful, Banks thought, but now her beauty was of a different kind altogether.

They sat, and Banks poured the wine. 'So,' he said, raising his glass. 'Here you are.'

'Here I am. How did you find me?'

'It's my job. Don't you remember what a great detective I am?'

Zelda managed a smile. 'Of course.'

'There were clues. Your past. Your books – the stories of abused women. The time you mentioned visiting an old friend in Croatia who ran a hostel for girls who had escaped sexual slavery. And this.' Banks handed her the Moleskine notebook.

'You read it?'

'Yes.'

Zelda flushed and set it down on the table.

'Keep it,' Banks said.

Zelda slipped the notebook in a pocket in her shift. 'So now you know all my secrets.'

'Hardly.'

Zelda hung her head. 'At least you know the very worst.'

Banks leaned forward and took her hand. She seemed surprised but didn't snatch it back. 'Zelda,' he said. 'I'm sorry to be the one to have to tell you this, but it's Ray. I'm afraid—'

'He's dead?'

'Yes. How did you know?'

'I didn't know. But I had a strange dream. What happened?'

'His heart. It happened quickly. There was nothing to be done.'

'The stubborn old fool,' she said. 'He would never go to the doctor. I told him many times. Those pains in his chest. The short breath. The coughing. He . . .' But the tears pouring down her face got in the way of talking, and soon her whole body was wracked with sobs. Banks let her cry. He had come forearmed and handed her a clean white handkerchief.

After a while, the sobbing ebbed away and she seemed to compose herself. She gulped down some wine. 'What's that package you brought?' she asked.

Banks handed her the tube. She opened it and unrolled Ray's last painting, the portrait of her. 'Annie wanted you to have it,' he said.

'Thank you.' Zelda studied the picture and put it aside, a strange sad smile on her face. 'How is she?'

'Surviving. It's hard.'

'Yes. I imagine so.' Zelda paused. 'I *was* going to go back, you know,' she said. 'One way or another. I didn't know when. But I was going to go back.'

Banks squeezed her hand. 'I know you were. It's one of those things beyond our control, Zelda. There was nothing to be done. Ray was Ray. He lived his life the way he wanted, and none of us would have changed him for anything. He was lucky to know you in these last few years. Lucky to know such happiness at the end. He knew that.'

Zelda regarded him with her damp eyes. '*I* was lucky to know *him*,' she said. 'You might think we had a strange relationship, that he was too old for me, but it worked. For both of us. We didn't ... you know ... I'm no use that way. But Raymond understood.'

'I don't judge you, Zelda, or your relationship. You know better than that.'

She gently disengaged her hand from his and patted his wrist to assure him it wasn't an angry gesture. 'I should do,' she said. 'And I'm Nelia now.' Then they both took a long sip of wine. It seemed to go straight to Banks's head, which was either something to do with its extraordinary strength, or the sun and sea. 'But you read the notebook,' she went on. 'You know about Darius and Goran. And later Petar and your enemy Keane. That's four people I've killed, Alan. I'm cursed. Bad to know.'

'I preferred to believe the notebook was a work of the imagination. Wishful thinking.'

Nelia gave him a sad smile. 'You're not that much of a fool. It was true. All of it. I killed them.'

'I went to Paris,' Banks said. 'A friend there told me about what happened with Darius.'

Nelia gave her head a slight shake. 'It was bad. I was stealing his blackmail material. Emile had asked me to. Promised me a

French passport. He was going to join me later wherever I went. Darius came in and caught me. He started beating me. There was a knife on the bar, one of those little ones you use to cut limes and lemons for drinks. I stabbed him, but it didn't penetrate very far, and he still kept coming, so I cut his throat. They almost had a scandal, made a quick cover-up, rushed me out of the country fast with a French passport. I think some of them wanted to kill me, but that didn't happen. I like to think Emile spoke up for me. He was true to his word. Later the Sûreté got me an interview for the job with the NCA. So they could keep an eye on me, I suppose. And Darius's musclemen killed Emile. That's what happened in Paris.'

'And London?'

'Goran Tadić? I drugged him in a hotel room and stabbed him to death. I assume his brother and colleagues got rid of the body. I never heard anything more about it until they abducted me from the cottage. They tracked me down through the Hotel Belgrade CCTV and taxi drivers. They also tortured Faye Butler, Keane's ex-girlfriend, until she told them what she knew. Then they killed her. But even when he took me, Petar Tadić didn't know who I was. He didn't remember that he had raped me when I was seventeen. I reminded him before I killed him. I don't know what you want me to say, but you won't get any apologies out of me. I have no regrets. Do what you wish, but I'm glad I killed them, all of them, and I'm glad they're dead. Raymond was worth more than all of them put together.'

'I can't say I disagree,' said Banks.

'And you a policeman.'

'Tell me, what happened at the treatment plant.'

'They kept me chained to the radiator upstairs, in a bare room. It looked like a disused office. It was always dark until they came to see me with their light.'

'How did you escape?'

'It doesn't matter. Petar Tadić made a mistake, and I took advantage. Then I took his keys after I killed him. I came down and saw Keane splashing petrol over you. You know the rest. I crept up on him and stabbed him and cut you free. Then I turned to fight him for the lighter, but he lit it. Pouff. It was so strange. This man, with the last movement in his life, he struck a cigarette lighter and started a big fire.'

'And afterwards?'

'There was a car parked outside the side entrance. Keane's car. The keys were still in the ignition. Tadić had told me that he had come back with my new passport and some money for the journey. They were taking me to a brothel in Dhaka. A terrible place. They told me I would die there slowly of disease and beatings. After I made sure you ran for the main exit, I went out of the side and drove away. I found the passport and money in the glove compartment. I drove to Newcastle and left the car at the airport, then I flew from there to Amsterdam. The passport was in the name of Frieda Mannheim, so I didn't expect any trouble, or run into any. That man Keane was a good forger. After that . . . I came here. It was easy to disappear, to lie low. Until now.'

'But why didn't you leave with me, the same way?'

'I think you know the answer to that. I had just killed two men, and you're a policeman.'

'Surely you know me better than that, Nelia? And it was self-defence.'

'Perhaps.' Nelia smiled. 'But I was hardly thinking any more clearly than you were.'

She stood up and walked to the edge of the promontory, carrying her wine. She made such a slight and vulnerable figure against the vast expanse of the darkening sea beyond that Banks found it hard to believe she had wreaked such havoc among the men who had stolen her youth. He knocked back the last of his wine and stood up. 'Raymond left you something else in his will,' he said.

'I don't want anything.'

Banks gestured to the house. 'It might help. With all your work here.'

Nelia nodded, her back to him.

'I'll see to it,' Banks said. 'I'll go now.'

Nelia turned to face him. 'Must you go so soon?' she said. 'It's not dark yet.'

'It's a long drive to Zagreb.'

'Are you going to arrest me?'

Banks looked at her for a long time, then shook his head. 'No,' he said. 'I've had enough of all that. More than enough.'

Then he turned away and walked back down the hill to his car.

ACKNOWLEDGEMENTS

There are many people to thank for helping me get this book ready for publication, starting with my wife Sheila Halladay, who read the first draft and sent me back to the manuscript with many helpful suggestions. At Hodder & Stoughton, I would especially like to thank my editor Carolyn Mays, her assistant Sorcha Rose and copy-editor Sharona. At McClelland and Stewart in Canada, thanks to Kelly Joseph and Jared Bland, and at William Morrow in the U.S.A., Emily Krump and Julia Elliott. It is also important to recognize the efforts of those whose work is yet to be done, especially publicists and sales reps, who will have a far more difficult task this time, for obvious reasons. Thank you in advance.

Also thanks to my agents Dominick Abel, David Grossman and Rosie and Jessica Buckman. I would also like to thank those overseas publishers, editors and translators who have stuck with me over the years. They know who they are. There are many others who contribute, including cover artists, book designers, proof-readers, booksellers and librarians, and I would like to thank all those people. Finally, thanks to my readers, without whom all our efforts would be pointless.

KT-433-808

FIRE AND FURY

ALSO BY MICHAEL WOLFF

Television Is the New Television:
The Unexpected Triumph of Old Media in the Digital Age

The Man Who Owns the News:
Inside the Secret World of Rupert Murdoch

Autumn of the Moguls:
My Misadventures with the Titans, Poseurs, and Money Guys
Who Mastered and Messed Up Big Media

Burn Rate:
How I Survived the Gold Rush Years on the Internet

Where We Stand

White Kids

FIRE AND FURY

INSIDE THE TRUMP WHITE HOUSE

MICHAEL WOLFF

Little, Brown

LITTLE, BROWN

First published in the United States in 2018 by Henry Holt and Company
First published in Great Britain in 2018 by Little, Brown

3 5 7 9 10 8 6 4

A CIP catalogue record for this book
is available from the British Library.

Hardback ISBN 978-1-4087-1140-8
Trade paperback 978-1-4087-1139-2

Designed by Meryl Sussman Levavi
Printed and bound in Great Britain by
Clays Ltd, St Ives plc

Papers used by Little, Brown are from well-managed forests
and other responsible sources.

Little, Brown
An imprint of
Little, Brown Book Group
Carmelite House
50 Victoria Embankment
London EC4Y 0DZ

An Hachette UK Company
www.hachette.co.uk

www.littlebrown.co.uk

For Victoria and Louise, mother and daughter

CONTENTS

AUTHOR'S NOTE

The reason to write this book could not be more obvious. With the inauguration of Donald Trump on January 20, 2017, the United States entered the eye of the most extraordinary political storm since at least Watergate. As the day approached, I set out to tell this story in as contemporaneous a fashion as possible, and to try to see life in the Trump White House through the eyes of the people closest to it.

This was originally conceived as an account of the Trump administration's first hundred days, that most traditional marker of a presidency. But events barreled on without natural pause for more than two hundred days, the curtain coming down on the first act of Trump's presidency only with the appointment of retired general John Kelly as the chief of staff in late July and the exit of chief strategist Stephen K. Bannon three weeks later.

The events I've described in these pages are based on conversations that took place over a period of eighteen months with the president, with most members of his senior staff—some of whom talked to me dozens of times—and with many people who they in turn spoke to. The first interview occurred well before I could have imagined a Trump White House, much less a book about it, in late May 2016 at Trump's home in Beverly Hills—the then candidate polishing off a pint of Häagen-Dazs vanilla as he happily and idly opined about a range of topics while his aides, Hope

Hicks, Corey Lewandowski, and Jared Kushner, went in and out of the room. Conversations with members of the campaign's team continued through the Republican Convention in Cleveland, when it was still hardly possible to conceive of Trump's election. They moved on to Trump Tower with a voluble Steve Bannon—before the election, when he still seemed like an entertaining oddity, and later, after the election, when he seemed like a miracle worker.

Shortly after January 20, I took up something like a semipermanent seat on a couch in the West Wing. Since then I have conducted more than two hundred interviews.

While the Trump administration has made hostility to the press a virtual policy, it has also been more open to the media than any White House in recent memory. In the beginning, I sought a level of formal access to this White House, something of a fly-on-the-wall status. The president himself encouraged this idea. But, given the many fiefdoms in the Trump White House that came into open conflict from the first days of the administration, there seemed no one person able to make this happen. Equally, there was no one to say "Go away." Hence I became more a constant interloper than an invited guest—something quite close to an actual fly on the wall—having accepted no rules nor having made any promises about what I might or might not write.

Many of the accounts of what has happened in the Trump White House are in conflict with one another; many, in Trumpian fashion, are baldly untrue. Those conflicts, and that looseness with the truth, if not with reality itself, are an elemental thread of the book. Sometimes I have let the players offer their versions, in turn allowing the reader to judge them. In other instances I have, through a consistency in accounts and through sources I have come to trust, settled on a version of events I believe to be true.

Some of my sources spoke to me on so-called deep background, a convention of contemporary political books that allows for a disembodied description of events provided by an unnamed witness to them. I have also relied on off-the-record interviews, allowing a source to provide a direct quote with the understanding that it was not for attribution. Other sources spoke to me with the understanding that the material in the interviews would not become public until the book came out. Finally, some sources spoke forthrightly on the record.

At the same time, it is worth noting some of the journalistic conundrums that I faced when dealing with the Trump administration, many of them the result of the White House's absence of official procedures and the lack of experience of its principals. These challenges have included dealing with off-the-record or deep-background material that was later casually put on the record; sources who provided accounts in confidence and subsequently shared them widely, as though liberated by their first utterances; a frequent inattention to setting any parameters on the use of a conversation; a source's views being so well known and widely shared that it would be risible not to credit them; and the almost samizdat sharing, or gobsmacked retelling, of otherwise private and deep-background conversations. And everywhere in this story is the president's own constant, tireless, and uncontrolled voice, public and private, shared by others on a daily basis, sometimes virtually as he utters it.

For whatever reason, almost everyone I contacted—senior members of the White House staff as well as dedicated observers of it—shared large amounts of time with me and went to great effort to help shed light on the unique nature of life inside the Trump White House. In the end, what I witnessed, and what this book is about, is a group of people who have struggled, each in their own way, to come to terms with the meaning of working for Donald Trump.

I owe them an enormous debt.

PROLOGUE: AILES AND BANNON

The evening began at six-thirty, but Steve Bannon, suddenly among the world's most powerful men and now less and less mindful of time constraints, was late.

Bannon had promised to come to this small dinner arranged by mutual friends in a Greenwich Village town house to see Roger Ailes, the former head of Fox News and the most significant figure in right-wing media and Bannon's sometime mentor. The next day, January 4, 2017—little more than two weeks before the inauguration of his friend Donald Trump as the forty-fifth president—Ailes would be heading to Palm Beach, into a forced, but he hoped temporary, retirement.

Snow was threatening, and for a while the dinner appeared doubtful. The seventy-six-year-old Ailes, with a long history of leg and hip problems, was barely walking, and, coming in to Manhattan with his wife Beth from their upstate home on the Hudson, was wary of slippery streets. But Ailes was eager to see Bannon. Bannon's aide, Alexandra Preate, kept texting steady updates on Bannon's progress extracting himself from Trump Tower.

As the small group waited for Bannon, it was Ailes's evening. Quite as dumbfounded by his old friend Donald Trump's victory as most everyone else, Ailes provided the gathering with something of a mini-seminar on the randomness and absurdities of politics. Before launching Fox

News in 1996, Ailes had been, for thirty years, among the leading political operatives in the Republican Party. As surprised as he was by this election, he could yet make a case for a straight line from Nixon to Trump. He just wasn't sure, he said, that Trump himself, at various times a Republican, Independent, and Democrat, could make the case. Still, he thought he knew Trump as well as anyone did and was eager to offer his help. He was also eager to get back into the right-wing media game, and he energetically described some of the possibilities for coming up with the billion or so dollars he thought he would need for a new cable network.

Both men, Ailes and Bannon, fancied themselves particular students of history, both autodidacts partial to universal field theories. They saw this in a charismatic sense—they had a personal relationship with history, as well as with Donald Trump.

Now, however reluctantly, Ailes understood that, at least for the moment, he was passing the right-wing torch to Bannon. It was a torch that burned bright with ironies. Ailes's Fox News, with its $1.5 billion in annual profits, had dominated Republican politics for two decades. Now Bannon's Breitbart News, with its mere $1.5 million in annual profits, was claiming that role. For thirty years, Ailes—until recently the single most powerful person in conservative politics—had humored and tolerated Donald Trump, but in the end Bannon and Breitbart had elected him.

Six months before, when a Trump victory still seemed out of the realm of the possible, Ailes, accused of sexual harassment, was cashiered from Fox News in a move engineered by the liberal sons of conservative eighty-five-year-old Rupert Murdoch, the controlling shareholder of Fox News and the most powerful media owner of the age. Ailes's downfall was cause for much liberal celebration: the greatest conservative bugbear in modern politics had been felled by the new social norm. Then Trump, hardly three months later, accused of vastly more louche and abusive behavior, was elected president.

* * *

Ailes enjoyed many things about Trump: his salesmanship, his showmanship, his gossip. He admired Trump's sixth sense for the public marketplace—or at least the relentlessness and indefatigability of his ceaseless attempts to win it over. He liked Trump's game. He liked Trump's impact and his shamelessness. "He just keeps going," Ailes had marveled to a friend after the first debate with Hillary Clinton. "You hit Donald along the head, and he keeps going. He doesn't even know he's been hit."

But Ailes was convinced that Trump had no political beliefs or backbone. The fact that Trump had become the ultimate avatar of Fox's angry common man was another sign that we were living in an upside-down world. The joke was on somebody—and Ailes thought it might be on him.

Still, Ailes had been observing politicians for decades, and in his long career he had witnessed just about every type and style and oddity and confection and cravenness and mania. Operatives like himself—and now, like Bannon—worked with all kinds. It was the ultimate symbiotic and codependent relationship. Politicians were front men in a complex organizational effort. Operatives knew the game, and so did most candidates and officeholders. But Ailes was pretty sure Trump did not. Trump was undisciplined—he had no capacity for any game plan. He could not be a part of any organization, nor was he likely to subscribe to any program or principle. In Ailes's view, he was "a rebel without a cause." He was simply "Donald"—as though nothing more need be said.

In early August, less than a month after Ailes had been ousted from Fox News, Trump asked his old friend to take over the management of his calamitous campaign. Ailes, knowing Trump's disinclination to take advice, or even listen to it, turned him down. This was the job Bannon took a week later.

After Trump's victory, Ailes seemed to balance regret that he had not seized the chance to run his friend's campaign with incredulity that Trump's offer had turned out to be the ultimate opportunity. Trump's rise to power, Ailes understood, was the improbable triumph of many things that Ailes and Fox News represented. After all, Ailes was perhaps the person most responsible for unleashing the angry-man currents of Trump's victory: he had invented the right-wing media that delighted in the Trump character.

Ailes, who was a member of the close circle of friends and advisers Trump frequently called, found himself hoping he would get more time with the new president once he and Beth moved to Palm Beach; he knew Trump planned to make regular trips to Mar-a-Lago, down the road from Ailes's new home. Still, though Ailes was well aware that in politics, winning changes everything—the winner is the winner—he couldn't quite get his head around the improbable and bizarre fact that his friend Donald Trump was now president of the United States.

* * *

At nine-thirty, three hours late, a good part of the dinner already eaten, Bannon finally arrived. Wearing a disheveled blazer, his signature pairing of two shirts, and military fatigues, the unshaven, overweight sixty-three-year-old joined the other guests at the table and immediately took control of the conversation. Pushing a proffered glass of wine away—"I don't drink"—he dived into a live commentary, an urgent download of information about the world he was about to take over.

"We're going to flood the zone so we have every cabinet member for the next seven days through their confirmation hearings," he said of the business-and-military 1950s-type cabinet choices. "Tillerson is two days, Session is two days, Mattis is two days. . . ."

Bannon veered from "Mad Dog" Mattis—the retired four-star general whom Trump had nominated as secretary of defense—to a long riff on torture, the surprising liberalism of generals, and the stupidity of the civilian-military bureaucracy. Then it was on to the looming appointment of Michael Flynn—a favorite Trump general who'd been the opening act at many Trump rallies—as the National Security Advisor.

"He's fine. He's not Jim Mattis and he's not John Kelly . . . but he's fine. He just needs the right staff around him." Still, Bannon averred: "When you take out all the never-Trump guys who signed all those letters and all the neocons who got us in all these wars . . . it's not a deep bench."

Bannon said he'd tried to push John Bolton, the famously hawkish diplomat, for the job as National Security Advisor. Bolton was an Ailes favorite, too.

"He's a bomb thrower," said Ailes. "And a strange little fucker. But you need him. Who else is good on Israel? Flynn is a little nutty on Iran. Tillerson"—the secretary of state designate—"just knows oil."

"Bolton's mustache is a problem," snorted Bannon. "Trump doesn't think he looks the part. You know Bolton is an acquired taste."

"Well, rumors were that he got in trouble because he got in a fight in a hotel one night and chased some woman."

"If I told Trump that, he might have the job."

* * *

Bannon was curiously able to embrace Trump while at the same time suggesting he did not take him entirely seriously. He had first met Trump, the on-again off-again presidential candidate, in 2010; at a meeting in Trump Tower, Bannon had proposed to Trump that he spend half a million dollars backing Tea Party–style candidates as a way to further his presidential ambitions. Bannon left the meeting figuring that Trump would never cough up that kind of dough. He just wasn't a serious player. Between that first encounter and mid-August 2016, when he took over the Trump campaign, Bannon, beyond a few interviews he had done with Trump for his Breitbart radio show, was pretty sure he hadn't spent more than ten minutes in one-on-one conversation with Trump.

But now Bannon's Zeitgeist moment had arrived. Everywhere there was a sudden sense of global self-doubt. Brexit in the UK, waves of immigrants arriving on Europe's angry shores, the disenfranchisement of the workingman, the specter of more financial meltdown, Bernie Sanders and his liberal revanchism—everywhere was backlash. Even the most dedicated exponents of globalism were hesitating. Bannon believed that great numbers of people were suddenly receptive to a new message: the world needs borders—or the world should return to a time when it had borders. When America was great. Trump had become the platform for that message.

By that January evening, Bannon had been immersed in Donald Trump's world for almost five months. And though he had accumulated a sizable catalogue of Trump's peculiarities, and cause enough for possible alarm about the unpredictability of his boss and his views, that did not detract from Trump's extraordinary, charismatic appeal to the right-wing, Tea Party, Internet meme base, and now, in victory, from the opportunity he was giving Steve Bannon.

* * *

"Does *he* get it?" asked Ailes suddenly, pausing and looking intently at Bannon.

He meant did Trump get it. This seemed to be a question about the right-wing agenda: Did the playboy billionaire really get the workingman populist cause? But it was possibly a point-blank question about the nature of power itself. Did Trump get where history had put him?

Bannon took a sip of water. "He gets it," said Bannon, after hesitating for perhaps a beat too long. "Or he gets what he gets."

With a sideways look, Ailes continued to stare him down, as though waiting for Bannon to show more of his cards.

"Really," Bannon said. "He's on the program. It's his program." Pivoting from Trump himself, Bannon plunged on with the Trump agenda. "Day one we're moving the U.S. embassy to Jerusalem. Netanyahu's all in. Sheldon"—Sheldon Adelson, the casino billionaire, far-right Israel defender, and Trump supporter—"is all in. We know where we're heading on this."

"Does Donald know?" asked a skeptical Ailes.

Bannon smiled—as though almost with a wink—and continued:

"Let Jordan take the West Bank, let Egypt take Gaza. Let them deal with it. Or sink trying. The Saudis are on the brink, Egyptians are on the brink, all scared to death of Persia . . . Yemen, Sinai, Libya . . . this thing is bad. . . . That's why Russia is so key. . . . Is Russia that bad? They're bad guys. But the world is full of bad guys."

Bannon offered all this with something like ebullience—a man remaking the world.

"But it's good to know the bad guys are the bad guys," said Ailes, pushing Bannon. "Donald may not know."

The real enemy, said an on-point Bannon, careful not to defend Trump too much or to dis him at all, was China. China was the first front in a new cold war. And it had all been misunderstood in the Obama years—what we thought we understood we didn't understand at all. That was the failure of American intelligence. "I think Comey is a third-rate guy. I think Brennan is a second-rate guy," Bannon said, dismissing the FBI director and the CIA director.

"The White House right now is like Johnson's White House in 1968. Susan Rice"—Obama's National Security Advisor—"is running the campaign against ISIS as a National Security Advisor. They're picking the targets, she's picking the drone strikes. I mean, they're running the war with just as much effectiveness as Johnson in sixty-eight. The Pentagon is totally disengaged from the whole thing. Intel services are disengaged from the whole thing. The media has let Obama off the hook. Take the ideology away from it, this is complete amateur hour. I don't know what Obama does. Nobody on Capitol Hill knows him, no business guys know him—what has he accomplished, what does he do?"

"Where's Donald on this?" asked Ailes, now with the clear implication that Bannon was far out ahead of his benefactor.

"He's totally on board."

"Focused?"

"He buys it."

"I wouldn't give Donald too much to think about," said an amused Ailes.

Bannon snorted. "Too much, too little—doesn't necessarily change things."

* * *

"What has he gotten himself into with the Russians?" pressed Ailes.

"Mostly," said Bannon, "he went to Russia and he thought he was going to meet Putin. But Putin couldn't give a shit about him. So he's kept trying."

"He's Donald," said Ailes.

"It's a magnificent thing," said Bannon, who had taken to regarding Trump as something like a natural wonder, beyond explanation.

Again, as though setting the issue of Trump aside—merely a large and peculiar presence to both be thankful for and to have to abide—Bannon, in the role he had conceived for himself, the auteur of the Trump presidency, charged forward:

"China's everything. Nothing else matters. We don't get China right, we don't get anything right. This whole thing is very simple. China is where Nazi Germany was in 1929 to 1930. The Chinese, like the Germans, are the most rational people in the world, until they're not. And they're gonna flip like Germany in the thirties. You're going to have a hypernationalist state, and once that happens you can't put the genie back in the bottle."

"Donald might not be Nixon in China," said Ailes, deadpan, suggesting that for Trump to seize the mantle of global transformation might strain credulity.

Bannon smiled. "Bannon in China," he said, with both remarkable grandiosity and wry self-deprecation.

"How's the kid?" asked Ailes, referring to Trump's son-in-law and paramount political adviser, thirty-six-year-old Jared Kushner.

"He's my partner," said Bannon, his tone suggesting that if he felt otherwise, he was nevertheless determined to stay on message.

"Really?" said a dubious Ailes.

"He's on the team."

"He's had lot of lunches with Rupert."

"In fact," said Bannon, "I could use your help here." Bannon then spent several minutes trying to recruit Ailes to help kneecap Murdoch. Ailes, since his ouster from Fox, had become only more bitter towards Murdoch. Now Murdoch was frequently jawboning the president-elect and encouraging him toward establishment moderation—all a strange inversion in the ever-stranger currents of American conservatism. Bannon wanted Ailes to suggest to Trump, a man whose many neuroses included a horror of forgetfulness or senility, that Murdoch might be losing it.

"I'll call him," said Ailes. "But Trump would jump through hoops for Rupert. Like for Putin. Sucks up and shits down. I just worry about who's jerking whose chain."

The older right-wing media wizard and the younger (though not by all that much) continued on to the other guests' satisfaction until twelve-thirty, the older trying to see through to the new national enigma that was Trump—although Ailes would say that in fact Trump's behavior was ever predictable—and the younger seemingly determined not to spoil his own moment of destiny.

"Donald Trump has got it. He's Trump, but he's got it. Trump is Trump," affirmed Bannon.

"Yeah, he's Trump," said Ailes, with something like incredulity.

1

ELECTION DAY

On the afternoon of November 8, 2016, Kellyanne Conway—Donald Trump's campaign manager and a central, indeed starring, personality of Trumpworld—settled into her glass office at Trump Tower. Right up until the last weeks of the race, the Trump campaign headquarters had remained a listless place. All that seemed to distinguish it from a corporate back office were a few posters with right-wing slogans.

Conway now was in a remarkably buoyant mood considering she was about to experience a resounding if not cataclysmic defeat. Donald Trump would lose the election—of this she was sure—but he would quite possibly hold the defeat to under 6 points. That was a substantial victory. As for the looming defeat itself, she shrugged it off: it was Reince Priebus's fault, not hers.

She had spent a good part of the day calling friends and allies in the political world and blaming Priebus. Now she briefed some of the television producers and anchors with whom she'd built strong relationships—and with whom, actively interviewing in the last few weeks, she was hoping to land a permanent on-air job after the election. She'd carefully courted many of them since joining the Trump campaign in mid-August and becoming the campaign's reliably combative voice and, with her spasmodic smiles and strange combination of woundedness and imperturbability, peculiarly telegenic face.

Beyond all of the other horrible blunders of the campaign, the real problem, she said, was the devil they couldn't control: the Republican National Committee, which was run by Priebus, his sidekick, thirty-two-year-old Katie Walsh, and their flack, Sean Spicer. Instead of being all in, the RNC, ultimately the tool of the Republican establishment, had been hedging its bets ever since Trump won the nomination in early summer. When Trump needed the push, the push just wasn't there.

That was the first part of Conway's spin. The other part was that despite everything, the campaign had really clawed its way back from the abyss. A severely underresourced team with, practically speaking, the worst candidate in modern political history—Conway offered either an eye-rolling pantomime whenever Trump's name was mentioned, or a dead stare—had actually done extraordinarily well. Conway, who had never been involved in a national campaign, and who, before Trump, ran a small-time, down-ballot polling firm, understood full well that, post-campaign, she would now be one of the leading conservative voices on cable news.

In fact, one of the Trump campaign pollsters, John McLaughlin, had begun to suggest within the past week or so that some key state numbers, heretofore dismal, might actually be changing to Trump's advantage. But neither Conway nor Trump himself nor his son-in-law Jared Kushner—the effective head of the campaign, or the designated family monitor of it—wavered in their certainty: their unexpected adventure would soon be over.

Only Steve Bannon, in his odd-man view, insisted the numbers would break in their favor. But this being Bannon's view—crazy Steve—it was quite the opposite of being a reassuring one.

Almost everybody in the campaign, still an extremely small outfit, thought of themselves as a clear-eyed team, as realistic about their prospects as perhaps any in politics. The unspoken agreement among them: not only would Donald Trump *not* be president, he should probably not be. Conveniently, the former conviction meant nobody had to deal with the latter issue.

As the campaign came to an end, Trump himself was sanguine. He had survived the release of the Billy Bush tape when, in the uproar that followed, the RNC had had the gall to pressure him to quit the race. FBI director James Comey, having bizarrely hung Hillary out to dry by saying he was reopening the investigation into her emails eleven days before the election, had helped avert a total Clinton landslide.

"I can be the most famous man in the world," Trump told his on-again, off-again aide Sam Nunberg at the outset of the campaign.

"But do you want to be president?" Nunberg asked (a qualitatively different question than the usual existential candidate test: "Why do you want to be president?"). Nunberg did not get an answer.

The point was, there didn't need to be an answer because he wasn't going to be president.

Trump's longtime friend Roger Ailes liked to say that if you wanted a career in television, first run for president. Now Trump, encouraged by Ailes, was floating rumors about a Trump network. It was a great future.

He would come out of this campaign, Trump assured Ailes, with a far more powerful brand and untold opportunities. "This is bigger than I ever dreamed of," he told Ailes in a conversation a week before the election. "I don't think about losing because it isn't losing. We've totally won." What's more, he was already laying down his public response to losing the election: *It was stolen!*

Donald Trump and his tiny band of campaign warriors were ready to lose with fire and fury. They were not ready to win.

* * *

In politics somebody has to lose, but invariably everybody thinks they can win. And you probably can't win unless you believe that you will win—except in the Trump campaign.

The leitmotif for Trump about his own campaign was how crappy it was and how everybody involved in it was a loser. He was equally convinced that the Clinton people were brilliant winners—"They've got the best and we've got the worst," he frequently said. Time spent with Trump on the campaign plane was often an epic dissing experience: everybody around him was an idiot.

Corey Lewandowski, who served as Trump's first more or less official campaign manager, was often berated by the candidate. For months Trump called him "the worst," and in June 2016 he was finally fired. Ever after, Trump proclaimed his campaign doomed without Lewandowski. "We're all losers," he would say. "All our guys are terrible, nobody knows what they're doing. . . . Wish Corey was back." Trump quickly soured on his second campaign manager, Paul Manafort, as well.

By August, trailing Clinton by 12 to 17 points and facing a daily firestorm of eviscerating press, Trump couldn't conjure even a far-fetched scenario for achieving an electoral victory. At this dire moment, Trump in some essential sense sold his losing campaign. The right-wing billionaire Bob Mercer, a Ted Cruz backer, had shifted his support to Trump with a $5 million infusion. Believing the campaign was cratering, Mercer and his daughter Rebekah took a helicopter from their Long Island estate out to a scheduled fundraiser—with other potential donors bailing by the second—at New York Jets owner and Johnson & Johnson heir Woody Johnson's summer house in the Hamptons.

Trump had no real relationship with either father or daughter. He'd had only a few conversations with Bob Mercer, who mostly talked in monosyllables; Rebekah Mercer's entire history with Trump consisted of a selfie taken with him at Trump Tower. But when the Mercers presented their plan to take over the campaign and install their lieutenants, Steve Bannon and Kellyanne Conway, Trump didn't resist. He only expressed vast incomprehension about why anyone would want to do that. "This thing," he told the Mercers, "is so fucked up."

By every meaningful indicator, something greater than even a sense of doom shadowed what Steve Bannon called "the broke-dick campaign"—a sense of structural impossibility.

The candidate who billed himself as a billionaire—ten times over—refused even to invest his own money in it. Bannon told Jared Kushner—who, when Bannon signed on to the campaign, had been off with his wife on a holiday in Croatia with Trump enemy David Geffen—that, after the first debate in September, they would need an additional $50 million to cover them until election day.

"No way we'll get fifty million unless we can guarantee him victory," said a clear-eyed Kushner.

"Twenty-five million?" prodded Bannon.

"If we can say victory is more than likely."

In the end, the best Trump would do is loan the campaign $10 million, provided he got it back as soon as they could raise other money. (Steve Mnuchin, then the campaign's finance chairman, came to collect the loan with the wire instructions ready to go, so Trump couldn't conveniently forget to send the money.)

There was in fact no real campaign because there was no real organization, or at best only a uniquely dysfunctional one. Roger Stone, the early de facto campaign manager, quit or was fired by Trump—with each man publicly claiming he had slapped down the other. Sam Nunberg, a Trump aide who had worked for Stone, was noisily ousted by Lewandowski, and then Trump exponentially increased the public dirty-clothes-washing by suing Nunberg. Lewandowski and Hope Hicks, the PR aide put on the campaign by Ivanka Trump, had an affair that ended in a public fight on the street—an incident cited by Nunberg in his response to Trump's suit. The campaign, on its face, was not designed to win anything.

Even as Trump eliminated the sixteen other Republican candidates, however far-fetched that might have seemed, it did not make the ultimate goal of winning the presidency any less preposterous.

And if, during the fall, winning seemed slightly more plausible, that evaporated with the Billy Bush affair. "I'm automatically attracted to beautiful—I just start kissing them," Trump told the NBC host Billy Bush on an open mic, amid the ongoing national debate about sexual harassment. "It's like a magnet. Just kiss. I don't even wait. And when you're a star they let you do it. You can do anything. . . . Grab them by the pussy. You can do anything."

It was an operatic unraveling. So mortifying was this development that when Reince Priebus, the RNC head, was called to New York from Washington for an emergency meeting at Trump Tower, he couldn't bring himself to leave Penn Station. It took two hours for the Trump team to coax him across town.

"Bro," said a desperate Bannon, cajoling Priebus on the phone, "I may never see you again after today, but you gotta come to this building and you gotta walk through the front door."

* * *

The silver lining of the ignominy Melania Trump had to endure after the Billy Bush tape was that now there was no way her husband could become president.

Donald Trump's marriage was perplexing to almost everybody around him—or it was, anyway, for those without private jets and many homes. He and Melania spent relatively little time together. They could go days at a time without contact, even when they were both in Trump Tower. Often she did not know where he was, or take much notice of that fact. Her husband moved between residences as he would move between rooms. Along with knowing little about his whereabouts, she knew little about his business, and took at best modest interest in it. An absentee father for his first four children, Trump was even more absent for his fifth, Barron, his son with Melania. Now on his third marriage, he told friends he thought he had finally perfected the art: live and let live—"Do your own thing."

He was a notorious womanizer, and during the campaign became possibly the world's most famous masher. While nobody would ever say Trump was sensitive when it came to women, he had many views about how to get along with them, including a theory he discussed with friends about how the more years between an older man and a younger woman, the less the younger woman took an older man's cheating personally.

Still, the notion that this was a marriage in name only was far from true. He spoke of Melania frequently when she wasn't there. He admired her looks—often, awkwardly for her, in the presence of others. She was, he told people proudly and without irony, a "trophy wife." And while he may not have quite shared his life with her, he gladly shared the spoils of it. "A happy wife is a happy life," he said, echoing a popular rich-man truism.

He also sought Melania's approval. (He sought the approval of all the women around him, who were wise to give it.) In 2014, when he first seriously began to consider running for president, Melania was one of the few who thought it was possible he could win. It was a punch line for his daughter, Ivanka, who had carefully distanced herself from the campaign. With a never-too-hidden distaste for her stepmother, Ivanka would say to friends: *All you have to know about Melania is that she thinks if he runs he'll certainly win.*

But the prospect of her husband's actually becoming president was, for Melania, a horrifying one. She believed it would destroy her carefully sheltered life—one sheltered, not inconsiderably, from the extended Trump family—which was almost entirely focused on her young son.

Don't put the cart before the horse, her amused husband said, even as he spent every day on the campaign trail, dominating the news. But her terror and torment mounted.

There was a whisper campaign about her, cruel and comical in its insinuations, going on in Manhattan, which friends told her about. Her modeling career was under close scrutiny. In Slovenia, where she grew up, a celebrity magazine, *Suzy*, put the rumors about her into print after Trump got the nomination. Then, with a sickening taste of what might be ahead, the *Daily Mail* blew the story across the world.

The *New York Post* got its hands on outtakes from a nude photo shoot that Melania had done early in her modeling career—a leak that everybody other than Melania assumed could be traced back to Trump himself.

Inconsolable, she confronted her husband. Is this the future? She told him she wouldn't be able to take it.

Trump responded in his fashion—*We'll sue!*—and set her up with lawyers who successfully did just that. But he was unaccustomedly contrite, too. Just a little longer, he told her. It would all be over in November. He offered his wife a solemn guarantee: there was simply no way he would win. And even for a chronically—he would say helplessly—unfaithful husband, this was one promise to his wife that he seemed sure to keep.

* * *

The Trump campaign had, perhaps less than inadvertently, replicated the scheme from Mel Brooks's *The Producers*. In that classic, Brooks's larcenous and dopey heroes, Max Bialystock and Leo Bloom, set out to sell more than 100 percent of the ownership stakes in the Broadway show they are producing. Since they will be found out only if the show is a hit, everything about the show is premised on its being a flop. Accordingly, they create a show so outlandish that it actually succeeds, thus dooming our heroes.

Winning presidential candidates—driven by hubris or narcissism or a preternatural sense of destiny—have, more than likely, spent a substantial part of their careers, if not their lives from adolescence, preparing for the role. They rise up the ladder of elected offices. They perfect a public face. They manically network, since success in politics is largely about who your allies are. They cram. (Even in the case of an uninterested George W. Bush, he relied on his father's cronies to cram for him.) And they clean up after themselves—or, at least, take great care to cover up. They prepare themselves to win and to govern.

The Trump calculation, quite a conscious one, was different. The candidate and his top lieutenants believed they could get all the benefits of *almost* becoming president without having to change their behavior or their fundamental worldview one whit: we don't have to be anything but who and what we are, because of course we won't win.

Many candidates for president have made a virtue of being Washington outsiders; in practice, this strategy merely favors governors over senators. Every serious candidate, no matter how much he or she disses Washington, relies on Beltway insiders for counsel and support. But with Trump, hardly a person in his innermost circle had ever worked in politics at the national level—his closest advisers had not worked in politics at all. Throughout his life, Trump had few close friends of any kind, but when he began his campaign for president he had almost no friends in politics. The only two actual politicians with whom Trump was close were Rudy Giuliani and Chris Christie, and both men were in their own way peculiar and isolated. And to say that he knew nothing—nothing at all—about the basic intellectual foundations of the job was a comic understatement. Early in the campaign, in a *Producers*-worthy scene, Sam Nunberg was sent to explain the Constitution to the candidate: "I got as far as the Fourth Amendment before his finger is pulling down on his lip and his eyes are rolling back in his head."

Almost everybody on the Trump team came with the kind of messy conflicts bound to bite a president or his staff. Mike Flynn, Trump's future National Security Advisor, who became Trump's opening act at campaign rallies and whom Trump loved to hear complain about the CIA and the haplessness of American spies, had been told by his friends that it had not been a good idea to take $45,000 from the Russians for a speech. "Well, it would only be a problem if we won," he assured them, knowing that it would therefore not be a problem.

Paul Manafort, the international lobbyist and political operative who Trump retained to run his campaign after Lewandowski was fired—and who agreed not to take a fee, amping up questions of quid pro quo—had spent thirty years representing dictators and corrupt despots, amassing millions of dollars in a money trail that had long caught the eye of U.S. investigators. What's more, when he joined the campaign, he was being pursued, his every financial step documented, by the billionaire Russian oligarch Oleg Deripaska, who claimed he stole $17 million from him in a crooked real estate scam.

For quite obvious reasons, no president before Trump and few politicians ever have come out of the real estate business: a lightly regulated market, based on substantial debt with exposure to frequent market fluctuations, it often depends on government favor, and is a preferred exchange currency for problem cash—money laundering. Trump's son-in-law Jared Kushner, Jared's father Charlie, Trump's sons Don Jr. and Eric, and his daughter Ivanka, as well as Trump himself, all supported their business enterprises to a greater or lesser extent working in the dubious limbo of international free cash flow and gray money. Charlie Kushner, to whose real estate business interests Trump's son-in-law and most important aide was wholly tied, had already spent time in a federal prison for tax evasion, witness tampering, and making illegal campaign donations.

Modern politicians and their staffs perform their most consequential piece of opposition research on themselves. If the Trump team had vetted their candidate, they would have reasonably concluded that heightened ethical scrutiny could easily put them in jeopardy. But Trump pointedly performed no such effort. Roger Stone, Trump's longtime political adviser, explained to Steve Bannon that Trump's psychic makeup made it impossible for him to take such a close look at himself. Nor could he tolerate knowing that somebody else would then know a lot about him—and therefore have something over him. And anyway, why take such a close and potentially threatening look, because what were the chances of winning?

Not only did Trump disregard the potential conflicts of his business deals and real estate holdings, he audaciously refused to release his tax returns. Why should he if he wasn't going to win?

What's more, Trump refused to spend any time considering, however hypothetically, transition matters, saying it was "bad luck"—but really meaning it was a waste of time. Nor would he even remotely contemplate the issue of his holdings and conflicts.

He wasn't going to win! Or losing was winning.

Trump would be the most famous man in the world—a martyr to crooked Hillary Clinton.

His daughter Ivanka and son-in-law Jared would have transformed themselves from relatively obscure rich kids into international celebrities and brand ambassadors.

Steve Bannon would become the de facto head of the Tea Party movement.

Kellyanne Conway would be a cable news star.

Reince Priebus and Katie Walsh would get their Republican Party back.

Melania Trump could return to inconspicuously lunching.

That was the trouble-free outcome they awaited on November 8, 2016. Losing would work out for everybody.

Shortly after eight o'clock that evening, when the unexpected trend—Trump might actually win—seemed confirmed, Don Jr. told a friend that his father, or DJT, as he called him, looked as if he had seen a ghost. Melania, to whom Donald Trump had made his solemn guarantee, was in tears—and not of joy.

There was, in the space of little more than an hour, in Steve Bannon's not unamused observation, a befuddled Trump morphing into a disbelieving Trump and then into a quite horrified Trump. But still to come was the final transformation: suddenly, Donald Trump became a man who believed that he deserved to be and was wholly capable of being the president of the United States.

2

TRUMP TOWER

On the Saturday after the election, Donald Trump received a small group of well-wishers in his triplex apartment in Trump Tower. Even his close friends were still shocked and bewildered, and there was a dazed quality to the gathering. But Trump himself was mostly looking at the clock.

Rupert Murdoch, heretofore doubtlessly certain Trump was a charlatan and a fool, said he and his new wife, Jerry Hall, would pay a call on the president-elect. But Murdoch was late—quite late. Trump kept assuring his guests that Rupert was on his way, coming soon. When some of the guests made a move to leave, Trump cajoled them to stay a little longer. *You'll want to stay to see Rupert.* (Or, one of the guests interpreted, you'll want to stay to see Trump with Rupert.)

Murdoch, who, with his then wife, Wendi, had often socialized with Jared and Ivanka, in the past made little effort to hide his lack of interest in Trump. Murdoch's fondness for Kushner created a curious piece of the power dynamic between Trump and his son-in-law, one that Kushner, with reasonable subtly, played to his advantage, often dropping Murdoch's name into conversations with his father-in-law. When, in 2015, Ivanka Trump told Murdoch that her father really, truly was going to run for president, Murdoch dismissed the possibility out of hand.

But now, the new president-elect—after the most astonishing upset in American history—was on tenterhooks waiting for Murdoch. "He's one of the greats," he told his guests, becoming more agitated as he waited. "Really, he's one of the greats, the last of the greats. You have to stay to see him."

It was a matched set of odd reversals—an ironic symmetry. Trump, perhaps not yet appreciating the difference between becoming president and elevating his social standing, was trying mightily to curry favor with the previously disdainful media mogul. And Murdoch, finally arriving at the party he was in more than one way sorely late to, was as subdued and thrown as everyone else, and struggling to adjust his view of a man who, for more than a generation, had been at best a clown prince among the rich and famous.

* * *

Murdoch was hardly the only billionaire who had been dismissive of Trump. In the years before the election, Carl Icahn, whose friendship Trump often cited, and who Trump had suggested he'd appoint to high office, openly ridiculed his fellow billionaire (whom he said was not remotely a billionaire).

Few people who knew Trump had illusions about him. That was almost his appeal: he was what he was. Twinkle in his eye, larceny in his soul.

But now he was the president-elect. And that, in a reality jujitsu, changed everything. So say whatever you want about him, he had done this. Pulled the sword from the stone. That meant something. *Everything.*

The billionaires had to rethink. So did everyone in the Trump orbit. The campaign staff, now suddenly in a position to snag West Wing jobs—career- and history-making jobs—had to see this odd, difficult, even ridiculous, and, on the face of it, ill-equipped person in a new light. He had been elected president. So he was, as Kellyanne Conway liked to point out, by definition, presidential.

Still, nobody had yet seen him be presidential—that is, make a public bow to political ritual and propriety. Or even to exercise some modest self-control.

Others were now recruited and, despite their obvious impressions of the man, agreed to sign on. Jim Mattis, a retired four-star general, one of the most respected commanders in the U.S. armed forces; Rex Tillerson, CEO of ExxonMobil; Scott Pruitt and Betsy DeVos, Jeb Bush loyalists—all of them were now focused on the singular fact that while he might be a peculiar figure, even an absurd-seeming one, he had been elected president.

We can make this work, is what everybody in the Trump orbit was suddenly saying. Or, at the very least, this *could possibly* work.

In fact, up close, Trump was not the bombastic and pugilistic man who had stirred rabid crowds on the campaign trail. He was neither angry nor combative. He may have been the most threatening and frightening and menacing presidential candidate in modern history, but in person he could seem almost soothing. His extreme self-satisfaction rubbed off. Life was sunny. Trump was an optimist—at least about himself. He was charming and full of flattery; he focused on you. He was funny—self-deprecating even. And incredibly energetic—*Let's do it* whatever it is, *let's do it.* He wasn't a tough guy. He was "a big warm-hearted monkey," said Bannon, with rather faint praise.

PayPal cofounder and Facebook board member Peter Thiel—really the only significant Silicon Valley voice to support Trump—was warned by another billionaire and longtime Trump friend that Trump would, in an explosion of flattery, offer Thiel his undying friendship. *Everybody says you're great, you and I are going to have an amazing working relationship, anything you want, call me and we'll get it done!* Thiel was advised not to take Trump's offer too seriously. But Thiel, who gave a speech supporting Trump at the Republican Convention in Cleveland, reported back that, even having been forewarned, he absolutely was certain of Trump's sincerity when he said they'd be friends for life—only never to basically hear from him again or have his calls returned. Still, power provides its own excuses for social lapses. Other aspects of the Trump character were more problematic.

Almost all the professionals who were now set to join him were coming face to face with the fact that it appeared he knew nothing. There was simply no subject, other than perhaps building construction, that he had substantially mastered. Everything with him was off the cuff. Whatever he knew he seemed to have learned an hour before—and that was mostly half-baked. But each member of the new Trump team was convincing him- or herself otherwise—because what did they know, the man had been elected president. He offered something, obviously. Indeed, while everybody in his rich-guy social circle knew about his wide-ranging ignorance—Trump, the businessman, could not even read a balance sheet, and Trump, who had campaigned on his deal-making skills, was, with his inattention to details, a terrible negotiator—they yet found him somehow *instinctive*. That was the word. He was a force of personality. He could make you believe.

"Is Trump a good person, an intelligent person, a capable person?" asked Sam Nunberg, Trump's longtime political aide. "I don't even know. But I know he's a star."

Trying to explain Trump's virtues and his attraction, Piers Morgan—the British newspaper man and ill-fated CNN anchor who had appeared on *Celebrity Apprentice* and stayed a loyal Trump friend—said it was all in Trump's book *The Art of the Deal*. Everything that made him Trump and that defined his savvy, energy, and charisma was there. If you wanted to know Trump, just read the book. But Trump had not written *The Art of the Deal*. His co-writer, Tony Schwartz, insisted that he had hardly contributed to it and might not even have read all of it. And that was perhaps the point. Trump was not a writer, he was a character—a protagonist and hero.

A pro wrestling fan who became a World Wrestling Entertainment supporter and personality (inducted into the WWE Hall of Fame), Trump lived, like Hulk Hogan, as a real-life fictional character. To the amusement of his friends, and unease of many of the people now preparing to work for him at the highest levels of the federal government, Trump often spoke of himself in the third person. Trump did this. The Trumpster did that. So powerful was this persona, or role, that he seemed reluctant, or unable, to give it up in favor of being president—or presidential.

However difficult he was, many of those now around him tried to justify his behavior—tried to find an explanation for his success in it, to understand it as an advantage, not a limitation. For Steve Bannon, Trump's unique political virtue was as an alpha male, maybe the last of the alpha males. A 1950s man, a Rat Pack type, a character out of *Mad Men*.

Trump's understanding of his own essential nature was even more precise. Once, coming back on his plane with a billionaire friend who had brought along a foreign model, Trump, trying to move in on his friend's date, urged a stop in Atlantic City. He would provide a tour of his casino. His friend assured the model that there was nothing to recommend Atlantic City. It was a place overrun by white trash.

"What is this 'white trash'?" asked the model.

"They're people just like me," said Trump, "only they're poor."

He looked for a license not to conform, not to be respectable. It was something of an outlaw prescription for winning—and winning, however you won, was what it was all about.

Or, as his friends would observe, mindful themselves not to be taken in, he simply had no scruples. He was a rebel, a disruptor, and, living outside the rules, contemptuous of them. A close Trump friend who was also a good Bill Clinton friend found them eerily similar—except that Clinton had a respectable front and Trump did not.

One manifestation of this outlaw personality, for both Trump and Clinton, was their brand of womanizing—and indeed, harassing. Even among world-class womanizers and harassers, they seemed exceptionally free of doubt or hesitation.

Trump liked to say that one of the things that made life worth living was getting your friends' wives into bed. In pursuing a friend's wife, he would try to persuade the wife that her husband was perhaps not what she thought. Then he'd have his secretary ask the friend into his office; once the friend arrived, Trump would engage in what was, for him, more or less constant sexual banter. *Do you still like having sex with your wife? How often? You must have had a better fuck than your wife? Tell me about it. I have girls coming in from Los Angeles at three o'clock. We can go upstairs and have a great time. I promise . . .* And all the while, Trump would have his friend's wife on the speakerphone, listening in.

Previous presidents, and not just Clinton, have of course lacked scruples. What was, to many of the people who knew Trump well, much more confounding was that he had managed to win this election, and arrive at this ultimate accomplishment, wholly lacking what in some obvious sense must be the main requirement of the job, what neuroscientists would call executive function. He had somehow won the race for president, but his brain seemed incapable of performing what would be essential tasks in his new job. He had no ability to plan and organize and pay attention and switch focus; he had never been able to tailor his behavior to what the goals at hand reasonably required. On the most basic level, he simply could not link cause and effect.

The charge that Trump colluded with the Russians to win the election, which he scoffed at, was, in the estimation of some of his friends, a perfect example of his inability to connect the dots. Even if he hadn't personally conspired with the Russians to fix the election, his efforts to curry favor with, of all people, Vladimir Putin had no doubt left a trail of alarming words and deeds likely to have enormous political costs.

Shortly after the election, his friend Ailes told him, with some urgency, "You've got to get right on Russia." Even exiled from Fox News, Ailes still maintained a fabled intelligence network. He warned Trump of potentially damaging material coming his way. "You need to take this seriously, Donald."

"Jared has this," said a happy Trump. "It's all worked out."

* * *

Trump Tower, next door to Tiffany and now headquarters of a populist revolution, suddenly seemed like an alien spaceship—the Death Star—on Fifth Avenue. As the great and good and ambitious, as well as angry protesters and the curious hoi polloi, began beating a path to the next president's door, mazelike barricades were hurriedly thrown up to shield him.

The Pre-Election Presidential Transition Act of 2010 established funding for presidential nominees to start the process of vetting thousands of candidates for jobs in a new administration, codifying policies that would determine the early actions of a new White House, and preparing for the handoff of bureaucratic responsibilities on January 20. During the campaign, New Jersey governor Chris Christie, the nominal head of the Trump transition office, had to forcefully tell the candidate that he couldn't redirect these funds, that the law required him to spend the money and plan for a transition—even one he did not expect to need. A frustrated Trump said he didn't want to hear any more about it.

The day after the election, Trump's close advisers—suddenly eager to be part of a process that almost everybody had ignored—immediately began blaming Christie for a lack of transition preparations. Hurriedly, the bare-bones transition team moved from downtown Washington to Trump Tower.

This was certainly some of the most expensive real estate ever occupied by a transition team (and, for that matter, a presidential campaign). And that was part of the point. It sent a Trump-style message: we're not only outsiders, but we're more powerful than you insiders. Richer. More famous. With better real estate.

And, of course, it was personalized: his name, fabulously, was on the door. Upstairs was his triplex apartment, vastly larger than the White House living quarters. Here was his private office, which he'd occupied since the 1980s. And here were the campaign and now transition floors—firmly in his orbit and not that of Washington and the "swamp."

Trump's instinct in the face of his unlikely, if not preposterous, success was the opposite of humility. It was, in some sense, to rub everybody's face in it. Washington insiders, or would-be insiders, would have to come to him. Trump Tower immediately upstaged the White House. Everybody who came to see the president-elect was acknowledging, or accepting, an outsider government. Trump forced them to endure what was gleefully called by insiders the "perp walk" in front of press and assorted gawkers. An act of obeisance, if not humiliation.

The otherworldly sense of Trump Tower helped obscure the fact that few in the thin ranks of Trump's inner circle, with their overnight responsibility for assembling a government, had almost any relevant experience. Nobody had a political background. Nobody had a policy background. Nobody had a legislative background.

Politics is a network business, a who-you-know business. But unlike other presidents-elect—all of whom invariably suffered from their own management defects—Trump did not have a career's worth of political and government contacts to call on. He hardly even had his own political organization. For most of the last eighteen months on the road, it had been, at its core, a three-person enterprise: his campaign manager, Corey Lewandowski (until he was forced out a month before the Republican National Convention); his spokesperson-bodyperson-intern, the campaign's first hire, twenty-six-year-old Hope Hicks; and Trump himself. Lean and mean and gut instincts—the more people you had to deal with, Trump found, the harder it was to turn the plane around and get home to bed at night.

The professional team—although in truth there was hardly a political professional among them—that had joined the campaign in August was a last-ditch bid to avoid hopeless humiliation. But these were people he'd worked with for just a few months.

Reince Priebus, getting ready to shift over from the RNC to the White House, noted, with alarm, how often Trump offered people jobs on the spot, many of whom he had never met before, for positions whose importance Trump did not particularly understand.

Ailes, a veteran of the Nixon, Reagan, and Bush 41 White Houses, was growing worried by the president-elect's lack of immediate focus on a White House structure that could serve and protect him. He tried to impress on Trump the ferocity of the opposition that would greet him.

"You need a son of a bitch as your chief of staff. And you need a son of a bitch who knows Washington," Ailes told Trump not long after the election. "You'll want to be your own son of a bitch, but you don't know Washington." Ailes had a suggestion: "Speaker Boehner." (John Boehner had been the Speaker of the House until he was forced out in a Tea Party putsch in 2011.)

"Who's that?" asked Trump.

Everybody in Trump's billionaire circle, concerned about his contempt for other people's expertise, tried to impress upon him the importance of the people, the many people, he would need with him in the White House, people who understood Washington. *Your people are more important than your policies. Your people* are *your policies.*

"Frank Sinatra was wrong," said David Bossie, one of Trump's longtime political advisers. "If you can make it in New York, you can't necessarily make it in Washington."

* * *

The nature of the role of the modern chief of staff is a focus of much White House scholarship. As much as the president himself, the chief of staff determines how the White House and executive branch—which employs 4 million people, including 1.3 million people in the armed services—will run.

The job has been construed as deputy president, or chief operating officer, or even prime minister. Larger-than-life chiefs have included Richard Nixon's H. R. Haldeman and Alexander Haig; Gerald Ford's Donald Rumsfeld and Dick Cheney; Jimmy Carter's Hamilton Jordan; Ronald Reagan's James Baker; George H. W. Bush's return of James Baker; Bill Clinton's Leon Panetta, Erskine Bowles, and John Podesta; George W. Bush's Andrew Card; and Barack Obama's Rahm Emanuel and Bill Daley. Anyone studying the position would conclude that a stronger chief of staff is better than a weaker one, and a chief of staff with a history in Washington and the federal government is better than an outsider.

Donald Trump had little, if any, awareness of the history of or the thinking about this role. Instead, he substituted his own management style and experience. For decades, he had relied on longtime retainers, cronies, and family. Even though Trump liked to portray his business as an empire, it was actually a discrete holding company and boutique enterprise, catering more to his peculiarities as proprietor and brand representative than to any bottom line or other performance measures.

His sons, Don Jr. and Eric—jokingly behind their backs known to Trump insiders as Uday and Qusay, after the sons of Saddam Hussein—wondered if there couldn't somehow be two parallel White House structures, one dedicated to their father's big-picture views, personal appearances, and salesmanship and the other concerned with day-to-day management issues. In this construct, they saw themselves tending to the day-to-day operations.

One of Trump's early ideas was to recruit his friend Tom Barrack—part of his kitchen cabinet of real estate tycoons including Steven Roth and Richard Lefrak—and make him chief of staff.

Barrack, the grandson of Lebanese immigrants, is a starstruck real estate investor of legendary acumen who owns Michael Jackson's former oddball paradise, Neverland Ranch. With Jeffrey Epstein—the New York financier who would become a tabloid regular after a guilty plea to one count of soliciting prostitution that sent him to jail in 2008 in Palm Beach for thirteen months—Trump and Barrack were a 1980s and '90s set of nightlife Musketeers.

The founder and CEO of the private equity firm Colony Capital, Barrack became a billionaire making investments in distress debt investments in real estate around the world, including helping to bail out his friend Donald Trump. More recently, he had helped bail out his friend's son-in-law, Jared Kushner.

He watched with amusement Trump's eccentric presidential campaign and brokered the deal to have Paul Manafort replace Corey Lewandowski after Lewandowski fell out of favor with Kushner. Then, as confounded as everyone else by the campaign's continuing successes, Barrack introduced the future president in warm and personal terms at the Republican National Convention in July (at odds with its otherwise dark and belligerent tone).

It was Trump's perfect fantasy that his friend Tom—an organizational whiz fully aware of his friend's lack of interest in day-to-day management—would sign on to run the White House. This was Trump's instant and convenient solution to the unforeseen circumstance of suddenly being president: to do it with his business mentor, confidant, investor, and friend, someone whom acquaintances of the two men describe as "being one of the best Donald handlers." In the Trump circle this was called the "two amigos" plan. (Epstein, who remained close to Barrack, had been whitewashed out of the Trump biography.)

Barrack, among the few people whose abilities Trump, a reflexive naysayer, didn't question, could, in Trump's hopeful view, really get things running smoothly and let Trump be Trump. It was, on Trump's part, an uncharacteristic piece of self-awareness: Donald Trump might not know what he didn't know, but he knew Tom Barrack knew. He would run the business and Trump would sell the product—making American great again. #MAGA.

For Barrack, as for everybody around Trump, the election result was a kind of beyond-belief lottery-winning circumstance—your implausible friend becoming president. But Barrack, even after countless pleading and cajoling phone calls from Trump, finally had to disappoint his friend, telling him "I'm just too rich." He would never be able to untangle his holdings and interests—including big investments in the Middle East—in a way that would satisfy ethics watchdogs. Trump was unconcerned or in denial about his own business conflicts, but Barrack saw nothing but hassle and cost for himself. Also, Barrack, on his fourth marriage, had no appetite for having his colorful personal life—often, over the years, conducted with Trump—become a public focus.

* * *

Trump's fallback was his son-in-law. On the campaign, after months of turmoil and outlandishness (if not to Trump, to most others, including his family), Kushner had stepped in and become his effective body man, hovering nearby, speaking only when spoken to, but then always offering a calming and flattering view. Corey Lewandowski called Jared the butler. Trump had come to believe that his son-in-law, in part because he seemed to understand how to stay out of his way, was uniquely sagacious.

In defiance of law and tone, and everybody's disbelieving looks, the president seemed intent on surrounding himself in the White House with his family. The Trumps, all of them—except for his wife, who, mystifyingly, was staying in New York—were moving in, all of them set to assume responsibilities similar to their status in the Trump Organization, without anyone apparently counseling against it.

Finally, it was the right-wing diva and Trump supporter Ann Coulter who took the president-elect aside and said, "Nobody is apparently telling you this. But you can't. You just can't hire your children."

Trump continued to insist that he had every right to his family's help, while at the same time asking for understanding. This is family, he said—"It's a *leettle, leettle* tricky." His staffers understood not only the inherent conflicts and difficult legal issues in having Trump's son-in-law run the White House, but that it would become, even more than it already was, family first for Trump. After a great deal of pressure, he at least agreed not to make his son-in-law the chief of staff—not officially, anyway.

* * *

If not Barrack or Kushner, then, Trump thought the job should probably go to New Jersey governor Chris Christie, who, with Rudy Giuliani, comprised the sum total of his circle of friends with actual political experience.

Christie, like most Trump allies, fell in and out of favor. In the final weeks of the campaign, Trump contemptuously measured Christie's increasing distance from his losing enterprise, and then, with victory, his eagerness to get back in.

Trump and Christie went back to Trump's days trying—and failing—to become an Atlantic City gaming mogul. *The* Atlantic City gaming mogul. (Trump had long been competitive with and in awe of the Las Vegas gaming mogul Steve Wynn, whom Trump would name finance chairman of the RNC.) Trump had backed Christie as he rose through New Jersey politics. He admired Christie's straight-talk style, and for a while, as Christie anticipated his own presidential run in 2012 and 2013—and as Trump was looking for a next chapter for himself with the fading of *The Apprentice*, his reality TV franchise—Trump even wondered whether he might be a vice presidential possibility for Christie.

Early in the campaign, Trump said he wouldn't have run against Christie but for the Bridgegate scandal (which erupted when Christie's associates closed traffic lanes on the George Washington Bridge to undermine the mayor of a nearby town who was a Christie opponent, and which Trump privately justified as "just New Jersey hardball"). When Christie dropped out of the race in February 2016 and signed on with the Trump campaign, he endured a torrent of ridicule for supporting his friend, whom he believed had promised him a clear track to the VP slot.

It had personally pained Trump not to be able to give it to him. But if the Republican establishment had not wanted Trump, they had not wanted Christie almost as much. So Christie got the job of leading the transition and the implicit promise of a central job—attorney general or chief of staff.

But when he was the federal prosecutor in New Jersey, Christie had sent Jared's father, Charles Kushner, to jail in 2005. Charlie Kushner, pursued by the feds for an income tax cheat, set up a scheme with a prostitute to blackmail his brother-in-law, who was planning to testify against him.

Various accounts, mostly offered by Christie himself, make Jared the vengeful hatchet man in Christie's aborted Trump administration career. It was a kind of perfect sweet-revenge story: the son of the wronged man (or, in this case—there's little dispute—the guilty-as-charged man) uses his power over the man who wronged his family. But other accounts offer a subtler and in a way darker picture. Jared Kushner, like sons-in-law everywhere, tiptoes around his father-in-law, carefully displacing as little air as possible: the massive and domineering older man, the reedy and pliant younger one. In the revised death-of-Chris-Christie story, it is not the deferential Jared who strikes back, but—in some sense even more satisfying for the revenge fantasy—Charlie Kushner himself who harshly demands his due. It was his daughter-in-law who held the real influence in the Trump circle, who delivered the blow. Ivanka told her father that Christie's appointment as chief of staff or to any other high position would be extremely difficult for her and her family, and it would be best that Christie be removed from the Trump orbit altogether.

* * *

Bannon was the heavy of the organization. Trump, who seemed awestruck by Bannon's conversation—a mix of insults, historical riffs, media insights, right-wing bons mots, and motivational truisms—now began suggesting Bannon to his circle of billionaires as chief of staff, only to have this notion soundly ridiculed and denounced. But Trump pronounced many people in favor of it anyway.

In the weeks leading up to the election, Trump had labeled Bannon a flatterer for his certainty that Trump would win. But now he had come to credit Bannon with something like mystical powers. And in fact Bannon, with no prior political experience, was the only Trump insider able to offer a coherent vision of Trump's populism—aka Trumpism.

The anti-Bannon forces—which included almost every non–Tea Party

Republican—were quick to react. Murdoch, a growing Bannon nemesis, told Trump that Bannon would be a dangerous choice. Joe Scarborough, the former congressman and cohost of MSNBC's *Morning Joe*, a favorite Trump show, privately told Trump "Washington will go up in flames" if Bannon became chief of staff, and, beginning a running theme, publicly denigrated Bannon on the show.

In fact, Bannon presented even bigger problems than his politics: he was profoundly disorganized, seemingly on the spectrum given what captured his single-minded focus to the disregard of everything else. Might he be the worst manager who ever lived? He might. He seemed incapable of returning a phone call. He answered emails in one word—partly a paranoia about email, but even more a controlling crypticness. He kept assistants and minders at constant bay. You couldn't really make an appointment with Bannon, you just had to show up. And somehow, his own key lieutenant, Alexandra Preate, a conservative fundraiser and PR woman, was as disorganized as he was. After three marriages, Bannon lived his bachelor's life on Capitol Hill in a row house known as the Breitbart Embassy that doubled as the Breitbart office—the life of a messy party. No sane person would hire Steven Bannon for a job that included making the trains run on time.

* * *

Hence, Reince Priebus.

For the Hill, he was the only reasonable chief among the contenders, and he quickly became the subject of intense lobbying by House Speaker Paul Ryan and Senate Majority Leader Mitch McConnell. If they were going to have to deal with an alien like Donald Trump, then best they do it with the help of a member of their own kind.

Priebus, forty-five, was neither politician nor policy wonk nor strategist. He was political machine worker, one of the oldest professions. A fundraiser.

A working-class kid originally from New Jersey and then Wisconsin, at thirty-two he made his first and last run for elective office: a failed bid for Wisconsin state senate. He became the chairman of the state party and then the general counsel of the Republican National Committee. In

2011 he stepped up to chairmanship of the RNC. Priebus's political cred came from appeasing the Tea Party in Wisconsin, and his association with Wisconsin governor Scott Walker, a rising Republican star (and, briefly—very briefly—the 2016 front-runner).

With significant parts of the Republican Party inalterably opposed to Trump, and with an almost universal belief within the party that Trump would go down to ignominious defeat, taking the party with him, Priebus was under great pressure after Trump captured the nomination to shift resources down the ticket and even to abandon the Trump campaign entirely.

Convinced himself that Trump was hopeless, Priebus nevertheless hedged his bets. The fact that he did not abandon Trump entirely became a possible margin of victory and made Priebus something of a hero (equally, in the Kellyanne Conway version, if they had lost, he would have been a reasonable target). He became the default choice for chief.

And yet his entry into the Trump inner circle caused Priebus his share of uncertainty and bewilderment. He came out of his first long meeting with Trump thinking it had been a disconcertingly weird experience. Trump talked nonstop and constantly repeated himself.

"Here's the deal," a close Trump associate told Priebus. "In an hour meeting with him you're going to hear fifty-four minutes of stories and they're going to be the same stories over and over again. So you have to have one point to make and you have to pepper it in whenever you can."

The Priebus appointment as chief of staff, announced in mid-November, also put Bannon on a coequal level. Trump was falling back on his own natural inclinations to let nobody have real power. Priebus, even with the top job, would be a weaker sort of figure, in the traditional mold of most Trump lieutenants over the years. The choice also worked well for the other would-be chiefs. Tom Barrack could easily circumvent Priebus and continue to speak directly to Trump. Jared Kushner's position as son-in-law and soon top aide would not be impeded. And Steve Bannon, reporting directly to Trump, remained the undisputed voice of Trumpism in the White House.

There would be, in other words, one chief of staff in name—the unimportant one—and various others, more important, in practice, ensuring both chaos and Trump's own undisputed independence.

Jim Baker, chief of staff for both Ronald Reagan and George H. W. Bush and almost everybody's model for managing the West Wing, advised Priebus not to take the job.

* * *

The transmogrification of Trump from joke candidate, to whisperer for a disaffected demographic, to risible nominee, to rent-in-the-fabric-of-time president-elect, did not inspire in him any larger sense of sober reflection. After the shock of it, he immediately seemed to rewrite himself as the inevitable president.

One instance of his revisionism, and of the new stature he now seemed to assume as president, involved the lowest point of the campaign—the Billy Bush tape.

His explanation, in an off-the-record conversation with a friendly cable anchor, was that it "really wasn't me."

The anchor acknowledged how unfair it was to be characterized by a single event.

"No," said Trump, "it wasn't me. I've been told by people who understand this stuff about how easy it is to alter these things and put in voices and completely different people."

He was the winner and now expected to be the object of awe, fascination, and favor. He expected this to be binary: a hostile media would turn into a fannish one.

And yet here he was, the winner who was treated with horror and depredations by a media that in the past, as a matter of course and protocol, could be depended on to shower lavish deference on an incoming president no matter who he was. (Trump's shortfall of three million votes continued to rankle and was a subject best avoided.) It was nearly incomprehensible to him that the same people—that is, the media—who had violently criticized him for saying he might dispute the election result were now calling *him* illegitimate.

Trump was not a politician who could parse factions of support and opprobrium; he was a salesman who needed to make a sale. "I won.

I am the winner. I am not the loser," he repeated, incredulously, like a mantra.

Bannon described Trump as a simple machine. The On switch was full of flattery, the Off switch full of calumny. The flattery was dripping, slavish, cast in ultimate superlatives, and entirely disconnected from reality: so-and-so was the best, the most incredible, the ne plus ultra, the eternal. The calumny was angry, bitter, resentful, ever a casting out and closing of the iron door.

This was the nature of Trump's particular salesmanship. His strategic belief was that there was no reason not to heap excessive puffery on a prospect. But if the prospect was ruled out as a buyer, there was no reason not to heap scorn and lawsuits on him or her. After all, if they don't respond to sucking up, they might respond to piling on. Bannon felt—perhaps with overconfidence—that Trump could be easily switched on and off.

Against the background of a mortal war of wills—with the media, the Democrats, and the swamp—that Bannon was encouraging him to wage, Trump could also be courted. In some sense, he wanted nothing so much as to be courted.

Amazon's Jeff Bezos, the owner of the *Washington Post*, which had become one of the many Trump media bêtes noires in the media world, nevertheless took pains to reach out not only to the president-elect but to his daughter Ivanka. During the campaign, Trump said Amazon was getting "away with murder taxwise" and that if he won, "Oh, do they have problems." Now Trump was suddenly praising Bezos as "a top-level genius." Elon Musk, in Trump Tower, pitched Trump on the new administration's joining him in his race to Mars, which Trump jumped at. Stephen Schwarzman, the head of the Blackstone Group—and a Kushner friend—offered to organize a business council for Trump, which Trump embraced. Anna Wintour, the *Vogue* editor and fashion industry queen, had hoped to be named America's ambassador to the UK under Obama and, when that didn't happen, closely aligned herself with Hillary Clinton. Now Wintour arrived at Trump Tower (but refused to do the perp walk) and suggested that she become Trump's ambassador to the Court of St. James's.

And Trump was inclined to entertain the idea. ("Fortunately," said Bannon, "there was no chemistry.")

On December 14, a high-level delegation from Silicon Valley came to Trump Tower to meet the president-elect, though Trump had repeatedly criticized the tech industry throughout the campaign. Later that afternoon, Trump called Rupert Murdoch, who asked him how the meeting had gone.

"Oh, great, just great," said Trump. "Really, really good. These guys really need my help. Obama was not very favorable to them, too much regulation. This is really an opportunity for me to help them."

"Donald," said Murdoch, "for eight years these guys had Obama in their pocket. They practically ran the administration. They don't need your help."

"Take this H-1B visa issue. They really need these H-1B visas."

Murdoch suggested that taking a liberal approach to H-1B visas might be hard to square with his immigration promises. But Trump seemed unconcerned, assuring Murdoch, "We'll figure it out."

"What a fucking idiot," said Murdoch, shrugging, as he got off the phone.

* * *

Ten days before Donald Trump's inauguration as the forty-fifth president, a group of young Trump staffers—the men in regulation Trump suits and ties, the women in the Trump-favored look of high boots, short skirts, and shoulder-length hair—were watching President Barack Obama give his farewell speech as it streamed on a laptop in the transition offices.

"Mr. Trump said he's never once listened to a whole Obama speech," said one of the young people authoritatively.

"They're so boring," said another.

While Obama bade his farewell, preparations for Trump's first press conference since the election, to be held the next day, were under way down the hall. The plan was to make a substantial effort to show that the president-elect's business conflicts would be addressed in a formal and considered way.

Up until now, Trump's view was that he'd been elected *because* of those conflicts—his business savvy, connections, experience, and brand—not in spite of them, and that it was ludicrous for anyone to think he could untangle himself even if he wanted to. Indeed, to reporters and anyone else who would listen, Kellyanne Conway offered on Trump's behalf a self-pitying defense about how great his sacrifice had already been.

After fanning the flames of his intention to disregard rules regarding conflicts of interest, now, in a bit of theater, he would take a generous new tack. Standing in the lobby of Trump Towner next to a table stacked high with document folders and legal papers, he would describe the vast efforts that had been made to do the impossible and how, henceforth, he would be exclusively focused on the nation's business.

But suddenly this turned out to be quite beside the point.

Fusion GPS, an opposition research company (founded by former journalists, it provided information to private clients), had been retained by Democratic Party interests. Fusion had hired Christopher Steele, a former British spy, in June 2016, to help investigate Trump's repeated brags about his relationship with Vladimir Putin and the nature of Trump's relationship with the Kremlin. With reports from Russian sources, many connected to Russian intelligence, Steele assembled a damaging report—now dubbed the "dossier"—suggesting that Donald Trump was being blackmailed by the Putin government. In September, Steele briefed reporters from the *New York Times*, the *Washington Post*, Yahoo! News, the *New Yorker*, and CNN. All declined to use this unverified information, with its unclear provenance, especially given that it was about an unlikely election winner.

But the day before the scheduled press conference, CNN broke details of the Steele dossier. Almost immediately thereafter, Buzzfeed published the entire report—an itemized bacchanal of beyond-the-pale behavior.

On the verge of Trump's ascendancy to the presidency, the media, with its singular voice on Trump matters, was propounding a conspiracy of vast proportions. The theory, suddenly presented as just this side of a likelihood, was that the Russians had suborned Donald Trump during a trip to Moscow with a crude blackmail scheme involving prostitutes and videotaped sexual acts pushing new boundaries of deviance (including "golden showers") with prostitutes and videotaped sex acts. The implicit conclusion: a compromised Trump had conspired with the Russians to steal the election and to install him in the White House as Putin's dupe.

If this was true, then the nation stood at one of the most extraordinary moments in the history of democracy, international relations, and journalism.

If it was not true—and it was hard to fathom a middle ground—then it would seem to support the Trump view (and the Bannon view) that the media, in also quite a dramatic development in the history of democracy, was so blinded by an abhorrence and revulsion, both ideological and personal, for the democratically elected leader that it would pursue any avenue to take him down. Mark Hemingway, in the conservative, but anti-Trump, *Weekly Standard*, argued the novel paradox of two unreliable narrators dominating American public life: the president-elect spoke with little information and frequently no factual basis, while "the frame the media has chosen to embrace is that everything the man does is, by default, unconstitutional or an abuse of power."

On the afternoon of January 11, these two opposing perceptions faced off in the lobby of Trump Tower: the political antichrist, a figure of dark but buffoonish scandal, in the pocket of America's epochal adversary, versus the would-be revolutionary-mob media, drunk on virtue, certainty, and conspiracy theories. Each represented, for the other side, a wholly discredited "fake" version of reality.

If these character notes seemed comic-book in style, that was exactly how the press conference unfolded.

First Trump's encomiums to himself:

"I will be the greatest jobs producer that God ever created. . . ."

A smattering of the issues before him:

"Veterans with a little cancer can't see a doctor until they are terminal. . . ."

Then the incredulity:

"I was in Russia years ago with the Ms. Universe contest—did very very well—I tell everyone be careful, because you don't want to see yourself on television—cameras all over the place. And again, not just Russia, all over. So would anyone really believe that story? I'm also very much of a germaphobe, by the way. Believe me."

Then the denial:

"I have no deals in Russia, I have no deal that could happen in Russia because we've stayed away, and I have no loans with Russia. I have to say one thing . . . Over the weekend I was offered two billion dollars to do a deal in Dubai and I turned it down. I didn't have to turn it down, because as you know I have a no-conflict situation as president. I didn't know about that until three months ago but it's a nice thing to have. But I didn't want to take advantage of something. I have a no-conflict-of-interest provision as president. I could actually run my business, run my business and run government at the same time. I don't like the way that looks but I would be able to do that if I wanted to. I could run the Trump organization, a great, great company, and I could run the country, but I don't want to do that."

Then the direct attack on CNN, his nemesis:

"Your organization is terrible. Your organization is terrible. . . . Quiet . . . quiet . . . don't be rude . . . Don't be. . . . No, I'm not going to give you a question . . . I'm not going to give you a question. . . . You are fake news. . . ."

And in summation:

"That report first of all should never have been printed because it's not worth the paper it's printed on. I will tell you that should never ever happen. Twenty-two million accounts were hacked by China. That's because we have no defense, because we're run by people who don't know what they're doing. Russia will have far greater respect for our country when I'm leading it. And not just Russia, China, which has taken total advantage of us. Russia, China, Japan, Mexico, all countries will respect us far more, far more than they do under past administrations. . . ."

Not only did the president-elect wear his deep and bitter grievances on his sleeve, but it was now clear that the fact of having been elected president would not change his unfiltered, apparently uncontrollable, utterly shoot-from-the-hip display of wounds, resentments, and ire.

"I think he did a fantastic job," said Kellyanne Conway after the news conference. "But the media won't say that. They never will."

3

DAY ONE

Jared Kushner at thirty-six prided himself on his ability to get along with older men. By the time of Donald Trump's inauguration he had become the designated intermediary between his father-in-law and the establishment, such as it was—more moderate Republicans, corporate interests, the New York rich. Having a line to Kushner seemed to offer an alarmed elite a handle on a volatile situation.

Several of his father-in-law's circle of confidants also confided in Kushner—often confiding their worries about their friend, the president-elect.

"I give him good advice about what he needs to do and for three hours the next day he does it, and then goes hopelessly off script," complained one of them to Trump's son-in-law. Kushner, whose pose was to take things in and not give much back, said he understood the frustration.

These powerful figures tried to convey a sense of real-world politics, which they all claimed to comprehend at some significantly higher threshold than the soon-to-be president. They were all concerned that Trump did not understand what he was up against. That there was simply not enough method to his madness.

Each of these interlocutors provided Kushner with something of a tutorial on the limitations of presidential power—that Washington was as much designed to frustrate and undermine presidential power as to accommodate it.

"Don't let him piss off the press, don't let him piss off the Republican Party, don't threaten congressmen because they will fuck you if you do, and most of all don't let him piss off the intel community," said one national Republican figure to Kushner. "If you fuck with the intel community they will figure out a way to get back at you and you'll have two or three years of a Russian investigation, and every day something else will leak out."

A vivid picture was painted for the preternaturally composed Kushner of spies and their power, of how secrets were passed out of the intelligence community to former members of the community or to other allies in Congress or even to persons in the executive branch and then to the press.

One of Kushner's now-frequent wise-men callers was Henry Kissinger. Kissinger, who had been a front-row witness when the bureaucracy and intelligence community revolted against Richard Nixon, outlined the kinds of mischief, and worse, that the new administration could face.

"Deep state," the left-wing and right-wing notion of an intelligence-network permanent-government conspiracy, part of the Breitbart lexicon, became the Trump team term of art: he's poked the deep state bear.

Names were put to this: John Brennan, the CIA director; James Clapper, the director of national intelligence; Susan Rice, the outgoing National Security Advisor; and Ben Rhodes, Rice's deputy and an Obama favorite.

Movie scenarios were painted: a cabal of intelligence community myrmidons, privy to all sorts of damning evidence of Trump's recklessness and dubious dealings, would, with a strategic schedule of wounding, embarrassing, and distracting leaks, make it impossible for the Trump White House to govern.

What Kushner was told, again and again, is that the president had to make amends. He had to reach out. He had to mollify. *These were forces not to be trifled with* was said with utmost gravity.

Throughout the campaign and even more forcefully after the election, Trump had targeted the American intelligence community—

the CIA, FBI, NSC, and, altogether, seventeen separate intelligence agencies—as incompetent and mendacious. (His message was "on auto pilot," said one aide.) Among the various and plentiful Trump mixed messages at odds with conservative orthodoxy, this was a particularly juicy one. His case against American intelligence included its faulty information about weapons of mass destruction that preceded the Iraq war, a litany of Obama Afghanistan-Iraq-Syria-Libya and other war-related intelligence failures, and, more recently, but by no means least of all, intelligence leaks regarding his purported Russian relationships and subterfuges.

Trump's criticism seemed to align him with the left in its half century of making a bogeyman of American intelligence agencies. But, in quite some reversal, the liberals and the intelligence community were now aligned in their horror of Donald Trump. Much of the left—which had resoundingly and scathingly rejected the intelligence community's unambiguous assessment of Edward Snowden as a betrayer of national secrets rather than a well-intentioned whistle-blower—now suddenly embraced the intelligence community's authority in its suggestion of Trump's nefarious relationships with the Russians.

Trump was dangerously out in the cold.

Hence, Kushner thought it was sensible to make a reach-out to the CIA among the first orders of the new administration's business.

* * *

Trump did not enjoy his own inauguration. He had hoped for a big blowout. Tom Barrack, the would-be showman—in addition to Michael Jackson's Neverland Ranch, he had bought Miramax Pictures from Disney with the actor Rob Lowe—may have declined the chief of staff job, but, as part of his shadow involvement with his friend's White House, he stepped up to raise the money for the inaugural and to create an event that—seemingly quite at odds with the new president's character, and with Steve Bannon's wish for a no-frills populist inauguration—he promised would have a "soft sensuality" and "poetic cadence." But Trump, imploring friends to use their influence to nail some of the A-level stars who were snubbing the event, started to get angry and hurt that stars were determined to embarrass him. Bannon, a soothing voice as well as a professional agitator, tried to argue the dialectical nature of what they had achieved (without using the word "dialectical"). Because Trump's success was beyond measure, or certainly beyond all expectations, the media and the liberals had to justify their own failure, he explained to the new president.

In the hours before the inauguration, the whole of Washington seemed to be holding its breath. On the evening before Trump was sworn in, Bob Corker, the Republican senator from Tennessee and the chairman of the Senate Foreign Relations Committee, opened his remarks as the featured speaker at a gathering at the Jefferson Hotel with the existential question, "Where are things going?" He paused for a moment and then answered, as though from some deep well of bewilderment, "I have no idea."

Later that evening, a concert at the Lincoln Memorial, part of an always awkward effort to import pop culture to Washington, ended up, absent any star power, with Trump himself taking the stage as the featured act, angrily insisting to aides that he could outdraw any star.

Dissuaded by his staff from staying at the Trump International Hotel in Washington and regretting his decision, the president-elect woke up on inaugural morning complaining about the accommodations at Blair House, the official guest residence across the street from the White House. Too hot, bad water pressure, bad bed.

His temper did not improve. Throughout the morning, he was visibly fighting with his wife, who seemed on the verge of tears and would return to New York the next day; almost every word he addressed to her was sharp and peremptory. Kellyanne Conway had taken up Melania Trump as a personal PR mission, promoting the new First Lady as a vital pillar of support for the president and a helpful voice in her own right, and was trying to convince Trump that she could have an important role in the White House. But, in general, the Trumps' relationship was one of those things nobody asked too many questions about—another mysterious variable in the presidential mood.

At the ceremonial meeting of the soon-to-be-new president and the soon-to-be-old president at the White House, which took place just before they set off for the swearing-in ceremony, Trump believed the Obamas acted disdainfully—"very arrogant"—toward him and Melania. Instead of wearing a game face, going into the inaugural events, the president-elect wore what some around him had taken to calling his golf face: angry and pissed off, shoulders hunched, arms swinging, brow furled, lips pursed. This had become the public Trump—truculent Trump.

An inauguration is supposed to be a love-in. The media gets a new and upbeat story. For the party faithful, happy times are here again. For the permanent government—the swamp—it's a chance to curry favor and seek new advantage. For the country, it's a coronation. But Bannon had three messages or themes he kept trying to reinforce with his boss: his presidency was going to be different—as different as any since Andrew Jackson's (he was supplying the less-than-well-read president-elect with Jackson-related books and quotes); they knew who their enemies were and shouldn't fall into the trap of trying to make them their friends, because they wouldn't be; and so, from day one, they should consider themselves on a war footing. While this spoke to Trump's combative "counterpuncher" side, it was hard on his eager-to-be-liked side. Bannon saw himself as managing these two impulses, emphasizing the former and explaining to his boss why having enemies here created friends somewhere else.

In fact, Trump's aggrieved mood became a perfect match for the Bannon-written aggrieved inaugural address. Much of the sixteen-minute speech was part of Bannon's daily *joie de guerre* patter—his take-back-the-country America-first, carnage-everywhere vision for the country. But it actually became darker and more forceful when filtered through Trump's disappointment and delivered with his golf face. The administration purposely began on a tone of menace—a Bannon-driven message to the other side that the country was about to undergo profound change. Trump's wounded feelings—his sense of being shunned and unloved on the very day he became president—helped send that message. When he came off the podium after delivering his address, he kept repeating, "Nobody will forget this speech."

George W. Bush, on the dais, supplied what seemed likely to become the historic footnote to the Trump address: "That's some weird shit."

* * *

Trump, despite his disappointment at Washington's failure to properly greet and celebrate him, was, like a good salesman, an optimist. Salesmen, whose primary characteristic and main asset is their ability to keep selling, constantly recast the world in positive terms. Discouragement for everyone else is merely the need to improve reality for them.

By the next morning, Trump was soliciting affirmation of his view that the inauguration had been a great success. "That crowd went all the way back. That were more than a million people at least, right?" He made a series of phone calls to friends who largely yes'd him on this. Kushner confirmed a big crowd. Conway did nothing to dissuade him. Priebus agreed. Bannon made a joke.

Among Trump's first moves as president was to have a series of inspirational photographs in the West Wing replaced with images of big crowd scenes at his inaugural ceremony.

Bannon had come to rationalize Trump's reality distortions. Trump's hyperbole, exaggerations, flights of fancy, improvisations, and general freedom toward and mangling of the facts, were products of the basic lack of guile, pretense, and impulse control that helped create the immediacy and spontaneity that was so successful with so many on the stump—while so horrifying to so many others.

For Bannon, Obama was the north star of aloofness. "Politics," said Bannon with an authority that belayed the fact that until the previous August he had never worked in politics, "is a more immediate game than he ever played it." Trump was, for Bannon, a modern-day William Jennings Bryan. (Bannon had long talked about the need for a new Williams Jennings Bryan in right-wing politics, with friends assuming Bannon meant himself.) At the turn of the twentieth century, Bryan had enthralled rural audiences with his ability to speak passionately and extemporaneously for apparently unlimited periods of time. Trump compensated—in the theory of some intimates, including Bannon—for his difficulties with reading, writing, and close focus with an improvisational style that produced, if not exactly a William Jennings Bryan effect, certainly close to the exact opposite of the Obama effect.

It was part hortatory, part personal testimony, part barstool blowhard, a rambling, disjointed, digressive, what-me-worry approach that combined aspects of cable television rage, big-tent religious revivalism, Borscht Belt tummler, motivational speaking, and YouTube vlogging. Charisma in American politics had come to define an order of charm, wit, and style—a coolness. But another sort of American charisma was more in the Christian evangelical vein, an emotional, experiential spectacle.

The Trump campaign had built its central strategy around great rallies regularly attracting tens of thousands, a political phenomenon that the Democrats both failed to heed and saw as a sign of Trump's limited appeal. For the Trump team, this style, this unmediated connection—his speeches, his tweets, his spontaneous phone calls to radio and television shows, and, often, to anyone who would listen—was revelatory, a new, personal, and inspirational politics. For the other side, it was clownishness that, at best, aspired to the kind of raw, authoritarian demagoguery that had long been discredited by and assigned to history and that, when it appeared in American politics, reliably failed.

While the advantages of this style for the Trump team were now very clear, the problem was that it often—in fact regularly—produced assertions that were not remotely true.

This had led increasingly to the two-different-realities theory of Trump politics. In the one reality, which encompassed most of Trump's supporters, his nature was understood and appreciated. He was the antiwonk. He was the counterexpert. His was the gut call. He was the everyman. He was jazz (some, in the telling, made it rap), everybody else an earnest folk music. In the other reality, in which resided most of his antagonists, his virtues were grievous if not mental and criminal flaws. In this reality lived the media, which, with its conclusion of a misbegotten and bastard presidency, believed it could diminish him and wound him (and wind him up) and rob him of all credibility by relentlessly pointing out how literally wrong he was.

The media, adopting a "shocked, shocked" morality, could not fathom how being factually wrong was not an absolute ending in itself. How could this not utterly shame him? How could his staff defend him? The facts were the facts! Defying them, or ignoring them, or subverting them, made you a liar—intending to deceive, bearing false witness. (A minor journalism controversy broke out about whether these untruths should be called inaccuracies or lies.)

In Bannon's view: (1) Trump was never going to change; (2) trying to get him to change would surely cramp his style; (3) it didn't matter to Trump supporters; (4) the media wasn't going to like him anyway; (5) it was better to play against the media than to the media; (6) the media's claim to be the protector of factual probity and accuracy was itself a sham; (7) the Trump revolution was an attack on conventional assumptions and expertise, so better to embrace Trump's behavior than try to curb it or cure it.

The problem was that, for all he was never going to stick to a script ("his mind just doesn't work that way" was one of the internal rationalizations), Trump craved media approval. But, as Bannon emphasized, he was never going to get the facts right, nor was he ever going to acknowledge that he got them wrong, so therefore he was not going to get that approval. This meant, next best thing, that he had to be aggressively defended against the media's disapproval.

The problem here was that the more vociferous the defense—mostly of assertions that could easily be proved wrong—the more the media redoubled its attacks and censure. What's more, Trump was receiving the censure of his friends, too. And it was not only calls from friends worried about him, but staffers calling people to call him and say *Simmer down.* "Who do you have in there?" said Joe Scarborough in a frantic call. "Who's the person you trust? Jared? Who can talk you through this stuff before you decided to act on it?"

"Well," said the president, "you won't like the answer, but the answer is me. Me. I talk to myself."

Hence, within twenty-four hours of the inauguration, the president had invented a million or so people who did not exist. He sent his new press secretary, Sean Spicer—whose personal mantra would shortly become "You can't make this shit up"—to argue his case in a media moment that turned Spicer, quite a buttoned-down political professional, into a national joke, which he seemed destined to never recover from. To boot, the president blamed Spicer for not making the million phantom souls seem real.

It was the first presidential instance of what the campaign regulars had learned over many months: on the most basic level, Trump just did not, as Spicer later put it, give a fuck. You could tell him whatever you wanted, but he knew what he knew, and if what you said contradicted what he knew, he simply didn't believe you.

The next day Kellyanne Conway, her aggressive posture during the campaign turning more and more to petulance and self-pity, asserted the new president's right to claim "alternative facts." As it happened, Conway meant to say "alternative information," which at least would imply there might be additional data. But as uttered, it certainly sounded like the new administration was claiming the right to recast reality. Which, in a sense, it was. Although, in Conway's view, it was the media doing the recasting, making a mountain (hence "fake news") out of a molehill (an honest minor exaggeration, albeit of vast proportions).

Anyway, the frequently asked question about whether Trump would continue his unsupervised and often inexplicable tweets now that he was officially in the White House and the president of the United States—a question as hotly asked inside the White House as out—was answered: he would.

This was his fundamental innovation in governing: regular, uncontrolled bursts of anger and spleen.

* * *

The president's immediate official business, however, was to make nice with the CIA.

On Saturday, January 21, in an event organized by Kushner, the president, in his first presidential act, paid a call on Langley to, in Bannon's hopeful description, "play some politics." In carefully prepared remarks in his first act as president, he would lay some of the famous Trump flattery on the CIA and the rest of the sprawling, and leaking, U.S. intelligence world.

Not taking off his dark overcoat, lending him quite a hulking gangster look, pacing in front of the CIA's wall of stars for its fallen agents, in front of a crowd of about three hundred agency personnel and a group of White House staffers, and, suddenly, in a mood of sleepless cockiness and pleasure at having a captive crowd, the new president, disregarding his text, launched into what we could confidently call some of the most peculiar remarks ever delivered by an American president.

"I know a lot about West Point, I'm a person who very strongly believes in academics. Every time I say I had an uncle who was a great professor at MIT for 35 years, who did a fantastic job in so many ways academically—he was an academic genius—and then they say, Is Donald Trump an intellectual? Trust me, I'm like a smart person."

Which was all somehow by way of praise for the new, soon-to-be-confirmed CIA director, Mike Pompeo, who had attended West Point and who Trump had brought with him to stand in the crowd—and who now found himself as bewildered as everyone else.

"You know when I was young. Of course I feel young—I feel like I was 30 . . . 35 . . . 39 . . . . Somebody said, Are you young? I said, I think I'm young. I was stopping in the final months of the campaign, four stops, five stops, seven stops—speeches, speeches in front of twenty-five, thirty thousand people . . . fifteen, nineteen thousand. I feel young—I think we're all so young. When I was young we were always winning things in this country. We'd win with trade, we'd win with wars—at a certain age I remembering hearing from one of my instructors, the United States has never lost a war. And then, after that, it's like we haven't won anything. You know the old expression, to the victor belongs the spoils? You remember I always say, keep the oil."

"*Who* should keep the oil?" asked a bewildered CIA employee, leaning over to a colleague in the back of the room.

"I wasn't a fan of Iraq, I didn't want to go into Iraq. But I will tell you when we were in we got out wrong and I always said in addition to that keep the oil. Now I said it for economic reasons, but if you think about it, Mike"—he called out across the room, addressing the soon-to-be director—"if we kept the oil we wouldn't have ISIS because that's where they made their money in the first place, so that's why we should have kept the oil. But okay—maybe you'll have another chance—but the fact is we should have kept the oil."

The president paused and smiled with evident satisfaction.

"The reason you are my first stop, as you know I have a running war with the media, they are among the most dishonest human beings on earth, and they sort of made it sound like I had a feud with the intelligence community and I just want to let you know the reason you're the number one stop is exactly the opposite, exactly, and they understand that. I was explaining about the numbers. We did, we did a thing yesterday at the speech. Did everybody like the speech? You had to like it. But we had a massive field of people. You saw them. Packed. I get up this morning, I turn on one of the networks, and they show an empty field and I say, Wait a minute, I made a speech. I looked out—the field was—it looked like a million, million and half people. They showed a field where there were practically nobody standing there. And they said Donald Trump did not draw well and I said it was almost raining, the rain should have scared them away, but God looked down and said we're not going to let it rain on your speech and in fact when I first started I said, Oooh no, first line I got hit by a couple of drops, and I said, Oh this is too bad, but we'll go right through it, the truth is it stopped immediately. . . ."

"No, it didn't," one of the staffers traveling with him said reflexively, then catching herself and, with a worried look, glancing around to see if she had been overheard.

". . . and then it became really sunny and I walked off and it poured right after I left. It poured but we have something amazing because—honestly it looked like a million, million and a half people, whatever it was it was, but it went all the way back to the Washington Monument and by mistake I get this network and it showed an empty field and it said we drew two hundred fifty thousand people. Now that's not bad, but it's a lie. . . . And we had another one yesterday which was interesting. In the Oval Office there's a beautiful statue of Dr. Martin Luther King and I also happen to like Churchill—Winston Churchill—I think most of us like Churchill, doesn't come from our country but had a lot to do with it, helped us, real ally, and as you know the Churchill statue was taken out. . . . So a reporter for *Time* magazine and I have been on the cover like fourteen or fifteen times. I think I have the all-time record in the history of *Time* magazine. Like if Tom Brady is on the cover it's one time because he won the Super Bowl or something. I've been on fifteen times this year. I don't think, Mike, that's a record that can ever be broken, do you agree with that . . . . What do you think?"

"No," said Pompeo in a stricken voice.

"But I will say that they said it was very interesting that 'Donald Trump took down the bust, the statue, of Dr. Martin Luther King,' and it was right there, there was a cameraman that was in front of it. So Zeke . . . Zeke . . . from *Time* magazine . . . writes a story that I took it down. I would never do that. I have great respect for Dr. Martin Luther King. But this is how dishonest the media is. Now big story, but the retraction was like this"—he indicated ever-so-small with his fingers. "Is it a line or do they even bother putting it in? I only like to say I love honesty, I like honest reporting. I will tell you, final time, although I will say it when you let in your thousands of other people who have been trying to come in, because I am coming back, we may have to get you a larger room, we may have to get you a larger room and maybe, *maybe*, it will be built by somebody that knows how to build and we won't have columns. You understand that? We get rid of the columns, but you know I just wanted to say that I love you, I respect you, there's nobody I respect more. You do a fantastic job and we're going to start winning again, and you're going to be leading the charge, so thank you all very much."

In a continuing sign of Trump's *Rashomon* effect—his speeches inspiring joy or horror—witnesses would describe his reception at the CIA as either a Beatles-like emotional outpouring or a response so confounded and appalled that, in the seconds after he finished, you could hear a pin drop.

4

BANNON

Steve Bannon was the first Trump senior staffer in the White House after Trump was sworn in. On the inauguration march, he had grabbed the newly appointed deputy chief of staff, Katie Walsh, Reince Priebus's deputy at the RNC, and together they had peeled off to inspect the now vacant West Wing. The carpet had been shampooed, but little else had changed. It was a warren of tiny offices in need of paint, not rigorously cleaned on a regular basis, the décor something like an admissions office at a public university. Bannon claimed the nondescript office across from the much grander chief of staff's suite, and he immediately requisitioned the white boards on which he intended to chart the first hundred days of the Trump administration. And right away he began moving furniture out. The point was to leave no room for anyone to sit. There were to be no meetings, at least no meetings where people could get comfortable. Limit discussion. Limit debate. This was war. This was a war room.

Many who had worked with Bannon on the campaign and through the transition shortly noticed a certain change. Having achieved one goal, he was clearly on to another. An intense man, he was suddenly at an even higher level of focus and determination.

"What's up with Steve?" Kushner began to ask. And then, "Is something wrong with Steve?" And then finally, "I don't understand. We were so close."

Within the first week, Bannon seemed to have put away the camaraderie of Trump Tower—including a willingness to talk at length at any hour—and become far more remote, if not unreachable. He was "focused on my shit." He was just getting things done. But many felt that getting things done was was more about him hatching plots against them. And certainly, among his basic character notes, Steve Bannon was a plotter. Strike before being struck. Anticipate the moves of others—counter them before they can make their moves. To him this was seeing things ahead, focusing on a set of goals. The first goal was the election of Donald Trump, the second the staffing of the Trump government. Now it was capturing the soul of the Trump White House, and he understood what others did not yet: this would be a mortal competition.

* * *

In the early days of the transition, Bannon had encouraged the Trump team to read David Halberstam's *The Best and the Brightest.* (One of the few people who seem actually to have taken him up on this reading assignment was Jared Kushner.) "A very moving experience reading this book. It makes the world clear, amazing characters and all true," Bannon enthused.

This was a personal bit of branding—Bannon made sure to exhibit the book to many of the liberal reporters he was courting. But he was also trying to make a point, an important one considering the slapdash nature of the transition team's staffing protocols: be careful who you hire.

Halberstam's book, published in 1972, is a Tolstoyan effort to understand how great figures of the academic, intellectual, and military world who had served during the Kennedy and Johnson years had so grievously misapprehended the nature of the Vietnam War and mishandled its prosecution. *The Best and the Brightest* was a cautionary tale about the 1960s establishment—the precursor of the establishment that Trump and Bannon were now so aggressively challenging.

But the book also served as a reverential guide to the establishment. For the 1970s generation of future policy experts, would-be world leaders, and Ivy League journalists aiming for big-time careers—though it was Bannon's generation, he was far outside this self-selected elite circle—*The Best and the Brightest* was a handbook about the characteristics of

American power and the routes to it. Not just the right schools and right backgrounds, although that, too, but the attitudes, conceits, affect, and language that would be most conducive to finding your way into the American power structure. Many saw the book as a set of prescriptions about how to get ahead, rather than, as intended, what not to do when you are ahead. *The Best and the Brightest* described the people who should be in power. A college-age Barack Obama was smitten with the book, as was Rhodes Scholar Bill Clinton.

Halberstam's book defined the look and feel of White House power. His language, resonant and imposing and, often, boffo pompous, had set the tone for the next half century of official presidential journalism. Even scandalous or unsuccessful tenants of the White House were treated as unique figures who had risen to the greatest heights after mastering a Darwinian political process. Bob Woodward, who helped bring Nixon down—and who himself became a figure of unchallengeable presidential mythmaking—wrote a long shelf of books in which even the most misguided presidential actions seemed part of an epochal march of ultimate responsibility and life-and-death decision making. Only the most hard-hearted reader would not entertain a daydream in which he or she was not part of this awesome pageant.

Steve Bannon was such a daydreamer.

* * *

But if Halberstam defined the presidential mien, Trump defied it—and defiled it. Not a single attribute would place him credibly in the revered circle of American presidential character and power. Which was, in a curious reversal of the book's premise, just what created Steve Bannon's opportunity.

The less likely a presidential candidate is, the more unlikely, and, often, inexperienced, his aides are—that is, an unlikely candidate can attract only unlikely aides, as the likely ones go to the more likely candidates. When an unlikely candidate wins—and as outsiders become ever more the quadrennial flavor of the month, the more likely an unlikely candidate is to get elected—ever more peculiar people fill the White House. Of course, a point about the Halberstam book and about the Trump campaign was that the most obvious players make grievous mistakes, too. Hence, in the Trump narrative, unlikely players far outside the establishment hold the true genius.

Still, few have been more unlikely than Steve Bannon.

At sixty-three, Bannon took his first formal job in politics when he joined the Trump campaign. Chief Strategist—his title in the new administration—was his first job not just in the federal government but in the public sector. ("*Strategist!*" scoffed Roger Stone, who, before Bannon, had been one of Trump's chief strategists.) Other than Trump himself, Bannon was certainly the oldest inexperienced person ever to work in the White House.

It was a flaky career that got him here.

Catholic school in Richmond, Virginia. Then a local college, Virginia Tech. Then seven years in the Navy, a lieutenant on ship duty and then in the Pentagon. While on active duty, he got a master's degree at Georgetown's School of Foreign Service, but then he washed out of his naval career. Then an MBA from Harvard Business School. Then four years as an investment banker at Goldman Sachs—his final two years focusing on the media industry in Los Angeles—but not rising above a midlevel position.

In 1990, at the age of thirty-seven, Bannon entered peripatetic entrepreneurhood under the auspices of Bannon & Co., a financial advisory firm to the entertainment industry. This was something of a hustler's shell company, hanging out a shingle in an industry with a small center of success and concentric rings radiating out of rising, aspiring, falling, and failing strivers. Bannon & Co., skirting falling and failing, made it to aspiring by raising small amounts of money for independent film projects—none a hit.

Bannon was rather a movie figure himself. A type. Alcohol. Bad marriages. Cash-strapped in a business where the measure of success is excesses of riches. Ever scheming. Ever disappointed.

For a man with a strong sense of his own destiny, he tended to be hardly noticed. Jon Corzine, the former Goldman chief and future United States senator and governor of New Jersey, climbing the Goldman ranks when Bannon was at the firm, was unaware of Bannon. When Bannon was appointed head of the Trump campaign and became an overnight press sensation—or question mark—his credentials suddenly included a convoluted story about how Bannon & Co. had acquired a stake in the megahit show *Seinfeld* and hence its twenty-year run of residual profits. But none of the Seinfeld principals, creators, or producers seem ever to have heard of him.

Mike Murphy, the Republican media consultant who ran Jeb Bush's PAC and became a leading anti-Trump movement figure, has the vaguest recollection of Bannon's seeking PR services from Murphy's firm for a film Bannon was producing a decade or so ago. "I'm told he was in the meeting, but I honestly can't get a picture of him."

The *New Yorker* magazine, dwelling on the Bannon enigma—one that basically translated to: How is it that the media has been almost wholly unaware of someone who is suddenly among the most powerful people in government?—tried to trace his steps in Hollywood and largely failed to find him. The *Washington Post* traced his many addresses to no clear conclusion, except a suggestion of possible misdemeanor voter fraud.

In the midnineties, he inserted himself in a significant role into Biosphere 2, a project copiously funded by Edward Bass, one of the Bass family oil heirs, about sustaining life in space, and dubbed by *Time* one of the hundred worst ideas of the century—a rich man's folly. Bannon, having to find his opportunities in distress situations, stepped into the project amid its collapse only to provoke further breakdown and litigation, including harassment and vandalism charges.

After the Biosphere 2 disaster, he participated in raising financing for a virtual currency scheme (MMORPGs, or MMOs) called Internet Gaming Entertainment (IGE). This was a successor company to Digital Entertainment Network (DEN), a dot-com burnout, whose principals included the former child star Brock Pierce (*The Mighty Ducks*) who went on to be the founder of IGE, but was then pushed out. Bannon was put in as CEO, and the company was subsumed by endless litigation.

Distress is an opportunistic business play. But some distress is better than others. The kinds of situations available to Bannon involved managing conflict, nastiness, and relative hopelessness—in essence managing and taking a small profit on dwindling cash. It's a living at the margins of people who are making a much better living. Bannon kept trying to make a killing but never found the killing sweet spot.

Distress is also a contrarian's game. And the contrarian's impulse—equal parts personal dissatisfaction, general resentment, and gambler's instinct—started to ever more strongly fuel Bannon. Part of the background for his contrarian impulse lay in an Irish Catholic union family, Catholic schools, and three unhappy marriages and bad divorces (journalists would make much of the recriminations in his second wife's divorce filings).

Not so long ago, Bannon might have been a recognizably modern figure, something of a romantic antihero, an ex-military and up-from-the-working-class guy, striving, through multiple marriages and various careers, to make it, but never finding much comfort in the establishment world, wanting to be part of it and wanting to blow it up at the same time—a character for Richard Ford, or John Updike, or Harry Crews. An American man's story. But now such stories have crossed a political line. The American man story is a right-wing story. Bannon found his models in political infighters like Lee Atwater, Roger Ailes, Karl Rove. All were larger-than-life American characters doing battle with conformity and modernity, relishing ways to violate liberal sensibilities.

The other point is that Bannon, however smart and even charismatic, however much he extolled the virtue of being a "stand-up guy," was not necessarily a nice guy. Several decades as a grasping entrepreneur without a satisfying success story doesn't smooth the hustle in hustler. One competitor in the conservative media business, while acknowledging his intelligence and the ambitiousness of his ideas, also noted, "He's mean, dishonest, and incapable of caring about other people. His eyes dart around like he's always looking for a weapon with which to bludgeon or gouge you."

Conservative media fit not only his angry, contrarian, and Roman Catholic side, but it had low barriers to entry—liberal media, by contrast, with its corporate hierarchies, was much harder to break into. What's more, conservative media is a highly lucrative target market category, with books (often dominating the bestseller lists), videos, and other products available through direct sales avenues that can circumvent more expensive distribution channels.

In the early 2000s, Bannon became a purveyor of conservative books products and media. His partner in this enterprise was David Bossie, the far-right pamphleteer and congressional committee investigator into the Clintons' Whitewater affair, who would join him as deputy campaign manager on the Trump campaign. Bannon met Breitbart News founder Andrew Breitbart at a screening of one of the Bannon-Bossie documentaries *In the Face of Evil* (billed as "Ronald Reagan's crusade to destroy the most tyrannical and depraved political systems the world has ever known"), which in turn led to a relationship with the man who offered Bannon the ultimate opportunity: Robert Mercer.

* * *

In this regard, Bannon was not so much an entrepreneur of vision or even business discipline, he was more simply following the money—or trying to separate a fool from his money. He could not have done better than Bob and Rebekah Mercer. Bannon focused his entrepreneurial talents on becoming courtier, Svengali, and political investment adviser to father and daughter.

Theirs was a consciously quixotic mission. They would devote vast sums—albeit still just a small part of Bob Mercer's many billions—to trying to build a radical free-market, small-government, homeschooling, antiliberal, gold-standard, pro-death-penalty, anti-Muslim, pro-Christian, monetarist, anti-civil-rights political movement in the United States.

Bob Mercer is an ultimate quant, an engineer who designs investment algorithms and became a co-CEO of one of the most successful hedge funds, Renaissance Technologies. With his daughter, Rebekah, Mercer set up what is in effect a private Tea Party movement, self-funding whatever Tea Party or alt-right project took their fancy. Bob Mercer is almost nonverbal, looking at you with a dead stare and either not talking or offering only minimal response. He had a Steinway baby grand on his yacht; after inviting friends and colleagues on the boat, he would spend the time playing the piano, wholly disengaged from his guests. And yet his political beliefs, to the extent they could be discerned, were generally Bush-like, and his political discussions, to the extent that you could get him to be responsive, were about issues involving ground game and data gathering. It was Rebekah Mercer—who had bonded with Bannon, and whose politics were grim, unyielding, and doctrinaire—who defined the family. "She's . . . like whoa, ideologically there is no conversation with her," said one senior Trump White House staffer.

With the death of Andrew Breitbart in 2012, Bannon, in essence holding the proxy of the Mercers' investment in the site, took over the Breitbart business. He leveraged his gaming experience into using Gamergate—a precursor alt-right movement that coalesced around an antipathy toward, and harassment of, women working in the online gaming industry—to build vast amounts of traffic through the virality of political memes. (After hours one night in the White House, Bannon would argue that he knew exactly how to build a Breitbart for the left. And he would have the key advantage because "people on the left want to win Pulitzers, whereas I want to *be* Pulitzer!")

Working out of—and living in—the town house Breitbart rented on Capitol Hill, Bannon became one of the growing number of notable Tea Party figures in Washington, the Mercers' consigliere. But a seeming measure of his marginality was that his big project was the career of Jeff Sessions—"Beauregard," Sessions's middle name, in Bannon's affectionate moniker and evocation of the Confederate general—among the least mainstream and most peculiar people in the Senate, whom Bannon tried to promote to run for president in 2012.

Donald Trump was a step up—and early in the 2016 race, Trump became the Breitbart totem. (Many of Trump's positions in the campaign were taken from the Breitbart articles he had printed out for him.) Indeed, Bannon began to suggest to people that he, like Ailes had been at Fox, was the true force behind his chosen candidate.

Bannon didn't much question Donald Trump's bona fides, or behavior, or electability, because, in part, Trump was just his latest rich man. The rich man is a fixed fact, which you have to accept and deal with in an entrepreneurial world—at least a lower-level entrepreneurial world. And, of course, if Trump had had firmer bona fides, better behavior, and clear electability, Bannon would not have had his chance.

However much a marginal, invisible, small-time hustler Bannon had been—something of an Elmore Leonard character—he was suddenly transformed inside Trump Tower, an office he entered on August 15, and for practical purposes, did not exit, save for a few hours a night (and not every night) in his temporary midtown Manhattan accommodations, until January 17, when the transition team moved to Washington. There was no competition in Trump Tower for being the brains of the operation. Of the dominant figures in the transition, neither Kushner, Priebus, nor Conway, and certainly not the president-elect, had the ability to express any kind of coherent perception or narrative. By default, everybody had to look to the voluble, aphoristic, shambolic, witty, off-the-cuff figure who was both ever present on the premises and who had, in an unlikely attribute, read a book or two.

And indeed who, during the campaign, turned out to be able to harness the Trump operation, not to mention its philosophic disarray, to a single political view: that the path to victory was an economic and cultural message to the white working class in Florida, Ohio, Michigan, and Pennsylvania.

* * *

Bannon collected enemies. Few fueled his savagery and rancor toward the standard-issue Republican world as much as Rupert Murdoch—not least because Murdoch had Donald Trump's ear. It was one of the key elements of Bannon's understanding of Trump: the last person Trump spoke to ended up with enormous influence. Trump would brag that Murdoch was always calling him; Murdoch, for his part, would complain that he couldn't get Trump off the phone.

"He doesn't know anything about American politics, and has no feel for the American people," said Bannon to Trump, always eager to point out that Murdoch wasn't an American. But Trump couldn't get enough of him. With his love of "winners"—and he saw Murdoch as the ultimate winner—Trump was suddenly bad-mouthing his friend Ailes as a "loser."

And yet in one regard Murdoch's message was useful to Bannon.

Having known every president since Harry Truman—as Murdoch took frequent opportunities to point out—and, he conjectured, as many heads of state as anyone living, Murdoch believed he understood better than younger men, even seventy-year-old Trump, that political power was fleeting. (This was in fact the same message he had imparted to Barack Obama.) A president really had only, max, six months to make an impact on the public and set his agenda, and he'd be lucky to get six months. After that it was just putting out fires and battling the opposition.

This was the message whose urgency Bannon himself had been trying to impress on an often distracted Trump. Indeed, in his first weeks in the White House, an inattentive Trump was already trying to curtail his schedule of meetings, limit his hours in the office, and keep his normal golf habits.

Bannon's strategic view of government was shock and awe. Dominate rather than negotiate. Having daydreamed his way into ultimate bureaucratic power, he did not want to see himself as a bureaucrat. He was of a higher purpose and moral order. He was an avenger. He was also, he believed, a straight shooter. There was a moral order in aligning language and action—if you said you were going to do something, you do it.

In his head, Bannon carried a set of decisive actions that would not just mark the new administration's opening days, but make it clear that nothing ever again would be the same. At the age of sixty-three, he was in a hurry.

* * *

Bannon had delved deeply into the nature of executive orders—EOs. You can't rule by decree in the United States, except you really can. The irony here was that it was the Obama administration, with a recalcitrant Republican Congress, that had pushed the EO envelope. Now, in something of a zero-sum game, Trump's EOs would undo Obama's EOs.

During the transition, Bannon and Stephen Miller, a former Sessions aide who had earlier joined the Trump campaign and then become Bannon's effective assistant and researcher, assembled a list of more than two hundred EOs to issue in the first hundred days.

But the first step in the new Trump administration had to be immigration, in Bannon's certain view. Foreigners were the ne plus ultra mania of Trumpism. An issue often dismissed as living on the one-track-mind fringe—Jeff Sessions was one of its cranky exponents—it was Trump's firm belief that a lot of people had had it up to here with foreigners. Before Trump, Bannon had bonded with Sessions on the issue. The Trump campaign became a sudden opportunity to see if nativism really had legs. And then when they won, Bannon understood there could be no hesitation about declaring their ethnocentric heart and soul.

To boot, it was an issue that made liberals bat-shit mad.

Laxly enforced immigration laws reached to the center of the new liberal philosophy and, for Bannon, exposed its hypocrisy. In the liberal worldview, diversity was an absolute good, whereas Bannon believed any reasonable person who was not wholly blinded by the liberal light could see that waves of immigrants came with a load of problems—just look at Europe. And these were problems borne not by cosseted liberals but by the more exposed citizens at the other end of the economic scale.

It was out of some instinctive or idiot-savant-like political understanding that Trump had made this issue his own, frequently observing, *Wasn't anybody an American anymore?* In some of his earliest political outings, even before Obama's election in 2008, Trump talked with bewilderment and resentment about strict quotas on European immigration and the deluge from "Asia and other places." (This deluge, as liberals would be quick to fact-check, was, even as it had grown, still quite a modest stream.) His obsessive focus on Obama's birth certificate was in part about the scourge of non-European foreignness—a certain race-baiting. *Who were these people? Why were they here?*

The campaign sometimes shared a striking graphic. It showed a map of the country reflecting dominant immigration trends in each state from fifty years ago—here was a multitude of countries, many European. Today, the equivalent map showed that every state in the United States was now dominated by Mexican immigration. This was the daily reality of the American workingman, in Bannon's view, the ever growing presence of an alternative, discount workforce.

Bannon's entire political career, such as it was, had been in political media. It was also in Internet media—that is, media ruled by immediate response. The Breitbart formula was to so appall the liberals that the base was doubly satisfied, generating clicks in a ricochet of disgust and delight. You defined yourself by your enemy's reaction. Conflict was the media bait—hence, now, the political chum. The new politics was not the art of the compromise but the art of conflict.

The real goal was to expose the hypocrisy of the liberal view. Somehow, despite laws, rules, and customs, liberal globalists had pushed a myth of more or less open immigration. It was a double liberal hypocrisy, because, sotto voce, the Obama administration had been quite aggressive in deporting illegal aliens—except don't tell the liberals that.

"People want their countries back," said Bannon. "A simple thing."

* * *

Bannon meant his EO to strip away the liberal conceits on an already illiberal process. Rather than seeking to accomplish his goals with the least amount of upset—keeping liberal fig leaves in place—he sought the most.

Why would you? was the logical question of anyone who saw the higher function of government as avoiding conflict.

This included most people in office. The new appointees in place at the affected agencies and departments, among them Homeland Security and State—General John Kelly, then the director of Homeland Security, would carry a grudge about the disarray caused by the immigration EO—wanted nothing more than a moment to get their footing before they might even consider dramatic and contentious new policies. Old appointees—Obama appointees who still occupied most executive branch jobs—found it unfathomable that the new administration would go out of its way to take procedures that largely already existed and to restate them in incendiary, red-flag, and ad hominem terms, such that liberals would have to oppose them.

Bannon's mission was to puncture the global-liberal-emperor-wears-no-clothes bubble, nowhere, in his view, as ludicrously demonstrated as the refusal to see the colossally difficult and costly effects of uncontrolled immigration. He wanted to force liberals to acknowledge that even liberal governments, even the Obama government, were engaged in the real politics of slowing immigration—ever hampered by the liberal refusal to acknowledge this effort.

The EO would be drafted to remorselessly express the administration's (or Bannon's) pitiless view. The problem was, Bannon really didn't know how to do this—change rules and laws. This limitation, Bannon understood, might easily be used to thwart them. Process was their enemy. But just doing it—the hell with how—and doing it immediately, could be a powerful countermeasure.

Just doing things became a Bannon principle, the sweeping antidote to bureaucratic and establishment ennui and resistance. It was the chaos of just doing things that actually got things done. Except, even if you assumed that not knowing how to do things didn't much matter if you just did them, it was still not clear who was going to do what you wanted to do. Or, a corollary, because nobody in the Trump administration really knew how to do anything, it was therefore not clear what anyone did.

Sean Spicer, whose job was literally to explain what people did and why, often simply could not—*because nobody really had a job, because nobody could do a job.*

Priebus, as chief of staff, had to organize meetings, schedules, and the hiring of staff; he also had to oversee the individual functions of the executive office departments. But Bannon, Kushner, Conway, and the president's daughter actually had no specific responsibilities—they could make it up as they went along. They did what they wanted. They would seize the day if they could—even if they really didn't know how to do what they wanted to do.

Bannon, for instance, even driven by his imperative just to get things done, did not use a computer. *How did he do anything?* Katie Walsh wondered. But that was the difference between big visions and small. Process was bunk. Expertise was the last refuge of liberals, ever defeated by the big picture. The will to get big things done was how big things got done. "Don't sweat the small stuff" was a pretty good gist of Donald Trump's—and Steve Bannon's—worldview. "Chaos was Steve's strategy," said Walsh.

Bannon got Stephen Miller to write the immigration EO. Miller, a fifty-five-year-old trapped in a thirty-two-year-old's body, was a former Jeff Sessions staffer brought on to the Trump campaign for his political experience. Except, other than being a dedicated far-right conservative, it was unclear what particular abilities accompanied Miller's political views. He was supposed to be a speechwriter, but if so, he seemed restricted to bullet points and unable to construct sentences. He was supposed to be a policy adviser but knew little about policy. He was supposed to be the house intellectual but was purposely unread. He was supposed to be a communications specialist, but he antagonized almost everyone. Bannon, during the transition, sent him to the Internet to learn about and to try to draft the EO.

By the time he arrived in the White House, Bannon had his back-of-the-envelope executive order on immigration and his travel ban, a sweeping, Trumpian exclusion of most Muslims from the United States, only begrudgingly whittled down, in part at Priebus's urging, to what would shortly be perceived as merely draconian.

In the mania to seize the day, with an almost total lack of knowing how, the nutty inaugural crowd numbers and the wacky CIA speech were followed, without almost anybody in the federal government having seen it or even being aware of it, by an executive order overhauling U.S. immigration policy. Bypassing lawyers, regulators, and the agencies and personnel responsible for enforcing it, President Trump—with Bannon's low, intense voice behind him, offering a rush of complex information—signed what was put in front of him.

On Friday, January 27, the travel ban was signed and took immediate effect. The result was an emotional outpouring of horror and indignation from liberal media, terror in immigrant communities, tumultuous protests at major airports, confusion throughout the government, and, in the White House, an inundation of lectures, warnings, and opprobrium from friends and family. *What have you done? Do you know what you're doing? You have to undo this! You're finished before you even start! Who is in charge there?*

But Steve Bannon was satisfied. He could not have hoped to draw a more vivid line between the two Americas—Trump's and liberals'—and between his White House and the White House inhabited by those not yet ready to burn the place down.

Why did we do this on a Friday when it would hit the airports hardest and bring out the most protesters? almost the entire White House staff demanded to know.

"Errr . . . that's why," said Bannon. "So the snowflakes would show up at the airports and riot." That was the way to crush the liberals: make them crazy and drag them to the left.

5

JARVANKA

On the Sunday after the immigration order was issued, Joe Scarborough and his cohost on the MSNBC show *Morning Joe*, Mika Brzezinski, came for lunch at the White House.

Scarborough is a former Republican congressman from Pensacola, Florida, and Brzezinski is the daughter of Zbigniew Brzezinski, a high-ranking aide in the Johnson White House and Jimmy Carter's National Security Advisor. *Morning Joe* had gone on the air in 2007 and developed a following among New York political and media types. Trump was a longtime devotee.

Early in the 2016 campaign, with a change of leadership at NBC News, it seemed likely that the show, its ratings falling, would be canceled. But Scarborough and Brzezinski embraced their relationship with Trump and became one of the few media outlets not only with a positive outlook on him, but that seemed to know his thinking. Trump became a frequent call-in guest and the show a way to speak more or less directly to him.

It was the kind of relationship Trump dreamed of: media people who took him seriously, talked about him often, solicited his views, provided him with gossip, and retailed the gossip he offered them. The effect was to make them all insiders together, which was exactly where Trump wanted to be. Though he branded himself as a political outsider, actually finding himself on the outside wounded him.

Trump believed that the media, which he propelled (in the case of Scarborough and Brzezinski, helping them keep their jobs), owed him something, and the media, giving him vast amounts of free coverage, believed he owed them, with Scarborough and Brzezinski seeing themselves as something like semiofficial advisers, if not the political fixers who had put him in his job.

In August, they had had a public spat, resulting in Trump's tweet: "Some day, when things calm down, I'll tell the real story of @JoeNBC and his very insecure long-time girlfriend, @morningmika. Two clowns!" But Trump's spats often ended in a tacit admission, however grudging, of mutual advantage, and in short order they were back on cordial terms again.

On their arrival at the White House, the ninth day of his presidency, Trump proudly showed them into the Oval Office and was momentarily deflated when Brzezinski said she had been there many times before with her father, beginning at age nine. Trump showed them some of the memorabilia and, eagerly, his new portrait of Andrew Jackson—the president whom Steve Bannon had made the totem figure of the new administration.

"So how do you think the first week has gone?" Trump asked the couple, in a buoyant mood, seeking flattery.

Scarborough, puzzled by Trump's jauntiness in the face of the protests spreading across the nation, demurred and then said, "Well, I love what you did with U.S. Steel and that you had the union guys come into the Oval Office." Trump had pledged to use U.S.-made steel in U.S. pipelines and, in a Trump touch, met at the White House with union representatives from building and sheet metal unions and then invited them back to the Oval Office—something Trump insisted Obama never did.

But Trump pressed his question, leaving Scarborough with the feeling that nobody had actually told Trump that he had had a very bad week. Bannon and Priebus, wandering in and out of the office, might actually have convinced him that the week had been a success, Scarborough thought.

Scarborough then ventured his opinion that the immigration order might have been handled better and that, all in all, it seemed like a rough period.

Trump, surprised, plunged into a long monologue about how well things had gone, telling Bannon and Priebus, with a gale of laughter, "Joe doesn't think we had a good week." And turning to Scarborough: "I could have invited Hannity!"

At lunch—fish, which Brzezinski doesn't eat—Jared and Ivanka joined the president and Scarborough and Brzezinski. Jared had become quite a Scarborough confidant and would continue to supply Scarborough with an inside view of the White House—that is, leaking to him. Scarborough subsequently became a defender of Kushner's White House position and view. But, for now, both son-in-law and daughter were subdued and deferential as Scarborough and Brzezinski chatted with the president, and the president—taking more of the air time as usual—held forth.

Trump continued to cast for positive impressions of his first week and Scarborough again reverted to his praise of Trump's handling of the steel union leadership. At which point, Jared interjected that reaching out to unions, a traditional Democratic constituency, was Bannon's doing, that this was "the Bannon way."

"Bannon?" said the president, jumping on his son-in-law. "That wasn't Bannon's idea. That was my idea. It's the Trump way, not the Bannon way."

Kushner, going concave, retreated from the discussion.

Trump, changing the topic, said to Scarborough and Brzezinski, "So what about you guys? What's going on?" He was referencing their not-so-secret secret relationship.

Scarborough and Brzezinski said it was all still complicated, and not public, officially, but it was good and everything was getting resolved.

"You guys should just get married," prodded Trump.

"I can marry you! I'm an Internet Unitarian minister," Kushner, otherwise an Orthodox Jew, said suddenly.

"What?" said the president. "What are you talking about? Why would they want *you* to marry them when *I* could marry them? When they could be married by the president! At Mar-a-Lago!"

* * *

Almost everybody advised Jared not to take the inside job. As a family member, he would command extraordinary influence from a position that no one could challenge. As an insider, a staffer, not only could his experience be challenged, but while the president himself might not yet be exposed, a family member on staff would be where enemies and critics might quite effectively start chipping from. Besides, inside Trump's West Wing, if you had a title—that is, other than son-in-law—people would surely want to take it from you.

Both Jared and Ivanka listened to this advice—from among others it came from Jared's brother, Josh, doubly making this case not only to protect his brother but also because of his antipathy to Trump—but both, balancing risk against reward, ignored it. Trump himself variously encouraged his son-in-law and his daughter in their new ambitions and, as their excitement mounted, tried to express his skepticism—while at the same time telling others that he was helpless to stop them.

For Jared and Ivanka, as really for everybody else in the new administration, quite including the president, this was a random and crazy turn of history such that how could you not seize it? It was a joint decision by the couple, and, in some sense, a joint job. Jared and Ivanka had made an earnest deal between themselves: if sometime in the future the time came, she'd be the one to run for president (or the first one of them to take the shot). The first woman president, Ivanka entertained, would not be Hillary Clinton, it would be Ivanka Trump.

Bannon, who had coined the Jarvanka conflation now in ever greater use, was horrified when the couple's deal was reported to him. "They didn't say that? Stop. Oh come on. They didn't actually say that? Please don't tell me that. Oh my god."

And the truth was that at least by then Ivanka would have more experience than almost anybody else now serving in the White House. She and Jared, or Jared, but by inference she, too, were in effect the real chief of staff—or certainly as much a chief of staff as Priebus or Bannon, all of them reporting directly to the president. Or, even more to the organizational point, Jared and Ivanka had a wholly independent standing inside the West Wing. A super status. Even as Priebus and Bannon tried, however diplomatically, to remind the couple of staff procedures and propriety, they would in turn remind the West Wing leadership of their overriding First Family prerogatives. In addition, the president had immediately handed Jared the Middle East portfolio, making him one of the significant international players in the administration—indeed, in the world. In the first weeks, this brief extended out to virtually every other international issue, about which nothing in Kushner's previous background would have prepared him for.

Kushner's most cogent reason for entering the White House was "leverage," by which he meant proximity. Quite beyond the status of being inside the family circle, anyone who had proximity to the president had leverage, the more proximity the more leverage. Trump himself you could see as a sort of Delphic oracle, sitting in place and throwing out pronouncements which had to be interpreted. Or as an energetic child, and whomever could placate or distract him became his favorite. Or as the Sun God (which is effectively how he saw himself), the absolute center of attention, dispensing favor and delegating power, which could, at any moment, be withdrawn. The added dimension was that this Sun God had little calculation. His inspiration existed in the moment, hence all the more reason to be there with him in the moment. Bannon, for one, joined Trump for dinner every night, or at least made himself available—one bachelor there for the effective other bachelor. (Priebus would observe that in the beginning everyone would try to be part of these dinners, but within a few months, they had become a torturous duty to be avoided.)

Part of Jared and Ivanka's calculation about the relative power and influence of a formal job in the West Wing versus an outside advisory role was the knowledge that influencing Trump required you to be all in. From phone call to phone call—and his day, beyond organized meetings, was almost entirely phone calls—you could lose him. The subtleties here were immense, because while he was often most influenced by the last person he spoke to, he did not actually listen to anyone. So it was not so much the force of an individual argument or petition that moved him, but rather more just someone's presence, the connection of what was going through his mind—and although he was a person of many obsessions, much of what was on his mind had no fixed view—to whomever he was with and their views.

Ultimately Trump may not be that different in his fundamental solipsism from anyone of great wealth who has lived most of his life in a highly controlled environment. But one clear difference was that he had acquired almost no formal sort of social discipline—he could not even attempt to imitate decorum. He could not really converse, for instance, not in the sense of sharing information, or of a balanced back-and-forth conversation. He neither particularly listened to what was said to him, nor particularly considered what he said in response (one reason he was so repetitive). Nor did he treat anyone with any sort of basic or reliable courtesy. If he wanted something, his focus might be sharp and attention lavish, but if someone wanted something from him, he tended to become irritable and quickly lost interest. He demanded you pay him attention, then decided you were weak for groveling. In a sense, he was like an instinctive, pampered, and hugely successful actor. Everybody was either a lackey who did his bidding or a high-ranking film functionary trying to coax out his attention and performance—and to do this without making him angry or petulant.

The payoff was his enthusiasm, quickness, spontaneity, and—if he departed for a moment from the nonstop focus on himself—an often incisive sense of the weaknesses of his opponents and a sense of their deepest desires. Politics was handicapped by incrementalism, of people knowing too much who were defeated by all the complexities and conflicting interests before they began. Trump, knowing little, might, Trumpers tried to believe, give a kooky new hope to the system.

Jared Kushner in quite a short period of time—rather less than a year—had crossed over from the standard Democratic view in which he was raised, to an acolyte of Trumpism, bewildering many friends and, as well, his own brother, whose insurance company, Oscar, funded with Kushner-family money, was destined to be dealt a blow by a repeal of Obamacare.

This seeming conversion was partly the result of Bannon's insistent and charismatic tutoring—a kind of real-life engagement with world-bending ideas that had escaped Kushner even at Harvard. And it was helped by his own resentments toward the liberal elites whom he had tried to court with his purchase of the *New York Observer*, an effort that had backfired terribly. And it was, once he ventured onto the campaign trail, about having to convince himself that close up to the absurd everything made sense—that Trumpism was a kind of unsentimental realpolitik that would show everybody in the end. But most of all, it was that they had won. And he was determined not to look a gift horse in the mouth. And, everything that was bad about Trumpism, he had convinced himself, he could help fix.

* * *

As much as it might have surprised him—for many years, he had humored Trump more than embraced him—Kushner was in fact rather like his father-in-law. Jared's father, Charlie, bore an eerie resemblance to Donald's father, Fred. Both men dominated their children, and they did this so completely that their children, despite their demands, became devoted to them. In both instances, this was extreme stuff: belligerent, uncompromising, ruthless men creating long-suffering offspring who were driven to achieve their father's approval. (Trump's older brother, Freddy, failing in this effort, and, by many reports, gay, drank himself to death; he died in 1981 at age forty-three.) In business meetings, observers would be nonplussed that Charlie and Jared Kushner invariably greeted each other with a kiss and that the adult Jared called his father Daddy.

Neither Donald nor Jared, no matter their domineering fathers, went into the world with humility. Insecurity was soothed by entitlement. Both out-of-towners who were eager to prove themselves or lay rightful claim in Manhattan (Kushner from New Jersey, Trump from Queens), they were largely seen as overweening, smug, and arrogant. Each cultivated a smooth affect, which could appear more comical than graceful. Neither, by choice nor awareness, could seem to escape his privilege. "Some people who are very privileged are aware of it and put it away; Kushner not only seemed in every gesture and word to emphasize his privilege, but also not to be aware of it," said one New York media executive who dealt with Kushner. Both men were never out of their circle of privilege. The main challenge they set for themselves was to enter further into the privileged circle. Social climbing was their work.

Jared's focus was often on older men. Rupert Murdoch spent a surprising amount of time with Jared, who sought advice from the older media mogul about the media business—which the young man was determined to break into. Kushner paid long court to Ronald Perelman, the billionaire financier and takeover artist, who later would host Jared and Ivanka in his private shul on Jewish high holy days. And, of course, Kushner wooed Trump himself, who became a fan of the young man and was uncharacteristically tolerant about his daughter's conversion to Orthodox Judaism when that became a necessary next step toward marriage. Likewise, Trump as a young man had carefully cultivated a set of older mentors, including Roy Cohn, the flamboyant lawyer and fixer who had served as right-hand man to the red-baiting Senator Joe McCarthy.

And then there was the harsh fact that the world of Manhattan and particular its living voice, the media, seemed to cruelly reject them. The media long ago turned on Donald Trump as a wannabe and lightweight, and wrote him off for that ultimate sin—anyway, the ultimate sin in media terms—of trying to curry favor with the media too much. His fame, such as it was, was actually reverse fame—he was famous for being infamous. It was joke fame.

To understand the media snub, and its many levels of irony, there is no better place to look than the *New York Observer*, the Manhattan media and society weekly that Kushner bought in 2006 for $10 million—by almost every estimate $10 million more than it was worth.

* * *

The *New York Observer* was, when it launched in 1987, a rich man's fancy, as much failed media often is. It was a bland weekly chronicle of the

Upper East Side, New York's wealthiest neighborhood. Its conceit was to treat this neighborhood like a small town. But nobody took any notice. Its frustrated patron, Arthur Carter, who made his money in the first generation of Wall Street consolidations, was introduced to Graydon Carter (no relation), who had started *Spy* magazine, a New York imitation of the British satirical publication *Private Eye*. *Spy* was part of a set of 1980s publications—*Manhattan, Inc.*, a relaunched *Vanity Fair*, and *New York*—obsessed with the new rich and what seemed to be a transformational moment in New York. Trump was both symbol of and punch line for this new era of excess and celebrity and the media's celebration of those things. Graydon Carter became the editor of the *New York Observer* in 1991 and not only refocused the weekly on big-money culture, but essentially made it a tip-sheet for the media writing about media culture, and for members of the big-money culture who wanted to be in the media. There may never have been such a self-conscious and self-referential publication as the *New York Observer*.

As Donald Trump, along with many others of this new-rich ilk, sought to be covered by the media—Murdoch's *New York Post* was the effective court recorder of this new publicity-hungry aristocracy—the *New York Observer* covered the process of him being covered. The story of Trump was the story of how he tried to make himself a story. He was shameless, campy, and instructive: if you were willing to risk humiliation, the world could be yours. Trump became the objective correlative for the rising appetite for fame and notoriety. Trump came to believe he understood everything about the media—who you need to know, what pretense you need to maintain, what information you could profitably trade, what lies you might tell, what lies the media expected you to tell. And the media came to believe it knew everything about Trump—his vanities, delusions, and lies, and the levels, uncharted, to which he would stoop for ever more media attention.

Graydon Carter soon used the *New York Observer* as his stepping-stone to *Vanity Fair*—where, he believed, he might have access to a higher level of celebrity than Donald Trump. Carter was followed at the *Observer* in 1994 by Peter Kaplan, an editor with a heightened sense of postmodern irony and ennui.

Trump, in Kaplan's telling, suddenly took on a new persona. Whereas he had before been the symbol of success and mocked for it, now he became, in a shift of zeitgeist (and of having to refinance a great deal of debt), a symbol of failure and mocked for it. This was a complicated reversal, not just having to do with Trump, but of how the media was now seeing itself. Donald Trump became a symbol of the media's own self-loathing: the interest in and promotion of Donald Trump was a morality tale about the media. Its ultimate end was Kaplan's pronouncement that Trump should not be covered anymore because every story about Donald Trump had become a cliché.

An important aspect of Kaplan's *New York Observer* and its self-conscious inside media baseball was that the paper became the prime school for a new generation of media reporters flooding every other publication in New York as journalism itself became ever more self-conscious and self-referential. To everyone working in media in New York, Donald Trump represented the ultimate shame of working in media in New York: you might have to write about Donald Trump. Not writing about him, or certainly not taking him at face value, became a moral stand.

In 2006, after Kaplan had edited the paper for fifteen years, Arthur Carter sold the *Observer*—which had never made a profit—to the then twenty-five-year-old Kushner, an unknown real estate heir interested in gaining stature and notoriety in the city. Kaplan was now working for someone twenty-five years his junior, a man who, ironically, was just the kind of arriviste he would otherwise have covered.

For Kushner, owning the paper soon paid off, because, with infinite ironies not necessarily apparent to him, it allowed him into the social circle where he met Donald Trump's daughter, Ivanka, whom he married in 2009. But the paper did not, irksomely for Kushner, pay off financially, which put him into increasing tension with Kaplan. Kaplan, in turn, began telling witty and devastating tales about the pretensions and callowness of his new boss, which spread, in constant retelling, among his many media protégés and hence throughout the media itself.

In 2009, Kaplan left the paper, and Kushner—making a mistake that many rich men who have bought vanity media properties are prone to making—tried to find a profit by cutting costs. In short order, the media world came to regard Kushner as the man who not only took Peter Kaplan's paper from him, but also ruined it, brutally and incompetently. And worse: in 2013, Kaplan, at fifty-nine, died of cancer. So, effectively, in the telling, Kushner had killed him, too.

Media is personal. It is a series of blood scores. The media in its often collective mind decides who is going to rise and who is going to fall, who lives and who dies. If you stay around long enough in the media eye, your fate, like that of a banana republic despot, is often an unkind one—a law Hillary Clinton was not able to circumvent. The media has the last word.

Long before he ran for president, Trump and his sidekick son-in-law Kushner had been marked not just for ignominy, but for slow torture by ridicule, contempt, and ever-more amusing persiflage. These people are nothing. They are media debris. For goodness' sake!

Trump, in a smart move, picked up his media reputation and relocated it from a hypercritical New York to a more value-free Hollywood, becoming the star of his own reality show, *The Apprentice*, and embracing a theory that would serve him well during his presidential campaign: in flyover country, there is no greater asset than celebrity. To be famous is to be loved—or at least fawned over.

The fabulous, incomprehensible irony that the Trump family had, despite the media's distaste, despite everything the media knows and understands and has said about them, risen to a level not only of ultimate consequence but even of immortality is beyond worst-case nightmare and into cosmic-joke territory. In this infuriating circumstance, Trump and his son-in-law were united, always aware and yet never quite understanding why they should be the butt of a media joke, and now the target of its stunned outrage.

* * *

The fact that Trump and his son-in-law had many things in common did not mean they operated on a common playing field. Kushner, no matter how close to Trump, was yet a member of the Trump entourage, with no more ultimate control of his father-in-law than anybody else now in the business of trying to control Trump.

Still, the difficulty of controlling him had been part of Kushner's self-justification or rationalization for stepping beyond his family role and taking a senior White House job: to exercise restraint on his father-in-law and even—a considerable stretch for the inexperienced young man—to help lend him some gravitas.

If Bannon was going to pursue as his first signature White House statement the travel ban, then Kushner was going to pursue as his first leadership mark a meeting with the Mexican president, whom his father-in-law had threatened and insulted throughout the campaign.

Kushner called up the ninety-three-year-old Kissinger for advice. This was both to flatter the old man and to be able to drop his name, but it was also actually for real advice. Trump had done nothing but cause problems for the Mexican president. To bring the Mexican president to the White House would be, despite Bannon's no-pivot policy from the campaign's harshness, a truly meaningful pivot for which Kushner would be able to claim credit (although don't call it a pivot). It was what Kushner believed he should be doing: quietly following behind the president and with added nuance and subtlety clarifying the president's real intentions, if not recasting them entirely.

The negotiation to bring Mexican president Enrique Peña Nieto to the White House had begun during the transition period. Kushner saw the chance to convert the issue of the wall into a bilateral agreement addressing immigration—hence a tour de force of Trumpian politics. The negotiations surrounding the visit reached their apogee on the Wednesday after the inaugural, with a high-level Mexican delegation—the first visit by any foreign leader to the Trump White House—meeting with Kushner and Reince Priebus. Kushner's message to his father-in-law that afternoon was that Peña Nieto had signed on to a White House meeting and planning for the visit could go forward.

The next day Trump tweeted: "The U.S. has a 60 billion dollar trade deficit with Mexico. It has been a one-sided deal from the beginning of NAFTA with massive numbers . . ." And he continued in the next tweet . . . "of jobs and companies lost. If Mexico is unwilling to pay for the badly needed wall, then it would be better to cancel the upcoming meeting . . ."

At which point Peña Nieto did just that, leaving Kushner's negotiation and statecraft as so much scrap on the floor.

* * *

On Friday, February 3, at breakfast at the Four Seasons hotel in Georgetown, an epicenter of the swamp, Ivanka Trump, flustered, came down the stairs and entered the dining room, talking loudly on her cell phone: "Things are so messed up and I don't know how to fix it. . . ."

The week had been overwhelmed by continuing fallout from the immigration order—the administration was in court and headed to a brutal ruling against it—and more embarrassing leaks of two theoretically make-nice phone calls, one with the Mexican president ("bad hombres") and the other with the Australian prime minister ("my worst call by far"). What's more, the day before, Nordstrom had announced that it was dropping Ivanka Trump's clothing line.

The thirty-five-year-old was a harried figure, a businesswoman who had had to abruptly shift control of her business. She was also quite overwhelmed by the effort of having just moved her three children into a new house in a new city—and having to do this largely on her own. Asked how his children were adjusting to their new school several weeks after the move, Jared said that yes, they were indeed in school—but he could not immediately identify where.

Still, in another sense, Ivanka was landing on her feet. Breakfast at the Four Seasons was a natural place for her. She was among everyone who was anyone. In the restaurant that morning: House Minority Leader Nancy Pelosi; Blackstone CEO Stephen Schwarzman; Washington fixture, lobbyist, and Clinton confidant Vernon Jordan; labor secretary nominee Wilbur Ross; Bloomberg Media CEO Justin Smith; *Washington Post* national reporter Mark Berman; and a table full of women lobbyists and fixers, including the music industry's longtime representative in Washington, Hillary Rosen; Elon Musk's D.C. adviser, Juleanna Glover; Uber's political and policy executive, Niki Christoff; and Time Warner's political affairs executive, Carol Melton.

In some sense—putting aside both her father's presence in the White House and his tirades against draining the swamp, which might otherwise include most everyone here, this was the type of room Ivanka had worked hard to be in. Following the route of her father, she was crafting her name and herself into a multifaceted, multiproduct brand; she was also transitioning from her father's aspirational male golf and business types to aspirational female mom and business types. She had, well before her father's presidency could have remotely been predicted, sold a book, *Women Who Work: Rewriting the Rules for Success*, for $1 million.

In many ways, it had been an unexpected journey, requiring more discipline than you might expect from a contented, distracted, run-of-the-mill socialite. As a twenty-one-year-old, she appeared in a film made by her then boyfriend, Jamie Johnson, a Johnson & Johnson heir. It's a curious, even somewhat unsettling film, in which Johnson corrals his set of rich-kid friends into openly sharing their dissatisfactions, general lack of ambition, and contempt for their families. (One of his friends would engage in long litigation with him over the portrayal.) Ivanka, speaking with something like a Valley Girl accent—which would transform in the years ahead into something like a Disney princess voice—seems no more ambitious or even employed than anyone else, but she is notably less angry with her parents.

She treated her father with some lightness, even irony, and in at least one television interview she made fun of his comb-over. She often described the mechanics behind it to friends: an absolutely clean pate—a contained island after scalp reduction surgery—surrounded by a furry circle of hair around the sides and front, from which all ends are drawn up to meet in the center and then swept back and secured by a stiffening spray. The color, she would point out to comical effect, was from a product called Just for Men—the longer it was left on, the darker it got. Impatience resulted in Trump's orange-blond hair color.

Father and daughter got along almost peculiarly well. She was the real mini-Trump (a title that many people now seemed to aspire to). She accepted him. She was a helper not just in his business dealings, but in his marital realignments. She facilitated entrances and exits. If you have a douchebag dad, and if everyone is open about it, then maybe it becomes fun and life a romantic comedy—sort of.

Reasonably, she ought to be much angrier. She grew up not just in the middle of a troubled family but in one that was at all times immersed in bad press. But she was able to bifurcate reality and live only in the uppermost part of it, where the Trump name, no matter how often tarnished, nevertheless had come to be an affectionately tolerated presence. She resided in a bubble of other wealthy people who thrived on their relationship with one another—at first among private school and Upper East Side of Manhattan friends, then among social, fashion, and media contacts. What's more, she tended to find protection as well as status in her boyfriends' families, aggressively bonding with a series of wealthy suitors' families—including Jamie Johnson's before the Kushners—over her own.

The Ivanka-Jared relationship was shepherded by Wendi Murdoch, herself a curious social example (to nobody so much as to her then husband, Rupert). The effort among a new generation of wealthy women was to recast life as a socialite, turning a certain model of whimsy and noblesse oblige into a new status as a power woman, a kind of postfeminist socialite. In this, you worked at knowing other rich people, the best rich people, and of being an integral and valuable part of a network of the rich, and of having your name itself evoke, well . . . riches. You weren't satisfied with what you had, you wanted more. This required quite a level of indefatigability. You were marketing a product—yourself. You were your own start-up.

This was what her father had always done. This, more than real estate, was the family business.

She and Kushner then united as a power couple, consciously recasting themselves as figures of ultimate attainment, ambition, and satisfaction in the new global world and as representatives of a new eco-philanthropic-art sensibility. For Ivanka, this included her friendship with Wendi Murdoch and with Dasha Zhukova, the then wife of the Russian oligarch Roman Abramovich, a fixture in the international art world, and, just a few months before the election, attending a Deepak Chopra seminar on mediation with Kushner. She was searching for meaning—and finding it. This transformation was further expressed not just in ancillary clothing, jewelry, and footwear lines, as well as reality TV projects, but in a careful social media presence. She became a superbly coordinated everymom, who would, with her father's election, recast herself again, this time as royal family.

And yet, the larger truth was that Ivanka's relationship with her father was in no way a conventional family relationship. If it wasn't pure opportunism, it was certainly transactional. It was business. Building the brand, the presidential campaign, and now the White House—it was all business.

But what did Ivanka and Jared *really* think of their father and father-in-law? "There's great, great, great affection—you see it, you really do," replied Kellyanne Conway, somewhat avoiding the question.

"They're not fools," said Rupert Murdoch when asked the question.

"They understand him, I think truly," reflected Joe Scarborough. "And they appreciate his energy. But there's detachment." That is, Scarborough went on, they have tolerance but few illusions.

* * *

Ivanka's breakfast that Friday at the Four Seasons was with Dina Powell, the latest Goldman Sachs executive to join the White House.

In the days after the election, Ivanka and Jared had both met with a revolving door of lawyers and PR people, most of them, the couple found, leery of involvement, not least because the couple seemed less interested in bending to advice and more interested in shopping for the advice they wanted. In fact, much of the advice they were getting had the same message: surround yourself—*acquaint* yourselves—with figures of the greatest establishment credibility. In effect: you are amateurs, you need professionals.

One name that kept coming up was Powell's. A Republican operative who had gone on to high influence and compensation at Goldman Sachs, she was quite the opposite of anyone's notion of a Trump Republican. Her family emigrated from Egypt when she was a girl, and she is fluent in Arabic. She worked her way up through a series of stalwart Republicans, including Texas senator Kay Bailey Hutchison and House Speaker Dick Armey. In the Bush White House she served as chief of the personnel office and an assistant secretary of state for educational and cultural affairs. She went to Goldman in 2007 and became a partner in 2010, running its philanthropic outreach, the Goldman Sachs Foundation. Following a trend in the careers of many political operatives, she had become, as well as an über networker, a corporate public affairs and PR-type adviser—someone who knew the right people in power and had a keen sensitivity to how other people's power can be used.

The table of women lobbyists and communications professionals in the Four Seasons that morning was certainly as interested in Powell, and her presence in the new administration, as they were in the president's daughter. If Ivanka Trump was a figure more of novelty than of seriousness, the fact that she had helped bring Powell into the White House and was now publicly conferring with her added a further dimension to the president's daughter. In a White House seeming to pursue a dead-set Trumpian way, this was a hint of an alternative course. In the assessment of the other fixers and PR women at the Four Seasons, this was a potential shadow White House—Trump's own family not assaulting the power structure but expressing an obvious enthusiasm for it.

Ivanka, after a long breakfast, made her way through the room. Between issuing snappish instructions on her phone, she bestowed warm greetings and accepted business cards.

6

AT HOME

Within the first weeks of his presidency a theory emerged among Trump's friends that he was not acting presidential, or, really, in any way taking into account his new status or restraining his behavior—from early morning tweets, to his refusal to follow scripted remarks, to his self-pitying calls to friends, details of which were already making it into the press—because he hadn't taken the leap that others before him had taken. Most presidents arrived in the White House from more or less ordinary political life, and could not help but be awed and reminded of their transformed circumstances by their sudden elevation to a mansion with palacelike servants and security, a plane at constant readiness, and downstairs a retinue of courtiers and advisers. But this would not have been that different from Trump's former life in Trump Tower, which was more commodious and to his taste than the White House, with servants, security, courtiers, and advisers always on the premises and a plane at the ready. The big deal of being president was not so apparent to him.

But another theory of the case was exactly opposite: he was totally off-kilter here because everything in his orderly world had been thrown on its head. In this view, the seventy-year-old Trump was a creature of habit at a level few people without despotic control of their environment could ever imagine. He had lived in the same home, a vast space in Trump

Tower, since shortly after the building was completed in 1983. Every morning since, he had made the same commute to his office a few floors down. His corner office was a time capsule from the 1980s, the same gold-lined mirrors, the same *Time* magazine covers fading on the wall; the only substantial change was the substitution of Joe Namath's football for Tom Brady's. Outside the doors to his office, everywhere he looked there were the same faces, the same retainers—servants, security, courtiers, the "yes people"—who had attended him basically always.

"Can you imagine how disruptive it would be if that's what you did every day and then suddenly you're in the White House?" marveled a longtime Trump friend, smiling broadly at this trick of fate, if not abrupt comeuppance.

Trump found the White House, an old building with only sporadic upkeep and piecemeal renovations—as well as a famous roach and rodent problem—to be vexing and even a little scary. Friends who admired his skills as a hotelier wondered why he just didn't remake the place, but he seemed cowed by the weight of the watchful eyes on him.

Kellyanne Conway, whose family had remained in New Jersey, and who had anticipated that she could commute home when the president went back to New York, was surprised that New York and Trump Tower were suddenly stricken from his schedule. Conway thought that the president, in addition to being aware of the hostility in New York, was making a conscious effort to be "part of this great house." (But, acknowledging the difficulties inherent in his change of circumstances and of adapting to presidential lifestyle, she added, "How often will he go to Camp David?"—the Spartan, woodsy presidential retreat in Catoctin Mountain Park in Maryland—"How 'bout never.")

At the White House, he retreated to his own bedroom—the first time since the Kennedy White House that a presidential couple had maintained separate rooms (although Melania was spending scant time so far in the White House). In the first days he ordered two television screens in addition to the one already there, and a lock on the door, precipitating a brief standoff with the Secret Service, who insisted they have access to the room. He reprimanded the housekeeping staff for picking up his shirt from the floor: "If my shirt is on the floor, it's because I want it on the floor." Then he imposed a set of new rules: nobody touch anything, especially not his toothbrush. (He had a longtime fear of being poisoned, one reason why he liked to eat at McDonald's—nobody knew he was coming and the food was safely premade.) Also, he would let housekeeping know when he wanted his sheets done, and he would strip his own bed.

If he was not having his six-thirty dinner with Steve Bannon, then, more to his liking, he was in bed by that time with a cheeseburger, watching his three screens and making phone calls—the phone was his true contact point with the world—to a small group of friends, among them most frequently Tom Barrack, who charted his rising and falling levels of agitation through the evening and then compared notes with one another.

* * *

But after the rocky start, things started to look better—even, some argued, presidential.

On Tuesday, January 31, in an efficiently choreographed prime-time ceremony, an upbeat and confident President Trump announced the nomination of federal appellate judge Neil Gorsuch to the Supreme Court. Gorsuch was a perfect combination of impeccable conservative standing, admirable probity, and gold-standard legal and judicial credentials. The nomination not only delivered on Trump's promise to the base and to the conservative establishment, but it was a choice that seemed perfectly presidential.

Gorsuch's nomination was also a victory for a staff that had seen Trump, with this plum job and rich reward in his hand, waver again and again. Pleased by how the nomination was received, especially by how little fault the media could find with it, Trump would shortly become a Gorsuch fan. But before settling on Gorsuch, he wondered why the job wasn't going to a friend and loyalist. In the Trump view, it was rather a waste to give the job to someone he didn't even know.

At various points in the process he had run through almost all his lawyer friends—all of them unlikely, if not peculiar, choices, and, in almost every case, political nonstarters. The one unlikely, peculiar, and nonstarter choice that he kept returning to was Rudy Giuliani.

Trump owed Giuliani; not that he was so terribly focused on his debts, but this was one that was certainly unpaid. Not only was Giuliani a longtime New York friend, but when few Republicans were offering Trump their support, and almost none with a national reputation, Giuliani was there for him—and in combative, fiery, and relentless fashion. This was particularly true during the hard days following Billy Bush: when virtually everybody, including the candidate himself, Bannon, Conway, and his children, believed the campaign would implode, Giuliani barely allowed himself a break from his nonstop, passionate, and unapologetic Trump defense.

Giuliani wanted to be the secretary of state, and Trump had in so many words offered him the job. The resistance to Giuliani from the Trump circle derived from the same reason Trump was inclined to give him the job—Giuliani had Trump's ear and wouldn't let go. The staff whispered about his health and stability. Even his full-on pussygate defense now started to seem like a liability. He was offered attorney general, Department of Homeland Security, and director of national intelligence, but he turned them all down, continuing to hold out for State. Or, in what staffers took to be the ultimate presumption, or grand triangulation, the Supreme Court. Since Trump could not put someone openly pro-choice on the court without both sundering his base and risking defeat of his nominee, then, of course, he'd *have* to give Giuliani State.

When this strategy failed—Rex Tillerson got the secretary of state job—that should have been the end of it, but Trump kept returning to the idea of putting Giuliani on the court. On February 8, during the confirmation process, Gorsuch took public exception to Trump's disparagement of the courts. Trump, in a moment of pique, decided to pull his nomination and, during conversations with his after-dinner callers, went back to discussing how he should have given the nod to Rudy. He was the only loyal guy. It was Bannon and Priebus who kept having to remind him, and to endlessly repeat, that in one of the campaign's few masterful pieces of issue-defusing politics, and perfect courtship of the conservative base, it had let the Federalist Society produce a list of candidates. The campaign had promised that the nominee would come from that list—and needless to say, Giuliani wasn't on it.

Gorsuch was it. And Trump would shortly not remember when he had ever wanted anyone but Gorsuch.

* * *

On February 3, the White House hosted a carefully orchestrated meeting of one of the newly organized business councils, the president's Strategic and Policy Forum. It was a group of highly placed CEOs and weighty business types brought together by Blackstone chief Stephen Schwarzman. The planning for the event—with a precise agenda, choreographed seating and introductions, and fancy handouts—was more due to Schwarzman than to the White House. But it ended up being the kind of event that Trump did very well at and very much enjoyed. Kellyanne Conway, often referencing the Schwarzman gathering, would soon begin a frequent theme of complaint, namely that these kinds of events—Trump sitting down with serious-minded people and looking for solutions to the nation's problems—were the soul of Trump's White House and the media was giving them scant coverage.

Hosting business advisory councils was a Kushner strategy. It was an enlightened business approach, distracting Trump from what Kushner viewed as the unenlightened right-wing agenda. To an increasingly scornful Bannon, its real purpose was to allow Kushner himself to consort with CEOs.

Schwarzman reflected what to many was a surprising and sudden business and Wall Street affinity for Trump. Although few major-company CEOs had publicly supported him—with many, if not all, big companies planning for a Hillary Clinton victory and already hiring Clinton-connected public policy teams and with a pervasive media belief that a Trump victory would assure a market tailspin—there was suddenly an overnight warming. An antiregulatory White House and the promise of tax reform outweighed the prospect of disruptive tweeting and other forms of Trump chaos; besides, the market had not stopped climbing since November 9, the day after the election. What's more, in one-on-one meetings, CEOs were reporting good vibes from Trump's effusive and artful flattery—and the sudden relief of not having to deal with what some knew to be relentless Clinton-team hondling (what can you do for us today and can we use your plan?).

On the other hand, while there was a warming C-suite feeling for Trump, there was also rising concern about the consumer side of many big brands. The Trump brand was suddenly the world's biggest brand—the new Apple, except the opposite, since it was universally disdained (at least among many of the consumers who most top brands sought to court).

Hence, on inaugural morning, the employees of Uber, the ride sharing company, whose then CEO Travis Kalanick had signed on to the Schwarzman council, woke up to find people chained to the doors of their San Francisco headquarters. The charge was that Uber and Kalanick were "collaborating"—with its whiff of Vichy—a much different status than a business looking to sober forums with the president as a way to influence the government. Indeed, the protesters who believed they were seeing the company's relationship with Trump in political terms were actually seeing this in conventional brand terms and zooming in on the disconnect. Uber's customer base is strongly young, urban, and progressive, and therefore out of sync with the Trump base. Brand-conscious millennials saw this as beyond policy dickering and as part of an epic identity clash. The Trump White House stood less for government and the push-pull of competing interests and developing policies, and more, in a brand-savvy world, as a fixed and unpopular cultural symbol.

Uber's Kalanick resigned from the council. Disney CEO Bob Iger simply found that he was otherwise occupied on the occasion of the forum's first meeting.

But most of the people on the council—other than Elon Musk, the investor, inventor, and founder of Tesla (who would later resign)—were not from media or tech companies, with their liberal bent, but from old-line, when-America-was-great enterprises. They included Mary Barra, the CEO of General Motors; Ginni Rometty of IBM; Jack Welch, the former CEO of GE; Jim McNerney, the former CEO of Boeing; and Indra

Nooyi of PepsiCo. If the new right had elected Trump, it was the older Fortune 100 executives who most pleased him.

Trump attended the meeting with his full retinue—the circle that seemed always to move with him in lockstep, including Bannon, Priebus, Kushner, Stephen Miller, and National Economic Council chief Gary Cohn—but conducted it entirely himself. Each of the people at the table, taking a point of interest, spoke for five minutes, with Trump then asking follow-up questions. Though Trump appeared not to have particularly, or at all, prepared for any of the subjects being discussed, he asked engaged and interested questions, pursuing things he wanted to know more about, making the meeting quite an easy back-and-forth. One of the CEOs observed that this seemed like the way Trump preferred to get information—talking about what he was interested in and getting other people to talk about his interests.

The meeting went on for two hours. In the White House view, this was Trump at his best. He was most at home around people he respected—and these were "the most respected people in the country," according to Trump—who seemed to respect him, too.

This became a staff goal—to create situations in which he was comfortable, to construct something of a bubble, to wall him off from a mean-spirited world. Indeed, they sought to carefully replicate this formula: Trump in the Oval or in a larger West Wing ceremonial room presiding in front of a receptive audience, with a photo opportunity. Trump was often his own stage manager at these events, directing people in and out of the picture.

* * *

The media has a careful if selective filter when it comes to portraying real life in the White House. The president and First Family are not, at least not usually, subjected to the sort of paparazzi pursuit that in celebrity media results in unflattering to embarrassing to mocking photographs, or in endless speculation about their private lives. Even in the worst scandals, a businesslike suit-and-tie formality is still accorded the president. *Saturday Night Live* presidential skits are funny in part because they play on our belief that in reality, presidents are quite contained and buttoned-down figures, and their families, trotting not far behind, colorless and obedient. The joke on Nixon was that he was pitiably uptight—even at the height of Watergate, drinking heavily, he remained in his coat and tie, kneeling in prayer. Gerald Ford merely tripped coming off Air Force One, providing great hilarity in this break from formal presidential poise. Ronald Reagan, likely suffering the early effects of Alzheimer's, remained a carefully managed picture of calm and confidence. Bill Clinton, amid the greatest break in presidential decorum in modern history, was even so always portrayed as a man in control. George W. Bush, for all his disengagement, was allowed by the media to be presented as dramatically in charge. Barack Obama, perhaps to his disadvantage, was consistently presented as thoughtful, steady, and determined. This is partly a benefit of overweening image control, but it is also because the president is thought to be the ultimate executive—or because the national myth requires him to be.

That was actually the kind of image that Donald Trump had worked to project throughout most of his career. His is a 1950s businessman sort of ideal. He aspires to look like his father—or, anyway, not to displease his father. Except when he's in golf wear, it is hard to imagine him out of a suit and tie, because he almost never is. Personal dignity—that is, apparent uprightness and respectability—is one of his fixations. He is uncomfortable when the men around him are not wearing suit and ties. Formality and convention—before he became president, almost everybody without high celebrity or a billion dollars called him "Mr. Trump"—are a central part of his identity. Casualness is the enemy of pretense. And his pretense was that the Trump brand stood for power, wealth, arrival.

On the February 5, the *New York Times* published an inside-the-White-House story that had the president, two weeks into his term, stalking around in the late hours of the night in his bathrobe, unable to work the light switches. Trump fell apart. It was, the president not incorrectly saw, a way of portraying him as losing it, as Norma Desmond in the movie *Sunset Boulevard*, a faded or even senile star living in a fantasy world. (This was Bannon's interpretation of the *Times*'s image of Trump, which was quickly adopted by everyone in the White House.) And, of course, once again, it was a media thing—he was being treated in a way that no other president had ever been treated.

This was not incorrect. The *New York Times*, in its efforts to cover a presidency that it openly saw as aberrant, had added to its White House beat something of a new form of coverage. Along with highlighting White House announcements—separating the trivial from the significant—the paper would also highlight, often in front-page coverage, the sense of the absurd, the pitiable, and the all-too-human. These stories turned Trump into a figure of ridicule. The two White House reporters most consistently on this beat, Maggie Haberman and Glenn Thrush, would become part of Trump's constant refrain about the media being out to get him. Thrush would even become a fixture in *Saturday Night Live* sketches that mocked the president, his children, his press secretary Sean Spicer, and his advisers Bannon and Conway.

The president, while often a fabulist in his depiction of the world, was quite a literalist when it came to how he saw himself. Hence he rebutted this picture of him as a half-demented or seriously addled midnight stalker in the White House by insisting that he didn't own a bathrobe.

"Do I seem like a bathrobe kind of guy, really?" he demanded, not humorously, of almost every person with whom he spoke over the next forty-eight hours. "Seriously, can you see me in a bathrobe?"

Who had leaked it? For Trump, the details of his personal life suddenly became a far greater matter of concern than all the other kinds of leaks.

The *New York Times* Washington bureau, itself quite literal and worried by the possible lack of an actual bathrobe, reverse-leaked that Bannon was the source of the story.

Bannon, who styled himself as a kind of black hole of silence, had also become a sort of official black-hole voice, everybody's Deep Throat. He was witty, intense, evocative, and bubbling over, his theoretical discretion ever giving way to a constant semipublic commentary on the pretensions and fatuousness and hopeless lack of seriousness of most everyone else in the White House. By the second week of the Trump presidency, everybody in the White House seemed to be maintaining their own list of likely leakers and doing their best to leak before being leaked about.

But another likely leak source about his angst in the White House was

Trump himself. In his calls throughout the day and at night from his bed, he frequently spoke to people who had no reason to keep his confidences. He was a river of grievances—including about what a dump the White House was on close inspection—examples of which many recipients of his calls promptly spread throughout the ever attentive and merciless gossip world.

* * *

On February 6, Trump made one of his seething, self-pitying, and unsolicited phone calls without presumption of confidentiality to a passing New York media acquaintance. The call had no discernible point other than to express his bent-out-of-shape feelings about the relentless contempt of the media and the disloyalty of his staff.

The initial subject of his ire was the *New York Times* and its reporter Maggie Haberman, whom he called "a nut job." The *Times*'s Gail Collins, who had written a column unfavorably comparing Trump to Vice President Pence, was "a moron." But then, continuing under the rubric of media he hated, he veered to CNN and the deep disloyalty of its chief, Jeff Zucker. Zucker, who as the head of NBC had commissioned *The Apprentice*, had been "made by Trump," Trump said of himself in the third person. And Trump had "personally" gotten Zucker his job at CNN. "Yes, yes, I did," said Trump.

He then repeated a story that he was obsessively telling almost everyone he spoke to. He'd gone to a dinner, he didn't remember when, where he had sat next to "a gentleman named Kent"—undoubtedly Phil Kent, a former CEO of Turner Broadcasting, the Time Warner division that oversaw CNN—"and he had a list of four names." Three of them Trump had never heard of, but he knew Jeff Zucker because of *The Apprentice*. "Zucker was number four on the list, so I talked him up to number one. I probably shouldn't have because Zucker is not that smart but I like to show I can do that sort of thing." But Zucker, "a very bad guy who has done terrible with the ratings," had turned around after Trump had gotten him the job and had said, well, it's "unbelievably disgusting." This was the Russian "dossier" and the "golden shower" story—the practice CNN had accused him of being party to in the Moscow hotel suite with assorted prostitutes.

Having dispensed with Zucker, the president of the United States went on to speculate on what was involved with a golden shower. And how this was all just part of a media campaign that would never succeed in driving him from the White House. Because they were sore losers and hated him for winning, they spread total lies, 100 percent made-up things, totally untrue, for instance, the cover that week of *Time* magazine—which, Trump reminded his listeners, he had been on more than anyone in history—that showed Steve Bannon, a good guy, saying he was the real president. "How much influence do you think Steve Bannon has over me?" Trump demanded and repeated the question, and then repeated the answer: "Zero! Zero!" And that went for his son-in-law, too, who had a lot to learn.

The media was not only hurting him, he said—he was not looking for any agreement or really even any response—but hurting his negotiating capabilities, which hurt the nation. And that went for *Saturday Night Live*, too, which might think it was very funny but was actually hurting everybody in the country. And while he understood that *SNL* was there to be mean to him, they were being very, very mean. It was "fake comedy." He had reviewed the treatment of all other presidents in the media and there was nothing like this ever, even of Nixon who was treated very unfairly. "Kellyanne, who is very fair, has this all documented. You can look at it."

The point is, he said, that that very day, he had saved $700 million a year in jobs that were going to Mexico but the media was talking about him in his bathrobe, which "I don't have because I've never worn a bathrobe. And would never wear one, because I'm not that kind of guy." And what the media was doing was undermining this very dignified house, and "dignity is so important." But Murdoch, "who had never called me, never once," was now calling all the time. So that should tell people something.

The call went on for twenty-six minutes.

7

RUSSIA

Even before there was reason to suspect Sally Yates, they suspected her. The transition report said Trump wouldn't like the fifty-six-year-old Atlanta-born University of Georgia career Justice Department lawyer slated to step up to acting attorney general. There was something about a particular kind of Obama person. Something about the way they walked and held themselves. *Superiority.* And about a certain kind of woman who would immediately rub Trump the wrong way—Obama women being a good tip-off, Hillary women another. Later this would be extended to "DOJ women."

Here was an elemental divide: between Trump and career government employees. He could understand politicians, but he was finding it hard to get a handle on these bureaucrat types, their temperament and motives. He couldn't grasp what they wanted. Why would they, or anyone, be a permanent government employee? "They max out at what? Two hundred grand? Tops," he said, expressing something like wonder.

Sally Yates could have been passed over for the acting AG spot—to serve in place while the attorney-general-designate, Jeff Sessions, waited for confirmation—and before long Trump would be furious about why she wasn't. But she was the sitting deputy and she'd been confirmed by the Senate, and the acting AG job needed someone with Senate confirmation. And even though she seemed to see herself as something of a prisoner held in hostile territory, Yates accepted the job.

Given this context, the curious information she presented to White House counsel Don McGahn during the administration's first week—this was before, in the second week, she refused to enforce the immigration order and was thereupon promptly fired—seemed not only unwelcome but suspect.

The newly confirmed National Security Advisor, Michael Flynn, had brushed off reports in the *Washington Post* about a conversation with Russian ambassador Sergey Kislyak. It was a simple meet and greet, he said. He assured the transition team—among others, Vice President–elect Pence—that there were no discussions of Obama administration sanctions against the Russians, an assurance Pence publicly repeated.

Yates now told the White House that Flynn's conversation with Kislyak had actually been captured as part of an "incidental collection" of authorized wiretaps. That is, a wiretap had presumably been authorized on the Russian ambassador by the secret Foreign Intelligence Surveillance Court and, incidentally, picked up Flynn.

The FISA court had achieved a moment of notoriety after the Edward Snowden revelations briefly made it a bête noire for liberals who were angry about privacy incursions. Now it was achieving another moment, but this time as the friend of liberals, who hoped to use these "incidental" wiretaps as a way to tie the Trump camp to a wide-ranging conspiracy with Russia.

In short order, McGahn, Priebus, and Bannon, each with prior doubts about Flynn's reliability and judgment—"a fuck-up," according to Bannon—conferred about the Yates message. Flynn was asked again about his call with Kislyak; he was also told that a recording might exist. Again he scoffed at any suggestion that this was a meaningful conversation about anything.

In one White House view, Yates's tattling was little more than "like she found out her girlfriend's husband flirted with somebody else and, standing on principle, had to tell on him."

Of more alarm to the White House was how, in an incidental collection wherein the names of American citizens are supposedly "masked"—with complicated procedures required to "unmask" them—had Yates so handily and conveniently picked up Flynn? Her report would also seem to confirm that the leak to the *Post* about these recordings came from the FBI, DOJ, or Obama White House sources—part of the growing river of leaks, with the *Times* and the *Post* the leakers' favored destinations.

The White House in its assessment of the Yates message ended up seeing this as less a problem with an always hard-to-handle Flynn than as a problem with Yates, even as a threat from her: the Justice Department, with its vast staff of career and Obama-inclined prosecutors, had ears on the Trump team.

* * *

"It's unfair," said Kellyanne Conway, sitting in her yet undecorated second-floor office while representing the president's hurt feelings. "It's obviously unfair. It's very unfair. They lost. They didn't win. This is so unfair. So POTUS just doesn't want to talk about it."

There was nobody in the White House who wanted to talk about—or even anyone who had been officially delegated to talk about—Russia, the story that, evident to most, even before they entered the White House, was certain to overwhelm the first year of the Trump administration at the very least. Nobody was prepared to deal with it.

"There's no reason to even talk about it," said Sean Spicer, sitting on the couch in his office, firmly crossing his arms. "There's no reason to even talk about it," he said again, stubbornly.

For his part, the president did not use, though he might have, the word "Kafkaesque." He regarded the Russia story as senseless and inexplicable and having no basis in reality. They were just being sucked in.

They had survived scandal during the campaign—the Billy Bush weekend—which virtually no one in Trump's inner circle had thought they could survive, only to be hit by the Russia scandal. Compared to Pussygate, Russia seemed like the only-desperate-thing-left-gate. What seemed unfair now was that the issue still wasn't going away, and that, incomprehensibly, people took it seriously. When at best it was . . . nothing.

It was the media.

The White House had quickly become accustomed to media-led scandals, but they were also used to their passing. But now this one was, frustratingly, holding on.

If there was any single piece of proof not just of media bias but of the intention of the media to do anything it could to undermine this president, it was—in the view of the Trump circle—this, the Russia story, what the *Washington Post* termed "Russia's attack on our political system." ("So terribly, terribly unfair, with no proof of one vote changed," according to Conway.) It was insidious. It was, to them, although they didn't put it this way, similar to the kind of dark Clinton-like conspiracies that Republicans were more wont to accuse liberals of—Whitewater, Benghazi, Emailgate. That is, an obsessive narrative that leads to investigations, which lead to other investigations, and to more obsessive no-escape media coverage. This was modern politics: blood-sport conspiracies that were about trying to destroy people and careers.

When the comparison to Whitewater was made to Conway, she, rather proving thc point about obsessions, immediately began to argue the particulars involving Webster Hubbell, a mostly forgotten figure in the Whitewater affair, and the culpability of the Rose Law Firm in Arkansas, where Hillary Clinton was a partner. Everybody believed their side's conspiracies, while utterly, and righteously, rejecting the conspiracies leveled at them. To call something a conspiracy was to dismiss it.

As for Bannon, who had himself promoted many conspiracies, he dismissed the Russia story in textbook fashion: "It's just a conspiracy theory." And, he added, the Trump team wasn't capable of conspiring about anything.

* * *

The Russia story was—just two weeks into the new presidency—a dividing line with each side viewing the other as pushing fake news.

The greater White House wholly believed that the story was an invented construct of weak if not preposterous narrative threads, with a mind-boggling thesis: *We fixed the election with the Russians, OMG!* The anti-Trump world, and especially its media—that is, *the* media—believed that there was a high, if not overwhelming, likelihood that there was *something* significant there, and a decent chance that it could be brought home.

If the media, self-righteously, saw it as the Holy Grail and silver bullet of Trump destruction, and the Trump White House saw it, with quite some self-pity, as a desperate effort to concoct a scandal, there was also a range of smart money in the middle.

The congressional Democrats had everything to gain by insisting, Benghazi-like, that where there was smoke (even if they were desperately working the bellows) there was fire, and by using investigations as a forum to promote their minority opinion (and for members to promote themselves).

For Republicans in Congress, the investigations were a card to play against Trump's vengefulness and unpredictability. Defending him—or something less than defending him and, indeed, possibly pursuing him—offered Republicans a new source of leverage in their dealings with him.

The intelligence community—with its myriad separate fiefdoms as suspicious of Trump as of any incoming president in memory—would, at will, have the threat of drip-drip-drip leaks to protect its own interests.

The FBI and DOJ would evaluate the evidence—and the opportunity—through their own lenses of righteousness and careerism. ("The DOJ is filled with women prosecutors like Yates who hate him," said a Trump aide, with a curiously gender-biased view of the growing challenge.)

If all politics is a test of your opponent's strength, acumen, and forbearance, then this, regardless of the empirical facts, was quite a clever test, with many traps that many people might fall into. Indeed, in many ways the issue was not Russia but, in fact, strength, acumen, and forbearance, the qualities Trump seemed clearly to lack. The constant harping about a possible crime, even if there wasn't an actual crime—and no one was yet pointing to a specific act of criminal collusion, or in fact any other clear violation of the law—could force a cover-up which might then turn into a crime. Or turn up a perfect storm of stupidity and cupidity.

"They take everything I've ever said and exaggerate it," said the president in his first week in the White House during a late-night call. "It's all exaggerated. My exaggerations are exaggerated."

* * *

Franklin Foer, the Washington-based former editor of the *New Republic*, made an early case for a Trump-Putin conspiracy on July 4, 2016, in *Slate*. His piece reflected the incredulity that had suddenly possessed the media and political intelligentsia: Trump, the unserious candidate, had, however incomprehensibly, become a more or less serious one. And somehow, because of his prior unseriousness, and his what-you-see-is-what-you-get nature, the braggart businessman, with his bankruptcies, casinos, and beauty pageants, had avoided serious vetting. For Trump students—which, over his thirty years of courting attention, many in the media had become—the New York real estate deals were dirty, the Atlantic City ventures were dirty, the Trump airline was dirty, Mar-a-Lago, the golf courses, and the hotels all dirty. No reasonable candidate could have survived a recounting of even one of these deals. But somehow a genial amount of corruption had been figured into the Trump candidacy—that, after all, was the platform he was running on. *I'll do for you what a tough businessman does for himself.*

To really see his corruption, you had to see it on a bigger stage. Foer was suggesting a fabulous one.

Assembling a detailed road map for a scandal that did not yet exist, Foer, without anything resembling smoking guns or even real evidence, pulled together in July virtually all of the circumstantial and thematic threads and many of the various characters that would play out over the next eighteen months. (Unbeknownst to the public or even most media or political insiders, Fusion GPS had by this point hired the former British spy Christopher Steele to investigate a connection between Trump and the Russian government.)

Putin was seeking a resurgence of Russian power and, as well, to block encroachments by the European Union and NATO. Trump's refusal to treat Putin as a semi-outlaw—not to mention what often seemed like a man crush on him—meant, ipso facto, that Trump was sanguine about a return of Russian power and might actually be promoting it.

Why? What could possibly be in it for an American politician to publicly embrace—sycophantically embrace—Vladimir Putin and to encourage what the West saw as Russian adventurism?

Theory 1: Trump was drawn to authoritarian strongmen. Foer

recounted Trump's longtime fascination with Russia, including being duped by a Gorbachev look-alike who visited Trump Tower in the 1980s, and his many fulsome and unnecessary "odes to Putin." This suggested a lie-down-with-dogs-wake-up-with-fleas vulnerability: consorting with or looking favorably upon politicians whose power lies partly in their tolerance of corruption brings you closer to corruption. Likewise, Putin was drawn to populist strongmen in his own image: hence, Foer asked, "Why *wouldn't* the Russians offer him the same furtive assistance they've lavished on Le Pen, Berlusconi, and the rest?"

Theory 2: Trump was part of a less-than-blue-chip (much less) international business set, feeding off the rivers of dubious wealth that had been unleashed by all the efforts to move cash, much of it from Russia and China, out of political harm's way. Such money, or rumors of such money, became an explanation—still only a circumstantial one—in trying to assess all the Trump business dealings that largely remained hidden from view. (There were two contradictory theories here: he had hidden these dealings because he didn't want to admit their paucity, or he had hidden them to mask their disreputableness.) Because Trump is less than creditworthy, Foer was among many who concluded that Trump needed to turn to other sources—more or less dirty money, or money with other sorts of strings attached. (One way the process can work is, roughly speaking, as follows: an oligarch makes an investment in a more or less legitimate third-party investment fund, which, quid pro quo, makes an investment in Trump.) And while Trump would categorically deny that he had any loans or investments from Russia, one would, of course, not have dirty money on one's books.

As a subset of this theory, Trump—never very scrupulous about vetting his people—surrounded himself with a variety of hustlers working their own deals, and, plausibly, aiding Trump's deals. Foer identified the following characters as part of a possible Russian conspiracy:

- Tevfik Arif, a former Russian official who ran the Bayrock Group, a middleman in Trump financings with an office in Trump Tower.
- Felix Sater (sometimes spelled Satter), a Russian-born immigrant to Brighton Beach in Brooklyn, who had previously served time in

prison in connection with a fraud at a Mafia-run brokerage and who went to work for Bayrock and had a business card identifying him as senior adviser to Donald Trump. (When Sater's name later continued to surface, Trump assured Bannon he didn't know Sater at all.)

- Carter Page, a banker of uncertain portfolio who had spent time in Russia and billed himself as having advised the state-run oil company, Gazprom, and who showed up on a hastily assembled list of Trump foreign policy advisers and who, it would turn out, the FBI was closely monitoring in what it said was a Russian intelligence effort to turn him. (Trump would later deny ever meeting Page, and the FBI would say that it believed Russian intelligence had targeted Page in an effort to turn him.)
- Michael Flynn, the former head of the Defense Intelligence Agency—fired by Obama for unclear reasons—who had yet to emerge as Trump's key foreign policy counselor and future National Security Advisor, but who was accompanying him on many campaign trips and who earlier in the year had been paid a $45,000 speaking fee in Moscow and been photographed sitting at a dinner with Putin.
- Paul Manafort, whom, along with serving as Trump's campaign manager, Foer highlighted as a political operative and consultant who had generated substantial income advising Kremlin-backed Viktor Yanukovych, who successfully ran for the presidency of Ukraine in 2010, was later deposed in 2014, and had been in business with the Russian oligarch and Putin crony Oleg Deripaska.

More than a year later, each of these men would be part of the near-daily Russia-Trump news cycle.

Theory 3: The Holy Grail proposition was that Trump and the Russians—perhaps even Putin himself—had gotten together to hack the Democratic National Committee.

Theory 4: But then there was the those-that-know-him-best theory, some version of which most Trumpers would come to embrace. He was just star-fucking. He took his beauty pageant to Russia because he thought Putin was going to be his friend. But Putin couldn't have cared less, and in the end Trump found himself at the promised gala dinner seated on one side next to a guy who looked like he had never used a utensil and on the other side Jabba the Hutt in a golf shirt. In other words, Trump—however foolish his sucking-up might have been, and however suspicious it might look in hindsight—just wanted a little respect.

Theory 5: The Russians, holding damaging information about Trump, were blackmailing him. He was a Manchurian Candidate.

* * *

On January 6, 2017—nearly six months to the day after Foer's piece was published—the CIA, FBI, and NSA announced their joint conclusion that "Vladimir Putin ordered an influence campaign in 2016 aimed at the U.S. presidential election." From the Steele dossier, to the steady leaks from the U.S. intelligence community, to testimony and statements from the leadership of U.S. intelligence agencies, a firm consensus had emerged. There was a nefarious connection, perhaps an ongoing one, between Trump and his campaign and the Russian government.

Still, this could yet be seen as highly wishful thinking by Trump opponents. "The underlying premise of the case is that spies tell the truth," said the veteran intelligence community journalist Edward Jay Epstein. "Who knew?" And, indeed, the worry in the White House was not about collusion—which seemed implausible if not farcical—but what, if the unraveling began, would likely lead to the messy Trump (and Kushner) business dealings. On this subject every member of the senior staff shrugged helplessly, covering eyes, ears, and mouth.

This was the peculiar and haunting consensus—not that Trump was guilty of all that he was accused of, but that he was guilty of so much else. It was all too possible that the hardly plausible would lead to the totally credible.

* * *

On February 13, twenty-four days into the new administration, National Security Advisor Michael Flynn became the first actual link between Russia and the White House.

Flynn had really only one supporter in the Trump administration, and that was the president himself. They were best friends during the campaign—buddy movie stuff. Post-inauguration, this translated into a total-access relationship. On Flynn's part, it led to a set of misapprehensions that was common inside Trump's circle: that the president's personal endorsement indicated your status in the White House and that Trump's level of flattery was a convincing indication that you had an unbreakable bond with him and that you were, in his eyes, and in his White House, something close to omnipotent. Trump, with his love of generals, *had* even for a moment wanted to make Michael Flynn his vice president.

Intoxicated by Trump's flattery during the campaign, Flynn—a lower-tier general and quite a flaky one at that—had become something of a Trump dancing monkey. When former generals make alliances with political candidates, they customarily position themselves as providers of expertise and figures of a special maturity. But Flynn had become quite a maniacal partisan, part of the Trump traveling road show, one of the ranters and ravers opening Trump rallies. This all-in enthusiasm and loyalty had helped win him access to Trump's ear, into which he poured his anti-intelligence-community theories.

During the early part of the transition, when Bannon and Kushner had seemed joined at the hip, this was part of their bond: an effort to disintermediate Flynn and his often problematic message. A subtext in the White House estimation of Flynn, slyly insinuated by Bannon, was that Defense Secretary Mattis was a four-star general and Flynn but a three-star.

"I like Flynn, he reminds me of my uncles," said Bannon. "But that's the problem: he reminds me of my uncles."

Bannon used the general odor that had more and more attached to Flynn among everybody except the president to help secure a seat for himself on the National Security Council. This was, for many in the national security community, a signal moment in the effort by the nationalist right wing to seize power. But Bannon's presence on the council was just as much driven by the need to babysit the impetuous Flynn, prone to antagonizing almost everyone else in the national security community. (Flynn was "a colonel in a general's uniform," according to one senior intelligence figure.)

Flynn, like everyone around Trump, was besotted by the otherworldly sense of opportunity that came with, against all odds, being in the White House. And inevitably, he had been made more grandiose by it.

In 2014, Flynn had been roughly cashiered out of government, for which he blamed his many enemies in the CIA. But he had energetically set himself up in business, joining the ranks of former government officials profiting off the ever growing globalist corporate-financial-government policy and business networks. Then, after flirting with several other Republican presidential candidates, he bonded with Trump. Both Flynn and Trump were antiglobalists—or, anyway, they believed the United States was getting screwed in global transactions. Still, money was money, and Flynn, who, when he retired, had been receiving a few hundred thousand a year on his general's pension, was not turning any of it down. Various friends and advisers—including Michael Ledeen, a longtime anti-Iran and anti-CIA crony, and the coauthor of Flynn's book, whose daughter now worked for Flynn—advised Flynn that he ought not to accept fees from Russia or the larger "consulting" assignments from Turkey.

It was in fact the sort of carelessness that almost everyone in Trump's world, including the president and his family, was guilty of. They lived with parallel realities in which, while proceeding with a presidential campaign, they also had to live in a vastly more likely world—rather a certain world—in which Donald Trump would never be president. Hence, business as usual.

In early February, an Obama administration lawyer friendly with Sally Yates remarked with some relish and considerable accuracy: "It certainly is an odd circumstance if you live your life without regard for being elected and then get elected—and quite an opportunity for your enemies."

In this, there was not only the Russian cloud hanging over the administration, but a sense that the intelligence community so distrusted Flynn, and so blamed its bad blood with Trump on him, that Flynn was the target here. Within the White House there was even a feeling that a soft trade was being implicitly offered: Flynn for the goodwill of the intelligence community.

At the same time, in what some thought a direct result of the president's rage over the Russia insinuations—particularly the insinuation about the golden shower—the president seemed to bond even more strongly with Flynn, assuring his National Security Advisor over and over again that he had his back, that the Russia accusations, those related both to Flynn and to himself, were "garbage." After Flynn's dismissal, a narrative describing Trump's increasing doubts about his adviser would be offered to the press, but in fact the opposite was true: the more doubts gathered around Flynn, the more certain the president became that Flynn was his all-important ally.

* * *

The final or deadliest leak during Michael Flynn's brief tenure is as likely to have come from the National Security Advisor's antagonists inside the White House as from the Justice Department.

On Wednesday, February 8, the *Washington Post*'s Karen DeYoung came to visit Flynn for what was billed as an off-the-record interview. They met not in his office but in the most ornate room in the Eisenhower Executive Office Building—the same room where Japanese diplomats waited to meet with Secretary of State Cordell Hull as he learned of the attack on Pearl Harbor.

To all outward appearances, it was an uneventful background interview, and DeYoung, Columbo-like in her affect, aroused no suspicions when she broached the de rigueur question: "My colleagues asked me to ask you this: Did you talk to the Russians about sanctions?"

Flynn declared that he had had no such conversations, absolutely no conversation, he confirmed again, and the interview, attended by senior National Security Council official and spokesman Michael Anton, ended soon thereafter.

But later that day, DeYoung called Anton and asked if she could use Flynn's denial on the record. Anton said he saw no problem—after all, the White House wanted Flynn's denial to be clear—and notified Flynn.

A few hours later, Flynn called Anton back with some worries about the statement. Anton applied an obvious test: "If you knew that there might be a tape of this conversation that could surface, would you still be a hundred percent sure?"

Flynn equivocated, and Anton, suddenly concerned, advised him that if he couldn't be sure they ought to "walk it back."

The *Post* piece, which appeared the next day under three other bylines—indicating that DeYoung's interview was hardly the point of the story—contained new leaked details of the Kislyak phone call, which the *Post* now said had indeed dealt with the issue of sanctions. The article also contained Flynn's denial—"he twice said 'no' "—as well as his walk-back: "On Thursday, Flynn, through his spokesman, backed away from the denial. The spokesman said Flynn 'indicated that while he had no recollection of discussing sanctions, he couldn't be certain that the topic never came up.' "

After the *Post* story, Priebus and Bannon questioned Flynn again. Flynn professed not to remember what he had said; if the subject of sanctions came up, he told them, it was at most glossed over. Curiously, no one seemed to have actually heard the conversation with Kislyak or seen a transcript.

Meanwhile, the vice president's people, caught unaware by the sudden Flynn controversy, were taking particular umbrage, less about Flynn's possible misrepresentations than about the fact that they had been kept out of the loop. But the president was undisturbed—or, in one version, "aggressively defensive"—and, while the greater White House looked on askance, Trump chose to take Flynn with him to Mar-a-Lago for his scheduled weekend with Shinzō Abe, the Japanese prime minister.

That Saturday night, in a bizarre spectacle, the Mar-a-Lago terrace became a public Situation Room when President Trump and Prime Minister Abe openly discussed how to respond to North Korea's launch of a missile three hundred miles into the Sea of Japan. Standing right over the president's shoulder was Michael Flynn. If Bannon, Priebus, and Kushner believed that Flynn's fate hung in the balance, the president seemed to have no such doubts.

For the senior White House staff, the underlying concern was less about getting rid of Flynn than about the president's relationship with Flynn. What had Flynn, in essence a spy in a soldier's uniform, roped the president into? What might they have got up to together?

On Monday morning, Kellyanne Conway appeared on MSNBC and offered a firm defense of the National Security Advisor. "Yes," she said, "General Flynn does enjoy the full confidence of the president." And while this seemed to many an indication that Conway was out of the loop, it was more accurately an indication that she had been talking directly to the president.

A White House meeting that morning failed to convince Trump to fire Flynn. He was concerned about what it would look like to lose his National Security Advisor after just twenty-four days. And he was adamant about not wanting to blame Flynn for talking to the Russians, even about sanctions. In Trump's view, condemning his adviser would connect him to a plot where there was no plot. His fury wasn't directed toward Flynn but to the "incidental" wiretap that had surveilled him. Making clear his confidence in his adviser, Trump insisted that Flynn come to Monday's lunch with the Canadian prime minister, Justin Trudeau.

Lunch was followed by another meeting about the furor. There were yet more details of the phone call and a growing itemization of the money Flynn had been paid by various Russian entities; there was also increasing focus on the theory that the leaks from the intel community—that is, the *whole* Russia mess—was directed at Flynn. Finally, there was a new rationale that Flynn should be fired not because of his Russian contacts, but because he had lied about them to the vice president. This was a convenient invention of a chain of command: in fact, Flynn did not report to Vice President Pence, and he was arguably a good deal more powerful than Pence.

The new rationale appealed to Trump, and he at last agreed that Flynn had to go.

Still, the president did not waiver in his belief in Flynn. Rather, Flynn's enemies were his enemies. And Russia was a gun to his head. He might, however ruefully, have had to fire Flynn, but Flynn was still his guy.

Flynn, ejected from the White House, had become the first established direct link between Trump and Russia. And depending on what he might say to whom, he was now potentially the most powerful person in Washington.

8

ORG CHART

The White House, realized former naval officer Steve Bannon after a few weeks, was really a military base, a government-issue office with a mansion's façade and a few ceremonial rooms sitting on top of a secure installation under military command. The juxtaposition was striking: military hierarchy and order in the background, the chaos of the temporary civilian occupants in the fore.

You could hardly find an entity more at odds with military discipline than a Trump organization. There was no real up-and-down structure, but merely a figure at the top and then everyone else scrambling for his attention. It wasn't task-based so much as response-oriented—whatever captured the boss's attention focused everybody's attention. That was the way in Trump Tower, just as it was now the way in the Trump White House.

The Oval Office itself had been used by prior occupants as the ultimate power symbol, a ceremonial climax. But as soon as Trump arrived, he moved in a collection of battle flags to frame him sitting at his desk, and the Oval immediately became the scene of a daily Trump clusterfuck. It's likely that more people had easy access to this president than any president before. Nearly all meetings in the Oval with the president were invariably surrounded and interrupted by a long list of retainers—indeed, everybody strove to be in every meeting. Furtive people skulked around without clear purpose: Bannon invariably found some reason to study papers in the corner and then to have a last word; Priebus kept his eye on Bannon; Kushner kept constant tabs on the whereabouts of the others. Trump liked to keep Hicks, Conway, and, often, his old *Apprentice* sidekick Omarosa Manigault—now with a confounding White House title—in constant hovering presence. As always, Trump wanted an eager audience, encouraging as many people as possible to make as many attempts as possible to be as close to him as possible. In time, however, he would take derisive notice of those who seemed most eager to suck up to him.

Good management reduces ego. But in the Trump White House, it could often seem that nothing happened, that reality simply did not exist, if it did not happen in Trump's presence. This made an upside-down kind of sense: if something happened and he wasn't present, he didn't care about it and barely recognized it. His response then was often just a blank stare. It also fed one theory of why hiring in the West Wing and throughout the executive branch was so slow—filling out the vast bureaucracy was out of his view and thus he couldn't care less. Likewise, visitors with appointments were befuddled by the West Wing's own lack of staff: after being greeted with a smart military salute by the dress marine at the West Wing door, they discovered that the West Wing often lacked a political-appointee receptionist, leaving guests to find their own way through the warren that was the Western world's pinnacle of power.

Trump, a former military academy cadet—albeit not an enthusiastic one—had touted a return to military values and expertise. In fact, he most of all sought to preserve his personal right to defy or ignore his own organization. This, too, made sense, since not really having an organization was the most efficient way to sidestep the people in your organization and to dominate them. It was just one irony of his courtship of admired military figures like James Mattis, H. R. McMaster, and John Kelly: they found themselves working in an administration that was in every way inimical to basic command principles.

* * *

Almost from the beginning, the West Wing was run against the near-daily report that the person charged with running it, Chief of Staff Reince Priebus, was about to lose his job. Or, if he was not about to lose his job, the only reason he was keeping it was that he had not had it long enough to yet be fired from it. But no one in Trump's inner circle doubted that he would lose his job as soon as, practically speaking, his losing it would not embarrass the president too much. So, they reasoned, no one need pay any attention to him. Priebus, who, during the transition, doubted he would make it to the inauguration, and then, once in, wondered if he could endure the torture for the minimally respectable period of a year, shortly reduced his goal to six months.

The president himself, absent any organizational rigor, often acted as his own chief of staff, or, in a sense, elevated the press secretary job to the primary staff job, and then functioned as his own press secretary—reviewing press releases, dictating quotes, getting reporters on the phone—which left the actual press secretary as a mere flunky and whipping boy. Moreover, his relatives acted as ad hoc general managers of whatever areas they might choose to be general managers in. Then there was Bannon, conducting something of an alternate-universe operation, often launching far-reaching undertakings that no one else knew about. And thus Priebus, at the center of an operation that had no center, found it easy to think there was no reason for him to be there at all.

At the same time, the president seemed to like Priebus more and more quite for the reason that he seemed entirely expendable. He took Trump's verbal abuse about his height and stature affably, or anyway stoically. He was a convenient punching bag when things went wrong—and he didn't punch back, to Trump's pleasure and disgust.

"I love Reince," said the president, with the faintest praise. "Who else would do this job?"

Among the three men with effectively equal rank in the West Wing—Priebus and Bannon and Kushner—only a shared contempt kept them from ganging up on one another.

In the early days of Trump's presidency, the situation seemed clear to everybody: three men were fighting to run the White House, to be the real chief of staff and power behind the Trump throne. And of course there was Trump himself, who didn't want to relinquish power to anyone.

In these crosshairs was thirty-two-year-old Katie Walsh.

* * *

Walsh, the White House deputy chief of staff, represented, at least to herself, a certain Republican ideal: clean, brisk, orderly, efficient. A righteous bureaucrat, pretty but with a permanently grim expression, Walsh was a fine example of the many political professionals in whom competence and organizational skills transcend ideology. (To wit: "I would much rather be part of an organization that has a clear chain of command that I disagree with than a chaotic organization that might seem to better reflect my views.") Walsh was an inside-the-Beltway figure—a swamp creature. Her expertise was prioritizing Beltway goals, coordinating Beltway personnel, marshaling Beltway resources. A head-down-get-things-done kind of person was how she saw herself. And no nonsense.

"Any time someone goes into a meeting with the president there are like sixty-five things that have to happen first," she enumerated. "What cabinet secretary has to be alerted about what person is going in there; what people on the Hill should be consulted; the president needs a policy briefing, so who's owning the brief and getting it to appropriate staff members, oh and by the way you have to vet the guy. . . . Then you have to give it to comms and figure out if it's a national story, a regional story and are we doing op-eds, going on national TV . . . and that's before you get to political affairs or public liaison. . . . And for anybody who meets with the president, it has to be explained why other people are not meeting with him, or else they'll go out there and shit all over the last person who was in. . . ."

Walsh was what politics is supposed to be—or what it has been. A business supported by, tended to, and, indeed, ennobled, by a professional political class. Politics, evident in the sameness and particular joylessness of Washington dress, a determined anti-fashion statement, is about procedure and temperament. Flash passes. No flash stays in the game.

From an all-girl Catholic school in St. Louis (still wearing a diamond cross around her neck) and volunteer work on local political campaigns, Walsh went to George Washington University—D.C. area colleges being among the most reliable feeders of swamp talent (government is not really an Ivy League profession). Most government and political organizations are not run, for better or worse, by MBAs, but by young people distinguished only by their earnestness and public sector idealism and ambition. (It is an anomaly of Republican politics that young people motivated to work in the public sector find themselves working to limit the public sector.) Careers advance by how well you learn on the job and how well you get along with the rest of the swamp and play its game.

In 2008, Walsh became the McCain campaign's midwest regional finance director—having majored in marketing and finance at GW, she was trusted to hold the checkbook. Then on to deputy finance director of the National Republican Senatorial Committee, deputy finance director and then finance director of the Republican National Committee, and finally, pre–White House, chief of staff of the RNC and its chairman, Reince Priebus.

In retrospect, the key moment in saving the Trump campaign might be less the Mercer-led takeover and imposition of Bannon and Conway in mid-August than the acceptance that the bare-bones and still largely one-man organization would need to depend on the largesse of the RNC. The RNC had the ground game and the data infrastructure; other campaigns might not normally trust the national committee, with its many snakes in the grass, but the Trump campaign had chosen not to build this sort of organization or make this investment. In late August, Bannon and Conway, with Kushner's consent, made a deal with the deep-swamp RNC despite Trump's continued insistence that they'd gotten this far without the RNC, so why come crawling now?

Almost right away Walsh became a key player in the campaign, a dedicated, make-the-trains-run-on-time power centralizer—a figure without which few organizations can run. Commuting between RNC headquarters in Washington and Trump Tower, she was the quartermaster who made national political resources available to the campaign.

If Trump himself was often a disruption in the final months of the race and during the transition, the campaign around him, in part because its only option was to smoothly integrate with the RNC, was a vastly more responsive and unified organization than, say, the Hillary Clinton campaign with its significantly greater resources. Facing catastrophe and seeming certain humiliation, the Trump campaign pulled together—with Priebus, Bannon, and Kushner all starring in buddy-movie roles.

The camaraderie barely survived a few days in the West Wing.

* * *

To Katie Walsh, it became almost immediately clear that the common purpose of the campaign and the urgency of the transition were lost as soon as the Trump team stepped into the White House. They had gone from managing Donald Trump to the expectation of being managed by him—or at least through him and almost solely for his purposes. Yet the president, while proposing the most radical departure from governing and policy norms in several generations, had few specific ideas about how to turn his themes and vitriol into policy, nor a team that could reasonably unite behind him.

In most White Houses, policy and action flow down, with staff trying to implement what the president wants—or, at the very least, what the chief of staff says the president wants. In the Trump White House, policy making, from the very first instance of Bannon's immigration EO, flowed up. It was a process of suggesting, in throw-it-against-the-wall style, what the president might want, and hoping he might then think that he had thought of this himself (a result that was often helped along with the suggestion that he had in fact already had the thought).

Trump, observed Walsh, had a set of beliefs and impulses, much of them on his mind for many years, some of them fairly contradictory, and little of them fitting legislative or political conventions or form. Hence, she and everyone else was translating a set of desires and urges into a program, a process that required a lot of guess work. It was, said Walsh, "like trying to figure out what a child wants."

But making suggestions was deeply complicated. Here was, arguably, the central issue of the Trump presidency, informing every aspect of Trumpian policy and leadership: he didn't process information in any conventional sense—or, in a way, he didn't process it at all.

Trump didn't read. He didn't really even skim. If it was print, it might as well not exist. Some believed that for all practical purposes he was no more than semiliterate. (There was some argument about this, because he could read headlines and articles about himself, or at least headlines on articles about himself, and the gossip squibs on the *New York Post*'s Page Six.) Some thought him dyslexic; certainly his comprehension was limited. Others concluded that he didn't read because he just didn't have to, and that in fact this was one of his key attributes as a populist. He was postliterate—total television.

But not only didn't he read, he didn't listen. He preferred to be the person talking. And he trusted his own expertise—no matter how paltry or irrelevant—more than anyone else's. What's more, he had an extremely short attention span, even when he thought you were worthy of attention.

The organization therefore needed a set of internal rationalizations that would allow it to trust a man who, while he knew little, was entirely confident of his own gut instincts and reflexive opinions, however frequently they might change.

Here was a key Trump White House rationale: expertise, that liberal virtue, was overrated. After all, so often people who had worked hard to know what they knew made the wrong decisions. So maybe the gut was as good, or maybe better, at getting to the heart of the matter than the wonkish and data-driven inability to see the forest for the trees that often seemed to plague U.S. policy making. Maybe. *Hopefully.*

Of course, nobody really believed that, except the president himself.

Still, here was the basic faith, overriding his impetuousness and eccentricities and limited knowledge base: nobody became the president of the United States—that camel-through-the-eye-of-the-needle accomplishment—without unique astuteness and cunning. *Right?* In the early days of the White House, this was the fundamental hypothesis of the senior staff, shared by Walsh and everyone else: Trump must know what he was doing, his intuition must be profound.

But then there was the other aspect of his supposedly superb insight and apprehension, and it was hard to miss: he was often confident, but he was just as often paralyzed, less a savant in these instances than a figure of sputtering and dangerous insecurities, whose instinctive response was to lash out and behave as if his gut, however silent and confused, was in fact in some clear and forceful way telling him what to do.

During the campaign, he became a kind of vaunted action figure. His staff marveled at his willingness to keep moving, getting back on the plane and getting off the plane and getting back on, and doing rally after rally, with a pride in doing more events than anybody else—double Hillary's!—and ever ridiculing his opponent's slow pace. He *performed.* "This man never takes a break from being Donald Trump," noted Bannon, with a complicated sort of faint praise, a few weeks after joining the campaign full time.

It was during Trump's early intelligence briefings, held soon after he captured the nomination, that alarm signals first went off among his new campaign staff: he seemed to lack the ability to take in third-party information. Or maybe he lacked the interest; whichever, he seemed almost phobic about having formal demands on his attention. He stonewalled every written page and balked at every explanation. "He's a guy who really hated school," said Bannon. "And he's not going to start liking it now."

However alarming, Trump's way of operating also presented an opportunity to the people in closest proximity to him: by understanding him, by observing the kind of habits and reflexive responses that his business opponents had long learned to use to their advantage, they might be able to game him, to *move* him. Still, while he might be moved today, nobody underestimated the complexities of continuing to move him in the same direction tomorrow.

* * *

One of the ways to establish what Trump wanted and where he stood and what his underlying policy intentions were—or at least the intentions that you could convince him were his—came to involve an improbably close textual analysis of his largely off-the-cuff speeches, random remarks, and reflexive tweets during the campaign.

Bannon doggedly went through the Trump oeuvre highlighting possible insights and policy proscriptions. Part of Bannon's authority in the new White House was as keeper of the Trump promises, meticulously logged onto the white board in his office. Some of these promises Trump enthusiastically remembered making, others he had little memory of, but was happy to accept that he had said it. Bannon acted as disciple and promoted Trump to guru—or inscrutable God.

This devolved into a further rationalization, or Trump truth: "The president was very clear on what he wanted to deliver to the American public," said Walsh. He was "excellent in communicating this." At the same time, she acknowledged that it was not at all clear in any specific sense what he wanted. Hence, there was another rationalization: Trump was "inspirational not operational."

Kushner, understanding that Bannon's white board represented Bannon's agenda more than the president's agenda, got to wondering how much of this source text was being edited by Bannon. He made several attempts to comb through his father-in-law's words on his own before expressing frustration with the task and giving up.

Mick Mulvaney, the former South Carolina congressman now head of the Office of Management and Budget and directly charged with creating the Trump budget that would underlie the White House program, also fell back on the Trump spoken record. Bob Woodward's 1994 book, *The Agenda,* is a blow-by-blow account of the first eighteen months of the Clinton White House, most of it focused on creating the Clinton budget, with the single largest block of the president's time devoted to deep contemplation and arguments about how to allocate resources. In Trump's case, this sort of close and continuous engagement was inconceivable; budgeting was simply too small-bore for him.

"The first couple of times when I went to the White House, someone had to say, This is Mick Mulvaney, he's the budget director," said Mulvaney. And in Mulvaney's telling Trump was too scattershot to ever be of much help, tending to interrupt planning with random questions that seem to have come from someone's recent lobbying or by some burst of free association. If Trump cared about something, he usually already had a fixed view based on limited information. If he didn't care, he had no view and no information. Hence, the Trump budget team was also largely forced to return to Trump's speeches when searching for the general policy themes they could then fasten into a budget program.

* * *

Walsh, sitting within sight of the Oval Office, was located at something like the ground zero of the information flow between the president and his staff. As Trump's primary scheduler, her job was to ration the president's time and organize the flow of information to him around the priorities that the White House had set. In this, Walsh became the effective middle person among the three men working hardest to maneuver the president—Bannon, Kushner, and Priebus.

Each man saw the president as something of a blank page—or a scrambled one. And each, Walsh came to appreciate with increasing incredulity, had a radically different idea of how to fill or remake that page. Bannon was the alt-right militant. Kushner was the New York Democrat. And Priebus was the establishment Republican. "Steve wants to force a million people out of the country and repeal the nation's health law and lay on a bunch of tariffs that will completely decimate how we trade, and Jared wants to deal with human trafficking and protecting Planned Parenthood." And Priebus wanted Donald Trump to be another kind of Republican altogether.

As Walsh saw it, Steve Bannon was running the Steve Bannon White House, Jared Kushner was running the Michael Bloomberg White House, and Reince Priebus was running the Paul Ryan White House. It was a 1970s video game, the white ball pinging back and forth in the black triangle.

Priebus—who was supposed to be the weak link, thus allowing both Bannon and Kushner, variously, to be the effective chief of staff—was actually turning out to be quite a barking dog, even if a small one. In the Bannon world and in the Kushner world, Trumpism represented politics with no connection to the Republican mainstream, with Bannon reviling that mainstream and Kushner operating as a Democrat. Priebus, meanwhile, was the designated mainstream terrier.

Bannon and Kushner were therefore more than a little irritated to discover that the unimposing Priebus had an agenda of his own: heeding Senate leader Mitch McConnell's prescription that "this president will sign whatever is put in front of him," while also taking advantage of the White House's lack of political and legislative experience and outsourcing as much policy as possible to Capitol Hill.

In the early weeks of the administration, Priebus arranged for House

Speaker Paul Ryan, however much a Trumpist bête noire for much of the campaign, to come into the White House with a group of ranking committee chairmen. In the meeting, the president blithely announced that he had never had much patience for committees and so was glad someone else did. Ryan, henceforth, became another figure with unfettered access to the president—and to whom the president, entirely uninterested in legislative strategy or procedures, granted virtual carte blanche.

Almost nobody represented what Bannon opposed as well as Paul Ryan. The essence of Bannonism (and Mercerism) was a radical isolationism, a protean protectionism, and a determined Keynesianism. Bannon ascribed these principles to Trumpism, and they ran as counter to Republicanism as it was perhaps possible to get. What's more, Bannon found Ryan, in theory the House's policy whiz, to be slow-witted if not incompetent, and an easy and constant target of Bannon's under-his-breath ridicule. Still, if the president had unaccountably embraced Priebus-Ryan, he also could not do without Bannon.

Bannon's unique ability—partly through becoming more familiar with the president's own words than the president was himself, and partly through a cunning self-effacement (upended by his bursts of self-promotion)—was to egg the president on by convincing him that Bannon's own views were entirely derived from the president's views. Bannon didn't promote internal debate, provide policy rationale, or deliver PowerPoint presentations; instead, he was the equivalent of Trump's personal talk radio. Trump could turn him on at any moment, and it pleased him that Bannon's pronouncements and views would consistently be fully formed and ever available, a bracing, unified-field narrative. As well, he could turn him off, and Bannon would be tactically quiet until turned on again.

Kushner had neither Bannon's policy imagination nor Priebus's institutional ties. But, of course, he had family status, carrying its own high authority. In addition, he had billionaire status. He had cultivated a wide range of New York and international money people, Trump acquaintances and cronies, and, often, people whom Trump would have wished to like him better than they did. In this, Kushner became the representative in the White House of the liberal status quo. He was something like what used to be called a Rockefeller Republican and now might more properly be a Goldman Sachs Democrat. He—and, perhaps even more, Ivanka—was at diametric odds with both Priebus, the stout-right, Sun Belt–leaning, evangelical dependent Republican, and Bannon, the alt-right, populist, anti-party disruptor.

From their separate corners each man pursued his own strategy. Bannon did all he could to roll over Priebus and Kushner in an effort to prosecute the war for Trumpism/Bannonism as quickly as possible. Priebus, already complaining about "political neophytes and the boss's relatives," subcontracted his agenda out to Ryan and the Hill. And Kushner, on one of the steepest learning curves in the history of politics (not that everyone in the White House wasn't on a steep curve, but Kushner's was perhaps the steepest), and often exhibiting a painful naïveté as he aspired to be one of the world's savviest players, was advocating doing nothing fast and everything in moderation. Each had coteries opposed to the other: Bannonites pursued their goal of breaking everything fast, Priebus's RNC faction focused on the opportunities for the Republican agenda, Kushner and his wife did their best to make their unpredictable relative look temperate and rational.

And in the middle was Trump.

* * *

"The three gentlemen running things," as Walsh came to coolly characterize them, all served Trump in different ways. Walsh understood that Bannon provided the president with inspiration and purpose, while the Priebus-Ryan connection promised to do what to Trump seemed like the specialized work of government. For his part, Kushner best coordinated the rich men who spoke to Trump at night, with Kushner often urging them to caution him against both Bannon and Priebus.

The three advisers were in open conflict by the end of the second week following the immigration EO and travel ban debacle. This internal rivalry was the result of stylistic, philosophic, and temperamental differences; perhaps more important, it was the direct result of the lack of a rational org chart or chain of command. For Walsh, it was a daily process of managing an impossible task: almost as soon as she received direction from one of the three men, she would be countermanded by one or another of them.

"I take a conversation at face value and move forward with it," she defended herself. "I put what was decided on the schedule and bring in comms and build a press plan around it and bring in political affairs and office of public liaison. And then Jared says, Why did you do that. And I say, 'Because we had a meeting three days ago with you and Reince and Steve where you agreed to do this.' And he says, 'But that didn't mean I wanted it on the schedule. That's not why I had that conversation.' It almost doesn't matter what anyone says: Jared will agree, and then it will get sabotaged, and then Jared goes to the president and says, See, that was Reince's idea or Steve's idea."

Bannon concentrated on a succession of EOs that would move the new administration forward without having to wade through Congress. That focus was countermanded by Priebus, who was cultivating the Trump-Ryan romance and the Republican agenda, which in turn was countermanded by Kushner, who was concentrating on presidential bonhomie and CEO roundtables, not least because he knew how much the president liked them (and, as Bannon pointed out, because Kushner himself liked them). And instead of facing the inherent conflicts in each strategy, the three men recognized that the conflicts were largely irresolvable and avoided facing that fact by avoiding each other.

Each man had, in his own astute fashion, found his own way to appeal to the president and to communicate with him. Bannon offered a rousing fuck-you show of force; Priebus offered flattery from the congressional leadership; Kushner offered the approval of blue-chip businessmen. So strong were these particular appeals that the president typically preferred not to distinguish among them. They were all exactly what he wanted from the presidency, and he didn't understand why he couldn't have them all. He wanted to break things, he wanted a Republican Congress to give him bills to sign, and he wanted the love and respect of New York *macher*s and socialites. Some inside the White House perceived that Bannon's EOs were meant to be a workaround in response to Priebus's courtship of the party, and that Kushner's CEOs were appalled by

Bannon's EOs and resistant to much of the Republican agenda. But if the president understood this, it did not particularly trouble him.

* * *

Having achieved something like executive paralysis within the first month of the new administration—each of the three gentlemen was as powerful in his allure to the president as the others and each, at times, was equally annoying to the president—Bannon, Priebus, and Kushner all built their own mechanisms to influence the president and undermine the others.

Analysis or argument or PowerPoint did not work. But who said what to Trump and when often did. If, at Bannon's prodding, Rebekah Mercer called him, that had an effect. Priebus could count on Paul Ryan's clout with him. If Kushner set up Murdoch to call, that registered. At the same time, each successive call mostly canceled the others out.

This paralysis led the three advisers to rely on the other particularly effective way to move him, which was to use the media. Hence each man became an inveterate and polished leaker. Bannon and Kushner studiously avoided press exposure; two of the most powerful people in government were, for the most part, entirely silent, eschewing almost all interviews and even the traditional political conversations on Sunday morning television. Curiously, however, both men became the background voices to virtually all media coverage of the White House. Early on, before getting down to attacking each other, Bannon and Kushner were united in their separate offensives against Priebus. Kushner's preferred outlet was Joe Scarborough and Mika Brzezinski's *Morning Joe*, one of the president's certain morning shows. Bannon's first port of call was the alt-right media ("Bannon's Breitbart shenanigans," in Walsh's view). By the end of the first month in the White House, Bannon and Kushner had each built a network of primary outlets, as well as secondary ones to deflect from the obviousness of the primary ones, creating a White House that simultaneously displayed extreme animosity toward the press and yet great willingness to leak to it. In this, at least, Trump's administration was achieving a landmark transparency.

The constant leaking was often blamed on lower minions and permanent executive branch staff, culminating in late February with an all-hands meeting of staffers called by Sean Spicer—cell phones surrendered at the door—during which the press secretary issued threats of random phone checks and admonitions about the use of encrypted texting apps. Everybody was a potential leaker; everybody was accusing everybody else of being a leaker.

Everybody *was* a leaker.

One day, when Kushner accused Walsh of leaking about him, she challenged him back: "My phone records versus yours, my email versus yours."

But most of the leaks, certainly the juiciest ones, were coming from the higher-ups—not to mention from the person occupying the topmost echelon.

The president couldn't stop talking. He was plaintive and self-pitying, and it was obvious to everyone that if he had a north star, it was just to be liked. He was ever uncomprehending about why everyone did not like him, or why it should be so difficult to get everyone to like him. He might be happy throughout the day as a parade of union steel workers or CEOs trooped into the White House, with the president praising his visitors and them praising him, but that good cheer would sour in the evening after several hours of cable television. Then he would get on the phone, and in unguarded ramblings to friends and others, conversations that would routinely last for thirty or forty minutes, and could go much longer, he would vent, largely at the media and his staff. In what was termed by some of the self-appointed Trump experts around him—and everyone was a Trump expert—he seemed intent on "poisoning the well," in which he created a loop of suspicion, disgruntlement, and blame heaped on others.

When the president got on the phone after dinner, it was often a rambling affair. In paranoid or sadistic fashion, he'd speculate on the flaws and weaknesses of each member of his staff. Bannon was disloyal (not to mention he always looks like shit). Priebus was weak (not to mention he was short—a midget). Kushner was a suck-up. Spicer was stupid (and looks terrible too). Conway was a crybaby. Jared and Ivanka should never have come to Washington.

His callers, largely because they found his conversation peculiar, alarming, or completely contrary to reason and common sense, often overrode what they might otherwise have assumed to be the confidential nature of the calls and shared the content with someone else. Hence news about the inner workings of the White House went into free circulation. Except it was not so much the inner workings of the White House—although it would often be reported as such—but the perambulations of the president's mind, which changed direction almost as fast as he could express himself. Yet there were constant tropes in his own narrative: Bannon was about to be cast out, Priebus too, and Kushner needed his protection from the other bullies.

So if Bannon, Priebus, and Kushner were now fighting a daily war with one another, it was mightily exacerbated by something of a running disinformation campaign about them that was being prosecuted by the president himself. A chronic naysayer, he viewed each member of his inner circle as a problem child whose fate he held in his hand. "We are sinners and he is God" was one view; "We serve at the president's displeasure," another.

* * *

In the West Wing of every administration since at least that of Clinton and Gore, the vice president has occupied a certain independent power base in the organization. And yet Vice President Mike Pence—the fallback guy in an administration the length of whose term remained the subject of something like a national office betting pool—was a cipher, a smiling presence either resisting his own obvious power or unable to seize it.

"I do funerals and ribbon cuttings," he told a former Republican Hill colleague. In this, he was seen as either feigning an old-fashioned, what-me-worry, standard-issue veep identity lest he upset his patron or, in fact, honestly acknowledging who he was.

Katie Walsh, amid the chaos, saw the vice president's office as a point of calm in the storm. Pence's staff was not only known by people outside the White House for the alacrity with which it returned calls and for the ease with which it seemed to accomplish West Wing tasks, it also seemed to be comprised of people who liked each other and who were dedicated to a common goal: eliminating as much friction as possible around the vice president.

Pence started nearly every speech saying, "I bring greetings from our forty-fifth president of the United States, Donald J. Trump . . ."—a salutation directed more to the president than to the audience.

Pence cast himself as blandly uninteresting, sometimes barely seeming to exist in the shadow of Donald Trump. Little leaked out of the Pence side of the White House. The people who worked for the vice president, were, like Pence himself, people of few words.

In a sense, he had solved the riddle of how to serve as the junior partner to a president who could not tolerate any kind of comparisons: extreme self-effacement.

"Pence," said Walsh, "is not dumb."

Actually, well short of intelligent was exactly how others in the West Wing saw him. And because he wasn't smart, he was not able to provide any leadership ballast.

On the Jarvanka side, Pence became a point of grateful amusement. He was almost absurdly happy to be Donald Trump's vice president, happy to play the role of exactly the kind of vice president that would not ruffle Trump's feathers. The Jarvanka side credited Pence's wife, Karen, as the guiding hand behind his convenient meekness. Indeed, he took to this role so well that, later, his extreme submissiveness struck some as suspicious.

The Priebus side, where Walsh firmly sat, saw Pence as one of the few senior West Wing figures who treated Priebus as though he was truly the chief of staff. Pence often seemed like a mere staffer, the ever present note taker in so many meetings.

From the Bannon side, Pence garnered only contempt. "Pence is like the husband in *Ozzie and Harriet*, a nonevent," said one Bannonite.

Although many saw him as a vice president who might well assume the presidency someday, he was also perceived as the weakest vice president in decades and, in organizational terms, an empty suit who was useless in the daily effort to help restrain the president and stabilize the West Wing.

* * *

During that first month, Walsh's disbelief and even fear about what was happening in the White House moved her to think about quitting. Every day after that became its own countdown toward the moment she knew she wouldn't be able to take it anymore—which would finally come at the end of March. To Walsh, the proud political pro, the chaos, the rivalries, and the president's own lack of focus and lack of concern were simply incomprehensible.

In early March, Walsh confronted Kushner and demanded: "Just give me the three things the president wants to focus on. What are the three priorities of this White House?"

"Yes," said Kushner, wholly absent an answer, "we should probably have that conversation."

9

CPAC

On February 23, a 75-degree day in Washington, the president woke up complaining about an overheated White House. But for once, the president's complaints were not the main concern. The excited focus in the West Wing was organizing a series of car pools out to the Conservative Political Action Conference, the annual gathering of conservative movement activists, which had outgrown the accommodations of Washington hotels and moved to the Gaylord Resort on Maryland's National Harbor waterfront. CPAC, right of right-of-center and trying to hold steady there, ambivalent about all the conservative vectors that further diverged from that point, had long had an uncomfortable relationship with Trump, viewing him as an unlikely conservative, if not a charlatan. CPAC, too, saw Bannon and Breitbart as practicing an outré conservatism. For several years Breitbart had staged a nearby competitive conference dubbed "The Uninvited."

But the Trump White House would dominate or even subsume the conference this year, and everybody wanted to turn out for this sweet moment. The president, set to speak on the second day, would, like Ronald Reagan, address the conference in his first year in office, whereas both Bushes, wary of CPAC and conservative activists, had largely snubbed the gathering.

Kellyanne Conway, a conference opener, was accompanied by her assistant, two daughters, and a babysitter. Bannon was making his first official pubic appearance of the Trump presidency, and his retinue included Rebekah Mercer, the pivotal Trump donor and Breitbart funder, her young daughter, and Allie Hanley, a Palm Beach aristocrat, conservative donor, and Mercer friend. (The imperious Hanley, who had not met Bannon before, pronounced him "dirty" looking.)

Bannon was scheduled to be interviewed in the afternoon session by CPAC chairman Matt Schlapp, a figure of strained affability who seemed to be trying to embrace the Trump takeover of his conference. A few days before, Bannon had decided to add Priebus to the interview, as both a private gesture of goodwill and a public display of unity—a sign of a budding alliance against Kushner.

In nearby Alexandria, Virginia, Richard Spencer, the president of the National Policy Institute, which is sometimes described as a "white supremacist think tank," who had, peskily for the White House, adopted the Trump presidency as a personal victory, was organizing his trip to CPAC, which would be as much a victory march for him as it was for the Trump team. Spencer—who, in 2016, he had declared, "Let's party like it's 1933," as in the year Hitler came to power—provoked an outcry with his widely covered "Heil Trump" (or "Hail Trump," which of course amounts to the same thing) salute after the election, and then achieved a kind of reverse martyrdom by taking a punch from a protester on Inauguration Day that was memorialized on YouTube.

CPAC, organized by the remnants of the conservative movement after Barry Goldwater's apocalyptic defeat in 1964, had, with stoic indefatigability, turned itself into the backbone of conservative survival and triumph. It had purged John Birchers and the racist right and embraced the philosophic conservative tenets of Russell Kirk and William F. Buckley. In time, it endorsed Reagan-era small government and antiregulatory reform, and then added the components of the cultural wars—antiabortion, anti-gay-marriage, and a tilt toward evangelicals—and married itself to conservative media, first right-wing radio and later Fox News. From this agglomeration it spun an ever more elaborate and all-embracing argument of conservative purity, synchronicity, and intellectual weight. Part of the fun of a CPAC conference, which attracted a wide assortment of conservative young people (reliably mocked as the Alex P. Keaton crowd by the growing throng of liberal press that covered the conference), was the learning of the conservative catechism.

But after a great Clinton surge in the 1990s, CPAC started to splinter during the George W. Bush years. Fox News became the emotional center of American conservativism. Bush neocons and the Iraq War were increasingly rejected by the libertarians and other suddenly breakaway factions (among them the paleocons); the family values right, meanwhile, was more and more challenged by younger conservatives. In the Obama years, the conservative movement was increasingly bewildered by Tea Party rejectionism and a new iconoclastic right-wing media, exemplified by Breitbart News, which was pointedly excluded from the CPAC conference.

In 2011, professing conservative fealty, Trump lobbied the group for a speaking slot and, with reports of a substantial cash contribution, was awarded a fifteen-minute berth. If CPAC was supposedly about honing a certain sort of conservative party line, it was also attentive to a wide variety of conservative celebrities, including, over the years, Rush Limbaugh, Ann Coulter, and various Fox News stars. The year before Obama's reelection, Trump fell into this category. But he was viewed quite differently four years later. In the winter of 2016, during the still competitive Republican primary race, Trump—now eyed as much as a Republican apostate as a Republican crowd pleaser—decided to forgo CPAC and what he feared would be less than a joyous welcome.

This year, as part of its new alignment with the Trump-Bannon White House, CPAC's personality headliner was slated to be the alt-right figure Milo Yiannopoulos, a gay British right-wing provocateur attached to Breitbart News. Yiannopoulos—whose entire position, rather more like a circa-1968 left-wing provocateur, seemed to be about flouting political correctness and social convention, resulting in left-wing hysteria and protests against him—was as confounding a conservative figure as could be imagined. Indeed, there was a subtle suggestion that CPAC had chosen Yiannopoulos precisely to hoist Bannon and the White House on the implicit connection to him—Yiannopoulos had been something of a

Bannon protégé. When, two days before CPAC opened, a conservative blogger discovered a video of Yiannopoulos in bizarre revelry seeming to rationalize pedophilia, the White House made it clear he had to go.

Still, the White House presence at CPAC—which included, along with the president, Bannon, Conway, Education Secretary Betsy DeVos, and the oddball White House foreign policy adviser and former Breitbart writer Sebastian Gorka—seemed to push the Yiannopoulos mess to the side. If CPAC was always looking to leaven boring politicians with star power, Trump, and anyone connected him, were now the biggest stars. With her family positioned out in front of a full house, Conway was interviewed in Oprah-like style by Mercedes Schlapp (wife of Matt Schlapp—CPAC was a family affair), a columnist for the conservative *Washington Times* who would later join the White House communications staff. It was an intimate and inspirational view of a woman of high achievement, the kind of interview that Conway believed she would have been treated to on network and cable television if she were not a Trump Republican—the type of treatment, she'd point out, that had been given to Democratic predecessors like Valerie Jarrett.

At about the time that Conway was explaining her particular brand of antifeminist feminism, Richard Spencer arrived at the convention center hoping to attend the breakout session "The Alt-Right Ain't Right at All," a modest effort to reaffirm CPAC's traditional values. Spencer, who since the Trump victory had committed himself to full-time activism and press opportunities, had planned to position himself to get in the first question. But almost immediately upon arriving and paying his $150 registration fee, he had attracted first one reporter and then a growing circle, a spontaneous press scrum, and he responded by giving an ad hoc news conference. Like Yiannopoulos, and in many ways like Trump and Bannon, Spencer helped frame the ironies of the modern conservative movement. He was a racist but hardly a conservative—he doggedly supported single-payer health care, for instance. And the attention he received was somehow less a credit to conservatism than another effort by the liberal media to smear conservatism. Hence, as the scrum around him increased to as many as thirty people, the CPAC irony police stepped in.

"You're not welcome on the property," announced one of the security guards. "They want you off the property. They want you to cease. They want you off the property."

"Wow," said Spencer. "Can they?"

"Enough debate," the guard said. "This is private property and CPAC wants you off the property."

Relieved of his credentials, Spencer was ushered to the CPAC perimeter of the hotel, where, his pride not all that wounded, he turned, in the comfort of the atrium lounge area, to social media and to texting and emailing reporters on his contact list.

The point Spencer was making was that his presence here was not really so disruptive or ironic as Bannon's, or, for that matter, Trump's. He might be ejected, but in a larger historical sense it was the conservatives who were now being ejected from their own movement by the new cadre—which included Trump and Bannon—of what Spencer called the identitarians, proponents of "white interests, values, customs, and culture."

Spencer was, he believed, the true Trumper and the rest of CPAC now the outliers.

* * *

In the green room, after Bannon, Priebus, and their retinues had arrived, Bannon—in dark shirt, dark jacket, and white pants—stood off to the side talking to his aide, Alexandra Preate. Priebus sat in the makeup chair, patiently receiving a layer of foundation, powder, and lip gloss.

"Steve—" said Priebus, gesturing to the chair as he got up.

"That's okay," said Bannon. He put up his hand, making another of the continual small gestures meant, pointedly, to define himself as something other than every phony baloney in swampland politics—and something other than Reince Priebus, with his heavy powder foundation.

The significance of Bannon's first appearance in public—after days of apparent West Wing turmoil, a *Time* magazine cover story about him, nearly endless speculation about his power and true intentions, and his elevation at least in the media mind to the essential mystery of the Trump White House—could hardly be underestimated. For Bannon himself this was, in his own mind, a carefully choreographed moment. It was his victory walk. He had, he thought, prevailed in the West Wing. He had, again in his own mind, projected his superiority over both Priebus and the idiot son-in-law. And he would now dominate CPAC. But for the moment he attempted a shucks-nothing-to-it lack of self-consciousness even as, at the same time, he was unquestionably the preening man of the hour. Demurring about accepting makeup was not just a way to belittle Priebus, but also a way to say that, ever the commando, he went into battle fully exposed.

"You know what he thinks even when you don't know what he thinks," explained Alexandra Preate. "He's a bit like a good boy who everybody knows is a bad boy."

When the two men emerged onto the stage and appeared on the big-screen monitors, the contrast between them could hardly have been greater. The powder made Priebus look mannequin-like, and his suit with lapel pin, little-boyish. Bannon, the supposedly publicity-shy man, was eating up the camera. He was a country music star—he was Johnny Cash. He seized Priebus's hand in a power handshake, then relaxed in his chair as Priebus came too eagerly forward in his.

Priebus opened with traditional bromides. Bannon, taking his turn, went wryly for the dig: "I want to thank you for finally inviting me to CPAC."

"We decided to say that everybody is a part of our conservative family," said Matt Schlapp, resigned. He then welcomed "the back of the room," where the hundreds of reporters covering the event were positioned.

"Is that the opposition party?" asked Bannon, shielding his eyes.

Schlapp went to the setup question: "We read a lot about you two. Ahem . . ."

"It's all good," replied Priebus tightly.

"I'll bet not all of it's accurate," said Schlapp. "I'll bet there's things that don't get written correctly. Let me ask both of you, what's the biggest misconception about what's going on in the Donald Trump White House?"

Bannon responded with something just less than a smirk and said nothing.

Priebus offered a testimonial to the closeness of his relationship with Bannon.

Bannon, eyes dancing, lifted the microphone trumpetlike and made a joke about Priebus's commodious office—two couches and a fireplace—and his own rough-and-ready one.

Priebus hewed to the message. "It's, ahh . . . it's actually . . . something that you all have helped build, which is, when you bring together, and what this election shows, and what President Trump showed, and let's not kid ourselves, I can talk about data and ground game and Steve can talk about big ideas but the truth of the matter is Donald Trump, President Trump, brought together the party and the conservative movement, and I tell you if the party and the conservative movement are together"—Priebus knocked his fists—"similar to Steve and I, it can't be stopped. And President Trump is the one guy, he was the one person, and I can say this after overseeing sixteen people kill each other, it was Donald Trump who was able to bring this country, this party, and this movement together. And Steve and I know that and we live it every day and our job is to get the agenda of President Trump through the door and on pen and paper."

With Priebus gasping for breath, Bannon snatched the relay baton. "I think if you look at the opposition party"—throwing his hand out to the back of the room—"and how they portrayed the campaign, how they portrayed the transition, and now how they are portraying the administration, it's always wrong. I mean on the very first day that Kellyanne and I started, we reached out to Reince, Sean Spicer, Katie. . . . It's the same team, you know, that every day was grinding away at the campaign, the same team that did the transition, and if you remember, the campaign was the most chaotic, in the media's description, most chaotic, most disorganized, most unprofessional, had no earthly idea what they were doing, and then you saw 'em all crying and weeping that night on November 8."

Back in the White House, Jared Kushner, watching the proceedings casually and then more attentively, suddenly felt a rising anger. Thin-skinned, defensive, on guard, he perceived Bannon's speech as a message sent directly to him. Bannon has just credited the Trump victory to everybody else. Kushner was certain he was being taunted.

When Schlapp asked the two men to enumerate the accomplishments of the last thirty days, Priebus floundered and then seized on Judge Gorsuch and the deregulation executive orders, all things, said Priebus, "that"—he paused, struggling—"eighty percent of Americans agree with."

After a brief pause, as though waiting for the air to clear, Bannon raised the microphone: "I kind of break it down into three verticals, three buckets; the first, national security and sovereignty, and that's your intelligence, defense department, homeland security. The second line of work is what I refer to as economic nationalism, and that is Wilbur Ross at Commerce, Steve Mnuchin at Treasury, [Robert] Lighthizer at Trade, Peter Navarro, [and] Stephen Miller, who are rethinking how we are going to reconstruct our trade arrangements around the world. The third, broadly, line of work is deconstruction of the administrative state—" Bannon stopped for a moment; the phrase, which had never before been uttered in American politics, drew wild applause. "The way the progressive left runs is that if they can't get it passed they're just going to put it in some sort of regulation in an agency. That's all going to be deconstructed."

Schlapp fed another setup question, this one about the media.

Priebus grabbed it, rambled and fumphered for a while, and ended up, somehow, on a positive note: *We'll all come together.*

Lifting the microphone, once again Joshua-like, and with a sweeping wave of his hand, Bannon pronounced, "It's not only not going to get better, it's going to get worse every day"—his fundamental apocalyptic song—"and here's why—and by the way, the internal logic makes sense, corporatist, globalist media, that are adamantly opposed, adamantly opposed, to an economic nationalist agenda like Donald Trump has. And here's why it's going to get worse: because he's going to continue to press his agenda. And as economic conditions continue to get better, as more jobs get better, they're going to continue to fight. If you think they're going to give you your country back without a fight you are sadly mistaken. Every day it is going to be a fight. This is why I'm proudest of Donald Trump. All the opportunities he had to waver off this. All the people he had coming to him saying 'Oh, you got to moderate.'" Another dig at Kushner. "Every day in the Oval Office he tells Reince and me, 'I committed this to the American people. I promised this when I ran. And I'm going to deliver on this.'"

And then the final, agreed-upon-beforehand question: "Can this Trump movement be combined with what's happening at CPAC and other conservative movements for fifty years? Can this be brought together . . . and is this going to save the country?"

"Well, we have to stick together as a team," said Priebus. "It's gonna take all of us working together to make it happen."

As Bannon started into his answer, he spoke slowly, looking out at his captive and riveted audience: "I've said that there is a new political order being formed out of this and it's still being formed. If you look at the wide degree of opinions in this room, whether you are a populist, whether you're a limited-government conservative, whether you're a libertarian, whether you're an economic nationalist, we have wide and sometimes divergent opinions, but I think the center core of what we believe, that we're a nation with an economy, not an economy just in some global market place with open borders, but that we are a nation with a culture, and a reason for being. I think that's what unites us. And that's what's going to unite this movement going forward."

Bannon lowered the microphone to, after what might be interpreted as a beat of uncertainty, suddenly thunderous applause.

Watching from the White House, Kushner—who had come to believe that there was something insidious when Bannon used the words "borders," "global," "culture," and "unite," and who was more and more convinced that they were personally directed against him—was now in a rage.

* * *

Kellyanne Conway had increasingly been worrying about the seventy-year-old president's sleeplessness and his worn look. It was the president's indefatigability—a constant restlessness—that she believed carried the team. On the campaign trail, he would always add stops and speeches. He doubled his own campaign time. Hillary worked at half time; he worked at double time. He sucked in the energy from the crowds. Now that he was living alone in the White House, though, he had seemed to lose a step.

But today he was back. He had been under the sunlamp and lightened his hair, and when the climate-change-denying president woke up on another springlike morning, 77 degrees in the middle of winter, on the second day of CPAC, he seemed practically a different person, or anyway a noticeably younger one. At the appointed hour, to the locked-down ballroom at the Gaylord Resort, filled to capacity with all stripes of the conservative faithful—Rebekah Mercer and her daughter up front—and hundreds of media people in an SRO gallery, the president emerged onto the stage, not in an energetic television-style rush, but with a slow swagger to the low strains of "I'm Proud to Be an American." He came to the stage as a political strongman, a man occupying his moment, clapping—here he reverted to entertainer pose—as he slowly approached the podium, mouthing "Thank you," crimson tie dipping over his belt.

This would be Trump's fifth CPAC address. As much as Steve Bannon liked to see himself as the author of Donald Trump, he also seemed to find it proof of some added legitimacy—and somehow amazing in itself—that since 2011 Trump had basically come to CPAC with the same message. He wasn't a cipher, he was a messenger. The country was a "mess"—a word that had stood the Trump test of time. Its leaders were weak. Its greatness had been lost. The only thing different was that in 2011 he was still reading his speeches with only occasional ad-libs, and now he ad-libbed everything.

"My first major speech was at CPAC," the president began. "Probably five or six years ago. My first major political speech. You were there. I loved it. I loved the people. I loved the commotion. They did these polls where I went through the roof. I wasn't even running, right? But it gave me an idea! And I got a little bit concerned when I saw what was happening in the country so I said let's go to it. It was very exciting. I walked the stage at CPAC. I had very little notes and even less preparation." (In fact, he read his 2011 speech from a sheet of paper.) "So when you have practically no notes and no preparation and then you leave and everybody was thrilled. I said, I think I like this business."

This first preamble gave way to the next preamble.

"I want you all to know that we are fighting the fake news. It's phony.

Fake. A few days ago I called the fake news the enemy of the people. Because they have no sources. They just make 'em up when there are none. I saw one story recently where they said nine people have confirmed. There are no nine people. I don't believe there was one or two people. Nine people. And I said, Give me a break. I know the people. I know who they talk to. There were no nine people. But they say nine people. . . ."

A few minutes into the forty-eight-minute speech and it was already off the rails, riff sustained by repetition.

"Maybe they're just bad at polling. Or maybe they're not legit. It's one or the other. They're very smart. They're very cunning. And they're very dishonest. . . . Just to conclude"—although he would go on for thirty-seven minutes more—"it's a very sensitive topic and they get upset when we expose their false stories. They say we can't criticize their dishonest coverage because of the First Amendment. You know they always bring up"—he went into a falsetto voice—"*the First Amendment.* Now I love the First Amendment. Nobody loves it better than me. Nobody."

Each member of the Trump traveling retinue was now maintaining a careful poker face. When they did break it, it was as though on a delay, given permission by the crowd's cheering or laughter. Otherwise, they seemed not to know whether the president had in fact gotten away with his peculiar rambles.

"By the way, you folks in here, the place is packed, there are lines that go back six blocks"—there were no lines outside the crowded lobby—"I tell you that because you won't read about it. But there are lines that go back six blocks. . . .

"There is one allegiance that unites us all, to America, America. . . . We all salute with pride the same American flag . . . and we are all equal, equal in the eyes of Almighty God. . . . We're equal . . . and I want to thank, by the way, the evangelical community, the Christian community, communities of faith, rabbis and priests and pastors, ministers, because the support for me, as you know, was a record, not only numbers of people but percentages of those numbers who voted for Trump . . . an amazing outpouring and I will not disappoint you . . . as long as we have faith in each other and trust in God then there is no goal beyond our reach . . .

there is no dream too large . . . no task too great . . . we are Americans and the future belongs to us . . . America is roaring. It's going to be bigger and better and stronger than ever before. . . ."

Inside the West Wing, some had idly speculated about how long he would go on if he could command time as well as language. The consensus seemed to be forever. The sound of his own voice, his lack of inhibition, the fact that linear thought and presentation turned out not at all to be necessary, the wonder that this random approach seemed to command, and his own replenishing supply of free association—all this suggested that he was limited only by everyone else's schedule and attention span.

Trump's extemporaneous moments were always existential, but more so for his aides than for him. He spoke obliviously and happily, believing himself to be a perfect pitch raconteur and public performer, while everyone with him held their breath. If a wackadoo moment occurred on the occasions—the frequent occasions—when his remarks careened in no clear direction, his staff had to go into intense method-acting response. It took absolute discipline not to acknowledge what everyone could see.

* * *

As the president finished up his speech, Richard Spencer, who in less than four months from the Trump election was on his way to becoming the most famous neo-Nazi in America since George Lincoln Rockwell, had returned to a seat in the atrium of the Gaylord Resort to argue his affinity for Donald Trump—and, he believed, vice versa.

Spencer, curiously, was one of the few people trying to ascribe an intellectual doctrine to Trumpism. Between those taking him literally but not seriously, and those taking him seriously but not literally, there was Richard Spencer. Practically speaking, he was doing both, arguing the case that if Trump and Bannon were the pilot fish for a new conservative movement, Spencer himself—the owner of altright.com and, he believed, the purest exponent of the movement—was their pilot fish, whether they knew it or not.

As close to a real-life Nazi as most reporters had ever seen, Spencer was a kind of catnip for the liberal press crowded at CPAC. Arguably, he was offering as good an explanation of Trump's anomalous politics as anyone else.

Spencer had come up through writing gigs on conservative publications, but he was hardly recognizable in any sort of official Republican or conservative way. He was a post-right-wing provocateur but with none of the dinner party waspishness or bite of Ann Coulter or Milo Yiannopoulos. They were a stagey type of reactionary. He was a real one—a genuine racist with a good education, in his case UVA, the University of Chicago, and Duke.

It was Bannon who effectively gave Spencer flight by pronouncing Breitbart to be "the platform for the alt-right"—the movement Spencer claimed to have founded, or at least owned the domain name for.

"I don't think Bannon or Trump are identitarians or alt-rightists," Spencer explained while camped out just over CPAC's property line at the Gaylord. They were not, like Spencer, philosophic racists (itself different from a knee-jerk racist). "But they are open to these ideas. And open to the people who are open to these ideas. We're the spice in the mix."

Spencer was right. Trump and Bannon, with Sessions in the mix, too, had come closer than any major national politician since the Civil Rights movement to tolerating a race-tinged political view.

"Trump has said things that conservatives never would have thought.... His criticism of the Iraq War, bashing the Bush family, I couldn't believe he did that... but he did.... Fuck them... if at the end of the day an Anglo Wasp family produces Jeb and W then clearly that's a clear sign of denegation.... And now they marry Mexicans... Jeb's wife... he married his housekeeper or something.

"In Trump's 2011 CPAC address he specifically calls for a relaxation of immigration restrictions for Europeans... that we should re-create an America that was far more stable and more beautiful.... No other conservative politician would say those things... but on the other hand pretty much everyone thought it... so it's powerful to say it.... Clearly [there's] a normalization process going on."

"We are the Trump vanguard. The left will say Trump is a nationalist and an implicit or quasi-racialist. Conservatives, because they are just so douchey, say Oh, no, of course not, he's a constitutionalist, or whatever.

We on the alt-right will say, He is a nationalist and he is a racialist. His movement is a white movement. Duh."

Looking very satisfied with himself, Spencer paused and then said: "We give him a kind of permission."

* * *

Nearby, in the Gaylord atrium, Rebekah Mercer sat having a snack with her home-schooled daughter and her friend and fellow conservative donor Allie Hanley. Both women agreed that the president's CPAC speech showed him at his most gracious and charming.

10

GOLDMAN

The Jarvanka side of the White House increasingly felt that rumors leaked by Bannon and his allies were undermining them. Jared and Ivanka, ever eager to enhance their status as the adults in the room, felt personally wounded by these backdoor attacks. Kushner, in fact, now believed Bannon would do anything to destroy them. This was personal. After months of defending Bannon against liberal media innuendo, Kushner had concluded that Bannon was an anti-Semite. That was the bottom-line issue. This was a complicated and frustrating business—and quite hard to communicate to his father-in-law—because one of Bannon's accusations against Kushner, the administration's point person on the Middle East, was that he was not nearly tough enough in his defense of Israel.

After the election, the Fox News anchor Tucker Carlson with sly jocularity privately pointed out to the president that by offhandedly giving the Israel portfolio to his son-in-law—who would, Trump said, make peace in the Middle East—he hadn't really done Kushner any favors.

"I know," replied Trump, quite enjoying the joke.

Jews and Israel were a curious Trump subtext. Trump's brutish father was an often vocal anti-Semite. In the split in New York real estate between the Jews and non-Jews, the Trumps were clearly on the lesser side. The Jews were white shoe, and Donald Trump, even more than his father, was perceived as a vulgarian—after all, he put his name on his buildings, quite a déclassé thing to do. (Ironically, this proved to be a significant advance in real estate marketing and, arguably, Trump's greatest accomplishment as a developer—branding buildings.) But Trump had grown up and built his business in New York, the world's largest Jewish city. He had made his reputation in the media, that most Jewish of industries, with some keen understanding of media tribal dynamics. His mentor, Roy Cohn, was a demimonde, semiunderworld, tough-guy Jew. He courted other figures he considered "tough-guy Jews" (one of his accolades): Carl Icahn, the billionaire hedge funder; Ike Perlmutter, the billionaire investor who had bought and sold Marvel Comics; Ronald Perelman, the billionaire Revlon chairman; Steven Roth, the New York billionaire real estate tycoon; and Sheldon Adelson, the billionaire casino magnate. Trump had adopted a sort of 1950s Jewish uncle (tough-guy variety) delivery, with assorted Yiddishisms—Hillary Clinton, he declared, had been "shlonged" in the 2008 primary—helping to give an inarticulate man an unexpected expressiveness. Now his daughter, a de facto First Lady, was, through her conversion, the first Jew in the White House.

The Trump campaign and the White House were constantly supplying off-note messages about Jews, from their equivocal regard for David Duke to their apparent desire to tinker with Holocaust history—or at least tendency to stumble over it. At one point early in the campaign, Trump's son-in-law, challenged by his own staff at the *New York Observer* and feeling pressure about his own bona fides, as well as seeking to stand by his father-in-law, wrote an impassioned defense of Trump in an attempt to prove that he was not an anti-Semite. For his efforts, Jared was rebuked by various members of his own family, who clearly seemed worried about both the direction of Trumpism and Jared's opportunism.

There was also the flirtation with European populism. Whenever possible, Trump seemed to side with and stoke Europe's rising right, with its anti-Semitic associations, piling on more portent and bad vibes. And then there was Bannon, who had allowed himself to become—through his orchestration of right-wing media themes and stoking of liberal outrage—a winking suggestion of anti-Semitism. It was certainly good right-wing business to annoy liberal Jews.

Kushner, for his part, was the prepped-out social climber who had rebuffed all entreaties in the past to support traditional Jewish organizations. When called upon, the billionaire scion had refused to contribute. Nobody was more perplexed by the sudden rise of Jared Kushner to his new position as Israel's great protector than U.S. Jewish organizations. Now, the Jewish great and the good, the venerated and the tried, the mandarins and myrmidons, had to pay court to Jared Kushner . . . who until little more than a few minutes ago had truly been a nobody.

For Trump, giving Israel to Kushner was not only a test, it was a Jewish test: the president was singling him out for being Jewish, rewarding him for being Jewish, saddling him with an impossible hurdle for being Jewish—and, too, defaulting to the stereotyping belief in the negotiating powers of Jews. "Henry Kissinger says Jared is going to be the new Henry Kissinger," Trump said more than once, rather a combined compliment and slur.

Bannon, meanwhile, did not hesitate to ding Kushner on Israel, that peculiar right-wing litmus test. Bannon could bait Jews—globalist, cosmopolitan, Davoscentric liberal Jews like Kushner—because the farther right you were, the more correct you were on Israel. Netanyahu was an old Kushner family friend, but when, in the fall, the Israeli prime minister came to New York to meet with Trump and Kushner, he made a point of seeking out Steve Bannon.

On Israel, Bannon had partnered with Sheldon Adelson, titan of Las Vegas, big-check right-wing contributor, and, in the president's mind, quite the toughest tough-guy Jew (that is, the richest). Adelson regularly disparaged Kushner's motives and abilities. The president, to Bannon's great satisfaction, kept telling his son-in-law, as he strategized on Israel, to check with Sheldon and, hence, Bannon.

Bannon's effort to grab the stronger-on-Israel label was deeply confounding to Kushner, who had been raised as an Orthodox Jew. His closest lieutenants in the White House, Avi Berkowitz and Josh Raffel, were

Orthodox Jews. On Friday afternoons, all Kushner business in the White House stopped before sunset for the Sabbath observance.

For Kushner, Bannon's right-wing defense of Israel, embraced by Trump, somehow became a jujitsu piece of anti-Semitism aimed directly at him. Bannon seemed determined to make Kushner appear weak and inadequate—a cuck, in alt-right speak.

So Kushner had struck back, bringing into the White House his own tough-guy Jews—Goldman Jews.

* * *

Kushner had pushed for the then president of Goldman Sachs, Gary Cohn, to run the National Economic Council and to be the president's chief economic adviser. Bannon's choice had been CNBC's conservative anchor and commentator Larry Kudlow. For Trump, the Goldman cachet outdrew even a television personality.

It was a Richie Rich moment. Kushner had been a summer intern at Goldman when Cohn was head of commodities trading. Cohn then became president of Goldman in 2006. Once Cohn joined Trump's team, Kushner often found occasion to mention that the president of Goldman Sachs was working for him. Bannon, depending on whom he wanted to slight, either referred to Kushner as Cohn's intern or pointed out that Cohn was now working for his intern. The president, for his part, was continually pulling Cohn into meetings, especially with foreign leaders, just to introduce him as the former president of Goldman Sachs.

Bannon had announced himself as Trump's brain, a boast that vastly irritated the president. But in Cohn, Kushner saw a better brain for the White House: not only was it much more politic for Cohn to be Kushner's brain than Trump's, but installing Cohn was the perfect countermove to Bannon's chaos management philosophy. Cohn was the only person in the West Wing who had ever managed a large organization (Goldman has thirty-five thousand employees). And, not to put too fine a point on it—though Kushner was happy to do so—Bannon had rolled out of Goldman having barely reached midlevel management status, whereas Cohn, his contemporary, had continued on to the firm's highest level, making hundreds of millions of dollars in the process. Cohn—a Democrat globalist-cosmopolitan Manhattanite who voted for Hillary Clinton and who still spoke frequently to former Goldman chief and former Democratic New Jersey senator and governor Jon Corzine—immediately became Bannon's antithesis.

For Bannon, the ideologue, Cohn was the exact inverse, a commodities trader doing what traders do—read the room and figure out which way the wind is blowing. "Getting Gary to take a position on something is like nailing butterflies to the wall," commented Katie Walsh.

Cohn started to describe a soon-to-be White House that would be business-focused and committed to advancing center-right to moderate positions. In this new configuration, Bannon would be marginalized and Cohn, who was dismissive of Priebus, would be the chief of staff in waiting. To Cohn, it seemed like easy street. Of course it would work out this way: Priebus was a lightweight and Bannon a slob who couldn't run anything.

Within weeks of Cohn's arrival on the transition team, Bannon nixed Cohn's plan to expand the National Economic Council by as many as thirty people. (Kushner, not to be denied, nixed Bannon's plan to have David Bossie build and lead his staff.) Bannon also retailed the likely not-too-far-off-the-mark view (or, anyway, a popular view inside Goldman Sachs) that Cohn, once slated to become Goldman's CEO, had been forced out for an untoward Haig-like grasping for power—in 1981 then secretary of state Alexander Haig had tried to insist he held the power after Ronald Reagan was shot—when Goldman CEO Lloyd Blankfein underwent cancer treatment. In the Bannon version, Kushner had bought damaged goods. The White House was clearly Cohn's professional lifeline—why else would he have come into the Trump administration? (Much of this was retailed to reporters by Sam Nunberg, the former Trump factotum who was now doing duty for Bannon. Nunberg was frank about his tactics: "I beat the shit out of Gary whenever possible.")

It is a measure of the power of blood (or blood by marriage), and likely the power of Goldman Sachs, too, that in the middle of a Republican-controlled Washington and a virulent, if not anti-Semitic (at least toward liberal Jews), right-wing West Wing, the Kushner-Cohn Democrats appeared to be ascendant. Part of the credit went to Kushner, who showed an unexpected tenacity. Conflict averse—in the Kushner household, his father, monopolizing all the conflict, forced everyone else to be a mollifier—confronting neither Bannon nor his father-in-law, he began to see himself in a stoic sense: he was the last man of moderation, the true figure of self-effacement, the necessary ballast of the ship. This would all be made manifest by a spectacular accomplishment. He would complete the mission his father-in-law had foisted on him, the one he was more and more seeing as his, yes, destiny. He *would* make peace in the Middle East.

"He's going to make peace in the Middle East," Bannon said often, his voice reverent and his expression deadpan, cracking up all the Bannonites.

So in one sense Kushner was a figure of heightened foolishness and ridicule. In another, he was a man, encouraged by his wife and by Cohn, who saw himself on the world stage carrying out a singular mission.

Here was yet another battle to be won or lost. Bannon regarded Kushner and Cohn (and Ivanka) as occupying an alternative reality that had little bearing on the real Trump revolution. Kushner and Cohn saw Bannon as not just destructive but self-destructive, and they were confident he would destroy himself before he destroyed them.

In the Trump White House, observed Henry Kissinger, "it is a war between the Jews and the non-Jews."

* * *

For Dina Powell, the other Goldman hire in the West Wing, the main consideration when Ivanka pitched her on coming to work at the White House was the downside assessment of being associated with a Trump presidency. Powell ran the Goldman Sachs philanthropic arm, a public relations initiative as well as a courtship of the increasingly powerful pools of philanthropic money. Representing Goldman, she had become something of a legend at Davos, a supreme networker among the world's supreme networkers. She stood at an intersection of image and fortune, in a world increasingly swayed by private wealth and personal brands.

It was a function of both her ambition and Ivanka Trump's sales talents during swift meetings in New York and Washington that Powell, swallowing her doubts, had come on board. That, and the politically risky but high-return gamble that she, aligned with Jared and Ivanka, and working closely with Cohn, her Goldman friend and ally, could take over the White House. That was the implicit plan: nothing less. Specifically, the idea was that Cohn or Powell—and quite possibly both over the course of the next four or eight years—would, as Bannon and Priebus faltered, come to hold the chief of staff job. The president's own constant grumbling about Bannon and Priebus, noted by Ivanka, encouraged this scenario.

This was no small point: a motivating force behind Powell's move was the certain belief on the part of Jared and Ivanka (a belief that Cohn and Powell found convincing) that the White House was theirs to take. For Cohn and Powell, the offer to join the Trump administration was transmuted beyond opportunity and became something like duty. It would be their job, working with Jared and Ivanka, to help manage and shape a White House that might otherwise become the opposite of the reason and moderation they could bring. They could be instrumental in saving the place—and, as well, take a quantum personal leap forward.

More immediately for Ivanka, who was focused on concerns about women in the Trump White House, Powell was an image correction to Kellyanne Conway, whom, quite apart from their war with Bannon, Ivanka and Jared disdained. Conway, who continued to hold the president's favor and to be his preferred defender on the cable news shows, had publicly declared herself the face of the administration—and for Ivanka and Jared, this was a horrifying face. The president's worst impulses seem to run through Conway without benefit of a filter. She compounded Trump's anger, impulsiveness, and miscues. Whereas a presidential adviser was supposed to buffer and interpret his gut calls, Conway expressed them, doubled down on them, made opera out of them. She took Trump's demand for loyalty too literally. In Ivanka and Jared's view, Conway was a cussed, antagonistic, self-dramatizing cable head, and Powell, they hoped, would be a deliberate, circumspect, adult guest on the Sunday morning shows.

By late February, after the first helter-skelter month in the West Wing, the campaign by Jared and Ivanka to undermine Bannon seemed to be working. The couple had created a feedback loop, which included Scarborough and Murdoch, that reinforced the president's deep annoyance with and frustration about Bannon's purported importance in the White House. For weeks after the *Time* magazine cover story featuring Bannon, there was hardly a conversation in which Trump didn't refer to it bitterly. ("He views *Time* covers as zero sum," said Roger Ailes. "If someone else gets on it, he doesn't.") Scarborough, cruelly, kept up a constant patter about President Bannon. Murdoch forcefully lectured the president about the oddness and extremism of Bannonism, linking Bannon with Ailes: "They're both crazy," he told Trump.

Kushner also pressed the view to the president—ever phobic about any age-related weakness—that the sixty-three-year-old Bannon wouldn't hold up under the strain of working in the White House. Indeed, Bannon was working sixteen- and eighteen-hour days, seven days a week, and, for fear of missing a presidential summons or afraid that someone else might grab it, he considered himself on call pretty much all night. As the weeks went by, Bannon seemed physically to deteriorate in front of everybody's eyes: his face became more puffy, his legs more swollen, his eyes more bleary, his clothes more slept in, his attention more distracted.

* * *

As Trump's second month in office began, the Jared-Ivanka-Gary-Dina camp focused on the president's February 28 speech to the joint session of Congress.

"Reset," declared Kushner. "Total reset."

The occasion provided an ideal opportunity. Trump would have to deliver the speech in front of him. It was not only on the teleprompter but distributed widely beforehand. What's more, the well-mannered crowd wouldn't egg him on. His handlers were in control. And for this occasion at least, Jared-Ivanka-Gary-Dina were the handlers.

"Steve will take credit for this speech if there's even one word of his in it," Ivanka told her father. She knew well that for Trump, credit, much more than content, was the hot-button driver, and her comment ensured that Trump would keep it out of Bannon's hands.

"The Goldman speech," Bannon called it.

The inaugural, largely written by Bannon and Stephen Miller, had shocked Jared and Ivanka. But a particular peculiarity of the Trump White House, compounding its messaging problems, was its lack of a speech-writing team. There was the literate and highly verbal Bannon, who did not really do any actual writing himself; there was Stephen Miller, who did little more than produce bullet points. Beyond that, it was pretty much just catch as catch can. There was a lack of coherent message because there was nobody to write a coherent message—just one more instance of disregarding political craft.

Ivanka grabbed firm control of the joint session draft and quickly began pulling in contributions from the Jarvanka camp. In the event, the president behaved exactly as they hoped. Here was an upbeat Trump, a salesman Trump, a nothing-to-be-afraid-of Trump, a happy-warrior Trump. Jared, Ivanka, and all their allies judged it a magnificent night, agreeing that finally, amid the pageantry—*Mr. Speaker, the President of the United States*—the president really did seem presidential. And for once, even the media agreed.

The hours following the president's speech were Trump's best time in the White House. It was, for at least one news cycle, a different presidency. For a moment, there was even something like a crisis of conscience among parts of the media: Had this president been grievously misread? Had the media, the biased media, missed well-intentioned Donald Trump? Was he finally showing his better nature? The president himself spent almost two full days doing nothing but reviewing his good press. He had arrived, finally, at a balmy shore (with appreciative natives on the beach). What's more, the success of the speech confirmed the Jared and Ivanka strategy: look for common ground. It also confirmed Ivanka's understanding of her father: he just wanted to be loved. And, likewise, it confirmed Bannon's worst fear: Trump, in his true heart, was a marsh-mallow.

The Trump on view the night of the joint session was not just a new Trump, but a declaration of a new West Wing brain trust (which Ivanka was making plans to formally join in just a few weeks). Jared and Ivanka, with an assist from their Goldman Sachs advisers, were changing the message, style, and themes of the White House. "Reaching out" was the new theme.

Bannon, hardly helping his cause, cast himself as a Cassandra to anyone who would listen. He insisted that only disaster would come from trying to mollify your mortal enemies. You need to keep taking the fight to them; you're fooling yourself if you believe that compromise is possible. The virtue of Donald Trump—the virtue, anyway, of Donald Trump to Steve Bannon—was that the cosmopolitan elite was never going to accept him. He was, after all, Donald Trump, however much you shined him up.

11

WIRETAP

With three screens in his White House bedroom, the president was his own best cable curator. But for print he depended on Hope Hicks. Hicks, who had been his junior aide for most of the campaign and his spokesperson (although, as he would point out, he was really his own spokesperson), had been, many thought, pushed to the sidelines in the West Wing by the Bannonites, the Goldman wing, and the Priebus-RNC professionals. To the senior staff, she seemed not only too young and too inexperienced—she was famous among campaign reporters for her hard-to-maneuver-in short skirts—but a way-too-overeager yes woman, always in fear of making a mistake, ever tremulously second-guessing herself and looking for Trump's approval. But the president kept rescuing her—"Where's Hope?"—from any oblivion others tried to assign her to. Baffling to almost everyone, Hicks remained his closest and most trusted aide, with, perhaps, the single most important job in this White House: interpreting the media for him in the most positive way it could be interpreted, and buffering him from the media that could not be positively spun.

The day after his "reset" speech before the joint session of Congress presented a certain conundrum for Hicks. Here were the first generally good notices for the administration. But in the *Post*, the *Times*, and the

New Yorker that day, there was also an ugly bouquet of very bad news. Fortunately the three different stories had not quite sunk into cable, so there was yet a brief respite. And at least for the better part of the day, March 1, Hicks herself did not entirely seem to grasp how bad the news actually was.

The *Washington Post*'s story was built around a leak from a Justice Department source (characterized as a "former senior American official"—hence, most likely someone from the Obama White House) saying that the new attorney general, Jeff Sessions, had, on two occasions, met with the Russian ambassador, Sergey Kislyak.

When the president was shown the story, he didn't see its significance. "So what?" he said.

Well, during his confirmation, it was explained to the president, Sessions had said he didn't.

Facing Sessions at the January 10 hearing, Al Franken, the former comedian and Democratic senator from Minnesota, appeared to be casting blindly for an elusive fish in his efforts to find a question. Stopping and starting, slogging through his sentence construction, Franken, who had been handed a question based on the just-revealed Steele dossier, got to this end:

> These documents also allegedly say, quote, "There was a continuing exchange of information during the campaign between Trump's surrogates and intermediaries for the Russian government."
>
> Now, again, I'm telling you this as it's coming out, so you know. But if it's true, it's obviously extremely serious and if there is any evidence that anyone affiliated with the Trump campaign communicated with the Russian government in the course of this campaign, what will you do?

Instead of answering Franken's circuitous question—"What will you do?"—with an easy "We will of course investigate and pursue any and all illegal actions," a confused Sessions answered a question he wasn't asked.

> Senator Franken, I'm not aware of any of those activities. I have been called a surrogate at a time or two in that campaign and I didn't have—did not have communications with the Russians, and I'm unable to comment on it.

The president's immediate focus was on the question of why anyone believed that communicating with the Russians was bad. There *is* nothing wrong with that, Trump insisted. As in the past, it was hard to move him off this point and to the issue at hand: a possible lie to Congress. The *Post* story, to the extent that it registered at all, didn't worry him. Supported by Hicks, he saw it a way-long-shot effort to pin something on Sessions. And anyway, Sessions was saying he didn't meet with the Russians as *a campaign surrogate*. So? He didn't. Case closed.

"Fake news," said the president, using his now all-purpose rejoinder.

As for the bad *Times* story, as Hicks related it to the president, it appeared to him to be good news. Briefed by anonymous sources in the Obama administration (*more* anonymous Obama sources), the story revealed a new dimension to the ever growing suggestion of a connection between the Trump campaign and Russian efforts to influence the U.S. election:

> American allies, including the British and the Dutch, had provided information describing meetings in European cities between Russian officials—and others close to Russia's president, Vladimir V. Putin—and associates of President-elect Trump, according to three former American officials who requested anonymity in discussing classified intelligence.

And:

> Separately, American intelligence agencies had intercepted communications of Russian officials, some of them within the Kremlin, discussing contacts with Trump associates.

The story went on:

> Mr. Trump has denied that his campaign had any contact with Russian officials, and at one point he openly suggested that American spy agencies had cooked up intelligence suggesting that the Russian government had tried to meddle in the presidential election. Mr. Trump has accused the Obama administration of hyping the Russia story line as a way to discredit his new administration.

And then the real point:

> At the Obama White House, Mr. Trump's statements stoked fears among some that intelligence could be covered up or destroyed—or its sources exposed—once power changed hands. What followed was a push to preserve the intelligence that underscored the deep anxiety with which the White House and American intelligence agencies had come to view the threat from Moscow.

Here was more confirmation of a central Trump thesis: The previous administration, its own candidate defeated, was not just disregarding the democratic custom of smoothing the way for the winner of the election; rather, in the Trump White House view, Obama's people had plotted with the intelligence community to put land mines in the new administration's way. Secret intelligence was, the story suggested, being widely distributed across intelligence agencies so as to make it easier to leak, and at the same time to protect the leakers. This intelligence, it was rumored, consisted of spreadsheets kept by Susan Rice that listed the Trump team's Russian contacts; borrowing a technique from WikiLeaks, the documents were secreted on a dozen servers in different places. Before this broad distribution, when the information was held tightly, it would have been easy to identify the small pool of leakers. But the Obama administration had significantly expanded that pool.

So this was good news, right? Wasn't this proof, the president asked, that Obama and his people were out to get him? The *Times* story was a leak about a plan to leak—and it provided clear evidence of the deep state.

Hope Hicks, as always, supported Trump's view. The crime was leaking and the culprit was the Obama administration. The Justice Department, the president was confident, was now going to investigate the former president and his people. Finally.

* * *

Hope Hicks also brought to the president a big piece in the *New Yorker.* The magazine had just published an article by three authors—Evan Osnos, David Remnick, and Joshua Yaffa—attributing Russian aggressiveness to a new cold war. Remnick, the editor of the *New Yorker,* had, since the Trump election, propounded an absolutist view that Trump's election imperiled Democratic norms.

This 13,500-word story—handily connecting the dots of Russia's geopolitical mortification, Putin's ambition, the country's cyber talents, Trump's own nascent authoritarianism, and the U.S. intelligence community's suspicions about Putin and Russia—codified a new narrative as coherent and as apocalyptic as the one about the old cold war. The difference was that in this one, the ultimate result was Donald Trump—he was the nuclear bomb. One of the frequently quoted sources in the article was Ben Rhodes, the Obama aide who, Trump's camp believed, was a key leaker, if not one of the architects of the Obama administration's continued effort to connect Trump and his team to Putin and Russia. Rhodes, many in the White House believed, *was* the deep state. They also believed that every time a leak was credited to "former and current officials," Rhodes was the former official who was in close touch with current officials.

While the article was largely just a dire recapitulation of fears about Putin and Trump, it did, in a parenthesis toward the end of the article—quite burying the lead—connect Jared Kushner to Kislyak, the Russian ambassador, in a meeting in Trump Tower with Michael Flynn in December.

Hicks missed this point; later, it had to be highlighted for the president by Bannon.

Three people in the Trump administration—the former National Security Advisor, the current attorney general, and the president's senior adviser and son-in-law—had now been directly connected to the Russian diplomat.

To Kushner and his wife, this was less than innocent: they would, with a sense of deepening threat, suspect Bannon of leaking the information about Kushner's meeting with Kislyak.

* * *

Few jobs in the Trump administration seemed so right, fitting, and even destined to their holder as Jeff Sessions's appointment as the nation's top law enforcement officer. As he viewed his work as AG, it was his mandate to curb, circumscribe, and undo the interpretation of federal law that had for three generations undermined American culture and offended his own place in it. "This is his life's work," said Steve Bannon.

And Sessions was certainly not going to risk his job over the silly Russia business, with its growing collection of slapstick Trump figures. God knows what those characters were up to—nothing good, everybody assumed. Best to have nothing to do with it.

Without consulting the president or, ostensibly, anyone in the White House, Sessions decided to move as far as possible out of harm's way. On March 2, the day after the *Post* story, he recused himself from anything having to do with the Russia investigation.

The news of the attorney general's recusal exploded like an IED in the White House. Sessions was Trump's protection against an overly aggressive Russian investigation. The president just could not grasp the logic here. He railed to friends: Why would Sessions not want to protect him? What would Sessions gain? Did he think this stuff was real? Sessions needed to do his job!

In fact, Trump already had good reason to worry about the DOJ. The president had a private source, one of his frequent callers, who, he believed, was keeping him abreast of what was going on in the Justice Department—and, the president noted, doing a much better job of it than Sessions himself.

The Trump administration, as a consequence of the Russia story, was involved in a high-stakes bureaucratic push-pull, with the president going outside government to find out what was happening in his own government. The source, a longtime friend with his own DOJ sources—many of the president's rich and powerful friends had their own reasons to keep close tabs on what was happening at the Justice Department—fed the president a bleak picture of a Justice Department and an FBI run amok in its efforts to get him. "Treason" was a word that was being used, the president was told.

"The DOJ," the president's source told him, "was filled with women who hated him." It was an army of lawyers and investigators taking instructions from the former administration. "They want to make Watergate look like Pissgate," the president was told. This comparison confused Trump; he thought his friend was making a reference to the Steele dossier and its tale of the golden showers.

After the attorney general's recusal, the president, whose instinctive reaction to every problem was to fire someone, right away, thought he should just get rid of Sessions. At the same time, there was little doubt in his mind about what was happening here. He knew where this Russia stuff was coming from, and if these Obama people thought they were going to get away with it they had another think coming. He would expose them all!

* * *

One of Jared Kushner's many new patrons was Tony Blair, the former British prime minister, whom Kushner had gotten to know when, on the banks of the River Jordan in 2010, they both attended the baptism of Grace and Chloe Murdoch, the young daughters of Rupert Murdoch and his then wife, Wendi. Jared and Ivanka had also lived in the same Trump building on Park Avenue where the Murdochs lived (for the Murdochs it was a temporary rental apartment while their grand triplex on Fifth Avenue was renovated, but the renovation had lasted for four years), and during that period Ivanka Trump had become one of Wendi Murdoch's closest friends. Blair, godfather to Grace, would later be accused by Murdoch of having an affair with his wife, and of being the cause of their breakup (something Blair has categorically denied). In the divorce, Wendi got the Trumps.

But once in the White House, the president's daughter and son-in-law became the target of a renewed and eager cultivation by, with quite some irony, both Blair and Murdoch. Lacking a circle of influence in almost all of the many areas of government with which he was now involved, Kushner was both susceptible to cultivation and more than a little desperate for the advice his cultivators had to offer. Blair, now with philanthropic, private diplomatic, and varied business interests in the Middle East, was particularly intent on helping shepherd some of Jared's Middle East initiatives.

In February, Blair visited Kushner in the White House.

On this trip, the now freelance diplomat, perhaps seeking to prove his usefulness to this new White House, mentioned a juicy rumor: the possibility that the British had had the Trump campaign staff under surveillance, monitoring its telephone calls and other communications and possibly even Trump himself. This was, as Kushner might understand, the Sabbath goy theory of intelligence. On the Sabbath, observant Jews could not turn on the lights, nor ask someone else to turn on the lights. But if they expressed the view that it would be much easier to see with light, and if a non-Jew then happened to turn them on, that would be fine. So although the Obama administration would not have asked the British to spy on the Trump campaign, the Brits would have been led to understand how helpful it might be if they did.

It was unclear whether the information was rumor, informed conjecture, speculation, or solid stuff. But, as it churned and festered in the president's mind, Kushner and Bannon went out to CIA headquarters in Langley to meet with Mike Pompeo and his deputy director Gina Haspel to check it out. A few days later, the CIA opaquely reported back that the information was not correct; it was a "miscommunication."

* * *

Politics had seemed to become, even well before the age of Trump, a mortal affair. It was now zero-sum: When one side profited, another lost. One side's victory was another's death. The old notion that politics was a trader's game, an understanding that somebody else had something you wanted—a vote, goodwill, old-fashioned patronage—and that in the end the only issue was cost, had gone out of fashion. Now it was a battle between good and evil.

Curiously, for a man who seemed to have led a movement based in anger and retribution, Trump was very much (or believed he was very much) a politician of the old stripe—a let's-work-it-out guy. You scratch my back, I'll scratch yours. He was, in his mind, the ultimate tactician, always knowing what the other guy wanted.

Steve Bannon had pressed him to invoke Andrew Jackson as his populist model, and he had loaded up on Jackson books (they remained unread). But his real beau ideal was Lyndon Johnson. LBJ was a big man who could knock heads, do deals, and bend lesser men to his will. Trade it out so in the end everyone got something, and the better dealmaker got a little more. (Trump did not, however, appreciate the irony of where Lyndon Johnson ended up—one of the first modern politicians to have found himself on the wrong end of both mortal and moral politics.)

But now, after little more than seven weeks in office, Trump saw his own predicament as unique and overwhelming. Like no other president before (though he did make some allowances for Bill Clinton), his enemies were out to get him. Worse, the system was rigged against him. The bureaucratic swamp, the intelligence agencies, the unfair courts, the lying media—they were all lined up against him. This was, for his senior staff, a reliable topic of conversation with him: the possible martyrdom of Donald Trump.

In the president's nighttime calls, he kept coming back to how unfair this was, and to what Tony Blair had said—and others, too! It all added up. There was a plot against him.

Now, it was certainly true that Trump's closest staff appreciated his volatility, and, to a person, was alarmed by it. At points on the day's spectrum of adverse political developments, he could have moments of, almost everyone would admit, irrationality. When that happened, he was alone in his anger and not approachable by anyone. His senior staff largely dealt with these dark hours by agreeing with him, no matter what he said. And if some of them occasionally tried to hedge, Hope Hicks never did. She agreed absolutely with all of it.

At Mar-a-Lago on the evening of March 3, the president watched Bret Baier interview Paul Ryan on Fox. Baier asked the Speaker about a report on the online news site Circa—owned by Sinclair, the conservative broadcast group—involving allegations that Trump Tower had been surveilled during the campaign.

On March 4, Trump's early morning tweets began:

> Terrible! Just found out that Obama had my "wires tapped" in Trump Tower just before the victory. Nothing found. This is McCarthyism! (4:35 a.m.)

> Is it legal for a sitting President to be "wire tapping" a race for president prior to an election? Turned down by court earlier. A NEW LOW! (4:49 a.m.)

> How low has President Obama gone to tap my phones during the very sacred election process. This is Nixon/Watergate. Bad (or sick) guy! (5:02 a.m.)

At 6:40 he called Priebus, waking him up. "Did you see my tweet?" he asked. "We've caught them red-handed!" Then the president held his phone so Priebus could hear the playback of the Baier show.

He had no interest in precision, or even any ability to be precise. This was pure public exclamation, a window into pain and frustration. With his misspellings and his use of 1970s lingo—"wire tapping" called up an image of FBI agents crouched in a van on Fifth Avenue—it seemed kooky and farcical. Of the many tweets that Trump had seemed to hoist himself by, from the point of view of the media, intelligence community, and extremely satisfied Democrats, the wiretap tweets had pulled him highest and most left him dangling in ignorance and embarrassment.

According to CNN, "Two former senior U.S. officials quickly dismissed Trump's accusations out of hand. 'Just nonsense,' said one former senior U.S. intelligence official." Inside the White House, the "just nonsense" quote was thought to be from Ben Rhodes, offered in cat-that-swallowed-the-canary fashion.

Ryan, for his part, told Priebus he had no idea what Baier was talking about and that he was just BSing through the interview.

But if tapping Trump's phones wasn't literally true, there was a sudden effort to find something that might be, and a frantic White House dished up a Breitbart article that linked to a piece by Louise Mensch, a former British politician who, now living in the United States, had become a kind of conspiracy-central of the Trump-Russia connection.

There was a further effort to push aggressive incidental collection and unmasking back onto the Obama White House. But in the end, this was another—and to some quite the ultimate—example of how difficult it was for the president to function in a literal, definitional, lawyerly, cause-and-effect political world.

It was a turning point. Until now, Trump's inner circle had been mostly game to defend him. But after the wiretap tweets, everybody, save perhaps Hope Hicks, moved into a state of queasy sheepishness, if not constant incredulity.

Sean Spicer, for one, kept repeating his daily, if not hourly, mantra: "You can't make this shit up."

12

REPEAL AND REPLACE

A few days after the election, Steve Bannon told the president-elect—in what Katie Walsh would characterize with a raised eyebrow as more "Breitbart shenanigans"—that they had the votes to replace Paul Ryan as Speaker of the House with Mark Meadows, the head of the Tea Party–inspired Freedom Caucus and an early Trump supporter. (Meadows's wife had a particular place of regard in the Trump camp for continuing a campaign swing across the Bible Belt over Billy Bush weekend.)

Nearly as much as winning the presidency itself, removing Ryan—indeed, humiliating him—was an ultimate expression of what Bannon sought to accomplish and of the mind-meld of Bannonism and Trumpism. From the beginning, the Breitbart campaign *against* Paul Ryan was a central part of its campaign *for* Donald Trump. Its embrace of Trump, and Bannon's personal enlistment in the campaign fourteen months after it began, was in part because Trump, throwing political sense to the wind, was willing to lead the charge against Ryan and the GOP godfathers. Still, there was a difference between the way Breitbart viewed Ryan and the way Trump viewed him.

For Breitbart, the House rebellion and transformation that had driven the former Speaker, John Boehner, from office, and which, plausibly, was set to remake the House into the center of the new radical Republicanism had been halted by Ryan's election as Speaker. Mitt Romney's running mate, and a figure who had merged a conservative fiscal wonkishness—he had been the chairman of the House Ways and Means Committee and, as well, chairman of the House Budget Committee—with an old-fashioned idea of unassailable Republican rectitude, Ryan was the official last, best hope of the Republican Party. (Bannon, typically, had turned this trope into an official Trumpist talking point: "Ryan was created in a petri dish at the Heritage Foundation.") If the Republican Party had been moved further right by the Tea Party rebellion, Ryan was part of the ballast that would prevent it from moving further, or at least at a vastly slower pace. In this he represented an adult, older-brother steadiness in contrast to the Tea Party's ADD-hyper immaturity—and a stoic, almost martyr-like resistance to the Trump movement.

Where the Republican establishment had promoted Ryan into this figure of not only maturity but sagaciousness, the Tea Party–Bannon–Breitbart wing mounted an ad hominem campaign pushing an image of Ryan as uncommitted to the cause, an inept strategist and incompetent leader. He was the Tea Party–Bannon–Breitbart punch line: the ultimate empty suit, a hee-haw sort of joke and an embarrassment.

Trump's distaste for Ryan was significantly less structural. He had no views about Ryan's political abilities, and had paid no real attention to Ryan's actual positions. His view was personal. Ryan had insulted him—again and again. Ryan had kept betting against him. Ryan had become the effective symbol of the Republican establishment's horror and disbelief about Trump. Adding insult to injury, Ryan had even achieved some moral stature by dissing Trump (and, as usual, he considered anybody's gain at his expense a double insult). By the spring of 2016, Ryan was still, and by then the only, alternative to Trump as the nominee. Say the word, many Republicans felt, and the convention would stampede to Ryan. But Ryan's seemingly smarter calculation was to let Trump win the nomination, and then to emerge as the obvious figure to lead the party after Trump's historic defeat and the inevitable purge of the Tea Party–Trump–Breitbart wing.

Instead, the election destroyed Paul Ryan, at least in Steve Bannon's eyes. Trump had not only saved the Republican Party but had given it a powerful majority. The entire Bannon dream had been realized. The Tea Party movement, with Trump as its remarkable face and voice, had come to power—something like total power. It owned the Republican Party. Publicly breaking Paul Ryan was the obvious and necessary step.

But a great deal could fall into the chasm between Bannon's structural contempt for Ryan and Trump's personal resentment. If Bannon saw Ryan as being unwilling and unable to carry out the new Bannon-Trump agenda, Trump saw a chastened Ryan as suddenly and satisfyingly abject, submissive, and useful. Bannon wanted to get rid of the entire Republican establishment; Trump was wholly satisfied that it now seemed to bend to him.

"He's quite a smart guy," Trump said after his first postelection conversation with the Speaker. "A very serious man. Everybody respects him."

Ryan, "rising to a movie-version level of flattery and sucking-up painful to witness," according to one senior Trump aide, was able to delay his execution. As Bannon pressed his case for Meadows—who was significantly less yielding than Ryan—Trump dithered and then finally decided that not only was he *not* going to push for Ryan's ouster, but Ryan was going to be his man, his partner. In an example of the odd and unpredictable effects of personal chemistry on Trump—of how easy it can be to sell the salesman—Trump would now eagerly back Ryan's agenda instead of the other way around.

"I don't think that we quite calculated that the president would give him carte blanche," reflected Katie Walsh. "The president and Paul went from such a bad place during the campaign to such a romance afterward that the president was happy to go along with whatever he wanted."

It didn't exactly surprise Bannon when Trump flipped; Bannon understood how easy it was to bullshit a bullshitter. Bannon also recognized that the Ryan rapprochement spoke to Trump's new appreciation of where he found himself. It was not just that Ryan had been willing to bow to Trump, but that Trump was willing to bow to his own fears about how little he actually knew about being president. If Ryan could be counted on to handle Congress, thought the president, well, phew, that takes care of that.

* * *

Trump had little or no interest in the central Republican goal of repealing Obamacare. An overweight seventy-year-old man with various physical phobias (for instance, he lied about his height to keep from having a body mass index that would label him as obese), he personally found health care and medical treatments of all kinds a distasteful subject. The details of the contested legislation were, to him, particularly boring; his attention would begin wandering from the first words of a policy discussion. He would have been able to enumerate few of the particulars of Obamacare—other than expressing glee about the silly Obama pledge that everyone could keep his or her doctor—and he certainly could not make any kind of meaningful distinction, positive or negative, between the health care system before Obamacare and the one after.

Prior to his presidency, he had likely never had a meaningful discussion in his life about health insurance. "No one in the country, or on earth, has given less thought to health insurance than Donald," said Roger Ailes. Pressed in a campaign interview about the importance of Obamacare repeal and reform, Trump was, to say the least, quite unsure of its place on the agenda: "This is an important subject but there are a lot of important subjects. Maybe it is in the top ten. Probably is. But there is heavy competition. So you can't be certain. Could be twelve. Or could be fifteen. Definitely top twenty for sure."

It was another one of his counterintuitive connections to many voters: Obama and Hillary Clinton seemed actually to want to talk about health care plans, whereas Trump, like most everybody else, absolutely did not.

All things considered, he probably preferred the notion of more people having health insurance than fewer people having it. He was even, when push came to shove, rather more for Obamacare than for repealing Obamacare. As well, he had made a set of rash Obama-like promises, going so far as to say that under a forthcoming Trumpcare plan (he had to be strongly discouraged from using this kind of rebranding—political wise men told him that this was one instance where he might not want to claim ownership with his name), no one would lose their health insurance, and that preexisting conditions would continue to be covered. In fact, he probably favored government-funded health care more than any other Republican. "Why can't Medicare simply cover everybody?" he had impatiently wondered aloud during one discussion with aides, all of whom were careful not to react to this heresy.

It was Bannon who held the line, insisting, sternly, that Obamacare was a litmus Republican issue, and that, holding a majority in Congress, they could not face Republican voters without having made good on the by now Republican catechism of repeal. Repeal, in Bannon's view, was the pledge, and repeal would be the most satisfying, even cathartic, result. It would also be the easiest one to achieve, since virtually every Republican was already publicly committed to voting for repeal. But Bannon, seeing health care as a weak link in Bannonism-Trumpism's appeal to the workingman, was careful to take a back seat in the debate. Later, he hardly even made an effort to rationalize how he'd washed his hands of the mess, saying just, "I hung back on health care because it's not my thing."

It was Ryan who, with "repeal and replace," obfuscated the issue and won over Trump. Repeal would satisfy the Republican bottom line, while replace would satisfy the otherwise off-the-cuff pledges that Trump had made on his own. (Pay no attention to the likelihood that what the president construed as repeal and replace might be very different from what Ryan construed as repeal and replace.) "Repeal and replace" was a useful slogan, too, in that it came to have meaning without having any actual or specific meaning.

The week after the election, Ryan, bringing Tom Price—the Georgia congressman and orthopedist who had become Ryan's resident heath care expert—traveled to Trump's Bedminster, New Jersey, estate for a repeal and replace briefing. The two men summed up for Trump—who kept wandering off topic and trying to turn the conversation to golf—seven years of Republican legislative thinking about Obamacare and the Republican alternatives. Here was a perfect example of an essential Trump paradigm: he acceded to anyone who seemed to know more about any issue he didn't care about, or simply one whose details he couldn't bring himself to focus on closely. *Great!* he would say, punctuating every statement with a similar exclamation and regularly making an effort to jump from his chair. On the spot, Trump eagerly agreed to let Ryan run the health care bill and to make Price the Health and Human Services secretary.

Kushner, largely staying silent during the health care debate, publicly seemed to accept the fact that a Republican administration had to address Obamacare, but he privately suggested that he was personally against both repeal alone and repeal and replace. He and his wife took a conventional Democratic view on Obamacare (it was better than the alternatives; its problems could be fixed in the future) and strategically believed it was best for the new administration to get some easier victories under its belt before entering a hard-to-win or no-win fight. (What's more, Kushner's brother Josh ran a health insurance company that depended on Obamacare.)

Not for the last time, then, the White House would be divided along the political spectrum, Bannon taking an absolutist base position, Priebus aligned with Ryan in support of the Republican leadership, and Kushner maintaining, and seeing no contradiction in, a moderate Democratic view. As for Trump himself, here was a man who was simply trying to get out from under something he didn't especially care about.

Ryan and Priebus's salesmanship promised to get the president out from under other issues as well. Health care reform, according to the Ryan plan, was something of a magic bullet. The reform the Speaker would push through Congress would fund the tax cuts Trump had guaranteed, which, in turn, would make all that Trump-promised infrastructure investment possible.

On this basis—this domino theory that was meant to triumphantly carry the Trump administration through to the August recess and mark it as one of the most transformational presidencies in modern times—Ryan kept his job as Speaker, rising from hated campaign symbol to the administration's man on the Hill. In effect, the president, quite aware of his and his staff's inexperience in drafting legislation (in fact, nobody on his senior staff had any experience at all), decided to outsource his agenda—and to a heretofore archenemy.

Watching Ryan steal the legislative initiative during the transition, Bannon faced an early realpolitik moment. If the president was willing to cede major initiatives, Bannon would need to run a counteroperation and be ready with more Breitbart shenanigans. Kushner, for his part, developed a certain Zen—you just had to go with the president's whims. As for the president, it was quite clear that deciding between contradictory policy approaches was not his style of leadership. He simply hoped that difficult decisions would make themselves.

* * *

Bannon was not merely contemptuous of Ryan's ideology; he had no respect, either, for his craft. In Bannon's view, what the new Republican majority needed was a man like John McCormick, the Democratic Speaker of the House who had served during Bannon's teenage years and had shepherded Johnson's Great Society legislation. McCormick and other Democrats from the 1960s were Bannon's political heroes—put Tip O'Neill in that pantheon, too. An Irish Catholic working-class man was philosophically separate from aristocrats and gentry—and without aspirations to be either. Bannon venerated old-fashioned pols. He looked like one himself: liver spots, jowls, edema. And he hated modern politicians; they lacked, in addition to political talents, authenticity and soul. Ryan was an Irish Catholic altar boy who had stayed an altar boy. He had not grown up to be a thug, cop, or priest—or a true politician.

Ryan certainly wasn't a vote counter. He was a benighted figure who had no ability to see around corners. His heart was in tax reform, but as far as he could tell the only path to tax reform was through health care. But he cared so little about the issue that—just as the White House had outsourced health care to him—he outsourced the writing of the bill to insurance companies and K Street lobbyists.

In fact, Ryan had tried to act like McCormick or O'Neill, offering absolute assurances of his hold on the legislation. It was, he told the president during his several daily calls, a "done deal." Trump's trust in Ryan rose still higher, and it seemed to become in his own mind proof that he had achieved a kind of mastery over the Hill. If the president had been worried, he was worried no more. Done deal. The White House, having had to sweat hardly at all, was about to get a big victory, bragged Kushner, embracing the expected win over his dislike of the bill.

The sudden concern that the outcome might be otherwise began in early March. Katie Walsh, who Kushner now described as "demanding and petulant," began to sound the alarm. But her efforts to personally involve the president in vote collecting were blocked by Kushner in a set of increasingly tense face-offs. The unraveling had begun.

* * *

Trump still dismissively called it "the Russian thing—a whole lot of nothing." But on March 20, FBI director James Comey appeared before the House Intelligence Committee and tied the story up in a neat package:

> I have been authorized by the Department of Justice to confirm that the FBI, as part of our counterintelligence mission, is investigating the Russian government's efforts to interfere in the 2016 presidential election, and that includes investigating the nature of any links between individuals associated with the Trump campaign and the Russian government and whether there was any coordination between the campaign and Russia's efforts. As with any counter intelligence investigation, this will also include an assessment of whether any crimes were committed. Because it is an open, ongoing investigation and is classified I cannot say more about what we are doing and whose conduct we are examining.

He had, however, said quite enough. Comey converted rumor, leaks, theory, innuendo, and pundit hot air—and until this moment that was all there was, at best the hope of a scandal—into a formal pursuit of the White House. Efforts to pooh-pooh the narrative—the fake news label, the president's germaphobe defense against the golden shower accusations, the haughty dismissal of minor associates and hopeless hangers-on, the plaintive, if real, insistence that no crime had even been alleged, and the president's charge that he was the victim of an Obama wiretap—had failed. Comey himself dismissed the wiretap allegation. By the evening of Comey's appearance, it was evident to everyone that the Russia plot line, far from petering out, had a mighty and bloody life to come.

Kushner, ever mindful of his father's collision with the Justice Department, was especially agitated by Comey's increasing focus on the White House. Doing something about Comey became a Kushner theme. What can we do about him? was a constant question. And it was one he kept raising with the president.

Yet this was also—as Bannon, without too much internal success, tried to explain—a structural issue. It was an opposition move. You could express surprise at how fierce, creative, and diabolical the moves turned out to be, but you shouldn't be surprised that your enemies would try to hurt you. This was check, but far from checkmate, and you had to continue to play the game, knowing that it would be a very long one. The only way to win the game, Bannon argued, was with a disciplined strategy.

But the president, prodded here by his family, was an obsessive and not a strategist. In his mind, this was not a problem to address, this was a person to focus on: Comey. Trump eschewed abstractions and, ad hominem, zeroed in on his opponent. Comey had been a difficult puzzle for Trump: Comey had declined to have the FBI pursue charges against Clinton for her email dodge. Then, in October, Comey had single-handedly boosted Trump's fortunes with the letter reopening the Clinton email investigation.

In their personal interactions, Trump had found Comey to be a stiff—he had no banter, no game. But Trump, who invariably thought people found him irresistible, believed that Comey admired *his* banter and game. When pressed, by Bannon and others, to fire Comey as one of his early acts—an idea opposed by Kushner, and thus another bullet on Bannon's list of bad recommendations by Kushner—the president said, "Don't worry, I've got him." That is, he had no doubt that he could woo and flatter the FBI director into positive feeling for him, if not outright submission.

Some seducers are preternaturally sensitive to the signals of those they try to seduce; others indiscriminately attempt to seduce, and, by the law of averages, often succeed (this latter group of men might now be regarded as harassers). That was Trump's approach to women—pleased when he scored, unconcerned when he didn't (and, often, despite the evidence, believing that he had). And so it was with Director Comey.

In their several meetings since he took office—when Comey received a presidential hug on January 22; at their dinner on January 27, during which Comey was asked to stay on as FBI director; at their Valentine's Day chat after emptying the office of everybody else, including Sessions, Comey's titular boss—Trump was confident that he had laid on the moves. The president was all but certain that Comey, understanding that he, Trump, had his back (i.e., had let him keep his job), would have Trump's back, too.

But now this testimony. It made no sense. What *did* make sense to Trump was that Comey wanted it to be about him. He was a media whore—this Trump understood. All right, then, he, too, could play it this way.

Indeed, health care, a no-fun issue—suddenly becoming much less fun, if, as seemed increasingly possible, Ryan couldn't deliver—palled before the clarity of Comey, and the fury, enmity, and bitterness Trump, and Trump's relatives, now bore him.

Comey was the larger-than-life problem. Taking Comey down was the obvious solution. Getting Comey became the mission.

In Keystone Cops fashion, the White House enlisted House Intelligence Committee chairman Devin Nunes in a farcical effort to discredit Comey and support the wiretap theory. The scheme shortly collapsed in universal ridicule.

Bannon, taking a public hands-off with respect to both health care and Comey, began to advise reporters that the important story wasn't health care but Russia. This was cryptic advice: it was not clear whether he was trying to distract attention from the coming health care debacle, or couple it with this new dangerous variable, thus amping up the kind of chaos that he usually benefited from.

But Bannon was unequivocal about one thing. *As the Russia story unfolds*, he advised reporters, *keep your eye on Kushner.*

* * *

By mid-March, Gary Cohn had been drafted into the effort to salvage the faltering health care bill. This might have seemed like a form of hazing for Cohn, whose grasp of legislative matters was even more limited than that of most in the White House.

On Friday, March 24, the morning of the theoretical House vote for the Republican health care bill, Politico's *Playbook* characterized the chances of a vote actually coming to the floor as a "toss-up." In that morning's senior staff meeting, Cohn was asked for an assessment of where things stood and promptly said, "I think it's a toss-up."

"Really?" thought Katie Walsh. "That's what you think?"

Bannon, joining Walsh in a pitiless contempt for the White House effort, targeted Kushner, Cohn, Priebus, Price, and Ryan in a series of calls to reporters. Kushner and Cohn could, per Bannon, be counted on to run at the first sound of gunfire. (Kushner, in fact, had spent much of the week on a skiing holiday.) Priebus mouthed Ryan talking points and excuses. Price, supposedly the health care guru, was an oafish imposter; he would stand up in meetings and mumble nothing but nonsense.

These were the bad guys, setting up the administration to lose the House in 2018, thereby assuring the president's impeachment. This was vintage Bannon analysis: a certain and immediate political apocalypse that sat side by side with the potential for a half century of Bannonism-Trumpism rule.

Convinced he knew the direction of success, keenly aware of his own age and finite opportunities, and—if for no clear reason—seeing himself as a talented political infighter, Bannon sought to draw the line between believers and sell-outs, being and nothingness. For him to succeed, he needed to isolate the Ryan, Cohn, and Kushner factions.

The Bannon faction held tight on forcing a vote on the health care bill—even knowing defeat was inevitable. "I want it as a report on Ryan's job as Speaker," said Bannon. That is, a devastating report, an epic fail.

The day of the vote, Pence was sent to the Hill to make one last pitch to Meadows's Freedom Caucus. (Ryan's people believed that Bannon was secretly urging Meadows to hold out, though earlier in the week Bannon had harshly ordered the Freedom Caucus to vote for the bill—"a silly Bannon show," according to Walsh.) At three-thirty, Ryan called the president to say he was short fifteen to twenty votes and needed to pull the vote. Bannon, backed by Mulvaney, who had become the White House's Hill operative, continued to urge an immediate vote. A defeat here would be a major defeat for the Republican leadership. That suited Bannon just fine: let them fail.

But the president backed down. Faced with this singular opportunity to make the Republican leadership the issue, and to name them as the problem, Trump wobbled, provoking in Bannon a not-so-silent rage. Ryan then leaked that it was the president who had asked him to cancel the vote.

Over the weekend, Bannon called a long list of reporters and told them—off the record, but hardly—"I don't see Ryan hanging around a long time."

* * *

After the bill had been pulled that Friday, Katie Walsh, feeling both angry and disgusted, told Kushner she wanted out. Outlining what she saw as the grim debacle of the Trump White House, she spoke with harsh candor about bitter rivalries joined to vast incompetence and an uncertain mission. Kushner, understanding that she needed to be discredited immediately, leaked that she had been leaking and hence had to be pushed out.

On Sunday evening, Walsh had dinner with Bannon in his Capitol Hill redoubt, the Breitbart Embassy, during which, to no avail, he implored her to stay. On Monday she sorted out the details with Priebus—she would leave to work part time for the RNC and part time for the Trump (c)(4), the outside campaign group. By Thursday she was gone.

Ten weeks into the new administration, the Trump White House had lost, after Michael Flynn, its second senior staff member—and the one whose job it was to actually get things done.

13

BANNON AGONISTES

He, too, felt like a prisoner, he had told Katie Walsh when she came to tell him she was leaving.

By ten weeks in, Steve Bannon's mastery of the Trump agenda, or at least of Trump himself, appeared to have crumbled. His current misery was both Catholic in nature—the self-flagellation of a man who believed he lived on a higher moral plane than all others—and fundamentally misanthropic. As an antisocial, maladjusted, post-middle-aged man, he had to make a supreme effort to get along with others, an effort that often did not go well. Most especially, he was miserable because of Donald Trump, whose cruelties, always great even when they were casual, were unbearable when he truly turned against you.

"I hated being on the campaign, I hated the transition, I hate being here in the White House," said Bannon, sitting one evening in Reince Priebus's office, on an unseasonably warm evening in early spring, with the French doors open to the arbor-covered patio where he and Priebus, now firm friends and allies in their antipathy toward Jarvanka, had set an outdoor table.

But Bannon was, he believed, here for a reason. And it was his firm belief—a belief he was unable to keep to himself, thus continually undermining his standing with the president—that his efforts had brought everybody else here. Even more important, he was the only person showing up for work every day who was committed to the purpose of actually changing the country. Changing it quickly, radically, and truly.

The idea of a split electorate—of blue and red states, of two opposing currents of values, of globalists and nationalists, of an establishment and populist revolt—was media shorthand for cultural angst and politically roiled times, and, to a large degree, for business as usual. But Bannon believed the split was literal. The United States had become a country of two hostile peoples. One would necessarily win and the other lose. Or one would dominate while the other would become marginal.

This was modern civil war—Bannon's war. The country built on the virtue and the character and the strength of the American workingman circa 1955–65 was the ideal he meant to defend and restore: trade agreements, or *trade wars*, that supported American manufacturing; immigration policies that protected American workers (and, hence, American culture, or at least America's identity from 1955 to 1965); and an international isolation that would conserve American resources and choke off the ruling class's Davos sensibility (and also save working-class military lives). This was, in the view of almost everyone but Donald Trump and the alt-right, a crazy bit of voodoo economic and political nonsense. But it was, for Bannon, a revolutionary and religious idea.

For most others in the White House, it was Bannon's pipe dream. "Steve is . . . Steve," became the gentle term of art for tolerating him. "A lot of stuff goes on in his head," said the president, pursuing one of his reliable conversational themes, dismissing Bannon.

But it wasn't Bannon versus everybody else so much as it was Bannon Trump versus non-Bannon Trump. If Trump, in his dark, determined, and aggressive mood, could represent Bannon and his views, he could just as easily represent nothing at all—or represent solely his own need for instant gratification. That's what the non-Bannon people understood about Trump. If the boss was happy, then a normal, incremental, two-steps-forward-one-step-back approach to politics might prevail. Even a new sort of centrism, as inimical to Bannonism as it was possible to conceive, could emerge. Bannon's pronouncements about a fifty-year rule for Trumpism might then be supplanted by the rule of Jared, Ivanka, and Goldman Sachs.

By the end of March, this was the side that was winning. Bannon's efforts to use the epic health care fail as evidence that the establishment was the enemy had hopelessly backfired. Trump saw the health care failure as his own failure, but since he didn't have failures, it couldn't be a failure, and would in fact be a success—if not now, soon. So Bannon, a Cassandra on the sidelines, was the problem.

Trump rationalized his early embrace of Bannon by heaping scorn on him—and by denying that he had ever embraced him. If there was anything wrong with his White House, it was Steve Bannon. Maligning Bannon was Trump's idea of fun. When it came to Bannon, Trump rose to something like high analysis: "Steve Bannon's problem is PR. He doesn't understand it. Everybody hates him. Because . . . look at him. His bad PR rubs off on other people."

The real question, of course, was how Bannon, the fuck-the-system populist, had ever come to think that he might get along with Donald Trump, the use-the-system-to-his-own-advantage billionaire. For Bannon, Trump was the game he had to play. But in truth he hardly played it—or couldn't help undermining it. While ever proclaiming it Trump's victory, he would helplessly point out that when he had joined the campaign it was facing a polling deficit that no campaign, ten weeks from election day, had ever recovered from. Trump without Bannon, according to Bannon, was Wendell Willkie.

Bannon understood the necessity not to take what otherwise might be Trump's own spotlight; he was well aware that the president meticulously logged all claims against credit that he believed solely to be his. Both he and Kushner, the two most important figures in the White House after the president, seemed professionally mute. Still, Bannon seemed to be everywhere, and the president was convinced—rightly—that it was the result of Bannon's private press operation. More often than self-mockery could sustain, Bannon referred to himself as "President Bannon." A bitter Kellyanne Conway, regularly dissed for her own spotlight grabbing, confirmed the president's observation that Bannon stepped into as many White House photo ops as possible. (Everybody seemed to keep count of everybody else's photo bombs.) Bannon also did not much bother to disguise his innumerable blind quotes, nor to make much of an effort to temper his not-so-private slurs against Kushner, Cohn, Powell, Conway, Priebus, and even the president's daughter (often, most especially, the president's daughter).

Curiously, Bannon never expressed a sideways thought about Trump—not yet. Trump's own righteousness and soundness was perhaps too central to Bannon's construct of Trumpism. Trump was the idea you had to support. This could seem to approach the traditional idea of respecting the office. In fact, it was the inverse. The man was the vessel: there was no Bannon without Trump. However much he might stand on his unique, even magical-seeming, contributions to the Trump victory, Bannon's opportunity was wholly provided by Trump's peculiar talent. He was no more than the man behind the man—Trump's Cromwell, as he put it, even though he was perfectly aware of Cromwell's fate.

But his loyalty to the idea of Trump hardly protected him from the actual Trump's constant briefs against him. The president had assembled a wide jury to weigh Bannon's fate, putting before it, in an insulting Borscht Belt style, a long list of Bannon's annoyances: "Guy looks homeless. Take a shower, Steve. You've worn those pants for six days. He says he's made money, I don't believe it." (The president, notably, never much took issue with Bannon's policy views.) The Trump administration was hardly two months old, yet every media outlet was predicting Bannon's coming defenestration.

One particularly profitable transaction with the president was to bring him new, ever harsher criticism of his chief strategist, or reports of other people criticizing him. It was important to know not to say anything positive to Trump about Bannon. Even faint praise before the "but"—"Steve is obviously smart, but . . ."—could produce a scowl and pout if you didn't hurry to the "but." (Then again, saying anyone was "smart" invariably incurred Trump's annoyance.) Kushner enlisted Scarborough and Brzezinski in something of a regular morning television Bannon slag-a-thon.

H. R. McMaster, the three-star general who had replaced Michael Flynn as National Security Advisor, had secured the president's pledge that he could veto members of the NSC. Kushner, a supporter of McMaster's appointment, had quickly ensured that Dina Powell, a key player in the Kushner faction, would join the NSC and Bannon would be removed.

Bannonites would, with lowered voices and certain pity, ask each other how he seemed and how he was holding up; invariably they would agree about how bad he looked, the strain etching ever deeper into his already ruined face. David Bossie thought Bannon "looked like he would die."

"I now understand what it is like to be in the court of the Tudors," reflected Bannon. On the campaign trail, he recalled, Newt Gingrich "would come with all these dumb ideas. When we won he was my new best friend. Every day a hundred ideas. When"—by spring in the White House—"I got cold, when I went through my Valley of Death, I saw him one day in the lobby and he looks down, avoiding my eyes with a kind of mumbled 'Hey, Steve.' And I say, 'What are you doing here, let's get you inside,' and he says, 'No, no, I'm fine, I'm waiting for Dina Powell.'"

Having attained the unimaginable—bringing a fierce alt-right, anti-liberal ethnopopulism into a central place in the White House—Bannon found himself face to face with the untenable: undermined by and having to answer to rich, entitled Democrats.

* * *

The paradox of the Trump presidency was that it was both the most ideologically driven and the least. It represented a deeply structural assault on liberal values—Bannon's deconstruction of the administrative state meant to take with it media, academic, and not-for-profit institutions. But from the start it also was apparent that the Trump administration could just as easily turn into a country club Republican or a Wall Street Democrat regime. Or just a constant effort to keep Donald Trump happy. Trump had his collection of pet-peeve issues, test-marketed in various media rollouts and megarallies, but none seemed so significant as his greater goal of personally coming out ahead of the game.

As the drumbeat for Bannon's removal grew, the Mercers stepped in to protect their investment in radical government overthrow and the future of Steve Bannon.

In an age when all successful political candidates are surrounded by, if not at the beck and call of, difficult, rich people pushing the bounds of their own power—and the richer they were, the more difficult they might be—Bob and Rebekah Mercer were quite onto themselves. If Trump's ascent was unlikely, the Mercers' was all the more so.

Even the difficult rich—the Koch brothers and Sheldon Adelson on the right, David Geffen and George Soros on the left—are leavened and restrained by the fact that money exists in a competitive market. Obnoxiousness has its limits. The world of the rich is, in its fashion, self-regulating. Social climbing has rules.

But among the difficult and entitled rich, the Mercers cut a path through disbelief and incredulity. Unlike other people contributing vast sums to political candidates, they were willing not to win—ever. Their bubble was their bubble.

So when they did win, by the fluke alignment of the stars for Donald Trump, they were yet pure. Now, having found themselves—by odds that were perfect-storm outlandish—in power, they were not going to give it up because Steve Bannon had hurt feelings and wasn't getting enough sleep.

Toward the end of March, the Mercers organized a set of emergency meetings. At least one of them was with the president himself. It was exactly the kind of meeting Trump usually avoided: he had no interest in personnel problems, since they put the emphasis on other people. Suddenly he was being forced to deal with Steve Bannon, rather than the other way around. What's more, it was a problem he had in part created with his constant Bannon dissing, and now he was being asked to eat crow. Even though the president kept saying he could and should fire Bannon, he was aware of the costs—a right-wing backlash of unpredictable proportions.

Trump thought the Mercers were super-strange bedfellows too. He didn't like Bob Mercer looking at him and not saying a word; he didn't like being in the same room with Mercer or his daughter. But though he refused to admit that the Mercers' decision to back him and their imposition of Bannon on the campaign in August was, likely, the event without which he would not now be in the White House, he did understand that if crossed, the Mercers and Bannon were potential world-class troublemakers.

The complexity of the Bannon-Mercer problem prompted Trump to consult two contradictory figures: Rupert Murdoch and Roger Ailes. Even as the president did so, perhaps he knew he would come up with a zero-sum answer.

Murdoch, already briefed by Kushner, said getting rid of Bannon was the only way to deal with the dysfunction in the White House. (Murdoch, of course, made the assumption that getting rid of Kushner was not an option.) It was the inevitable outcome, so do it now. Murdoch's response made perfect sense: by now, he had become an active political supporter of the Kushner-Goldman moderates, seeing them as the people who would save the world from Bannon and, indeed, from Trump as well.

Ailes, blunt and declarative as always, said, "Donald, you can't do it. You've made your bed and Steve is in it. You don't have to listen to him, you don't have to even get along with him. But you're married to him. You can't handle a divorce right now."

Jared and Ivanka were gleeful at the prospect of Bannon's ouster. His departure would return the Trump organization to pure family control—the family and its functionaries, without an internal rival for brand meaning and leadership. From the family's point of view, it would also—at least in theory—help facilitate one of the most implausible brand shifts in history: Donald Trump to respectability. The dream, long differed, of the Trump pivot, might actually happen without Bannon. Never mind that this Kushner ideal—saving Trump from himself and projecting Jared and Ivanka into the future—was nearly as far-fetched and extreme as Bannon's own fantasy of a White House dedicated to the return of a pre-1965 American mythology.

If Bannon were to go, it also might cause the ultimate split in the already fractured Republican Party. Before the election, one theory suggested that a defeated Trump would take his embittered 35 percent and make hay with a rancorous minority. Now the alarming theory was that as Kushner tried to transform his father-in-law into the kind of latter-day Rockefeller that Trump, however implausibly, had on occasion dreamed of becoming (Rockefeller Center being an inspiration for his own real estate branding), Bannon could run off with some meaningful part of that 35 percent.

This was the Breitbart threat. The Breitbart organization remained under the control of the Mercers, and it could at any moment be handed back to Steve Bannon. And now, with Bannon's overnight transformation into political genius and kingmaker, and the triumph of the alt-right, Breitbart was potentially much more powerful. Trump's victory had, in some sense, handed the Mercers the tool with which to destroy him. As push came to shove and the mainstream media and swamp bureaucracy more and more militantly organized against him, Trump was certainly going to need the Mercer-backed alt-right standing up in his defense. What, after all, was he without them?

As the pressure mounted, Bannon—until now absolutely disciplined in his regard for Donald Trump as the ideal avatar of Trumpism (and Bannonism), rigidly staying in character as aide and supporter of a maverick political talent—began to crack. Trump, as almost anyone who had ever worked for him appreciated, was, despite what you hoped he might be, Trump—and he would invariably sour on everyone around him.

But the Mercers dug in. Without Bannon, they believed the Trump presidency, at least the Trump presidency they had imagined (and helped pay for), was over. The focus became how to make Steve's life better. They made him pledge to leave the office at a reasonable time—no more waiting around for Trump to possibly need a dinner companion. (Recently, Jared and Ivanka had been heading this off anyway.) The solution included a search for a Bannon's Bannon—a chief strategist for the chief strategist.

In late March, the Mercers came to an agreed-upon truce with the president: Bannon would not be fired. While this guaranteed nothing about his influence and standing, it did buy Bannon and his allies some time. They could regroup. A presidential aide was only as good as the last good advice he gave, and in this, Bannon believed the ineptness of his rivals, Kushner and his wife, would seal their fate.

* * *

Though the president agreed not to fire Bannon, he gave Kushner and his daughter something in exchange: he would enhance both their roles.

On March 27, the Office of American Innovation was created and Kushner was put in charge. Its stated mission was to reduce federal bureaucracy—that is, to reduce it by creating more of it, a committee to end committees. In addition, Kushner's new outfit would study the government's internal technology, focus on job creation, encourage and suggest policies about apprenticeships, enlist business in a partnership with government, and help with the opioid epidemic. It was, in other words, business as usual, albeit with a new burst of enthusiasm for the administrative state.

But its real import was that it gave Kushner his own internal White House staff, a team of people working not just on Kushner-supported projects—all largely antithetical to Bannon projects—but, more broadly, as Kushner explained to one staffer, "on expanding my footprint." Kushner even got his own "comms person," a dedicated spokesperson and Kushner promoter. It was a bureaucratic build-out meant not only to enhance Kushner but to diminish Steve Bannon.

Two days after the announcement about Jared's expanded power base, Ivanka was formally given a White House job, too: adviser to the president. From the beginning she had been a key adviser to her husband—and he to her. Still, it was an overnight consolidation of Trump family power in the White House. It was, quite at Steve Bannon's expense, a remarkable bureaucratic coup: a divided White House had now all but been united under the president's family.

His son-in-law and daughter hoped—they were even confident—that they could speak to DJT's better self, or at least balance Republican needs with progressive rationality, compassion, and good works. Further, they could support this moderation by routing a steady stream of like-minded CEOs through the Oval Office. And, indeed, the president seldom disagreed with and was often enthusiastic about the Jared and Ivanka program. "If they tell him the whales need to be saved, he's basically for it," noted Katie Walsh.

But Bannon, suffering in his internal exile, remained convinced that he represented what Donald Trump actually believed, or, more accurately, what the president felt. He knew Trump to be a fundamentally emotional man, and he was certain that the deepest part of him was angry and dark. However much the president wanted to support his daughter and her husband's aspirations, their worldview was not his. As Walsh saw it, "Steve believes he is Darth Vader and that Trump is called to the dark side."

Indeed, Trump's fierce efforts to deny Bannon's influence may well have been in inverse proportion to the influence Bannon actually had.

The president did not truly listen to anybody. The more you talked, the less he listened. "But Steve is careful about what he says, and there is something, a timbre in his voice and his energy and excitement, that the president can really hone in on, blocking everything else out," said Walsh.

As Jared and Ivanka were taking a victory lap, Trump signed Executive Order 13783, a change in environmental policy carefully shepherded by Bannon, which, he argued, effectively gutted the National Environmental Policy Act, the 1970 law that served as the foundation of modern environmental protections and that required all executive agencies to prepare environmental impact statements for agency actions. Among other impacts, EO 13783 removed a prior directive to consider climate change—a precursor to coming debates on the country's position regarding the Paris Climate Accord.

On April 3, Kushner unexpectedly turned up in Iraq, accompanying Gen. Joseph Dunford, chairman of the Joint Chiefs of Staff. According to the White House press office, Kushner was "traveling on behalf of the president to express the president's support and commitment to the government of Iraq and U.S. personnel currently engaged in the campaign." Kushner, otherwise a remote and clammed-up media presence, was copiously photographed throughout the trip.

Bannon, watching one of the many television screens that provided a constant background in the West Wing, glimpsed Kushner wearing a headset while flying in a helicopter over Baghdad. To no one in particular, recalling a foolish and callow George W. Bush in flight gear on the aircraft carrier USS *Abraham Lincoln* proclaiming the end of the Iraq War, he intoned, "Mission accomplished."

Gritting his teeth, Bannon saw the structure of the White House moving in the exact opposite direction from Trumpism-Bannonism. But even now, he was certain he perceived the real impulses of the administration coming his way. It was Bannon, stoic and resolute, the great if unheralded warrior, who, at least in his own mind, was destined to save the nation.

14

SITUATION ROOM

Just before seven o'clock on the morning of Tuesday, April 4, the seventy-fourth day of the Trump presidency, Syrian government forces attacked the rebel-held town of Khan Sheikhoun with chemical weapons. Scores of children were killed. It was the first time a major outside event had intruded into the Trump presidency.

Most presidencies are shaped by external crises. The presidency, in its most critical role, is a reactive job. Much of the alarm about Donald Trump came from the widespread conviction that he could not be counted on to be cool or deliberate in the face of a storm. He had been lucky so far: ten weeks in, and he had not been seriously tested. In part this might have been because the crises generated from inside the White House had overshadowed all outside contenders.

Even a gruesome attack, even one on children in an already long war, might not yet be a presidential game changer of the kind that everyone knew would surely come. Still, these were chemical weapons launched by a repeat offender, Bashar al-Assad. In any other presidency, such an atrocity would command a considered and, ideally, skillful response. Obama's consideration had in fact been less than skillful in proclaiming the use of chemical weapons as a red line—and then allowing it to be crossed.

Almost nobody in the Trump administration was willing to predict how the president might react—or even whether he would react. Did he think the chemical attack important or unimportant? No one could say.

If the Trump White House was as unsettling as any in American history, the president's views of foreign policy and the world at large were among its most random, uninformed, and seemingly capricious aspects. His advisers didn't know whether he was an isolationist or a militarist, or whether he could distinguish between the two. He was enamored with generals and determined that people with military command experience take the lead in foreign policy, but he hated to be told what to do. He was against nation building, but he believed there were few situations that he couldn't personally make better. He had little to no experience in foreign policy, but he had no respect for the experts, either.

Suddenly, the question of how the president might respond to the attack in Khan Sheikhoun was a litmus test for normality and those who hoped to represent it in Trump's White House. Here was the kind of dramatic juxtaposition that might make for a vivid and efficient piece of theater: people working in the Trump White House who were trying to behave normally.

* * *

Surprisingly, perhaps, there were quite a few such people.

Acting normal, embodying normality—doing things the way a striving, achieving, rational person would do them—was how Dina Powell saw her job in the White House. At forty-three, Powell had made a career at the intersection of the corporate world and public policy; she did well (very, very well) by doing good. She had made great strides in George W. Bush's White House and then later at Goldman Sachs. Returning to the White House at a penultimate level, with at least a chance of rising to one of the country's highest unelected positions, would potentially be worth enormous sums when she returned to the corporate world.

In Trumpland, however, the exact opposite could happen. Powell's carefully cultivated reputation, her brand (and she was one of those people who thought intently about their personal brand), could become inextricably tied to the Trump brand. Worse, she could become part of what might easily turn into historical calamity. Already, for many people who knew Dina Powell—and everybody who was anybody knew Dina Powell—the fact that she had taken a position in the Trump White House indicated either recklessness or seriously bad judgment.

"How," wondered one of her longtime friends, "does she rationalize this?" Friends, family, and neighbors asked, silently or openly, *Do you know what you're doing? And how* could *you? And why* would *you?*

Here was the line dividing those whose reason for being in the White House was a professed loyalty to the president from the professionals they had needed to hire. Bannon, Conway, and Hicks—along with an assortment of more or less peculiar ideologues that had attached themselves to Trump and, of course, his family, all people without clearly monetizable reputations before their association with Trump—were, for better or worse, hitched to him. (Even among dedicated Trumpers there was always a certain amount of holding their breath and constant reexamination of their options.) But those within the larger circle of White House influence, those with some stature or at least an imagined stature, had to work through significantly more complicated contortions of personal and career justification.

Often they wore their qualms on their sleeves. Mick Mulvaney, the OMB director, made a point of stressing the fact that he worked in the Executive Office Building, not the West Wing. Michael Anton, holding down Ben Rhodes's former job at the NSC, had perfected a deft eye roll (referred to as the Anton eye roll). H. R. McMaster seemed to wear a constant grimace and have perpetual steam rising from his bald head. ("What's wrong with him?" the president often asked.)

There was, of course, a higher rationale: the White House needed normal, sane, logical, adult professionals. To a person, these pros saw themselves bringing positive attributes—rational minds, analytic powers, significant professional experience—to a situation sorely lacking those things. They were doing their bit to make things more normal and, therefore, more stable. They were bulwarks, or saw themselves that way, against chaos, impulsiveness, and stupidity. They were less Trump supporters than an antidote to Trump.

"If it all starts going south—more south than it is already going—I have no doubt that Joe Hagin would himself take personal responsibility, and do what needed to be done," said a senior Republican figure in Washington, in an effort at self-reassurance, about the former Bush staffer who now served as Trump's deputy chief of staff for operations.

But this sense of duty and virtue involved a complicated calculation about your positive effect on the White House versus its negative effect on you. In April, an email originally copied to more than a dozen people went into far wider circulation when it was forwarded and reforwarded. Purporting to represent the views of Gary Cohn and quite succinctly summarizing the appalled sense in much of the White House, the email read:

> It's worse than you can imagine. An idiot surrounded by clowns. Trump won't read anything—not one-page memos, not the brief policy papers; nothing. He gets up halfway through meetings with world leaders because he is bored. And his staff is no better. Kushner is an entitled baby who knows nothing. Bannon is an arrogant prick who thinks he's smarter than he is. Trump is less a person than a collection of terrible traits. No one will survive the first year but his family. I hate the work, but feel I need to stay because I'm the only person there with a clue what he's doing. The reason so few jobs have been filled is that they only accept people who pass ridiculous purity tests, even for midlevel policy-making jobs where the people will never see the light of day. I am in a constant state of shock and horror.

Still, the mess that might do serious damage to the nation, and, by association, to your own brand, might be transcended if you were seen as the person, by dint of competence and professional behavior, taking control of it.

Powell, who had come into the White House as an adviser to Ivanka Trump, rose, in weeks, to a position on the National Security Council, and was then, suddenly, along with Cohn, her Goldman colleague, a contender for some of the highest posts in the administration.

At the same time, both she and Cohn were spending a good deal of time with their ad hoc outside advisers on which way they might jump out of the White House. Powell could eye seven-figure comms jobs at various Fortune 100 companies, or a C-suite future at a tech company—Facebook's Sheryl Sandberg, after all, had a background in corporate philanthropy and in the Obama administration. Cohn, on his part, already a centamillionaire, was thinking about the World Bank or the Fed.

Ivanka Trump—dealing with some of the same personal and career considerations as Powell, except without a viable escape strategy—was quite in her own corner. Inexpressive and even botlike in public but, among friends, discursive and strategic, Ivanka had become both more defensive about her father and more alarmed by where his White House was heading. She and her husband blamed this on Bannon and his let-Trump-be-Trump philosophy (often interpreted as let Trump be Bannon). The couple had come to regard him as more diabolical than Rasputin. Hence it was their job to keep Bannon and the ideologues from the president, who, they believed, was, in his heart, a practical-minded person (at least in his better moods), swayed only by people preying on his short attention span.

In mutually codependent fashion, Ivanka relied on Dina to suggest management tactics that would help her handle her father and the White House, while Dina relied on Ivanka to offer regular assurances that not everyone named Trump was completely crazy. This link meant that within the greater West Wing population, Powell was seen as part of the much tighter family circle, which, while it conferred influence, also made her the target of ever sharper attacks. "She will expose herself as being totally incompetent," said a bitter Katie Walsh, seeing Powell as less a normalizing influence than another aspect of the abnormal Trump family power play.

And indeed, both Powell and Cohn had privately concluded that the job they both had their eye on—chief of staff, that singularly necessary White House management position—would always be impossible to perform if the president's daughter and son-in-law, no matter how much they were allied to them, were in de facto command whenever they wanted to exert it.

Dina and Ivanka were themselves spearheading an initiative that, otherwise, would have been a fundamental responsibility of the chief of staff: controlling the president's information flow.

* * *

The unique problem here was partly how to get information to someone who did not (or could not or would not) read, and who at best listened only selectively. But the other part of the problem was how best to qualify the information that he liked to get. Hope Hicks, after more than a year at this side, had honed her instincts for the kind of information—the clips—that would please him. Bannon, in his intense and confiding voice, could insinuate himself into the president's mind. Kellyanne Conway brought him the latest outrages against him. There were his after-dinner calls—the billionaire chorus. And then cable, itself programmed to reach him—to court him or enrage him.

The information he did not get was formal information. The data. The details. The options. The analysis. He didn't do PowerPoint. For anything that smacked of a classroom or of being lectured to—"professor" was one of his bad words, and he was proud of never going to class, never buying a textbook, never taking a note—he got up and left the room.

This was a problem in multiple respects—indeed, in almost all the prescribed functions of the presidency. But perhaps most of all, it was a problem in the evaluation of strategic military options.

The president liked generals. The more fruit salad they wore, the better. The president was very pleased with the compliments he got for appointing generals who commanded the respect that Mattis and Kelly and McMaster were accorded (pay no attention to Michael Flynn). What the president did not like was *listening* to generals, who, for the most part, were skilled in the new army jargon of PowerPoint, data dumps, and McKinsey-like presentations. One of the things that endeared Flynn to the president was that Flynn, quite the conspiracist and drama queen, had a vivid storytelling sense.

By the time of the Syrian attack on Khan Sheikhoun, McMaster had been Trump's National Security Advisor for only about six weeks. Yet his efforts to inform the president had already become an exercise in trying to tutor a recalcitrant and resentful student. Recently Trump's meetings with McMaster had ended up in near acrimony, and now the president was telling several friends that his new National Security Advisor was too boring and that he was going to fire him.

McMaster had been the default choice, a fact that Trump kept returning to: Why had he hired him? He blamed his son-in-law.

After the president fired Flynn in February, he had spent two days at Mar-a-Lago interviewing replacements, badly taxing his patience.

John Bolton, the former U.S. ambassador to the United Nations and Bannon's consistent choice, made his aggressive light-up-the-world, go-to-war pitch.

Then Lt. Gen. Robert L. Caslen Jr., superintendent of the United States Military Academy at West Point, presented himself with what Trump viewed positively as old-fashioned military decorum. *Yes, sir. No, sir. That's correct, sir. Well, I think we know China has some problems, sir.* And in short order it seemed that Trump was selling Caslen on the job.

"That's the guy I want," said Trump. "He's got the look."

But Caslen demurred. He had never really had a staff job. Kushner thought he might not be ready.

"Yeah, but I liked that guy," pressed Trump.

Then McMaster, wearing a uniform with his silver star, came in and immediately launched into a wide-ranging lecture on global strategy. Trump was soon, and obviously, distracted, and as the lecture continued he began sulking.

"That guy bores the shit out of me," announced Trump after McMaster left the room. But Kushner pushed him to take another meeting with McMaster, who the next day showed up without his uniform and in a baggy suit.

"He looks like a beer salesman," Trump said, announcing that he would hire McMaster but didn't want to have another meeting with him.

Shortly after his appointment, McMaster appeared on *Morning Joe*. Trump saw the show and noted admiringly, "The guy sure gets good press."

The president decided he had made a good hire.

* * *

By midmorning on April 4, a full briefing had been assembled at the White House for the president about the chemical attacks. Along with his daughter and Powell, most members of the president's inner national security circle saw the bombing of Khan Sheikhoun as a straightforward opportunity to register an absolute moral objection. The circumstance was unequivocal: Bashar al-Assad's government, once again defying international law, had used chemical weapons. There was video documenting the attack and substantial agreement among intelligence agencies about Assad's responsibility. The politics were right: Barack Obama failed to act when confronted with a Syrian chemical attack, and now Trump could. The downside was small; it would be a contained response. And it had the added advantage of seeming to stand up to the Russians, Assad's effective partners in Syria, which would score a political point at home.

Bannon, at perhaps his lowest moment of influence in the White House—many still felt that his departure was imminent—was the only voice arguing against a military response. It was a purist's rationale: keep the United States out of intractable problems, and certainly don't increase our involvement in them. He was holding the line against the rising business-as-usual faction, making decisions based on the same set of assumptions, Bannon believed, that had resulted in the Middle East quagmire. It was time to break the standard-response pattern of behavior, represented by the Jarvanka-Powell-Cohn-McMaster alliance. Forget normal—in fact, to Bannon, normal was precisely the problem.

The president had already agreed to McMaster's demand that Bannon be removed from the National Security Council, though the change wouldn't be announced until the following day. But Trump was also drawn to Bannon's strategic view: Why do anything, if you don't have to? Or, why would you do something that doesn't actually get you anything? Since taking office, the president had been developing an intuitive national security view: keep as many despots who might otherwise screw you as happy as possible. A self-styled strongman, he was also a fundamental appeaser. In this instance, then, why cross the Russians?

By the afternoon, the national security team was experiencing a sense of rising panic: the president, in their view, didn't seem to be quite registering the situation. Bannon wasn't helping. His hyperrationalist approach obviously appealed to the not-always-rational president. A chemical attack didn't change the circumstances on the ground, Bannon argued; besides, there had been far worse attacks with far more casualties than this one. If you were looking for broken children, you could find them anywhere. Why these broken children?

The president was not a debater—well, not in any Socratic sense. Nor was he in any conventional sense a decision maker. And certainly he was not a student of foreign policy views and options. But this was nevertheless turning into a genuine philosophical face-off.

"Do nothing" had long been viewed as an unacceptable position of helplessness by American foreign policy experts. The instinct to do something was driven by the desire to prove you were not limited to nothing. You couldn't do nothing and show strength. But Bannon's approach was very much "A pox on all your houses," it was not our mess, and judging by all recent evidence, no good would come of trying to help clean it up. That effort would cost military lives with no military reward. Bannon, believing in the need for a radical shift in foreign policy, was proposing a new doctrine: Fuck 'em. This iron-fisted isolationism appealed to the president's transactional self: What was in it for us (or for him)?

Hence the urgency to get Bannon off the National Security Council. The curious thing is that in the beginning he was thought to be much more reasonable than Michael Flynn, with his fixation on Iran as the source of all evil. Bannon was supposed to babysit Flynn. But Bannon, quite to Kushner's shock, had not just an isolationist worldview but an apocalyptic one. Much of the world would burn and there was nothing you could do about it.

The announcement of Bannon's removal was made the day after the attack. That in itself was a rather remarkable accomplishment on the part of the moderates. In little more than two months, Trump's radical, if not screwball, national security leadership had been replaced by so-called reasonable people.

The job was now to bring the president into this circle of reason.

* * *

As the day wore on, both Ivanka Trump and Dina Powell were united in their determination to persuade the president to react . . . normally. At the very minimum, an absolute condemnation of the use of chemical weapons, a set of sanctions, and, ideally, a military response—although not a big one. None of this was in any way exceptional. Which was sort of the point: it was critical not to respond in a radical, destabilizing way—including a radical nonresponse.

Kushner was by now complaining to his wife that her father just didn't get it. It had even been difficult to get a consensus on releasing a firm statement about the unacceptability of the use of chemical weapons at the noon press briefing. To both Kushner and McMaster it seemed obvious that the president was more annoyed about having to think about the attack than by the attack itself.

Finally, Ivanka told Dina they needed to show the president a different kind of presentation. Ivanka had long ago figured out how to make successful pitches to her father. You had to push his enthusiasm buttons. He may be a businessman, but numbers didn't do it for him. He was not a spreadsheet jockey—his numbers guys dealt with spreadsheets. He liked big names. He liked the big picture—he liked *literal* big pictures. He liked to see it. He liked "impact."

But in one sense, the military, the intelligence community, and the White House's national security team remained behind the times. Theirs was a data world rather than a picture world. As it happened, the attack on Khan Sheikhoun had produced a wealth of visual evidence. Bannon might be right that this attack was no more mortal than countless others, but by focusing on this one and curating the visual proof, this atrocity became singular.

Late that afternoon, Ivanka and Dina created a presentation that Bannon, in disgust, characterized as pictures of kids foaming at the mouth.

When the two women showed the presentation to the president, he went through it several times. He seemed mesmerized.

Watching the president's response, Bannon saw Trumpism melting before his eyes. Trump—despite his visceral resistance to the establishment ass-covering and standard-issue foreign policy expertise that had pulled the country into hopeless wars—was suddenly putty. After seeing all the horrifying photos, he immediately adopted a completely conventional point of view: it seemed inconceivable to him that we couldn't do something.

That evening, the president described the pictures in a call to a friend—the foam, all that foam. *These are just kids.* He usually displayed a consistent contempt for anything but overwhelming military response; now he expressed a sudden, wide-eyed interest in all kinds of other military options.

On Wednesday, April 5, Trump received a briefing that outlined multiple options for how to respond. But again McMaster burdened him with detail. He quickly became frustrated, feeling that he was being manipulated.

The following day, the president and several of his top aides flew to Florida for a meeting with the Chinese president, Xi Jinping—a meeting organized by Kushner with the help of Henry Kissinger. While aboard Air Force One, he held a tightly choreographed meeting of the National Security Council, tying into the staff on the ground. By this point, the decision about how to respond to the chemical attack had already been made: the military would launch a Tomahawk cruise missile strike at Al Shayrat airfield. After a final round of discussion, while on board, the president, almost ceremonially, ordered the strike for the next day.

With the meeting over and the decision made, Trump, in a buoyant mood, came back to chat with reporters traveling with him on Air Force One. In a teasing fashion, he declined to say what he planned to do about Syria. An hour later, Air Force One landed and the president was hustled to Mar-a-Lago.

The Chinese president and his wife arrived for dinner shortly after five o'clock and were greeted by a military guard on the Mar-a-Lago driveway. With Ivanka supervising arrangements, virtually the entire White House senior staff attended.

During a dinner of Dover sole, haricots verts, and thumbelina carrots—Kushner seated with the Chinese first couple, Bannon at the end of the table—the attack on Al Shayrat airfield was launched.

Shortly before ten, the president, reading straight off the teleprompter, announced that the mission had been completed. Dina Powell arranged a for-posterity photo of the president with his advisers and national security team in the makeshift situation room at Mar-a-Lago. She was the only woman in the room. Steve Bannon glowered from his seat at the table, revolted by the stagecraft and the "phoniness of the fucking thing."

It was a cheerful and relieved Trump who mingled with his guests among the palm trees and mangroves. "That was a big one," he confided to a friend. His national security staff were even more relieved. The unpredictable president seemed almost predictable. The unmanageable president, manageable.

15

MEDIA

On April 19, Bill O'Reilly, the Fox anchor and the biggest star in cable news, was pushed out by the Murdoch family over charges of sexual harassment. This was a continuation of the purge at the network that had begun nine months before with the firing of its chief, Roger Ailes. Fox achieved its ultimate political influence with the election of Donald Trump, yet now the future of the network seemed held in a peculiar Murdoch family limbo between conservative father and liberal sons.

A few hours after the O'Reilly announcement, Ailes, from his new oceanfront home in Palm Beach—precluded by his separation agreement with Fox from any efforts to compete with it for eighteen months—sent an emissary into the West Wing with a question for Steve Bannon: *O'Reilly and Hannity are in, what about you?* Ailes, in secret, had been plotting his comeback with a new conservative network. Currently in internal exile inside the White House, Bannon—"the next Ailes"—was all ears.

This was not just the plotting of ambitious men, seeking both opportunity and revenge; the idea for a new network was also driven by an urgent sense that the Trump phenomenon was about, as much as anything else, right-wing media. For twenty years, Fox had honed its populist message: liberals were stealing and ruining the country. Then, just at the moment that many liberals—including Rupert Murdoch's sons, who were increasingly in control of their father's company—had begun to believe that the Fox audience was beginning to age out, with its anti-gay-marriage, anti-abortion, anti-immigrant social message, which seemed too hoary for younger Republicans, along came Breitbart News. Breitbart not only spoke to a much younger right-wing audience—here Bannon felt he was as much in tune with this audience as Ailes was with his—but it had turned this audience into a huge army of digital activists (or social media trolls).

As right-wing media had fiercely coalesced around Trump—readily excusing all the ways he might contradict the traditional conservative ethos—mainstream media had become as fiercely resistant. The country was divided as much by media as by politics. Media was the avatar of politics. A sidelined Ailes was eager to get back in the game. This was his natural playing field: (1) Trump's election proved the power of a significantly smaller but more dedicated electoral base—just as, in cable television terms, a smaller hardcore base was more valuable than a bigger, less committed one; (2) this meant an inverse dedication by an equally small circle of passionate enemies; (3) hence, there would be blood.

If Bannon was as finished as he appeared in the White House, this was his opportunity, too. Indeed, the problem with Bannon's $1.5 million a year Internetcentric Breitbart News was that it couldn't be monetized or scaled up in a big way, but with O'Reilly and Hannity on board, there could be television riches fueled by, into the foreseeable future, a new Trump-inspired era of right-wing passion and hegemony.

Ailes's message to his would-be protégé was plain: Not just the rise of Trump, but the fall of Fox could be Bannon's moment.

In reply, Bannon let Ailes know that for now, he was trying to hold on to his position in the White House. But yes, the opportunity was obvious.

* * *

Even as O'Reilly's fate was being debated by the Murdochs, Trump, understanding O'Reilly's power and knowing how much O'Reilly's audience overlapped with his own base, had expressed his support and approval—"I don't think Bill did anything wrong. . . . He is a good person," he told the *New York Times*.

But in fact a paradox of the new strength of conservative media was Trump himself. During the campaign, when it suited him, he had turned on Fox. If there were other media opportunities, he took them. (In the recent past, Republicans, particularly in the primary season, paid careful obeisance to Fox over other media outlets.) Trump kept insisting that he was bigger than just conservative media.

In the past month, Ailes, a frequent Trump caller and after-dinner adviser, had all but stopped speaking to the president, piqued by the constant reports that Trump was bad-mouthing him as he praised a newly attentive Murdoch, who had, before the election, only ever ridiculed Trump.

"Men who demand the most loyalty tend to be the least loyal pricks," noted a sardonic Ailes (a man who himself demanded lots of loyalty).

The conundrum was that conservative media saw Trump as its creature, while Trump saw himself as a star, a vaunted and valued product of all media, one climbing ever higher. It was a cult of personality, and he was the personality. He was the most famous man in the world. Everybody loved him—or ought to.

On Trump's part this was, arguably, something of a large misunderstanding about the nature of conservative media. He clearly did not understand that what conservative media elevated, liberal media would necessarily take down. Trump, goaded by Bannon, would continue to do the things that would delight conservative media and incur the wrath of liberal media. That was the program. The more your supporters loved you, the more your antagonists hated you. That's how it was supposed to work. And that's how it was working.

But Trump himself was desperately wounded by his treatment in the mainstream media. He obsessed on every slight until it was overtaken by the next slight. Slights were singled out and replayed again and again, his mood worsening with each replay (he was always rerunning the DVR). Much of the president's daily conversation was a repetitive rundown of what various anchors and hosts had said about him. And he was upset not only when he was attacked, but when the people around him were attacked. But he did not credit their loyalty, or blame himself or the nature of liberal media for the indignities heaped on his staffers; he blamed them and their inability to get good press.

Mainstream media's self-righteousness and contempt for Trump helped provide a tsunami of clicks for right-wing media. But an often raging, self-pitying, tormented president had not gotten this memo, or had failed to comprehend it. He was looking for media love everywhere. In this, Trump quite profoundly seemed unable to distinguish between his political advantage and his personal needs—he thought emotionally, not strategically.

The great value of being president, in his view, was that you're the most famous man in the world, and fame is always venerated and adored by the media. Isn't it? But, confusingly, Trump was president in large part because of his particular talent, conscious or reflexive, to alienate the media, which then turned him into a figure reviled by the media. This was not a dialectical space that was comfortable for an insecure man.

"For Trump," noted Ailes, "the media represented power, much more so than politics, and he wanted the attention and respect of its most powerful men. Donald and I were really quite good friends for more than 25 years, but he would have preferred to be friends with Murdoch, who thought he was a moron—at least until he became president."

* * *

The White House Correspondents' Dinner was set for April 29, the one hundredth day of the Trump administration. The annual dinner, once an insiders' event, had become an opportunity for media organizations to promote themselves by recruiting celebrities—most of whom had nothing to do with journalism or politics—to sit at their tables. This had resulted in a notable Trump humiliation when, in 2011, Barack Obama singled out Trump for particular mockery. In Trump lore, this was the insult that pushed him to make the 2016 run.

Not long after the Trump team's arrival in the White House, the Correspondents' Dinner became a cause for worry. On a winter afternoon in Kellyanne Conway's upstairs West Wing office, Conway and Hope Hicks engaged in a pained discussion about what to do.

The central problem was that the president was neither inclined to make fun of himself, nor particularly funny himself—at least not, in Conway's description, "in that kind of humorous way."

George W. Bush had famously resisted the Correspondents' Dinner and suffered greatly at it, but he had prepped extensively, and every year he pulled out an acceptable performance. But neither woman, confiding their concerns around the small table in Conway's office to a journalist they regarded as sympathetic, thought Trump had a realistic chance of making the dinner anything like a success.

"He doesn't appreciate cruel humor," said Conway.

"His style is more old-fashioned," said Hicks.

Both women, clearly seeing the Correspondents' Dinner as an intractable problem, kept characterizing the event as "unfair," which, more generally, is how they characterized the media's view of Trump. "He's unfairly portrayed." "They don't give him the benefit of the doubt." "He's just not treated the way other presidents have been treated."

The burden here for Conway and Hicks was their understanding that the president did not see the media's lack of regard for him as part of a political divide on which he stood on a particular side. Instead, he perceived it as a deep personal attack on him: for entirely unfair reasons, ad hominem reasons, the media just did not like him. Ridiculed him. Cruelly. Why?

The journalist, trying to offer some comfort, told the two women there was a rumor going around that Graydon Carter—the editor of *Vanity Fair* and host of one of the most important parties of the Correspondents' Dinner weekend, and, for decades, one of Trump's key tormentors in the media—was shortly going to be pushed out of the magazine.

"Really?" said Hicks, jumping up. "Oh my God, can I tell him? Would that be okay? He'll want to know this." She headed quickly downstairs to the Oval Office.

* * *

Curiously, Conway and Hicks each portrayed a side of the president's alter ego media problem. Conway was the bitter antagonist, the mud-in-your-eye messenger who reliably sent the media into paroxysms of outrage against the president. Hicks was the confidante ever trying to get the president a break and some good ink in the only media he really cared about—the media that most hated him. But as different as they were in their media functions and temperament, both women had achieved remarkable influence in the administration by serving as the key lieutenants responsible for addressing the president's most pressing concern, his media reputation.

While Trump was in most ways a conventional misogynist, in the workplace he was much closer to women than to men. The former he confided in, the latter he held at arm's length. He liked and needed his office wives, and he trusted them with his most important personal issues. Women, according to Trump, were simply more loyal and trustworthy than men. Men might be more forceful and competent, but they were also more likely to have their own agendas. Women, by their nature, or Trump's version of their nature, were more likely to focus their purpose on a man. A man like Trump.

It wasn't happenstance or just casting balance that his *Apprentice* sidekick was a woman, nor that his daughter Ivanka had become one of his closest confidants. He felt women understood him. Or, the kind of women he liked—positive-outlook, can-do, loyal women, who also looked good—understood him. Everybody who successfully worked for him understood that there was always a subtext of his needs and personal tics that had to be scrupulously attended to; in this, he was not all that different from other highly successful figures, just more so. It would be hard to imagine someone who expected a greater awareness of and more catering to his peculiar whims, rhythms, prejudices, and often inchoate desires. He needed special—extra special—handling. Women, he explained to one friend with something like self-awareness, generally got this more precisely than men. In particular, women who self-selected themselves as tolerant of or oblivious to or amused by or steeled against his casual misogyny and constant sexual subtext—which was somehow, incongruously and often jarringly, matched with paternal regard—got this.

* * *

Kellyanne Conway first met Donald Trump at a meeting of the condo board for the Trump International Hotel, which was directly across the street from the UN and was where, in the early 2000s, she lived with her husband and children. Conway's husband, George, a graduate of Harvard College and Yale Law School, was a partner at the premier corporate mergers and acquisitions firm Wachtell, Lipton, Rosen & Katz. (Though Wachtell was a Democratic-leaning firm, George had played a behind-the-scenes role on the team that represented Paula Jones in her pursuit of Bill Clinton.) In its professional and domestic balance, the Conway family was organized around George's career. Kellyanne's career was a sidelight.

Kellyanne, who in the Trump campaign would use her working-class biography to good effect, grew up in central New Jersey, the daughter of a trucker, raised by a single mother (and, always in her narrative, her grandmother and two unmarried aunts). She went to George Washington law school and afterward interned for Reagan's pollster, Richard Wirthlin. Then she became the assistant to Frank Luntz, a curious figure in the Republican Party, known as much for his television deals and toupee as for his polling acumen. Conway herself began to make appearances on cable TV while working for Luntz.

One virtue of the research and polling business she started in 1995 was that it could adapt to her husband's career. But she never much rose above a midrank presence in Republican political circles, nor did she become more than the also-ran behind Ann Coulter and Laura Ingraham on cable television—which is where Trump first saw her and why he singled her out at the condo board meeting.

In a real sense, however, her advantage was not meeting Trump but being taken up by the Mercers. They recruited Conway in 2015 to work on the Cruz campaign, when Trump was still far from the conservative ideal, and then, in August 2016, inserted her into the Trump campaign.

She understood her role. "I will only ever call you Mr. Trump," she told the candidate with perfect-pitch solemnity when he interviewed her for the job. It was a trope she would repeat in interview after interview—Conway was a catalog of learned lines—a message repeated as much for Trump as for others.

Her title was campaign manager, but that was a misnomer. Bannon was the real manager, and she was the senior pollster. But Bannon shortly replaced her in that role and she was left in what Trump saw as the vastly more important role of cable spokesperson.

Conway seemed to have a convenient On-Off toggle. In private, in the Off position, she seemed to regard Trump as a figure of exhausting exaggeration or even absurdity—or, at least, if you regarded him that way, she seemed to suggest that she might, too. She illustrated her opinion of her boss with a whole series of facial expressions: eyes rolling, mouth agape, head snapping back. But in the On position, she metamorphosed into believer, protector, defender, and handler. Conway is an antifeminist (or, actually, in a complicated ideological somersault, she sees feminists as being antifeminists), ascribing her methods and temperament to her being a wife and mother. She's instinctive and reactive. Hence her role as the ultimate Trump defender: she verbally threw herself in front of any bullet coming his way.

Trump loved her defend-at-all-costs shtick. Conway's appearances were on his schedule to watch live. His was often the first call she got after coming off the air. She channeled Trump: she said exactly the kind of Trump stuff that would otherwise make her put a finger-gun to her head.

After the election—Trump's victory setting off a domestic reordering in the Conway household, and a scramble to get her husband an administration job—Trump assumed she would be his press secretary. "He and my mother," Conway said, "because they both watch a lot of television, thought this was one of the most important jobs." In Conway's version, she turned Trump down or demurred. She kept proposing alternatives in which she would be the key spokesperson but would be more as well. In fact, almost everyone else was maneuvering Trump around his desire to appoint Conway.

Loyalty was Trump's most valued attribute, and in Conway's view her kamikaze-like media defense of the president had earned her a position of utmost primacy in the White House. But in her public persona, she had pushed the boundaries of loyalty too far; she was so hyperbolic that even Trump loyalists found her behavior extreme and were repelled. None were more put off than Jared and Ivanka, who, appalled at the shamelessness of her television appearances, extended this into a larger critique of Conway's vulgarity. When referring to her, they were particularly partial to using the shorthand "nails," a reference to her Cruella de Vil–length manicure treatments.

By mid-February she was already the subject of leaks—many coming from Jared and Ivanka—about how she had been sidelined. She vociferously defended herself, producing a list of television appearances still on her schedule, albeit lesser ones. But she also had a teary scene with Trump in the Oval Office, offering to resign if the president had lost faith in her. Almost invariably, when confronted with self-abnegation, Trump offered copious reassurances. "You will always have a place in my administration," he told her. "You will be here for eight years."

But she had indeed been sidelined, reduced to second-rate media, to being a designated emissary to right-wing groups, and left out of any meaningful decision making. This she blamed on the media, a scourge that further united her in self-pity with Donald Trump. In fact, her relationship with the president deepened as they bonded over their media wounds.

* * *

Hope Hicks, then age twenty-six, was the campaign's first hire. She knew the president vastly better than Conway did, and she understood that her most important media function was not to be in the media.

Hicks grew up in Greenwich, Connecticut. Her father was a PR executive who now worked for the Glover Park Group, the Democratic-leaning communications and political consulting firm; her mother was a former staffer for a democratic congressman. An indifferent student, Hicks went to Southern Methodist University and then did some modeling before getting a PR job. She first went to work for Matthew Hiltzik, who ran a small New York–based PR firm and was noted for his ability to work with high-maintenance clients, including the movie producer Harvey Weinstein (later pilloried for years of sexual harassment and abuse—accusations that Hiltzik and his staff had long helped protect him from) and the television personality Katie Couric. Hiltzik, an active Democrat who had worked for Hillary Clinton, also represented Ivanka Trump's fashion line; Hicks started to do some work for the account and then joined Ivanka's company full time. In 2015, Ivanka seconded her to her father's campaign; as the campaign progressed, moving from novelty project to political factor to juggernaut, Hicks's family increasingly, and incredulously, viewed her as rather having been taken captive. (Following the Trump victory and her move into the White House, her friends and intimates talked with great concern about what kind of therapies and recuperation she would need after her tenure was finally over.)

Over the eighteen months of the campaign, the traveling group usually consisted of the candidate, Hicks, and the campaign manager, Corey Lewandowski. In time, she became—in addition to an inadvertent participant in history, about which she was quite as astonished as anyone—a kind of Stepford factotum, as absolutely dedicated to and tolerant of Mr. Trump as anyone who had ever worked for him.

Shortly after Lewandowski, with whom Hicks had an on-and-off romantic relationship, was fired in June 2016 for clashing with Trump family members, Hicks sat in Trump Tower with Trump and his sons, worrying about Lewandowski's treatment in the press and wondering aloud how she might help him. Trump, who otherwise seemed to treat Hicks in a protective and even paternal way, looked up and said, "Why? You've already done enough for him. You're the best piece of tail he'll ever have," sending Hicks running from the room.

As new layers began to form around Trump, first as nominee and then as president-elect, Hicks continued playing the role of his personal PR woman. She would remain his constant shadow and the person with the best access to him. "Have you spoken to Hope?" were among the words most frequently uttered in the West Wing.

Hicks, sponsored by Ivanka and ever loyal to her, was in fact thought of as Trump's real daughter, while Ivanka was thought of as his real wife. More functionally, but as elementally, Hicks was the president's chief media handler. She worked by the president's side, wholly separate from the White House's forty-person-strong communications office. The president's personal message and image were entrusted to her—or, more accurately, she was the president's agent in retailing that message and image, which he trusted to no one but himself. Together they formed something of a freelance operation.

Without any particular politics of her own, and, with her New York PR background, quite looking down on the right-wing press, she was the president's official liaison to the mainstream media. The president had charged her with the ultimate job: a good write-up in the *New York Times*.

That, in the president's estimation, had yet failed to happen, "but Hope tries and tries," the president said.

On more than one occasion, after a day—one of the countless days—of particularly bad notices, the president greeted her, affectionately, with "You must be the world's worst PR person."

* * *

In the early days of the transition, with Conway out of the running for the press secretary job, Trump became determined to find a "star." The conservative radio host Laura Ingraham, who had spoken at the convention, was on the list, as was Ann Coulter. Fox Business's Maria Bartiromo was also under consideration. (This was television, the president-elect said, and it ought to be a good-looking woman.) When none of those ideas panned out, the job was offered to Fox News's Tucker Carlson, who turned it down.

But there was a counterview: the press secretary ought to be the opposite of a star. In fact, the entire press operation ought to be downgraded. If the press was the enemy, why pander to it, why give it more visibility? This was fundamental Bannonism: stop thinking you can somehow get along with your enemies.

As the debate went on, Priebus pushed for one of his deputies at the Republican National Committee, Sean Spicer, a well-liked forty-five-year-old Washington political professional with a string of posts on the Hill in the George W. Bush years as well as with the RNC. Spicer, hesitant to take the job, kept anxiously posing the question to colleagues in the Washington swamp: "If I do this, will I ever be able to work again?"

There were conflicting answers.

During the transition, many members of Trump's team came to agree with Bannon that their approach to White House press management ought to be to push it off—and the longer the arm's length the better. For the press, this initiative, or rumors of it, became another sign of the incoming administration's antipress stance and its systematic efforts to cut off the information supply. In truth, the suggestions about moving the briefing room away from the White House, or curtailing the briefing schedule, or limiting broadcast windows or press pool access, were variously discussed by other incoming administrations. In her husband's White House, Hillary Clinton had been a proponent of limiting press access.

It was Donald Trump who was not able to relinquish this proximity to the press and the stage in his own house. He regularly berated Spicer for his ham-handed performances, often giving his full attention to them. His response to Spicer's briefings was part of his continuing belief that nobody could work the media like he could, that somehow he had been stuck with an F-Troop communications team that was absent charisma, magnetism, and proper media connections.

Trump's pressure on Spicer—a constant stream of directorial castigation and instruction that reliably rattled the press secretary—helped turn the briefings into a can't-miss train wreck. Meanwhile, the real press operation had more or less devolved into a set of competing press organizations within the White House.

There was Hope Hicks and the president, living in what other West Wingers characterized as an alternative universe in which the mainstream media would yet discover the charm and wisdom of Donald Trump. Where past presidents might have spent portions of their day talking about the needs, desires, and points of leverage among various members of Congress, the president and Hicks spent a great deal of time talking about a fixed cast of media personalities, trying to second-guess the real agendas and weak spots among cable anchors and producers and *Times* and *Post* reporters.

Often the focus of this otherworldly ambition was directed at *Times* reporter Maggie Haberman. Haberman's front-page beat at the paper, which might be called the "weirdness of Donald Trump" beat, involved producing vivid tales of eccentricities, questionable behavior, and shit the president says, told in a knowing, deadpan style. Beyond acknowledging that Trump was a boy from Queens yet in awe of the *Times*, nobody in the West Wing could explain why he and Hicks would so often turn to Haberman for what would so reliably be a mocking and hurtful portrayal. There was some feeling that Trump was returning to scenes of past success: the *Times* might be against him, but Haberman had worked at the *New York Post* for many years. "She's very professional," Conway said, speaking in defense of the president and trying to justify Haberman's extraordinary access. But however intent he remained on getting good ink in the *Times*, the president saw Haberman as "mean and horrible." And yet, on a near-weekly basis, he and Hicks plotted when next to have the *Times* come in.

* * *

Kushner had his personal press operation and Bannon had his. The leaking culture had become so open and overt—most of the time everybody could identify everybody else's leaks—that it was now formally staffed.

Kushner's Office of American Innovation employed, as its spokesperson, Josh Raffel, who, like Hicks, came out of Matthew Hiltzik's PR shop. Raffel, a Democrat who had been working in Hollywood, acted as Kushner and his wife's personal rep—not least of all because the couple felt that Spicer, owing his allegiance to Priebus, was not aggressively representing them. This was explicit. "Josh is Jared's Hope," was his internal West Wing job description.

Raffel coordinated all of Kushner and Ivanka's personal press, though there was more of this for Ivanka than for Kushner. But, more importantly, Raffel coordinated all of Kushner's substantial leaking, or, as it were, his off-the-record briefings and guidance—no small part of it against Bannon. Kushner, who with great conviction asserted that he never leaked, in part justified his press operation as a defense against Bannon's press operation.

Bannon's "person," Alexandra Preate—a witty conservative socialite partial to champagne—had previously represented Breitbart News and other conservative figures like CNBC's Larry Kudlow, and was close friends with Rebekah Mercer. In a relationship that nobody seemed quite able to explain, she handled all of Bannon's press "outreach" but was not employed by the White House, although she maintained an office, or at least an officelike presence, there. The point was clear: her client was Bannon and not the Trump administration.

Bannon, to Jared and Ivanka's continued alarm, had unique access to Breitbart's significant abilities to change the right-wing mood and focus. Bannon insisted he had cut his ties to his former colleagues at Breitbart, but that strained everybody's credulity—and everybody figured nobody was supposed to believe it. Rather, everybody was supposed to fear it.

There was, curiously, general agreement in the West Wing that Donald Trump, the media president, had one of the most dysfunctional communication operations in modern White House history. Mike Dubke, a Republican PR operative who was hired as White House communications director, was, by all estimations, from the first day on his way out the door. In the end he lasted only three months.

* * *

The White House Correspondents' Dinner rose, as much as any other challenge for the new president and his team, as a test of his abilities. He wanted to do it. He was certain that the power of his charm was greater than the rancor that he bore this audience—or that they bore him.

He recalled his 2015 *Saturday Night Live* appearance—which, in his view, was entirely successful. In fact, he had refused to prepare, had kept saying he would "improvise," no problem. Comedians don't actually improvise, he was told; it's all scripted and rehearsed. But this counsel had only marginal effect.

Almost nobody except the president himself thought he could pull off the Correspondents' Dinner. His staff was terrified that he would die up there in front of a seething and contemptuous audience. Though he could dish it out, often very harshly, no one thought he could take it. Still, the president seemed eager to appear at the event, if casual about it, too—with Hicks, ordinarily encouraging his every impulse, trying not to.

Bannon pressed the symbolic point: the president should not be seen currying the favor of his enemies, or trying to entertain them. The media was a much better whipping boy than it was a partner in crime. The Bannon principle, the steel stake in the ground, remained: don't bend, don't accommodate, don't meet halfway. And in the end, rather than implying that Trump did not have the talent and wit to move this crowd, that was a much better way to persuade the president that he should not appear at the dinner.

When Trump finally agreed to forgo the event, Conway, Hicks, and virtually everybody else in the West Wing breathed a lot easier.

* * *

Shortly after five o'clock on the one hundredth day of his presidency—a particularly muggy one—while twenty-five hundred or so members of news organizations and their friends gathered at the Washington Hilton for the White House Correspondents' Dinner, the president left the West Wing for Marine One, which was soon en route to Andrews Air Force Base. Accompanying him were Steve Bannon, Stephen Miller, Reince Priebus, Hope Hicks, and Kellyanne Conway. Vice President Pence and his wife joined the group at Andrews for the brief flight on Air Force One to Harrisburg, Pennsylvania, where the president would give a speech. During the flight, crab cakes were served, and *Face the Nation*'s John Dickerson was granted a special hundredth-day interview.

The first Harrisburg event was held at a factory that manufactured landscaping and gardening tools, where the president closely inspected a line of colorful wheelbarrows. The next event, where the speech would be delivered, was at a rodeo arena in the Farm Show Complex and Expo Center.

And that was the point of this little trip. It had been designed both to remind the rest of the country that the president was not just another phony baloney in a tux like those at the White House Correspondents' Dinner (this somehow presupposed that the president's base cared about or was even aware of the event) and to keep the president's mind off the fact that he was missing the dinner.

But the president kept asking for updates on the jokes.

16

COMEY

"It's impossible to make him understand you can't stop these investigations," said Roger Ailes in early May, a frustrated voice in the Trump kitchen cabinet. "In the old days, you could say leave it alone. Now you say leave it alone and you're the one who gets investigated. He can't get this through his head."

In fact, as various members of the billionaires' cabinet tried to calm down the president during their evening phone calls, they were largely egging him on by expressing deep concern about his DOJ and FBI peril. Many of Trump's wealthy friends saw themselves as having particular DOJ expertise. In their own careers, they had had enough issues with the Justice Department to prompt them to develop DOJ relationships and sources, and now they were always up on DOJ gossip. Flynn was going to throw him in the soup. Manafort was going to roll. And it wasn't just Russia. It was Atlantic City. And Mar-a-Lago. And Trump SoHo.

Both Chris Christie and Rudy Giuliani—each a self-styled expert on the DOJ and the FBI, and ever assuring Trump of their inside sources—encouraged him to take the view that the DOJ was resolved against him; it was all part of a holdover Obama plot.

Even more urgent was Charlie Kushner's fear, channeled through his son and daughter-in-law, that the Kushner family's dealings were getting wrapped up in the pursuit of Trump. Leaks in January had put the kibosh on the Kushners' deal with the Chinese financial colossus Anbang Insurance Group to refinance the family's large debt in one of its major real estate holdings, 666 Fifth Avenue. At the end of April, the *New York Times*, supplied with leaks from the DOJ, linked the Kushner business in a front-page article to Beny Steinmetz—an Israeli diamond, mining, and real estate billionaire with Russian ties who was under chronic investigation around the world. (The Kushner position was not helped by the fact that the president had been gleefully telling multiple people that Jared could solve the Middle East problem because the Kushners knew all the best people in Israel.) During the first week of May, the *Times* and the *Washington Post* covered the Kushner family's supposed efforts to attract Chinese investors with the promise of U.S. visas.

"The kids"—Jared and Ivanka—exhibited an increasingly panicked sense that the FBI and DOJ were moving beyond Russian election interference and into finances. "Ivanka is terrified," said a satisfied Bannon.

Trump turned to suggesting to his billionaire chorus that he fire FBI director Comey. He had raised this idea many times before, but always, seemingly, at the same time and in the same context that he brought up the possibility of firing everybody. *Should I fire Bannon? Should I fire Reince? Should I fire McMaster? Should I fire Spicer? Should I fire Tillerson?* This ritual was, everyone understood, more a pretext to a discussion of the power he held than it was, strictly, about personnel decisions. Still, in Trump's poison-the-well fashion, the should-I-fire-so-and-so question, and any consideration of it by any of the billionaires, was translated into agreement, as in: *Carl Icahn thinks I should fire Comey (or Bannon, or Priebus, or McMaster, or Tillerson).*

His daughter and son-in-law, their urgency compounded by Charlie Kushner's concern, encouraged him, arguing that the once possibly charmable Comey was now a dangerous and uncontrollable player whose profit would inevitably be their loss. When Trump got wound up about something, Bannon noted, someone was usually winding him up. The family focus of discussion—insistent, almost frenzied—became wholly about Comey's ambition. He would rise by damaging them. And the drumbeat grew.

"That son of a bitch is going to try to fire the head of the FBI," said Ailes.

During the first week of May, the president had a ranting meeting with Sessions and his deputy Rod Rosenstein. It was a humiliating meeting for both men, with Trump insisting they couldn't control their own people and pushing them to find a reason to fire Comey—in effect, he blamed them for not having come up with that reason months ago. (It was their fault, he implied, that Comey hadn't been fired right off the bat.)

Also that week, there was a meeting that included the president, Jared and Ivanka, Bannon, Priebus, and White House counsel Don McGahn. It was a closed-door meeting—widely noted because it was unusual for the Oval Office door ever to be closed.

All the Democrats hate Comey, said the president, expressing his certain and self-justifying view. *All the FBI agents hate him, too—75 percent of them can't stand him.* (This was a number that Kushner had somehow alighted on, and Trump had taken it up.) *Firing Comey will be a huge fundraising advantage*, declared the president, a man who almost never talked about fundraising.

McGahn tried to explain that in fact Comey himself was not running the Russia investigation, that without Comey the investigation would proceed anyway. McGahn, the lawyer whose job was necessarily to issue cautions, was a frequent target of Trump rages. Typically these would begin as a kind of exaggeration or acting and then devolve into the real thing: uncontrollable, vein-popping, ugly-face, tantrum stuff. It got primal. Now the president's denunciations focused in a vicious fury on McGahn and his cautions about Comey.

"Comey was a rat," repeated Trump. There were rats everywhere and you had to get rid of them. *John Dean, John Dean*, he repeated. "Do you know what John Dean did to Nixon?"

Trump, who saw history through personalities—people he might have liked or disliked—was a John Dean freak. He went bananas when a now gray and much aged Dean appeared on talk shows to compare the Trump-Russia investigation to Watergate. That would bring the president to instant attention and launch an inevitable talk-back monologue to the screen about loyalty and what people would do for media attention. It might also be accompanied by several revisionist theories Trump had about Watergate and how Nixon had been framed. And always there were rats. A rat was someone who would take you down for his own advantage. If you had a rat, you needed to kill it. And there were rats all around.

(Later, it was Bannon who had to take the president aside and tell him that John Dean had been the White House counsel in the Nixon administration, so maybe it would be a good idea to lighten up on McGahn.)

As the meeting went on, Bannon, from the doghouse and now, in their mutual antipathy to Jarvanka, allied with Priebus, seized the opportunity to make an impassioned case opposing any move against Comey—which was also, as much, an effort to make the case against Jared and Ivanka and their allies, "the geniuses." ("The geniuses" was one of Trump's terms of derision for anybody who might annoy him or think they were smarter than him, and Bannon now appropriated the term and applied it to Trump's family.) Offering forceful and dire warnings, Bannon told the president: "This Russian story is a third-tier story, but you fire Comey and it'll be the biggest story in the world."

By the time the meeting ended, Bannon and Priebus believed they had prevailed. But that weekend, at Bedminster, the president, again listening to the deep dismay of his daughter and son-in-law, built up another head of steam. With Jared and Ivanka, Stephen Miller was also along for the weekend. The weather was bad and the president missed his golf game, dwelling, with Jared, on his Comey fury. It was Jared, in the version told by those outside the Jarvanka circle, that pushed for action, once more winding up his father-in-law. With the president's assent, Kushner, in this version, gave Miller notes on why the FBI director should be fired and asked him to draft a letter that could set out the basis for immediate dismissal. Miller—less than a deft drafting hand—recruited Hicks to help, another person without clearly relevant abilities. (Miller would later be admonished by Bannon for letting himself get tied up, and potentially implicated, in the Comey mess.)

The letter, in the panicky draft assembled by Miller and Hicks, either from Kushner's directions or on instructions directly coming from the president, was an off-the-wall mishmash containing the talking points—Comey's handling of the Hillary Clinton investigation; the assertion (from Kushner) that the FBI itself had turned against Comey; and, the president's key obsession, the fact that Comey wouldn't publicly acknowledge that the president wasn't under investigation—that would form the Trump family's case for firing Comey. That is, everything but the fact that Comey's FBI was investigating the president.

The Kushner side, for its part, bitterly fought back against any characterization of Kushner as the prime mover or mastermind, in effect putting the entire Bedminster letter effort—as well as the determination to get rid of Comey—entirely on the president's head and casting Kushner as passive bystander. (The Kushner side's position was articulated as follows: "Did he [Kushner] support the decision? Yes. Was he told this was happening? Yes. Did he encourage it? No. Was he fighting for it [Comey's ouster] for weeks and months? No. Did he fight [the ouster]? No. Did he say it would go badly? No.")

Horrified, McGahn quashed sending it. Nevertheless, it was passed to Sessions and Rosenstein, who quickly began drafting their own version of what Kushner and the president obviously wanted.

"I knew when he got back he might blow at any moment," said Bannon after the president returned from his Bedminster weekend.

* * *

On Monday morning, May 8, in a meeting in the Oval Office, the president told Priebus and Bannon that he had made his decision: he would fire Director Comey. Both men again made heated pleas against the move, arguing for, at the very least, more discussion. Here was a key technique for managing the president: delay. Rolling something forward likely meant that something else—an equal or greater fiasco—would come along to preempt whatever fiasco was currently at hand. What's more, delay worked advantageously with Trump's attention span; whatever the issue of the moment, he would shortly be on to something else. When the meeting ended, Priebus and Bannon thought they had bought some breathing room.

Later that day, Sally Yates and former director of National Intelligence James Clapper appeared before the Senate Judiciary Committee's Crime and Terrorism subcommittee—and were greeted by a series of furious tweets from the president.

Here was, Bannon saw again, the essential Trump problem. He hopelessly personalized everything. He saw the world in commercial and show business terms: someone else was always trying to one-up you, someone else was always trying to take the limelight. The battle was between you and someone else who wanted what you had. For Bannon, reducing the political world to face-offs and spats belittled the place in history Trump and his administration had achieved. But it also belied the real powers they were up against. Not people—institutions.

To Trump, he was just up against Sally Yates, who was, he steamed, "such a cunt."

Since her firing on January 30, Yates had remained suspiciously quiet. When journalists approached her, she, or her intermediaries, explained that per her lawyers she was shut down on all media. The president believed she was merely lying in wait. In phone calls to friends, he worried about her "plan" and "strategy," and he continued to press his after-dinner sources for what they thought she and Ben Rhodes, Trump's favorite Obama plotter, had "up their sleeves."

For each of his enemies—and, actually, for each of his friends—the issue for him came down, in many ways, to their personal press plan. The media was the battlefield. Trump assumed everybody wanted his or her fifteen minutes and that everybody had a press strategy for when they got them. If you couldn't get press directly for yourself, you became a leaker. There was no happenstance news, in Trump's view. All news was manipulated and designed, planned and planted. All news was to some extent fake—he understood that very well, because he himself had faked it so many times in his career. This was why he had so naturally cottoned to the "fake news" label. "I've made stuff up forever, and they always print it," he bragged.

The return of Sally Yates, with her appointment before the Senate Judiciary Committee, marked the beginning, Trump believed, of a sustained and well-organized media rollout for her. (His press view was confirmed later in May by a lavish, hagiographic profile of Yates in the *New Yorker*.

"How long do you think she was planning this?" he asked, rhetorically. "You know she was. It's her payday.") "Yates is only famous because of me," the president complained bitterly. "Otherwise, who is she? Nobody."

In front of Congress that Monday morning, Yates delivered a cinematic performance—cool, temperate, detailed, selfless—compounding Trump's fury and agitation.

* * *

On the morning of Tuesday, May 9, with the president still fixated on Comey, and with Kushner and his daughter behind him, Priebus again moved to delay: "There's a right way to do this and a wrong way to do this," he told the president. "We don't want him learning about this on television. I'm going to say this one last time: this is not the right way to do this. If you want to do this, the right way is to have him in and have a conversation. This is the decent way and the professional way." Once more, the president seemed to calm down and become more focused on the necessary process.

But that was a false flag. In fact, the president, in order to avoid embracing conventional process—or, for that matter, any real sense of cause and effect—merely eliminated everybody else from *his* process. For most of the day, almost no one would know that he had decided to take matters into his own hands. In presidential annals, the firing of FBI director James Comey may be the most consequential move ever made by a modern president acting entirely on his own.

As it happened, the Justice Department—Attorney General Sessions and Deputy Attorney General Rod Rosenstein—were, independent of the president's own course, preparing their case against Comey. They would take the Bedminster line and blame Comey for errors of his handling of the Clinton email mess—a problematic charge, because if that was truly the issue, why wasn't Comey dismissed on that basis as soon as the Trump administration took office? But in fact, quite regardless of the Sessions and Rosenstein case, the president had determined to act on his own.

Jared and Ivanka were urging the president on, but even they did not know that the axe would shortly fall. Hope Hicks, Trump's steadfast shadow, who otherwise knew everything the president thought—not least because he was helpless not to express it out loud—didn't know. Steve Bannon, however much he worried that the president might blow, didn't know. His chief of staff didn't know. And his press secretary didn't know. The president, on the verge of starting a war with the FBI, the DOJ, and many in Congress, was going rogue.

At some point that afternoon Trump told his daughter and son-in-law about his plan. They immediately became coconspirators and firmly shut out any competing advice.

Eerily, it was a notably on-time and unruffled day in the West Wing. Mark Halperin, the political reporter and campaign chronicler, was waiting in the reception area for Hope Hicks, who fetched him a bit before 5:00 p.m. Fox's Howard Kurtz was there, too, waiting for his appointment with Sean Spicer. And Reince Priebus's assistant had just been out to tell his five o'clock appointment it would be only a few more minutes.

Just before five, in fact, the president, having not too long before notified McGahn of his intention, pulled the trigger. Trump's personal security guard, Keith Schiller, delivered the termination letter to Comey's office at the FBI just after five o'clock. The letter's second sentence included the words "You are hereby terminated and removed from office, effective immediately."

Shortly thereafter, most of the West Wing staff, courtesy of an erroneous report from Fox News, was for a brief moment under the impression that Comey had resigned. Then, in a series of information synapses throughout the offices of the West Wing, it became clear what had actually happened.

"So next it's a special prosecutor!" said Priebus in disbelief, to no one in particular, when he learned shortly before five o'clock what was happening.

Spicer, who would later be blamed for not figuring out how to positively spin the Comey firing, had only minutes to process it.

Not only had the decision been made by the president with almost no consultation except that of his inner family circle, but the response, and explanation, and even legal justifications, were also almost exclusively managed by him and his family. Rosenstein and Sessions's parallel rationale for the firing was shoehorned in at the last minute, at which point, at Kushner's direction, the initial explanation of Comey's firing became that the president had acted solely on their recommendation. Spicer was forced to deliver this unlikely rationale, as was the vice president. But this pretense unraveled almost immediately, not least because most everyone in the West Wing, wanting nothing to do with the decision to fire Comey, was helping to unravel it.

The president, along with his family, stood on one side of the White House divide, while the staff—mouths agape, disbelieving and speechless—stood on the other.

But the president seemed also to want it known that he, aroused and dangerous, personally took down Comey. Forget Rosenstein and Sessions, it *was* personal. It was a powerful president and a vengeful one, in every way galled and affronted by those in pursuit of him, and determined to protect his family, who were in turn determined to have him protect them.

"The daughter will take down the father," said Bannon, in a Shakespearian mood.

Within the West Wing there was much replaying of alternative scenarios. If you wanted to get rid of Comey, there were surely politic ways of doing it—which had in fact been suggested to Trump. (A curious one—an idea that later would seem ironic—was to get rid of General Kelly at Homeland Security and move Comey into that job.) But the point really was that Trump had wanted to confront and humiliate the FBI director. Cruelty was a Trump attribute.

The firing had been carried out publicly and in front of his family—catching Comey entirely off guard as he gave a speech in California. Then the president had further personalized the blow with an ad hominem attack on the director, suggesting that the FBI itself was on Trump's side and that it, too, had only contempt for Comey.

The next day, as though to further emphasize and delight in both the insult and his personal impunity, the president met with Russian bigwigs in the Oval Office, including Russia's Ambassador Kislyak, the very focus of much of the Trump-Russia investigation. To the Russians he said: "I just fired the head of the FBI. He was crazy, a real nut job. I faced great pressure because of Russia. That's taken off." Then, to boot, he revealed information supplied to the United States by Israel from its agent in place in Syria about ISIS using laptops to smuggle bombs onto airlines—revealing enough information to compromise the Israeli agent. (This incident did not help Trump's reputation in intelligence circles, since, in spycraft, human sources are to be protected above all other secrets.)

"It's Trump," said Bannon. "He thinks he can fire the FBI."

* * *

Trump believed that firing Comey would make him a hero. Over the next forty-eight hours he spun his side to various friends. It was simple: he had stood up to the FBI. He proved that he was willing to take on the state power. The outsider against the insiders. After all, that's why he was elected.

At some level he had a point. One reason presidents don't fire the director of the FBI is that they fear the consequences. It's the Hoover syndrome: any president can be hostage to what the FBI knows, and a president who treats the FBI with something less than deference does so at his own peril. But this president had stood up to the feds. One man against the unaccountable power that the left had long railed against—and that more recently the right had taken as a Holy Grail issue, too. "Everybody should be rooting for me," the president said to friends, more and more plaintively.

Here was another peculiar Trump attribute: an inability to see his actions the way most others saw them. Or to fully appreciate how people expected him to behave. The notion of the presidency as an institutional and political concept, with an emphasis on ritual and propriety and semiotic messaging—statesmanship—was quite beyond him.

Inside the government, the response to Comey's firing was a kind of bureaucratic revulsion. Bannon had tried to explain to Trump the essential nature of career government officials, people whose comfort zone was in their association with hegemonic organizations and a sense of a higher cause—they were different, very different, from those who sought individual distinction. Whatever else Comey might be, he was first and foremost a bureaucrat. Casting him ignominiously out was yet another Trump insult to the bureaucracy.

Rod Rosenstein, the author of the letter that ostensibly provided the justification for firing Comey, now stood in the line of fire. The fifty-two-year-old Rosenstein, who, in rimless glasses, seemed to style himself as a bureaucrat's bureaucrat, was the longest-serving U.S. attorney in the country. He lived within the system, all by the book, his highest goal seeming to be to have people say he did things by the book. He was a straight shooter—and he wanted everyone to know it.

All this was undermined by Trump—trashed, even. The brow-beating and snarling president had hectored the country's two top law enforcement officials into an ill-considered or, at the very least, an ill-timed indictment of the director of the FBI. Rosenstein was already feeling used and abused. And then he was shown to have been tricked, too. He was a dupe.

The president had forced Rosenstein and Sessions to construct a legal rationale, yet then he could not even maintain the bureaucratic pretense of following it. Having enlisted Rosenstein and Sessions in his plot, Trump now exposed their efforts to present a reasonable and aboveboard case as a sham—and, arguably, a plan to obstruct justice. The president made it perfectly clear that he hadn't fired the director of the FBI because he did Hillary wrong; he fired Comey because the FBI was too aggressively investigating him and his administration.

Hyper-by-the-book Rod Rosenstein—heretofore the quintessential apolitical player—immediately became, in Washington eyes, a hopeless Trump tool. But Rosenstein's revenge was deft, swift, overwhelming, and (of course) by the book.

Given the decision of the attorney general to recuse himself from the Russia investigation, it fell under the authority of the deputy attorney general to determine whether a conflict existed—that is, whether the deputy attorney general, because of self-interest, might not be able to act objectively—and if, in his sole discretion, he judged a conflict to exist, to appoint an outside special counsel with wide powers and responsibilities to conduct an investigation and, potentially, a prosecution.

On May 17, twelve days after FBI director Comey was fired, without consulting the White House or the attorney general, Rosenstein appointed former FBI director Robert Mueller to oversee the investigation of Trump's, his campaign's, and his staff's ties to Russia. If Michael Flynn had recently become the most powerful man in Washington for what he might reveal about the president, now Mueller arguably assumed that position because he had the power to make Flynn, and all other assorted Trump cronies and flunkies, squeal.

Rosenstein, of course, perhaps with some satisfaction, understood that he had delivered what could be a mortal blow to the Trump presidency.

Bannon, shaking his head in wonder about Trump, commented drily: "He doesn't necessarily see what's coming."

17

ABROAD AND AT HOME

On May 12, Roger Ailes was scheduled to return to New York from Palm Beach to meet with Peter Thiel, an early and lonely Trump supporter in Silicon Valley who had become increasingly astonished by Trump's unpredictability. Ailes and Thiel, both worried that Trump could bring Trumpism down, were set to discuss the funding and launch of a new cable news network. Thiel would pay for it and Ailes would bring O'Reilly, Hannity, himself, and maybe Bannon to it.

But two days before the meeting, Ailes fell in his bathroom and hit his head. Before slipping into a coma, he told his wife not to reschedule the meeting with Thiel. A week later, Ailes, that singular figure in the march from Nixon's silent majority to Reagan's Democrats to Trump's passionate base, was dead.

His funeral in Palm Beach on May 20 was quite a study in the currents of right-wing ambivalence and even mortification. Right-wing professionals remained passionate in their outward defense of Trump but were rattled, if not abashed, among one another. At the funeral, Rush Limbaugh and Laura Ingraham struggled to parse support for Trumpism even as they distanced themselves from Trump himself.

The president had surely become the right wing's meal ticket. He was the ultimate antiliberal: an authoritarian who was the living embodiment of resistance to authority. He was the exuberant inverse of everything the right wing found patronizing and gullible and sanctimonious about the left. And yet, obviously, Trump was Trump—careless, capricious, disloyal, far beyond any sort of control. Nobody knew that as well as the people who knew him best.

Ailes's wife, Beth, had militantly invited only Ailes loyalists to the funeral. Anyone who had wavered in her husband's defense since his firing or had decided that a better future lay with the Murdoch family was excluded. This put Trump, still enthralled by his new standing with Murdoch, on the other side of the line. Hours and then days—carefully tracked by Beth Ailes—ticked off without a condolence call from the president.

The morning of the funeral, Sean Hannity's private plane took off for Palm Beach from Republic Airport in Farmingdale, Long Island. Accompanying Hannity was a small group of current and former Fox employees, all Ailes and Trump partisans. But each felt some open angst, or even incredulity, about Trump being Trump: first there was the difficulty of grasping the Comey rationale, and now his failure to give even a nod to his late friend Ailes.

"He's an idiot, obviously," said the former Fox correspondent Liz Trotta.

Fox anchor Kimberly Guilfoyle spent much of the flight debating Trump's entreaties to have her replace Sean Spicer at the White House. "There are a lot of issues, including personal survival."

As for Hannity himself, his view of the right-wing world was shifting from Foxcentric to Trumpcentric. He did not think much more than a year would pass before he, too, would be pushed from the network, or find it too inhospitable to stay on. And yet he was pained by Trump's slavish attentions to Murdoch, who had not only ousted Ailes but whose conservatism was at best utilitarian. "He was for Hillary!" said Hannity.

Ruminating out loud, Hannity said he would leave the network and go work full time for Trump, because nothing was more important than that Trump succeed—"in spite of himself," Hannity added, laughing.

But he was pissed off that Trump hadn't called Beth. "Mueller," he concluded, drawing deeply on an electronic cigarette, had distracted him.

Trump may be a Frankenstein creation, but he was the right wing's creation, the first, true, right-wing original. Hannity could look past the Comey disaster. And Jared. And the mess in the White House.

Still, he hadn't called Beth.

"What the fuck is wrong with him?" asked Hannity.

* * *

Trump believed he was one win away from turning everything around. Or, perhaps more to the point, one win away from good press that would turn everything around. The fact that he had largely squandered his first hundred days—whose victories should have been the currency of the next hundred days—was immaterial. You could be down in the media one day and then the next have a hit that made you a success.

"Big things, we need big things," he said, angrily and often. "This isn't big. I need big. Bring me big. Do you even know what big is?"

Repeal and replace, infrastructure, true tax reform—the rollout Trump had promised and then depended on Paul Ryan to deliver—was effectively in tatters. Every senior staff member was now maintaining that they shouldn't have done health care, the precursor to the legislative rollout, in the first place. Whose idea was that, anyway?

The natural default might be to do smaller things, incremental versions of the program. But Trump showed little interest in the small stuff. He became listless and irritable.

So, okay, it would have to be peace in the Middle East.

For Trump, as for many showmen or press release entrepreneurs, the enemy of everything is complexity and red tape, and the solution for everything is cutting corners. Bypass or ignore the difficulties; just move in a straight line to the vision, which, if it's bold enough, or grandiose enough, will sell itself. In this formula, there is always a series of middlemen who will promise to help you cut the corners, as well as partners who will be happy to piggyback on your grandiosity.

Enter the Crown Prince of the House of Saud, Mohammed bin Salman bin Abdulaziz Al Saud, age thirty-one. Aka MBS.

The fortuitous circumstance was that the king of Saudi Arabia,

MBS's father, was losing it. The consensus in the Saudi royal family about a need to modernize was growing stronger (somewhat). MBS—an inveterate player of video games—was a new sort of personality in the Saudi leadership. He was voluble, open, and expansive, a charmer and an international player, a canny salesman rather than a remote, taciturn grandee. He had seized the economic portfolio and was pursuing a vision—quite a Trumpian vision—to out-Dubai Dubai and diversify the economy. His would be a new, modern—well, a bit more modern—kingdom (yes, women would soon be allowed to drive—so thank God self-driving cars were coming!). Saudi leadership was marked by age, traditionalism, relative anonymity, and careful consensus thinking. The Saudi royal family, on the other hand, whence the leadership class comes, was often marked by excess, flash, and the partaking of the joys of modernity in foreign ports. MBS, a man in a hurry, was trying to bridge the Saudi royal selves.

Global liberal leadership had been all but paralyzed by the election of Donald Trump—indeed, by the very *existence* of Donald Trump. But it was an inverted universe in the Middle East. The Obama truculence and hyperrationalization and micromanaging, preceded by the Bush moral militarism and ensuing disruptions, preceded by Clinton deal making, quid pro quo, and backstabbing, had opened the way for Trump's version of realpolitik. He had no patience with the our-hands-are-tied ennui of the post–cold war order, that sense of the chess board locked in place, of incremental movement being the best-case scenario—the alternative being only war. His was a much simpler view: Who's got the power? Give me his number.

And, just as basically: The enemy of my enemy is my friend. If Trump had one fixed point of reference in the Middle East, it was—mostly courtesy of Michael Flynn's tutoring—that Iran was the bad guy. Hence everybody opposed to Iran was a pretty good guy.

After the election, MBS had reached out to Kushner. In the confusion of the Trump transition, nobody with foreign policy stature and an international network had been put in place—even the new secretary of state designate, Rex Tillerson, had no real experience in foreign policy. To bewildered foreign secretaries, it seemed logical to see the president-elect's son-in-law as a figure of stability. Whatever happened, he would be there. And for certain regimes, especially the familycentric Saudis, Kushner, the son-in-law, was much more reassuring than a policy person. He wasn't in his job because of his ideas.

Of the many Trump gashes in modern major-power governing, you could certainly drive a Trojan horse through his lack of foreign policy particulars and relationships. This presented a do-over opportunity for the world in its relationship with the United States—or it did if you were willing to speak the new Trump language, whatever that was. There wasn't much of a road map here, just pure opportunism, a new transactional openness. Or, even more, a chance to use the powers of charm and seduction to which Trump responded as enthusiastically as he did to offers of advantageous new deals.

It was Kissingeresque realpolitik. Kissinger himself, long familiar with Trump by way of the New York social world and now taking Kushner under his wing, was successfully reinserting himself, helping to organize meetings with the Chinese and the Russians.

Most of America's usual partners, and even many antagonists, were unsettled if not horrified. Still, some saw opportunity. The Russians could see a free pass on the Ukraine and Georgia, as well as a lifting of sanctions, in return for giving up on Iran and Syria. Early in the transition, a high-ranking official in the Turkish government reached out in genuine confusion to a prominent U.S. business figure to inquire whether Turkey would have better leverage by putting pressure on the U.S. military presence in Turkey or by offering the new president an enviable hotel site on the Bosporus.

There was something curiously aligned between the Trump family and MBS. Like the entire Saudi leadership, MBS had, practically speaking, no education outside of Saudi Arabia. In the past, this had worked to limit the Saudi options—nobody was equipped to confidently explore new intellectual possibilities. As a consequence, everybody was wary of trying to get them to imagine change. But MBS and Trump were on pretty much equal footing. Knowing little made them oddly comfortable with each other. When MBS offered himself to Kushner as his guy in the Saudi kingdom, that was "like meeting someone nice at your first day of boarding school," said Kushner's friend.

Casting aside, in very quick order, previously held assumptions—in fact, not really aware of those assumptions—the new Trump thinking about the Middle East became the following: There are basically four players (or at least we can forget everybody else)—Israel, Egypt, Saudi Arabia, and Iran. The first three can be united against the fourth. And Egypt and Saudi Arabia, given what they want with respect to Iran—and anything else that does not interfere with the United States' interests—will pressure the Palestinians to make a deal. Voilà.

This represented a queasy-making mishmash of thought. Bannon's isolationism (a pox on all your houses—and keep us out of it); Flynn's anti-Iranism (of all the world's perfidy and toxicity, there is none like that of the mullahs); and Kushner's Kissingerism (not so much Kissingerism as, having no point of view himself, a dutiful attempt to follow the ninety-four-year-old's advice).

But the fundamental point was that the last three administrations had gotten the Middle East wrong. It was impossible to overstate how much contempt the Trump people felt for the business-as-usual thinking that had gotten it so wrong. Hence, the new operating principle was simple: do the opposite of what they (Obama, but the Bush neocons, too) would do. Their behavior, their conceits, their ideas—in some sense even their backgrounds, education, and class—were all suspect. And, what's more, you don't really have to know all that much yourself; you just do it differently than it was done before.

The old foreign policy was based on the idea of nuance: facing an infinitely complex multilateral algebra of threats, interests, incentives, deals, and ever evolving relationships, we strain to reach a balanced future. In practice, the new foreign policy, an effective Trump doctrine, was to reduce the board to three elements: powers we can work with, powers we cannot work with, and those without enough power whom we can functionally disregard or sacrifice. It was cold war stuff. And, indeed, in the larger Trump view, it was during the cold war that time and circumstance gave the United States its greatest global advantage. That was when America was great.

* * *

Kushner was the driver of the Trump doctrine. His test cases were China, Mexico, Canada, and Saudi Arabia. He offered each country the opportunity to make his father-in-law happy.

In the first days of the administration, Mexico blew its chance. In transcripts of conversations between Trump and Mexican president Enrique Peña Nieto that would later become public, it was vividly clear that Mexico did not understand or was unwilling to play the new game. The Mexican president refused to construct a pretense for paying for the wall, a pretense that might have redounded to his vast advantage (without his having to actually pay for the wall).

Not long after, Canada's new prime minister, Justin Trudeau, a forty-five-year-old globalist in the style of Clinton and Blair, came to Washington and repeatedly smiled and bit his tongue. And that did the trick: Canada quickly became Trump's new best friend.

The Chinese, who Trump had oft maligned during the campaign, came to Mar-a-Lago for a summit advanced by Kushner and Kissinger. (This required some tutoring for Trump, who referred to the Chinese leader as "Mr. X-i"; the president was told to think of him as a woman and call him "she.") They were in an agreeable mood, evidently willing to humor Trump. And they quickly figured out that if you flatter him, he flatters you.

But it was the Saudis, also often maligned during the campaign, who, with their intuitive understanding of family, ceremony, and ritual and propriety, truly scored.

The foreign policy establishment had a long and well-honed relationship with MBS's rival, the crown prince, Mohammed bin Nayef (MBN). Key NSA and State Department figures were alarmed that Kushner's discussions and fast-advancing relationship with MBS would send a dangerous message to MBN. And of course it did. The foreign policy people believed Kushner was being led by MBS, whose real views were entirely untested. The Kushner view was either, naïvely, that he wasn't being led, or, with the confidence of a thirty-six-year-old assuming the new prerogatives of the man in charge, that he didn't care: let's embrace anybody who will embrace us.

The Kushner/MBS plan that emerged was straightforward in a way that foreign policy usually isn't: If you give us what we want, we'll give you what you want. On MBS's assurance that he would deliver some seriously good news, he was invited to visit the White House in March. (The Saudis arrived with a big delegation, but they were received at the White House by only the president's small circle—and the Saudis took particular note that Trump ordered Priebus to jump up and fetch him things during the meeting.) The two large men, the older Trump and much younger MBS—both charmers, flatterers, and country club jokers, each in their way—grandly hit it off.

It was an aggressive bit of diplomacy. MBS was using this Trump embrace as part of his own power play in the kingdom. And the Trump White House, ever denying this was the case, let him. In return, MBS offered a basket of deals and announcements that would coincide with a scheduled presidential visit to Saudi Arabia—Trump's first trip abroad. Trump would get a "win."

Planned before the Comey firing and Mueller hiring, the trip had State Department professionals alarmed. The itinerary—May 19 to May 27—was too long for any president, particularly such an untested and untutored one. (Trump himself, full of phobias about travel and unfamiliar locations, had been grumbling about the burdens of the trip.) But coming immediately after Comey and Mueller it was a get-out-of-Dodge godsend. There couldn't have been a better time to be making headlines far from Washington. A road trip could transform everything.

Almost the entire West Wing, along with State Department and National Security staff, was on board for the trip: Melania Trump, Ivanka Trump, Jared Kushner, Reince Priebus, Stephen Bannon, Gary Cohn, Dina Powell, Hope Hicks, Sean Spicer, Stephen Miller, Joe Hagin, Rex Tillerson, and Michael Anton. Also included were Sarah Huckabee Sanders, the deputy press secretary; Dan Scavino, the administration's social media director; Keith Schiller, the president's personal security adviser; and Wilbur Ross, the commerce secretary. (Ross was widely ridiculed for never missing an Air Force One opportunity—as Bannon put it, "Wilbur is Zelig, every time you turn around he's in a picture.") This trip and the robust American delegation was the antidote, and alternate universe to the Mueller appointment.

The president and his son-in-law could barely contain their confidence and enthusiasm. They felt certain that they had set out on the road to peace in the Middle East—and in this, they were much like a number of other administrations that had come before them.

Trump was effusive in his praise for Kushner. "Jared's gotten the Arabs totally on our side. Done deal," he assured one of his after-dinner callers before leaving on the trip. "It's going to be beautiful."

"He believed," said the caller, "that this trip could pull it out, like a twist in a bad movie."

* * *

On the empty roads of Riyadh, the presidential motorcade passed billboards with pictures of Trump and the Saudi king (MBS's eighty-one-year-old father) with the legend TOGETHER WE PREVAIL.

In part, the president's enthusiasm seemed to be born out of—or perhaps had caused—a substantial exaggeration of what had actually been agreed to during the negotiations ahead of the trip. In the days before his departure, he was telling people that the Saudis were going to finance an entirely new military presence in the kingdom, supplanting and even replacing the U.S. command headquarters in Qatar. And there would be "the biggest breakthrough in Israel-Palestine negotiations ever." It would be "*the* game changer, major like has never been seen."

In truth, his version of what would be accomplished was a quantum leap beyond what was actually agreed, but that did not seem to alter his feelings of zeal and delight.

The Saudis would immediately buy $110 billion's worth of American arms, and a total of $350 billion over ten years. "Hundreds of billions of dollars of investments into the United States and jobs, jobs, jobs," declared the president. Plus, the Americans and the Saudis would together "counter violent extremist messaging, disrupt financing of terrorism, and advance defense cooperation." And they would establish a center in Riyadh to fight extremism. And if this was not exactly peace in the Middle East, the president, according to the secretary of state, "feels like there's a moment in time here. The president's going to talk with Netanyahu about the process going forward. He's going to be talking to President Abbas about what he feels is necessary for the Palestinians to be successful."

It was all a Trumpian big deal. Meanwhile, the First Family—POTUS, FLOTUS, and Jared and Ivanka—were ferried around in gold golf carts, and the Saudis threw a $75 million party in Trump's honor, with Trump getting to sit on a thronelike chair. (The president, while receiving an honor from the Saudi king, appeared in a photograph to have bowed, arousing some right-wing ire.)

Fifty Arab and Muslim nations were summoned by the Saudis to pay the president court. The president called home to tell his friends how natural and easy this was, and how, inexplicably and suspiciously, Obama had messed it all up. There "has been a little strain, but there won't be strain with this administration," the president assured Hamad bin Isa Al Khalifa, the king of Bahrain.

Abdel Fattah el-Sisi, the Egyptian strongman, ably stroked the president and said, "You are a unique personality that is capable of doing the impossible." (To Sisi, Trump replied, "Love your shoes. Boy, those shoes. Man. . . .")

It was, in dramatic ways, a shift in foreign policy attitude and strategy—and its effects were almost immediate. The president, ignoring if not defying foreign policy advice, gave a nod to the Saudis' plan to bully Qatar. Trump's view was that Qatar was providing financial support to terror groups—pay no attention to a similar Saudi history. (Only *some* members of the Saudi royal family had provided such support, went the new reasoning.) Within weeks of the trip, MBS, detaining MBN quite in the dead of night, would force him to relinquish the Crown Prince title, which MBS would then assume for himself. Trump would tell friends that he and Jared had engineered this: "We've put our man on top!"

From Riyadh, the presidential party went on to Jerusalem, where the president met with Netanyahu and, in Bethlehem, with Abbas, expressing ever greater certainty that, in his third-person guise, "Trump will make peace." Then to Rome to meet the pope. Then to Brussels, where, in character, he meaningfully drew the line between Western-alliance-based foreign policy, which had been firmly in place since World War II, and the new America First ethos.

In Trump's view, all this should have been presidency-shaping stuff. He couldn't believe his dramatic accomplishments weren't getting bigger play. He was simply in denial, Bannon, Priebus, and others noted, about the continuing and competing Comey and Mueller headlines.

One of Trump's deficiencies—a constant in the campaign and, so far, in the presidency—was his uncertain grasp of cause and effect. Until now, whatever problems he might have caused in the past had reliably been supplanted by new events, giving him the confidence that one bad story can always be replaced by a better, more dramatic story. He could always change the conversation. The Saudi trip and his bold campaign to upend the old foreign policy world order should have accomplished exactly that. But the president continued to find himself trapped, incredulously on his part, by Comey and Mueller. Nothing seemed to move on from those two events.

After the Saudi leg of the trip, Bannon and Priebus, both exhausted by the trip's intense proximity to the president and his family, peeled off and headed back to Washington. It was now their job to deal with what had become, in the White House staff's absence, the actual, even ultimate, presidency-shaping crisis.

* * *

What did the people around Trump actually think of Trump? This was not just a reasonable question, it was the question those around Trump most asked themselves. They constantly struggled to figure out what they themselves actually thought and what they thought everybody else was truly thinking.

Mostly they kept their answers to themselves, but in the instance of Comey and Mueller, beyond all the usual dodging and weaving rationalizations, there really wasn't anybody, other than the president's family, who didn't very pointedly blame Trump himself.

This was the point at which an emperors-new-clothes threshold was crossed. Now you could, out loud, rather freely doubt his judgment, acumen, and, most of all, the advice he was getting.

"He's not only crazy," declared Tom Barrack to a friend, "he's stupid."

But Bannon, along with Priebus, had strongly opposed the Comey firing, while Ivanka and Jared had not only supported it, but insisted on it. This seismic event prompted a new theme from Bannon, repeated by him widely, which was that every piece of advice from the couple was bad advice.

Nobody now believed that firing Comey was a good idea; even the president seemed sheepish. Hence, Bannon saw his new role as saving Trump—and Trump would always need saving. He might be a brilliant actor but he could not manage his own career.

And for Bannon, this new challenge brought a clear benefit: when Trump's fortune sank, Bannon's rose.

On the trip to the Middle East, Bannon went to work. He became focused on the figure of Lanny Davis, one of the Clinton impeachment lawyers who, for the better part of two years, became a near round-the-clock spokesperson and public defender of the Clinton White House. Bannon judged Comey-Mueller to be as threatening to the Trump White House as Monica Lewinsky and Ken Starr were to the Clinton White House, and he saw the model for escaping a mortal fate in the Clinton response.

"What the Clintons did was to go to the mattresses with amazing discipline," he explained. "They set up an outside shop and then Bill and Hillary never mentioned it again. They ground through it. Starr had them dead to rights and they got through it."

Bannon knew exactly what needed to be done: seal off the West Wing and build a separate legal and communications staff to defend the president. In this construct, the president would occupy a parallel reality, removed from and uninvolved with what would become an obvious partisan blood sport—as it had in the Clinton model. Politics would be relegated to its nasty corner, and Trump would conduct himself as the president and as the commander in chief.

"So we're going to do it," insisted Bannon, with *joie de guerre* and manic energy, "the way they did it. Separate war room, separate lawyers, separate spokespeople. It's keeping that fight over there so we can wage this other fight over here. Everybody gets this. Well, maybe not Trump so much. Not clear. Maybe a little. Not what he imagined."

Bannon, in great excitement, and Priebus, grateful for an excuse to leave the president's side, rushed back to the West Wing to begin to cordon it off.

It did not escape Priebus's notice that Bannon had in mind to create a rear guard of defenders—David Bossie, Corey Lewandowski, and Jason Miller, all of whom would be outside spokespeople—that would largely be loyal to him. Most of all, it did not escape Priebus that Bannon was asking the president to play a role entirely out of character: the cool, steady, long-suffering chief executive.

And it certainly didn't help that they were unable to hire a law firm with a top-notch white-collar government practice. By the time Bannon and Priebus were back in Washington, three blue-chip firms had said no. All of them were afraid they would face a rebellion among the younger staff if they represented Trump, afraid Trump would publicly humiliate them if the going got tough, and afraid Trump would stiff them for the bill.

In the end, nine top firms turned them down.

18

BANNON REDUX

Bannon was back, according to the Bannon faction. According to Bannon himself: "I'm good. I'm *good.* I'm back. I said don't do it. You don't fire the director of the FBI. The geniuses around here thought otherwise."

Was Bannon back? asked the worried other side of the house—Jared and Ivanka, Dina Powell, Gary Cohn, Hope Hicks, H. R. McMaster.

If he was back, that meant he had successfully defied the organizational premise of the Trump White House: the family would always prevail. Steve Bannon had, even in his internal exile, not stopped his running public verbal assault on Jared and Ivanka. Off the record became Bannon's effective on the record. These were bitter, sometimes hilarious, denunciations of the couple's acumen, intelligence, and motives: "They think they're defending him, but they are always defending themselves."

Now he declared they were finished as a power center—destroyed. And if not, they would destroy the president with their terrible and self-serving advice. Even worse than Jared was Ivanka. "She was a nonevent on the campaign. She became a White House staffer and that's when people suddenly realized she's dumb as a brick. A little marketing savvy and has a look, but as far as understanding actually how the world works and what politics is and what it means—nothing. Once you expose that, you lose such credibility. Jared just kind of flits in and does the Arab stuff."

The folks on the Jarvanka side seemed more and more genuinely afraid of what might happen if they crossed the Bannon side. Because the Bannonites, they truly seemed to fear, were assassins.

On the flight to Riyadh, Dina Powell approached Bannon about a leak involving her to a right-wing news site. She told him she knew the leak had come from Julia Hahn, one of Bannon's people and a former Breitbart writer.

"You should take it up with her," said an amused Bannon. "But she's a beast. And she will come at you. Let me know how it works out."

Among Bannon's many regular targets, Powell had become a favorite. She was often billed as Deputy National Security Advisor; that was her sometime designation even in the *New York Times*. Actually, she was Deputy National Security Advisor *for Strategy*—the difference, Bannon pointed out, between the COO of a hotel chain and the concierge.

Coming back from the overseas trip, Powell began to talk in earnest to friends about her timetable to get out of the White House and back into a private-sector job. Sheryl Sandberg, she said, was her model.

"Oh my fucking god," said Bannon.

On May 26, the day before the presidential party returned from the overseas trip, the *Washington Post* reported that during the transition, Kushner and Sergey Kislyak, the Russian ambassador, had, at Kushner's instigation, discussed the possibility of having the Russians set up a private communications channel between the transition team and the Kremlin. The *Post* cited "U.S. officials briefed on intelligence reports." The Jarvanka side believed that Bannon was the source.

Part of the by now deep enmity between the First Family couple and their allies and Bannon and his team was the Jarvanka conviction that Bannon had played a part in many of the reports of Kushner's interactions with the Russians. This was not, in other words, merely an internal policy war; it was a death match. For Bannon to live, Kushner would have to be wholly discredited—pilloried, investigated, possibly even jailed.

Bannon, assured by everyone that there was no winning against the

Trump family, hardly tried to hide his satisfied belief that he was going to outplay them. In the Oval Office, in front of her father, Bannon openly attacked her. "You," he said, pointing at her as the president watched, "are a fucking liar." Ivanka's bitter complaints to her father, which in the past had diminished Bannon, were now met by a hands-off Trump: "I told you this is a tough town, baby."

* * *

But if Bannon was back, it was far from clear what being back meant. Trump being Trump, was this true rehabilitation, or did he feel an even deeper rancor toward Bannon for having survived his initial intention to kill him? Nobody really thought Trump forgot—instead, he dwelled and ruminated and chewed. "One of the worst things is when he believes you've succeeded at his expense," explained Sam Nunberg, once on the inside of the Trump circle, then cast to the outside. "If your win is in any way perceived as his loss, phew."

For his part, Bannon believed he was back because, at a pivotal moment, his advice had proved vastly better than that of the "geniuses." Firing Comey, the solve-all-problems Jarvanka solution, had indeed unleashed a set of terrible consequences.

The Jarvanka side believed that Bannon was in essence blackmailing the president. As Bannon went, so went the virulence of right-wing digital media. Despite his apparent obsession with the "fake news" put out by the *New York Times*, the *Washington Post*, and CNN, for the president the threat of fake news was actually greater on the right. Though he would never call out fake news on Fox, Breitbart, and the others, these outlets—which could conceivably spew a catchall of conspiracies in which a weak Trump sold out to a powerful establishment—were potentially far more dangerous than their counterparts on the left.

Bannon, too, was seen to be rectifying an earlier bureaucratic mistake. Where initially he had been content to be the brains of the operation—confident that he was vastly smarter than everybody else (and, indeed, few tried to challenge him for that title)—and not staff up, now he was putting his organization and loyalists firmly in place. His off-balance-sheet communications staff—Bossie, Lewandowski, Jason

Miller, Sam Nunberg (even though he had long fallen out with Trump himself), and Alexandra Preate—formed quite a private army of leakers and defenders. What's more, whatever breach there had been between Bannon and Priebus came smoothly together over their mutual loathing of Jared and Ivanka. The professional White House was united against the amateur family White House.

Adding to Bannon's new bureaucratic advantage, he had maximum influence on the staffing of the new firewall team, the lawyers and comm staff who would collectively become the Lanny Davis of the Trump defense. Unable to hire prestige talent, Bannon turned to one of the president's longtime hit-man lawyers, Marc Kasowitz. Bannon had previously bonded with Kasowitz when the attorney had handled a series of near-death problems on the campaign, including dealing with a vast number of allegations and legal threats from an ever growing list of women accusing Trump of molesting and harassing them.

On May 31, the Bannon firewall plan went into effect. Henceforth, all discussion related to Russia, the Mueller and congressional investigations, and other personal legal issues would be entirely handled by the Kasowitz team. The president, as Bannon described the plan in private and as he urged his boss, would no longer be addressing any of these areas. Among the many, many efforts to force Trump into presidential mode, this was the latest.

Bannon then installed Mark Corallo, a former Karl Rove communications staffer, as the firewall spokesperson. He was also planning to put in Bossie and Lewandowski as part of the crisis management team. And at Bannon's prompting, Kasowitz attempted to further insulate the president by giving his client a central piece of advice: send the kids home.

Bannon was indeed back. It was his team. It was his wall around the president—one that he hoped would keep Jarvanka out.

Bannon's formal moment of being back was marked by a major milestone. On June 1, after a long and bitter internal debate, the president announced that he had decided to withdraw from the Paris Climate Agreement. For Bannon, it was a deeply satisfying slap in the face of liberal rectitude—Elon Musk and Bob Iger immediately resigned from

Trump's business council—and confirmation of Trump's true Bannonite instincts.

It was, likewise, the move that Ivanka Trump had campaigned hardest against in the White House.

"Score," said Bannon. "The bitch is dead."

* * *

There are few modern political variables more disruptive than a dedicated prosecutor. It's the ultimate wild card.

A prosecutor means that the issue under investigation—or, invariably, cascading issues—will be a constant media focus. Setting their own public stage, prosecutors are certain leakers.

It means that everybody in a widening circle has to hire a lawyer. Even tangential involvement can cost six figures; central involvement quickly rises into the millions.

By early summer, there was already an intense seller's market in Washington for top criminal legal talent. As the Mueller investigation got under way, White House staffers made a panicky rush to get the best firm before someone else got there first and created a conflict.

"Can't talk about Russia, nothing, can't go there," said Katie Walsh, now three months removed from the White House, on advice of her new counsel.

Any interviews or depositions given to investigators risked putting you in jeopardy. What's more, every day in the White House brought new dangers: any random meeting you might find yourself in exposed you more.

Bannon kept insisting on the absolute importance of this point—and for him the strategic importance. If you didn't want to find yourself getting wrung out in front of Congress, your career and your net worth in jeopardy, be careful who you spoke to. More to the point: you must not under any circumstances speak to Jared and Ivanka, who were now Russia toxic. It was Bannon's widely advertised virtue and advantage: "I've never been to Russia. I don't know anybody from Russia. I've never spoken to any Russians. And I'd just as well not speak to anyone who has."

Bannon observed a hapless Pence in a lot of "wrong meetings," and helped to bring in the Republican operative Nick Ayers as Pence's chief of staff, and to get "our fallback guy" out of the White House and "running around the world and looking like a vice president."

And beyond the immediate fears and disruption, there was the virtually certain outcome that a special prosecutor delegated to find a crime would find one—likely many. Everybody became a potential agent of implicating others. Dominos would fall. Targets would flip.

Paul Manafort, making a good living in international financial gray areas, his risk calculation based on the long-shot odds that an under-the-radar privateer would ever receive close scrutiny, would now be subjected to microscopic review. His nemesis, Oleg Deripaska—still pursuing his $17 million claim against Manafort and himself looking for favorable treatment from federal authorities who had restricted his travel to the United States—was continuing his own deep investigation into Manafort's Russian and Ukrainian business affairs.

Tom Barrack, privy to the president's stream of consciousness as well as his financial history, was suddenly taking stock of his own exposure. Indeed, all the billionaire friends with whom Trump got on the phone and gossiped and rambled were potential witnesses.

In the past, administrations forced to deal with a special prosecutor appointed to investigate and prosecute matters with which the president might have been involved usually became consumed by the effort to cope. Their tenure broke into "before" and "after" periods—with the "after" period hopelessly bogged down in the soap opera of G-man pursuit. Now it looked like the "after" period would be almost the entirety of the Trump administration.

The idea of formal collusion and artful conspiracy—as media and Democrats more or less breathlessly believed or hoped had happened between Trump and the Russians—seemed unlikely to everybody in the White House. (Bannon's comment that the Trump campaign was not organized enough to collude with its own state organizations became everybody's favorite talking point—not least because it was true.) But nobody was vouching for the side deals and freelance operations and otherwise nothing-burger stuff that was a prosecutor's daily bread and the likely detritus of the Trump hangers-on. And everybody believed that if the investigation moved into the long chain of Trump financial transactions, it would almost certainly reach the Trump family and the Trump White House.

And then there was the president's insistent claim that he could do something. *I can fire him*, he would say. Indeed, it was another of his repetitive loops: I can fire him. I *can* fire him. Mueller. The idea of a showdown in which the stronger, more determined, more intransigent, more damn-the-consequences man prevails was central to Trump's own personal mythology. He lived in a mano a mano world, one in which if your own respectability and sense of personal dignity were not a paramount issue—if you weren't weak in the sense of needing to seem like a reasonable and respectable person—you had a terrific advantage. And if you made it personal, if you believed that when the fight really mattered that it was kill or be killed, you were unlikely to meet someone willing to make it as personal as you were.

This was Bannon's fundamental insight about Trump: he made *everything* personal, and he was helpless not to.

* * *

Dissuaded by everyone from focusing his anger on Mueller (at least for now), the president focused on Sessions.

Sessions—"Beauregard"—was a close Bannon ally, and in May and June the president's almost daily digs against the attorney general—beyond even his loyalty and resolve, Trump issued scathing criticism of his stature, voice, and dress—provided a sudden bit of good news for the anti-Bannon side of the house. Bannon, they reasoned, couldn't really be on top if his key proxy was now being blamed for everything bad in Trump's life. As always, Trump's regard or scorn was infectious. If you were in favor, then whatever and whomever he associated with you was also in favor. If you weren't, then everything associated with you was poisonous.

The brutality of Trump's dissatisfaction kept increasing. A small man with a Mr. Magoo stature and an old-fashioned Southern accent, Sessions was bitterly mocked by the president, who drew a corrosive portrait of physical and mental weakness. Insult trauma radiated out of the Oval Office. You could hear it when passing by.

Bannon's efforts to talk the president down—reminding Trump of the difficulties they would encounter during another attorney general confirmation, the importance of Sessions to the hard conservative base, the loyalty that Sessions had shown during the Trump campaign—backfired. To the anti-Bannon side's satisfaction, they resulted in another round of Trump's dissing Bannon.

The attack on Sessions now became, at least in the president's mind, the opening salvo in an active effort to replace Sessions as attorney general. But there were only two candidates to run the Justice Department from whom Trump believed he could extract absolute loyalty, Chris Christie and Rudy Giuliani. He believed they would both perform kamikaze acts for him—just as everyone else knew they would almost certainly never be confirmed.

* * *

As James Comey's testimony before the Senate Intelligence Committee approached—it would take place on June 8, twelve days after the presidential traveling party returned home from the long trip to the Middle East and Europe—there began among senior staffers an almost open inquiry into Trump's motives and state of mind.

This seemed spurred by an obvious question: Why hadn't he fired Comey during his first days of office, when it would likely have been seen as a natural changing of the guard with no clear connection to the Russian investigation? There were many equivocal answers: general disorganization, the fast pace of events, and a genuine sense of innocence and naïveté about the Russian charges. But now there seemed to be a new understanding: Donald Trump believed he had vastly more power, authority, and control than in fact he had, and he believed his talent for manipulating people and bending and dominating them was vastly greater than it was. Pushing this line of reasoning just a little further: senior staff believed the president had a problem with reality, and reality was now overwhelming him.

If true, this notion directly contravened the basic premise of the support for Trump among his staff. In some sense, not too closely questioned, they believed he had almost magical powers. Since his success was not explainable, he must have talents beyond what they could fathom. His instincts. Or his salesman's gifts. Or his energy. Or just the fact that he was the opposite of what he was supposed to be. This was out-of-the-ordinary politics—shock-to-the-system politics—but it could work.

But what if it didn't? What if they were all profoundly wrong?

Comey's firing and the Mueller investigation prompted a delayed reckoning that ended months of willing suspension of disbelief. These sudden doubts and considerations—at the highest level of government—did not quite yet go to the president's ability to adequately function in his job. But they did, arguably for the first time in open discussions, go to the view that he was hopelessly prone to self-sabotaging his ability to function in the job. This insight, scary as it was, at least left open the possibility that if all the elements of self-sabotage were carefully controlled—his information, his contacts, his public remarks, and the sense of danger and threat to him—he might yet be able to pull it together and successfully perform.

Quite suddenly, this became the prevailing view of the Trump presidency and the opportunity that still beckoned: you can be saved by those around you or brought down by them.

Bannon believed the Trump presidency would fail in some more or less apocalyptic fashion if Kushner and his wife remained Trump's most influential advisers. Their lack of political or real-world experience had already hobbled the presidency, but since the Comey disaster it was getting worse: as Bannon saw it, they were now acting out of personal panic.

The Kushner side believed that Bannon or Bannonism had pushed the president into a harshness that undermined his natural salesman's abilities to charm and reach out. Bannon and his ilk had made him the monster he more and more seemed to be.

Meanwhile, virtually everybody believed that a large measure of the fault lay in Reince Priebus, who had failed to create a White House that could protect the president from himself—or from Bannon or from his own children. At the same time, believing that the fundamental problem lay in Priebus was easy scapegoating, not to mention little short of risible:

with so little power, the chief of staff simply wasn't capable of directing either Trump or those around him. Priebus himself could, not too helpfully, argue only that no one had any idea how much worse all this would have been without his long-suffering mediation among the president's relatives, his Svengali, and Trump's own terrible instincts. There might be two or three debacles a day, but without Priebus's stoic resolve, and the Trump blows that he absorbed, there might have been a dozen more.

* * *

On June 8, from a little after ten in the morning to nearly one in the afternoon, James Comey testified in public before the Senate Intelligence Committee. The former FBI director's testimony, quite a tour de force of directness, moral standing, personal honor, and damning details, left the country with a simple message: the president was likely a fool and certainly a liar. In the age of modern media politesse, few presidents had been so directly challenged and impugned before Congress.

Here it was, stark in Comey's telling: the president regarded the FBI director as working directly for him, of owing his job to him, and now he wanted something back. "My common sense," said Comey, "again, I could be wrong, but my common sense told me what's going on here is he's looking to get something in exchange for granting my request to stay in the job."

In Comey's telling, the president wanted the FBI to lay off Michael Flynn. And he wanted to stop the FBI from pursuing its Russia-related investigation. The point could hardly have been clearer: if the president was pressuring the director because he feared that an investigation of Michael Flynn would damage him, then this was an obstruction of justice.

The contrast between the two men, Comey and Trump, was in essence the contrast between good government and Trump himself. Comey came across as precise, compartmentalized, scrupulous in his presentation of the details of what transpired and the nature of his responsibility—he was as by-the-book as it gets. Trump, in the portrait offered by Comey, was shady, shoot-from-the-hip, heedless or even unaware of the rules, deceptive, and in it for himself.

After the hearing ended, the president told everybody he had not watched it, but everybody knew he had. To the extent that this was, as Trump saw it, a contest between the two men, it was as direct a juxtaposition as might be imagined. The entire point of the Comey testimony was to recast and contradict what the president had said in his angry and defensive tweets and statements, and to cast suspicion on his actions and motives—and to suggest that the president's intention was to suborn the director of the FBI.

Even among Trump loyalists who believed, as Trump did, that Comey was a phony and this was all a put-up job, the nearly universal feeling was that in this mortal game, Trump was quite defenseless.

* * *

Five days later, on June 13, it was Jeff Sessions's turn to testify before the Senate Intelligence Committee. His task was to try to explain the contacts he had had with the Russian ambassador, contacts that had later caused him to recuse himself—and made him the president's punching bag. Unlike Comey, who had been invited to the Senate to show off his virtue—and had seized the opportunity—Sessions had been invited to defend his equivocation, deception, or stupidity.

In an often testy exchange, the attorney general provided a squirrelly view of executive privilege. Though the president had not in fact evoked executive privilege, Sessions deemed it appropriate to try to protect it anyway.

Bannon, watching the testimony from the West Wing, quickly became frustrated. "Come on, Beauregard," he said.

Unshaven, Bannon sat at the head of the long wooden conference table in the chief of staff's office and focused intently on the flat-screen monitor across the room.

"They thought the cosmopolitans would like it if we fired Comey," he said, with "they" being Jared and Ivanka. "The cosmopolitans would be cheering for us for taking down the man who took Hillary down." Where the president saw Sessions as the cause of the Comey fiasco, Bannon saw Sessions as a victim of it.

A sylphlike Kushner, wearing a skinny gray suit and skinny black tie, slipped into the room. (Recently making the rounds was a joke about

Kushner being the best-dressed man in Washington, which is quite the opposite of a compliment.) On occasion the power struggle between Bannon and Kushner seemed to take physical form. Bannon's demeanor rarely changed, but Kushner could be petulant, condescending, and dismissive—or, as he was now, hesitating, abashed, and respectful.

Bannon ignored Kushner until the younger man cleared his throat. "How's it going?"

Bannon indicated the television set: as in, *Watch for yourself.*

Finally Bannon spoke. "They don't realize this is about institutions, not people."

"They" would appear to be the Jarvanka side—or an even broader construct referring to all those who mindlessly stood with Trump.

"This town is about institutions," Bannon continued. "We fire the FBI director and we fire the whole FBI. Trump is a man against institutions, and the institutions know it. How do you think that goes down?"

This was shorthand for a favorite Bannon riff: In the course of the campaign, Donald Trump had threatened virtually every institution in American political life. He was a clown-prince version of Jimmy Stewart in *Mr. Smith Goes to Washington*. Trump believed, offering catnip to deep American ire and resentment, that one man could be bigger than the system. This analysis presupposed that the institutions of political life were as responsive as those in the commercial life that Trump was from—and that they yearned to meet the market and find the Zeitgeist. But what if these institutions—the media, the judiciary, the intelligence community, the greater executive branch itself, and the "swamp" with its law firms, consultants, influence peddlers, and leakers—were in no way eager to adapt? If, by their nature, they were determined to endure, then this accidental president was up against it.

Kushner seemed unpersuaded. "I wouldn't put it like that," he said.

"I think that's the lesson of the first hundred days that some people around here have learned," said Bannon, ignoring Kushner. "It's not going to get better. This is what it's like."

"I don't know," said Kushner.

"Know it," said Bannon.

"I think Sessions is doing okay," said Kushner. "Don't you?"

19

MIKA WHO?

The media had unlocked the value of Donald Trump, but few in the media had unlocked it more directly and personally than Joe Scarborough and Mika Brzezinski. Their MSNBC breakfast show was an ongoing soap-opera-ish or possibly Oprahesque drama about their relationship with Trump—how he had disappointed them, how far they had come from their original regard for him, and how much and how pathetically he regularly embarrassed himself. The bond he once had with them, forged through mutual celebrity and a shared proprietary sense of politics (Scarborough, the former congressman, seemed to feel that he ought reasonably to be president as much as Donald Trump felt he should be), had distinguished the show during the campaign; now its public fraying became part of the daily news cycle. Scarborough and Brzezinski lectured him, channeled the concerns of his friends and family, upbraided him, and openly worried about him—that he was getting the wrong advice (Bannon) and, too, that his mental powers were slipping. They also staked a claim at representing the reasonable center-right alternative to the president, and indeed were quite a good barometer of both the center-right's efforts to deal with him and its day-to-day difficulties of living with him.

Trump, believing he had been used and abused by Scarborough and Brzezinski, claimed he'd stopped watching the show. But Hope Hicks, every morning, quaking, had to recount it for him.

Morning Joe was a ground-zero study in the way the media had overinvested in Trump. He was the whale against which media emotions, self-regard, ego, *joie de guerre*, career advancement, and desire to be at the center of the story, too, all churned in nearly ecstatic obsession. In reverse regard, the media was the same whale, serving the same function, for Trump.

To this Trump added another tic, a lifelong sense that people were constantly taking unfair advantage of him. This perhaps came from his father's cheapness and lack of generosity, or from his own overawareness of being a rich kid (and, no doubt, his insecurities about this), or from a negotiator's profound understanding that it is never win-win, that where there is profit there is loss. Trump simply could not abide the knowledge that somebody was getting a leg up at his expense. His was a zero-sum ecosystem. In the world of Trump, anything that he deemed of value either accrued to him or had been robbed from him.

Scarborough and Brzezinski had taken their relationship with Trump and amply monetized it, while putting no percentage in his pocket—and in this instance, he judged his commission should be slavishly favorable treatment. To say this drove him mad would be an understatement. He dwelled and fixated on the perceived injustice. *Don't mention Joe or Mika to him* was a standing proscription.

His wounded feelings and incomprehension at the failure of people whose embrace he sought to, in return, embrace him was "deep, crazy deep," said his former aide Sam Nunberg, who had run afoul of his need for 100 percent approbation and his bitter suspicion of being profited from.

* * *

Out of this accumulated rage came his June 29 tweet about Mika Brzezinski.

It was classic Trump: there was no mediation between off-the-record language and the public statement. Referring to "low I.Q. Crazy Mika" in one tweet, he wrote in another that she was "bleeding badly from a face-lift" when she and Scarborough visited Trump at Mar-a-Lago on the previous New Year's Eve. Many of his tweets were not, as they might seem, spontaneous utterances, but constant ones. Trump's rifts often began as insult comedy and solidified as bitter accusations and then, in an uncontainable moment, became an official proclamation.

The next step, in his tweet paradigm, was universal liberal opprobrium. Almost a week of social media fury, cable breast-beating, and front-page condemnation followed his tweet about Brzezinski. That was accompanied by the other part of the Trump tweet dynamic: by unifying liberal opinion against him, he unified its opposite for him.

In truth, he was often neither fully aware of the nature of what he had said nor fully cognizant of why there should be such a passionate reaction to it. As often as not, he surprised himself. "What did I say?" he would ask after getting severe blowback.

He wasn't serving up these insults for effect—well, not entirely. And his behavior wasn't carefully calculated; it was tit for tat, and he likely would have said what he'd said even if no one was left standing with him. (This very lack of calculation, this inability to be political, was part of his political charm.) It was just his good luck that the Trumpian 35 percent—that standing percentage of people who, according to most polls, seemed to support him no matter what (who would, in his estimation, let him get away with shooting someone on Fifth Avenue)—was largely unfazed and maybe even buoyed by every new expression of Trumpness.

Now, having expressed himself and gotten in the last word, Trump was cheery again.

"Mika and Joe totally love this. It's big ratings for them," said the president, with certain satisfaction and obvious truth.

* * *

Ten days later, a large table of Bannonites was having dinner at the Bombay Club, a high-end Indian restaurant two blocks from the White House. One of the group—Arthur Schwartz, a PR consultant—asked a question about the Mika and Joe affair.

Perhaps it was the noise, but it was also a fitting measure of the speed of events in the Trump era: Bannon lieutenant Alexandra Preate replied, with genuine fogginess, "Who?"

The operetta of the Mika tweets—the uncouthness and verbal abuse demonstrated by the president, his serious lack of control and judgment, and the worldwide censure heaped upon him for it—had already far receded, wholly overshadowed by more Trump eruptions and controversy.

But before moving on to the next episode of ohmygodness, it is worth considering the possibility that this constant, daily, often more than once-a-day, pileup of events—each one canceling out the one before—is the true aberration and novelty at the heart of the Trump presidency.

Perhaps never before in history—not through world wars, the overthrow of empires, periods of extraordinary social transformation, or episodes of government-shaking scandal—have real-life events unfolded with such emotional and plot-thickening impact. In the fashion of binge-watching a television show, one's real life became quite secondary to the public drama. It was not unreasonable to say *Whoa, wait just a minute: public life doesn't happen like this.* Public life in fact lacks coherence and drama. (History, by contrast, attains coherence and drama only in hindsight.)

The process of accomplishing the smallest set of tasks within the sprawling and resistant executive branch is a turtle process. The burden of the White House is the boredom of bureaucracy. All White Houses struggle to rise above that, and they succeed only on occasion. In the age of hypermedia, this has not gotten easier for the White House, it's gotten harder.

It's a distracted nation, fragmented and preoccupied. It was, arguably, the peculiar tragedy of Barack Obama that even as a transformational figure—and inspirational communicator—he couldn't really command much interest. As well, it might be a central tragedy of the news media that its old-fashioned and even benighted civic-minded belief that politics is the highest form of news has helped transform it from a mass business to a narrow-cast one. Alas, politics itself has more and more become a discrete business. Its appeal is B-to-B—business-to-business. The real swamp is the swamp of insular, inbred, incestuous interests. This isn't corruption so much as overspecialization. It's a wonk's life. Politics has gone one way, the culture another. The left-right junkies might pretend otherwise, but the great middle doesn't put political concerns at the top of their minds.

And yet, contravening all cultural and media logic, Donald Trump produced on a daily basis an astonishing, can't-stop-following-it narrative. And this was not even because he was changing or upsetting the fundamentals of American life. In six months as president, failing to master almost any aspect of the bureaucratic process, he had, beyond placing his nominee on the Supreme Court, accomplished, practically speaking, nothing. And yet, *OMG!!!* There almost was no other story in America—and in much of the world. That was the radical and transformational nature of the Trump presidency: it held everybody's attention.

Inside the White House, the daily brouhaha and world's fascination was no cause for joy. It was, in the White House staff's bitter view, the media that turned every day into a climactic, dastardly moment. And, in a sense, this was correct: every development cannot be climactic. The fact that yesterday's climax would soon, compared to the next climax, be piddling, rather bore out the disproportion. The media was failing to judge the relative importance of Trump events: most Trump events came to naught (arguably all of them did), and yet all were greeted with equal shock and horror. The White House staff believed that the media's Trump coverage lacked "context"—by this, they meant that people ought to realize that Trump was mostly just huffing and puffing.

At the same time, few in the White House did not assign blame to Trump for this as well. He seemed to lack the most basic understanding that a president's words and actions would, necessarily, be magnified to the nth power. In some convenient sense, he failed to understand this because he wanted the attention, no matter how often it disappointed him. But he also wanted it because again and again the response surprised him—and, as though every time was the first time, he could not modify his behavior.

Sean Spicer caught the brunt of the daily drama, turning this otherwise reasonable, mild-mannered, process-oriented professional into a joke figure standing at the White House door. In his daily out-of-body experience, as a witness to his own humiliation and loss for words, Spicer understood after a while—although he began to understand this beginning his first day on the job when dealing with the dispute about the inaugural audience numbers—that he had "gone down a rabbit hole." In this disorienting place, all public artifice, pretense, proportion, savvy, and self-awareness had been cast off, or—possibly another result of Trump never really intending to be president—never really figured into the state of being president.

On the other hand, constant hysteria did have one unintended political virtue. If every new event canceled out every other event, like some wacky news-cycle pyramid scheme, then you always survived another day.

* * *

Donald Trump's sons, Don Jr., thirty-nine, and Eric, thirty-three, existed in an enforced infantile relationship to their father, a role that embarrassed them, but one that they also professionally embraced. The role was to be Donald Trump's heirs and attendees. Their father took some regular pleasure in pointing out that they were in the back of the room when God handed out brains—but, then again, Trump tended to scorn anyone who might be smarter than he was. Their sister Ivanka, certainly no native genius, was the designated family smart person, her husband Jared the family's smooth operator. That left Don and Eric to errands and admin. In fact, the brothers had grown into reasonably competent family-owned-company executives (this is not saying all that much) because their father had little or no patience for actually running his company. Of course, quite a good amount of their professional time was spent on the whims, projects, promotions, and general way of life of DJT.

One benefit of their father's run for president was that it kept him away from the office. Still, the campaign's administration was largely their responsibility, so when the campaign went from caprice to a serious development in the Trump business and family, it caused a disruption in the family dynamic. Other people were suddenly eager to be Donald Trump's key lieutenants. There were the outsiders, like Corey Lewandowski, the campaign manager, but there was also the insider, brother-in-law Jared. Trump, not unusually for a family-run company, made everybody compete for his favor. The company was about him; it existed because of his name, personality, and charisma, so the highest standing in the company was reserved for those who could best serve him. There wasn't all that much competition for this role before he ran for president, but in early 2016, with the Republican Party collapsing and Trump rising, his sons faced a new professional and family situation.

Their brother-in-law had been slowly drawn into the campaign, partly at his wife's urging because her father's lack of constraint might actually affect the Trump business if they didn't keep an eye on him. And then he, with his brothers-in-law, was pulled in by the excitement of the campaign itself. By late spring 2016, when the nomination was all but clinched, the Trump campaign was a set of competing power centers with the knives out.

Lewandowski regarded both brothers and their brother-in-law with rolling-on-the-floor contempt: not only were Don Jr. and Eric stupid, and Jared somehow both supercilious and obsequious (the butler), but nobody knew a whit about politics—indeed, there wasn't an hour of political experience among them.

As time went on, Lewandowski became particularly close to the candidate. To the family, especially to Kushner, Lewandowski was an enabler. Trump's worst instincts flowed through Lewandowski. In early June, a little more than a month before the Republican National Convention, Jared and Ivanka decided that what was needed—for the sake of the campaign, for the sake of the Trump business—was an intervention.

Making common cause with Don Jr. and Eric, Jared and Ivanka pushed for a united front to convince Trump to oust Lewandowski. Don Jr., feeling squeezed not only by Lewandowski but by Jared, too, seized the opportunity. He would push out Lewandowski and become his replacement—and indeed, eleven days later Lewandowski would be gone.

All this was part of the background to one of the most preposterous meetings in modern politics. On June 9, 2016, Don Jr., Jared, and Paul Manafort met with a movieworthy cast of dubious characters in Trump Tower after having been promised damaging information about Hillary Clinton. Don Jr., encouraged by Jared and Ivanka, was trying to impress his father that he had the stuff to rise in the campaign.

When this meeting became public thirteen months later, it would, for the Trump White House, encapsulate both the case against collusion with the Russians and the case for it. It was a case, or the lack of one, not of masterminds and subterfuge, but of senseless and benighted people so guileless and unconcerned that they enthusiastically colluded in plain sight.

* * *

Walking into Trump Tower that June day were a well-connected lawyer from Moscow, who was a likely Russian agent; associates of the Azerbaijani Russian oligarch Aras Agalarov; a U.S. music promoter who managed Agalarov's son, a Russian pop star; and a Russian government lobbyist in Washington. Their purpose in visiting the campaign headquarters of a presumptive major party nominee for president of the United States was to meet with three of the most highly placed people on the campaign. This meeting was preceded by an email chain addressed to multiple recipients inside the Trump campaign of almost joyful intent: the Russians were offering a dump of negative or even incriminating information about their opponent.

Among the why-and-how theories of this imbecilic meeting:

- The Russians, in organized or freelance fashion, were trying to entrap the Trump campaign into a compromising relationship.
- The meeting was part of an already active cooperation on the part of the Trump campaign with the Russians to obtain and distribute damaging information about Hillary Clinton—and, indeed, within days of the Don Jr. meeting, WikiLeaks announced that it had obtained Clinton emails. Less than a month later, it started to release them.
- The wide-eyed Trump campaign, largely still playacting at running for president—and with no thought whatsoever of actually winning the election—was open to any and all entreaties and offers, because it had nothing to lose. Dopey Don Jr. (Fredo, as Steve Bannon would dub him, in one of his frequent *Godfather* borrowings) was simply trying to prove he was a player and a go-to guy.
- The meeting included the campaign chairman, Paul Manafort, and the campaign's most influential voice, Jared Kushner, because: (a) a

high-level conspiracy was being coordinated; (b) Manafort and Kushner, not taking the campaign very seriously, and without a thought of any consequence here, were merely entertained by the possibility of dirty tricks; (c) the three men were united in their plan to get rid of Lewandowski—with Don Jr. as the hatchet man—and, as part of this unity, Manafort and Kushner need to show up at Don Jr.'s silly meeting.

Whatever the reason for the meeting, no matter which of the above scenarios most accurately describes how this comical and alarming group came together, a year later, practically nobody doubted that Don Jr. would have wanted his father to know that he seized the initiative.

"The chance that Don Jr. did not walk these jumos up to his father's office on the twenty-sixth floor is zero," said an astonished and derisive Bannon, not long after the meeting was revealed.

"The three senior guys in the campaign," an incredulous Bannon went on, "thought it was a good idea to meet with a foreign government inside Trump Tower in the conference room on the twenty-fifth floor—with no lawyers. *They didn't have any lawyers.* Even if you thought that this was not treasonous, or unpatriotic, or bad shit, and I happen to think it's all of that, you should have called the FBI immediately. Even if you didn't think to do that, and you're totally amoral, and you wanted that information, you do it in a Holiday Inn in Manchester, New Hampshire, with your lawyers who meet with these people and go through everything and then they verbally come and tell another lawyer in a cut-out, and if you've got something, then you figure out how to dump it down to Breitbart or something like that, or maybe some other more legitimate publication. You never see it, you never know it, because you don't need to. . . . But that's the brain trust that they had."

All of the participants would ultimately plead that the meeting was utterly inconsequential, whatever the hope for it might have been, and admit that it was hapless. But even if that was true, a year later the revelation of the meeting had three profound and probably transformational effects:

First, the constant, ever repeated denials about there having been no discussion between campaign officials and the Russians connected to the Kremlin about the campaign, and, indeed, no meaningful contact between campaign officials and the Russian government, were exploded.

Second, the certainty among the White House staff that Trump himself would have not only been apprised of the details of this meeting, but have met the principals, meant that the president was caught out as a liar by those whose trust he most needed. It was another inflection point between hunkered-in-the-bunker and signed-on-for-the-wild-ride, and get-me-out-of-here.

Third, it was now starkly clear that everyone's interests diverged. The fortunes of Don Jr., Paul Manafort, and Jared Kushner hung individually in the balance. Indeed, the best guess by many in the West Wing was that the details of the meeting had been leaked by the Kushner side, thus sacrificing Don Jr. in an attempt to deflect responsibility away from themselves.

* * *

Even before word of the June 2016 meeting leaked out, Kushner's legal team—largely assembled in a rush since the appointment of Mueller, the special counsel—had been piecing together a forensic picture of both the campaign's Russian contacts and Kushner Companies' finances and money trail. In January, ignoring almost everybody's caution against it, Jared Kushner had entered the White House as a senior figure in the administration; now, six months later, he faced acute legal jeopardy. He had tried to keep a low profile, seeing himself as a behind-the-scenes counselor, but now his public position was not only endangering himself but the future of his family's business. As long as he remained exposed, his family was effectively blocked from most financial sources. Without access to this market, their holdings risked becoming distress debt situations.

Jared and Ivanka's self-created fantasylike life—two ambitious, well-mannered, well-liked young people living at the top of New York's social and financial world after having, in their version of humble fashion, accepted global power—had now, even with neither husband nor wife in office long enough to have taken any real action at all, come to the precipice of disgrace.

Jail was possible. So was bankruptcy. Trump may have been talking defiantly about offering pardons, or bragging about his power to give them, but that did not solve Kushner's business problems, nor did it provide a way to mollify Charlie Kushner, Jared's choleric and often irrational father. What's more, successfully navigating through the eye of the legal needle would require a careful touch and nuanced strategic approach on the part of the president—quite an unlikely development.

Meanwhile, the couple blamed everyone else in the White House. They blamed Priebus for the disarray that had produced a warlike atmosphere that propelled constant and damaging leaks, they blamed Bannon for leaking, and they blamed Spicer for poorly defending their virtue and interests.

They *needed* to defend themselves. One strategy was to get out of town (Bannon had a list of all the tense moments when the couple had taken a convenient holiday), and it happened that Trump would be attending the G20 summit Hamburg, Germany, on July 7 and 8. Jared and Ivanka accompanied the president on the trip, and while at the summit they learned that word of Don Jr.'s meeting with the Russians—and the couple kept pointedly presenting it as Don Jr.'s meeting—had leaked. Worse, they learned that the story was about to break in the *New York Times*.

Originally, Trump's staff was expecting details of the Don Jr. meeting to break on the website *Circa*. The lawyers, and spokesperson Mark Corallo, had been working to manage this news. But while in Hamburg, the president's staff learned that the *Times* was developing a story that had far more details about the meeting—quite possibly supplied by the Kushner side—which it would publish on Saturday, July 8. Advance knowledge of this article was kept from the president's legal team for the ostensible reason that it didn't involve the president.

In Hamburg, Ivanka, knowing the news would shortly get out, was presenting her signature effort: a World Bank fund to aid women entrepreneurs in developing countries. This was another instance of what White House staffers saw as the couple's extraordinarily off-message direction. Nowhere in the Trump campaign, nowhere on Bannon's white boards, nowhere in the heart of this president was there an interest in women entrepreneurs in developing countries. The daughter's agenda was singularly at odds with the father's—or at least the agenda that had elected him. Ivanka, in the view of almost every White House staffer, profoundly misunderstood the nature of her job and had converted traditional First Lady noblesse oblige efforts into White House staff work.

Shortly before boarding Air Force One for the return trip home, Ivanka—with what by now was starting to seem like an almost anarchic tone deafness—sat in for her father between Chinese president Xi Jinping and British prime minister Theresa May at the main G20 conference table. But this was mere distraction: as the president and his team huddled on the plane, the central subject was not the conference, it was how to respond to the *Times* story about Don Jr.'s and Jared's Trump Tower meeting, now only hours away from breaking.

En route to Washington, Sean Spicer and everybody else from the communications office was relegated to the back of the plane and excluded from the panicky discussions. Hope Hicks became the senior communications strategist, with the president, as always, her singular client. In the days following, that highest political state of being "in the room" was turned on its head. *Not* being in the room—in this case, the forward cabin on Air Force One—became an exalted status and get-out-of-jail-free card. "It used to hurt my feelings when I saw them running around doing things that were my job," said Spicer. "Now I'm glad to be out of the loop."

Included in the discussion on the plane were the president, Hicks, Jared and Ivanka, and their spokesperson, Josh Raffel. Ivanka, according to the later recollection of her team, would shortly leave the meeting, take a pill, and go to sleep. Jared, in the telling of his team, might have been there, but he was "not taking a pencil to anything." Nearby, in a small conference room watching the movie *Fargo*, were Dina Powell, Gary Cohn, Stephen Miller, and H. R. McMaster, all of whom would later insist that they were, however physically close to the unfolding crisis, removed from it. And, indeed, anyone "in the room" was caught in a moment that would shortly receive the special counsel's close scrutiny, with the relevant question being whether one or more federal employees had induced other federal employees to lie.

An aggrieved, unyielding, and threatening president dominated the discussion, pushing into line his daughter and her husband, Hicks, and Raffel. Kasowitz—the lawyer whose specific job was to keep Trump at arm's length from Russian-related matters—was kept on hold on the phone for an hour and then not put through. The president insisted that the meeting in Trump Tower was purely and simply about Russian adoption policy. That's what was discussed, period. Period. Even though it was likely, if not certain, that the *Times* had the incriminating email chain—in fact, it was quite possible that Jared and Ivanka and the lawyers *knew* the *Times* had this email chain—the president ordered that no one should let on to the more problematic discussion about Hillary Clinton.

It was a real-time example of denial and cover-up. The president believed, belligerently, what he believed. Reality was what he was convinced it was—or should be. Hence the official story: there was a brief courtesy meeting in Trump Tower about adoption policy, to no result, attended by senior aides and unaffiliated Russian nationals. The crafting of this manufactured tale was a rogue operation by rookies—always the two most combustible elements of a cover-up.

In Washington, Kasowitz and the legal team's spokesperson, Mark Corallo, weren't informed of either the *Times* article or the plan for how to respond to it until Don Jr.'s initial statement went out just before the story broke that Saturday.

Over the course of next seventy-two hours or so, the senior staff found itself wholly separate from—and, once again, looking on in astonishment at—the actions of the president's innermost circle of aides. In this, the relationship of the president and Hope Hicks, long tolerated as a quaint bond between the older man and a trustworthy young woman, began to be seen as anomalous and alarming. Completely devoted to accommodating him, she, his media facilitator, was the ultimate facilitator of unmediated behavior. His impulses and thoughts—unedited, unreviewed, unchallenged—not only passed through him, but, via Hicks, traveled out into the world without any other White House arbitration.

"The problem isn't Twitter, it's Hope," observed one communication staffer.

On July 9, a day after publishing its first story, the *Times* noted that the Trump Tower meeting was specifically called to discuss the Russian offer of damaging material about Clinton. The next day, as the *Times* prepared to publish the full email chain, Don Jr. hurriedly dumped it himself. There followed an almost daily count of new figures—all, in their own way, peculiar and unsettling—who emerged as participants in the meeting.

But the revelation of the Trump Tower meeting had another, perhaps even larger dimension. It marked the collapse of the president's legal strategy: the demise of Steve Bannon's Clinton-emulating firewall around the president.

The lawyers, in disgust and alarm, saw, in effect, each principal becoming a witness to another principal's potential misdeeds—all conspiring with one another to get their stories straight. The client and his family were panicking and running their own defense. Short-term headlines were overwhelming any sort of long-term strategy. "The worst thing you can do is lie to a prosecutor," said one member of the legal team. The persistent Trump idea that it is not a crime to lie to the media was regarded by the legal team as at best reckless and, in itself, potentially actionable: an explicit attempt to throw sand into the investigation's gears.

Mark Corallo was instructed not to speak to the press, indeed not to even answer his phone. Later that week, Corallo, seeing no good outcome—and privately confiding that he believed the meeting on Air Force One represented a likely obstruction of justice—quit. (The Jarvanka side would put it out that Corallo was fired.)

"These guys are not going to be second-guessed by the kids," said a frustrated Bannon about the firewall team.

Likewise, the Trump family, no matter its legal exposure, was not going to be run by its lawyers. Jared and Ivanka helped to coordinate a set of lurid leaks—alleging drinking, bad behavior, personal life in disarray—about Marc Kasowitz, who had advised the president to send the couple home. Shortly after the presidential party returned to Washington, Kasowitz was out.

* * *

Blame continued to flow. The odor of a bitter new reality, if not doom, that attached to the Comey-Mueller debacle was compounded by everyone's efforts not to be tagged by it.

The sides in the White House—Jared, Ivanka, Hope Hicks, and an increasingly ambivalent Dina Powell and Gary Cohn on one side, and almost everyone else, including Priebus, Spicer, Conway, and most clearly Bannon, on the other—were most distinguished by their culpability in or distance from the Comey-Mueller calamity. It was, as the non-Jarvanka side would unceasingly point out, a calamity *of their own making.* Therefore it became an effort of the Jarvankas not only to achieve distance for themselves from the causes of the debacle—such involvement as they had they now cast as strictly passive involvement or just following orders—but to suggest that their adversaries were at least equally at fault.

Shortly after the Don Jr. story broke, the president not unsuccessfully changed the subject by focusing the blame for the Comey-Mueller mess on Sessions, even more forcefully belittling and threatening him and suggesting that his days were numbered.

Bannon, who continued to defend Sessions, and who believed that he had militantly—indeed with scathing attacks on the Jarvankas for their stupidity—walled himself off from the Comey smashup, was now suddenly getting calls from reporters with leaks that painted him as an engaged participant in the Comey decision.

In a furious phone call to Hicks, Bannon blamed the leaks on her. In time, he had come to see the twenty-eight-year-old as nothing more than a hapless presidential enabler and poor-fish Jarvanka flunky—and he believed she had now deeply implicated herself in the entire disaster by participating in the Air Force One meeting. The next day, with more inquiries coming from reporters, he confronted Hicks inside the cabinet room, accusing her of doing Jared and Ivanka's dirty work. The face-off quickly escalated into an existential confrontation between the two sides of the White House—two sides on a total war footing.

"*You don't know what you're doing,*" shouted a livid Bannon at Hicks, demanding to know who she worked for, the White House or Jared and

Ivanka. "*You don't know how much trouble you are in*," he screamed, telling her that if she didn't get a lawyer he would call her father and tell him he had better get her one. "*You are dumb as a stone!*" Moving from the cabinet room across the open area into the president's earshot, "a loud, scary, clearly threatening" Bannon, in the Jarvanka telling, yelled, "*I am going to fuck you and your little group!*" with a baffled president plaintively wanting to know, "What's going on?"

In the Jarvanka-side account, Hicks then ran from Bannon, hysterically sobbing and "visibly terrified." Others in the West Wing marked this as the high point of the boiling enmity between the two sides. For the Jarvankas, Bannon's rant was also a display that they believed they could use against him. The Jarvanka people pushed Priebus to refer the matter to the White House counsel, billing this as the most verbally abusive moment in the history of the West Wing, or at least certainly up among the most abusive episodes ever.

For Bannon, this was just more Jarvanka desperation—they were the ones, not him, saddled with Comey-Mueller. They were the ones panicking and out of control.

For the rest of his time in the White House, Bannon would not speak to Hicks again.

20

MCMASTER AND SCARAMUCCI

Trump was impetuous and yet did not like to make decisions, at least not ones that seemed to corner him into having to analyze a problem. And no decision hounded him so much—really from the first moment of his presidency—as what to do about Afghanistan. It was a conundrum that became a battle. It involved not only his own resistance to analytic reasoning, but the left brain/right brain divide of his White House, the split between those who argued for disruption and those who wanted to uphold the status quo.

In this, Bannon became the disruptive and unlikely White House voice for peace—or anyway a kind of peace. In Bannon's view, only he and the not-too-resolute backbone of Donald Trump stood between consigning fifty thousand more American soldiers to hopelessness in Afghanistan.

Representing the status quo—and, ideally, a surge on top of the status quo—was H. R. McMaster, who, next to Jarvanka, had become Bannon's prime target for abuse. On this front, Bannon forged an easy bond with the president, who didn't much hide his contempt for the PowerPoint general. Bannon and the president enjoyed trash-talking McMaster together.

McMaster was a protégé of David Petraeus, the former CENTCOM and Afghanistan commander who became Obama's CIA director before resigning in a scandal involving a love affair and the mishandling of classified information. Petraeus and now McMaster represented a kind of business-as-usual approach in Afghanistan and the Middle East. A stubborn McMaster kept proposing to the president new versions of the surge, but at each pitch Trump would wave him out of the Oval Office and roll his eyes in despair and disbelief.

The president's distaste and rancor for McMaster grew on pace with the approaching need to finally make a decision on Afghanistan, a decision he continued to put off. His position on Afghanistan—a military quagmire he knew little about, other than that it was a quagmire—had always been a derisive and caustic kiss-off of the sixteen-year war. Having inherited it did not make his feelings warmer or inspire him to want to dwell on it further. He knew the war was cursed and, knowing that, felt no need to know more. He put the responsibility for it on two of his favorite people to blame: Bush and Obama.

For Bannon, Afghanistan represented one more failure of establishment thinking. More precisely, it represented the establishment's inability to confront failure.

Curiously, McMaster had written a book on exactly this subject, a scathing critique of the unchallenged assumptions with which military leaders pursued the Vietnam War. The book was embraced by liberals and the establishment, with whom, in Bannon's view, McMaster had become hopelessly aligned. And now—ever afraid of the unknown, intent on keeping options open, dedicated to stability, and eager to protect his establishment cred—McMaster was recommending a huge troop surge in Afghanistan.

* * *

By early July, the pressure to make a decision was approaching the boiling point. Trump had already authorized the Pentagon to deploy the troop resources it believed were needed, but Defense Secretary Mattis refused to act without a specific authorization from the president. Trump would finally have to make the call—unless he could find a way to put it off again.

Bannon's thought was that the decision could be made for the president—a way the president liked to have decisions made—if Bannon could get rid of McMaster. That would both head off the strongest voice for more troops and also avenge Bannon's ouster by McMaster's hand from the NSC.

With the president promising that he would make up his mind by August, and McMaster, Mattis, and Tillerson pressing for a decision as soon as possible, Bannon-inspired media began a campaign to brand McMaster as a globalist, interventionist, and all around not-our-kind-of-Trumper—and, to boot, soft on Israel.

It was a scurrilous, albeit partly true, attack. McMaster was in fact talking to Petraeus often. The kicker was the suggestion that McMaster was giving inside dope to Petraeus, a pariah because of his guilty plea regarding his mishandling of classified information. It was also the case that McMaster was disliked by the president and on the point of being dismissed.

It was Bannon, riding high again, enjoying himself in a moment of supreme overconfidence.

Indeed, in part to prove there were other options beyond more troops or humiliating defeat—and logically there probably weren't more options—Bannon became a sponsor of Blackwater-founder Erik Prince's obviously self-serving idea to replace the U.S. military force with private contractors and CIA and Special Operations personnel. The notion was briefly embraced by the president, then ridiculed by the military.

By now Bannon believed McMaster would be out by August. He was sure he had the president's word on this. Done deal. "McMaster wants to send more troops to Afghanistan, so we're going to send *him*," said a triumphal Bannon. In Bannon's scenario, Trump would give McMaster a fourth star and "promote" him to top military commander in Afghanistan.

As with the chemical attack in Syria, it was Dina Powell—even as she made increasingly determined efforts to get herself out of the White House, either on a Sheryl Sandberg trajectory or, stopping first at a way station, as ambassador to the United Nations—who struggled to help support the least disruptive, most keep-all-options-open approach. In this, both because the approach seemed like the safest course and because it was the opposite of Bannon's course, she readily recruited Jared and Ivanka.

The solution Powell endorsed, which was designed to put the problem and the reckoning off for another year or two or three, was likely to make the United States' position in Afghanistan even more hopeless. Instead of sending fifty or sixty thousand troops—which, at insupportable cost and the risk of national fury, might in fact win the war—the Pentagon would send some much lower number, one which would arouse little notice and merely prevent us from losing the war. In the Powell and Jarvanka view, it was the moderate, best-case, easiest-to-sell course, and it struck just the right balance between the military's unacceptable scenarios: retreat and dishonor or many more troops.

Before long, a plan to send four, five, six, or (tops) seven thousand troops became the middle-course strategy supported by the national security establishment and most everyone else save for Bannon and the president. Powell even helped design a PowerPoint deck that McMaster began using with the president: pictures of Kabul in the 1970s when it still looked something like a modern city. It could be like this again, the president was told, if we are resolute!

But even with almost everyone arrayed against him, Bannon was confident he was winning. He had a united right-wing press with him, and, he believed, a fed-up, working-class Trump base—its children the likely Afghanistan fodder. Most of all, he had the president. Pissed off that he was being handed the same problem and the same options that were handed Obama, Trump continued to heap spleen and mockery on McMaster.

Kushner and Powell organized a leak campaign in McMaster's defense. Their narrative was not a pro-troops defense; instead, it was about Bannon's leaks and his use of right-wing media to besmirch McMaster, "one of the most decorated and respected generals of his generation." The issue was not Afghanistan, the issue was Bannon. In this narrative, it was McMaster, a figure of stability, against Bannon, a figure of disruption. It was the *New York Times* and the *Washington Post*, who came to the defense of McMaster, against Breitbart and its cronies and satellites.

It was the establishment and never-Trumpers against the America-first Trumpkins. In many respects, Bannon was outgunned and outnumbered, yet he still thought he had it nailed. And when he won, not only would another grievously stupid chapter in the war in Afghanistan be avoided, but Jarvanka, and Powell, their factotum, would be further consigned to irrelevance and powerlessness.

* * *

As the debate moved toward resolution, the NSC, in its role as a presenter of options rather than an advocate for them (although of course it was advocating, too), presented three: withdrawal; Erik Prince's army of contractors; and a conventional, albeit limited, surge.

Withdrawal, whatever its merits—and however much a takeover of Afghanistan by the Taliban could be delayed or mitigated—still left Donald Trump with having lost a war, an insupportable position for the president.

The second option, a force of contractors and the CIA, was largely deep-sixed by the CIA. The agency had spent sixteen years successfully avoiding Afghanistan, and everyone knew that careers were not advanced in Afghanistan, they died in Afghanistan. So please keep us out of it.

That left McMaster's position, a modest surge, argued by Secretary of State Tillerson: more troops in Afghanistan, which, somehow, slightly, would be there on a different basis, somewhat, with a different mission, subtly, than that of troops sent there before.

The military fully expected the president to sign off on the third option. But on July 19, at a meeting of the national security team in the situation room at the White House, Trump lost it.

For two hours, he angrily railed against the mess he had been handed. He threatened to fire almost every general in the chain of command. He couldn't fathom, he said, how it had taken so many months of study to come up with this nothing-much-different plan. He disparaged the advice that came from generals and praised the advice from enlisted men. If we have to be in Afghanistan, he demanded, why can't we make money off it? China, he complained, has mining rights, but not the United States. (He was referring to a ten-year-old U.S.-backed deal.) This is just like the

21 Club, he said, suddenly confusing everyone with this reference to a New York restaurant, one of his favorites. In the 1980s, 21 closed for a year and hired a large number of consultants to analyze how to make the restaurant more profitable. In the end, their advice was: Get a bigger kitchen. *Exactly what any waiter would have said*, Trump shouted.

To Bannon, the meeting was a high point of the Trump presidency to date. The generals were punting and waffling and desperately trying to save face—they were, according to Bannon, talking pure "gobbledygook" in the situation room. "Trump was standing up to them," said a happy Bannon. "Hammering them. He left a bowel movement in the middle of their Afghan plans. Again and again, he came back to the same point: we're stuck and losing and nobody here has a plan to do much better than that."

Though there was still no hint of a viable alternative strategy in Afghanistan, Bannon, his Jarvanka frustration cresting, was sure he was the winner here. McMaster was toast.

* * *

Later on the day of the Afghanistan briefing, Bannon heard about yet another harebrained Jarvanka scheme. They planned to hire Anthony Scaramucci, aka "the Mooch."

After Trump had clinched the nomination more than a year before, Scaramucci—a hedge funder and go-to Trump surrogate for cable business news (mostly Fox Business Channel)—had become a reliable presence at Trump Tower. But then, in the last month of the campaign, with polls predicting a humiliating Trump defeat, he was suddenly nowhere to be seen. The question "Where's the Mooch?" seemed to be just one more indicator of the campaign's certain and pitiless end.

But on the day after the election, Steve Bannon—soon to be named chief strategist for the forty-fifth president-elect—was greeted as he arrived midmorning in Trump Tower by Anthony Scaramucci, holding a Starbucks coffee for him.

Over the next three months, Scaramucci, although no longer needed as a surrogate and without anything else particularly to do, became a constant hovering—or even lurking—presence at Trump Tower. Ever unflagging, he interrupted a meeting in Kellyanne Conway's office in early January just to make sure she knew that her husband's firm, Wachtell, Lipton, was representing him. Having made that point, name-dropping and vastly praising the firm's key partners, he then helped himself to a chair in Conway's meeting and, for both Conway's and her visitor's benefit, offered a stirring testimonial to the uniqueness and sagacity of Donald Trump and the working-class people—speaking of which, he took the opportunity to provide a résumé of his own Long Island working-class bona fides—who had elected him.

Scaramucci was hardly the only hanger-on and job seeker in the building, but his method was among the most dogged. He spent his days looking for meetings to be invited into, or visitors to engage with—this was easy because every other job seeker was looking for someone with whom to chat it up, so he soon became something like the unofficial offi cial greeter. Whenever possible, he would grab a few minutes with any senior staffer who would not rebuff him. As he waited to be offered a high White House position, he was, he seemed personally certain, reaffirming his loyalty and team spirit and unique energy. He was so confident about his future that he made a deal to sell his hedge fund, Skybridge Capital, to HNA Group, the Chinese megaconglomerate.

Political campaigns, substantially based on volunteer help, attract a range of silly, needy, and opportunistic figures. The Trump campaign perhaps scraped lower in the barrel than most. The Mooch, for one, might not have been the most peculiar volunteer in the Trump run for president, but many figured him to be among the most shameless.

It was not just that before he became a dedicated supporter of Donald Trump, he was a dedicated naysayer, or that he had once been an Obama and Hillary Clinton supporter. The problem was that, really, nobody liked him. Even for someone in politics, he was immodest and incorrigible, and followed by a trail of self-serving and often contradictory statements made to this person about that person, which invariably made it back to whatever person was being most negatively talked about.

He was not merely a shameless self-promoter; he was a *proud* self-promoter. He was, by his own account, a fantastic networker. (This boast was surely true, since Skybridge Capital was a fund of funds, which is less a matter of investment acumen than of knowing top fund managers and being able to invest with them.) He had paid as much as half a million dollars to have his firm's logo appear in the movie *Wall Street 2* and to buy himself a cameo part in the film. He ran a yearly conference for hedge funders at which he himself was the star. He had a television gig at Fox Business Channel. He was a famous partier every year at Davos, once exuberantly dancing alongside the son of Muammar Gaddafi.

As for the presidential campaign, when signing on with Donald Trump—after he had bet big against Trump—he billed himself as a version of Trump, and he saw the two of them as a new kind of showman and communicator set to transform politics.

Although his persistence and his constant on-the-spot personal lobbying might not have endeared him to anybody, it did prompt the "What to do with Scaramucci?" question, which somehow came to beg an answer. Priebus, trying to deal with the Mooch problem and dispose of him at the same time, suggested that he take a money-raising job as finance director of the RNC—an offer Scaramucci rebuffed in a blowup in Trump Tower, loudly bad-mouthing Priebus in vivid language, a mere preview of what was to come.

While he wanted a job with the Trump administration, the Mooch specifically wanted one of the jobs that would give him a tax break on the sale of his business. A federal program provides for deferred payment of capital gains in the event of a sale of property to meet ethical requirements. Scaramucci needed a job that would get him a "certificate of divestiture," which is what an envious Scaramucci knew Gary Cohn had received for the sale of his Goldman stock.

A week before the inaugural he was finally offered such a job: director of the White House Office of Public Engagement and Intergovernmental Affairs. He would be the president's representative and cheerleader before Trump-partial interest groups.

But the White House ethics office balked—the sale of his business would take months to complete and he would be directly negotiating with an entity that was at least in part controlled by the Chinese government. And because Scaramucci had little support from anybody else, he was effectively blocked. It was, a resentful Scaramucci noted, one of the few instances in the Trump government when someone's business conflicts interfered with a White House appointment.

And yet with a salesman's tenacity, the Mooch pressed on. He appointed himself a Trump ambassador without portfolio. He declared himself Trump's man on Wall Street, even if, practically speaking, he wasn't a Trump man and he was exiting his firm on Wall Street. He was also in constant touch with anybody from the Trump circle who was willing to be in touch with him.

The "What to do with the Mooch" question persisted. Kushner, with whom Scaramucci had exercised a rare restraint during the campaign, and who had steadily heard from other New York contacts about Scaramucci's continued loyalty, helped push the question.

Priebus and others held Scaramucci at bay until June and then, as a bit of a punch line, Scaramucci was offered and, degradingly, had to accept, being named senior vice president and chief strategy officer for the U.S. Export-Import Bank, an executive branch agency Trump had long vowed to eliminate. But the Mooch was not ready to give up the fight: after yet more lobbying, he was offered, at Bannon's instigation, the post of ambassador to the Organization for Economic Co-operation and Development. The job came with a twenty-room apartment on the Seine, a full staff, and—Bannon found this part particularly amusing—absolutely no influence or responsibilities.

* * *

Meanwhile, another persistent question, "What to do with Spicer," seemed to somehow have been joined to the disaster involving the bungled response to the news of the June 2016 meeting between Don Jr., Jared, and the Russians. Since the president, while traveling on Air Force One, had actually dictated Don Jr.'s response to the initial *Times* report about the meeting, the blame for this should have been laid at the feet of Trump and Hope Hicks: Trump dictated, Hicks transcribed. But because no disasters could be laid at the president's feet, Hicks herself was spared. And, even though he had been pointedly excluded from the Trump Tower crisis, the blame for the episode was now put at Spicer's feet, precisely because, his loyalty in doubt, he and the communications staff *had* to be excluded.

In this, the comms team was judged to be antagonistic if not hostile to the interests of Jared and Ivanka; Spicer and his people had failed to mount an inclusive defense for them, nor had the comms team adequately defended the White House. This of course homed in on the essential and obvious point: although the junior first couple were mere staffers and not part of the institutional standing of the White House, they thought and acted as if they were part of the presidential entity. Their ire and increasing bitterness came from some of the staff's reluctance—really, a deep and intensifying resistance—to treat them as part and parcel of the presidency. (Once Priebus had to take Ivanka aside to make sure she understood that in her official role, she was just a staffer. Ivanka had insisted on the distinction that she was a staffer-slash-First Daughter.)

Bannon was their public enemy; they expected nothing of him. But Priebus and Spicer they regarded as functionaries, and their job was to support the White House's goals, which included their goals and interests.

Spicer, ever ridiculed in the media for his cockamamie defense of the White House and a seeming dumb loyalty, had been judged by the president, quite from the inauguration, to be not loyal enough and not nearly as aggressive as he should be in Trump's defense. Or, in Jared and Ivanka's view, in his family's defense. "What does Spicer's forty-member comm staff actually *do*?" was a persistent First Family question.

* * *

Almost from the beginning, the president had been interviewing potential new press secretaries. He appeared to have offered the job to various people, one of whom was Kimberly Guilfoyle, the Fox News personality and cohost of *The Five*. Guilfoyle, the former wife of California Democrat Gavin Newsom, was also reported to be Anthony Scaramucci's girlfriend, a rumor he denied. Unbeknownst to the White House, Scaramucci's personal life was in dramatic free fall. On July 9, nine months pregnant with their second child, Scaramucci's wife filed for divorce.

Guilfoyle, knowing that Spicer was on his way out but having decided not to take his job—or, according to others in the White House, never having been offered it—suggested Scaramucci, who set to work convincing Jared and Ivanka that theirs was largely a PR problem and that they were ill served by the current communications team.

Scaramucci called a reporter he knew to urge that an upcoming story about Kushner's Russian contacts be spiked. He followed up by having another mutual contact call the reporter to say that if the story was spiked it would help the Mooch get into the White House, whereupon the reporter would have special Mooch access. The Mooch then assured Jared and Ivanka that he had, in this clever way, killed the story.

Now Scaramucci had their attention. *We need some new thinking*, the couple thought; *we need somebody who is more on our side*. The fact that Scaramucci was from New York, and Wall Street, and was rich, reassured them that he understood what the deal was. And that he would understand the stakes and know that an aggressive game needed to be played.

On the other hand, the couple did not want to be perceived as being heavy-handed. So, after bitterly accusing Spicer of not defending them adequately, they suddenly backed off and suggested that they were just looking to add a new voice to the mix. The job of White House communications director, which had no precise purview, had been vacant since May, when Mike Dubke, whose presence at the White House had hardly registered, resigned. Scaramucci could take this job, the couple figured, and in that role he could be their ally.

"He's good on television," Ivanka told Spicer when she explained the rationale for hiring a former hedge fund manager as White House communications director. "Maybe he can help us."

It was the president who, meeting with Scaramucci, was won over by the Mooch's cringeworthy Wall Street hortatory flattery. ("I can only hope to realize a small part of your genius as a communicator, but you are my example and model" was one report of the gist of the Scaramucci supplication.) And it was Trump who then urged that Scaramucci become the true communications chief, reporting directly to the president.

On July 19, Jared and Ivanka, through intermediaries, put a feeler out to Bannon: What would he think about Scaramucci's coming on board in the comms job?

So preposterous did this seem to Bannon—it was a cry of haplessness, and certain evidence that the couple had become truly desperate—that he refused to consider or even reply to the question. Now he was sure: Jarvanka was losing it.

21

BANNON AND SCARAMUCCI

Bannon's apartment in Arlington, Virginia, a fifteen-minute drive from downtown Washington, was called the "safe house." This seemed somehow to acknowledge his transience and to nod, with whatever irony, to the underground and even romantic nature of his politics—the roguish and *joie de guerre* alt-right. Bannon had decamped here from the Breitbart Embassy on A Street on Capitol Hill. It was a one-bedroom graduate-student sort of apartment, in a mixed-use building over a mega-McDonald's—quite belying Bannon's rumored fortune—with five or six hundred books (emphasis on popular history) stacked against the wall without benefit of shelving. His lieutenant, Alexandra Preate, also lived in the building, as did the American lawyer for Nigel Farage, the right-wing British Brexit leader who was part of the greater Breitbart circle.

On the evening on Thursday, July 20, the day after the contentious meeting about Afghanistan, Bannon was hosting a small dinner—organized by Preate, with Chinese takeout. Bannon was in an expansive, almost celebratory, mood. Still, Bannon knew, just when you felt on top of the world in the Trump administration, you could probably count on getting cut down. That was the pattern and price of one-man leadership—insecure-man leadership. The other biggest guy in the room always had to be reduced in size.

Many around him felt Bannon was going into another bad cycle. In his first run around the track, he'd been punished by the president for his *Time* magazine cover and for the *Saturday Night Live* portrayal of "President Bannon"—that cruelest of digs to Trump. Now there was a new book, *The Devil's Bargain*, and it claimed, often in Bannon's own words, that Trump could not have done it without him. The president was again greatly peeved.

Still, Bannon seemed to feel he had broken through. Whatever happened, he had clarity. It was such a mess inside in the White House that, if nothing else, this clarity would put him on top. His agenda was front and center, and his enemies sidelined. Jared and Ivanka were getting blown up every day and were now wholly preoccupied with protecting themselves. Dina Powell was looking for another job. McMaster had screwed himself on Afghanistan. Gary Cohn, once a killer enemy, was now desperate to be named Fed chairman and currying favor with Bannon—"licking my balls," Bannon said with a quite a cackle. In return for supporting Cohn's campaign to win the Fed job, Bannon was extracting fealty from him for the right-wing trade agenda.

The geniuses were fucked. Even POTUS might be fucked. But Bannon had the vision and the discipline—he was sure he did. "I'm cracking my shit every day. The nationalist agenda, we're fucking owning it. I'll be there for the duration."

Before the dinner, Bannon had sent around an article from the *Guardian*—though one of the leading English-language left-leaning newspapers, it was nevertheless Bannon's favorite paper—about the backlash to globalization. The article, by the liberal journalist Nikil Saval, both accepted Bannon's central populist political premise—"the competition between workers in developing and developed countries . . . helped drive down wages and job security for workers in developed countries"—and elevated it to the epochal fight of our time. Davos was dead and Bannon was very much alive. "Economists who were once ardent proponents of globalization have become some of its most prominent critics," wrote Saval. "Erstwhile supporters now concede, at least in part, that it has produced inequality, unemployment and downward pressure on wages. Nuances and criticisms that economists only used to raise in private seminars are finally coming out in the open."

"I'm starting to get tired of winning" was all that Bannon said in his email with the link to the article.

Now, restless and pacing, Bannon was recounting how Trump had dumped on McMaster and, as well, savoring the rolling-on-the-floor absurdity of the geniuses' Scaramucci gambit. But most of all he was incredulous about something else that had happened the day before.

Unbeknownst to senior staff, or to the comms office—other than by way of a pro forma schedule note—the president had given a major interview to the *New York Times*. Jared and Ivanka, along with Hope Hicks, had set it up. The *Times*'s Maggie Haberman, Trump's bête noire ("very mean, and not smart") and yet his go-to journalist for some higher sort of approval, had been called in to see the president with her colleagues Peter Baker and Michael Schmidt. The result was one of the most peculiar and ill-advised interviews in presidential history, from a president who had already, several times before, achieved that milestone.

In the interview, Trump had done his daughter and son-in-law's increasingly frantic bidding. He had, even if to no clear end and without certain strategy, continued on his course of threatening the attorney general for recusing himself and opening the door to a special prosecutor. He openly pushed Sessions to resign—mocking and insulting him and daring him to try to stay. However much this seemed to advance no one's cause, except perhaps that of the special prosecutor, Bannon's incredulity—"Jefferson Beauregard Sessions is not going to go anywhere"—was most keenly focused on another remarkable passage in the interview: the president had admonished the special counsel not to cross the line into his family's finances.

"Ehhh . . . ehhh . . . ehhh!" screeched Bannon, making the sound of an emergency alarm. "Don't look here! Let's tell a prosecutor what *not* to look at!"

Bannon then described the conversation he'd had with the president earlier that day: "I went right into him and said, 'Why did you say that?' And he says, 'The Sessions thing?' and I say, 'No, that's bad, but it's another day at the office.' I said, 'Why did you say it was off limits to go after your family's finances?' And he says, 'Well, it is . . . .' I go, 'Hey, they are going to determine their mandate. . . . You may not like it, but you just guaranteed if you want to get anybody else in [the special counsel] slot, every senator will make him swear that the first thing he's going to do is come in and subpoena your fucking tax returns.' "

Bannon, with further disbelief, recounted the details of a recent story from the *Financial Times* about Felix Sater, one of the shadiest of the shady Trump-associated characters, who was closely aligned with Trump's longtime personal lawyer, Michael Cohen (reportedly a target of the Mueller investigation), and a key follow-the-money link to Russia. Sater, "get ready for it—I know this may shock you, but wait for it"—had had major problems with the law before, "caught with a couple of guys in Boca running Russian money through a boiler room." And, it turns out, "Brother Sater" was prosecuted by—"wait"—*Andrew Weissmann.* (Mueller had recently hired Weissmann, a high-powered Washington lawyer who headed the DOJ's criminal fraud division.) "You've got the LeBron James of money laundering investigations on you, Jarvanka. My asshole just got so tight!"

Bannon quite literally slapped his sides and then returned to his conversation with the president. "And he goes, 'That's not their mandate.' Seriously, dude?"

Preate, putting out the Chinese food on a table, said, "It wasn't their mandate to put Arthur Andersen out of business during Enron, but that didn't stop Andrew Weissmann"—one of the Enron prosecutors.

"You realize where this is going," Bannon continued. "This is all about *money laundering.* Mueller chose Weissmann first and he is a money laundering guy. Their path to fucking Trump goes right through Paul Manafort, Don Jr., and Jared Kushner . . . It's as plain as a hair on your face. . . . It goes through all the Kushner shit. They're going to roll those two guys up and say play me or trade me. But . . . '*executive privilege!*' " Bannon mimicked. " 'We've got executive privilege!' There's no executive privilege! We proved that in Watergate."

An expressive man, Bannon seemed to have suddenly exhausted himself. After a pause, he added wearily: "They're sitting on a beach trying to stop a Category Five."

With his hands in front of him, he mimed something like a force field that would isolate him from danger. "It's not my deal. He's got the five geniuses around him: Jarvanka, Hope Hicks, Dina Powell, and Josh Raffel." He threw up his hands again, this time as if to say *Hands off.* "I know no Russians, I don't know nothin' about nothin'. I'm not being a witness. I'm not hiring a lawyer. It is not going to be my ass in front of a microphone on national TV answering questions. Hope Hicks is so fucked she doesn't even know it. They are going to lay her out. They're going to crack Don Junior like an egg on national TV. Michael Cohen, cracked like an egg. He"—the president—"said to me everybody would take that Don Junior meeting with the Russians. I said, 'Everybody would *not* take that meeting.' I said, 'I'm a naval officer. I'm not going to take a meeting with Russian nationals, and do it in headquarters, are you fucking insane?' and he says, 'But he's a good boy.' There were no meetings like that after I took over the campaign."

Bannon's tone veered from ad absurdum desperation to resignation.

"If he fires Mueller it just brings the impeachment quicker. Why not, let's do it. Let's get it on. Why not? What am I going to do? Am I going to go in and save him? He's Donald Trump. He's always gonna do things. He wants an unrecused attorney general. I told him if Jeff Sessions goes, Rod Rosenstein goes, and then Rachel Brand"—the associate attorney general, next in line after Rosenstein—"goes, we'll be digging down into Obama career guys. An Obama guy will be acting attorney general. I said you're not going to get Rudy"—Trump had again revived a wish for his loyalists Rudy Giuliani or Chris Christie to take the job—"because he was on the campaign and will have to recuse himself, and Chris Christie, too, so those are masturbatory fantasies, get those out of your brain. And, for anybody to get confirmed now, they are going to have to swear and ensure that things will go ahead and they won't fire anybody, because you said yesterday—*Ehhh . . . ehhh . . . .ehhh!*—'my family finances are off limits,' and they're going to demand that, whoever he is, he promises and commits to make the family finances part of this investigation. I told him as night follows day that's a lock, so you better hope Sessions stays around."

"He was calling people in New York last night asking what he should do," added Preate. (Almost everybody in the White House followed Trump's thinking by tracking whom he had called the night before.)

Bannon sat back and, with steam-rising frustration—almost a cartoon figure—he outlined his Clinton-like legal plan. "They went to the mattresses with amazing discipline. They ground through it." But that *was* about discipline, he emphasized, and Trump, said Bannon, noting the obvious, was the least disciplined man in politics.

It was clear where Mueller and his team were going, said Bannon: they would trace a money trail through Paul Manafort, Michael Flynn, Michael Cohen, and Jared Kushner and roll one or all of them on the president.

It's Shakespearean, he said, enumerating the bad advice from his family circle: "It's the geniuses, the same people who talked him into firing Comey, the same people on Air Force One who cut out his outside legal team, knowing the email was out there, knowing that email existed, put the statement out about Don Junior, that the meeting was all about adoptions . . . the same geniuses trying to get Sessions fired.

"Look, Kasowitz has known him for twenty-five years. Kasowitz has gotten him out of all kinds of jams. Kasowitz on the campaign—what did we have, a hundred women? Kasowitz took care of all of them. And now he's out in, what, four weeks? He's New York's toughest lawyer. Mark Corallo, toughest motherfucker I ever met, just can't do it."

Jared and Ivanka believe, said Bannon, that if they advocate prison reform and save DACA—the program to protect the children of illegal immigrants—the liberals will come to their defense. He digressed briefly to characterize Ivanka Trump's legislative acumen, and her difficulty—which had become quite a White House preoccupation—in finding sponsorship for her family leave proposal. "Here's why, I keep telling her: there's no political constituency in it. You know how easy it is to get a bill sponsored, any schmendrick can do it. You know why your bill has no sponsorship? Because people realize how *dumb* it is." In fact, said, Bannon, eyes rolling and mouth agape, it was the Jarvanka idea to try to trade off amnesty for the border wall. "If not the dumbest idea in Western civilization, it's up there in the top three. Do these geniuses even know who we are?"

Just then Bannon took a call, the caller telling him that it looked as if Scaramucci might indeed be getting the job of communications director. "Don't fuck with me, dude," he laughed. "Don't fuck with me like that!"

He got off the phone expressing further wonder at the fantasy world of the geniuses—and added, for good measure, an extra dollop of dripping contempt for them. "I literally do not talk to them. You know why? I'm doing my shit, and they got nothing to do with it, and I don't care what they're doing . . . I don't care. . . . I'm not going to be alone with them, I'm not going to be in a room with them. Ivanka walked into the Oval today . . . [and] as soon as she walked in, I looked at her and walked right out. . . . I won't be in a room . . . don't want to do it. . . . Hope Hicks walked in, I walked out."

"The FBI put Jared's father in jail," said Preate. "Don't they understand you don't mess—"

"Charlie Kushner," said Bannon, smacking his head again in additional disbelief. "He's going crazy because they're going to get down deep in his shit about how he's financed everything. . . . all the shit coming out of Israel . . . and all these guys coming out of Eastern Europe . . . all these Russian guys . . . and guys in Kazakhstan. . . . And he's frozen on 666 [Fifth Avenue]. . . . [If] it goes under next year, the whole thing's cross-collateralized . . . he's wiped, he's gone, he's done, it's over. . . . Toast."

He held his face in his hands for a moment and then looked up again.

"I'm pretty good at coming up with solutions, I came up with a solution for his broke-dick campaign in about a day, but I don't see this. I don't see a plan for getting through. Now, I gave him a plan, I said you seal the Oval Office, you send those two kids home, you get rid of Hope, all these deadbeats, and you listen to your legal team—Kasowitz, and Mark Dowd, and Jay Sekulow, and Mark Corallo, these are all professionals who have done this many times. You listen to those guys and never talk about this stuff again, you just conduct yourself as commander in chief and then you can be president for eight years. If you don't, you're not, simple. But he's the president, he gets a choice, and he's clearly choosing to go down another path . . . and you can't stop him. The guy is going to call his own plays. He's Trump. . . ."

And then another call came, this one from Sam Nunberg. He, too, was calling about Scaramucci, and his words caused something like stupefaction in Bannon: "No fucking, fucking way."

Bannon got off the phone and said, "Jesus. Scaramucci. I can't even respond to this. It's Kafkaesque. Jared and Ivanka needed somebody to represent their shit. It's madness. He'll be on that podium for two days and he'll be so chopped he'll bleed out everywhere. He'll literally blow up in a week. This is why I don't take this stuff seriously. Hiring Scaramucci? He's not qualified to do anything. He runs a fund of funds. Do you know what a fund of funds is? It's not a fund. Dude, it's sick. We look like buffoons."

* * *

The ten days of Anthony Scaramucci, saw, on the first day, July 21, the resignation of Sean Spicer. Oddly, this seemed to catch everyone unawares. In a meeting with Scaramucci, Spicer, and Priebus, the president—who in his announcement of Scaramucci's hire as communications director had promoted Scaramucci not only over Spicer, but in effect over Priebus, his chief of staff—suggested that the men ought to be able to work it out together.

Spicer went back to his office, printed out his letter of resignation, and then took it back to the nonplussed president, who said again that he really wanted Spicer to be a part of things. But Spicer, surely the most mocked man in America, understood that he had been handed a gift. His White House days were over.

For Scaramucci, it was now payback time. Scaramucci blamed his six humiliating months out in the cold on nobody so much as Reince Priebus—having announced his White House future, having sold his business in anticipation of it, he had come away with nothing, or at least nothing of any value. But now, in a reversal befitting a true master of the universe—befitting, actually, Trump himself—Scaramucci was in the White House, bigger, better, and grander than even he had had the gall to imagine. And Priebus was dead meat.

That was the signal the president had sent Scaramucci—deal with the mess. In Trump's view, the problems in his tenure so far were just problems about the team. If the team went, the problems went. So Scaramucci had his marching orders. The fact that the president had been saying the same stuff about his rotten team from the first day, that this riff had been a constant from the campaign on, that he would often say he wanted everybody to go and then turn around and say he *didn't* want everybody to go—all that rather went over Scaramucci's head.

Scaramucci began taunting Priebus publicly, and inside the West Wing he adopted a tough-guy attitude about Bannon—"I won't take his bullshit." Trump seemed delighted with this behavior, which led Scaramucci to feel that the president was urging him on. Jared and Ivanka were pleased, too; they believed they had scored with Scaramucci and were confident that he would defend them against Bannon and the rest.

Bannon and Priebus remained not just disbelieving but barely able not to crack up. For both men, Scaramucci was either a hallucinatory episode—they wondered whether they ought to just shut their eyes while it passed—or some further march into madness.

* * *

Even as measured against other trying weeks in the Trump White House, the week of July 24 was a head-slammer. First, it opened the next episode in what had become a comic-opera effort to repeal Obamacare in the Senate. As in the House, this had become much less about health care than a struggle both among Republicans in Congress and between the Republican leadership and the White House. The signature stand for the Republican Party had now become the symbol of its civil war.

On that Monday, the president's son-in-law appeared at the microphones in front of the West Wing to preview his statement to Senate investigators about the Trump campaign's connections to Russia. Having almost never spoken before in public, he now denied culpability in the Russian mess by claiming feckless naïveté; speaking in a reedy, self-pitying voice, he portrayed himself as a Candide-like figure who had become disillusioned by a harsh world.

And that evening, the president traveled to West Virginia to deliver a speech before the Boy Scouts of America. Once more, his speech was tonally at odds with time, place, and good sense. It prompted an immediate apology from the Boy Scouts to its members, their parents, and the country at large. The quick trip did not seem to improve Trump's mood: the next morning, seething, the president again publicly attacked his attorney general and—for good measure and no evident reason—tweeted his ban of transgender people in the military. (The president had been presented with four different options related to the military's transgender policy. The presentation was meant to frame an ongoing discussion, but ten minutes after receiving the discussion points, and without further consultation, Trump tweeted his transgender ban.)

The following day, Wednesday, Scaramucci learned that one of his financial disclosure forms seemed to have been leaked; assuming he'd been sabotaged by his enemies, Scaramucci blamed Priebus directly, implicitly accusing him of a felony. In fact, Scaramucci's financial form was a public document available to all.

That afternoon, Priebus told the president that he understood he should resign and they should start talking about his replacement.

Then, that evening, there was a small dinner in the White House, with various current and former Fox News people, including Kimberly Guilfoyle, in attendance—and this was leaked. Drinking more than usual, trying desperately to contain the details of the meltdown of his personal life (being linked to Guilfoyle wasn't going to help his negotiation with his wife), and wired by events beyond his own circuits' capacity, Scaramucci called a reporter at the *New Yorker* magazine and unloaded.

The resulting article was surreal—so naked in its pain and fury, that for almost twenty-four hours nobody seemed to be able to quite acknowledge that he had committed public suicide. The article quoted Scaramucci speaking bluntly about the chief of staff: "Reince Priebus—if you want to leak something—he'll be asked to resign very shortly." Saying that he had taken his new job "to serve the country" and that he was "not trying to build my brand," Scaramucci also took on Steve Bannon: "I'm not Steve Bannon. I'm not trying to suck my own cock." (In fact, Bannon learned about the piece when fact-checkers from the magazine called him for comment about Scaramucci's accusation that he sucked his own cock.)

Scaramucci, who had in effect publicly fired Priebus, was behaving so bizarrely that it wasn't at all clear who would be the last man standing. Priebus, on the verge of being fired for so long, realized that he might have agreed to resign too soon. He might have gotten the chance to fire Scaramucci!

On Friday, as health care repeal cratered in the Senate, Priebus joined the president on board Air Force One for a trip to New York for a speech. As it happened, so did Scaramucci, who, avoiding the *New Yorker* fall-out, had said he'd gone to New York to visit his mother but in fact had been hiding out at the Trump Hotel in Washington. Now here he was, with his bags (he would indeed now stay in New York and visit his mother), behaving as though nothing had happened.

On the way back from the trip, Priebus and the president talked on the plane and discussed the timing of his departure, with the president urging him to do it the right way and to take his time. "You tell me what works for you," said Trump. "Let's make it good."

Minutes later, Priebus stepped onto the tarmac and an alert on his phone said the president had just tweeted that there was a new chief of staff, Department of Homeland Security chief John Kelly, and that Priebus was out.

The Trump presidency was six months old, but the question of who might replace Priebus had been a topic of discussion almost from day one. Among the string of candidates were Powell and Cohn, the Jarvanka favorites; OMB director Mick Mulvaney, one of the Bannon picks; and Kelly.

In fact, Kelly—who would soon abjectly apologize to Priebus for the basic lack of courtesy in the way his dismissal was handled—had not been consulted about his appointment. The president's tweet was the first he knew of it.

But indeed there was no time to waste. Now the paramount issue before the Trump government was that somebody would have to fire Scaramucci. Since Scaramucci had effectively gotten rid of Priebus—the person who logically should have fired *him*—the new chief of staff was needed, more or less immediately, to get rid of the Mooch.

And six days later, just hours after he was sworn in, Kelly fired Scaramucci.

Chastened themselves, the junior first couple, the geniuses of the Scaramucci hire, panicked that they would, deservedly, catch the blame for one of the most ludicrous if not catastrophic hires in modern White House history. Now they rushed to say how firmly they supported the decision to get rid of Scaramucci.

"So I punch you in the face," Sean Spicer noted from the sidelines, "and then say, 'Oh my god, we've got to get you to a hospital!' "

22

GENERAL KELLY

On August 4, the president and key members of the West Wing left for Trump's golf club in Bedminster. The new chief of staff, General Kelly, was in tow, but the president's chief strategist, Steve Bannon, had been left behind. Trump was grouchy about the planned seventeen-day trip, bothered by how diligently his golf dates were being clocked by the media. So this was now dubbed a "working" trip—another piece of Trump vanity that drew shrugs, eye rolling, and head shaking from a staff that had been charged with planning events that looked like work even as they were instructed to leave yawning expanses of time for golf.

During the president's absence, the West Wing would be renovated—Trump, the hotelier and decorator, was "disgusted" by its condition. The president did not want to move over to the nearby Executive Office Building, where the West Wing business would temporarily be conducted—and where Steve Bannon sat waiting for his call to go to Bedminster.

He was about to leave for Bedminster, Bannon kept telling everyone, but no invitation came. Bannon, who claimed credit for bringing Kelly into the administration in the first place, was unsure where he stood with the new chief. Indeed, the president himself was unsure about where he himself stood; he kept asking people if Kelly liked him. More generally,

Bannon wasn't entirely clear *what* Kelly was doing, other than his duty. Where exactly did the new chief of staff fit in Trumpworld?

While Kelly stood somewhere right of center on the political spectrum and had been a willing tough immigration enforcer at Homeland Security, he was not anywhere near so right as Bannon or Trump. "He's not hardcore" was Bannon's regretful appraisal. At the same time, Kelly was certainly not close in any way to the New York liberals in the White House. But politics was not his purview. As director of Homeland Security he had watched the chaos in the White House with disgust and thought about quitting. Now he had agreed to try to tame it. He was sixty-seven, resolute, stern, and grim. "Does he ever smile?" asked Trump, who had already begun to think that he had somehow been tricked into the hire.

Some Trumpers, particularly those with over-the-transom access to the president, believed that he had been tricked into some form of very-much-not-Trump submission. Roger Stone, one of those people whose calls Kelly was now shielding the president from, spread the dark scenario that Mattis, McMaster, and Kelly had agreed that no military action would ever be taken unless the three were in accord—and that at least one of them would always remain in Washington if the others were away.

After Kelly dispatched Scaramucci, his two immediate issues, now on the table in Bedminster, were the president's relatives and Steve Bannon. One side or the other obviously had to go. Or perhaps both should go.

It was far from clear whether a White House chief of staff who saw his function as establishing command process and enforcing organizational hierarchy—directing a decision funnel to the commander in chief—could operate effectively or even exist in a White House where the commander in chief's children had special access and overriding influence. As much as the president's daughter and son-in-law were now offering slavish regard for the new command principals, they would, surely, by habit and temperament, override Kelly's control of the West Wing. Not only did they have obvious special influence with the president, but important members of the staff saw them as having this juice, and hence believed that they were the true north of West Wing advancement and power.

Curiously, for all their callowness, Jared and Ivanka had become quite a fearsome presence, as feared by others as the two of them feared Bannon. What's more, they had become quite accomplished infighters and leakers—they had front-room *and* back-channel power—although, with great woundedness, they insisted, incredibly, that they never leaked. "If they hear someone talking about them, because they are so careful about their image and have crafted this whole persona—it's like anyone who tries to pierce it or say something against it is like a big problem," said one senior staffer. "They get very upset and will come after you."

On the other hand, while "the kids" might make Kelly's job all but impossible, keeping Bannon on board didn't make a lot of sense, either. Whatever his gifts, he was a hopeless plotter and malcontent, bound to do an end run around any organization. Besides, as the Bedminster hiatus—working or otherwise—began, Bannon was once more on the president's shit list.

The president continued to stew about *The Devil's Bargain*, the book by Joshua Green that gave Bannon credit for the election. Then, too, while the president tended to side with Bannon against McMaster, the campaign to defend McMaster, supported by Jared and Ivanka, was having an effect. Murdoch, enlisted by Jared to help defend McMaster, was personally lobbying the president for Bannon's head. Bannonites felt they had to defend Bannon against an impulsive move by the president: so now, not only did they brand McMaster as weak on Israel, they persuaded Sheldon Adelson to lobby Trump—Bannon, Adelson told the president, was the only person he trusted on Israel in the White House. Adelson's billions and implacability always impressed Trump, and his endorsement, Bannon believed, significantly strengthened his hand.

But overriding the management of the harrowing West Wing dysfunction, Kelly's success—or even relevance, as he was informed by almost anyone who was in a position to offer him an opinion—depended on his rising to the central challenge of his job, which was how to manage Trump. Or, actually, how to live with not managing him. His desires, needs, and impulses had to exist—*necessarily* had to exist—outside the organizational structure. Trump was the one variable that, in management terms, simply could not be controlled. He was like a recalcitrant two-year-old. If you tried to control him, it would only have the opposite effect. In this, then, the manager had to most firmly manage his own expectations.

In an early meeting with the president, General Kelly had Jared and Ivanka on his agenda—how the president saw their role; what he thought was working and not working about it; how he envisioned it going forward. It was all intended to be a politic way of opening a discussion about getting them out. But the president was, Kelly soon learned, delighted with all aspects of their performance in the West Wing. Maybe at some point Jared would become secretary of state—that was the only change the president seemed to foresee. The most Kelly could do was to get the president to acknowledge that the couple should be part of a greater organizational discipline in the West Wing and should not so readily jump the line.

This, at least, was something that the general could try to enforce. At a dinner in Bedminster—the president dining with his daughter and son-in-law—the First Family were confused when Kelly showed up at the meal and joined them. This, they shortly came to understand, was neither an attempt at pleasant socializing nor an instance of unwarranted over-familiarity. It was enforcement: Jared and Ivanka needed to go through him to talk to the president.

But Trump had made clear his feeling that the roles played by the kids in his administration needed only minor adjustment, and this now presented a significant problem for Bannon. Bannon really had believed that Kelly would find a way to send Jarvanka home. How could he not? Indeed, Bannon had convinced himself that they represented the largest danger to Trump. They would take the president down. As much, Bannon believed that *he* could not remain in the White House if they did.

Beyond Trump's current irritation with Bannon, which many believed was just the usual constant of Trump resentment and complaint, Bannonites felt that their leader had, at least policywise, gained the upper hand. Jarvanka was marginalized; the Republican leadership, after health care, was discredited; the Cohn-Mnuchin tax plan was a hash. Through one window, the future looked almost rosy for Bannon.

Sam Nunberg, the former Trump loyalist who was now wholly a Bannon loyalist, believed that Bannon would stay in the White House for two years and then leave to run Trump's reelection campaign. "If you can get this idiot elected twice," Nunberg marveled, you would achieve something like immortality in politics.

But through another window, Bannon couldn't possibly remain in place. He seemed to have moved into a heightened state that allowed him to see just how ridiculous the White House had become. He could barely hold his tongue—indeed, he couldn't hold it. Pressed, he could not see the future of the Trump administration. And, while many Bannonites argued the case for Jarvanka ineffectiveness and irrelevance—just ignore them, they said—Bannon, with mounting ferocity and pubic venom, could abide them less and less every day.

Bannon, continuing to wait for his call to join the president in Bedminster, decided that he would force the situation and offered his resignation to Kelly. But this was in fact a game of chicken: he wanted to stay. On the other hand, he wanted Jarvanka to go. And that became an effective ultimatum.

* * *

At lunch on August 8, in the Clubhouse at Bedminster—amid Trumpish chandeliers, golf trophies, and tournament plaques—the president was flanked by Tom Price, the secretary of health and human services, and his wife, Melania. Kellyanne Conway was at the lunch; so were Kushner and several others. This was one of the "make-work" events—over lunch, there was a discussion of the opioid crisis, which was then followed by a statement from the president and a brief round of questions from reporters. While reading the statement in a monotone, Trump kept his head down, propping it on his elbows.

After taking some humdrum questions about opioids, he was suddenly asked about North Korea, and, quite as though in stop-action animation, he seemed to come alive.

North Korea had been a heavy-on-detail, short-on-answers problem that that he believed was the product of lesser minds and weaker resolve—and that he had trouble paying attention to. What's more, he had increasingly personalized his antagonism with North Korean leader Kim Jong-un, referring to him often with derogatory epithets.

His staff had not prepared him for this, but, in apparent relief that he could digress from the opioid discussion, as well as sudden satisfaction at the opportunity to address this nagging problem, he ventured out, in language that he'd repeated often in private—as he repeated everything often—to the precipice of an international crisis.

"North Korea best not make any more threats to the United States. They will be met with the fire and the fury like the world has never seen. He has been very threatening beyond a normal state, and as I said they will be met with fire and fury and frankly power, the likes of which this world has never seen before. Thank you."

* * *

North Korea, a situation the president had been consistently advised to downplay, now became the central subject of the rest of the week—with most senior staff occupied not so much by the topic itself, but by how to respond to the president, who was threatening to "blow" again.

Against this background, almost no one paid attention to the announcement by the Trump supporter and American neo-Nazi Richard Spencer that he was organizing a protest at the University of Virginia, in Charlottesville, over the removal of a statue of Robert E. Lee. "Unite the Right," the theme of the rally called for Saturday, August 12, was explicitly designed to link Trump's politics with white nationalism.

On August 11, with the president in Bedminster continuing to threaten North Korea—and also, inexplicably to almost everyone on his staff, threatening military intervention in Venezuela—Spencer called for an evening protest.

At 8:45 p.m.—with the president in for the night in Bedminster—about 250 young men dressed in khaki pants and polo shirts, quite a Trump style of dress, began an organized parade across the UVA campus while carrying kerosene torches. Parade monitors with headsets directed the scene. At a signal, the marchers began chanting official movement slogans: "Blood and soil!" "You will not replace us!" "Jews will not replace us!" Soon, at the center of campus, near a statue of UVA's founder, Thomas Jefferson, Spencer's group was met by a counterprotest. With virtually no police presence, the first of the weekend's melees and injuries ensued.

Beginning again at eight o'clock the next morning, the park near the Lee statue became the battleground of a suddenly surging white racist movement, with clubs, shields, mace, pistols, and automatic rifles (Virginia is an "open carry" state)—a movement seemingly, and to liberal horror, born out of the Trump campaign and election, as in fact Richard Spencer intended it to seem. Opposing the demonstrators was a hardened, militant left called to the barricades. You could hardly have better set an end-times scene, no matter the limited numbers of protesters. Much of the morning involved a series of charges and countercharges—a rocks-and-bottles combat, with a seemingly hands-off police force standing by.

In Bedminster, there was still little awareness of the unfolding events in Charlottesville. But then, at about one o'clock in the afternoon, James Alex Fields Jr., a twenty-year-old would-be Nazi, plunged his Dodge Charger into a group of counterprotesters, killing thirty-two-year-old Heather Heyer and injuring a score of others.

In a tweet hurriedly composed by his staff, the president declared: "We ALL must be united & condemn all that hate stands for. There is no place for this kind of violence in America. Lets come together as one!"

Otherwise, however, it was largely business as usual for the president—Charlottesville was a mere distraction, and indeed, the staff's goal was to keep him off North Korea. The main event in Bedminster that day was the ceremonial signing of an act extending the funding of a program that let veterans obtain medical care outside VA hospitals. The signing was held in a big ballroom at the Clubhouse two hours after Alex Field's attack.

During the signing, Trump took a moment to condemn the "hatred, bigotry, and violence on many sides" in Charlottesville. Almost immediately, the president came under attack for the distinction he had appeared to refuse to draw between avowed racists and the other side. As Richard Spencer had correctly understood, the president's sympathies were muddled.

However easy and obvious it was to condemn white racists—even self-styled neo-Nazis—he instinctively resisted.

It wasn't until the next morning that the White House finally tried to clarify Trump's position with a formal statement: "The President said very strongly in his statement yesterday that he condemns all forms of violence, bigotry, and hatred. Of course that includes white supremacists, KKK neo-Nazi and all extremist groups. He called for national unity and bringing all Americans together."

But in fact he hadn't condemned white supremacists, KKK, and neo-Nazis—and he continued to be stubborn about not doing it.

In a call to Bannon, Trump sought help making his case: "Where does this all end? Are they going to take down the Washington Monument, Mount Rushmore, Mount Vernon?" Bannon—still not receiving his summons to Bedminster—urged this to be the line: the president should condemn violence and misfits and also defend history (even with Trump's weak grasp of it). Stressing the literal issue of monuments would bedevil the left and comfort the right.

But Jared and Ivanka, with Kelly backing them, urged presidential behavior. Their plan was to have Trump return to the White House and address the issue with a forceful censure of hate groups and racial politics—exactly the unambiguous sort of position Richard Spencer had strategically bet Trump would not willingly take.

Bannon, understanding these same currents in Trump, lobbied Kelly and told him that the Jarvanka approach would backfire: *It will be clear his heart's not in it*, said Bannon.

The president arrived shortly before eleven o'clock on Monday morning at a White House under construction and a wall of shouted questions about Charlottesville: "Do you condemn the actions of neo-Nazis? Do you condemn the actions of white supremacists?" Some ninety minutes later he stood in the Diplomatic Reception Room, his eyes locked on to the teleprompter, and delivered a six-minute statement.

Before getting to the point: "Our economy is now strong. The stock market continues to hit record highs, unemployment is at a sixteen-year low, and businesses are more optimistic than ever before. Companies are moving back to the United States and bringing many thousands of jobs with them. We have already created over one million jobs since I took office."

And only then: "We must love each other, show affection for each other and unite together in condemnation of hatred, bigotry and violence. . . . We must rediscover the bonds of love and loyalty that bring us together as Americans. . . . Racism is evil. And those who cause violence in its name are criminals and thugs including the KKK, neo-Nazis, white supremacists, and other hate groups that are repugnant to everything we hold dear as Americans."

It was a reluctant mini-grovel. It was something of a restaging of the take-it-back birther speech about Obama during the campaign: much distraction and obfuscation, then a mumbled acknowledgment. Similarly, he looked here, trying to tow the accepted line on Charlottesville, like a kid called on the carpet. Resentful and petulant, he was clearly reading forced lines.

And in fact he got little credit for these presidential-style remarks, with reporters shouting questions about why it had taken him so long to address the issue. As he got back on Marine One to head to Andrews Air Force Base and on to JFK and then into Manhattan and Trump Tower, his mood was dark and I-told-you-so. Privately, he kept trying to rationalize why someone would be a member of the KKK—that is, they might not actually believe what the KKK believed, and the KKK probably does not believe what it used to believe, and, anyway, who really knows what the KKK believes now? In fact, he said, his own father was accused of being involved with the KKK—not true. (In fact, yes, true.)

The next day, Tuesday, August 15, the White House had a news conference scheduled at Trump Tower. Bannon urged Kelly to cancel it. It was a nothing conference anyway. Its premise was about infrastructure—about undoing an environmental regulation that could help get projects started faster—but it was really just another effort to show that Trump was working and not just on a holiday. So why bother? What's more, Bannon told Kelly, he could see the signs: the arrow on the Trump pressure cooker was climbing, and before long he'd blow.

The news conference went ahead anyway. Standing at the lectern in the lobby of Trump Tower, the president stayed on script for mere minutes.

Defensive and self-justifying, he staked out a contrition-is-bunk, the-fault-lies-everywhere-else position and then dug in deep. He went on without an evident ability to adjust his emotions to political circumstance or, really, even to make an effort to save himself. It was yet one more example, among his many now, of the comic-absurd, movielike politician who just says whatever is on his mind. Unmediated. Crazylike.

"What about the alt-left that came charging at the, as you say, alt-right? Do they have any semblance of guilt? What about the fact they came charging with clubs in their hands? As far as I'm concerned that was a horrible, horrible day. . . . I think there's blame on both sides. I have no doubt about it, you don't have any doubt about it. If you reported it accurately, you would see."

Steve Bannon, still waiting in his temporary office in the EOB, thought, *Oh my god, there he goes. I told you so.*

* * *

Outside of the portion of the electorate that, as Trump once claimed, would let him shoot someone on Fifth Avenue, the civilized world was pretty much universally aghast. Everybody came to a dumbfounded moral attention. Anybody in any position of responsibility remotely tied to some idea of establishment respectability had to disavow him. Every CEO of a public company who had associated him- or herself with the Trump White House now needed to cut the ties. The overriding issue might not even be what unreconstructed sentiments he actually seemed to hold in his heart—Bannon averred that Trump was not in fact anti-Semitic, but on the other count he wasn't sure—but that he flat-out couldn't control himself.

In the wake of the immolating news conference, all eyes were suddenly on Kelly—this was his baptism of Trump fire. Spicer, Priebus, Cohn, Powell, Bannon, Tillerson, Mattis, Mnuchin—virtually the entire senior staff and cabinet of the Trump presidency, past and present, had traveled through the stages of adventure, challenge, frustration, battle, self-justification, and doubt, before finally having to confront the very real likelihood that the president they worked for—whose presidency they bore some official responsibility for—didn't have the wherewithal to adequately function in his job. Now, after less than two weeks on the job, it was Kelly's turn to stand at that precipice.

The debate, as Bannon put it, was not about whether the president's situation was bad, but whether it was Twenty-Fifth-Amendment bad.

* * *

To Bannon, if not to Trump, the linchpin of Trumpism was China. The story of the next generation, he believed, had been written, and it was about war with China. Commercial war, trade war, cultural war, diplomatic war—it would be an all-encompassing war that few in the United States now understood needed to be fought, and that almost nobody was prepared to fight.

Bannon had compiled a list of "China hawks" that crossed political lines, going from the Breitbart gang, to former *New Republic* editor Peter Beinart—who regarded Bannon only with scorn—and orthodox liberal-progressive stalwart Robert Kuttner, the editor of the small, public policy magazine *American Prospect*. On Wednesday, August 16, the day after the president's news conference in Trump Tower, Bannon, out of the blue, called Kuttner from his EOB office to talk China.

By this point, Bannon was all but convinced that he was on the way out of the White House. He had received no invitation to join the president in Bedminster, a withering sign. That day, he had learned of the appointment of Hope Hicks as interim communications director—a Jarvanka victory. Meanwhile, the steady whisper from the Jarvanka side continued about his certain demise; it had become a constant background noise.

He was still not sure he would be fired, yet Bannon, in only the second on-the-record interview he had given since the Trump victory, called Kuttner and in effect sealed his fate. He would later maintain that the conversation was not on the record. But this was the Bannon method, in which he merely tempted fate.

If Trump was helplessly Trump in his most recent news conference, Bannon was helplessly Bannon in his chat with Kuttner. He tried to prop up what he made sound like a weak Trump on China. He corrected, in mocking fashion, the president's bluster on North Korea—"ten million people in Seoul" will die, he declared. And he insulted his internal enemies—"they're wetting themselves."

If Trump was incapable of sounding like a president, Bannon had matched him: he was incapable of sounding like a presidential aide.

* * *

That evening, a group of Bannonites gathered near the White House for dinner. The dinner was called for the bar at the Hay-Adams hotel, but Arthur Schwartz, a Bannonite PR man, got into an altercation with the Hay-Adams bartender about switching the television from CNN to Fox, where his client, Blackstone's Stephen Schwarzman, the chairman of one of the president's business councils, was shortly to appear. The business council was hemorrhaging its CEO members after the president's Charlottesville news conference, and Trump, in a tweet, had announced that he was disbanding it. (Schwarzman had advised the president that the council was collapsing and that the president ought to at least make it look as if shutting it down was his decision.)

Schwartz, in high dudgeon, announced that he was checking out of the Hay-Adams and moving to the Trump Hotel. He also insisted that the dinner be moved two blocks away to Joe's, an outpost of Miami's Joe's Stone Crab. Matthew Boyle, the Washington political editor of Breitbart News, was swept into Schwartz's furious departure, with Schwartz upbraiding the twenty-nine-year-old for lighting a cigarette. "I don't know anyone who smokes," he sniffed. Although Schwartz was firmly in the Bannon camp, this seemed to be a general dig at the Breitbart people for being low-class.

Both dedicated Bannonites debated the effect of Bannon's interview, which had caught everybody in the Bannon universe off guard. Neither man could understand why he would have given an interview.

Was Bannon finished?

No, no, no, argued Schwartz. He might have been a few weeks ago when Murdoch had ganged up with McMaster and gone to the president and pressed him to dump Bannon. But then Sheldon had fixed it, Schwartz said.

"Steve stayed home when Abbas came," said Schwartz. "He wasn't going to breathe the air that a terrorist breathed." This was the precise line Schwartz would hand out to reporters in the coming days in a further effort to establish Bannon's right-wing virtue.

Alexandra Preate, Bannon's lieutenant, arrived at Joe's out of breath. Seconds later, Jason Miller, another PR man in the Bannon fold, arrived. During the transition, Miller had been slated to be the communications director, but then it had come out that Miller had had a relationship with another staff member who announced in a tweet she was pregnant by Miller—as was also, at this point, Miller's wife. Miller, who had lost his promised White House job but continued serving as an outside Trump and Bannon voice, was now, with the recent birth of the child—with the recent birth of both of his children by different women—facing another wave of difficult press. Still, even he was obsessively focused on what Bannon's interview might mean.

By now the table was buzzing with speculation.

How would the president react?

How would Kelly react?

Was this curtains?

For a group of people in touch with Bannon on an almost moment-by-moment basis, it was remarkable that nobody seemed to understand that, forcibly or otherwise, he would surely be moving out of the White House. On the contrary, the damaging interview was, by consensus, converted into a brilliant strategic move. Bannon was not going anywhere—not least because there was no Trump without Bannon.

It was an excited dinner, a revved-up occasion involving a passionate group of people all attached to the man who they believed was the most compelling figure in Washington. They saw him as some sort of irreducible element: Bannon was Bannon was Bannon.

As the evening went on, Matt Boyle got in a furious text-message fight with Jonathan Swan, a White House reporter who had written a story about Bannon being on the losing side in the Bannon-McMaster showdown. Soon almost every well-connected reporter in the city was checking in with somebody at the table. When a text came in, the recipient would hold up his or her phone if it showed a notable reporter's name.

At one point, Bannon texted Schwartz some talking points. Could it be that this was just one more day in the endless Trump drama?

Schwartz, who seemed to regard Trump's stupidity as a political given, offered a vigorous analysis of why Trump could not do without Bannon. Then, seeking more proof of his theory, Schwartz said he was texting Sam Nunberg, generally regarded as the man who understood Trump's whims and impulses best, and who had sagely predicted Bannon's survival at each doubtful moment in the past months.

"Nunberg always knows," said Schwartz.

Seconds later, Schwartz looked up. His eyes widened and for a moment he went silent. Then he said: "Nunberg says Bannon's dead."

And, indeed, unbeknownst to the Bannonites, even those closest to him, Bannon was at that moment finalizing his exit with Kelly. By the next day, he would be packing up his little office, and on Monday, when Trump would return to a refurbished West Wing—a paint job, new furniture, and new rugs, its look tilting toward the Trump Hotel—Steve Bannon would be back on Capitol Hill at the Breitbart Embassy, still, he was confident, the chief strategist for the Trump revolution.

EPILOGUE: BANNON AND TRUMP

On a sweltering morning in October 2017, the man who had more or less single-handedly brought about the U.S. withdrawal from the Paris climate accord, stood on the steps of the Breitbart town house and said, with a hearty laugh, "I guess global warming is real."

Steve Bannon had lost twenty pounds since his exit from the White House six weeks before—he was on a crash all-sushi diet. "That building," said his friend David Bossie, speaking about all White Houses but especially the Trump White House, "takes perfectly healthy people and turns them into old, unhealthy people." But Bannon, who Bossie had declared on virtual life support during his final days in the West Wing, was again, by his own description, "on fire." He had moved out of the Arlington "safe house" and reestablished himself back at the Breitbart Embassy, turning it into a headquarters for the next stage of the Trump movement, which might not include Trump at all.

Asked about Trump's leadership of the nationalist-populist movement, Bannon registered a not inconsiderable change in the country's political landscape: "*I* am the leader of the national-populist movement."

One cause of Bannon's boast and new resolve was that Trump, for no reason that Bannon could quite divine, had embraced Mitch McConnell's establishment candidate in the recent Republican run-off in Alabama rather than support the nat-pop choice for the Senate seat vacated by now attorney general Jeff Sessions. After all, McConnell and the president were barely on speaking terms. From his August "working holiday" in Bedminster, the president's staff had tried to organize a makeup meeting with McConnell, but McConnell's staff had sent back word that it wouldn't be possible because the Senate leader would be getting a haircut.

But the president—ever hurt and confused by his inability to get along with the congressional leadership, and then, conversely, enraged by their refusal to get along with him—had gone all-in for the McConnell-backed Luther Strange, who had run against Bannon's candidate, the right-wing firebrand Roy Moore. (Even by Alabama standards, Moore was far right: he had been removed as chief justice of the Alabama Supreme Court for defying a federal court order to take down a monument of the Ten Commandments in the Alabama judicial building.)

For Bannon, the president's political thinking had been obtuse at best. He was unlikely to get anything from McConnell—and indeed Trump had demanded nothing for his support for Luther Strange, which came via an unplanned tweet in August. Strange's prospects were not only dim, but he was likely to lose in a humiliating fashion. Roy Moore was the clear candidate of the Trump base—and he was Bannon's candidate. Hence, that would be the contest: Trump against Bannon. In fact, the president really didn't have to support anyone—no one would have complained if he'd stayed neutral in a primary race. Or, he could have tacitly supported Strange and not doubled down with more and more insistent tweets.

For Bannon, this episode was not only about the president's continuing and curious confusion about what he represented, but about his mercurial, intemperate, and often cockamamie motivations. Against all political logic, Trump had supported Luther Strange, he told Bannon, because "Luther's my friend."

"He said it like a nine-year-old," said Bannon, recoiling, and noting that there was no universe in which Trump and Strange were actually friends.

For every member of the White House senior staff this would be the lasting conundrum of dealing with President Trump: the "why" of his often baffling behavior.

"The president fundamentally wants to be liked" was Katie Walsh's analysis. "He just fundamentally needs to be liked so badly that it's always . . . everything is a struggle for him."

This translated into a constant need to win something—anything. Equally important, it was essential that he *look* like a winner. Of course, trying to win without consideration, plan, or clear goals had, in the course of the administration's first nine months, resulted in almost nothing but losses. At the same time, confounding all political logic, that lack of a plan, that impulsivity, that apparent *joie de guerre*, had helped create the disruptiveness that seemed to so joyously shatter the status quo for so many.

But now, Bannon thought, that novelty was finally wearing off.

For Bannon, the Strange-Moore race had been a test of the Trump cult of personality. Certainly Trump continued to believe that people were following *him*, that he was the movement—and that his support was worth 8 to 10 points in any race. Bannon had decided to test this thesis and to do it as dramatically as possible. All told, the Senate Republican leadership and others spent $32 million on Strange's campaign, while Moore's campaign spent $2 million.

Trump, though aware of Strange's deep polling deficit, had agreed to extend his support in a personal trip. But his appearance in Huntsville, Alabama, on September 22, before a Trump-size crowd, was a political flatliner. It was a full-on Trump speech, ninety minutes of rambling and improvisation—the wall would be built (now it was a see-through wall), Russian interference in the U.S. election was a hoax, he would fire anybody on his cabinet who supported Moore. But, while his base turned out en masse, still drawn to Trump the novelty, his cheerleading for Luther Strange drew at best a muted response. As the crowd became restless, the event threatened to become a hopeless embarrassment.

Reading his audience and desperate to find a way out, Trump suddenly threw out a line about Colin Kaepernick taking to his knee while the national anthem played at a National Football League game. The line got a standing ovation. The president thereupon promptly abandoned Luther Strange for the rest of the speech. Likewise, for the next week he continued to whip the NFL. Pay no attention to Strange's resounding defeat five days after the event in Huntsville. Ignore the size and scale of Trump's rejection and the Moore-Bannon triumph, with its hint of new disruptions to come. Now Trump had a new topic, and a winning one: the Knee.

* * *

The fundamental premise of nearly everybody who joined the Trump White House was, *This can work. We can help make this work.* Now, only three-quarters of the way through just the first year of Trump's term, there was literally not one member of the senior staff who could any longer be confident of that premise. Arguably—and on many days indubitably—most members of the senior staff believed that the sole upside of being part of the Trump White House was to help prevent worse from happening.

In early October, Secretary of State Rex Tillerson's fate was sealed—if his obvious ambivalence toward the president had not already sealed it—by the revelation that he had called the president "a fucking moron."

This—insulting Donald Trump's intelligence—was both the thing you could not do and the thing—drawing there-but-for-the-grace-of-God guffaws across the senior staff—that everybody was guilty of. Everyone, in his or her own way, struggled to express the baldly obvious fact that the president did not know enough, did not know what he didn't know, did not particularly care, and, to boot, was confident if not serene in his unquestioned certitudes. There was now a fair amount of back-of-the-classroom giggling about who had called Trump what. For Steve Mnuchin and Reince Priebus, he was an "idiot." For Gary Cohn, he was "dumb as shit." For H. R. McMaster he was a "dope." The list went on.

Tillerson would merely become yet another example of a subordinate who believed that his own abilities could somehow compensate for Trump's failings.

Aligned with Tillerson were the three generals, Mattis, McMasters, and Kelly, each seeing themselves as representing maturity, stability, and restraint. And each, of course, was resented by Trump for it. The suggestion that any or all of these men might be more focused and even tempered than Trump himself was cause for sulking and tantrums on the president's part.

The daily discussion among senior staffers, those still there and those now gone—all of whom had written off Tillerson's future in the Trump administration—was how long General Kelly would last as chief of staff. There was something of a virtual office pool, and the joke was that Reince Priebus was likely to be Trump's longest-serving chief of staff. Kelly's distaste for the president was open knowledge—in his every word and gesture he condescended to Trump—the president's distaste for Kelly even more so. It was sport for the president to defy Kelly, who had become the one thing in his life he had never been able to abide: a disapproving and censorious father figure.

* * *

There really were no illusions at 1600 Pennsylvania Avenue. Kelly's long-suffering antipathy toward the president was rivaled only by his scorn for the president's family—"Kushner," he pronounced, was "insubordinate." Cohn's derisive contempt for Kushner as well as the president was even greater. In return, the president heaped more abuse on Cohn—the former president of Goldman Sachs was now a "complete idiot, dumber than dumb." In fact, the president had also stopped defending his own family, wondering when they would "take the hint and go home."

But, of course, this was still politics: those who could overcome shame or disbelief—and, despite all Trumpian coarseness and absurdity, suck up to him and humor him—might achieve unique political advantage. As it happened, few could.

By October, however, many on the president's staff took particular notice of one of the few remaining Trump opportunists: Nikki Haley, the UN ambassador. Haley—"as ambitious as Lucifer," in the characterization of one member of the senior staff—had concluded that Trump's tenure would last, at best, a single term, and that she, with requisite submission, could be his heir apparent. Haley had courted and befriended Ivanka, and Ivanka had brought her into the family circle, where she had become a particular focus of Trump's attention, and he of hers.

Haley, as had become increasingly evident to the wider foreign policy and national security team, was the family's pick for secretary of state after Rex Tillerson's inevitable resignation. (Likewise, in this shuffle, Dina Powell would replace Haley at the UN.)

The president had been spending a notable amount of private time with Haley on Air Force One and was seen to be grooming her for a national political future. Haley, who was much more of a traditional Republican, one with a pronounced moderate streak—a type increasingly known as a Jarvanka Republican—was, evident to many, being mentored in Trumpian ways. The danger here, offered one senior Trumper, "is that she is so much smarter than him."

What now existed, even before the end of the president's first year, was an effective power vacuum. The president, in his failure to move beyond daily chaos, had hardly seized the day. But, as sure as politics, someone would.

In that sense, the Trumpian and Republican future was already moving beyond this White House. There was Bannon, working from the outside and trying to take over the Trump movement. There was the Republican leadership in Congress, trying to stymie Trumpism—if not slay it. There was John McCain, doing his best to embarrass it. There was the special counsel's office, pursuing the president and many of those around him.

The stakes were very clear to Bannon. Haley, quite an un-Trumpian figure, but by far the closest of any of his cabinet members to him, might, with clever political wiles, entice Trump to hand her the Trumpian revolution. Indeed, fearing Haley's hold on the president, Bannon's side had—the very morning that Bannon had stood on the steps of the Breitbart town house in the unseasonable October weather—gone into overdrive to push the CIA's Mike Pompeo for State after Tillerson's departure.

This was all part of the next stage of Trumpism—to protect it from Trump.

* * *

General Kelly was conscientiously and grimly trying to purge the West Wing chaos. He had begun by compartmentalizing the sources and nature of the chaos. The overriding source, of course, was the president's own eruptions, which Kelly could not control and had resigned himself to accepting. As for the ancillary chaos, much of it had been calmed by the elimination of Bannon, Priebus, Scaramucci, and Spicer, with the effect of making it quite a Jarvanka-controlled West Wing.

Now, nine months in, the administration faced the additional problem that it was very hard to hire anyone of stature to replace the senior people who had departed. And the stature of those who remained seemed to be more diminutive by the week.

Hope Hicks, at twenty-eight, and Stephen Miller, at thirty-two, both of whom had begun as effective interns on the campaign, were now among the seniormost figures in the White House. Hicks had assumed command of the communications operation, and Miller had effectively replaced Bannon as the senior political strategist.

After the Scaramucci fiasco, and the realization that the position of communications director would be vastly harder to fill, Hicks was assigned the job as the "interim" director. She was given the interim title partly because it seemed implausible that she was qualified to run an already battered messaging operation, and partly because if she *was* given the permanent job everyone would assume that the president was effectively calling the daily shots. But by the middle of September, interim was quietly converted to permanent.

In the larger media and political world, Miller—who Bannon referred to as "my typist"—was a figure of ever increasing incredulity. He could hardly be taken out in public without engaging in some screwball, if not screeching, fit of denunciation and grievance. He was the de facto crafter of policy and speeches, and yet up until now he had largely only taken dictation.

Most problematic of all, Hicks and Miller, along with everyone on the Jarvanka side, were now directly connected to actions involved in the Russian investigation or efforts to spin it, deflect it, or, indeed, cover it up. Miller and Hicks had drafted—or at least typed—Kushner's version of the first letter written at Bedminster to fire Comey. Hicks had joined with Kushner and his wife to draft on Air Force One the Trump-directed press release about Don Jr. and Kushner's meeting with the Russians in Trump Tower.

In its way, this had become the defining issue for the White House staff: who had been in what inopportune room. And even beyond the general chaos, the constant legal danger formed part of the high barrier to getting people to come work in the West Wing.

Kushner and his wife—now largely regarded as a time bomb inside the White House—were spending considerable time on their own defense and battling a sense of mounting paranoia, not least about what members of the senior staff who had already exited the West Wing might now say about them. Kushner, in the middle of October, would, curiously, add to his legal team Charles Harder, the libel lawyer who had defended both Hulk Hogan in his libel suit against Gawker, the Internet gossip site, and Melania Trump in her suit against the *Daily Mail*. The implied threat to media and to critics was clear. Talk about Jared Kushner at your peril. It also likely meant that Donald Trump was yet managing the White House's legal defense, slotting in his favorite "tough guy" lawyers.

Beyond Donald Trump's own daily antics, here was the consuming issue of the White House: the ongoing investigation directed by Robert Mueller. The father, the daughter, the son-in-law, his father, the extended family exposure, the prosecutor, the retainers looking to save their own skins, the staffers who Trump had rewarded with the back of his hand—it all threatened, in Bannon's view, to make Shakespeare look like Dr. Seuss.

Everyone waited for the dominoes to fall, and to see how the president, in his fury, might react and change the game again.

* * *

Steve Bannon was telling people he thought there was a 33.3 percent chance that the Mueller investigation would lead to the impeachment of the president, a 33.3 percent chance that Trump would resign, perhaps in the wake of a threat by the cabinet to act on the Twenty-Fifth Amendment (by which the cabinet can remove the president in the event of his incapacitation), and a 33.3 percent chance that he would limp to the end of his term. In any event, there would certainly not be a second term, or even an attempt at one.

"He's not going to make it," said Bannon at the Breitbart Embassy. "He's lost his stuff."

Less volubly, Bannon was telling people something else: he, Steve Bannon, was going to run for president in 2020. The locution, "If I were president . . ." was turning into, "When I am president . . ."

The top Trump donors from 2016 were in his camp, Bannon claimed: Sheldon Adelson, the Mercers, Bernie Marcus, and Peter Thiel. In short order, and as though he had been preparing for this move for some time, Bannon had left the White House and quickly thrown together a rump campaign organization. The heretofore behind-the-scenes Bannon was methodically meeting with every conservative leader in the country—doing his best, as he put it, to "kiss the ass and pay homage to all the gray-beards." And he was keynoting a list of must-attend conservative events.

"Why is Steve speaking? I didn't know he spoke," the president remarked with puzzlement and rising worry to aides.

Trump had been upstaged in other ways as well. He had been scheduled for a major *60 Minutes* interview in September, but this was abruptly canceled after Bannon's *60 Minutes* interview with Charlie Rose on September 11. The president's advisers felt he shouldn't put himself in a position where he would be compared with Bannon. The worry among staffers—all of them concerned that Trump's rambling and his alarming repetitions (the same sentences delivered with the same expressions minutes apart) had significantly increased, and that his ability to stay focused, never great, had notably declined—was that he was likely to suffer by such a comparison. Instead, the interview with Trump was offered to Sean Hannity—with a preview of the questions.

Bannon was also taking the Breitbart opposition research group—the same forensic accountant types who had put together the damning *Clinton Cash* revelations—and focusing it on what he characterized as the "political elites." This was a catchall list of enemies that included as many Republicans as Democrats.

Most of all, Bannon was focused on fielding candidates for 2018. While the president had repeatedly threatened to support primary challenges against his enemies, in the end, with his aggressive head start, it was Bannon who would be leading these challenges. It was Bannon spreading fear in the Republican Party, not Trump. Indeed, Bannon was willing to pick outré if not whacky candidates—including former Staten Island congressman Michael Grimm, who had done a stint in federal prison—to demonstrate, as he had demonstrated with Trump, the scale, artfulness, and menace of Bannon-style politics. Although the Republicans in the 2018 congressional races were looking, according to Bannon's numbers, at a 15-point deficit, it was Bannon's belief that the more extreme the right-wing challenge appeared, the more likely the Democrats would field left-wing nutters even less electable than right-wing nutters. The disruption had just begun.

Trump, in Bannon's view, was a chapter, or even a detour, in the Trump revolution, which had always been about weaknesses in the two major parties. The Trump presidency—however long it lasted—had created the opening that would provide the true outsiders their opportunity. Trump was just the beginning.

Standing on the Breitbart steps that October morning, Bannon smiled and said: "It's going to be wild as shit."

ACKNOWLEDGMENTS

I am grateful to Janice Min and Matthew Belloni at the *Hollywood Reporter*, who, eighteen months ago, got me up one morning to jump on a plane in New York and that evening interview the unlikely candidate in Los Angeles. My publisher, Stephen Rubin, and editor, John Sterling, at Henry Holt have not only generously supported this book but shepherded it with enthusiasm and care on an almost daily basis. My agent, Andrew Wylie, made this book happen, as usual, virtually overnight.

Michael Jackson at Two Cities TV, Peter Benedek at UTA, and my lawyers, Kevin Morris and Alex Kohner, have patiently pushed this project forward.

A libel reading can be like a visit to the dentist. But in my long experience, no libel lawyer is more nuanced, sensitive, and strategic than Eric Rayman. Once again, almost a pleasure.

Many friends, colleagues, and generous people in the greater media and political world have made this a smarter book, among them Mike Allen, Jonathan Swan, John Homans, Franklin Foer, Jack Shafer, Tammy Haddad, Leela de Kretser, Stevan Keane, Matt Stone, Edward Jay Epstein, Simon Dumenco, Tucker Carlson, Joe Scarborough, Piers Morgan, Juleanna Glover, Niki Christoff, Dylan Jones, Michael Ledeen, Mike Murphy, Tim Miller, Larry McCarthy, Benjamin Ginsberg, Al

From, Kathy Ruemmler, Matthew Hiltzik, Lisa Dallos, Mike Rogers, Joanna Coles, Steve Hilton, Michael Schrage, Matt Cooper, Jim Impoco, Michael Feldman, Scott McConnell, and Mehreen Maluk.

My appreciation to fact-checkers Danit Lidor, Christina Goulding, and Joanne Gerber.

My greatest thanks to Victoria Floethe, for her support, patience, and insights, and for her good grace in letting this book take such a demanding place in our lives.

INDEX

ABOUT THE AUTHOR

MICHAEL WOLFF has received numerous awards for his work, including two National Magazine Awards. He has been a regular columnist for *Vanity Fair*, *New York*, *The Hollywood Reporter*, British *GQ*, *USA Today*, and *The Guardian*. He is the author of six prior books, including the bestselling *Burn Rate* and *The Man Who Owns the News*. He lives in Manhattan and has four children.